Grace Livingston Hill Collection #6

Grace Livingston Hill (1865–1947) remains popular more than fifty years after her death. She wrote dozens of books that carry her unique style for combining Christian faith with tasteful and exciting romance.

Isabella Alden (1841–1930), an aunt of Grace Livingston Hill, was a gifted storyteller and prolific author as well, often using her writing to teach lessons espoused by her husband, Gustavus R. Alden, a minister. She also helped her niece Grace get started in her career as a bestselling inspirational novelist.

The Best Man, Grace Livingston Hill
When Secret Service agent Cyril Gordon is assigned to steal back a coded message stolen from the government, he never expects to be hindered from carrying out his commission by a wedding. His chief told him only a matter of life and death should stand in the way, and that is what he faces—for himself and for another.

The Big Blue Soldier, Grace Livingston Hill
Miss Marilla Chadwick, disappointed by her nephew's unwillingness to visit after the war, invites the next soldier she sees to dinner. To save face in front of her neighbor, Marilla asks the soldier to pretend to be her nephew. Mary Amber is certain the stranger is deceiving Marilla and decides to uncover the truth. But what she learns changes her life, Marilla's and the soldier's forever.

The Witness, Grace Livingston Hill
Star athlete, A student and fraternity president Paul Courtland watches while a college classmate falls to an untimely death. Struck by his own part in the tragedy, he seeks solace in the classmate's peaceful room— and in the Presence he has met. A friend introduces him to a young woman who is certain to bring him out of his somber mood—and into trouble. After yet another tragedy, Paul must choose: to follow his emotions or his Guide.

As in a Mirror, Isabella Alden
John Stuart King, noted author and scholar, poses as a tramp to find out how people will treat him and thus write about his experiences. He hires on at the Elliott farm and there meets Truth embodied in the farmer's daughter Hilda. Known for her integrity, she serves as a mirror for those around her, compelling them to see their own falseness, whether intentional or just for "fun." The search for truth deepens when a will is changed and then lost.

Grace Livingston Hill

COLLECTION NO. 6

FOUR COMPLETE NOVELS

Updated for today's reader

BARBOUR
PUBLISHING, INC.
Uhrichsville, Ohio

Edited and updated for today's reader by Deborah Cole.

ISBN 1-57748-726-5

Published by Barbour Publishing, Inc., P.O. Box 719, Uhrichsville, Ohio 44683
http://www.barbourbooks.com

ecpa Member of the
Evangelical Christian
Publishers Association

Printed in the United States of America

The Best Man

Chapter 1

Cyril Gordon had been seated at his desk only ten minutes and was deep in the morning's mail when an urgent message came from his chief, summoning him to the inner office.

The chief had keen blue eyes and shaggy eyebrows. He never wasted words; yet those words when spoken had more weight than those of most other men in Washington.

His nod and glance held the briefest of good-morning gleams, and he said merely, "Gordon, can you take the Pennsylvania train for New York that leaves the station in thirty-two minutes?"

The young man was used to abrupt questions from his chief, but he caught his breath, mentally surveying his day's schedule. "Why, sir, I suppose I could—if it's necessary—"

"It's necessary," said the chief, as if that settled the matter.

"But—half an hour!" exclaimed Gordon in dismay. "I could hardly get to my rooms and back to the station. I don't see how—isn't there a train a little later?"

"Later train won't do. Phone your man. Tell him to pack your bag and meet you at the station in twenty minutes. You'll need evening clothes. Can you depend on your man to get your things quickly without fail?"

Something in the chief's tone caused Gordon to make no further demur.

"Sure!" he responded with his usual businesslike tone, as he strode off to the phone. His daze was passing. "Evening clothes?" he questioned, as if he might not have heard right.

"Yes, evening clothes, and everything you'll need for daytime for a respectable gentleman of leisure—a tourist, you understand."

Gordon perceived he was being given a mission of trust and importance, not unmixed with mystery. He was new in the Secret Service, and it had been his ambition to rise in his chief's good graces. He rang the telephone bell furiously and called up the number of his own apartments, giving his man orders in a breezy, decisive tone that caused a look of satisfaction to settle in the wrinkles around the chief's eyes.

Gordon looked at his watch and told his man on just what car he must leave the apartments for the station. The chief noted it was two cars ahead of what would have been necessary. His gray head nodded almost imperceptibly, and his eyes showed he was content with his selection of a man.

"Now, sir," said Gordon, as he hung up the receiver, "I'm ready for orders."

"Well, you're to go to New York and take a cab for the Cosmopolis Hotel— your room there is already secured by wire. Your name is John Burnham. The name of the hotel and the number of your room are on this memorandum. You'll find awaiting you an invitation to dine this evening with a Mr. Holman, who knows of you as an expert in code-reading. Our men met him on the train an hour ago and arranged for him to invite you. He didn't know whom they represented, of course. He's already tried to phone you at the hotel about coming to dinner tonight. He knows you're expected there before evening. Here's a letter of introduction to him from a man he knows. Our men got that also. It's genuine, of course.

"Last night a message of national importance, written in cipher, was stolen from one of our men before it had been read. This is now in Holman's hands; he's hoping to have you decipher it for him and a few guests who'll also be present at dinner. They wish to use it for their own purposes. Your commission is to get hold of the message and bring it to us as soon as possible. Another message, of very different import, written on the same kind of paper, is in this envelope, with a translation for you to use in case you have to substitute a message. You'll have to use your own wits and judgment. The main thing is, *get the paper and get back with it,* with as little delay as possible. Undoubtedly your life will be in danger if it's discovered you've made off with it. Spare no care to protect yourself *and the message* at all hazards. Remember: I said '*and the message,*' young man! It means much to the country.

"In this envelope is money—all you'll probably need. Telegraph or phone this address if you're in trouble. Draw on us for more, if necessary, through this same address. Here's the code you can use in case you need to telegraph. Your ticket is already bought. I've sent Clarkson to the station for it, and he'll meet you at the train. You can give him instructions in case you forget anything. Take your mail with you and telegraph back orders to your stenographer. I think that's all. Oh, yes, tonight, while you're at dinner, you'll be called to the phone by one of our men. If you're in trouble, this may give you an opportunity to get away and let us know. You'll find a motor at the door now, waiting to take you to the station. If your man doesn't get there with your things, take the train anyway and buy some more when you get to New York. Don't turn aside from your commission for anything. Don't let *anything* hinder you! Make it a matter of life and death! Good morning and good luck!"

The chief held out a big, hairy hand that was surprisingly warm and soft considering the hardness of his face and voice. The young man grasped it, feeling as if he were suddenly being plunged into waves of unknown depth and needed to hold on to this strong hand.

He went out of the office quietly enough, and the keen old eyes watched him knowingly, understanding the mingled elation and dread. But there was no hesitancy when the nature of the commission was made known. The young man was "game." He would do. Not even an eyelash had flickered at the hint of danger. The chief felt he'd be faithful even in the face of possible death.

Gordon's man rushed into the station just after he reached there himself. Clarkson was already there with the ticket. Gordon had time to scribble a message to Julia Bentley, whose perfumed scrawl he'd read on the way down. Julia had invited him over for the evening. He couldn't tell whether he was relieved or sorry to tell her he couldn't come. It began to look to him as if he'd ask Julia

Bentley to marry him someday, when she tired of playing the others against him and he made up his mind to surrender his freedom to any woman.

He bought a paper and settled himself in the parlor car, but his interest wasn't in the paper. His strange commission engaged his thoughts. He took out the envelope containing instructions and reviewed the matter, looking curiously at the cipher message and its translation, which, however, told him nothing. It was the old chief's way of keeping the business to himself until he chose to explain. Doubtless it was safer for both message and messenger that he didn't know the full import of what he was undertaking.

Gordon carefully jotted down everything his chief had told him, comparing it with the written instructions in the envelope. Then he arranged in his mind how he'd proceed when he reached New York and tried to plan how to recover the stolen message. He knew, however, he'd have to trust the inspiration of the moment. Then it occurred to him to clear his overcoat pockets of any letters or other tell-tale articles and stow them in his suitcase. He might have to leave his overcoat behind. It would be well to have no clues for anyone to follow.

After arranging these matters and preparing a few letters with notes for his stenographer, to be mailed back to her from Philadelphia, he reread Julia Bentley's note. When every angular line of her tall script was imprinted on his memory, he tore the note into tiny pieces and dropped them from the car window.

The question was, did he or didn't he want to ask Julia Bentley to become his wife? He had no doubt as to what her answer would be. Julia had made it plain to him she'd rather have him than any of her other admirers, though she liked to keep them all attendant upon her. Well, that was her right so long as she was unmarried. He had no fault to find with her. She was a fine girl, and everybody liked her. Also, she was of a good family and with a modest fortune in her own right. Everybody assumed they liked each other. It was time he was married and had a real home, he supposed, whatever that was—that seemed to have such a great charm for all his friends. To his eyes it had as yet taken on no alluring mirage effect. He'd never known a real home, more than his quiet bachelor apartments were to him now, where his man ordered everything as he was told and the meals were sent up when wanted. He had money enough from his inheritance to make things more than comfortable, and he was deeply interested in his profession.

Still, if he was ever going to marry, it was high time, of course. But did he want Julia? He couldn't quite think pleasantly of her in his rooms when he came home tired at night; she would always want to attend her endless theater parties and receptions and dances, always demand his attention. She was bright and handsome and well dressed, but he had never expressed love to her. He couldn't imagine himself doing so. How did men express love anyway? Could one call it love when it was "made" love? These questions followed one another idly through his brain as the landscape whirled past him. If he had stayed at home, he'd have spent the evening with Julia, as she requested in her note, and probably stayed a quiet half hour after other callers left, as he'd been doing lately, and tried to find out whether he really cared for her or not.

Suppose, for instance, they were married and she sat beside him now. Would he feel deep joy as he looked at her beautiful face and realized she was his? He looked over toward the next chair and tried to imagine that the stout old woman with the double chin and the youthful purple hat was Julia, but that wouldn't work. He whirled his chair about and tried it on an empty chair. That went better; but still no thrill lifted him out of this strange uncertainty. He couldn't help thinking about trying details. The way Julia looked when she was vexed. Did one mind that in the woman one loved? The way she ordered her coachman about. Would she ever speak so to her husband? She had a charming smile, but her frown was—well—unbecoming, to say the least.

He tried to keep up the fallacy of her presence. He bought a magazine he knew she liked and imagined reading a story to her. He could easily tell how her black eyes would snap at certain phrases she disliked. He knew just what her comment would be on the heroine's conduct. It was an old disputed point between them. He knew how she'd criticize the hero, and somehow he felt himself in the hero's place every time she did. The story wasn't a success, and he felt weariness as he laid the magazine aside at the call for dinner from the dining car.

Before he finished eating he began to feel that although Julia might think now that she'd like to marry him, the truth was she wouldn't enjoy the actual life together any better than he would. Were all marriages like that? Did people lose the glamour and just settle down to endure each other's faults and make the most of each other's pleasant side and not have anything more? Or was he getting cynical? Had he lived alone too long, as his friends sometimes told him, and so was losing the ability to love anybody but himself? He knit his brows and got up to go out and see why the train had stopped so long in this little country settlement.

A wrecked freight appeared to be ahead and would delay them. No one knew just how long; it would depend on how soon the wrecking train arrived to help.

Gordon walked up and down the grass at the side of the track, looking each way for sign of the wrecking train. The thought of Julia occurred to him, but he put it away, for he knew just how poorly Julia would bear a delay on a journey even in his company. He had been with her once when the engine got off the track on a short trip down to a Virginia house party, and she was the most impatient creature alive, although it didn't matter to the rest of the party whether they made merry on the train or at their friend's house. And yet, if Julia were anything at all to him, wouldn't he like the thought of her companionship now?

A great white dog hobbled up to him and stood wagging its tail as he turned to go back to the train, and he laid his hand on the animal's head and noted the wistful eyes on its face. Gordon stood for a moment petting it. Then he turned impatiently and tramped back to his car again. But when he reached the steps, the dog had followed him.

Gordon frowned, half in annoyance, half in amusement, and sitting down on a log by the wayside he took the dog's nose in his hands, caressing the white fur above it.

The dog whined happily, and Gordon meditated. How long would the train wait? Would he miss getting to New York in time for the dinner? Would he miss the chance to rise in his chief's good graces? The chief would expect him to get to New York some other way if the train were delayed. How long should he wait?

All at once he saw the conductor and trainmen coming back hurriedly. Evidently the train was about to start. With a final stroke of the white head, he called a workman nearby, handed him half a dollar to hold the dog and sprang on board.

He had scarcely settled himself into his chair, however, before the dog came rushing up the aisle from the other end of the car and threw itself muddily and noisily upon him.

With haste and perturbation Gordon hurried the dog to the door and tried to fling it off, but the poor creature pulled back and clung to the platform yelping piteously.

Just then the conductor came from the other car and looked at him curiously.

"No dogs allowed in these cars," he said gruffly.

"Well, if you know how to enforce that rule I wish you would," said Gordon. "I'm sure I don't know what to do with it."

"Where's it been since you left Washington?" asked the grim conductor with suspicion in his eyes.

"I certainly haven't had a dog of that size secreted about me," remarked the young man dryly. "Besides, it isn't my dog. I never saw it till he followed me at the station. I'm as anxious to be rid of it as it is to stay."

The conductor eyed the young man keenly and then allowed a grim sense of humor to appear in one corner of his mouth.

"Got a chain or a rope for it?" he asked more sympathetically.

"Well, no," remarked the unhappy attaché of the dog. "Since I didn't have an appointment with the dog I didn't provide myself with a leash for him."

"Take it into the baggage car," said the conductor briefly and slammed his way into the next car.

There seemed nothing else to do, but it was annoying to be forced to parade in front of his fellow travelers with this dog in tow, when his commission required him to be as inconspicuous as possible.

At Jersey City he hoped to escape and leave the dog to the baggage man's tender mercies. But that official was craftily waiting for him and handed the animal over to its unwilling master with a satisfaction ill-proportioned to the fee he received for caring for it.

Then began a series of misfortunes. Disappointment and suspicion stalked beside him, and behind him a voice continually whispered his chief's last injunction: "Don't let anything hinder you!"

Frantically he tried one place and then another, but to no avail. Nobody apparently wanted to care for a stray white dog, and his very haste aroused suspicion. Once he came near being arrested as a dog thief. He couldn't get rid of that dog! Yet he mustn't let it follow him! Would he have to have the animal sent home to Washington as the only solution? Then an odd notion seized him that in some such way Miss Julia Bentley had shadowed his days for nearly three years; and he had actually this day been considering calmly whether he mightn't have to marry her just because she was so persistent in possessing him. Not that she was unladylike, of course—no, indeed! She was stately and beautiful and had never offended. But she had always quietly, persistently, taken it for granted that he would be her attendant whenever she chose; and she always chose whenever he was in the least inclined to enjoy any other woman's company.

He frowned at himself. Was there something weak about his character that a woman or a dog could so easily master him? Would any other employee in the office, once trusted with that great commission, have allowed a dog to hinder him?

Gordon couldn't afford to waste any more time. He must get rid of it at once!

The express office wouldn't take a dog without a collar and chain unless it was crated; and the delays and exasperating hindrances seemed to be interminable. But at last, following a kind officer's advice, he took the dog to an institution in New York where, he was told, dogs were boarded and cared for and where he finally disposed of him, having first paid ten dollars for the privilege. As he settled back in a taxicab with his watch in his hand, he congratulated himself that he still had ample time to reach his hotel and get into evening clothes before he must present himself for his work.

Within three blocks of the hotel the cab came to such a sudden standstill that Gordon was thrown to his knees.

Chapter 2

They were surrounded immediately by a crowd in which policemen were a prominent feature. The chauffeur seemed dazed in the officers' hands.

A barefoot, white-faced figure huddled limply in the midst showed Gordon what had happened, and there were menacing glances toward him and a show of lifted stones. He heard one boy say, "You bet he's in a hurry to git away. Them kind allus is. They don't care who they kills!"

A great horror seized him. The cab had run over a newsboy and perhaps killed him. Yet instantly came the remembrance of his commission: "Don't let anything hinder you. Make it a matter of life and death!" Well, it looked as if this was a matter of death hindering him now.

They bundled the moaning boy into the taxicab. Gordon saw no escape through the tightly packed crowd, who eyed him suspiciously, so he climbed in beside the grimy scrap of unconscious humanity, and they were off to the hospital to the tune of "Don't let anything hinder you! Don't let anything hinder you!" He felt that if it didn't stop soon he'd go crazy. He considered opening the cab door and escaping in spite of their speed, but a vision of broken legs and a hospital bed for himself held him to his seat. One of the policemen had climbed on in front with the chauffeur, and now and again he glanced back as if he were conveying a couple of prisoners to jail. It was vexatious beyond anything! And all because of that white dog! Could anything be more ridiculous than the whole performance?

His annoyance and irritation almost made him forget that his progress through the streets had silenced this little fellow beside him. But as he looked at his watch for the fifth time the boy opened his eyes and moaned, and in those eyes he saw a striking resemblance to the look in the dog's eyes.

Gordon started. In spite of himself it seemed as if the dog were reproaching him through the child's eyes. Suddenly the boy spoke.

"Will yous stay by me till I'm mended?" whispered the weak voice.

Gordon's heart leaped in horror again, and it came to him that he was being tried out this day to see if he had the right stuff in him for hard tasks. The appeal in the boy's eyes reached him as no request had ever done, and yet he might not answer it. Duty—life-and-death duty—called him elsewhere, and he must leave the fellow he'd involuntarily caused injury to, to suffer and perhaps to die. It cut him not to respond to that appeal.

Was it because he was weary that he was visited just then by a vision of Julia Bentley with her handsome lips curled scornfully? Julia Bentley wouldn't have approved of his stopping to carry a boy to the hospital, any more than to care for a dog's comfort.

"Look here, kiddie," he said gently, leaning over the child. "I'd stay by you if I could, but I've already made myself late for an appointment by coming so far with you. Do you know what duty is?"

The child nodded sorrowfully.

"Don't yous mind me," he murmured weakly. "Just yous go. I'm game all right." Then the voice trailed off into silence again, and the eyelids fluttered down upon the grimy, unconscious face.

Gordon went into the hospital for a moment to leave money in the authorities' hands for the boy's benefit and a message that he'd return in a week or two if possible; then he hurried away.

Back in the cab, he felt as if he'd killed a man and left him lying by the roadside while he continued his unswerving march toward the hideous duty which was growing more portentous. He closed his eyes and tried to think. But all the time the child's white face appeared before him, and Julia Bentley's mocking eyes tantalized him, as if she were telling him he'd spoiled all his chances—and hers—by his foolish soft-heartedness. But what else could he do? he asked himself fiercely.

He looked at his watch. It was at least a ten-minute ride to the hotel. Thanks to his man the process of dressing for evening wouldn't take long, for he knew everything would be in place and he wouldn't be hindered. But there was his suitcase. He shouldn't leave it at the hotel, neither must he take it with him to the house where he was to be a guest. He could only go around by the station where it would have to be checked. That meant a longer ride and more delay, but it must be done.

He arrived at the hotel at last, and in the act of signing the unaccustomed "John Burnham" in the hotel registry, a call came to the telephone.

With a hand that trembled from excitement he took the receiver. His breath went from him as though he'd just run up five flights of stairs. "Yes? Hello! Oh, Mrs. Holman. Yes! Burnham. I've just arrived. I was delayed. A wreck ahead of the train. Very kind of you to invite me. Yes, I'll be there in a few moments, as soon as I can freshen up. Thank you. Good-bye."

It all sounded commonplace to the clerk, who was making out bills, but as Gordon hung up the receiver he looked around furtively as if expecting to see a dozen detectives ready to seize him. It was the first time he'd ever undertaken a commission under an assumed name, and he felt as if he were shouting his commission through the New York streets.

Gordon dressed in a hurry. As he was leaving the hotel a telegram was handed him. It was from his chief and so worded that to the operator who copied it down it read like a hasty call to Boston; but to his code-enlightened eyes it was merely a blind to cover his exit from the hotel and from New York and set any possible hunters on a wrong scent. He marveled at the wonderful mind of his chief, who thought out every detail of an important campaign and didn't forget one point where difficulty might arise.

Gordon had a nervous feeling as he again stepped into a taxicab and gave his order. He wondered how many stray dogs and newsboys with broken legs would attach themselves to him on the way to dinner. Whenever the speed slowed down or cars and autos halted them, his heart pounded painfully, lest something new had happened. But he arrived safely and swiftly at the station, checked his suitcase and took another cab to Mr. Holman's residence without further incident.

The other guests were waiting for him, and after the introductions they went immediately to the dining room. Gordon took his seat feeling he'd bungled everything hopelessly and arrived so late there was no hope of his doing what he'd been sent to do. For the first few minutes his thoughts were jumbled and his eyes dazed with the brilliant lights of the room. He couldn't distinguish the faces of the people present. It seemed as if those near him could hear his heartbeat. He found himself starting and stammering when he was addressed as "Mr. Burnham." His thoughts were mingled with white dogs, newsboys and ladies with scornful smiles.

He was seated on the right of his hostess, and gradually her gentle manners calmed him. He began to gain control of himself, and now he seemed to see afar his chief's keen eye testing him. His heart swelled to meet this new demand, to rise above all obstacles and conquer in spite of circumstances, to forget everything else.

From that moment the dancing lights in the glittering silver and cut glass of the table began to settle into order. And slowly, one by one, the conglomeration of faces around the board resolved into individuals.

There was the pretty, pale hostess, whose gentle ways seemed hardly to fit with her large, boisterous, though polished, husband. Unscrupulousness was written all over his ruddy features, with a certain unhidden craftiness which passed for geniality among his kind.

Two others had faces full of cunning, both men of wealth and culture. Whatever refinement they might possess was dominated by the guile that on this occasion, at least, sat unmasked on their countenances. They had outwitted an enemy and were openly exultant.

Of the other guests, one was very young and sleek, with eyes that had early learned to evade; one was old and weary-looking, with a hunted expression; one was thickset, with little eyes set close in a fleshy face. Gordon began to understand that these three did the others' bidding. They listened to the conversation merely from a business standpoint and not with any personal interest. They were there because they were needed, not desired.

One bond they seemed to hold in common: an alert readiness to combine for their mutual safety. This didn't manifest itself in anything tangible, but the guest felt it was there and ready to spring upon him at any instant.

All this came gradually to the young man as the meal with its pleasant formalities began. As yet nothing had been said about the reason for his being there.

"Did you tell me you were in a wreck?" suddenly asked the hostess sweetly, turning to him.

The table talk hushed instantly while the host asked, "A wreck! Was it serious?"

Gordon perceived his mistake at once. With instant caution he replied, smiling, "Oh, nothing serious, a little breakdown on a freight ahead, requiring time to patch up. It reminded me—." And then he launched boldly into one of the bright dinner stories for which he was noted among his companions at home. His heart was beating wildly, but he succeeded in turning the table's attention to his joke, instead of letting them ask where he'd come from and on what road. Questions about him were dangerous he saw, if he were to get possession of the valued paper and get away without leaving a trail behind him. He succeeded in one thing more, which, though he didn't know it, was what his chief had hoped he'd do when he chose him instead of a man with wider experience. He made every man at the table feel that he was delightful, a man to be thoroughly trusted and enjoyed and who would never suspect them of having any ulterior motives in anything they were doing.

The conversation rippled with bright stories and repartee, and Gordon began to feel almost as if he were merely enjoying a social dinner at home, with Julia Bentley down the table listening and haughtily smiling her approval. The incidents of the dog and the newsboy were forgotten, and the young man felt his self-respect rising. His heart was acting normal again, and he could control his thoughts. Then suddenly the crisis arrived.

The soup and fish courses had been disposed of, and the table was being prepared for the entrée. The host leaned back genially in his chair. "By the way, Mr. Burnham, did you know I had an axe to grind in asking you here this evening? That sounds inhospitable, doesn't it? But I'm sure we're all grateful to the axe that has given us the opportunity of meeting you. We're delighted at having discovered you."

Gordon bowed, smiling at the compliment, and the murmurs of hearty assent around the table showed him he'd begun well. If only he could keep it up! But *how* was he to get that magic bit of paper and take it away with him?

"Mr. Burnham, I was delighted to learn through a friend that you're an expert in code-reading. Did the message from my friend Mr. Sims this morning give you any intimation I wanted you to do me a favor?"

Gordon bowed again. "Yes, it was intimated to me you had some message you'd like deciphered, and I also have a letter of introduction from Mr. Sims."

Here Gordon took the letter of introduction from his pocket and handed it across the table to his host, who opened it genially, as if it were hardly necessary to read what was written within since they already knew so delightfully the man it introduced. The duplicate cipher writing in Gordon's pocket crackled knowingly when he settled his coat about him again, as if to say, "My time's coming! It's almost here now."

The young man wondered how he was to get it out without being seen, in case he'd want to use it, but he smiled pleasantly at his host with no sign of perturbation.

"You see," went on Mr. Holman, "we have an important message we can't read, and our expert who understands these matters is out of town and can't return for some time. We need to know as soon as possible the import of this writing."

While he was speaking Mr. Holman drew from his pocket a long, soft leather wallet and took from it a folded paper Gordon at once recognized as the duplicate of the one he carried in his pocket. His head seemed to reel and the lights go dark before him as he reached a cold hand out for the paper. He saw in it his own advancement coming to his eager grasp; yet when he got it could he hold it? Something of the coolness of a man facing a terrible danger came to him now. By sheer force of will he steadied his trembling fingers as he took the bit of paper and opened it carelessly, as if he'd never heard of it before.

"I'll do my best," he said.

A sudden silence fell as every eye was fixed upon him while he unfolded the paper. He gave one swift glance about the table before he dropped his eyes to the task. Every face held the intensity of almost terrible eagerness, and on every one but that of the gentle hostess sat cunning—craft that would stop at nothing to serve its own ends. It was a moment of almost awful import.

The next instant Gordon's glance went to the paper in his hand, and his brain and heart were seized in the grip of fright. No other word could describe his feeling. The message before him was clearly written in the home office code, and the words stared at him plainly without the necessity of study. Their import was the revelation of one of the most momentous questions concerning the Secret Service work, the answer to which had puzzled the entire department for weeks. That answer he now held in his hand, and he knew that if it became known by those outside before it had done its work through the department it would result in dire calamity to the cause of righteousness in the country and incidentally crush the inefficient messenger who allowed it to become known. For the instant Gordon felt unequal to the task before him. How could he keep these bloodhounds at bay—for such they were, he perceived from the import of the message, bloodhounds who were getting ill-gotten gains from innocent and unsuspecting victims—some of them little children.

But the old chief had picked his man well. Only for an instant the glittering lights darkened before his eyes and the cold perspiration started. Then he rallied his forces and looked up. The welfare of a nation's honor was in his hands, and he would be true. It was a matter of life and death, and he would save it or lose his own life if need be.

He summoned his ready smile.

"I'll be glad to serve you if I can," he said. "Of course I'd like to look this over a few minutes before attempting to read it. Codes are different, you know, from one another, but there's a key to them all if one can just find it out. This looks as if it might be simple."

The spell of breathlessness was broken. The guests relaxed and continued with their dinner.

Gordon, meanwhile, tried coolly to keep up a pretense of eating, the paper held in one hand while he seemed to be studying it. Once he turned it over and looked on the back. A large cross mark appeared in red ink at the upper end. He looked at it curiously and then instinctively at his host.

"That's my own mark," said Mr. Holman. "I put it there to distinguish it from other papers." He was smiling politely, but he might as well have said, "I put it there to identify it in case of theft." Everyone at the table, unless it might be his wife, understood that was what he meant. Gordon felt it and was conscious of the other paper in his vest pocket. The way would be difficult.

Among the articles in the envelope the chief had given him before leaving Washington were a pair of shell-rimmed eyeglasses, a false mustache, a goatee and a pair of eyebrows. He'd laughed at the suggestion of high tragedy in the disguise but brought them with him for a possible emergency. The eyeglasses were tucked into the vest pocket beside the duplicate paper. He thought of them now. Could he, under cover of taking them out, manage to exchange the papers? And if so, how about that red ink mark across the back? Would anyone notice its absence? It was well to exchange the papers as soon as possible before the writing had been studied by those at the table, for he knew the other message, though resembling this one in general words, differed enough to attract a close observer's attention. Dared he risk their noticing the absence of the red cross on the back?

Slowly, cautiously, under cover of the conversation, he got that duplicate paper out of his pocket and under the napkin in his lap. This he did with one hand, all the time ostentatiously holding the code message in the other hand, with its back to the people at the table. This hand meanwhile also held his coat lapel out so he might more easily search his vest pockets for the glasses. It all looked natural. The hostess was engaged in a whispered conversation with the maid at the moment. The host and other guests were finishing the delicious patties on their plates, and the precious code message was safely in evidence, red cross and all. They saw no reason to be suspicious about the stranger's hunt for his glasses.

"Oh, here they are!" he said and put on the glasses to look more closely at the paper, spreading it smoothly on the tablecloth before him and wondering how he'd get it into his lap in place of the one now lying quietly under his napkin.

The host and the guests politely refrained from talking to Gordon and told each other the day's incidents in low tones that indicated the nonimportance of what they were saying—while they waited for the hour's real business.

Then the butler removed the plates, pausing beside Gordon and waiting punctiliously with his silver tray to brush away the crumbs.

This was just what Gordon waited for. It had come to him as the only way. Courteously he drew aside, lifting the paper from the table and putting it in his lap, for just the instant while the butler did his work. But in that instant the paper with the red cross was slipped under the napkin, and the other paper took its place on the table, back down so that its lack of a red cross couldn't be noted.

So far, so good, but how long could this be kept up? And the paper under the napkin—how would it get into his pocket? His hands were like ice now, and his brain seemed to be at boiling heat as he sat back and realized the deed was done and could not be undone. If anyone picked up that paper from the table and discovered the lack of the red mark, it would be all up with him. He looked up for an instant to meet the gaze of the six men upon him. They had nothing better to do now than look at him until the next course arrived. He realized that not one of them would have mercy upon him if they knew what he'd done, not unless it might be the tired, old-looking one, and he wouldn't dare interfere.

Still Gordon was enabled to smile and say some pleasant nothings to his hostess when she passed him the salted almonds. His hand lay carelessly guarding the secret of the paper on the table, innocently, as though he just *happened* to lay it on the paper.

Sitting thus with the real paper in his lap under his large damask napkin, the false paper under his hand on the table where he from time to time perused it and his eyeglasses which made him look distinguished still on his nose, he heard the distant telephone bell ring.

He remembered his chief's words and sat rigid. From his position he could see the tall clock in the hall, and its gilded hands pointed to ten minutes before seven. It was about the time his chief said he'd be called on the telephone. What should he do with the two papers?

He had only an instant to think until the well-trained butler returned and announced that someone wished to speak with Mr. Burnham on the telephone. His resolve was taken. He'd have to leave the substitute paper on the table. To carry it away might arouse suspicion, and, further, he couldn't easily manage both without being noticed. The real paper must be put safely away at all hazards, and he must take the chance that the absence of the red mark would remain unnoticed until his return.

Deliberately he laid a heavy silver spoon across one edge of the paper on the table and an ice cream fork across the other, as if to hold it in place until his return. Then, rising with apologies, he gathered his napkin, paper and all in his hand, holding it against his coat naturally, as if he'd forgotten he had it, and strode into the front hall, where in an alcove was the telephone. As he passed the hat rack he swept his coat and hat off with his free hand and bore them with him, hoping he wasn't being watched from the dining room. Could he possibly get from the telephone out the front door without being seen? Hastily he hid the cipher message in an inner pocket. The napkin he dropped on the telephone table and, taking up the receiver, said, "Hello! Yes! Oh, good evening! You don't say! How did that happen?" He made his voice purposely clear, so it might be heard in the dining room if anyone was listening. Then glancing in that direction he saw, to his horror, his host lean over and lift the cipher paper he'd left on the table and hand it to the guest on his right.

The messenger at the other end had given his agreed-upon sentence, and he'd replied according to the sentences laid down by the chief in his instructions. The other end had said good-bye and hung up, but Gordon's voice spoke, cool and clear in the little alcove, despite his excitement. "All right. Certainly I can take time to write it down. Wait until I get my pencil. Now I'm ready. Do you have it there? I'll wait a minute until you get it."

His heart beat wildly. The blood surged through his ears like rushing waters. Would they look for the red mark? The soft clink of spoons and dishes and the murmur of conversation continued, but he had no doubt it would be only seconds before his theft would be discovered. He must make an instant dash for liberty while he could. Cautiously, stealthily, like a shadow from the alcove, with one eye on the dining room, he stole to the door and turned the knob. Yet even as he did so he saw his recent host rise excitedly from his seat and fairly snatch the paper from the man who held it. His last glimpse of the room where he had three minutes before enjoyed the hospitality of the house was of the entire company starting up and pointing to him even as he slid from sight. There was no longer need for silence. He had been discovered and must fight for his life. He shut the door quickly, his nerves so tense it seemed as if something must break soon. He opened and slammed the outer door and was out in the great whirling city under the electric lamps with only the chance of a second of time before his pursuers would be upon him.

He came down the steps with the air of one who could scarcely take time to touch his feet to the ground but must fly.

Chapter 3

Almost in front of the house stood a closed carriage with two fine horses, but the coachman was looking up anxiously toward the next building. The sound of the closing door drew the man's attention, and, catching Gordon's eye, he started to jump down and throw open the door of the carriage. Quick as a flash, Gordon saw he'd been mistaken for the man the carriage awaited, and he determined to use the circumstance.

"Don't get down," he called to the man. "It's very late already. I'll open the door. Drive for all you're worth."

He jumped in and slammed the carriage door behind him, and in a second more the horses were flying down the street. A glance from the back window showed an excited group of his fellow guests standing at the open door of the mansion he had just left pointing toward his carriage and wildly gesticulating. He surmised that his host was already at the telephone calling for his own private detective.

Gordon could scarcely believe he'd accomplished his mission and flight so far, and yet he knew his situation was precarious. Where he was going he neither knew nor cared. When he was sure he was far enough from the house he'd call to the driver and give him directions, but first he must make sure the precious paper was safely stowed away, in case he was caught and searched. They might be coming after him with motorcycles in a minute or two.

Carefully rolling the paper, he slipped it into a hollow gold case among the things in the envelope the chief had given him. A fine chain was attached to the case, and the whole looked innocently like a gold pencil. The chain he slipped about his neck, dropping the case down inside his collar. That done he breathed more freely. Only from his dead body should they take that away. Then he hastily put on the false eyebrows, mustache and goatee provided for his disguise and, pulling on a pair of light gloves, felt more fit to evade detection.

He was just thinking what he should say to the driver about taking him to the station, for it was important that he get out of the city at once. Glancing out of the window to see what part of the city he was being taken through, he became aware of an auto close beside the carriage, keeping pace with it, and two men stretching their necks as if to peer into the carriage window at him. He withdrew to the shadow instantly so they couldn't see him, but his one quick glance made him sure that one of his pursuers was the short, thickset man with the cruel jaw who had sat across from him at dinner a few minutes before. If so, he had practically no chance at all of escape, for what was a carriage against a swift moving car, and what was he against a whole city full of strangers and enemies? If he attempted to drop from the carriage on the other side and escape into the darkness, he had one chance in a thousand of not being seen, and he couldn't hope to get away and hide in this unknown part of the city. Yet he must take his chance somehow, for the carriage must sooner or later get somewhere and he be obliged to face his pursuers.

To make matters worse, at the instant when he'd decided to jump at the next dark place and was measuring the distance with his eye, with his hand stretched out to grasp the door handle, a blustering motorcycle burst forth where he'd intended to jump, with a man in uniform riding it. He dodged back into the darkness of the carriage, and the motorcycle came so near that its rider turned and looked in. He felt that his time had come and his cause was lost.

It hadn't occurred to him that the men pursuing him wouldn't likely call in municipal aid in their search, lest their own duplicity be discovered. He reasoned that he was dealing with desperate men who'd stop at nothing to get back the original cipher paper and silence him. He was well aware that only death would be considered a sufficient silencer for him after what he'd seen at Mr. Holman's dinner table, for the evidence he could give would involve the honor of every man who had sat there. He saw in a flash that the two henchmen he was sure were riding in the car on his right had been at the table to silence him if he showed any signs of giving trouble.

The wonder was a stranger was called in on a matter of such grave import which meant ruin to them all if they were found out, but probably they reasoned that every man had his price and intended to offer him a share of the booty. The chief had likely caused them to understand he was the right kind of man for their purpose.

Yet, of course, they'd taken precautions, and now they had him caught, an auto on one side, a motorcycle on the other and no telling how many more behind! He was a fool to get into this carriage. He might have known it would only trap him to his death. There seemed absolutely no escape now—yet he must fight to the last. He put his hand on his revolver to make sure it was easy to get and tried to think whether it wouldn't be better to chew up and swallow that cipher message rather than risk its falling again into the enemy's hands. He decided he must carry it intact to his chief if possible and dash for safety at once.

Just then the carriage turned into a wide driveway, and the attendant auto and motorcycle dropped behind as if puzzled at the move. The carriage stopped short, and a bright light from an open doorway was flung into his face. High stone walls seemed to be on one side, and the lighted doorway on the other evidently led into a great stone building. He could hear the car and cycle puffing just behind. A wild notion that the carriage had been placed in front of the house to trap him in case he tried to escape and that he'd been brought to prison flitted through his mind.

His hand was on his revolver as the coachman jumped down to fling open the carriage door, for he intended to fight for his liberty to the last.

He glanced back through the carriage window, and the auto lights glared in his face. The short, thickset man was getting out of the car, and the motorcyclist had stood his machine up against the wall and was coming toward the carriage. Escape would be practically impossible. He had a wild thought of dashing out the opposite side of his carriage, seizing the motorcycle and making off on it, and then the door on his left was flung open and the carriage surrounded by six excited men in evening clothes talking at once.

"Here you are at last!" they choerused.

"Where's the best man?" shouted someone from the doorway. "Hasn't he come either?"

As if in answer one of the men by the carriage door wheeled and called excitedly, "He's come! Tell him—tell Jeff—he's come." Then turning once more to Gordon he seized him by the arm and cried, "Come on quickly! There isn't a minute to wait. The organist is frantic. Everybody's been as nervous as could be. We couldn't go on without you—you know. But don't let that worry you. It's all right now you've come. Forget it, old man, and hustle."

Dimly Gordon perceived above the subdued hubbub that an organ was playing, and even as he listened it burst into the joyous notes of the wedding march. It dawned upon him this wasn't a prison he'd come to but a church—not a courtroom but a wedding. And, horror of horrors, they took him for the best man! His disguise had been his undoing. How would he get out of this scrape? And with his pursuers just behind!

"Let me explain—" he began and wondered what he could explain.

"There's no time for explanations now, man. I tell you the organ has begun the march. We're expected to be marching down that middle aisle this very minute, and Jeff's waiting for us in the chapel. I signalled the bride and the organist the minute we sighted you. Come on! Everybody knows your boat was late coming in. You don't need to explain a thing till afterward."

At that moment one of the ushers moved aside, and the short, thickset man stepped between, the light shining full upon his face, and Gordon knew him for the man who sat opposite him at the table earlier. He was peering eagerly into the carriage door, and Gordon saw his only escape was into the church. With his heart pounding like a trip hammer he yielded himself to the six ushers, who swept the pursuer aside as if he'd been a fly and literally bore Gordon up the steps and through the church door.

A burst of music filled his senses, and dazzling lights and glimpses of flowers, palms and beautiful garments bewildered him. His one thought was to escape his pursuers. Would they follow him into the church and drag him out in the presence of all these people, or would they be thrown off the track for a while and give him opportunity to get away? He looked around wildly for an exit, but he was in the insistent ushers' hands. One of them chattered to him in a low, growling whisper, such as men use on solemn occasions.

"It must have been rough on you being anxious like this about getting here, but never mind now. It'll go all right. Come on. Here's our cue, and Jefferson's over there. You and he go in with the minister, you know. The groom and the best man, you understand—they'll tell you when. Jeff has the ring all right, so you won't need to bother about that. There's absolutely nothing for you to do but stand where you're put and go out when the rest do. You needn't feel a bit nervous."

Didn't these people recognize their mistake even here in the bright light? Couldn't they see his mustache was stuck on and one eyebrow was crooked? Didn't they know their best man well enough to recognize his voice? Surely someone would discover the mistake soon—that man Jeff over there who was eyeing him so intently. He'd be sure to know this wasn't his friend. Yet every minute they continued to think so was a distinct gain for Gordon, puzzling his pursuers and giving himself time to think and plan and study his strange surroundings.

And now they were drawing him forward, and a turn of his head gave him a vision of the stubbed head of the thickset man peering in at the chapel door and watching him eagerly. He must fool him if possible.

"But I don't know anything about the arrangements," faltered Gordon, reflecting that the best man might not be well known to the ushers and perhaps he resembled him.

It wasn't the first time he'd been taken for another man—and with his present makeup and all, perhaps it was natural. Could he bluff it out for a few minutes until the ceremony was over and then escape? It would be the best way to throw that impudent man in the doorway off his track. If the real best man would stay away long enough it wouldn't be difficult. The original man might turn up after he was gone and create a pleasant mystery, but nobody would be injured thereby. All this passed through his mind while the usher kept up his sepulchral whisper.

"Just the usual arrangements, you know—nothing new. You and Jeff go in after the ushers have reached the back of the church and opened the door. Then you just stand there till Celia and her uncle come up the aisle. The ceremony follows—very brief. Celia had all that repeating after the minister cut out because of not being able to rehearse. It's to be just the simplest service, not the usual lengthy affair. Don't worry—you'll be all right, old man. Hurry! They're calling you. Leave your hat here. Now I must go. Keep cool. It'll soon be over."

The breathless usher hurried through the door and settled into a sort of exalted hobble to the time of the wonderful Lohengrin music. Gordon turned, thinking even yet to escape; but his pursuer's eagle eye was on him, and the man Jefferson was by his side.

"Here we are!" he said, grabbing Gordon's hat and coat and dumping them on a chair. "I'll look after everything. Just come along. It's time we went in. The doctor is motioning for us. Awfully glad to see you at last. Too bad you had to rush so. How many years is it since I saw you? Ten! You've changed some, but you're looking fine. No need to worry about anything. It'll soon be over and the knot tied."

Mechanically Gordon fell into place beside the pleasant-faced youth, well-groomed and handsome. Looking furtively at his finely cut, happy features, Gordon wondered if he'd feel as glad as this youth seemed to be, when he walked down the aisle to meet his bride. How, by the way, would he feel if he were going to be married now—facing this great company of well-dressed people to meet Miss Julia Bentley and be joined to her for life? Instinctively his soul shrank within him at the thought.

But now the door was wide open, the organ pealing its best, and he suddenly became aware of many eyes and of wondering how long his eyebrows would withstand the perspiration trickling down his forehead. His mustache—ridiculous appendage! Why hadn't he removed it? Was it awry? Dared he put up his hand to see? His gloves! Would anyone notice they weren't as fresh as a best man's should be? Then he took his first step to the music, and it was like being pulled from a delicious morning nap and plunged into a tub of icy water.

He walked with feet that suddenly felt like lead, across a church that looked to be miles in width, before swarms of curious eyes. These people were all strangers to him, he reflected. They weren't looking at him, anyway, but at the bridegroom by his side, and it mattered little what he did, as long as he kept still and braved it out—if only the real best man didn't turn up until he was out of the church. Then he could vanish in the dark and go by some back way to a car or taxicab and so to the station. The thought of the paper inside the gold pencil case elated him. If only he could get out of this dreadful church, he'd probably get away safely. Perhaps the wedding might even protect him, for they'd never seek him in a crowded church at a fashionable wedding.

The man by his side managed him admirably, giving him a whispered hint, a shove or a push now and then, and getting him into the proper position. It seemed as if the best man had to occupy a place of too much importance in the church; but since they put him there, of course it was right. He glanced furtively over the faces near the front, and they all looked satisfied, as if everything was going as it should. So he settled down to his fate, his strained face partly hidden by the abundant mustache and eyebrows.

People whispered softly how handsome he looked, and some suggested he wasn't as stout as when they last saw him ten years before. His stay in a foreign land must have done him good. One woman even told her daughter he was far more distinguished-looking than she ever thought he could become.

The music stole onward. And slowly, like the opening of buds into flowers, the bridal party inched up the middle aisle until at last the bride in all the mystery of her white veil arrived, and all the maidens in their flowers and many colored gauzes were suitably positioned about her.

The feeble old man on whose arm the bride had leaned as she came up the aisle dropped out of the procession, taking a front seat, and Gordon found himself standing beside the bride. He felt sure something must be wrong about it and looked at his young guide to change places with him.

But the man named Jefferson held him in place with a warning eye. "You're all right. Just stay where you are," he whispered.

Gordon stayed, reflecting on the strange fashions of weddings and wondering why he'd never noticed how a wedding party came in and stood and got out again. If he were only out of this, how glad he'd be. It seemed one had to be an all-around man to be a member of the Secret Service.

The organ had hushed its voice to a sort of exultant sobbing, filled with dreams of joys and hints of sorrow, and the minister in a voice both impressive and musical began the ceremony. Gordon stood doggedly and wondered if that really was one eyebrow coming down over his eye or only a drop of perspiration.

Another full second passed, and he decided that if he ever got out of this situation alive he would never, no, *never* get married himself.

During the next second that crawled by he became supremely conscious of the creature in white by his side. A desire possessed him to look at her and see if she was like Julia Bentley. It was a nightmare haunting his dreams that she *was* Julia Bentley somehow transported to New York and being married to him willy-nilly. He couldn't shake it off, and the other eyebrow began to feel shaky. He was sure it was sailing down over his eye. If he only dared press its adhesive a little tighter to his flesh!

Sometime during the situation came a prayer, interminable to his excited imagination, as all the other ceremonies.

Under cover of the hush and the bowed heads, Gordon turned desperately toward the bride. He must see her and drive this phantasm from his brain. He turned, half expecting to see Julia's tall, handsome form, though telling himself he was a fool and wondering why he so dreaded the idea. Then his gaze was held fascinated.

She was a little creature, slender and young and beautiful, with a beauty a deathly pallor only enhanced. Her face was delicately cut and set in a frame of fine dark hair, the whole made exquisite by the mist of white tulle that breathed itself about her like real mist over a flower. But the lovely head drooped, the coral lips had a look of unutterable sadness, and the long lashes swept over the white cheeks. He couldn't take his eyes from her now that he'd looked. How lovely, and how fitting for the delightful youth by his side! Now that he thought of it she was like him, only smaller and more delicate, of course. A sudden fierce, ridiculous feeling of envy filled Gordon's heart. Why couldn't he have known and loved a girl like that? Why had Julia Bentley been forever in his pathway as the girl laid out for his choice?

He looked at her with such intensity that one dear old sister, listening to the prayer with her eyes open, whispered to the other beside her: "Just see him look at her! How he must love her! Wasn't it wonderful he came right from the steamer to the church and never saw her till now, for the first time in ten long years. It's so romantic!"

"Yes," whispered the other, "and I believe it'll last. He looks at her that way. Only I do dislike that way of arranging the hair on his face. But then it's foreign, I suppose. He'll probably get over it if they stay in this country."

A severe old lady in front of them turned a reprimanding chin toward them, and they subsided. Still Gordon continued to gaze.

Then the bride became aware of his look, raised her eyes and—they were full of tears!

They gave him one reproachful glance that shot through his soul like a sword, and her lashes dropped again. By some mysterious control over the laws of gravity, the tears remained unshed, and the man's gaze was turned aside; but that look had done its mighty work.

All the day's experiences rushed over him and seemed to culminate in that one look, as if the reproach of all things had come upon him. The hurt in the white dog's eyes had touched him, the perfect courage in the appeal of the child's eyes had called forth his deepest sympathy, but the tears of this exquisite woman wrung his heart. He saw that the appeal of the dog and the child had been the opening wedge for a woman's look which tore self from him and flung it at her feet for her to walk upon; and when the prayer was ended he found he was trembling.

He looked vindictively at the innocent youth beside him, as the rustle of the audience and the breath of relief from the bridal party indicated the next stage in the ceremony. How had this innocent-looking youth caused tears in those lovely eyes? Was she marrying him against her will? He was only a boy. What right had he to suppose he could care for a delicate creature like that? He was making her cry already and seemed utterly unconscious of it. What could be the matter? Gordon wanted to kick him.

Then it occurred to him that inadvertently *he* might have caused her tears— he, supposedly the best man, who was late and held up the wedding. Of course it wasn't really his fault; but by proxy it was, for he now was masquerading as that unlucky best man, and she was likely reproaching him for what she supposed was his stupidity. He'd heard that women cried sometimes from vexation, disappointment or excitement.

Yet in his heart he couldn't set those tears, that look, down to such a trivial cause. They'd reached his soul, and he felt something deeper was there than mere vexation. There was bitter reproach for a deep wrong done. The glance told him that. His manhood rose to defend her against the one who'd hurt her. He longed to get one more look into her eyes to make sure; and then, if appeal was still there, his soul must answer it.

For the moment his commission, his ridiculous situation, the real peril to his life and trust, were forgotten.

The man Jefferson had produced a ring and was nudging him. It appeared the best man had some part to play with that ring. He dimly remembered somewhere hearing the best man must hand the ring to the bridegroom at the proper moment. But it was absurd for them to do that when the bridegroom already held the golden circlet in his fingers! Why didn't he step up like a man and put it on the outstretched hand—that little hand just in front of him there, so timidly held out with its glove fingers tucked back, like a dove crept out from its covert unwillingly?

But that Jefferson-man still held out the ring stupidly to him and evidently expected him to take it. Silly youth! He'd have to take it and hand it back, of course. He must do as he was told and hasten that awful ceremony to its close. He took the ring and held it out, but the young man didn't take it again.

Instead he whispered, "Put it on her finger!"

Gordon frowned. Could he be hearing right? Why didn't the fellow put the ring on his own bride? If he were being married, he'd knock down any man who dared to put his wife's wedding ring on for him. Could that be the silly custom now, to have the best man put the bride's ring on? How out of place! But he mustn't make a scene.

The hand, slender and white, came a shade nearer as if to help, and the ring finger separated itself from the others.

He looked at the smooth circlet. It seemed too tiny for any woman's finger. Then, reverently, he slipped it on, with a strange longing to touch the hand. While he was thinking himself a fool and enjoying one of his intermittent visions of Julia Bentley's expressive countenance interpolated on the present scene, a peculiar thing happened.

There were some low murmurs and motions he hadn't noticed because he thought his part of this uncomfortable affair was about concluded. Then, lo and behold, the minister and the young man by his side both began fumbling for his hand, and among them they managed to bring it into position and place in its astonished grasp the hand he'd just crowned with its ring.

As his fingers closed over the bride's hand, his touch conveyed such reverence, such tenderness, that the girl's eyes were raised once more to his face, this time with the conquered tears retreating but the pain and appeal still there. He looked and involuntarily pressed her hand closer, as if to promise whatever she asked. Then, with her hand in his and realizing that they two were detached as it were from the rest of the wedding party, standing in a center of their own, his senses returned to him, and he perceived as in a flash of understanding that *they* were being married!

Some terrible, unexplainable mistake had been made, and he was stupidly standing in another man's place, taking life vows upon himself! The thing had passed from an adventure of little moment into the matter of a life tragedy, two life tragedies perhaps! What should he do?

With the question came the words, "I pronounce you husband and wife," and "let no man put asunder."

Chapter 4

What had he done? Had he unconsciously committed some unnamed, unheard-of crime? Could anyone understand or excuse such stupidity? Could he ever hold up his head again, though he fled to the remotest part of the globe? Could nothing save the situation? Now, before they left the church, couldn't he declare the truth and set things right, undo the words spoken in the presence of all these witnesses and send out to find the real bridegroom? Surely neither law nor gospel could endorse a bond made in the ignorance of either participant. It would, of course, be a terrible thing for the bride, but better now than later. Besides, he was pledged by that handclasp to answer the appeal in her eyes and protect her. This, then, was what it had meant!

But his commission! What of that? "A matter of life and death!" Ah! But this was *more* than life or death!

While these rapid thoughts were flashing through his brain, the benediction was being pronounced, and with the last word the organ pealed forth its triumphant lay. The audience stirred excitedly, anticipating the final view of the wedding procession.

The bride turned to take her bouquet from the maid of honor, and the movement broke the spell under which Gordon had been held.

He turned to the young man by his side and spoke hurriedly in a low tone. "An awful mistake has been made," he said, and the organ drowned everything but the word "mistake." "I don't know what to do."

But young Jefferson hastened to reassure him, "Not a bit of it, old chap. Nobody noticed that hitch about the ring. It was only a second. Everything went off slick. You haven't anything more to do now but take my sister out. Look alive there! She looks as if she might faint! She hasn't been a bit well all day! Steady her quick, can't you? She'll stick it out till she gets to the air, but hurry, for goodness' sake!"

Gordon turned in alarm. Already the frail white bride had a claim on him. His first duty was to get her out of this crowd. Perhaps she'd discovered he wasn't the right man, and that was the meaning of her tears and appeal. Yet she'd held her own and allowed things to go through to the finish, and perhaps he had no right to reveal to the assembled multitudes what she evidently wanted kept quiet. He must wait till he could ask her. He must do as this other man said—this—this brother of hers—who was of course the best man. O fool and blind! Why didn't he understand at the beginning and get out of this fix before it was too late? And what should he do when he reached the door? How could he ever explain? His commission! He dared not breathe a word of that! What explanation could he possibly offer for his—yes—his *criminal* conduct? Why, no such thing was ever heard of in the history of mankind as what had happened to him. From start to finish it was—it was—he couldn't think of words to express what it was. He was by this time meandering jerkily down the aisle, attempting to keep time to the music and look the part she evidently expected him to play. But his eyes were on her face, whiter now and, if possible, lovelier than before.

"Oh, just see how devoted he is," murmured the elder of the two dear old sisters, and he caught the sense of her words as he passed and wondered.

Then, immediately before him, retreating backward down the aisle with scornful eyes upon him he seemed to feel Miss Julia Bentley's presence leading onward toward the church door. But he wouldn't take his eyes from the face of the bride on his arm. He somehow knew if he could hold out without looking up, until he reached that door, Julia's power over him would be exorcised forever.

Out into the vacant vestibule, under the tented canopy, alone together for the moment, he felt her gentle weight grow heavy on his arm and knew her footsteps were lagging. Instinctively, lest others should gather around them, he almost lifted her and bore her down the carpeted steps, through the covered pathway, to the luxurious motorcar waiting with open door, and placed her on the cushions. Someone closed the car door, and almost immediately they were in motion.

She settled back with a sigh, as if she couldn't have borne one instant more of strain. Sitting opposite he adjusted the window to give her air. She seemed grateful but said nothing. Her eyes were closed, and the whole droop of her figure showed utter exhaustion. It seemed a desecration to speak to her; yet he must have some kind of understanding before they reached their destination.

"An explanation is due you—" he began, without knowing just what he was going to say. But she put out her hand with a weary protest.

"Oh, please don't!" she pleaded. "I know—the boat was late! It doesn't matter in the least."

He sat back appalled! She didn't know then that she'd married the wrong man!

"But you don't understand," he protested.

"Never mind," she moaned. "I don't want to understand. Nothing can change things. Just let me be quiet till we get to the house, or I can never go through with the rest of it."

Her words ended with almost a sob, and he sat silent for an instant, with a mingling of emotions, uppermost of which was a desire to take the girl into his arms and comfort her. "Nothing can change things!" That sounded as if she knew but thought it too late to undo the great mistake, now that it had been made. He must let her know he hadn't understood until the ceremony was over. While he sat helplessly looking at her in the dim car where she looked so small and misty huddled beside her great bouquet, she opened her eyes and looked at him. She seemed to understand he was about to speak again. By the great arc light they were passing he saw tears in her eyes again.

Her voice held a childlike pleading as she uttered one word: "Don't!"

It hurt him like a knife; he didn't know why. But he couldn't resist the appeal. Duty or no duty, he couldn't disobey her command.

"Very well," he said quietly, almost tenderly, and sat back with folded arms. After all, what explanation could he give her that she'd believe? He might not breathe a word of his commission or the message. What other reason could he give for his extraordinary appearance at her wedding and by her side?

The promise in his voice seemed to relieve her. She closed her eyes. He must just keep still and have his eyes open for a chance to escape when the carriage reached its destination.

Thus silently they threaded through unknown streets, strange thoughts in the heart of each. The bride was struggling with her burden, and the man was trying to think his way out of the maze into which he'd unwittingly wandered. He tried to set his thoughts in order and find out what to do. First of all, of course, came his commission, but somehow every time the bride took first place in his mind. Could he serve both? What *would* serve both, and what would serve *either?* As for him, he was free to confess that no room was left to consider his own interests.

Whatever was good in him must go now to set matters right in which he'd blundered. He must do the best he could for the girl who had so strangely crossed his pathway and return to his commission. But when he tried to realize the importance of his commission and set it against the girl-bride's interests, his mind became confused. He couldn't think of slipping away and leaving her without further words, even if an opportunity offered itself. Perhaps he was wrong. Doubtless his many friends might tell him so if they were consulted, but he didn't intend to consult them. He intended to see this troubled soul to some place of safety and look out for his commission as best he could afterward. One thing he didn't fully realize, and that was that Miss Julia Bentley's vision troubled him no longer. He was free. Only one woman in the world concerned him, and that was the one who sat opposite to him and whom he'd just married.

Just married! He! The thought brought with it a thrill of wonder and something else that wasn't unpleasant. What if he really had? Of course he hadn't. Of course such a thing couldn't hold good. But what if he had? Just for an instant he entertained the thought—would he be glad or sorry? He didn't know her, of course—had heard her speak only a few words, had looked into her face plainly but once—and yet suppose she were his! His heart answered the question with a joyous overflowing that astonished him, and all his former ideas of real love were swept from his mind in a breath. He knew that, stranger though she was, he could take her to his heart—cherish her, love her and bear with her—as he never could have done Julia Bentley.

All at once he realized his thoughts were dwelling on a woman who by all that was holy belonged to another man, and he'd doubtless have to deal with that other man soon. He must prepare himself for a new phase of the situation. Should he escape from the automobile's opposite door while the bride was being assisted from her seat? No, he couldn't, for he'd be expected to get out first and help her out. Besides, too many would be around, and he couldn't possibly get away. But, greater than any such reason, the thing binding him was the look in her eyes through the tears. He simply couldn't leave her until he knew she no longer needed him. And yet there was his commission! Well, he must see her in the hands of those who'd care for her at least. Such he'd done even for the white dog, and then, too, surely she was worth as much of his time as he gave the injured child of the streets. If only he could explain to her now!

The thought of his message, with its terrible significance, safe in his possession, sent shivers through his frame! Suppose he'd be caught and it taken from him, all because of this incident! What scorn would be his! How would he ever explain to his chief? Would anyone believe a man in his senses could marry a stranger before a whole church full of people and not know he was until the deed was done—and then not do anything about it after it was done? That's what he was doing now. He should be explaining something somehow to that creature in the shadow of the carriage. Perhaps in some way it might relieve her sorrow if he did, and yet when he looked at her and tried to speak, his mouth was hopelessly closed. He might not tell her anything!

He sifted his immediate actions down to two necessities: get his companion to a safe place where her friends could care for her, and escape as soon as possible. It was awful to leave her without telling her anything—when she evidently believed him to be the man she'd promised to marry—but the real bridegroom would surely turn up soon and make matters right. Anyhow, the least he could do was take himself out of her way and get his trust to its owners at once.

The car halted suddenly before a brightly lighted mansion, whose tented entrance effectually shut out the gaze of alien eyes and made the transit from car to domicile entirely private. There was no opportunity here to disappear. The sidewalk and road were thick with curious onlookers. He stepped from the car first and helped the lady out. He bore her heavy bouquet because she looked too frail to carry it further.

In the doorway she was surrounded by servants, foremost among whom her old nurse greeted her with tears and smiles and many "Miss-Celia-my-dears." Gordon stood entranced, watching the play of loving-kindness in the bride's face. As soon as he could lay down those flowers inconspicuously, he'd be on the alert for an escape. It surely would be found through some back or side entrance of the house.

But even as the thought came to him the old nurse stepped back to let the other servants greet the bride with stiff bows and embarrassed words of blessing, and he felt a hand laid heavily on his arm.

He started as he turned, thinking instantly again of his commission and expecting to see a policeman in uniform by his side, but it was only the old nurse, with tears of devotion still in her faded eyes.

"Mister George, ye hevn't forgot me, hev ye?" she asked earnestly. "You usen't to like me verra well, I mind, but ye was awful for the teasin', an' I was always for my Miss Celie! But bygones is bygones now, an' I wish ye well. Yer growed a man, an' I know ye must be worthy o' her, or she'd never hev consented to take ye. Yev got a gude wife an' no mistake, an' I know ye'll be the happiest man alive. Ye won't hold it against me, Mister George, that I used to tell yer uncle on your masterful tricks, will ye? You mind I was only carin' fer my baby girl, an' ye were but a boy."

She paused as if expecting an answer, and Gordon embarrassedly assured her he'd never think of holding such a trifling matter against her. He cast a look of reverent admiration and tenderness toward the beautiful girl who was smiling on her loyal subjects like a queen, roused from her sorrow to give joy to others. Even her old nurse was satisfied.

"Ah, ye luve her, Mister George, don't ye?" the nurse questioned. "I don't wonder. Everybody what lays eyes on her luves her. She's that dear—." Here the tears got the better of the good woman, and she forgot herself and pulled at the skirt of her new black dress thinking it was an apron and wishing to wipe her eyes.

Then suddenly Gordon found his lips uttering strange words, as if his heart had suddenly taken things in hand and determined to do as it pleased without consulting his judgment.

"Yes, I love her," he was saying, and to his amazement he found the words were true.

This discovery complicated matters still more.

"Then ye'll promise me something, Mister George, won't ye?" said the nurse anxiously. "Ye'll promise me never to make her feel bad anymore? She's cried a lot these last three months, an' nobody knows but me. She could hide it from them all but her old nurse that's loved her so long. But she's been that sorrowful, enough fer a whole lifetime. Promise ye'll do all in yer power to make her happy always."

"I will do all in my power to make her happy," he said solemnly, as if uttering a vow, and wondered how short-lived that power was to be.

Chapter 5

The wedding party had arrived in full force now. Carriages and automobiles were unloading; cheerful voices and laughter filled the house. The servants disappeared to their places, and the bride, with only a motioning look toward Gordon, led the way to where they were to stand under an arch of roses, lilies and palms, in a room with drooping ferns and white carnations hung from the ceiling on invisible threads of silver wire.

Gordon could only follow, as his way was blocked by the incoming guests, and he foresaw that his exit would have to be made from some other door than the front if he were to escape. As he stepped into the flower-scented room, he was conscious of moving from the world of ordinary things into one of wonder, beauty and mysterious joy. But all the time he knew he was an imposter, with no right in this place of honor.

Yet there he stood bowing, shaking hands and smirking behind his false mustache, which threatened every minute to betray him.

People told him he was looking well and congratulated him on his bride. Some said he was stouter than when he left the country, and some said he was thinner. They asked him questions about relatives and friends living and dead, and he ran constant risk of getting into hopeless difficulties. His only safety was in smiling and saying little, seeming not to hear some questions and answering others with another question. It wasn't hard after he got started because there were so many people, and they kept coming one after another, so no one had much time to talk. Then supper with its formalities was accomplished somehow, though to Gordon, with his already satisfied appetite and his hampering mustache, it seemed an endless ordeal.

"Jeff," as they called him, was everywhere, attending to everything, and he slipped up to the unwilling bridegroom just as he was having to answer a difficult question about his vessel's lateness and their passage in crossing. By this time Gordon had discovered he was supposed to have been ten years abroad, and his steamer was late in landing. But where he came from or what he was doing over there were still to be found out; and it was extremely puzzling to be asked from what port he sailed and how he came to be there when he was supposed to have been in St. Petersburg the week before. His state of mind was anything but enviable. Besides all this, Gordon was just reflecting that he'd last seen his hat and coat in the church. What had become of them, and how could he go to the station without a hat? Then "Jeff" arrived.

"Your train leaves at 10:03," he said in a low, business-like tone, as if he enjoyed the importance of making the arrangements. "I've secured the stateroom as you cabled me to do, and here are the tickets and checks. The trunks are down there checked. Celia didn't want any nonsense about their being tied up with white ribbon. She hates all that. We've arranged for you to slip out by the fire escape and down through the next neighbor's backyard, where a motor, just a plain, regular one from the station, will be waiting around the corner in the shadow. Celia knows where it is. None of the party will know you're gone until you're well under way. The car they think you'll take is being adorned with white at the front door now, but you won't have any trouble. I've fixed everything up. Your coat and hat are out on the fire escape, and as soon as Celia's ready I'll show you the way."

Gordon thanked him. There was nothing else to do, but his countenance grew blank. Was there, then, no escape? Must he actually take another man's bride with him in order to get away? And how was he to get away from her? Where was the real bridegroom, and why didn't he appear on the scene? And yet what complications that might bring. He looked wildly about for a chance to flee at once, for how could he possibly run away with a bride on his hands? If only someone were going with them to the station he could slip away with a clear conscience, leaving her in good hands. He'd rid himself of a lonely dog and a suffering child, though it anguished him to do so; but leave this lovely woman for whom he at least appeared to have become responsible, he could not, until he was sure she would come to no harm through him.

"Don't let anything hinder you! Don't let anything hinder you!"

This refrain had apparently not ceased since it began but had chimed its message through music, ceremony, prayer and reception without interruption. It acted like a goad upon his conscience now. He must do something that would free him to return to Washington. An inspiration came to him.

"Wouldn't you like to go to the station with us?" he asked the young man. "I'm sure your sister would like to have you."

The boy's face lit up. "Oh, wouldn't you mind? I'd like it awfully, and—if it's all the same to you, I wish Mother could go too. It's the first time Celia and she were separated, and I know she hates to say good-bye with the house full of folks this way. But she doesn't expect it, and really it isn't fair to you, when you haven't seen Celia alone yet, and it's your wedding trip—"

"There'll be plenty of time for us," said the compulsory bridegroom and felt as if he'd perjured himself. It wasn't in his nature to enjoy a serious masquerade of this kind.

"I'll be glad to have you both come," he added earnestly. "I really want you. Tell your mother."

The boy grasped his hand. "I say, you're all right! I don't mind confessing I've hated the thought of you for a whole three months, ever since Celia told us she promised to marry you. You see, I never really knew you when I was a little chap, but I didn't used to like you for some reason. I suppose kids often take irrational dislikes like that. But ever since I laid eyes on you tonight, I liked you all the way through. I like your eyes. It isn't a bit as I remembered you. I used to think your eyes had a deceitful look. Awful to tell you, isn't it? But I felt as if I wanted to have it off my conscience, for I see now you're nothing of the kind. You've got the most honest eyes I ever saw on a man, and

I'd stake my last cent you wouldn't cheat a church mouse. You're true as steel, and I'm mighty glad you're my brother-in-law. I know you'll be good to Celia."

The slow color mounted under Gordon's disguise until it reached his burnished brown hair. His eyes *were* honest eyes. They were always so—until today. Into what a world of deceit he'd entered! How he'd like to make a clean breast of it all to this nice, frank boy, but he mustn't! There was his trust! For an instant he was about to explain that he wasn't the true bridegroom and get young Jefferson to help him set matters right, but an influx of newly arrived guests broke in on their privacy.

He could only press the boy's hand and say in embarrassed tones: "Thank you! I'll try to be worthy of your good opinion!"

It was over at last, and the bride slipped from his side to prepare for the journey. He looked hastily around, feeling that his first opportunity had come for escape. If an open window had presented itself, he'd have vaulted through, trusting to luck and his heels to get away, but there was no window, and every door was blocked by staring, admiring people. He thought of the fire escape where his hat and coat waited and wondered if he could find it.

With smiling apologies, he broke away from those around him, murmuring something about being needed, and worked his way toward the stairs and the back halls. Coming at last upon an open window, he slipped through, his heart beating wildly. He thought he was there ahead of the others; but a dark form loomed ahead, and he perceived someone coming up from outside. Another second, and he saw it was his newly acquired brother-in-law.

"Say, this is great!" was his greeting. "How did you manage to find your way up alone? I was just coming down after you. I wanted to leave you there till the last minute so no one would suspect, but now you're here we can hustle off at once. I just took Mother and Celia down. It was pretty stiff for Mother to climb down, for she was a little afraid; but she was game all right and was so pleased to go. They're waiting for us down there in the court. Here, let me help you with your overcoat. Now I'll pull down this window, so no one will suspect us and follow. That's all right now—come on! You go ahead. Just hold on to the railing and go slow. I'll keep close to you. I know the way. I've played fire here many a year and could climb down in my sleep."

Gordon found himself wishing this delightful brother-in-law were really his. There was evidently to be no escape here. He considered getting away in the dark when they reached the foot of the stairs; much as he hated to leave that way, he felt he must do so if he had any chance at all. But when they reached the ground he saw that was hopeless. The car to take them to the station was drawn up close to the spot, and the chauffeur stood beside it.

"Your mother says fer you to hurry, Mister Jefferson," he called. "They're coming out around the block to watch. Get in as quick as you can."

The burly chauffeur stood below Gordon, helped him to alight on his feet from the fire escape and hustled him into the darkness of the conveyance.

They were very quiet until they'd left the dark court and were speeding away down the avenue.

Then the bride's mother laid two gentle hands upon Gordon's, leaning across from her seat to do so, and said, "My son, I'll never forget this! It was dear of you to give me these last few minutes with my darling!"

Gordon, deeply touched, mumbled something about being glad to have her, and Jefferson relieved the situation by pouring forth a volume of information and questions, fortunately not pausing long enough to have the latter answered. The bride sat with one hand clasped in her mother's and said nothing. Gordon was haunted by the thought of tears in her eyes.

With little opportunity for thinking, Gordon made a hasty plan. He decided to get his party out to the train and then remember his suitcase, which he'd left checked in the station. Jefferson would probably insist upon going for it, but he'd insist more strenuously that the brother and sister would want to have this last minute together. Then he could get away in the crowd and disappear, coming later for his suitcase perhaps or sending a porter from his own train for it. The only drawback to this arrangement was that it seemed a dishonorable way to leave these people who would in the nature of things be left in a trying position by his disappearance, especially the sad bride. But it couldn't be helped, and his staying would only complicate things still further, for he would have to explain who he was, and that was practically impossible because of his commission. It wouldn't do to run risks until his mission was accomplished and his message delivered. After that he could confess and make whatever reparation a man in his strange position would render.

The plan worked very well. The brother of course urged that he be allowed to go back for the suitcase, but Gordon, with well-feigned thoughtfulness, said in a low tone, "Your sister will want you for a minute to herself."

A tender look came into the boy's eyes, and he turned back smiling to the stateroom where his mother and sister were having a wordless farewell. Gordon jumped from the train and sprinted down the platform, feeling meaner than he ever remembered feeling and with a strange heaviness about his heart. He forgot he needed to be on his guard against possible detectives sent by Mr. Holman. Even the importance of the message he carried seemed to weigh less, now that he was free. His feet had a strange unwillingness to hurry and without a constant pressure of the will would have lagged in spite of him. His heart wanted to let suitcase and commission and everything else go to the winds and take him back to the stateroom where he'd left his bride of an hour. She wasn't his, and he might not go, but he knew he'd never be the same again. He would always wonder where she was, wishing he could have saved her from whatever troubled her; wishing she were his bride and not another's.

He passed back through the station gate, and a man in evening clothes eyed him sharply. He imagined he saw a resemblance to one of the men at the Holman dinner table, but he dared not look again lest a glance should cost him recognition. He wondered blindly which way to take and if it would be safe to go at once to the checking window or whether he should go in hiding until he was sure young Jefferson would no longer look for him.

Then a hand touched his shoulder, and a voice that was strangely welcome shouted, "This way, George! The checking place is over to the right!"

He turned, and there stood Jefferson, smiling and panting.

"You see, the little mother had something to say to Celia alone, so I saw I was *de trop* and thought I better come with you," he declared as soon as he could get his breath.

"Say, but you can run!" added the panting youth. "What's the hurry? It's ten whole minutes before the train leaves. I couldn't waste all that time kicking my heels on the platform, when I might be enjoying my new brother-in-law's company. I say, are you really going to live permanently in Chicago? I do wish you'd decide to come back to New York. Mother'll miss Celia no end. I don't know how she's going to stand it."

Walking airily by Gordon's side, he talked, apparently not noticing the sudden start and look of mingled anxiety and relief that spread over his brother-in-law's countenance.

Then another man walked by them and, turning, looked in their faces. Gordon was sure it was the thickset man from Holman's. He eyed Gordon keenly.

Suddenly all other questions stepped into the background, and the only immediate matter that concerned him was his message, to get it safely to its destination. With real relief he saw this had been his greatest concern all the time, underneath all hindrances, and that there hadn't been at any moment any escape from the crowding circumstances other than what he'd taken, step by step. If he had been beset by thieves and blackguards and thrown into prison for a time, he wouldn't have felt shame at the delay, for those things he couldn't help. He saw with new illumination that there was no more shame to him from these trivial and peculiar circumstances he'd been hemmed in with since his start to New York than if he'd been checked by more tragic obstacles. His only real misgiving was about his marriage. It seemed his fault, and he felt there should be some way to confess his part at once—but how—without putting his message in jeopardy—for no one would believe unless they knew all.

But the time of danger was at hand, he plainly saw. The man he dared not look closely at had turned again and was walking parallel to them, glancing now and again in their direction. He was watching Gordon furtively; not a motion escaped him.

There was a moment's delay at the checking counter while the attendant searched for the suitcase, and Gordon was convinced the man stopped a few steps away merely to watch him.

He dared not look around or notice the man, but he was sure he followed them back to the train. He felt his presence clearly.

But Gordon was cool and collected now. It was as if the last two hours' experiences, with their embarrassing predicaments, had been wiped off the calendar and he were back at the moment when he left the Holman house. He knew as well as if he'd watched them follow him that they'd discovered his—theft—treachery—whatever it should be called—and he was being searched for; and, because of what was at stake, those men would track him to death if they could. But he knew also that his disguise and his companion were for the moment puzzling this sleuthhound.

This was probably not the only watcher about the station. Detectives, too, perhaps, were hired hastily and ready to seize a suspect.

He marveled he could walk so deliberately, swinging his suitcase in his gloved hand at so momentous a time. He smiled and talked easily with the pleasant fellow who walked by his side and answered his questions with little idea of what he was saying; making promises his heart would like to keep, but which he now saw no way of making good.

Thus they entered the train and came to the car where the bride and her mother waited. Tears were on the girl's face, and she turned to the window to hide them. Gordon's eyes followed her wistfully, and down through the double glass, unnoticed by her absent gaze, he saw the face of the man who had followed him, sharply watching him.

Realizing his hat was a partial disguise, he kept it on in spite of the ladies' presence. The color rose in his cheeks that he had to seem so discourteous. To cover his embarrassment, he insisted on taking the elder lady to the platform, as it was almost time for the train to start, and so he went deliberately out to act the bridegroom's part in the face of his recognized foe.

The mother and Gordon stood for a moment on the platform, while Jefferson bade his sister good-bye and tried to soothe her distress at parting from her mother.

"He's all right, Celie—indeed he is," said the young fellow, laying his hand on his sister's bowed head. "He's going to be awfully good to you; he cares a lot for you, and he's promised to do lots of nice things. He says he'll bring you back soon, and he'd never stand in the way of your being with us a lot. He did indeed! What do you think of that? Isn't it quite different from what you thought he'd say? He doesn't seem to think he's got to spend the rest of his days in Chicago either. He says something might turn up to enable him to change his plans. Isn't that great?"

Celia tried to look up and smile through her tears, while the man outside studied the situation and then strolled back to watch Gordon and the elder woman.

"You'll be good to my little girl," the woman pleaded. "She's always been guarded, and she'll miss us all, even though she has you."

The voice went through Gordon like a knife. To stand much more of this and not denounce himself for a blackguard would be impossible. Neither could he keep his hat on in the presence of this wonderful mother, who appealed to him even more since he never knew a mother of his own and had always longed for one.

He put up his hand and lifted his hat slightly, guarding as much as possible his own face from the view of the man on the platform, who was still walking up and down, often passing near enough to hear what they were saying.

In this reverent attitude Gordon said, as though he were uttering a sacred vow: "I'll guard her as if she were—as if I were—*you*"—then he paused a moment and added tenderly—"Mother!"

He wondered if it weren't desecration to utter such words when he couldn't perform them in the way the mother meant. "Imposter!" was the word ringing in his ears now. The clamor about being hindered had ceased, for he was doing his best and not letting even a woman's happiness stand in the way of his duty.

Yet his heart had dictated the words he spoke, while his mind and judgment were busy with his perilous position. He felt that in every way he would guard and care for the girl who would be in his keeping at least for a few minutes until he could contrive some way to return her to her friends without him.

The train whistle was sounding now, and the brakemen were shouting, "All aboard!"

He helped the elderly woman down the steps, and she reached up her face to kiss him. He bent and took the caress, the first time a woman's lips had touched his face since he was a child.

"I won't let anything harm her," he whispered.

"My boy, I can trust you!"

Then he put her into her son's care, pulled himself up on the train as the wheels started moving and hurried back to the bride. On the platform, walking beside the train, he still saw the man. Going to the weeping girl, Gordon stooped over her gently, touched her on the shoulder and reached up to draw the window shade down. The last face he saw outside was that of the baffled man, who was turning back, but why? Would he report to others, and would they stop again before leaving the city, where officers or detectives might board the train? He should be ready to get off and run for his life if so. The only way appeared to fee the porter to look after his companion and leave her, despicable as it seemed! Yet his honor told him he could never do that, no matter what was at stake.

Then, without warning, a new situation was thrust upon him. The bride, who had been standing with bowed head and her handkerchief up to her eyes, as her brother had left her, tottered and fell into his arms, limp and white. Instantly his senses were called into action, and he forgot the man on the platform; forgot the possible next stop in the city and the explanation he was about to make to the girl; forgot even his mission's importance and the fact that the train he was on was headed toward Chicago, instead of Washington; forgot everything but the fact that the loveliest girl he'd ever seen, with the saddest look a human face might wear, was lying apparently lifeless in his arms.

Outside the window the man had turned back and was now running excitedly along with the train trying to see into the window. And down the platform, not ten yards behind, came a frantic man with English-looking clothes, a thick mustache and goatee, shaggy eyebrows and a sensual face, striding angrily along as fast as his heavy body would carry him.

But Gordon saw none of them.

Chapter 6

Five hours earlier, the man who was hurling himself furiously after the retreating train had driven calmly through the city. He came from the pier of the White Star Line to the apartment of a man he met abroad, who had offered him the use of his place during his absence. The rooms were in the fourth story of a fine apartment house. The returning exile noted with satisfaction the irreproachable neighborhood, as he slowly descended from the carriage, paid his fee and entered the door, to present his letter of introduction to the janitor in charge.

He opened the steamer trunk he'd brought with him in the cab, took out his wedding garments and hung these carefully in the closet.

Then he telephoned his best man, Jefferson Hathaway, to tell him the boat was late arriving at the dock, but he was here at last. He gave him a few directions concerning some errands and agreed to be at the church a half-hour before the ceremony, so he could see the arrangements. He was told his bride was very tired and was resting and agreed it would be as well not to disturb her; they would have time enough to talk afterward, and there wasn't anything to say but what he'd already written. He'd have about all he could do to get there on time now. He asked if Jefferson had called for the ring he ordered and if the carriage would be sent for him in time and then closed the interview. He and Jefferson weren't fond of one another, though Jefferson was the beloved brother of his bride-to-be.

He hung up the receiver and rang for a brandy and soda to brace himself for the coming ordeal which was to bind to him a woman whom for years he'd tried to get in his power and might have loved if she hadn't scorned him for the evil she knew was in him. At last he found a way to subdue her and bring her with her ample fortune to his feet, and he felt the conqueror's exultation as he prepared for the evening.

As he dressed, a smile of satisfaction played on his flabby face. He was naturally a selfish person and always knew how to make other people attend to bothersome details for him while he enjoyed himself. He was comfortable and self-complacent as he posed before the mirror to smooth his mustache and note how well he was looking. Then he went to the closet for his coat.

It was most peculiar, the way it happened, but somehow, as he stepped into that closet to take down his coat, which hung at the back where the space was widest, the opening at the wrist of his shirtsleeve caught for just an instant in the little knob of the closet latch. The gold button which held the cuff to the wristband slipped its hold, and the man was free almost at once, but the angry twitch he made at the slight detention gave the door an impetus which set it silently moving on its hinges. (George Hayne was always impatient at the slightest detention.) He'd scarcely put his hand on his wedding coat when a soft steel click, followed by utter darkness, warned him that his impatience had entrapped him. He put out his hand and pushed at the door, but the catch had settled into place. It was a strong catch, and it did its work well. The man was a prisoner.

At first he was only annoyed and gave the door an angry kick or two, as if of course it would release him meekly. But then he thought of his polished wedding shoes and desisted. He tried to find a knob and shake the door, but the only knob was the tiny brass one on the outside of the catch. Then he set his massive, flabby shoulder against the door and pressed with all his might, till his bulky linen shirt front creaked, and his wedding collar wilted. But the door stood like adamant. It was massive, like the man, but it wasn't flabby. The wood of which it was composed had spent its early life in the open air, drinking sunshine and sparkling air, wet with the dews of heaven, and exercising against the north blast. It was nothing for it to hold out against this pillow of a man, who had been nurtured in the dissipation and folly of a great city. The door held its own.

He was there, safe and fast, in the still dark, with time for reflection. And certain things in his life called for reflection, having never had him at an advantage.

In due time, after exhausting his breath and strength in fruitless pushing and his vocabulary in foolish curses, he lifted up his voice and roared. No other word would quite describe the sound that issued from his throat. But the city roared placidly below him, and no one minded him in the least.

He sacrificed the shiny toes of his shoes and added resounding kicks on the door to the general hubbub. He changed the roar to a bellow like a mad bull, but still the silence succeeding it was as deep and monotonous as ever. He tried going to the back of the closet and hurling himself against the door, but he only hurt his soft muscles with the effort. Finally he sat down on the closet floor.

Now the janitor's wife, who occupied an overcrowded apartment, had surreptitiously borrowed the use of this closet the week before, in order to hang in it her Sunday gown, whose front was covered with grease spots, overlaid with French chalk. The French chalk had done its work and removed the grease spots and now lay on the closet floor. The imprisoned bridegroom didn't know that, of course, and sat down to rest from his unusual exertions and reflect on what could be done next.

The immediate present passed rapidly in review. He couldn't afford more than ten minutes to get out of this hole. He should be on the way to the church at once. There was no telling what nonsense Celia might get into her head if he delayed. He'd known her since childhood, and she'd always scorned him. His hold on her now was like a rope of sand, but he alone knew that. If he could only knock that old door down! If he only hadn't hung up his coat in the closet! If the man who built the house hadn't put such a fool catch on the door! When he got out he'd chop it off! If only he had a little more room and a little more air! It was stifling! Great beads of perspiration rolled down his hot forehead, and his wet collar made a cool band about his neck. He wondered if he had another clean collar like that with him. If he *only* could get out of this accursed place! Where were all the people? Why was everything so still? Would they never come and let him out?

He recalled telling the janitor he'd occupy the room with his baggage for two or three weeks perhaps, but he expected to go away on a trip this very evening. The janitor wouldn't think it strange if he didn't appear. How would it be to stay here and die? Horrible thought!

He jumped up from the floor and began his howlings and gyrations once more, but soon desisted and sat down to be entertained by a panorama of his past life which is always unpleasantly in evidence at such times. Fine and clear in the closet's darkness stood out the nicely laid scheme of deviltry by which he contrived to be at last within reach of a coveted fortune.

Occasionally the frantic thought came that just through this mishap of a clothespress catch he might lose it. The fraud and trickery by which he had an heiress in his power didn't trouble him so much as the thought of losing her— at least of losing the fortune. He must have that fortune, for he was deep in debt, and—but then he would refuse to think and stand up to batter at his prison door again.

Four hours his prison walls enclosed him, with inky blackness all around except for a faint glimmer of light, which marked the well-fitted base of the door as the night outside drew on. He had lighted the gas when he began dressing, for the room was already filled with shadows, and now that streak of flickering gaslight seemed to be the only thing that saved him from losing his mind.

Somewhere from out of the dim shadows a face evolved itself and gazed at him, a haggard face with hollow eyes and despair written on it. It reproached him with a sin he thought long forgotten. He shrank back in horror, and the cold perspiration stood out on his forehead, for the eyes were the eyes of the man whose name he forged on a note involving trust money fifteen years before. The man, quiet and unsuspecting, had suffered the penalty in a prison cell until his death five years ago.

Sometimes at night in the first years after his crime, that face had haunted him, appearing at odd intervals when he was plotting some shady means of adding to his income. Then he resolved to turn over a new leaf and gave up one or two schemes as being too unscrupulous, thus acquiring a feeling of being virtuous. But it was a long time since the face had appeared. He'd settled it in his mind that the forgery was merely a patch of wild oats he had sown in his youth, something to be regretted but not too severely blamed for. Thus forgiving himself he felt it was more the world's fault for not giving him what he wanted than his for putting a harmless old man in prison. Of the shame that had killed the old man he knew nothing, nor could he understand. The actual punishment itself was all that appealed to him. He was one who had to be taught with the lash and then only kept straight with it in sight.

But the face was very near and vivid here in the thick darkness. It was like a cell, this closet, bare, cold, black. The eyes in the gloom seemed to pierce him with the thought: "This is what you made me suffer. It is your turn now!" Nearer they came looking into his own, until they saw into his sinful soul and drew back, appalled at the smallness and meanness of what they saw.

Then for the first time in his whole selfish life George Hayne knew shame, for the eyes read to him all they saw.

Closer and thicker grew the air of the small closet; fiercer grew the rage and shame and horror of the man incarcerated.

Now from out of the shadows stared other eyes that had never haunted him before, eyes of victims to whom he'd never cast half a thought. Eyes of men and women he'd robbed by his artful, gentlemanly craft; eyes of innocent girls whose wrecked lives had contributed to his selfish scheme of living; even the great reproachful eyes of little children who had looked to him for pity and found none. Last, above them all, were the eyes of the lovely girl he was to have married.

He had always loved Celia Hathaway more than he could have loved anyone or anything else besides himself, and it ate into him that he could never make her bow to him; not even by torture could he bring her to her knees. Stung by the years of her scorn he'd stooped lower and lower in dealing with her until he employed the tools of slow torture upon her soul so he might diminish her pride and put her fortune and her very self within his power. The strength with which she withheld him until the time of her surrender had turned his selfish love into hate with contemplations of revenge.

But now her eyes seemed to taunt him with his foolish defeat at this last minute before the final triumph.

Undoubtedly the brandy had gone to his head. Was he going mad that he couldn't get away from all those terrible eyes?

He felt sure he was dying when at last the janitor came up to the fourth floor on his inspection round, noticed the light flaring from the transom over the door occupied by the stranger who said he would leave on a trip almost immediately and went in to investigate. The eyes vanished at his step. The man in the closet lost no time in making his presence known, and the janitor cautiously and with great deliberation investigated the reason for this disturbance and finally let him out, after being promised a reward which never materialized.

The stranger flew to the telephone in frantic haste and called up the house of his affianced bride, shouting wildly at the operator for all undue delays. When he finally succeeded in getting someone to the phone, it was only to be told that neither Mrs. Hathaway nor her son was there. Were they at the church?

"Oh, no," the servant answered, "they came back from the church long ago. There's a wedding in the house and a great many people. They're making so much noise I can't hear. Speak louder, please!"

He shouted and raved at the servant, asking futile questions and demanding information, but the louder he raved the less the servant understood. Finally George hung up the receiver and dashed about the room like an insane creature, tearing off his wilted collar, grabbing at another, jerking on his fine coat, snatching his hat and overcoat, and dashing down the stairs, regardless of the janitor's demand for the promised reward of freedom.

Out in the street he rushed back and forth blindly in search of some conveyance, found a taxicab at last and, plunging in, ordered it to the Hathaway address at once.

When he arrived there, he presented an enlivening spectacle to the guests, who were still making merry. His trousers were covered with French chalk; his collar had slipped from its confining button in front and curved gracefully about one fat cheek; his high hat was a crush indeed, having been rammed down on his head in his excitement. He talked so fast and loud they thought he was crazy and tried to put him out, but he shook his fist angrily in the footman's face and demanded to know where Miss Hathaway was. When they told him she was married and gone, he turned livid with wrath and told them that was impossible, since he was the bridegroom.

By this time the guests had gathered in curious groups in the hall and on the stairs, listening, and when he claimed to be the bridegroom they shouted with laughter, thinking this must be some practical joke or else the man was insane.

But one older gentleman, a family friend, stepped up to the excited visitor and said in a calming voice: "My friend, you've made a mistake! Miss Hathaway has this evening been married to Mr. George Hayne, just arrived from abroad, and they're on their way to take the train. You've come too late to see her, or else you have the wrong address and are speaking of some other Miss Hathaway. That's likely the explanation."

George looked around on the company with helpless rage, then rushed to his taxicab and gave the order for the station.

Arriving at the station, he saw he was within half a minute of the Chicago train's departure, and none knew better than he what time that train was to depart. Hadn't he given minute directions regarding the arrangements to his future brother-in-law? What did it all mean anyway? Had Celia somehow carried out the wedding without him to hide her mortification at his nonappearance? Or had she run away? He was too excited to use his reason. He could merely urge his heavy bulk onward toward the fleeing train. He dashed up the platform, overcoat streaming from his arm, coattails flying, hat crushed down on his head, his bechalked legs rumbling heavily after him. He passed Jefferson and his mother, watching the retreating train.

Jefferson laughed at the funny spectacle, but the mother didn't notice and only said absently, "I think he'll be good to her, don't you, Jeff? He has nice eyes. I don't remember his eyes seeming so pleasant and so—deferential."

Then they turned to go back to their car, and the train moved faster out of the station. It would presently rush out into the night, leaving the two pursuers to face each other, baffled.

Both of them realized this at the same instant, and the thickset man with sudden decision turned again and, plunging along with the train, caught at the rail and swung himself with dangerous precipitation to the last platform of the last car with a half-frightened triumph. Looking back he saw the other man with a frantic effort sprint forward, try to do the same thing and, failing, sprawl flat on the platform, to the amusement of two trainmen standing near.

George Hayne, having thus come to a full stop in his headlong career, lay prostrate for a moment, stunned and shaken. Then, gathering himself up slowly, he gazed after the departing train. After all, if he caught it what could he have done? It was incredible that Celia could marry and go on her wedding trip without him. If she eloped with someone else and they were on that train, what could he have done? Kill the bridegroom and force the bride to return with him and be married all over again? Yes, but that might have been awkward, and he had enough awkward situations to his account already. Besides, Celia wasn't likely married yet. Those people at the house had been fooled somehow, and she'd run away. Perhaps her mother and brother had gone with her. The same threats that had made her bend to him once should follow her wherever she went. She would marry him yet and pay for this folly a hundredfold. He lifted a shaking hand of curse toward the train which by this time was vanishing into the dark opening at the end of the station, where signal lights like red berries festooned themselves in an arch against the blackness, and the lights of the last car paled and vanished like a forgotten dream.

Then he turned and hobbled slowly back to the gates regardless of the merriment he was arousing in the genial trainmen. He was spent and bruised, and his appearance was anything but dignified. No member of the wedding company, had they seen him at this juncture, would have recognized in him any resemblance to the handsome gentleman who had played his part in the wedding ceremony. No one would have thought he could be Celia Hathaway's bridegroom.

Slowly back to the gate he crept, haggard, dishevelled, crestfallen: his hair in its several isolated locks over his forehead, his collar wilted, his clothes smeared with chalk and dust, his overcoat dragging forlornly behind him. He was trying to decide what to do next and realizing the torment of a perpetual thirst when a hand was laid suddenly upon him and a voice that somehow had a familiar twang said: "You will come with me, sir."

He looked up and there before him in the flesh were the eyes of the man who had haunted him for years, the very eyes grown younger and filled with more than reproach. They were piercing him with the keenness of retribution. They said, as plainly as those eyes in the closet had spoken a brief hour before, "Your time is over. My time has come. You have sinned. You shall suffer. Come now and meet your reward."

He started back in horror. His hands trembled, and his brain reeled. He wished for another cocktail to help him meet this extraordinary emergency. Surely something had happened to his nerves that he was seeing these eyes in reality and hearing the voice, that old man's voice made young, bidding him come with him. It couldn't be, of course. He was unnerved with all he'd been through. The man had mistaken him for someone—or perhaps it wasn't a man after all. He glanced quickly around to see if others saw him and at once realized a crowd was collecting about them.

The man with the strange eyes and the familiar voice was dressed in plain clothes, but he seemed to have full assurance he was a real live man and had a right to dictate. George Hayne couldn't shake away his grasp. A determination about it struck terror to his soul, and he had a weak desire to scream and hide his eyes. Could he be coming down with delirium tremens? That brandy must have been unusually strong to have lasted so long in its effects. Then he made a weak effort to speak, but his voice sounded small and frightened. The eyes took his assurance from him.

"Who are you?" he asked. "What right have *you* to dictate to *me?*" he meant to add. But the words died away in his throat, for the plainclothesman had opened his coat and disclosed a badge that shone straight into his eyes.

"I am Norman Brand," answered the voice, "and I want you for what you did to my father. It's time you paid your debt. You were the cause of his humiliation and death. I've been watching you for years. I saw the notice of your wedding in the paper and was tracking you. It was for this I entered the service. Come with me."

With a cry of horror George Hayne wrenched away from his captor and turned to flee. Instantly three revolvers were leveled at him, and he found two policemen in brass buttons stationed behind him and the crowd closing in about him. Wherever he turned he looked into a gun barrel, with no escape in any direction.

They led him away to the patrol wagon, the erstwhile bridegroom, and in place of the immaculate linen he had searched so frantically for in his apartment they put on his wrists cuffs of iron. They put him in a cell and left him with the old man's eyes for company and the haunting likeness of his son's voice filling him with frenzy.

The unquenchable thirst came upon him, and he begged for brandy and soda, but none came to slake his thirst. He had crossed the great gulf, and justice at last had him in her grasp.

Chapter 7

Meanwhile the man on the steps of the last car of the Chicago Limited was having his doubts about whether he should have boarded that train. He realized the fat traveler who was hurling himself after the train had stirred in him a sudden impulse half-formed before, and he had obeyed it. Perhaps he was following a wrong scent and would lose the reward he knew was his if he brought the code-writing thief, dead or alive, to his employer. He was half inclined to jump off again now before it was too late. Looking down he saw they were already speeding over a network of tracks, and trains were flying by in every direction. By the time they were out of this the speed would be too great for him to jump. It was even now risky, and he was no longer agile. He must do it at once if he did it at all.

He looked ahead tentatively to see if the track he must jump on was clear, and the great eye of an engine stabbed him in the face as it bore down upon him. The next instant it swept by, its hot breath fanning his cheek, and he drew back, shuddering involuntarily. It was no use. He couldn't jump here. Perhaps they'd slow up or stop, and, anyway, should he jump or stay on board?

He sat down on the upper step to get the situation in hand. Perhaps in a minute more the way would be clearer to jump off if he decided not to go on. Thus he vacillated. It was rather unlike him not to know his own mind.

There appeared to be something here to follow, and yet perhaps he was mistaken. He was the first man of the company at the front door after Mr. Holman turned the paper over and they all noticed the absence of the red mark. It was simultaneous with the door latch clicking, and he'd covered the ground from his seat to the door sooner than anyone else. He could swear he saw the man get into the cab that stood almost in front of the house. He lost no time in getting into his own car, detailed for such an emergency, and in signalling the officer on a motorcycle who was also ready for a quick call. The carriage had barely turned the corner when they followed—no other like it was in sight either way—and he'd followed it closely. It must have been the right carriage. And yet, when the man got out at the church he was much changed in appearance, so that he'd looked twice into the empty carriage to make sure the man he searched for wasn't still in there hiding. Then he followed him into the church, saw him married and stood close at hand when he put his bride into a big car. He followed the car to the house where the reception was held, mingling with the guests and watching until the bridal couple left for the train. He stood in the shadowed alley, the only guest who found how the bride was really going away, and again he followed to the station.

He walked close enough to the bridegroom in the station to be almost sure that mustache and those heavy eyebrows were false, and yet he couldn't figure it out. How could a man about to be married in a church full of fashionable people flirt with chance by accepting an invitation to a dinner where he might not get away for hours? What would have happened if he hadn't arrived in time? Could these two men be identical? Everything but the likeness and his following the man so closely pointed out the impossibility.

The thickset man trusted his inner impressions thoroughly, and in this case his inner impression was that he must watch this peculiar bridegroom and be sure he wasn't the right man before he forever got away from him. And yet he might be missing the right man by doing it. But he'd come so far and risked a good deal already in following and in throwing himself on that fast-moving train. He would stay a little longer and be sure. He'd try to get a seat where he could watch him, and in an hour he should know if he was really the man who stole the code-writing. If he could avoid the conductor for now he'd simply profess to have taken the wrong train by mistake and maybe get put off somewhere near home, in case he discovered he was barking up the wrong tree. He'd stick to the train for a while, since there seemed no safe way of getting off at present.

After deciding so much, he gave one last glance toward the city's twinkling lights rushing past and sauntered into the train, keeping an eye out for the conductor. He meant to burn no bridges behind him. He was well provided with money for any kind of trip and mileage books and passes. He knew where to send a telegram that would bring him instant assistance in case of need, and even now he knew the motorcycle officer had reported to his employer that he'd boarded this train. He had no immediate need to worry. He was after big game, and one must take risks accordingly. Thus he entered the sleeper to make good the impression of his inner senses.

ঌ

Gordon had never held anything so precious, so sweet and beautiful and frail-looking, in his arms. He felt that he should lay her down; yet he longed to draw her closer and shield her from every trouble.

But she wasn't his—only a precious trust to be guarded and cared for as vigilantly as the message he carried hidden about his neck. She belonged to another, somewhere, and was a sacred trust until circumstances enabled him to return her to her rightful husband. Just what all this might mean to him, to the woman in his arms and to the man she was to have married, Gordon hadn't as yet had time to think. Nor had he as yet disentangled himself from the conflicting factors and determined what was his fault and what he should do about it.

He laid her gently on the couch of the drawing room and opened the door of the private dressing room. There would be cold water in there.

He knew very little about caring for sick people—he'd always been well and strong himself—but they used cold water for people who fainted, he was sure. He wouldn't call in anyone to help, unless it was necessary. He closed the stateroom door and went after the water. As he passed the mirror, he started at the curious vision in it. One false eyebrow had come loose and was hanging over his eye, and his goatee was crooked. Had it been so all the time? He snatched the loose eyebrow off and then the other, but the mustache and goatee were more tightly affixed, and it was painful to remove them. He glanced back, and the girl's pale, limp look frightened him. Why was he stopping over his appearance when she might be dying, and as for pain—he tore the false hair roughly from him and, stuffing it into his pocket, filled a glass with water and went back to the couch. His chin and upper lip smarted, but he didn't notice it or know the plaster mark was all about his face. He only knew she lay there apparently lifeless, and he must bring the soul back into those eyes. It was strange, wonderful, how his feeling had grown for the girl he'd never seen till three hours before.

He held the glass to her lips and tried to make her drink, then poured water on his handkerchief and awkwardly bathed her forehead. One hand drooped over the side of the couch and touched his. It seemed so soft and cold and lifeless!

He blamed himself for having no remedies in his suitcase. Why hadn't he thought to carry something—a simple restorative? Other people might need it. No man should travel without something for life-saving in an emergency. He might even have needed it himself in case of a railroad accident or something.

He slipped his arm tenderly under her head and tried to raise it so she could drink, but the lips didn't move or attempt to swallow.

Then a panic seized him. Suppose she was dying? Not until later, when he had quiet and opportunity for thought, did it occur to him what a terrible responsibility he'd taken upon himself in letting her people leave her with him. What a fearful position he'd be in if she died. At the moment his whole thought was one of anguish at the idea of losing her—anxiety to save her precious life—and not for himself.

Forgetting his own need for quiet and obscurity, he laid her gently back on the couch and rushed from the stateroom out into the aisle of the sleeper. The conductor was just making his rounds, and he hurried to him.

"Is there a doctor on board or perhaps a nurse? There's a lady"—he hesitated, and the color mounted in his face—"that is, my wife." He spoke the word unwillingly, having at the instant of speaking realized he must say this to protect her good name. It seemed like uttering a falsehood or stealing another man's property. Technically, though, it was true, and for her sake he must acknowledge it.

"My wife," he began again more connectedly, "is ill—unconscious."

The conductor looked up at him sharply. He'd sized them up as a wedding party when they came down the platform toward the train. The young man's blush confirmed his supposition.

"I'll see!" he said briefly. "Go back to her, and I'll bring someone."

Just as Gordon turned back, the thickset man entered the car from the other end and met him face to face. But Gordon was too distraught to notice him; furthermore, his mind was put to rest about his pursuer as soon as the train started.

Not so with the pursuer, however. His keen eyes took in the white, anxious face with the sticking plaster smeared about the mouth and eyebrows and instantly knew his man. His instincts hadn't failed him after all.

He put out a pair of brawny fists to catch at him, but a lurch of the train and Gordon's swift stride outdid him. By the time the thickset man had righted his footing, Gordon was disappearing into the stateroom, and the conductor with another man was in the aisle behind him waiting to pass. He stepped back and watched. At least he'd driven his prey to quarry, and there was no possible escape now until the train stopped. He'd watch that door as a cat watches a mouse and perhaps send a telegram for help before he made any move. It was as well his impulse to take the man then and there had come to nothing. What would the other passengers have thought of him? He must move cautiously. What a blunder he'd almost made. He didn't intend to make public his errand. The men who were behind him didn't wish to be known or have their business known.

With narrowing eyes he watched the stateroom door as the conductor and doctor came and went. He gathered from a few questions asked by a passenger that someone was sick, probably the lady he saw faint as the train started. It occurred to him this might be his opportunity, and when the conductor came out of the drawing room the second time he inquired if any assistance was needed and implied that doctoring was his profession, though it would be a sorry patient who had only his attention. If he had one accomplishment, however, it was bluffing, and he never stopped at any profession that suited his needs.

The conductor was annoyed at the interruptions and answered him brusquely that they had all the help necessary, and nothing was the matter anyway.

The man could only wait. He subsided with his eye on the stateroom door and later secured a berth in plain sight of that door, but he gave no order to have it made up until every other passenger in the car was gone to what rest a sleeping car provides. He kept his vigil well but was rewarded with no sight of his prey that night. At last with a sense of duty well done and a deftly worded telegraphic message to Mr. Holman to be sent from a station they would pass after midnight, he crept to his well-earned rest and slept. And the train thundered on its way into the night.

Gordon meanwhile had hurried back from his appeal to the conductor and looked helplessly down at the delicate girl as she lay there so pale and seemingly lifeless. Her traveling dress set off the exquisite face finely, and her glorious hair seemed to crown her.

The conductor hurried in presently, followed by a grave elderly man with a professional air. He touched a practiced finger to the limp wrist, looked closely into the face and then, taking a small bottle from his case, called for a glass.

The liquid was poured between the closed lips, the throat reluctantly swallowed it, the eyelids presently fluttered, a long breath that was scarcely more than a sigh hovered between the lips, and then the blue eyes opened.

She looked about, bewildered, looking longest at Gordon, then closed her eyes wearily, as if she wished they hadn't brought her back, and lay still.

The physician still knelt beside her, and Gordon, with time now to think, considered the possible consequences of his deeds. With anxious face he stood watching, reflecting bitterly that he might not claim even a look of recognition from those sweet eyes and wishing with all his heart that his marriage had been genuine. A passing memory of his morning ride to New York in company with Miss Bentley's conjured vision brought wonder to his eyes. It all seemed so long ago and so strange that he ever could have entertained for a moment the thought of marrying Julia. She was a good girl, of course, fine and handsome and all that—but—and here his eyes sought the face on the couch. His heart suffered for the trouble he saw and for the trouble he must yet give her when he told her who he was, or rather who he was not. He must tell her and soon. It wouldn't do to go on in her company—nor to Chicago! And yet how could he leave her in this condition?

But no revelations were to be given that night.

The physician administered another draught and ordered the porter to make up the berth immediately. Then with skillful hands and strong arms he laid the young girl upon the pillows and made her comfortable. Gordon meanwhile stood awkwardly by, wanting to help but not knowing how.

"She'd better not be disturbed anymore than necessary tonight," said the doctor, as he patted the traveling dress about the girl's ankles with professional hands. "Don't let her yield to any nonsense about putting up her hair or removing that dress for fear she'll rumple it. She needs to lie perfectly quiet. It's a case of utter exhaustion, and I'd say a long strain of some kind—anxiety, worry perhaps." He looked keenly at the sheepish bridegroom. "Has she had any trouble?"

Gordon lifted honest eyes.

"I'm afraid so," he answered contritely, as if it must have been his fault some way.

"Well, don't let her have any more," said the elder man briskly. "She's a fragile bit of womanhood, young man, and you'll have to handle her carefully or she'll blow away. Make her *happy,* young man! People can't have too much happiness in this world. It's the best thing, after all, to keep them well. Don't be afraid to give her plenty."

"Thank you!" said Gordon fervently, wishing it were in his power to do what the physician ordered.

The kind physician, the assiduous porter and the brusque but good-hearted conductor went away at last, and Gordon was left with his precious charge, who to all appearances was sleeping quietly. The light was turned low, and the curtains of the berth were a little apart. He could see the dim outline of drapery about her and one shadowy hand lying limp at the edge of the couch, in weary relaxation.

Above her, in the upper berth, which he'd told the porter not to make up, lay a sheaf of lilies of the valley from her bouquet. It seemed so strange for him to be there.

He locked the door, so no one would disturb the sleeper, and stepped into the private dressing room. For a full minute he looked into the mirror at his own weary, soiled face and wondered if he, Cyril Gordon, before honored and self-respecting, had really done in the last twelve hours all he was crediting himself with doing! And the question was, how did it happen? Did he take leave of his senses, or did circumstances become too much for him? Did he lose the power of judging between right and wrong? Could he have helped anything that came upon him? How? What should he do now? Was he a criminal beyond redemption? Had he spoiled the life of the woman out there in her berth, or could he make amends for what he'd done? And was he as badly to blame as he felt?

After a minute he rallied and realized his face was dirty. He washed the marks of adhesive plaster away and then, not satisfied with the result, brought his shaving things from his suitcase and shaved. He felt more like himself after that and slipped back into the darkened drawing room and stretched himself wearily on the couch, which, according to his directions, wasn't made up, but merely furnished with pillows and a blanket.

The night settled into the noisy quiet of an express train, and each revolution of the wheels, as they whirled Chicago-ward, resolved into the old refrain, "Don't let anything hinder you! Don't let anything hinder you!"

He certainly wasn't taking the most direct route from New York to Washington, though it might eventually prove that the longest way around was the shortest way home, because of its comparative safety.

As he settled to the quiet of his couch, several things became more clear to him. One was that they'd safely passed the New York outskirts without interference and must by this time be speeding toward Albany, unless they were on a road that took them more directly west. He hadn't thought to look at the tickets for knowledge of his bearings, and the light was too dim for him to distinguish any monograms or letterings on inlaid wood panels or transoms, even if he knew enough about New York railroads to gain information from them. One thing was certain: Even if he was mistaken about his supposed pursuers, by morning someone would surely be searching for him. The duped Holman combination would stop at nothing when they discovered his theft of the paper, and he couldn't hope that so sharp-eyed a man as Mr. Holman seemed to be would be long in discovering the absence of his private mark on the paper. Undoubtedly he knew it already.

As for the frantic bridegroom, Gordon dreaded meeting him. It must be put off until the message was safe with his chief. Then, if he had to answer with his life for carrying off another man's bride, he could at least feel he left no duty to his government undone. His present situation was plainly dangerous from two points of view: The bridegroom would have no difficulty in finding out what train he and the lady had taken, and he was satisfied that an emissary of Holman had more than a suspicion of his identity.

The obvious thing to do was get off that train at the first opportunity and get across country to another railroad line. But how could he do that with a sick lady on his hands? Of course he could leave her to herself. She probably had taken journeys before and would know how to get back. She could at least telegraph her friends to come for her. He could leave her money and a note explaining his involuntary villainy, and her indignation with him would probably be a sufficient stimulant to keep her from dying of chagrin at her plight. But from the first, every nerve and fiber in him rejected this suggestion. It would be cowardly, unmanly, horrible! Undoubtedly it might be the wise thing to do from many standpoints, but—*never!* He could no more leave her that way than he could run off to save his life and leave the message he carried. She was a trust as much as that. He got into this, and he must get out somehow, but he wouldn't desert the lady or neglect his duty.

Toward morning it occurred to him he should have deserted the bride while she was still unconscious, jumping off the train at the short stop they made soon after she fell into his arms. She would then have been cared for by someone, after his absence was discovered, and she would have been put off the train and her friends sent for at once. But it would have been dastardly to desert her that way and not know if she still lived.

It was a terrible muddle, right and wrong juggled in such a mysterious and unusual way. He never remembered coming to a spot where it was difficult to know which of two things was right to do. There were always such clearly defined divisions. He'd supposed that people who professed not to know what was right wished to be blinded on the subject because they wished to do wrong and think it right. But now he saw he'd judged such too harshly.

Perhaps his brain had been strained with the day's excitement and annoyances, and he wasn't quite in a condition to judge what was right. He should snatch a few minutes' sleep, and then his mind would be clearer, for something must be done and soon. It wouldn't do to risk entering a large city where detectives and officers with full details might even now be watching for him. He was too familiar with the workings of retribution in this progressive age not to know his danger. But he really must get some sleep.

At last he yielded to the drowsiness that was stealing over him—just for a moment, he thought—and the wheels hummed on their monotonous song: "Don't let anything hinder! Don't let anything—! Don't let—! Don't! Hin-der-r-r-r!"

Chapter 8

The man slept, and the train rushed on. The night waned. The dawn grew purple in the east and streaked itself with gold; then later got out a fillet of crimson and drew over its cloudy forehead. The breath of lilies filled the room with delicate fragrance and mingled strange scenes in the dreams of the man and the woman so strangely united.

The bride grew restless and stirred, but the man on the couch didn't hear her. He was dreaming of a shooting affray, in which he carried a bride in a gold pencil and was shot for stealing a sandwich out of Mr. Holman's vest pocket.

The morning light grew clearer. The east had put on a vesture of gold above her purple robe, and its reflection shone softly in at the window, for the train was at that moment rushing northward, though its general course was west.

The sleeper behind the thick green curtains stirred again and became aware, as in many days past, of her sorrowful burden. Always at first waking, the realization of it sat upon her as though it would crush the life from her body. She fought back waking consciousness as she'd learned to do in the last three months, yet knew it was futile while she was doing it.

The sun shot up between the crimson bars, like a topaz on a lady's gown that crowns the whole beautiful costume. The piercing, jeweled light lay across the pale face, touching the lips with warm fingers, and the troubled soul knew all that had passed.

She lay quiet, letting the torrent sweep over her with its sickening realization. She was married! It was over—with the painful parting from dear ones. She was away from them all. The new life she so dreaded had begun, and how was she to face it—the life with one she feared and didn't respect? How could she ever have done it except for the love of her dear ones?

Gradually she remembered the night before—the parting with her mother and her brother; the things that brought the tears again to her eyes. Then all was blankness. She must have fainted. She didn't often faint, but it must be— yes, she remembered opening her eyes and seeing men's faces about her, and George—could it have been George?—with a kinder look in his eyes than she ever thought to see there. Then she must have fainted again—or had she? No, someone lifted her into this berth, and she drank something and went to sleep. What happened? Where was everybody? It was good to be left alone. She grudgingly gave her unloved husband a fragment of gratitude for not talking to her. In the carriage on the way he seemed determined to begin a long argument of some kind. She didn't want to argue anymore. She had written tomes on the subject and said all she had to say.

He wasn't deceived. He knew she didn't love him and would never have married him but for her mother's sake and for the sake of her beloved father's memory. What was the use of saying more? Let it rest. The deed was done, and they were married. Now let him have his way and make her suffer as he chose.

If he would let her suffer in silence and not inflict his bitter tongue upon her, she would try to bear it. And perhaps—oh, perhaps she wouldn't live long, and it would soon be all over.

As the daylight grew, the girl felt inclined to find out whether her husband was near. Cautiously she lifted her head and, drawing back a corner of the curtain, peered out.

He lay quietly on the couch, one hand under his cheek against the pillow, the other across his breast, as if to guard something. He was in the still sleep of the weary. He scarcely seemed to be breathing.

Celia dropped the curtain and put her hand to her throat. It startled her to find him so near and so still. She lay down again and closed her eyes. She mustn't awaken him. She would have as long a time to herself as was possible and try to think of her dear mother and her precious brother. Oh, if she were just going away from them alone, how well she could bear it! But to be going with one she'd always almost hated—

Her brother's happy words about George suddenly came to her mind. Jefferson thought him fine. Well, of course the dear boy knew nothing about it. He hadn't read all those awful letters. He didn't know the threats—the terrible language. She shuddered as she thought of it. But in the same breath she was glad her brother had been deceived. She wouldn't have it otherwise. Her dear ones must never know what she'd gone through to save them from disgrace and loss of fortune—disgrace, of course, being the first and greatest. She'd feared George would let them see through his veneer of manners and leave them troubled, but he appeared better than she'd hoped. The years had made a greater change in him than she expected. He really wasn't as bad as her conjured image of him.

Then a sudden desire to look at him again seized her, to know once for all just how he really seemed. She wouldn't want to notice him awake any more than she could help or dare, lest he presume upon her sudden interest, to act as if he'd never offended. If she looked at him now as he lay asleep, she might study his face and see what she really had to expect.

She fought the desire to peer at him again, but finally it gained possession of her, and she drew back the curtain.

He was lying as quietly as before. His heavy hair, a little disordered on the pillow, gave him a noble, interesting appearance. He didn't seem at all a fellow to fear. It was incredible he could have written those letters.

She tried to trace in his features a likeness to the youth of ten years ago, whom she knew when she was a little girl, who tied her braids to her chair and put raw oysters and caterpillars down her back or stretched invisible cords to trip her feet in dark places. He'd never failed to mortify her on all possible occasions, and once—but the memories were too horrible as they crowded one upon another! Let them be forgotten!

She watched the face before her keenly, critically, yet she could see no trace of any such character as she'd imagined the boy George must have developed as a man—of which his letters had given her ample proof. This man's face was finely cut and sensitive. She saw nothing coarse in its lines. The long, dark eyelashes lay above dark circles of weariness and gave the boyish look that touches the maternal chord in a woman's heart. George used to have a puffy, self-indulgent look under his eyes even when he was a boy. She imagined from his last photograph that he'd be much stouter, more bombastic. But, then, in his sleep, perhaps those things fell from a man.

She tried to turn away indifferently, but something in his face held her. She studied it. If he'd been any other man, any stranger, she would have said from looking at him critically that kindness was written on the face before her. There was fine, firm modeling about the lips and the clean-shaven chin; yet she thought she knew the man before her to be the opposite. How deceptive were looks! She would probably be envied rather than pitied by all who saw her. Well, perhaps that was better. She could more easily keep her trouble to herself. But stay—what about this man seemed different? The smooth face? Yes. She had the dim impression that last night he wore a mustache. She must have been mistaken, of course. She'd only looked at him when necessary, and her brain was in such a whirl. But still something seemed different about him.

Her eyes wandered to the hand that lay across his breast. It was the fine, clean hand of a professional man. There was nothing flabby about it. George as a boy used to have big, stumpy fingers and nails chewed down to the quick. She could remember how she used to hate to look at them when she was a little girl and yet somehow couldn't keep her eyes away. She saw with relief that the nails on his hands were well cared for.

He looked very handsome and attractive as he lay there. The sun shot one of its early bolts of light across his hair as the train turned in its course and lurched northward around a curve. He had the kind of hair that makes a woman's hand instinctively long to touch it.

Celia wondered at the curious thoughts that crowded through her mind, knowing that when this man awakened she would think of nothing but his hateful personality as she'd known it through the years. And she was his wife! How strange! How terrible! How impossible to live with the thought through interminable weary years! Oh, that she might die at once before her strength failed and her mother found out her sorrow!

She lay back again on her pillows and tried to think, but somehow a pleasant image of him, her husband, lingered in her memory. Would she ever see anything pleasant in him? Ever endure the days of his companionship? Ever come to the point where she could overlook his outrageous conduct toward her, forgive him and even tolerate him? Sharp memories crowded upon her, and the smarting tears stung their way into her eyes, answering and echoing in her heart, "No, no, a thousand times, no!" She had paid his price and gained redemption for her own, but—forget what he'd done? *Never!*

The long strain of weariness and the monotony of the onrushing train lulled her half into unconsciousness again, and the man on the couch slumbered on.

He came to himself suddenly, with all his senses alert, as the thumping noise and the motion of the train ceased, and a sudden silence of open country succeeded, broken now and again by distant oncoming and receding voices.

He caught the fragment of a sentence from some train official.

"It's a half-hour late, and maybe more. We'll just have to lie by, that's all. Here, you, Jim, take this flag and run up to the switch—" The voice trailed into the distance, ended by the metallic note of a hammer doing something mysterious to the car's underpinning.

Gordon sat up suddenly, his hand still across his chest, where his waking thought had been to see if the little pencil case was safe.

Glancing toward the curtains of the berth and perceiving no motion, he concluded the girl still slept.

He slipped his feet into his shoes and stood up looking toward the curtains. He wanted to go out and see where they were stopping, but dared he go without knowing she was all right?

He stooped and brought his face close to the opening in the curtains. Celia felt his eyes on her. Her own were closed, and by a superhuman effort she controlled her breathing, gently, as if she were asleep.

He looked for a long moment, thrilled by the delicate beauty of her sleeping face, eager to see that her lips were no longer white. Turning away, he unlocked the door and stepped out.

The car's other occupants were still wrapped in slumber. Loud snores of various kinds and qualities testified to that. A dim light at the further end contended luridly, and losingly, with the daylight now flooding the outside world and creeping into the transoms.

Gordon closed the compartment door noiselessly and walked down the aisle to the end of the car.

A door was open, and he could hear voices outside. The conductor stood talking with two brakemen. He heard the words "three-quarters of an hour at least." Then the men walked off toward the engine.

Gordon looked across the country, and for the first time since he started on his journey remembered it was springtime and May.

A bitter wind had blown the night before, with a hint of rain in the air. In fact, it had rained during the ride to the hospital with the hurt child, but he was so perturbed he'd scarcely noticed the weather. But this was a radiant morning.

The sun was in one of its most charming moods, when it touches everything with glory after the long winter of darkness and cold. Every tree trunk in the distance seemed to stand out clearly, every blade of grass was set with a glowing jewel, and the winding stream across a narrow valley fairly blazed with brightness. The road with its deep, clean wheel-grooves seemed like a well-taken photograph.

The air had an alluring softness mingled with its winter tang that made one long to walk anywhere out into the world, just for the joy of being and doing. A meadowlark shot up from somewhere to a telegraph pole, let go a blithe note and hurried on. The exhilaration filled Gordon's blood.

And here was the chance he craved to slip away from the train before it reached a place where he could be discovered. If he'd only thought to bring his suitcase! He could slip back now without being noticed and get it! He could even go without it! But—he couldn't leave her that way—could he? Perhaps he should—but it wouldn't do to leave his suitcase with her, for it contained letters addressed to his real name. An explanation would be demanded, and he could never satisfy a loving mother and brother for leaving a helpless girl in such a situation—even if he could satisfy his own conscience, which he knew he never could. He simply couldn't leave her, and yet he *must* get away from that train as soon as possible. Perhaps this was the only opportunity he'd have before reaching Buffalo, and it was risky, indeed dangerous, to enter Buffalo. It was a foregone conclusion that private detectives would be ready to meet the train in Buffalo with full descriptions and details and only too ready to make away with him if they could do so without being found out. He looked nervously back at the car door. Dared he attempt to waken her and say they'd made a mistake and must change cars? Was she well enough? And where could they go?

He looked off toward the landscape for answer to his question.

They were decidedly in the country. The train stood at the top of a high embankment of cinders, below which a smooth country road ran parallel to the railroad for some distance. Then it met another road at right angles to it, which stretched away between thrifty meadowlands to a nestling village. The glorified stream he'd first noticed far up the valley glinted narrower here in the morning light, with a suggestion of watercress and forget-me-nots in its fringes as it veered away under a bridge toward the village and hid itself in a tangle of willows and cattails.

How easy it would be to slide down that embankment and walk out that road over the bridge to the village, where of course a conveyance could be hired to bear him to another railroad town and then to—Pittsburgh, perhaps, where he could easily get a train to Washington. How easy if only he weren't held by some invisible hands to care for the sleeper inside the car! But, for her sake as well as his own, he must do something and speedily.

He was standing thus in deep meditation, looking off at the village which seemed so near and yet would be so far for her to walk, when he was pervaded with that strange sense of someone near. For an instant he resisted the desire to lift his eyes and prove to himself no one was present in a doorway he knew was unoccupied a moment before. Then, frowning at his own nervousness, he turned.

She stood there in all the beauty of her fresh young girlhood, a delicate pallor on her cheeks and a deep sadness in her great dark eyes, fixed upon him intently in a sort of puzzled study. She was fully dressed, even to her hat and gloves. Every wave of her hair lay exquisitely in place under her hat, as though she might have taken an hour or two to dress; yet she had accomplished it with excited haste and trembling fingers, determined to finish before the dreaded man returned.

She had sprung from her berth the instant he closed the door upon her and fastened the little catch to bar him out. She dashed cold water onto her face, fastened her garments hurriedly and tossed her hair into place with a few touches. Then putting on her hat, coat and gloves, she'd followed him into the outer air. She felt she must have air to breathe or she'd suffocate. A wild desire filled her to go alone into the great outdoors. Oh, if she only dared run away from him! But she might not do that, for he'd probably make good his threats on her dear mother and brother. No, she must be patient and bear to the end what was set down for her. But she'd get out and breathe a little before he returned. He'd likely gone into the smoker. She remembered the George of old was an inveterate cigarette smoker. She would have time to taste the morning while he had his smoke. And if he returned and found her gone what did it matter? The inevitable beginning of conversations she dreaded would be delayed for a time.

She never expected to come upon him standing alone, looking off at the morning beauty as if he enjoyed it. The sight of him held her, watching, as his sleeping face had held her gaze earlier. How different he was! How the ten years had changed him! One could almost imagine it might have changed his spirit also—but for those letters—those terrible letters! The writer of those letters could not change, except for the worse!

And yet he was handsome, intellectual looking, kind in his bearing, appreciative of the beauty about him—she couldn't deny it. It was astonishing. He'd lost that baggy look under his eyes and the weak, cruel pout of lip she remembered so keenly.

Then he turned, and a smile of delight and welcome lit up his face. In spite of herself she couldn't keep an answering smile from glimmering faintly in her own.

"What! You up and out here?" he said, hastening closer to the step. "How are you feeling this morning? Better, I'm sure, or you wouldn't be here so early."

"Oh, I had to get out to the air," she said. "I couldn't stand the car another minute. I wish we could walk the rest of the way."

"Do you?" he said, with a quick, surprised appreciation in his voice. "I was just wishing something like that myself. Do you see that straight road down there? I was longing to slide down this bank and walk over to that village for breakfast. Then we could get an auto, perhaps, or a carriage to take us to another train. If you hadn't been so ill last night, I might have proposed it."

"Could we?" she asked earnestly. "I'd like it so much. What a lovely morning!" Her eyes were wistful, like the eyes of those who weep and wonder why they may not laugh, since the sunshine is still yellow.

"Of course we could," he said, "if you're only able."

"Oh, I'm able enough. I'd much rather do that than go back into that stuffy car. But wouldn't they think it awfully odd of us to run away from the train this way?"

"They needn't know anything about it," he declared, like a boy about to play truant. "I'll slip back in the car and get our suitcases. Is there any danger of leaving something of yours behind?"

"No, I put everything in my suitcase before I came out," she said listlessly, as though she'd already lost her desire to go.

"I'm afraid you're not able," he said, pausing as he scaled the steps.

She was surprised at his interest in her welfare.

"Why, of course I am," she said. "I've often taken longer walks than that looks, and I'll feel much better for being out. I really feel as if I couldn't stand it any longer in there."

"Good! Then we'll try it!"

He hurried in for the baggage and left her standing on the cinder roadbed beside the train, looking off at the opening morning.

Chapter 9

At that instant the thickset man in his berth not ten feet away became broadly conscious of the cessation of motion that had lulled him to such sound repose. So does a tiny, sharp sound strike upon our senses and bring them into life again from sleep, making us aware of a state of things that has been going on for some time, perhaps without our realization. The sound that rousing him may have been the click of the stateroom latch as Gordon opened the door.

The shades were down in the man's berth and the curtains drawn close. The daylight hadn't yet penetrated through their thickness. But once awake his senses were alert. He yawned, stretched and suddenly arrested another yawn to analyze the stillness about him. A sonorous snore emphasized the car's quiet and made him aware of the occupants of those curtained apartments. His mind went over a quick résumé of the night before and detailed him at once to duty.

Another soft clicking of the latch set him to listening, and his bristly shocked head was stuck instantly out between the curtains into the aisle, eyes toward the stateroom door, just in time to see a man stealing quietly down the passageway out the end door, carrying two suitcases and an umbrella. It was his man. He was sure instantly, and his mind grew frantic. Almost he'd outdone himself through foolish sleep.

He half sprang from his berth, then remembered he was partly dressed and jerked back to grab his clothes, stopping to yank up his window shade with an impatient click and flatten his face against the windowpane.

Yes, there they were on the ground outside the train—man, woman, baggage—slipping away from him while he slept peacefully and let them go! The language of his mind at that point was hot with invectives.

Gordon had made his way back to the girl's side without meeting any porters or wakeful fellow passengers. But a distant rumbling greeted his ears. The waited-for express was coming. If they were to get away, it must be done at once, or their flight would be discovered and perhaps even prevented. It certainly was better not to have it known where they got off. He'd closed the stateroom door behind him, and so it might be some time before their absence would be discovered. Perhaps there'd be other stops before the train reached Buffalo, in which case their track wouldn't be easily followed. He had no idea his pursuer's evil eye was even then upon him.

Celia was already on the ground, looking off toward the village wistfully. Just how it was to make her lot any brighter to get out of the train and run away to a strange village she didn't explain to herself, but it seemed to relieve her pent-up feelings. She was half afraid George might raise some new objection when he returned.

Gordon swung himself down on the cinder path, scanning the track either way. The conductor and brakemen weren't in sight. In the distance a black speck was rushing down upon them. Gordon could hear the vibration of the rail of the second track, on which he placed his foot as he helped Celia across. In a moment more the train would pass. They must be down the embankment, out of sight. Wouldn't the girl be afraid of the steep incline?

She hesitated an instant at the top, for it was very steep. Then, looking up at him, she saw he expected her to go down with him. She gave a little gasp, set her lips and started.

He held her as well as he could with two suitcases and an umbrella clutched in his other hand. Finally, as the grade grew steeper, he let the baggage slide down by itself, while he devoted himself to steadying the girl's now inevitable and swift descent.

It certainly wasn't an ideal way of traveling, but it landed them without delay, though much shaken and scratched and divested of every vestige of dignity. It was impossible not to laugh, and Celia's voice rang out merrily, showing she hadn't always wept and looked sorrowful.

"Are you hurt much?" asked Gordon anxiously, holding her hands and looking down at her tenderly.

Before she could reply, the express train roared above them, drowning their voices and laughter. When it was past they saw their own train take up its interrupted way and move off. If the passengers on those two trains hadn't been deeply wrapped in slumber, they might have been surprised to see two fashionably attired young persons, with hats awry and clasped hands, laughing in a country road at five o'clock on a May morning. But only one was awake, and by the time the two in the road below remembered to look up and notice, the trains were disappearing.

The girl was deeply impressed with Gordon's solicitude for her. It was so out of keeping with his letters. He'd never seemed to care whether she suffered or not. In all the arrangements he said what *he* wanted, indeed what he *would have*, with an implied threat in his sentence in case she demurred. Never was there any expression of desire for her happiness. Therefore she was surprised to find him so gentle and thoughtful of her. Perhaps, after all, he wouldn't prove so terrible to live with as she'd feared. And yet—how could anyone who wrote those letters have any alleviating qualities? It couldn't be. She must harden herself against him. Still, if he would be outwardly decent to her, it would make her lot easier, of course.

But her mental reasoning was interrupted by his stout denunciations of himself.

"I shouldn't have let you slide down there," he declared. "It was terrible, after what you went through last night. I didn't realize how steep and rough it was. Indeed I didn't. I don't see how you ever can forgive me."

"Why, I'm not hurt," she said gently, astonished at his solicitation. A strange lump arose in her throat by his kindness, threatening tears. Why should kindness from an unexpected quarter bring tears?

"I'm only a little shaken up," she continued as she saw anxiety in his brown eyes, "and I don't mind it in the least. I think it was rather fun, don't you?"

A faint glimmer of a smile wavered over the corners of her mouth, and Gordon experienced a sudden desire to take her in his arms and kiss her. It was a strange new feeling. He'd never had any such thought about Julia Bentley.

"Why, I—why, yes, I guess so, if you're sure you're not hurt."

"Not a bit," she said, and then, for some unexplained reason, they both began to laugh. After that they felt better.

"If your shoes are as full of these miserable cinders as mine are, they need emptying," declared Gordon, shaking first one well-shod foot and then the other, and looking ruefully at her velvet boots.

"Suppose you sit down," he said, looking about for a seat, but the dewy grass was the only resting place visible. He put the suitcases together and improvised a chair. "Now sit down and let me take them off for you."

He knelt in the road at her feet as she protested that she could do it for herself. But he won out and awkwardly unbuttoned the tiny buttons, holding the little foot firmly, almost reverently, against his knee.

He drew the velvet shoe off and, turning it upside down, shook out the intruding cinders and put a clumsy finger in to make sure they were all gone. Then he passed his hand over the sole of the silk-stockinged foot that rested so lightly on his knee, to make sure no cinders clung to it. The sight and touch of that foot stirred him. He'd never been called upon to render such intimate service to any woman, and he did it now with a half-averted gaze and the utmost respect in his manner. He tried to speak about the morning, the departing train, the annoying cinders, anything to make their unusual position seem natural and unstrained. He felt deeply embarrassed, the more so because of his own double part in this odd masquerade.

Celia sat watching him, strangely stirred. Her wonder over his kindness grew with each moment, and her prejudices almost dissolved. She couldn't understand it. He must want something more of her, for George Hayne had never been kind unless he wanted something of her. She dreaded lest she'd soon find it out. Yet he didn't look like a man who was deceiving her. She drew a deep sigh. If only it were true, and he were good and kind and had never written those awful letters! How dear it would be to be tenderly cared for this way! Gordon looked up in great distress.

"You're tired!" he declared, pausing in his attempt to fasten the pearl buttons. "I've been cruel to let you get off the train!"

"Indeed I'm not," said the girl, brightening with sudden effort. At least, she wouldn't spoil the kindness while it lasted. It was surely better than what she'd feared.

"You never can button those shoes with your fingers," she said and laughed, as he redoubled his efforts to capture a tiny disc of pearl and set it into its small velvet socket. "Here! I have a buttonhook in my handbag. Try this."

She produced a small silver instrument from a gold-link bag on her arm and handed it to him. He took it helplessly, trying first one end and then the other, succeeding with neither.

"Here, let me show you," she said, laughing and pulling off one glove. Her fingers grasped the silver buttonhook and flashed in and out of the velvet holes, knitting the shoe to the foot in no time. He watched the process in humble wonder, and she was flattered with his interest and admiration. For a minute she forgot who and what he was and let her laugh ring out merrily. So with shy audacity he assayed to take off the other shoe.

They felt well acquainted, as if they were going on a day's picnic, when they finally gathered up their belongings and started down the road. Gordon summoned his ready wit and intellect to brighten the walk for her, though he found himself again and again almost referring to his Washington life or some other personal matter that would have brought a wondering question to her lips. He'd decided he mustn't tell her who he was until he could put her in an independent position, where she could get away from him at once if she chose. He was bound to look after her until then, and it was better to carry it out leaving her to think what she pleased until he could tell her everything. If all went well, they might be able to catch a Pittsburgh train that night and be in Washington the next day. Then, his message delivered, he'd tell her the whole story. Until then he must hold his peace.

They walked cheerfully down the road, the girl's pale cheeks flushing with the morning and the exercise. She wasn't naturally delicate, and her faint the night before had resulted from a series of heavy strains on a heart burdened with terrible fear. The morning and his kindness had made her forget she was supposed to be walking into a world of dread and sacrifice.

> The year's at the spring,
> The day's at the morn.

quoted Gordon lightly,

> Morning's at seven;
> The hillside's dew-pearled—

He waved an umbrella off to where a hill flashed back a thousand lights from its jeweled grass blades thickly set.

> The lark's on the wing;
> The snail's on the thorn,

continued Celia, catching his spirit and pointing to a lark that darted up into the blue with a morning trill in his throat.

Gordon turned appreciative eyes upon her. It was good to have her take up his favorite poet in that tone of voice—a tone that showed that she too knew and loved Browning.

God's in his heaven,
All's right with the world.

He finished in a quieter voice, looking straight into her eyes. "That seems true today, doesn't it?"

The blue eyes wavered with a shadow in them as they looked back into the brown ones.

"Almost—perhaps," she faltered.

The young man wished he dared go behind that "almost—perhaps" and find out what she meant, but he concluded it was better to bring back the smile and help her forget for a little while at least.

Down by the brook they paused to rest, under a weeping willow whose green-tinged plumes were dabbling in the brook. Gordon arranged the suitcases for her to sit upon, then climbed down to the brookside and gathered a great bunch of forget-me-nots, blue as her eyes, and brought them to her.

She looked at them in wonder, to think they grew out here, wild, untended. She'd never seen them before, except in pots in florists' windows. She touched them delicately with the tips of her fingers, as if they were too ethereal for earth, then fastened them in the breast of her dress.

"They exactly match your eyes!" he exclaimed involuntarily.

Then he wished he hadn't spoken, for she flushed and paled under his glance, until he felt he'd been unduly bold. He wondered why he said it. He wasn't in the habit of saying pretty things to girls, but this girl somehow called it from him. It was genuine. He sat a moment abashed, not knowing what to say next, as if he were a shy boy, and she didn't help him. She seemed unable to carry off the situation. He wasn't sure if she was displeased or not.

Her heart had thrilled strangely as he spoke, and she was vexed with herself that it should be so. A man who had bullied and threatened her for three terrible months and forced her to marry him had no right to a thrill of her heart or a look from her eyes, be he ever so kind for the moment. He certainly was nice and pleasant when he chose to be; she must watch herself, for never must she yield to his smooth overtures. Well she knew him. He had some reason for all this pleasantness. It would surely be revealed soon.

She stiffened her lips and tried to look away from him to the purply-green hills. But the echo of his words came upon her again, and again her heart thrilled at them. What if—oh, what if he were all right, and she might accept the admiration in his voice? And yet how could that be? The color returned to her cheeks, and the tears flew to her eyes, till they looked all sky and dew, and she dared not turn back to him.

The silence remained unbroken, until a lark in the willow copse behind them burst forth into song.

"Are you offended at what I said?" he asked. "I'm sorry if you didn't like it. The words said themselves without my stopping to think whether you might not like it. Will you forgive me?"

"Oh," she said, lifting her eyes to his, "I'm not offended. There's nothing to forgive. It was—beautiful!"

Then his eyes spoke the compliment over again, and the thrill started anew in her heart, till her cheeks grew rosy, and she buried her face in the coolness of the tiny flowers to hide her confusion.

"It was true," he said in a low, loverlike voice that sounded like a caress.

"Shouldn't we hurry to catch our train?" said Celia, suddenly springing to her feet. "I'm quite rested now." She felt if she stayed there another moment she would yield to the spell he'd cast on her.

With a dull thud of consciousness the man got to his feet and reminded himself this was another man's promised wife to whom he'd been letting his soul go out.

"Don't let anything hinder you! Don't let anything hinder you!" suddenly babbled out the little brook, and he gathered up his suitcases and started on.

"I'll carry my suitcase," declared a decided voice behind him, and a small hand seized hold of its handle.

"I beg your pardon—you are not!" declared Gordon in a much more determined voice.

"But they're too heavy for you—both of them—and the umbrella too," she protested. "Give me the umbrella then."

But he wouldn't give her even the umbrella, rejoicing in his strength to shield her and bear her burdens. As she walked beside him, she remembered vividly a morning when George Hayne had made her carry two heavy baskets, that his hands might be free to shoot birds. Could this be the same George Hayne?

Altogether it was a happy walk and far shorter than either had expected it to be, though Gordon worried about his companion before they reached the village outskirts. He kept begging her to sit down and rest again, but she wouldn't. She was excited about the strange village to which they were coming. Its outlying farmhouses were clean and white, with green blinds folded placidly over their front windows and only their back doors astir. The cows looked peaceful, and the dogs seemed friendly.

They walked up the village street, shaded in patches with sunshine flecks through the young leaves. If anyone had told Celia Hathaway the night before that she would walk and talk thus today with her bridegroom, she would have laughed him to scorn. But now unconsciously she'd drifted into friendliness with the man she'd expected to hate the rest of her life.

One long, straight, maple-lined street, running parallel to the stream, comprised the village. They walked to the center of it and still saw no signs of a restaurant. A post office, a couple of stores and a bakery made up the town's business portion, and inquiry revealed there was no public eating house. The one hotel had been sold at auction the week before because of the owner's death. The early village loungers stared at the city folks with their luggage and no apparent means of transit except their two delicately shod feet. It presented a problem too grave to be solved unassisted, and they shook their heads solemnly.

At last one asked, "Hed a runaway?"

"Oh, no!" laughed Gordon pleasantly. "We didn't travel with horses."

"Hed a puncture then," stated another, shifting from one foot to the other.

"Wal, you come the wrong direction to git help," said a languid listener. "Thur ain't no garridge here. The feller what uset to keep it skipped out with Sam Galt's wife a month ago. You'd ought to'a' turned back to Ashville. They got a good blacksmith there can tinker ye up."

"Is that so?" said Gordon interestedly. "Well, now, that's too bad, but since it can't be helped we'll have to forget it. What's the next town on ahead and how far?"

"Sugar Grove's two mile further on, and Milton's five. They've got a garridge and a rest'rant to Milton, but that's only sence the railroad built a junction there."

"Has anyone here a conveyance I could hire to take us to Milton?" questioned Gordon, looking anxiously about the indolent group.

"I wouldn't want to drive to Milton for less'n five dollars," declared a lazy youth after a suitable pause.

"Very well," said Gordon. "How soon can you be ready, and what sort of rig do you have? Will it be comfortable for the lady?"

The youth eyed the graceful woman in her dainty city dress. His own lass was dressed far prettier to his mind. But her eyes so blue, like the little weed-flowers at her breast, went to his head. His tongue was suddenly tied.

"It's all right! It's as good's you'll get!" volunteered a sullen-faced man half-sitting on a sugar barrel. He was the sort who preferred to see fashionable ladies uncomfortable.

The youth departed for his "team," and after some inquiries Gordon found he might persuade the owner of the tiny white colonial house across the street to prepare a "snack" for him and his companion. So they crossed the street and waited fifteen minutes in a dank little parlor adorned in funeral wreaths and embroidered doilies, for a delicious breakfast of poached eggs, coffee, homemade bread, butter like roses and a comb of amber honey. To each the experience was a new one, and they enjoyed it together like two children, letting their eyes speak volumes of comments in the midst of the old lady's volubility. Unconsciously by their experiences they were being brought closer to each other.

The "rig," when it arrived at the door driven by the blushing youth, proved to be a high spring wagon with two seats. In the front seat the youth lounged without thinking of assisting his passengers. Gordon swung the baggage up and then lifted the girl into the back seat, taking the place beside her and planting a firm hand and arm behind the backless seat so she might feel more secure.

That ride, with his arm behind her, was just one more link in the pretty chain of closeness being welded about these two. Without realizing, she began to droop, until she grew very tired, and he seemed to know at once.

"Just lean against my arm," he said. "You must be tired, and it will help you bear the jolting." He spoke as if his arm were made of wood or iron and was merely one of his belongings, like an umbrella or suitcase. He made it seem natural for her to lean against him.

If he'd claimed it as her right and privilege as wife, she would have recoiled from him for recalling to her the hated relation and would have sat straight as a beanpole the rest of the way. But, as it was, she sank back a bit deprecatingly and realized it was a great help. In her heart she thanked him for enabling her to rest without entirely compromising her attitude toward him. Nothing about it suggested anything loverlike; it seemed just a common courtesy.

Yet the strong arm almost trembled as he felt the precious weight against it, and he wished the way were ten miles instead of five. Once, as Celia leaned forward to point to an especially lovely view that opened up as they wound around a curve in the road, they ran over a stone, and the wagon gave an unexpected jolt. Gordon reached his hand out to steady her, and she settled back to his arm with a pleasant sense of safety and being cared for. Looking up shyly, she saw his eyes upon her, with that deep look of admiration and something more, and again that strange thrill of joy that had come when he gave her the forget-me-nots swept through her.

She felt almost as if she were harboring a sinful thought when she remembered the letters he'd written. But the day's happiness for even a moment, when she'd been sad for so long, was so welcome that she let herself enjoy it, refusing to think evil of him now, here, in this bright day.

Thus like children on a picnic, they passed through Sugar Grove and arrived at the town of Milton. There they bade their driver good-bye, rewarding him with a crisp five-dollar bill. He drove home with a vision of smiles in forget-me-not eyes and a marked inability to tell anything about his wonderful passengers who had filled the village with awe and amazement and given no clue to anyone as to who or what they were.

Chapter 10

Meanwhile, the pursuer, in his berth, baffled and frantic and raging, with hands that fumbled because of eagerness, sought to get into his garments and find his shoes from the melée of blankets and other articles in the berth. All the time he kept one eye looking out the window. He mustn't let his prey get away from him now. He must watch and see what they'd do. How fortunate he awakened in time. At least he'd have a clue. Where was this? A station?

He stopped operations once more to gaze off at the landscape, a desolate country scene to his city-hardened eyes. Not a house in sight or a station. The distant village spires seemed like a mirage to him. This couldn't be a station. What were those two doing down there anyway? Dared he risk calling the conductor and having him hold them? No, this must be kept absolutely quiet. Mr. Holman had said that if a breath of the matter came out it was worse than death for all concerned. He must just get off this train as fast as he could and follow them if they were getting away. He might get the man in a lonely place—it would be easy enough to watch his chance and gag the lady—he'd done such things before. He felt far more at home in such an affair than he had the night before at the Holman dinner table. What a pity one of the others hadn't come along. It would be mere child's play for two to handle those two who looked as if they'd turn frightened at the first threat. But he felt confident he could manage alone.

He panted with haste and succeeded in getting the wrong legs into his trousers and having to begin all over again, his efforts greatly hampered by needing to watch out the window.

Then came the distant rumble of an oncoming train and an answering scream from his own engine. The two on the ground had crossed quickly over the second track and were looking down the steep embankment. Were they going down there? What fate that he wasn't ready to follow them at once! The train coming would pass—their own would start—and he couldn't get out. His opportunity was leaving him, and he couldn't find his shoes!

Well, what of it? He would go without! What were shoes in a time like this? Surely he could get along barefoot and beg a pair at some farmhouse or buy a pair at a country store. He must get out at any cost, shoes or no shoes. Grasping his coat which contained his money and valuables he sprang from his berth straight into the arms of the porter who was hurrying back to his car after gossiping outside with a brakeman over the delay.

"What's de mattah, sah?" asked the astonished porter, rallying quickly from the shock and assuming his habitual courtesy.

"My shoes!" roared the irate traveler. "What have you done with my shoes?"

"Quiet, sah, please, sah—you'll wake de whole cyah," said the porter. "I put yoh shoes under de berth, sah, right whar I allus puts 'em aftah blackin', sah."

The porter stooped and extracted the shoes from beneath the curtain, and the traveler, whose experience in Pullmans was small, grabbed them and made for the door, shoes in hand. With a snort and a lurch and a preliminary jar the train had taken up its motion, and a loud rushing outside proclaimed that the other train was passing.

The porter, feeling he was treated with injustice, gazed reproachfully after the man for a full minute before he followed to tell him the washroom was at the other end of the car and not down past the drawing room as he evidently supposed.

He found the man in stocking feet on the cold iron platform, his head out of the opening left in the vestibuled train, for when the porter came in he'd shut the outer door and slammed down the movable platform, making it impossible for anyone to get out. Only the little opening the size of a window was left above the grating guard, and the man clung to it as if he'd jump over it if he dared. He was looking back over the track, and his face wasn't good to see.

He turned wildly upon the porter.

"I want you to stop this train and let me off!" he shouted. "I lost something valuable back there on the track. Stop the train quick, I tell you, or I'll sue the railroad!"

"What was it you lost?" asked the porter respectfully. He wondered if the man was still half asleep.

"It was a—my—why, it was a very valuable paper. It means a fortune to me and several other people, and I must go back and get it. Stop the train at once, I tell you, or I'll jump out!"

"I can't stop the train, sah. You'll hev to see the conductah 'bout that. But I specks there's mighty little prospec' o' gettin' this train stopped foh it gits to its destinashun. We's one hour a'hind time now, sah, an' he's gotta make up foh we gits to Buff'lo."

The excited passenger railed and stormed until several sleepers were awakened and stuck curious sleepy countenances out from the curtains of their berths. But the porter was obdurate and wouldn't take any measures to stop the train or even call the conductor until the passenger promised to return quietly to his berth.

The thickset man wasn't used to obeying, but he saw he was only hindering himself and finally hurried back to his berth where he hastily parted the curtains, craning his neck to see back along the track and over the green valley growing smaller in the distance. He could just make out two specks moving on the white ribbon of the road. He felt sure he knew the direction they were taking. If he only could get off the train he could catch them, for they'd have no idea he was coming and would take no precautions. If he'd only awakened a few seconds sooner he'd be following them now.

Fully ten minutes he argued with the conductor, showing a wide incongruity between his language and his gentlemanly attire, but the conductor only promised to set him down at a water tower ten miles ahead where they had to slow up for water. He said sue or no sue he had his orders, and the thickset man didn't inspire him either to sympathy or confidence. The conductor had been many years on the road and generally knew when to stop his train and when to let it go on.

Sullenly the thickset man accepted the conductor's decision and prepared to leave the train at the water tower, his eye out for the landmarks along the way as he finished dressing.

He was in no pleasant frame of mind, having missed a good amount of his accustomed stimulants the night before and seeing little prospect of either stimulants or breakfast before him. He wasn't built for a ten-mile walk over the cinders, and his flabby muscles already ached at the prospect. But then, of course, he wouldn't have to go far before he found an automobile or some kind of conveyance to help him. He looked eagerly from the window for indications of garages or stables, but the river wound its silver way among the gray-green willow fringes, and the new grass shone a placid emerald plain with nothing more alive than a few cows grazing here and there. Not even a horse that might be borrowed without his owner's knowledge. It was a strange, forsaken spot, ten whole miles and no sign of any public livery! Off to the right and left he could see villages, but most were too far from the track to help. It began to look as if he must just foot it all the way. Now and then a small shanty or tiny dwelling whizzed by near at hand, but nothing that would relieve his situation.

It occurred to him to go into the dining car for breakfast, but even as he thought of it the conductor told him he must be ready to get off, for they didn't stop long.

He certainly looked a harmless creature, as he stood alone on the cinder elevation and surveyed the landscape. Ten miles from his quarry, alone on a stretch of endless ties and rails with a gleaming river mocking him down in the valley and a laughing sky jeering overhead. He started down the shining track with his temper a wreck, his mind in chaos, his soul at war with the world. The worst of it was that the whole fault was his for going to sleep. He began to fear he'd lost his chance. Then he set his jaw and strode ahead.

The morning sun poured down on the man on his pilgrimage and waxed hotter until noon. Trains whizzed mercilessly by and gave him no succor. Weary, faint and fiercely thirsty he came at last to the spot where he was satisfied his quarry had escaped. He could see the marks of their rough descent in the steep cinder bank and assaying the same himself came upon a shred of purple silk caught on a bramble at the foot.

Puffing and panting, bruised and footsore, he sat down at the very place where Celia had stopped to have her shoes fastened and mopped his purple brow. But triumph gleamed in his eye, and after a few moment's rest he trudged onward. That town over there should yield both conveyance and food as well as information concerning those he sought. He would catch them. They could never get away from him. He was on their track again, though hours behind. He'd get them yet, and no man should take his reward from him.

Almost spent, he came at last to the village and ate a surprisingly large dish of beef and vegetable stew at the quaint house where Celia and Gordon had breakfasted. But the old lady who served it to them was shy about talking, and though admitting a couple of people had been there that morning she was non-committal about their appearance. They might have been young and good-looking and worn feathers in their hats, and they might not. She wasn't one for noticing people's appearance if they treated her civilly and paid their bills. Would he have another cup of coffee? He would and two more pieces of pie, but he got little further information.

At the corner store where he searched for something stronger than coffee, he further pursued his investigations.

The loungers were still there. It was their only business in life, and they were diligent at it. They eyed the newcomer with relish and settled back on their various barrels and boxes to enjoy whatever entertainment might relieve their monotonous existence.

A house divided against itself cannot stand. This man's elegant garments didn't fit the rest of his general appearance, which had been accentuated by his long, hot, dusty trek. The high evening hat was jammed on the back of his head and bore a decided dent from rolling down the cinder embankment; his collar was wilted and lifeless, his coat awry, and his fine patent leather shoes, which pinched, were covered with dust. Moreover, again the speech of the man betrayed him, and the keen-minded old gossips who were eyeing him suspiciously sized him up the minute he opened his mouth.

"Saw anything of a couple of young folks walking down this way?" he inquired casually, pausing to light a cigar with which he was reinforcing himself for further travel.

One man allowed such people might have passed that day. He hardly seemed willing to commit himself. But another vouchsafed the information that "Joe here driv two parties of thet description to Milton this mornin'—jes' got back. Mebbe he could answer fer 'em."

Joe frowned. He didn't like the thickset man's looks. He still remembered the forget-me-not eyes.

But the stranger instantly asked to be driven to Milton, offering ten dollars for the same when he found the driver was reluctant and that Milton was a railroad center. A few keen questions made him sure his man had gone to Milton.

Joe haggled, allowing his horse was tired and he didn't care about the trip twice in one day, but finally agreed to take the man for fifteen dollars and sauntered off to get a fresh horse. He had no mind to be in a hurry. He had his own opinion about letting those two "parties" get out of the way before the third put in an appearance, but he didn't intend to lose fifteen dollars. It would help to buy the ring he coveted for his girl.

In due time Joe rode leisurely up, and the impatient traveler climbed into the high spring wagon and was driven away from the apathetic gaze of the country loungers. They stared unblinkingly and took in the fact that Joe was headed toward Ashville and evidently meant to take his fare to Milton by way of that village, a thirty-mile drive at least. The man would get his money's worth in the ride, or would he? A grim twinkle sat in their several eyes as the spring wagon turned the curve in the road and was lost to sight, and after due silence an old stager spoke up.

"Do you reckon that there was their shofur?" he requested languidly.

"Naw!" replied a farmer's son vigorously. "He wouldn't try to showf all dolled up like that. He's the rich dad comin' after the runaways. Joe don't intend he shell get 'em yet awhile. I reckon the ceremony'll be over 'fore he steps in to interfere." This lad went twice a month to Milton to the "movies" and was regarded as an authority on matters of romance. A pause showed that his theory had taken root in his auditors' minds.

"Wal, I reckon Joe thinks the longest way 'round is the shortest way home," declared the old stager. "Joe never did like them codfish swells—but how do you 'count fer that gal's style? She wasn't like this orn'ry un you say's her dad."

"Oh, she's ben to collidge, I 'spose," declared the youth. "They get all that off'n collidge."

"Serves the old man right fer sendin' his gal to a fool collidge when she shoulda' ben home learnin' to housekeep. I hope she gits off with her young man all right," said a grim old lounger.

A cackle of laughter went around the group, which presently broke up, for this had been a strenuous day, and all felt their need of rest. Besides they wanted to get home and tell the news before some neighbor got ahead of them.

All this time Celia and Gordon were touring Milton, serenely unconscious of danger near or of a guardian angel named Joe.

Investigation disclosed that a train was leaving for Pittsburgh about three in the afternoon. Gordon sent a code telegram to his chief, assuring him of the safety of the message and of his own intention to proceed to Washington as fast as steam could carry him. Then he took the girl to a restaurant, where they mounted two high stools and partook with an unusually ravenous appetite of nearly everything on the menu—corn soup, roast beef, baked trout, stewed tomatoes, cole slaw, custard, apple and mince pies, with a cup of good country coffee and real cream—all for twenty-five cents apiece.

It was a merry meal. Celia felt somehow as if for the time all memory of the past had been taken from her and she were free to think and act happily in the present, without any great problems to solve or decisions to make. They were just two young people off having a good time, at least until that afternoon train came.

After dinner they walked to a tiny park where two white ducks disported themselves on a seven-by-nine pond, spanned by a rustic bridge where lovers had cut their initials. Gordon took out his knife and idly cut C. H. in the rough bark of the upper rail, while his companion sat on the board seat and watched him. She was pondering the fact that he cut her initials and not his own. It would have been like the George of old to cut his own and never once think of hers. And now he put only one H. Probably he thought of her now as Celia Hayne, without the Hathaway, or else he was so used to writing her name Celia Hathaway that he wasn't thinking at all.

Those letters! How they haunted her and clouded every bright experience she grasped and tried to hold for a little while.

They were silent now, while he worked and she thought. He finished the C. H. and was cutting another C, but instead of making another H, he carefully carved out the letter G. What was that for? C. G.? Who was C. G.? Oh, how stupid! George, of course. He had started a C by mistake. But he didn't add the expected H. Instead he snapped his knife shut, laid his hand over the carving and leaned over the rail.

"Sometime, perhaps, we'll come here again and remember," he said and then realized he had no right to hope for any such anniversary.

"Oh!" She looked up into his eyes, startled, troubled, the shadow of fear in her eyes.

He looked into them and read her trouble, and his own eyes looked back his desire to comfort her.

His look carried further than he meant it should. For the third time that day a thrill of delight passed over her and left her fearful with a strange joy she felt she should put from her.

It was only an instant, that look, but it brought the bright color to both faces and made Gordon feel the need to change the subject.

"See those little fish down there," he said, pointing to the pond below them.

Through a blur of tears, the girl looked down and saw the tiny, sharp-finned creatures darting here and there in a sunbeam like a small searchlight set to show them off.

She moved her hand on the rail to lean further over, and her fingers touched his hand. She wouldn't draw them away quickly, lest she hurt him. Why, she didn't know, but she could not—would not—hurt him. Not now! The two hands lay side by side for a full minute, and the touch to Gordon was as if a rose leaf had kissed his soul. He'd never felt anything sweeter. He longed to gather the hand into his clasp and feel its pulses trembling there as he felt it in the church the night before, but she wasn't his. He might not touch her till she had her choice of what to do, and she would never choose him when she knew how he had deceived her.

That one supreme moment they had of perfect awareness of the drawing of soul to soul, of the sweetness of that hovering touch of hands, of the longing to know and understand each other.

Then a sharp whistle sounded, and a farmer's boy with a new rake and a sack of corn on his shoulder came sauntering down the road to the bridge. Instantly they drew apart, and Celia felt she'd been on the verge of disloyalty to her true self.

They walked silently back to the station, busy with their own thoughts, each conscious of that one moment when the other had come so near.

Chapter 11

A lot of people were at the station. They'd gone to a family gathering of some sort from their remarks, and they talked loudly and much. Thus the two stood apart—for the seats were all occupied—and had no opportunity for conversation, except a quiet smiling comment now and then on the chatter about them or the odd remarks they heard.

A constraint had come upon them, each withdrawing, each aware of something separating. Gordon struggled to prevent it, but he seemed helpless. Celia smiled in answer to his quiet remarks, but it was a smile of distance, such as she wore early in the morning. She'd found her former standing ground, with its fence of prejudice, and was repairing the breaks through which she'd gone over to the enemy during the day. She was bracing herself with dire reminders and snatches from those terrible letters written in fiery characters in her heart. Never could she care for a man who had done what this man had. She'd forgotten those terrible things he said of her dear dead father. How could she forget for an instant! How could she let her hand lie close to the hand that had defiled itself by writing such things!

By the time they were seated in the train, she was freezing in her attitude, and poor Gordon sat miserably beside her and tried to think how he had offended her. It wasn't his fault her hand lay near his on the rail. She put it there herself. Perhaps she expected him to put his over it, to show her he cared as a bridegroom should care—as he did, in reality, if he only had the right. And perhaps she was hurt that he stood coolly and said or did nothing. But he couldn't help it.

Much to Gordon's relief, the train carried a parlor car, and it happened this day to be almost deserted except for a deaf old man who slumbered audibly at the further end from the two chairs Gordon selected. He established his companion comfortably, disposed of the baggage and sat down, but the girl ignored him. She stared out the window, her eyes seeming to see nothing. For two hours she sat; he made occasional remarks, to which she made little or no reply, until he lapsed into silence, looking at her with troubled eyes. Finally, as they neared the Pittsburgh outskirts, he leaned forward and touched her coat-sleeve, to attract her attention.

"Have I offended—hurt—you in any way?" he asked gently. She turned toward him, and her eyes were brimming full of tears.

"No," she said, and her lips were trembling. "No, you've been—most—kind—but—I can't forget *those letters!*" She ended with a sob and raised her handkerchief to stifle it.

"Letters?" he asked helplessly. "What letters?"

"The letters you wrote me. All the letters of the last five months. I can't forget them. I can *never* forget them! How do you *think* I could?"

He looked at her anxiously, not knowing what to say, and yet he must say something. The time had come when some kind of understanding, some clearing up of facts, must take place. He must go cautiously, but he must find out what was the matter. He couldn't see her suffer so. There must be some way to let her know that as far as he was concerned she need suffer nothing further and he'd do all in his power to set her right with her world.

But letters! He wrote no letters. His face lighted up with the certainty of one thing: She still thought him the man she'd intended to marry. She wasn't therefore troubled about that phase of the question. It was strange, almost unbelievable, but he wasn't responsible for the trouble in her eyes. What trouble she might feel when she knew all, he had yet to find out, but it was a great relief to be sure of so much. Still, something must be said.

"Letters!" he repeated again stupidly. "Would you mind telling me just what was in the letters that hurt you?" he added with a perplexed tone.

She turned astonished eyes on him.

"How can you ask?" she said almost bitterly. "You surely must know how terrible they were! You couldn't be the man you've seemed today if you didn't understand what you were doing to me in making those terrible threats. You must know how cruel they were."

"I'm afraid I don't understand," he said earnestly, the trouble still apparent in his eyes. "Would you mind being a little more explicit? Would you mind telling me exactly what you think I wrote you that sounded like a threat?"

He asked the question half hesitatingly, because he wasn't sure whether he was justified in thus obtaining private information under false pretenses. Yet he felt he must know what troubled her or he could never help her. He was sure if she knew he was an utter stranger, even a kind one, those gentle lips would never open to inform him upon her torturer. As it was she could tell him her trouble with a perfectly clear conscience, thinking she was telling it to the man who knew all about it. But his hesitation about prying into a stranger's private affairs, even with a good motive, gave him an air of troubled dignity and anxiety to know his fault that puzzled the girl more than all that had gone before.

"I can't understand how you can ask such a question, since it's been the constant subject of discussion in all our letters!" she replied, sitting up with asperity and drying her tears. She was on the verge of growing angry with him for his petty, willful misunderstanding of words whose meaning she felt he must know well.

"I do ask it," he said quietly, "and, believe me, I have a good motive in doing so."

She looked at him in surprise. It was impossible to be angry with those kind eyes, even though he persisted in willful stupidity.

"Well, then, since you wish it stated once more I'll tell you," she declared, the tears welling again into her eyes. "You first demanded I marry you—demanded—without any pretense whatever of caring for me—with a hidden threat in your demand that if I did not, you'd bring some dire calamity upon me by means already in your power. You took me for the same foolish girl you teased for years before you went abroad to live. And when I refused, you told me not only could you take from my mother all the property she inherited from her brother, by a will made just before my uncle's death and unknown except to his lawyer and you, but you could and would blacken my dear dead father's name and honor and show that every cent belonging to Mother and Jefferson and me was stolen property.

"When I challenged you to prove any such thing against my honored father, you threatened to bring out a terrible story and prove it with witnesses who would swear to anything you said. You knew my father's life—you as much as admitted your charges were false—and yet you dared send me a letter from a vile creature who pretended she was his first wife and said she could prove he'd spent much time in her company. You knew the whole thing was a falsehood, but you threatened to publicize this through the newspapers if I didn't marry you. You realized I knew that, even though few people and no friends would believe that of my father, such a report in the papers—false though it was—would crush my mother to death. You knew I'd give my life to save her, and so you had me in your power, as you have me now. You've always wanted me in your power, just because you love to torture, and now you have me. But you can't make me forget what you've done. I've given my life, but I cannot give anymore. If it isn't sufficient, you'll have to do your worst."

She dropped her face into the wet handkerchief, and Gordon sat with pale, drawn countenance and clenched hands. He was trembling with indignation toward the villain who had thus imposed upon this delicate flower of womanhood. He longed to search the world over for the false bridegroom and, finding him, give him his just dues.

And what should he do or say? Tell her at once who he was and trust to her kind heart to forgive his terrible blunder and keep his secret till the message was safely delivered? Had he any right? No, the secret wasn't his to divulge either for his own benefit or for any other's. He must keep that to himself. But he must help her in some way.

At last he spoke, scarcely knowing what to say: "It is *terrible* what you've told me. To have written such things to one like you—in fact, to anyone on earth—seems unforgivable. It's the most inhuman cruelty I've ever heard of. You're fully justified in hating and despising the man who wrote such words to you."

"Then why did you write them?" she burst forth. "And how can you sit there calmly and talk that way about it, as if you had nothing to do with the matter?"

"Because I never wrote those letters," he said, looking her steadily, earnestly, in the eyes.

"You never wrote them!" she exclaimed. "You deny it?"

"I deny it." His voice was quiet, earnest, convincing.

She looked at him dazed, bewildered, indignant, sorrowful. "But you can't deny it," she said, her fragile frame trembling with excitement. "I have the letters in my suitcase. You cannot deny your own handwriting. I have the last awful one—the one in which you threatened Father's good name—here in my handbag. I dared not put it with the rest, and I had no opportunity to destroy it before leaving home. I felt as if I must always keep it with me, lest its awful secret got out. There it is. Read it and see your own name signed to the words you say you did not write!"

While she talked, her trembling fingers had taken a folded, crumpled letter from her little handbag, and this she reached over and laid on the arm of his chair.

"Read it," she said. "Read it and see that you can't deny it."

"I'd rather not read it," he said. "I don't need to read it to deny I ever wrote such things to you."

"But I insist you read it," said the girl.

"If you insist, I'll read it," he said, taking the letter reluctantly and opening it.

She watched him furtively through the tears while he read, saw the angry flush steal into his cheeks as the villainy of a fellow man was revealed to him through the brief, coarse, cruel epistle and mistook the flush for one of shame.

Then his true brown eyes looked up and met her tearful gaze steadily, a fine anger burning in them.

"And you think I wrote that!" he said, with something in his voice she couldn't understand.

"What else could I think? It bears your signature," she answered coldly.

"The letter is vile," he said, "and the man who wrote it is a blackguard and deserves the utmost the law allows for such offenses. With your permission I'll make it my business to see he gets it."

"What do you mean?" she said wide-eyed. "How could you punish yourself? You can't still deny you wrote the letter."

"I still deny I wrote it or ever saw it until you handed it to me just now."

The girl looked at him, nonplussed, more than half convinced, in spite of reason.

"But isn't that your handwriting?"

"It isn't. Look!"

He took out his fountain pen and, holding the letter on the arm of her chair, wrote rapidly in his natural hand her own name and address beneath the address on the envelope, then held it up to her.

"Do they look alike?"

The two writings were as unlike as possible, the letter being addressed in an almost unreadable scrawl and the fresh writing standing fine and clear. Even a child could see at a glance that the two weren't written by the same hand—and yet, of course, it might have been practiced to deceive. This thought flashed through both their minds even as he held it out for her to look.

She looked from the envelope to his eyes and back to the letter, startled, not knowing what to think.

But before either of them had time for another word the conductor, the porter and several people from the car behind hurried through. They realized that while they talked the train had stopped, amid the blazing electric lights of a great city station.

"Why," said Gordon, startled, "we must have reached Pittsburgh. Is this Pittsburgh?" he called out to the vanishing porter.

"Yas, sah!" yelled the porter, putting his head around the curve of the passageway. "You bettah hurry, sah, foh this train goes on to Cincinnati pretty quick. We's late gittin' in, you see."

Neither of them noticed a man in rough clothes with slouched hat and hands in his pockets who boarded the train a few miles back and walked through the car several times eyeing them. He stuck his head in at the door now and drew back quickly out of sight.

Gordon gathered up the baggage, and they went out of the car, while the porter rushed back as they reached the door to assist them and get a last tip. They had no opportunity to say anything more, as they mingled with the crowd. The man with the slouched hat followed and stood unobtrusively behind them.

Gordon looked down at the girl's pale, drawn face, and his heart was touched with compassion for her trouble. He must make some satisfactory explanation at once that would set her heart at rest, but he couldn't do it here, for every seat about them was filled with noisy, chattering folk.

He stooped and whispered low and tenderly: "Don't worry, little girl! Just try to trust me, and I'll explain it all."

"Can you explain it?" she asked anxiously, as if catching at a rope thrown out to save her life.

"Perfectly," he said, "if you'll be patient and trust me. But we can't talk here. Just wait in this seat until I see if I can get a stateroom on the sleeper."

He left her with his courteous bow, and she watched his tall figure as he threaded his way among the crowds to the Pullman window, her heart filled with mingling emotions. In spite of her reason, a tiny bit of hope for the future was springing up in her heart, and without her will she found herself inclined to trust him. At least it was all she could do at present.

Chapter 12

Back at Milton an hour before, when the shades of dusk were falling and a slender moon hung timidly on the horizon's edge, a horse drawing a spring wagon ambled deliberately into town and came to a reluctant halt beside the railroad station, having made a wide detour through the larger part of the county on the way to that metropolis.

The sun was hot, and the road was rough. The jolts over stones and bumps hadn't added to the comfort of the thickset man, already bruised and weary from his travels. Joe's conversation hadn't ceased. He'd given his guest a wide range of topics, discoursing on the buckwheat crop and the blight that might assail the cherry trees. He pointed out certain portions of land infested with rattlesnakes and told blood-curdling stories of experiences with stray bears and wildcats in a maple grove they passed through. The passenger looked furtively behind him and urged the driver on.

Joe, seeing his gullibility, only made his stories of country life bigger, for the thickset man, bold as a lion in his own city haunts, was a coward in unknown country.

When the traveler, looking at his watch, urged Joe to make haste and asked how many miles further Milton was, Joe managed for the horse to stumble on a stony bit of road. Then climbing down from the wagon he examined the horse's feet each in turn, shaking his head over the left fore foot.

"Jes' 'z I 'sposed," he meditated. "Stone bruise! Lame horse! Don't believe I should go on. Sorry, but it'll be the horse's ruination. You ain't in a hurry, I hope."

The passenger in great excitement promised to double the fare if the young man would get another horse and hurry him forward. After great professions of doubt Joe gave in and said he'd try the horse, but it wouldn't do to work him hard. They'd have to let him take his time. He couldn't on any account leave the horse behind anywhere and get a fresh one because it belonged to his best friend and he promised to bring it back safe and sound. They'd just take their time and go slow and see if the horse could stand it. He wouldn't think of trying if it weren't for needing the extra money.

So the impatient traveler was dragged fuming along weary hour after weary hour, through the monotonous glory of a spring afternoon of which he saw nothing but road dust as he tried to count the endless miles. Every mile or two Joe descended from the wagon seat and fussed around the leg of the horse, who undisturbed by such attention, dozed cozily by the roadside during this process. And so was the traveler brought to his destination ten minutes after the last train stopping at Milton that night had passed the station.

The telegraph office wasn't closed, however. Without waiting to haggle, the passenger paid his thirty dollars for the longest journey he ever took and disappeared into the station.

Meanwhile, Joe, whipping up his petted animal and whistling cheerily,

Where did you get that girl—

rattled home down the shortcut from Milton at a surprising pace for a lame horse. He was eating his supper at home in little more than an hour, and the horse seemed to have miraculously recovered from his stone bruise. Joe was wondering how his girl would look in a hat with plumes like the blue-eyed lady's and thinking of his thirty dollars with a chuckle.

It was surprising how much that thickset man, weary and desperate though he was, could accomplish, when once he reached the telegraph station and sent his messages flying on their way. In less than three minutes after his arrival he extracted from the station agent the fact that two people, man and woman, answering the description he gave, bought tickets for Pittsburgh and took the afternoon train for that city. The agent noticed them because they looked as if they came from the city. He especially noticed the plumes, the like of which he'd never seen before. He'd taken every minute he could get off from selling tickets and sending telegrams to watch the lady through his little window. They didn't wear hats like that in Milton.

In ten minutes the thickset man had one message on its way to a Pittsburgh crony he kept in constant touch with for just such occasions as this, stirring him to strenuous action. Another message was winging its mysterious way to Mr. Holman, giving him the main facts in the case. A third message caught another crony thirty miles north of Pittsburgh and ordered him to board the evening express at his own station, hunt up the parties described and shadow them to their destination, if possible getting in touch with the Pittsburgh crony when he reached the city.

The pursuer then ate a ham sandwich with liberal washings of liquid fire while he awaited replies to some of his messages. When he was satisfied he'd set justice in motion, he hired an automobile and started across country to catch a midnight express to Pittsburgh. He'd given orders that his man and accompanying lady should be held in Pittsburgh until his arrival. He had no doubt the orders would be carried out, so sure was he of being on the right track and that his cronies would be able and willing to follow his orders.

When the young travelers reached Pittsburgh, an excursion was going on, and the place was crowded. The trainmen kept calling off specials, and crowds hurried out of the waiting room, only to be replaced by other crowds, all eager, pushing, talking, laughing. They were mostly men, but a good many women and some children seemed to be of the number. The noise and excitement worried Celia after her own exciting afternoon. She longed to lie down and sleep, but the seat was narrow and hard, and people were pressing on every side. That disagreeable man in the slouched hat stood too near. He was repulsive looking, though he didn't seem aware of her presence.

Gordon had a long wait before he finally secured the coveted stateroom and started back to her, when suddenly a familiar face loomed up in the crowd and startled him. It was the face of a private detective well known about Washington but headquartered in New York.

It hadn't occurred to him to fear watchers so far south and west as Pittsburgh. The other bridegroom wouldn't think to track him here. As for the Holman contingent, they wouldn't likely make a public disturbance about his disappearance, lest a connection be found between them and the first theft of government property. They could have watchers only through private means, and they must have been wily indeed if they anticipated his move through Pittsburgh to Washington. Still, it was the natural move for him to make to get home as quickly as possible and escape them. And this man in the crowd was the one they'd have likely picked for their work. He was as slippery in his dealings as they must be and no doubt in league with them. He knew the man and his ways and didn't intend to fall into his hands.

Whether he was seen by the detective yet or not, he couldn't tell, but he suspected he had been by the way the man avoided recognizing him. Not an instant could be lost! The stateroom must go untenanted. He must make a dash for liberty. Liberty! Ah, East Liberty! What odd things our brains are! He knew Pittsburgh a little. He remembered catching a train at East Liberty Station once when he had no time to come down to the station to take it. Perhaps he might get the same train at East Liberty. It was nearly two hours before it left.

Swooping down on the baggage, he murmured in the girl's ear: "Can you hurry a little? We must catch a car right away."

She followed him closely through the crowd. He was stooping as if to look down at his suitcase, so his height might not attract the man's attention. In a moment more they were out in the lighted blackness of the streets. One glance backward showed his supposed enemy stretching his neck above the crowd, as if searching for someone, as he hurried toward the doorway they'd just passed. Behind them shadowed the man in the slouched hat and with a curious motion of his hand signalled another like him, the Pittsburgh crony, who skulked in the darkness outside. Instantly this man gave another signal, and out of the street's gloom a carriage drew up at the curb before the door, the cabman looking eagerly for patronage.

Gordon put both suitcases in one hand and, taking Celia's arm as gently as he could in his haste, hurried her toward the carriage. It was the very refuge he sought. He placed her inside and gave the order for East Liberty Station, drawing a long breath of relief at being safely out of the station. He didn't see the shabby one who mounted the box beside the driver and gave his directions in guttural whispers, or the man with the slouched hat who watched from the doorway and followed them on the nearest car. He only felt how good it was to be by themselves once more where they could talk without interruption.

But conversation wasn't easy under the circumstances. The noise of wagons, trains and cars was so great at the station that they could think of nothing but the din. When they'd threaded their way out of the tangle and started rattling over the pavement, the driver went at such a furious pace they could still only converse by shouting. It seemed strange that any cabman should drive at such a rapid rate within the city limits, but as Gordon was anxious to get away from the station and the keen-eyed detective as fast as possible he thought nothing of it at first. After a shouted word or two they ceased to talk, and Gordon, half shyly, reached out a reassuring hand and laid it on the girl's shrinking one in her lap. He'd meant to keep it there only a second, to make her understand all was well and he could soon explain things. But since she didn't seem to resent it or draw her own away, he yielded to the temptation and kept the small gloved hand in his.

The carriage rattled on over rough places, around corners, tilting now and then sideways, and Celia, half frightened, was forced to cling to her protector to keep from being thrown on the floor of the cab.

"Oh, are we running away?" she breathed into his ear.

"I think not—dear," he answered back, the last word inaudible. "The driver thinks we're in a hurry, but he didn't need to go at this furious pace. I'll tell him."

He leaned forward and tapped on the glass, but the driver paid no attention except to drive faster. Could he have lost control of his horse, or hadn't he heard? Gordon tried again and accompanied the knocking with a shout, but to no avail. The cab rattled steadily on.

Gordon discovered two men on the box instead of one, and a sudden premonition sent a thrill of alarm through him. What if that detective's presence had been a warning, and he unheeding walked into a trap? What a fool he was to get into a carriage where he was at the driver's mercy. He should have stayed in open places where kidnapping was impossible. Now that he thought of it he felt convinced this was what the enemy would try to do—kidnap him. The more fruitless he found his efforts to make the driver hear him, the more he felt convinced something was wrong. He tried to open the door next to him and found it stuck. He put all his strength forth to turn the catch, but it held fast.

Then a cold sweat broke out on him, and horror filled his mind. His commission with its large significance to the country was in imminent jeopardy. His own life was probably hanging in the balance, but most of all he felt the awful peril of the girl by his side. What terrible experiences might be hers within the next hour if his brain and right arm couldn't protect her. Instinctively his hand went to the pocket where he'd kept his revolver ready since leaving Washington. Danger shouldn't find him utterly unprepared.

He realized, too, that his alarms could be unfounded, that the driver was really taking them to the East Liberty station and the door merely stuck. He must keep a steady head and not let his companion see he was nervous. The first thing was to find out where they were, but that was difficult. The street they rattled over was dark with the gloom of a smoky city added to the night. The only streetlights were at wide intervals, and the buildings appeared to be blank walls of darkness, probably warehouses. The way was narrow and entirely unknown. Gordon couldn't tell if he'd ever been there. He was sure from his knowledge of the stations they'd gone much farther than East Liberty, and the darkness and loneliness of the region they were passing through filled him again with vague alarm.

It occurred to him he might get the window sash down and speak to the driver, and he struggled with the one on his own side for awhile, with little result, for it seemed plugged up with paper wads all around. This fact renewed his anxiety. There appeared to be intention in sealing up that carriage. He leaned over and felt around the opposite door's sash and found paper wads there also. There certainly was intention. Not to alarm Celia he straightened back and worked again at his own window sash, cautiously pulling out the paper until at last he could let down the glass.

A rush of dank air rewarded his efforts, and the girl drew a breath of relief. Gordon never knew how near she'd been to fainting at that moment. She was sitting perfectly quiet in her corner watching him, her fears kept to herself, though her heart was beating wildly. She was convinced the horse was running away.

Gordon leaned his head out of the window, but immediately he caught the gleam of a revolver in a hand that hung at the side of the driver's box, pointed downward straight toward his face, as if ready in case of need. The hand's owner wasn't looking toward him but was talking in muffled tones to the driver. They evidently hadn't heard the window let down but were ready for the first sign of an attempt by their victims to escape.

Quietly Gordon drew in his head and speculated on wrenching that revolver out of its owner's hand. He could do it from where he sat, but would it be wise? They were probably locked in a trap, and the driver was likely armed also. What chance would he have to save Celia if he brought on a desperate fight? If he were alone he might knock that revolver out of the man's hand and spring from the window, taking his chance of getting away, but now he had Celia to think of. Not for a universe of governments could he leave a woman in such desperate straits. She must be considered first, even ahead of the message. This was life and death.

He wondered at his own coolness as he sat back in the carriage and quietly lifted the glass frame back into place. Then he laid a steady hand on Celia's again and stooping close whispered into her ear.

"I'm afraid something's wrong with our driver. Can you be a little brave—dear?" He didn't know he'd used the last word this time, but Celia knew and felt her heart thrill to trust him.

"Oh, yes," she breathed close to his face. "You don't think he's been drinking, do you?"

"Well, perhaps," said Gordon, relieved at the explanation. "But keep calm. I think we can get out of this all right. Suppose you change seats with me and let me see if that door will open easily. We might want to get out in a hurry in case he slows up somewhere soon."

Celia slipped into Gordon's seat, and he applied himself with all his strength and ingenuity, gently manipulating the latch and pressing his shoulder against the door. At last it gave way and swung open. He'd worked carefully; otherwise, the sudden giving of the latch would have thrown him out of the carriage and alarmed the driver. He was thoroughly convinced by this time that he was being kidnapped, perhaps to be murdered, and every sense was alert. It was his characteristic to be exceedingly cool during a crisis. It was this quality the chief had valued most in him and the final reason why he was selected for this difficult task instead of an older, more experienced man who at times lost his head.

With the door to the outside world open Gordon surveyed the enemy from that side. He saw no gleaming weapon here. The man sat grimly enough, laying on the whip and muttering curses to his bony horse who galloped recklessly on as if partaking of his master's desperate desires. In the distance Gordon could hear the rumbling of an oncoming train. The street was still dark with scarcely a vehicle or person to be seen. There seemed no help at hand and no opportunity to get out, for they were still rushing at a tremendous pace. An attempt to jump now would likely result in broken limbs, leaving them in a worse plight. He slipped back to his own seat and put Celia next to the free door again. She must be where she could get out first if the opportunity presented itself. Also, he must throw out the suitcases if possible because of the letters and valuables they contained.

Instinctively his hand sought Celia's in the darkness again, and hers nestled into it in a frightened way as if his strength gave her comfort.

Then, before they could speak, there came the rushing sound of a train almost upon them, and the cab halted with a jerk, the driver pulling the horse far back on his haunches to stop him. The shock almost threw Celia to the floor, but Gordon's arm steadied her, and instantly he was on the alert.

Chapter 13

Glancing through the window he saw they were in front of a railroad track on which a long freight train was rushing madly along at a giddy pace. The driver had evidently hoped to pass this point before the train got there but failed. The train had an exultant sound as if it knew and had outwitted the driver.

On one side of the street were high buildings and on the other a great lumberyard, between which and their carriage stood a team of horses hitched to a covered wagon, from the back of which some boards protruded. This was on the side next to Celia where the door would open! Gordon's heart leaped up with hope and wonder over the miracle of their opportunity. The best thing about their situation was that their driver stopped in back of the covered wagon, so their door would open to the street directly behind the wagon. It enabled them to slip across without getting too near the driver. Nothing could have been better arranged for their escape, and the clatter of the empty freight cars drowned all sounds.

Without delay Gordon softly unlatched the door and swung it open whispering to Celia: "Go! Quick! Over there by the fence in the shadow. Don't look around or speak! Quick! I'll come!"

Trembling in every limb yet with brave eyes, Celia slipped like a wraith from the carriage, stole behind the boards and melted into the shadow of the lumberyard's fence. Grasping the suitcases, Gordon moved instantly after her, silently closing the carriage door and dropping into the shadows behind the big wagon, scarcely able to believe they'd escaped.

Ten feet back along the sidewalk was a gateway with tall, thick posts. The gate itself was closed, but it hung a few inches inside the fence line. Into this depression the two stepped softly and stood, flattening themselves back against the gate as closely as possible, scarcely daring to breathe, while the long freight clattered and rambled on its way.

Gordon saw the driver look down at the window below him and glance back hastily over his shoulder, and the man on the other side of the box looked down on his side. The glitter of something in his hand shone for an instant in the signal light glare over the track. Then the horse lurched forward, and the cab began its crazy gait over the track and up the cobbled street. They'd started onward without getting down to look in the carriage and see if all was safe with their prisoners, and they didn't even look back to see if they'd escaped. They evidently trusted in their means to lock the carriage doors and heard no sounds of their escaping. It was incredible but true.

Gordon drew a long breath of relief and relaxed from his strained position. The next thing was to get out of that neighborhood as swiftly as possible before those men discovered their birds had flown. They would of course know at once where their departure had taken place and return to search for them, with perhaps more men to help. A second escape would be impossible.

Gordon snatched up the suitcases with one hand and with the other drew Celia's arm within his.

"Now we must hurry with all our might," he said softly. "Are you all right?"

"Yes." Her breath was coming in a sob, but her eyes were shining bravely.

"Poor child!" His voice was tender. "Were you much frightened?"

"A little," she answered more bravely now.

"I'll have hard work to forgive myself for all this," he said. "But we mustn't talk. We have to get out of this quickly, or they may come back after us. Lean on me and walk as fast as you can."

Celia bent her efforts to take long, springing strides, and together they fairly skimmed the pavements, turning first this corner, then that, in the general direction from which Gordon thought they'd come. At last, three blocks away they caught the welcome whirr of a trolley and, breathless, flew onward, just catching a car. They didn't care where it went as long as they were safe in a bright light with other people. The trolley conductor rang up their fares and answered Gordon's questions about how to get to East Liberty station, and the two sighed in unison as they found a seat.

Gordon watched her lovingly, glad she didn't know how terrible her danger had been. His heart was still beating wildly at their marvelous escape and his own present responsibility. He must run no further risks. They would keep to crowded trolleys and trust to hiding in the open. The main thing was to get out of the city on the first train they could board.

When they reached East Liberty station a long train was just coming in, all sleepers, and they could hear the echo of a stentorian voice: "Special for Harrisburg, Baltimore and Washington! All aboard!" At the further end of the platform Gordon saw the lank form of the detective he'd tried to avoid an hour before at the other station.

Without thinking he hurried Celia forward, and they sprang aboard. Not until they were fairly in the cars and the wheels moving under them did it occur to him that his companion had had nothing to eat since about twelve o'clock. She must be famished and could become ill again. What a fool he was not to have thought! They could have stopped in some obscure restaurant along the way and taken a later train, and yet it was safer to get away at once. Without doubt watchers were at East Liberty, too, and he was lucky to be on the train without a challenge; he was sure the detective's face lighted strangely as he looked his way. A buffet might be attached to the train. At least he'd investigate. If not, they must get off at the next stop—there must surely be another stop near the city.

They had to wait some time to get the conductor's attention. He was having trouble with some disgruntled passengers who each claimed to have the same berth. Gordon finally got his ear and showing his stateroom tickets asked if they could be used on this train.

"No," growled the worried conductor. "You're on the wrong train. This is a special, and every berth in the train is taken now but one upper."

"Then we'll have to get off at the next stop, I suppose, and take the other train," said Gordon dismally.

"There isn't another stop till somewhere in the middle of the night. I tell you this is a special, and we're scheduled to go straight through. East Liberty's the last stop."

"Then what shall we do?" asked Gordon inanely.

"I'm sure I don't know," snapped the conductor. "I've enough to do without mending other people's mistakes. Stay aboard, I suppose, unless you want to jump off and commit suicide."

"But I have a lady with me who isn't at all well," said Gordon with dignity.

"So much the worse for the lady," replied the conductor. "I told you there's one upper berth."

"An upper berth wouldn't do for her," said Gordon. "She isn't well."

"Suit yourself!" snapped the official. "I reckon it's better than nothing. You may not have it long. I'm likely to be asked for it the next half minute."

"Is that so? And is there absolutely nothing else?"

"Young man, I can't waste words on you. I haven't time. Take it or let it alone. It's all one to me. There's maybe some standing room left in the day coach."

"I'll take it," said Gordon meekly, wishing he could go back and undo the last half hour. How was he to tell Celia he could provide her nothing better than an upper berth?

She was sitting with her back to him, her face resting wearily on her hand against the window. Two men with checked suits, big seal rings and diamond scarfpins sat in the opposite seat. He knew it was unpleasant for her. A nondescript woman with a large hat and thick powder on her face shared Celia's seat. He reflected that "specials" didn't always bear a select company.

"Is there nothing you can do?" he pleaded with the conductor, as he took the bit of pasteboard entitling him to the last vacant berth. "Don't you suppose you could get some man to change and give her a lower berth? It'll be hard for her. She isn't used to upper berths."

His eyes rested wistfully on the bowed head. Celia had taken off her hat, and the fitful light of the car played with the burnished flecks in her hair. The conductor's grim eye softened as he looked.

"That the lady? I'll see what I can do," he said briefly and stumped off to the next car.

Gordon went over to Celia and told her quietly that he hoped to have arrangements for her soon, so she could be comfortable. She must be fearfully tired with the excitement and fright and hurry. He added that he'd blundered in getting on this train, and now there might not be a chance to get off for several hours and probably no supper to be had.

"Oh, it doesn't matter in the least," said Celia wearily. "I'm not at all hungry."

What she wanted was to have her mind relieved about the letters, but she saw there was no opportunity now. She even seemed sorry at his troubled look and tried to smile through the settled sadness in her eyes.

He could see she was weary, and he felt like a great brute in care of a child and mentally berated himself for his thoughtlessness.

Gordon started off in search of food for her and was more successful than he'd hoped. The newsboy had two chicken sandwiches left, and these, with some oranges and ice water, Gordon presently brought to her and was rewarded by a smile this time, almost as warm as those she'd given him during their beautiful day.

But he couldn't sit beside her, for the places were all taken, and he couldn't stand in the aisle and talk, for the porter was constantly running back and forth making up the berths. The whole train seemed congested; every seat was full, with men standing in the aisles. He noticed they all wore badges of some fraternal order—doubtless a delegation to some convention, upon which they'd intruded. They were a good-natured, noisy, happy crowd, but not anywhere among them was to be found a quiet spot where he and Celia could continue their suddenly interrupted conversation.

Presently the conductor came to him and said he had found a gentleman who would give the lady his lower berth and take her upper one. It was already made up, and the lady might take possession at once.

Gordon exchanged the tickets and immediately escorted Celia to it. He found her glad to go, for she was now quite weary and longed to get away from the light and noise about her.

He led the way with the suitcases, hoping that in the other car there would be some spot where they could talk for a few minutes. But he was disappointed. It was even fuller than the first car. He arranged everything for her comfort as far as possible, disposed of her hat and fixed her suitcase so she could open it. Even then people were crowding by, and private conversation was impossible. He stepped back when all was arranged and held the curtain aside so she might sit on the edge of her berth.

Then stooping over he whispered, "Try to trust me until morning. I'll explain it all to you then, so that you'll understand how I've had nothing to do with those letters. Forget it and try to rest. Will you?"

His tone was wistful. He'd never wanted to do anything so much as to stoop and kiss those sweet lips and the lovely eyes that looked up at him out of the dusky shadows of the berth. They looked more than ever like the blue tired flowers that drooped from her dress. But he held himself with a firm hand. She wasn't his to kiss. When she knew how he deceived her, she'd probably never give him the right to kiss her.

"I'll try," she murmured in answer to his question and then added, "but where will you be? Is your berth nearby?"

"Not far away—that is, I had to take a place in another car; they're so crowded."

"Oh!" she said a little anxiously. "Are you sure you have a good comfortable place?"

"Oh, yes, I'll be all right," he answered. It was wonderful to have her care whether he was comfortable or not.

The porter was making up the opposite berth, and there was no room to stand longer, so he bade her good night. She extended her hand for a farewell. For an instant he held it close, with gentle pressure, as if to reassure her. Then he went to the day coach and settled down into a hard corner at the back of the car, drawing his cap over his eyes and letting his heart beat wildly over that touch of her dear hand. Wave after wave of sweetness thrilled his soul with a joy he'd never known before.

And this was love! What kind of wretch was he, presuming to love like this a woman who was the promised bride of another man! Ah, but such a man! A villain! A brute, who had used his power over her to make her suffer tortures! Had a man like that a right to claim her? His whole being answered no.

Then the memory of the look in her eyes would thrill his heart anew, and he would forget the wretch who stood between him and this lovely girl he knew now he loved as he'd never dreamed a man could love.

Gradually his mind steadied itself under the sweet intoxication, and he wondered what he should say to her in the morning. It was good he hadn't had further opportunity to talk with her that night, for he couldn't have told her everything. Now if all went well they'd be in Washington in the morning, and he might make some excuse till after he'd delivered his message. Then he could tell the whole story and lay his case before her for decision. His heart throbbed at the thought of her forgiving him, and yet it seemed most unlikely. Sometimes he let his wild longings imagine how it would be if she could be induced to let the marriage stand. But he told himself at the same time that it could never be. Likely there was someone else in New York her heart would turn to if she were free from the scoundrel who had threatened her into a compulsory marriage. He would promise to help and protect her from the man who was evidently using blackmail to get her into his power, probably to control her property. At least it would be some comfort to help her out of her trouble. Yet would she ever trust a man who had even unwittingly let her be bound by the sacred tie of marriage to a stranger?

And thus, amid hope and fear, the night whirled itself away. Forward in the sleeper the girl lay wide awake for a long time. In the middle of the night a thought suddenly evolved itself out of the blackness of her curtained berth. She sat upright alertly and stared into the darkness, as if it were something she could catch and handle and examine. The thought was born out of a dreamy vision of the crisp brown waves, almost curls if they hadn't been so short and thick, covering the head of the man who had lain sleeping outside her curtains the previous morning. It came to her with sudden force that it wasn't at all like the hair of the boy George Hayne, who used to trouble her girlish days. His was thin and black and oily, collecting naturally into isolated strings and giving him the appearance of a kitten who had been out in the rain. One lock—how well she remembered that lock!—on the crown of his head had always refused to lie down, no matter how much persuasion was brought to bear upon it. It was the one point on which the self-satisfied George was pregnable, that lock that would always rise stiffly, oilily, from the top of his head. The hair she admired that other morning in the rising sun's dawning crimson hadn't been that way. It had clung to the shape of the fine head as if it loved to go that way. It was beautiful and fine with a sense of life and vigor in its every wave. Could hair change in ten years? Could it grow brown where it had been black? Could it glow without being oily? Could it take on the signs of natural wave where it had been as straight as a die? Could it grow like fur where it had been so thin?

The girl couldn't solve the problem, but the thought was startling and brought with it many suggestive, disturbing possibilities. Yet gradually out of the darkness she drew a sort of comfort in her dawning enlightenment. Two things she had to go on in her strange premises: He said he didn't write the letters, and his hair wasn't the same. Who then was he? Her husband now undoubtedly, but who? And if deeds and hair could change so materially, why not spirits? At least he wasn't the same she had feared and dreaded. There was so much comfort.

And at last she lay down and slept.

Chapter 14

They were late coming into Washington, for the special had been side-tracked in the night for several express trains, and the noisy crowd that kept one another awake till after midnight made up by sleeping into the morning.

Three times Gordon journeyed three cars forward to see if his companion of yesterday was awake and needed anything. But each time he found the curtains drawn and still, and each time he went slowly back to his seat in the crowded day coach.

Not until the white dome of the Capitol and the tall needle of the monument were painted soft and vision-like against the sky, reminding one of pictures of the heavenly city in the story of *Pilgrim's Progress*, did he seek her again and find her fully ready, standing in the aisle while the porter put up the berth. Beneath the brim of her hat she lifted her eyes to him, as if she were both glad and frightened to see him. And then that ecstasy shot through him again, as he realized suddenly what it would be to have her for his life companion, to feel her glad looks were all for him and have the right to remove all fright from her.

They could only smile at each other for good morning, for everybody was standing up and being brushed, pushing here and there for suitcases and lost umbrellas, and talking loudly about how late the train was. Then at last they were there and could get out and walk silently side by side in the noisy procession through the station to the sidewalk.

What little things sometimes change a lifetime and make for our safety or our destruction! That very morning three keen watchers were set to guard that Washington station to hunt out the government spy who had stolen back the stolen message and take him, message and all, dead or alive, back to New York. The man who could testify against the Holman combination was not to be allowed to live if getting him out of the way was possible. But they never thought to watch the special which was supposed to carry only delegates to the great convention. He couldn't be on that! They knew he was coming from Pittsburgh, for they were so advised by telegram the evening before by one of their company who saw him buying a sleeper ticket for Washington. But they felt safe about that special, for they inquired and were told no one but delegates could come on it. They did their work thoroughly and were on hand with every possible plan perfected for bagging their game. But they took the time when the Pittsburgh Special was expected to arrive for eating a hearty breakfast in the restaurant across the street from the station. Two of them emerged from the restaurant doorway in time to meet the next Pittsburgh train, just as Gordon, having placed the lady in a closed carriage, was getting in himself.

If the carriage had stood in any other spot along the pavement in front of the station, they never would have seen him, but, as it was, they had a full view of him. Because they were Washington men and experts in their line, they recognized him at once and knew their plans had failed. Only by extreme measures could they hope to prevent the delivery of the message which would mean downfall and disaster to them and their schemes.

As Gordon shut the carriage door, he caught a vision of his two enemies pointing excitedly toward him, and he knew the bloodhounds were on the scent.

His heart beat wildly. His anxiety was divided between the message and the lady. What should he do? Drive at once to his chief's home and deliver the message, or leave the girl at his rooms, phone for a faster conveyance and trust to getting to his chief ahead of his pursuers?

"Don't let anything hinder you! Don't let anything hinder you! Make it a matter of life and death!" rang the words in his ears, and now it seemed as if he must go straight ahead with the message. And yet—"a matter of life and death!" He must not take the lady with him into danger. If he must be in danger of death he didn't want to die having exposed an innocent stranger to the same.

Then another point needed to be considered.

He'd already told the driver to take him to his apartments as rapidly as possible. It wouldn't do to stop him now and change directions, for a pistol shot could easily reach him. And, coming from a crowd, who would be suspected? His enemies were standing on the threshold of a place where they had many of their kind to protect them, and none of his friends knew of his coming. It would be a race for life from now to the finish.

Celia was looking out with interest at the streets, recognizing landmarks with wonder, and didn't notice Gordon's set face and burning eyes as he strained his vision to note how fast the horse was going. Oh, if the driver would only turn off at the next corner into the side street they couldn't watch the carriage so far, but it wasn't likely, for this was the most direct road, and yet— yes, he turned! Joy! The street here was so crowded he'd sought the narrower, less crowded way so he might go faster.

It seemed an age to him before they stopped at his apartments. To Celia, it was a short ride, in which familiar scenes had brought her pleasure, for she recognized she wasn't in strange Chicago, but in Washington, a city often visited. Somehow she felt it was an omen of a better future than she'd feared.

"Oh, why didn't you tell me?" she smiled to Gordon. "It's Washington, dear old Washington."

Somehow he controlled the tumult in his heart and smiled back, saying in a natural voice, "I'm so glad you like it."

She seemed to understand they couldn't talk until they reached a quiet place somewhere, and she didn't trouble him with questions. Instead, she looked from the window or watched him furtively, comparing him with her memory of George Hayne and wondering in her own thoughts. She was glad to have them to herself for this bit, for now that the morning had come she was almost afraid of what revelation might bring forth. And so they took the swift ride in more or less silence, and neither thought it strange.

As the carriage stopped, he spoke with a low, hurried voice, tense with excitement; but her own nerves were strained also, and she didn't notice.

"We get out here."

He had the fare ready for the driver and, stepping out, hurried Celia into the shelter of the hallway. An elevator had just come down, so in a second more they were up safe in the hall before his own apartment.

Taking a latchkey from his pocket, he inserted it in the door, flung it open and ushered Celia to a large leather chair in the middle of the room. Then, stepping quickly to the side of the room, he touched a bell and from it went to the telephone, with an "Excuse me, please—this is necessary" to the girl, who sat astonished, wondering at the homelikeness of the room and at the "at-home-ness" of the man. She'd expected to be taken to a hotel. This seemed to be a private apartment with which he was perfectly acquainted. Perhaps it belonged to some friend. But how, after an absence of years, could he remember just where to go, which door and which elevator to take, and how to fit the key so easily? Then her attention was arrested by his voice.

"Give me 254 L, please. Is this 254 L? . . . Is Mr. Osborne in? . . . You say he has *not* gone to the office yet? . . . May I speak with him? . . . Is this Mr. Osborne? . . . I didn't expect you to know my voice. . . . Yes, sir, just arrived and all safe so far. Shall I bring it to the house or the office? . . . The house? . . . All right, sir. Immediately. . . . By the way, I'm sure Hale and Burke are on my track. They saw me at the station. . . . To your house? . . . You'll wait until I come? . . . All right, sir. Yes, immediately. . . . Sure, I'll take precautions. . . . Good-bye."

With the closing words came a tap at the door.

"Come in, Henry," he answered, as the astonished girl turned toward the door. "Henry, you'll go down, please, to the restaurant and bring up a menu card. This lady will select what she'd like to have, and you'll serve breakfast for her in this room as soon as possible. I'll be out for perhaps an hour, and, meanwhile, you'll obey any orders she may give you."

He didn't introduce her as his wife, but she didn't notice the omission. She'd suddenly become aware of a strange, distraught haste in his manner, and when he said he was going out, alarm seized her; she couldn't tell why.

The man bowed to his master, looked his admiration and devotion to the lady, waited long enough to say, "I'm mighty glad to see you safe back, sir," and disappeared to obey orders.

Celia turned toward Gordon for an explanation, but he was already at the telephone again.

"Forty-six! . . . Is this the garage? . . . This is the Harris Apartments. . . . Can you send Thomas with a closed car to the rear door immediately? . . . Yes. . . . No, I want Thomas and a car that can speed. . . . Yes, the rear door, *rear,* and at once. . . . What? . . . What's that? . . . But I *must.* . . . It's *official* business. . . . Well, I thought so. Hurry them up. Good-bye."

He turned and saw her troubled gaze following him with growing fear in her eyes.

"What's the matter?" she asked anxiously. "Has something happened?"

He paused one moment and, coming to her, laid his hands on hers tenderly.

"Nothing the matter at all," he said soothingly. "At least nothing that need worry you. It's just a matter of pressing business. I'm sorry to leave you for a little while, but it's necessary. I can't explain until I return. You'll trust me? You won't worry?"

"I will try!"

Her lips were quivering, and her eyes were filled with tears. Again he felt that intense longing to lay his lips on hers and comfort her, but he put it from him.

"There's nothing to feel sad about," he said, smiling gently. "It's nothing tragic, but there's need for haste, for if I wait, I may fail yet—. It's something that means a great deal to me. When I come back I'll explain all."

"Go!" she said, putting out her hands in resignation, as if she'd hurry him from her. And though she was burning to know what it all meant, something about him compelled her to trust him and wait.

Then his control almost left him. He nearly took those hands in his and kissed them, but he didn't. Instead he walked swiftly to his bedroom door, threw open a chiffonier drawer and took out something small and sinister. She could see the gleam of its polished metal and sensed a strange little menace in the click as he did something to it—she couldn't see what, because his back was to her. He came out with his hand in his pocket, as if he'd just hidden something there.

She wasn't familiar with firearms. Her mother had been afraid of them, and her brother had never displayed any around the house. Yet she knew by instinct that Gordon possessed some weapon of defense; and a nameless horror rose in her heart and shone from her blue eyes, but she wouldn't speak a word to let him know it. If he hadn't been in such haste, he would have seen. Her horror would have been still greater if she knew he already carried one loaded revolver and was taking a second in case of emergency.

"Don't worry," he called as he hurried out the door. "Henry will get anything you need, and I'll soon be back."

The door closed, and he was gone. She heard his quick step down the hall, heard the elevator door slide and slam again, and then she knew he'd gone down. Outside an automobile sounded, and she seemed to hear again his words at the phone, "The rear door." Why had he gone to the rear door? Was he in hiding? Was he flying from someone? What did it mean?

Without stopping to reason it out, she flew across the room and opened the door of the bedroom he'd just left, then through it passed swiftly to a bathroom beyond. Yes, there was a window. Would it be the one? Could she see him? And what good would it do her if she could?

She crowded close to the window. It had a heavy sash with stained glass, but she selected a clear bit of yellow and put her eye close. Yes, a closed automobile was just below her, and it had started away from the building. He'd gone then. Where?

Her mind was a blank for a few minutes. She went slowly back to the other room without noticing anything about her, sat down in the chair, putting her hands to her temples, and tried to think. Back to the moment in the church where he appeared at her side and the service began. Something told her then that he was different, and yet there were those letters, and how could he not have written them?

He was gone on some dangerous business. Of that she felt sure. The man he first phoned gave him some caution. He promised to take precaution—that meant the wicked, gleaming thing in his pocket. Perhaps some harm would come to him, and she would never know.

She stared at the opposite wall. Well, and suppose it did? Why did she care? Wasn't he the man whose power over her two short days ago made her welcome death as her deliverer? Why was all changed now? Just because he smiled on her and was kind? Gave her a few wildflowers and said her eyes were like them? Had hair that waved instead of being straight and thin?

Where was her loyalty to her dear dead father's memory? How could she worry about danger coming to one who threatened to tell terrible lies that would stain her father in the thoughts of people who had loved him? Had she forgotten the letters? Was she willing to forgive all just because he declared he didn't write them? How foolish! He said he could prove he didn't, but of course that was nonsense. He must have written them. And yet the wave in his hair and the kindness in his eyes. . . . And he'd looked terrible things when he read that letter; as if he'd like to wreak vengeance on the man who wrote it. Could a man masquerade that way?

And then a new solution to the problem came to her. Suppose this—whoever he was—this man who had married her, had gone out to find and punish George Hayne? Suppose—but then she covered her eyes with her hands and shuddered. Yet why should she care? But she did. Suppose *he* should be killed! Who was he, if not George Hayne, and how did he come to take his place? Was it just another of George's terrible tricks on her?

A quick vision came of their bringing him back to her. He would lie, perhaps, on that crimson leather couch over there, as he lay in the train's stateroom, with his hands hanging limp and one perhaps across his chest, as if he were guarding something, and his bright waves of brown hair lying heavy about his forehead—only his forehead would be so white and cold, with a little blue mark in his temple perhaps.

Henry's footsteps brought her back to the present again. She smiled at him pleasantly as he entered and answered his questions about what she'd have for breakfast. But he selected the menu, not she, and after he'd gone she couldn't have told what she ordered. She couldn't get away from the vision on the couch. She closed her eyes and pressed her cold fingers against her lids to drive it away, but still her bridegroom seemed to lie there before her.

The man came back presently with a loaded tray and set it down on a little table he wheeled before her, as though he'd done it many times before. She thanked him and said she didn't need anything else, so he went away.

She toyed with the cup of delicious coffee he poured for her, and the few swallows she took gave her new heart. She broke a piece from a hot roll and ate a little of the delicious steak. Still her mind was working, and her heart was full of nameless anxiety.

He went away without any breakfast himself and had eaten little supper the night before. She got up and walked about the room, trying to shake off the horror and the dread of what morning might bring. Ordinarily she'd have thought of sending a message to her mother and brother, but her mind was so troubled now that it never occurred to her.

The walls of the room were tinted a soft greenish gray, and above the picture molding they blended into a woodsy landscape with a hint of water and blue sky through interlacing branches. It reminded her of the village they saw as they started from the train in the early morning light.

Two or three fine pictures were hung in good lights. She studied them and knew that the one who had selected and hung them was a judge of true art. They didn't hold her attention long, for as yet she hadn't connected the room with the man she was waiting for.

A handsome mahogany desk stood open in a broad space by the window. She was attracted by a painted miniature of a woman. She took it up and studied the face. It was fine and sweet, with brown hair dressed low and eyes that reminded her of the man who had brought her there. Was this, then, the home of some relative he came to stop with for a day or two, and, if so, where was the relative? The dress in the miniature was from a quarter of a century past, yet the face was young and sweet, as young, perhaps, as she. She wondered who it was. She put the miniature back in place tenderly. She felt she'd like to know this woman with the sweet eyes. She wished her here now, that she might tell her all her anxiety.

Her eyes wandered to the pile of letters, some of them official-looking ones, one or two in square, perfumed envelopes, with high, angular writing. They were all addressed to Mr. Cyril Gordon. That was strange! Who was Mr. Cyril Gordon? What had they—what had she—to do with him? Was he a friend whom George—whom they—were visiting for a few days? It was bewildering.

Then the telephone rang.

Her heart beat wildly, and she looked toward it as if it had been a human voice speaking and she had no power to answer. What should she do? Should she answer? Or should she wait for the man to come? Could the man hear the telephone bell, or was she perhaps expected to answer? And yet if Mr. Cyril Gordon—well, somebody should answer. The phone rang insistently again and still a third time. What if *he* should be calling her! Perhaps he was in distress. This thought sent her flying to the phone.

She took down the receiver and called, "Hello!" Her voice sounded far away even to her.

"Is this Mr. Gordon's apartment?"

"Yes," she answered, for her eyes were resting on the pile of letters close at hand.

"Is Mr. Gordon there?"

"No, he isn't," she answered, growing more confident now and almost wishing she hadn't answered a stranger's phone.

"Why, I just phoned the office, and they told me he'd returned," said a voice with an imperious note in it. "Are you sure he isn't there?"

"Quite sure," she replied.

"Who is this, please?"

"I beg your pardon," said Celia, trying to make time and not knowing how to reply. She was no longer Miss Hathaway. Who was she? Mrs. Hayne? She shrank from the name. It filled her with horror. "Who is this, I said," snapped the other voice now. "Is this the chambermaid? Because if it is I'd like you to look around and inquire and be quite sure Mr. Gordon isn't there. I wish to speak with him about something very important."

Celia smiled. "No, this isn't the chambermaid," she said sweetly, "and I'm quite sure Mr. Gordon isn't here."

"How long before he'll be there?"

"I don't know, for I've just come myself."

"Who is this?"

"Why—just a friend," she answered, wondering if that was the best thing to say.

"Oh!" There was a long and contemplative pause at the other end.

"Well, could you give Mr. Gordon a message when he comes in?"

"Why, certainly, I think so. Who is this?"

"Miss Bentley. Julia Bentley. He'll know," replied the imperious one eagerly now. "And tell him, please, that he's expected here for dinner tonight. We need him to complete the number, and he simply mustn't fail me. I'll excuse him for going off in such a rush if he comes early and tells me all about it. Now you won't forget, will you? You got the name, Bentley, did you? B-E-N-T-L-E-Y. And you'll tell him the minute he comes in?"

"Yes."

"Thank you! What did you say your name was?"

But Celia had hung up. Somehow the message annoyed her; she couldn't tell why. She wished she hadn't answered the phone. Whoever Mr. Cyril Gordon was, what should she do if he suddenly appeared? As for this imperious lady and her message she hoped she'd never have to deliver it. On second thought why not write it and leave it on his desk with the pile of letters? It would pass away a few of these dreadful minutes that lagged so distressfully.

She sat down and wrote: "Miss Bentley wishes Mr. Gordon to dine with her this evening. She'll pardon his running away the other day if he'll come early." She laid it beside the high angular writing on the square perfumed letters and returned to the leather chair, too restless to rest yet too weary to stand up.

She went presently to the back windows to look out and then to the side ones. Across the housetops she glimpsed domes and buildings. She saw the

Congressional Library, which usually delighted her with its exquisite tones of gold and brown and white. But she had no eyes for it now. Beyond were more buildings, all set in the lovely foliage which was much further developed than it had been in New York. From another window she could get a glimpse of the Potomac shining in the morning sun.

She wandered to the front windows and looked out. People were passing and repassing. It was a busy street, but she couldn't make out whether she knew it. Two men were walking back and forth on the opposite side. They went no further than the street corner either way. They looked across at the windows sometimes and pointed up, when they met, and once one of them took something out of his pocket and flashed it under his coat at his side, as if to have it ready for use. It reminded her of the thing he'd held in his hand in the bedroom, and she shuddered. She watched them, fascinated.

Now and then she went to the rear window, to look for any sign of the automobile returning, and then hurried back to the front to see if the men were still there. Once she returned to the chair and, lying back, shut her eyes and let yesterday's memory sweep over her in all its details. She began to feel that some dreadful mistake had been made somewhere, and he was surely all right. He couldn't have written those terrible letters. Then again the details of their wild carriage ride in Pittsburgh and miraculous escape haunted her. Something strange and unexplained about that she must understand.

Chapter 15

Meanwhile, Gordon was speeding away to another part of the city by the fastest time an experienced chauffeur dared to make. About the time they turned the first corner into the avenue, two burly policemen sauntered into the square in front of the house where the Secret Service chief lived. Nothing about their demeanor showed they were detailed there by special urgency. And three men who hurried to the park across the street from the house couldn't know the policemen's careless stroll resulted from the chief's hurried telephone message to police headquarters immediately after his message from Gordon.

The policemen strolled by the house, greeted each other and walked on around the square across the park. They eyed the three men sitting idly on a bench and passed leisurely on. They disappeared around a corner and to the three men were out of the way. The latter didn't know the hidden places where the officers took up their watch. When an automobile appeared, and the three got up from their park bench and distributed themselves among the shrubbery near the walk, they didn't know their every movement was observed. But they wondered how those two policemen seemed to spring out of the ground suddenly, just as the auto halted in front of the chief's house.

Gordon bounded out and up the steps, and the door opened before him as if he were expected. The two grim and apparently indifferent policemen stood outside like two stone images on guard, while up the street in rhythm rode two mounted police, also halting before the house as if for a purpose. The three men in the bushes hid their death instruments and would have slunk away had there been a chance. Turning to make a hasty flight, they were met by three more policemen. The crack of a revolver sounded as one of the three desperadoes tried a last reckless dash for freedom—and failed. The wretch went to justice with his right arm hanging limp by his side.

Inside the house Gordon was delivering up his message. As he laid it before his chief and stood silent while the elder man read and pondered its tremendous import, it occurred to him for the first time that his chief would require some report of his journey and the hindrances that made him a whole day late in getting back to Washington. His heart stood still with sudden panic. What should he do? What right had he to tell of his marriage to an unknown woman? A marriage that perhaps wasn't a marriage. He couldn't know the outcome until he told the girl everything. As far as he was concerned he knew the great joy of his life had come to him in her. Yet he couldn't hope it would be so with her. And he must think of her and protect her good name in every way. If she ever consented to remain with him and be his wife, he must never let a soul know other than that the marriage was planned long ago. It wouldn't be fair to her. It would make life intolerable for them either together or apart. And while he might be and doubtless was safe in confiding in his chief and asking him to keep silence about the matter, still he felt even that would be a breach of faith with Celia. He must close his lips until he could talk with her and know her wishes. He drew a sigh of weariness. He'd come a long, hard way, and it wasn't over. The worst ordeal would be his confession to the bride who wasn't his wife.

The chief looked up.

"Could you make this out, Gordon?" he asked, noting keenly the young man's weary eyes, the strained, tense look about his mouth.

"Oh, yes, sir—I saw it at once. I was almost afraid my eyes might betray the secret before I got away with it."

"Then you know what you've saved the country and what you've been worth to the service."

The young man flushed with pleasure.

"Thank you, sir," he said, looking down. "I understood it was important, and I'm glad I could accomplish the errand without failing."

"Have you reason to think you were followed, except for what you saw at the station in this city?"

"Yes, sir, I'm sure detectives were after me as I was leaving New York. They were suspicious of me. I saw one of the men who'd been at the dinner with me watching me. The disguise—and—some circumstances—threw him off. He wasn't sure. Then there was a man—you know him, Balder—at Pittsburgh?—"

"Pittsburgh!"

"Yes, you wonder how I got to Pittsburgh. You see, I was shadowed almost from the first, I suspect. When I reached the station in New York I was sure I recognized the man who sat opposite me a few minutes before. I suppose my disguise, which you so thoughtfully provided, bothered him; he followed me at a little distance, but he didn't speak to me. I had to get on the first train circumstances permitted, and perhaps the fact it was a Chicago train made him think he was mistaken. Anyhow I saw no more of him after the train left the station. Rather unexpectedly I found I could get the drawing room compartment and went into immediate retirement, leaving the train at daylight where it was delayed on a side track, and walked across country till I found a conveyance that took me to a Pittsburgh train. It didn't seem feasible to get away from the Chicago train any sooner since the train made no more stops, and it was late at night when I boarded it. I thought I'd run less risk by detouring. I never dreamed they'd have watchers for me at Pittsburgh, and I can't think how they got on my track. But almost the first minute I landed I spied Balder stretching his neck over the crowds. I bolted from the station at once and, finding a carriage drawn up before the door ready for me, got in and ordered them to drive me to East Liberty station.

"I'm afraid I'll always be suspicious of handy closed carriages after this experience. I certainly have reason to be. The door was no sooner closed on me than the driver raced like mad through the streets. I didn't think much of it until he'd been going long enough to reach East Liberty, and the horse was still rushing like a locomotive. Then I saw we were in a lonely, unfamiliar district of the city. That alarmed me, and I tapped on the window and called to the driver. He paid no attention. Then I found the doors fastened shut and the windows plugged so they wouldn't open.

"I discovered an armed man rode beside the driver. I got one door open after a good deal of work and escaped when we stopped for a freight train to pass. But I'm satisfied I was being kidnapped and if I hadn't escaped when I did you'd never have heard of me again or the message. I finally reached East Liberty station and jumped on the first train, but I glimpsed Balder stretching his neck over the crowd. He must have seen me and had Hale and Burke on the watch when I got here. They just missed me by a half second. They went over to the restaurant—didn't expect me on a special—but I got away and am mighty glad to get that paper into your possession and out of mine. It's rather a long story to tell the whole, but I think you have the main facts."

A suspicious glitter shone in the old chief's eyes as he extended his hand and grasped Gordon's in a hearty shake. But all he said was, "And you're all worn out—I'll guarantee you didn't sleep much last night."

"Well, no," said Gordon, "I had to sit up in a day coach and share the seat with another man. Besides, I was rather excited."

"Of course, of course!" puffed the chief, coughing vigorously and showing by his gruff attitude that he was deeply affected. "Well, young man, this won't be forgotten by the department. Now you go home and get a good sleep. Take the whole day off, if you wish, and then come down tomorrow morning and tell me all about it. Do I need to know anything more now so justice may be done?"

"I believe not," said Gordon, sighing with relief. "There's a list of the men who were at the dinner with me. I wrote them down from memory last night when I couldn't sleep. I also wrote a few scraps of conversation, which will show you how deep the plot had gone. If I hadn't read the message and known its import, I wouldn't have understood what they were talking about."

"H-m! Yes. If we'd had more time before you started I might have told you all about it. Still it seemed desirable for you to appear as comfortable as possible. I thought this would be best accomplished by your knowing nothing of the import of the writing when you first met the people."

"I suppose it was as well I didn't know more than I did. You're a great chief, sir! I was deeply impressed anew with that fact as I saw how wonderfully you planned for every possible emergency. It was great, sir."

"Pooh! Get home to bed," the chief said brusquely.

He touched a bell, and a man appeared.

"Jessup, is the coast clear?" he asked.

"Yessah," declared the man. "They've jest hed a couple o' shots in the pahk, an' now they tuk the villains off to the p'lice station. The officers is out ther' waitin' to 'scort the gemman."

"Get home, Gordon, and don't come to the office till ten in the morning. Then come straight to my private room."

Gordon thanked him and left the room preceded by the gray-haired servant. He was surprised to find the policemen outside and wondered that one was going in front and the other behind him as he rode along. He was greatly relieved not to be asked for the whole story. His heart was filled with anxiety now to return to the girl and tell her everything. Yet he dreaded it more than anything he'd ever faced. He sat back on cushions and, covering his face with his hands, tried to think how to begin, but he could see only her sweet eyes filled with tears and think of nothing but how she looked and smiled during the beautiful morning they'd spent together in the beautiful town of Milton. Would he ever see it again?

Celia at her window grew more nervous as an hour and then another half hour slipped away, and still he didn't come. Then two mounted policemen rode down the street following an automobile.

She had no eyes now for the men lurking across the way, and when she looked for them again, she saw them running in the opposite direction as fast as they could, gesturing wildly for a car to stop for them.

She stood by the window and saw Gordon get out of the car and disappear into the building below; saw the car wheel and curve away and the mounted police take up their stand on either corner. She heard the elevator clang as it started up and the door clash as it stopped at that floor; heard steps coming toward the door and the key in the latch. Then she turned and looked at him, her hands clasped before her and her eyes yearning, glad and fearful all at once.

"Oh, I've been so frightened about you! I'm so glad you've come!" she said and caught her voice in a sob as she took a step toward him.

He threw his hat on the floor, wherever it might land, and went to meet her, a great light glowing in his tired eyes, his arms outstretched to hers.

"And did you care?" he asked in a voice of almost awe. "Dear, did you *care* what became of *me?*"

He had come quite close to her now.

"Oh, yes, I *cared!* I couldn't help it." Her voice held a real sob now, though her eyes were shining.

His arms circled her, as if he would draw her to him in spite of everything. Yet he kept them around her without touching her.

Looking down into her face he breathed softly, "Oh, my dear, it seems as if I must hold you close and kiss you!"

She looked up and, with a lovely gesture of surrender, whispered, "I can trust you."

"Not until you know all," he said and put her gently from him into the armchair, with a look of reverence and self-abnegation she felt she would never forget.

"Then tell me quickly," she said, a swift fear weakening her from head to foot. She laid her hand across her heart, as if to steady its beating.

He wheeled the leather couch forward opposite her chair and sat down, his head drooping, his eyes down. He dreaded beginning.

She waited for the revelation, her eyes on his bowed head.

Finally he lifted his eyes and saw her look, and a tender light entered his face.

"It's a strange story," he said. "I don't know what you'll think of me after it's told, but I want you to know that, blundering, stupid, even criminal, though you may think me, I'd sooner die this minute than cause you one more breath of suffering."

Her eyes lit up with a wonderful light, and the ready tears sprang into them, tears that sparkled through the great joy illumining her face.

"Please go on," she said gently, adding, "I believe you."

But even with those words in his ears the beginning wasn't easy. Gordon drew a deep breath and launched forth.

"I'm not the man you think," he said, looking at her to see how she'd take it. "My name is not George Hayne. My name is Cyril Gordon."

He sent his truth home to her understanding and waited in breathless silence, hoping against hope that this might not turn her against him.

"Oh!" she breathed softly, as if some puzzle were solving itself. "Oh!"—this time not altogether in surprise nor as if the fact were displeasing. She looked at him expectantly for further revelation, and he plunged into his story.

"I'm a member of the Secret Service—headquarters here in Washington—and day before yesterday I was sent to New York on an important errand. A message of great import written in a private code had been stolen from one of our men. I was sent to get it before they could decipher it. The message involved such significant matters that I was ordered to go under an assumed name and not to let anyone know of my mission. My orders were to get the message and let nothing hinder me in bringing it to Washington. I went understanding fully I might even risk my life."

He looked up. The girl sat wide-eyed, with hands clasped together at her throat.

He hurried on, not to cause her any needless anxiety.

"I won't weary you with details. A good many annoying hindrances came in the way, making me nervous, but I carried out my chief's program, got the message and escaped from the house of the man who'd stolen it. As I closed the door behind me, knowing it could be only a few seconds before six furious men would be on my track and stop at nothing to get back what I took from them, I saw a carriage standing almost before the house. The driver took me for the man he awaited, and I lost no time in taking advantage of his mistake. I jumped in, telling him to drive as fast as he could. I intended to give him further directions, but he had evidently had them from another quarter, and I thought I could call to him as soon as we were out of the dangerous neighborhood.

"To add to my situation I soon became sure an automobile and a motorcycle were following me. I recognized a man in the car as the one who sat opposite me at the table a few minutes before. My coachman drove like mad, while I hurried to secure the message, so if I were caught it wouldn't be found, and to put on a slight disguise—some eyebrows and things the chief had given me. Before I knew where I was, the carriage had stopped before a building. At first I thought it was a prison—and the car and motorcycle stopped behind me. I felt pretty well trapped."

The girl gave a low moan, and Gordon, not daring to look up, hurried on with his story.

"There isn't much more to tell that you don't already know. I soon discovered the building was a church, not a prison. What happened afterward resulted from my extreme perturbation of mind, I suppose. I can't account for my stupidity and subsequent cowardice in any other way. Neither could I explain matters satisfactorily at any time during the whole mix-up, because of the trust I carried and which I couldn't reveal even in confidence or jeopardize in the slightest. Naturally at first my commission and how to get safely through it was the only important thing to me. If you keep this in mind, perhaps you can judge me less harshly.

"My only thought when the carriage stopped was how to escape those two pursuers, and that more or less pervaded my mind during what followed. Ordinary matters, which would have been clear another time, meant nothing. You see, the instant that carriage came to a standstill someone threw open the door and I heard a voice call, 'Where is the best man?' Then another voice said, 'Here he is!' I took it they thought I was the best man but would soon discover I wasn't when I came into the light. I had no chance to slip away or would have vanished in the dark, but everybody surrounded me and seemed to think I was all right.

"The two men who followed were close behind eyeing me. I'm satisfied they were to blame for that wild ride we took in Pittsburgh!

"I soon saw by the remarks that the man I was supposed to be had been away from this country for ten years, and of course then they wouldn't be very critical. I tried twice to explain there was a mistake, but both times they misunderstood me and thought I was saying I couldn't go in the processional because I hadn't practiced.

"I don't know how I came to be in such a dreadful mess. It should have been easy to say I got into the wrong carriage and they must excuse me, that I wasn't their man. But they gave me no time to think or speak. They just turned me over from one man to another and took everything for granted. I realized I'd have to break loose and flee before their eyes to escape and decided there'd be no harm in marching down the aisle as best man in a delayed wedding, if that's all I had to do. I could disappear as soon as the ceremony was over, and no one would be the wiser. The real best man would probably turn up, and then they might wonder as they pleased, for I'd be far away. And perhaps this was as good a place as any to hide for half an hour until my pursuers were baffled and seeking elsewhere for me. I can see now I made a grave mistake in allowing even so much deception, but I didn't see any harm in it then, and they all seemed in great distress for the ceremony to go forward.

"Bear in mind also that I was entirely taken up with the importance of hiding my message until I could take it safely to my chief. Nothing else seemed to matter much. If the real best man was late to the wedding and they were willing to use me in his place, what harm could come from it? He certainly deserved it for being late, and if he came in during the ceremony he'd think someone else was put in his place. They introduced me to your brother—Jefferson. I thought he was the bridegroom, and I thought so until they laid your hand in mine!"

"Oh!" she moaned, covering her face.

"I knew it!" he said bitterly. "I knew you'd feel that way as soon as you knew. I don't blame you. I deserve it! I was a fool, a villain, a dumb brute—whatever you have a mind to call me! You can't begin to understand how I've suffered for you since this happened and how I've blamed myself."

He got up suddenly and strode over to the window, frowning down into the sunlit street and wondering how everybody seemed to be going on in exactly the same hurry as ever, when for him life had suddenly come to a standstill.

Chapter 16

The room was still. The girl didn't even sob. He turned after a moment and went back to that bowed head there in the deep crimson chair.

"Look here," he said. "I know you can't ever forgive me. I don't expect it or deserve it! But please don't feel so awfully about it. I'll explain it to everyone. I'll make it all right for you. I'll take every bit of blame on myself and get plenty of witnesses to prove it—"

The girl looked up with sorrow and surprise in her wet eyes.

"Why, I don't blame you," she said mournfully. "I can't see how you were to blame. It was no one's fault. It was just an unusual happening—a strange set of circumstances. I couldn't blame you. There's nothing to forgive, and if there were I'd gladly forgive it!"

"Then what on earth makes you look so pale and feel so distressed?" he asked in a distracted voice, as a man will sometimes look and talk to the woman he loves when she becomes a tearful problem of despair to his obtuse eyes.

"Oh, don't you know?"

"No, I don't," he said. "You're surely not mourning for that brute of a man you promised to sacrifice your life to?"

She shook her head and buried her face in her hands again. He could see the tears dropping between her fingers, and they seemed to fall red hot upon his heart.

"Then what is it?" His tone was almost sharp in its demand, but she only cried the harder. Her slender shoulders were shaking with her grief now.

He put his hand down softly and touched her bowed head.

"Won't you tell me, dear?" he breathed and, stooping, knelt beside her.

The sobs ceased, and she was quite still for a moment while his hand still lay on her hair with that gentle, pleading touch.

"It's—because you married me—in—that way—without knowing—oh, can't you see how terrible—"

Oh, the folly and blindness of love! Gordon got up from his knees as if she'd stung him.

"You needn't feel bad about that anymore," he said in a hurt tone. "Didn't I tell you I'd set you free at once? Surely no one in his senses could call you bound after such circumstances."

She was still, as if he'd struck her, and then she raised her head and her eyes suddenly grown haughty.

"You mean *I* will set *you* free!" she said coldly. "I couldn't think of letting you be bound by a misunderstanding when you were under great stress of mind. You were in no wise to blame. *I* will set *you* free."

"As you please," he retorted bitterly, turning toward the window again. "It all amounts to the same thing. There's nothing for you to feel bad about."

"Yes, there is," she answered, with a quick rush of feeling that broke through her assumed haughtiness. "I'll always feel I broke in upon your life. You've had a very trying experience with me, and you never can quite forget it. Things won't be the same—"

She paused, and the quiet tears chased each other down her face.

"No," said Gordon still bitterly, "things will never be the same for me. I'll always see you sitting there in my chair. I'll always miss you from it! But I'm glad. I'd never have known what I missed if it hadn't been for this." He spoke almost savagely.

He didn't look around, but she was staring at him in astonishment, her blue eyes suddenly alight.

"What do you mean?" she asked softly.

He wheeled around. "I mean I'll never forget you, and I don't want to forget you. I'd rather have had these two days of your sweet company than all my lifetime with anyone else."

"Oh!" she breathed. "Then why—why did you say what you did about being free?"

"I didn't say anything about being free that I remember. You said that."

"I said I'd set you free. I couldn't, of course, hold you to a bond you didn't want—"

"But I didn't say I didn't want it. I said I wouldn't hold you if *you* didn't want to stay."

"Do you mean that if you'd known me a little—that is, just as much as you know me now—and had come in there and found out your mistake before it was too late, that you would have *wanted* to go on with it?"

She waited for his answer breathlessly.

"If you'd known me as much as you do now and had looked up and seen it was I and not George Hayne you were marrying, would *you* have wanted to go on and be married?"

Her cheeks grew rosy and her eyes confused.

"I asked you first," she said, with just a flicker of a smile.

He caught the shimmer of light in her eyes and came toward her eagerly, his own face all aglow now with a dawning understanding.

"Darling," he said, "I can go further than you've asked. From the minute my eyes rested on your face under that white veil I wished with all my heart I might have known you before any other man had found and won you. When you turned and looked at me with that deep sorrow in your eyes, you pledged me with every fiber of my being to fight for you. I was yours from that instant. And when your hand was laid in mine, my heart went out in longing to have it stay in mine forever. I know now that the real reason I didn't reveal my identity then was not because I was afraid of anything that might happen or any scene I might make. It was because my heart was fighting for the right to keep what was given me out of the unknown. You're my wife, by every law of heaven and earth, if your heart will say yes. I love you, as I never knew a man could love, and yet if you don't want to stay with me I'll set you free. But I'd never be the same, for I'm married to you in my heart and always shall be. Darling, look up and answer my question now."

He stood before her with outstretched arms, and for answer she rose and walked to him slowly, with downcast eyes.

"I don't want to be set free," she said.

Then gently he folded his arms about her, as if she were too precious to handle roughly, and laid his lips on hers.

The shrill, insistent clang of the telephone bell broke in on their bliss. For a moment Gordon let it ring, but its merciless clatter wouldn't be denied. Drawing Celia close within his arm, he made her come with him to the phone.

To his annoyance, Julia Bentley's haughty voice answered him.

His arm was about Celia, and she felt his whole body stiffen with formality.

"Oh, Miss Bentley! Good morning! Your message? Why, no! Ah! Well, I've just come in—"

A pause allowed Celia, panic-stricken, to hand him the paper on which she'd written Julia's message.

"Ah! Oh, yes, I have the message. Yes, it's very kind of you—," he murmured stiffly, "but you'll have to excuse me. No, really. It's impossible! I have another engagement." His arm stole closer around Celia's waist and caught her hand, squeezing it. He smiled, with a grimace toward the telephone, which gladdened her heart. "Pardon me, I didn't hear that," he went on. . . . "Oh, give up my engagement and come? . . . It isn't possible!" His voice rang with a glad, decided force, and he held still closer the soft fingers in his hand. . . . "Well, I'm sorry you feel that way about it. I'm certainly not trying to be disagreeable. No, I couldn't come tomorrow night either. . . . I can't make any plans for the next few days. . . . I may have to leave town again—possibly return to New York. Yes, business has been very pressing. I hope you'll excuse me. I'm sorry to disappoint you. No, of course I didn't do it on purpose. I'll have some pleasant news to tell you when I see you again—or—perhaps I'll find a way to let you know of it before I see you."

The color rose in Celia's cheeks, and she moved in closer to him.

"No, I couldn't tell it over the phone. No, it'll keep. Good things will always keep if they're well cared for, you know. No, I can't. And I'm sorry to disappoint you tonight, but it can't be helped. . . . Good-bye."

He hung up the receiver with a sigh of relief.

"Who is Miss Bentley?" asked Celia, with a natural interest. She was pleased he hadn't addressed her as "Julia."

"Why, she's—a friend—I suppose you'd call her. She's been taking my time lately, more than I enjoyed. Still, she's a nice girl. You'll like her, I think. But I hope you'll never get too intimate. I wouldn't like to have her around continually. She—," he paused and finished, laughing, "she makes me tired."

"I was afraid, from her tone when she phoned you, that she was a very dear friend—that she might be someone you cared for. She had a sort of proprietorship in her tone."

"Yes, that's the word, 'proprietorship,' " he laughed. "I couldn't care for her. I never did. I tried to consider her in that light one day, because I'd been told repeatedly I should settle down. But the thought of having her with me always was—well—intolerable. The fact is, you reign supreme in a heart that has never loved another girl. I didn't know such a thing existed as love like this. I knew I lacked something, but I didn't know what it was. This is greater than all the gifts of life, this gift of your love. And that it should come to me in this beautiful, unsought way seems too good to be true!"

He drew her to him once more and looked down into her lovely face, as if he couldn't drink enough of its sweetness.

"And to think you're willing to be my wife! My wife!" He folded her close again.

A discreet tap on the door announced Henry's arrival, and Gordon roused to the need for ordering lunch.

He stepped to the door with a happy smile and held it open.

"Come in a minute, Henry," he said. "This is my wife. I hope you'll take her wishes as your special charge and do for her as you've done so faithfully for me."

The man's eyes shone with pleasure as he bowed low before the gentle lady.

"I'm very glad to hear it, sir, and I offer you my congratulations, and the lady, too. She can't find no better man in the whole United States than Mars' Gordon. I'm mighty glad you got ma'ied, sir, an' I hope you both have a mighty fine life."

The luncheon was served in Henry's best style, and his face shone as he stepped noiselessly about, putting silver and china and glass in place and casting admiring glances at the lady, who held the miniature in her hand.

"Your mother, you say? How dear she is! And she died so long ago! You never knew her? Oh, how strange and sweet and pitiful to have a beautiful girl-mother like that!"

She put out her hand to his in the shelter of the deep window, and they thought Henry didn't see the look and touch that passed between them. But he discreetly averted his eyes and smiled benignly at the salt cellars and the celery he was arranging. Then he hurried out to a florist's next door and returned with a dozen white roses, which he arranged in a small crystal pitcher, one of the few articles of his mother's that Gordon possessed. It had never been used before, except to stand on the mantel.

After they finished their luncheon, and Henry cleared the table and left the room, Gordon remarked, "I wonder what's become of George Hayne. Do you suppose he means to try to make trouble?"

Celia's hands fluttered to her throat.

"Oh!" she said. "I'd forgotten him! How terrible! He'll do *something*, of course. He'll do *everything*. He'll probably carry out all his threats. How could I have forgotten! Perhaps Mama is now in great distress. What can we do? What can *I* do?"

She looked up at him, and his heart bounded at the thought that she was his to protect as long as life should last and that she already depended upon him.

"Don't be frightened," he soothed her. "He can't do anything very dreadful, and if he tries we'll soon silence him. He's written blackmail in those letters! He's simply a big coward, who'll run and hide as soon as he's exposed. He thought you didn't understand law and took advantage of you. I'm sure I can silence him."

"Oh, do you think so? But poor Mama! It will kill her! And George will stop at nothing when he's crossed. I've known him too long. It will be *terrible* if he carries out his threat." Tears were in his eyes and agony in her face.

"We must telephone your mother at once and set her heart at rest. Then we can find out just what should be done," said Gordon. "It was unforgivably thoughtless of me not to have done it before."

Celia's face was radiant at the thought of speaking to her mother.

"Oh, how beautiful! Why didn't I think of that before! What perfectly dear things telephones are!"

With one accord they went to the telephone table.

"Shall you call them up, or shall I?" he asked.

"You call, and then I'll speak to Mama," she said, her eyes shining. "I want them to hear your voice again. They can't help knowing you're all right when they hear your voice."

For that, he gave her a glance worth having.

"Then why didn't you think I was all right yesterday afternoon? I sensed that you didn't. I used my voice to the best of my ability, but it did no good then."

"Well, you see, that was different! There were those letters to be accounted for. Mama and Jeff don't know anything about the letters."

"And what are you going to tell them now?"

She hesitated for a minute.

"You'd better find out how much they already know," he suggested. "If this George Hayne hasn't turned up yet, perhaps you can wait until you can write, or we might go up tomorrow and explain it ourselves."

"Oh, could we? How lovely!"

"I think we could," said Gordon. "I'm sure I can make it possible. Of course, you know a wedding journey isn't exactly in the Secret Service program, but I might be able to work them for one. I surely can in a few days if this Holman business doesn't hold me up. I may be needed for a witness. I'll talk with the chief first."

"Oh, how wonderful! Then you call them up and just say something pleasant—anything, you know, and then say I'll speak to Mama."

She gave him the number, and in a few minutes a voice from New York said, "Hello!"

"Hello!" called Gordon. "Is this Mr. Jefferson Hathaway? . . . Well, this is your new brother-in-law. How are you all? . . . Your mother recovered from all the excitement and weariness? . . . That's good. . . . What's that? . . . You've been trying to phone us in Chicago? . . . But we're not in Chicago. We changed our minds and came to Washington instead. . . . Yes, we're in Washington—the Harris Apartments. We've been selfish not to communicate with you sooner. At least I have. Celia hasn't had any choice in the matter. I've kept her so busy. Yes, she's very well and looks happy. She wants to speak for herself. I'll try to bring her up tomorrow for a visit. I want to see you too. We have a lot of things to explain to you. . . . Here's Celia. She wants to speak to you."

Celia, her eyes shining, her lips quivering with suppressed excitement, took the receiver.

"Oh, Jeff, dear, it's good to hear your voice," she said. "Is everything all right? Yes, I've been having a perfectly beautiful time, and I've something fine to tell you. All those nice things you said to me just before you got off the train are true. Yes, he's just as nice as you said and a great deal nicer besides. Oh, yes, I'm very happy, and I want to speak to Mama, please. Jeff, is she all right? Is she *perfectly* well and not fretting a bit? You know you promised to tell me. What's that? She thought I looked sad? Well, I did, but that's all gone now. Everything's wonderful. Tell Mother to come to the phone, please—I want to make her understand."

"I'm going to tell her, dear," she whispered, looking up at Gordon. "I'm afraid George will get there before we do and make her worry."

For answer he stooped and kissed her, his arm encircling her and drawing her close. "Whatever you think best, dearest," he whispered back.

"Is that you, Mama?" With a happy smile she turned back to the phone. "Dear Mama! Yes, I'm safe and happy, and I'm sorry you've worried. We won't let you do it again. But listen—I've something to tell you, a surprise— Mama, I didn't marry George Hayne at all. No, I say I *did not* marry George Hayne at all. George Hayne is a wicked man. I can't tell you about it over the phone, but that's why I looked sad. Yes, I was *married* all right, but not to George. He's so different, Mother. He's right here beside me now, and, Mother, he's dear—you'd be very happy about him if you could see him. What did you say? Didn't I mean to marry George? Why, Mother, I never wanted to. I was awfully unhappy about it, and I knew I made you feel so too, though I tried not to. But I'll explain. You'll be perfectly satisfied when you know about it. . . . No, there's nothing whatever for you to worry about. Everything is right now, and life looks more beautiful to me than it ever did. What's his name? Oh!" She looked up at Gordon with a funny expression of dismay. She'd forgotten, and he whispered it in her ear.

"Cyril—"

"It's Cyril, Mother! Isn't that a nice name! Which name? Oh, the first name, of course. The last name?"

"Gordon," he supplied in her ear again.

"Cyril Gordon, Mother," she said, giggling in spite of herself at her strange predicament. "Yes, Mother. I couldn't be happier unless I had you and Jeff, too, and"—she paused, hesitating at the unaccustomed name—"Cyril says we're coming to visit you tomorrow. We'll come up and see you and explain everything. And you're not to worry about George Hayne if he comes. Just let Jeff put him off by telling him you've sent for me or something, and don't pay any attention to what he says. What? You say he came? How strange—and he hasn't been back? I'm so thankful. He's dreadful. Oh, Mother, you don't know what I've escaped! And Cyril is good and dear. What? You want to speak to him? All right. He's right here. Good-bye, Mother, dear, till tomorrow. And you'll promise not to worry about anything? All right. Here's—Cyril."

Gordon took the receiver.

"Mother, I'm taking good care of her, just as I promised, and I'm bringing her for a flying visit to see you tomorrow. Yes, I'll take good care of her. She's very dear to me. The best thing that ever came into my life."

Then a mother's blessing came thrilling over the wires and touched the handsome, manly face with tenderness.

"Thank you," he said. "I'll try always to make you glad you said those words."

They returned to looking in each other's eyes, after the receiver was hung up, as if they'd been parted a long time. It seemed somehow as if their joy must be greater than any other married couple, because they had all their courting yet to do. It was beautiful to think of what was before them.

They both had so much to tell and tell again because they'd only told half. And they had so many hopes and experiences to exchange, so many opinions to compare and rejoice over because they were alike on many essentials. Then they went through the rooms and looked at and talked about Gordon's pictures and favorite books and touched lightly upon plans for the future.

The apartment would do until they could look about and get a house, Gordon said. His heart swelled with pride that at last he'd have a real home, like his other married friends, with a real princess to preside over it.

Then Celia told the horror of the last three months, with the preceding years' unpleasant shadows behind it. She told this in the evening dusk, before Henry came in to light up and they realized it was almost dinnertime, with her face hidden on her husband's shoulder and his arms about her, to comfort her at each revelation of the story. They tried also to plan what to do about George Hayne. Then there was the whole story of Gordon's journey and commission from the time the old chief called him into the office until he stood beside her at the church altar and they were married. It was told in careful detail with all the comical, exasperating and pitiful incidents of the white dog and the little newsboy. Strangest of all was Gordon never said one word about Julia Bentley and her imaginary presence with him that first day, and he never even knew he left out an important detail.

Celia laughed over the white dog and declared they must bring him home to live with them. And she cried over the brave little newsboy and was eager to visit him in New York, promising herself pleasure in taking him gifts and permanently bettering his condition. In this way Gordon incidentally learned his wife had a fortune in her own right, a fact that for a time gave him great uneasiness of mind, since Gordon was an independent creature and had ideas about supporting his wife by his own work.

Celia laughed at him about this. Her fortune hadn't spoiled her, and she soon made him see it had always been a mere incident in her scheme of living—a comfortable and pleasant incident to be sure, but still an incident to be kept always in the background and never cause for self-gratulation or pride.

Gordon found himself dreading the explanation when he reached New York and faced his wife's mother and brother. Celia had worked through his explanations and slowly come to accept them. Somehow by the spirit's beautiful ways, her soul was finding and believing in his soul before the truth was made known to her, but could her mother and brother also believe? He planned with Celia just how he should tell the story. This led to his bringing out letters and papers that would be worthwhile showing as credentials. At every step of the way, as Celia glimpsed into his past, her face shone with joy, and her heart leaped with the assurance that her lot had been cast in goodly places. She perceived not only that this man was honored and respected in high places, but that his early life had been good and true.

The strange loneliness that had surrounded his young manhood seemed suddenly to have faded into the past and was replaced by the exciting, yet comforting, companionship of one peculiarly fitted to fill the need in his life.

Chapter 17

The next morning quite early the phone called Gordon to the office. The chief's secretary said the matter was urgent.

He hurried away leaving Celia somewhat uneasy lest their plans for going to New York that day couldn't be carried out. But she made up her mind not to fret if the trip had to be put off a little.

Gordon entered his chief's office anxiously, for he felt that in justice to his wife he should take her right back to New York and get matters there adjusted. But he feared business would hold him at home until the Holman matter was settled.

The chief greeted him affably and bade him sit down.

"I'm sorry to have called you up so early," he said, "but we need you. The fact is, they've arrested Holman and five other men, and you're needed to identify them. Would it be asking too much of an already overworked man to send you back to New York today?"

Gordon almost sprang from his seat in pleasure.

"It exactly fits my plans or, rather, my wishes," he said, smiling. "I have several matters I'd like to attend to in New York and which, of course, I didn't have time for."

He paused and looked at his chief, marveling that the way had so miraculously opened for him to keep silence a little longer about his marriage. Perhaps the chief need never be told the marriage ceremony took place on the day of the Holman dinner.

"That's good," said the chief, smiling. "You certainly have earned the right to attend to your own affairs. Then we don't need to feel so bad at sending you back. Can you go on the afternoon train? Good! Then let's hear your account of the trip briefly, to see if we missed any points yesterday. But, first, step here a moment. I have something to show you."

He flung open the door to the next office.

"You knew Ferry left the department because of ill health? I've taken the liberty of having your things moved in here. This will be your headquarters, and you'll be next to me in the department."

Gordon turned in amazement and gazed at the kind old face. Promotion he'd hoped for, but such promotion, right over his elders and superiors, he never dreamed of receiving. He could have taken the chief in his arms.

"Pooh!" said the chief, when Gordon tried to blunder out some words of appreciation. "You deserve it! By the way, you know someone has to run across the water to look after that Stanhope matter. That will fall to you, I'm afraid. Sorry to keep you globe-trotting, but perhaps you'll like to make a little vacation of it. The department will give you some time if you want it. Oh, don't thank me! It's simply the reward of doing your duty, to have more duties given you and higher ones. You've done well, young man. I have here all the papers in the Stanhope case and full directions written out. Then if you can plan for it you needn't return but go on over, unless it suits your pleasure. You understand the matter as fully as I do already. And now for business. Let's hurry through. We have one or two little matters to talk over, and I know you'll want to hurry back and get ready for your journey."

And so the account of Gordon's extraordinary escape and eventful journey home was retold, yet not all of it, and became one of the department's classics.

At parting the chief pressed Gordon's hand heartily and ushered him out into the hall, with the same brusque manner he used to close all business interviews, and Gordon found himself hurrying through the familiar halls in a daze of happiness. The secret of his unexpected marriage was still his own—and hers.

Celia was watching at the window when his key clicked in the lock and he let himself into the apartment, his face alight with joy in meeting her again after the brief absence. She turned in a quiver of pleasure at his coming.

"Well, get ready," he said. "We're ordered off to New York on the afternoon train with a wedding trip to Europe in the bargain. And I'm promoted to the next place to the chief. What do you think of that for a morning's surprise?"

He tossed up his hat like a boy, came over to where she stood and stooping laid reverent lips upon her brow and eyes.

"Oh, beautiful! Lovely!" cried Celia. "Come and sit down on the couch and tell me all about it. We can work faster afterward if we get it off our minds. Was your chief shocked you were married without his permission or knowledge?"

"Why, that was the best of all. I didn't have to tell him I was married. And he's not to know until just as I sail. He need never know how it happened. It isn't his business, and it would be hard to explain. No one need ever know except your mother and brother unless you wish them to, dear."

"Oh, I'm so glad and relieved," said Celia. "I've been worrying about that a little—what people would think of us—for of course we couldn't explain it as it is to us. They'd always be watching us to see if we really cared for each other and suspecting we didn't. It would be horrid. It's our own precious secret, and nobody but Mama and Jeff have a right to know—don't you think so?"

"I certainly do, and I was trying to figure out as I went into the office how I could manage not to tell the chief, when what did he do but spring a proposition on me to go at once to New York and identify those men. He apologized tremendously for sending me right back again but said it was necessary. I told him it just suited me for I had affairs I hadn't had time to attend to when I was there and would be glad to go back and see to them. That let me out on the wedding question, for I'd only need to tell him I was married when I got back. He'd never ask when."

"But the announcements," said Celia, "I never thought of that. We'll need some kind of announcements, or my friends won't understand about my new name. And we'll have to send him one, won't we?"

"Why, I don't know. Couldn't we get along without announcements? You can explain to your intimate friends, and the others won't ever remember the name after a few months—we'll not likely meet many of them right away. I'll write to my chief and tell him informally leaving out the date entirely. He won't miss it. If we have announcements at all, we needn't send him one. He wouldn't likely see one any other way or notice the date. I think we can manage that matter. We'll talk it over with your—with *Mother*," he added tenderly. "How good it sounds to say that. I never knew my mother, you know."

Celia nestled her hands in his and murmured, "Oh, I'm so happy! But I don't understand how you got a wedding trip without telling your chief about our marriage."

"Easy as anything. He asked me if I'd mind running across the water to attend to a matter for the service and said I might have extra time while there for a vacation. He never suspects that vacation is to be used as a wedding trip. I'll write him or phone him the night we leave New York. I may have to stay in the city two or three days to get this Holman matter settled, and then we can be off. In the meantime you can spend the time reconciling your mother to her new son. Do you think we'll have a hard time explaining matters to her?"

"Not a bit," said Celia. "She never liked George. My marrying him was the only thing we ever disagreed about. She suspected all the time I wasn't happy and couldn't understand why I insisted on marrying him when I hadn't seen him for ten years. She begged me to wait until he'd been back in the country for a year or two, but he wouldn't hear it and threatened to carry out his worst at once."

Gordon's heart suddenly contracted with righteous wrath over the cowardliness of the man who sought to gain his own ends by intimidating a woman—and this woman, so dear and lovely in her nature. The man's heart seemed indeed dark to have done what he did. He mentally resolved to search him out and bring him to justice as soon as he reached New York. It puzzled him to understand how easily he seemed to have abandoned his purposes. Perhaps after all he was more of a coward than they thought and hadn't dared to remain in the country when he found Celia had braved his wrath and married another man. He'd find out about him and set the girl's heart at rest as soon as possible, to avoid any future embarrassment. Gordon stooped and kissed his wife again.

But it suddenly occurred to the two that trains didn't wait for lovers' long loitering, and with one accord they went to work. Celia of course had few preparations. Her trunk was probably in Chicago and would need to be wired for. Gordon attended to that first, looking up the check number and ordering it back to New York by telegraph. Turning from the telephone he rang for Henry and asked Celia to order lunch while he gathered some things he must take with him. A stay of several weeks would necessitate more baggage than he'd taken to New York.

He walked into the bedroom and began pulling out things to pack. When Celia turned from giving her directions, she found him standing in the bedroom doorway with an old-fashioned velvet jewel case in his hand. He'd just taken it from the little safe in his room. His face wore a wonderful tender light as if he'd just discovered something precious.

"Dear," he said, "I wonder if you'll care for these. They were Mother's. Perhaps this ring will do until I can buy you a new one. See if it will fit you."

He held out a ring containing a diamond of singular purity and brilliance in a quaint old-fashioned setting.

Celia put out her hand with its wedding ring, the ring he placed on her finger at the altar, and he slipped the other jeweled one above it. It fit perfectly.

"It's a beauty," breathed Celia, holding out her hand to admire it, "and I would far rather have it than a new one. Your dear little mother!"

"There's not much else here but a little string of pearls and a pin or two. I've always kept them near me. Somehow they seemed like a link between me and Mother. I was keeping them for—," he said, hesitating, and then giving her a rare smile, finished, "I was keeping them for you."

Her answering look needed no words, which was well, for Henry appeared just then to serve lunch and remind his master that his train left in two hours. They had no further time for sentiment.

And yet, these two, it seemed, couldn't be practical that day. They idled over their luncheon and dawdled over their packing, stopping to look at this and that picture or bric-a-brac that Gordon had picked up in his travels. Henry finally took matters in his own hands, packed them off and sent their baggage after them. Henry was a capable man and rejoiced to see the devotion of his master and his new mistress, but he was practical and knew where his part came in.

Chapter 18

The journey back to New York seemed brief for the two whose lives had just been blended so unexpectedly, and every mile was filled with a new, sweet discovery in one another. When they reached the city they rushed in on Mrs. Hathaway and Jeff like two children who had so much to tell they didn't know where to begin.

Mrs. Hathaway settled the matter by insisting on their having dinner immediately and leaving all explanations until afterward. With the servants present, of course, little could be said about the matter each one had uppermost in their hearts. But with a spirit of deep happiness in the atmosphere one couldn't entertain any fears amid the radiant smiles passing between mother and daughter, husband and wife, brother and sister.

As soon as the meal was concluded the mother led them up to her sitting room, and closing the door she faced them. Half breathless with excitement they stood in a row before her.

"My three dear children!" she murmured.

Gordon's eyes lit with joy, and his heart thrilled with the wonder of it all. Then the mother stepped up to him and led him to the couch and made him sit beside her, while the brother and sister sat together nearby.

"Now, Cyril, my new son," she said, her eyes resting on his face, "you may tell me your story. I see my girl has lost both head and heart to you, and I doubt if she could tell it connectedly."

While Celia and Jeff were laughing at this, Gordon set about winning a mother—and an eager-eyed young brother who was more than half committed to his cause already.

Celia watched proudly as her handsome husband took out his credentials and began his explanation.

"First, I must tell you who I am, and these papers will do it better than I could. Will you look at them, please?"

He handed her a few letters and papers.

"These papers on the top show the rank and position my father and my grandfather held with the government and in the army. This is a letter from the president to my father congratulating him on his approaching marriage to my mother. That paper contains my mother's family tree, and the letters with it will give you an idea of the honor in which my mother's family was held in Washington and in Virginia, her old home. I know these matters aren't important and say nothing whatever about what I am myself, but they're things you'd likely have known about my family if you'd known me all my life. At least they'll tell you my family was respectable."

Mrs. Hathaway examined the papers and suddenly looked up, exclaiming, "My dear! My father knew your grandfather. I think I saw him once when he came to our home in New York. It was years ago, and I was a young girl, but I remember he was a fine-looking man with keen dark eyes and a heavy head of iron gray hair."

She looked at Gordon. "I wonder if your eyes aren't like his. It was long ago, of course."

"They used to say I looked like him. I don't remember him. He died when I was very young."

The mother looked up with a pleased smile. "Now tell me about yourself," she said and laid a gentle hand on his.

Gordon looked down, an embarrassed flush spreading over his face.

"There's nothing great to tell," he said. "I've always tried to live a straight true life, and I've never been in love with any girl before—." He flashed a smile at Celia.

"I was left alone in the world when young and have lived around in boarding schools and college. I graduated from Harvard and have traveled a little. Some money was left from my father's estate, not much. I'm not rich. I'm a Secret Service man, and I love my work. I get a good salary and was this morning promoted to the position next in rank to my chief, so now I'll have more money. I can make your daughter comfortable and give her some of the luxuries, if not all, to which she's been accustomed."

"My dear boy, that part isn't what I'm anxious about—," interrupted the mother.

"I know," said Gordon, "but it's a detail you have a right to be told. I understand you care far more what I am than how much money I can make, and I promise you I'm going to try to be all you'd want your daughter's husband to be. Perhaps the best thing I can say for myself is that I love her better than my life, and I mean to make her happiness the dearest thing in life to me."

The mother's understanding look answered him more eloquently than words, and after a moment she spoke again.

"But I don't understand how you could have known one another, and yet I never have heard of you. Celia isn't good at keeping things from her mother, though the last three months she's had a sadness I couldn't fathom. She seemed so insistent upon having this marriage just as George planned it—and I was so afraid she'd regret not waiting. How could you have known one another all this time and she never talked to me about it, and why did George Hayne have any part whatever in it if you two loved one another? Just how long have you known each other? Did it begin when you visited in Washington last spring, Celia?"

With dancing eyes Celia shook her head.

"No, Mama. If I'd met him then, George Hayne would never have had anything to do with the matter, for Cyril would have known how to help me out of my difficulty."

"I'll tell you the whole story from my standpoint and from the beginning," said Gordon, dreading now that the crisis was upon him, what the outcome would be. "I wanted you to know who and what I was before you know the story, so you might judge me as kindly as possible and know that however I may have been to blame it was through no intention of mine. My story may sound rather impossible. I know it will seem improbable, but it's true. May I hope to be believed?"

"I think you may," answered the mother, searching his face anxiously.

"Thank you," he said and, gathering his courage, plunged into his story.

Mrs. Hathaway was watching him with interest. Jeff had drawn his chair up close and could scarcely restrain his excitement.

When Gordon told of his commission Jeff burst forth: "Say, that was a great stunt! I wish I could've been with you! You must be great to be trusted with a thing like that!"

But his mother gently reproved him. "Hush, son. Let's hear the story."

Celia watched her husband with pride, two bright spots of color in her cheeks and her hands clasping each other tightly. She was hearing many new details now.

When Gordon mentioned the dinner at Holman's, Jeff interrupted: "Holman! Not J. P.? Why, of course—we know him! Celia was one of his daughter's bridesmaids last spring! The old lynx! I always thought he was crooked! People hint a lot of things about him—"

"Jeff, dear, let's hear the story," insisted his mother, and the story continued.

Gordon had been looking down as he talked. He dreaded seeing their faces as the truth dawned on them. But when he'd told all, he lifted honest eyes to the mother.

"I hope you'll believe me that not until they laid your daughter's hand in mine did I know I was supposed to be the bridegroom. If I hadn't been so distraught and trying so hard to think how to escape, I probably would have noticed I was standing next to her and that everything was peculiar about the whole matter, but I didn't. And then when I suddenly knew she and I were being married, what should I have done? Do you think I should have stopped the ceremony then and there and made a scene before all those people? What was right to do? Suppose my commission had been entirely out of the question, and I'd had no duty toward the government to keep entirely quiet about myself, do you think I should have made a scene? Would you have wanted me to for your daughter's sake? Tell me, please," he insisted gently.

While she hesitated he added, "I did some pretty hard thinking during that first quarter of a second when I realized what was happening, and I tell you honestly I didn't know what was the right thing to do. It seemed awful for her sake to make a scene, and to tell you the truth I worshipped her from the moment my eyes rested upon her. There was something sad and appealing as she looked at me that seemed to pledge my life to save her from trouble. Tell me, do you think I should have stopped the ceremony at the first moment I realized I was being married?"

The mother's face had softened as she watched him and listened to his tender words about Celia, and now she answered gently, "I'm not sure—perhaps not! It was a grave question to face. I don't know that I can blame you for doing nothing. It would have been terrible for her and us and everybody and have made it all so public. Oh, I think you did right not to do anything publicly—perhaps—and yet—it's terrible to think you've been forced to marry my daughter that way."

"Please don't say forced—*Mother*—," Gordon said, laying both hands earnestly upon hers and looking into her eyes. "One thing that held me back from doing anything was that I so earnestly desired that what I was passing through might be real and lasting. I've never seen anyone like her before. I know that if the mistake had been righted and she'd gone out of my life, I'd never have felt the same again. I'm glad with all my heart that she's mine, and—Mother!—I think she's glad too!"

The mother turned toward her daughter, and Celia with starry eyes came and knelt before them and laid her hands in her husband's.

"Yes, dear little Mother, I'm happier than I've ever been."

And kneeling thus, with her husband's arm about her, her face against his shoulder and both her hands clasped in his, she told her mother about the tortures George Hayne had put her through. Her mother turned white with horror at what her beloved child had endured, and the brother got up and stormed across the floor, vowing vengeance on George Hayne's luckless head.

Then after the mother had given her blessing to the two and Jeff had added his own original one, the couple told about the eventful wedding trip until the hour grew late and the mother sent them all off to bed.

The next few days were both busy and happy ones for the two. They visited the hospital and cheered up the little newsboy with fruit, toys and many promises. And they brought home a happy white dog from his boarding place, and Jeff adopted him. Gordon had a trying hour or two at court with his one-time dinner host, the scoundrel who stole the cipher message. And, in prison where he went in search of George Hayne, he saw the thickset man glaring at him from a cell window as he passed along a corridor.

For many reasons Gordon desired to find the lost bridegroom as soon as possible and asked one of the men working on the Holman case to help.

"Oh, you won't have to search for him," declared the man with a smile. "He was safely landed in prison three days ago. He was neatly caught by the son of the man whose name he forged several years ago. It was a big corporation's trust money, and the man died in his place in a prison cell. But the son means to see the real culprit punished."

And so Gordon, in the capacity of Celia's lawyer, went to the prison to talk with George Hayne. That miserable man found no excuse for his sins when the searching talk was over. Gordon didn't let the man know who he was but informed him Celia was married and if he made her any further trouble, the whole thing would be exposed, and he'd have to answer a grave charge of blackmail.

The days passed rapidly, and at last the New York matter for which Gordon's presence was needed was finished, and he was free to sail away with his bride.

On the morning of their departure Gordon's voice rang out over the miles of telephone wires to his old chief in Washington: "I'm married and am just starting on my wedding trip. Don't you want to congratulate me?"

And the chief's gruff voice sounded back: "Good work, old man! Congratulations for you both. She may or may not be the best girl in the world—I haven't had a chance to see yet—but she's a lucky girl, for she's got *the best man I know*. Tell her that for me! Bless you both! I'm glad she's going with you. It won't be so lonesome."

Gordon gave her the message that afternoon as they sailed straight into the sunshine of a new and beautiful life together.

"Dear," he said, as he arranged her steamer rug more comfortably about her, "has it occurred to you that you're probably the only bride who ever married the best man at her wedding?"

Celia smiled and after a minute replied mischievously, "I suppose every bride *thinks* her husband is the best man."

The Big Blue Soldier

Chapter 1

A nd you don't think I should have had lemon custard to go with the pumpkin instead of the mince?"

Miss Marilla Chadwick turned from her anxious watching at the kitchen window to search Mary Amber's clear young eyes for the truth, the whole truth, and nothing but the truth.

"Oh, no, I think mince is much better. All men like mince pie. It's so—comprehensive, you know."

Miss Marilla turned back to her window, satisfied.

"If he came on that train, he should be in sight around the bend of the road in about three minutes," she said tensely. "I've timed it often when folks were coming out from town, and it always takes just six minutes to get around the bend of the road."

Throughout the months of the Great War, Marilla Chadwick had knit and bandaged and canteened and helped with an eager, wistful look in her gray eyes. Many sweaters had gone to some needy lad with the thrilling remark as she handed it over to the committee: "I keep thinking, what if my nephew Dick should be needing one, and this just came along in time?"

But when the war was over, most people started using pink and blue wool on their needles or else cast them aside altogether and tried to forget there ever was a war. And the price of turkeys went up so high that people forgot to be thankful the war was over. But Miss Marilla still held that wistful look in her eyes and spoke of her nephew Dick with bated breath and a sigh. For wasn't Dick among those favored few who were to remain and do patrol work for an indefinite time in enemy territory, while others were gathered to their waiting homes and eager loved ones? Marilla spoke of Dick as of one who still lingered on the borderland of terror and laid his young life down as a continuous sacrifice for the good of the great world.

A paragraph to that effect appeared in *The Springhaven Chronicle,* a local sheet that offered scant news items and fat platitudes at an ever-increasing rate to a gullible and conceited populace, who supported it because it was the only way to know what one's neighbors were doing. The paragraph was the reluctant work of Mary Amber, the young girl who lived next door to Marilla. She had been her devoted friend since the age of four, when Marilla baked sugar cookies for her in the form of stodgy men with currant eyes and outstretched arms.

Mary Amber remembered the nephew Dick as a young imp of nine who made a whole long, beautiful summer ugly with his torments. She also knew that the neighbors all around had memories of that summer when Dick's parents went on a Western trip and left him with his aunt Marilla. Mary Amber shrank from exposing her dear friend to the criticisms of those readers of *The Springhaven Chronicle* who remembered their cats being tortured, their chickens chased, their flower beds trampled, their children bullied and their windows broken by the youthful Dick.

But time had softened the memories of that fateful summer in Marilla's mind, and, besides, she needed a hero. Mary Amber didn't have the heart to refuse to write the paragraph, but she made it as conservative as circumstances allowed.

But now at last Lieutenant Richard Chadwick's division was coming home! Marilla read in the paper what day they would sail and that they were expected to arrive no later than the twenty-ninth. As she read, she conceived a wild and daring plan. Why shouldn't she have a real, live hero herself? A bit belated, of course, but all the more distinguished for that. And why shouldn't Mary Amber have a whole devoted soldier boy of her own for the village to see and admire? Not that she told Mary Amber that—oh, no! But she could see herself, Mary Amber and Dick going together to church on Sunday morning, the bars on his uniform gleaming like the light in Mary's hazel eyes.

Marilla felt one pang of fear when she thought he might not wear his uniform home, since everybody else was in citizen's clothing. Then her sweet faith in the wholesomeness of all things rescued her, and she smiled. Of course he'd wear it home; it would be too outrageous not to when he was a hero. Of course he would wear it the first few days. And that was a good reason why she must invite him at once instead of waiting until he went to his home and was discharged. She *must* have him in his uniform. She wanted the glory of it for her own brief share in the inspiration and sacrifice that was fast becoming history.

So Marilla had hurried into the city to consult a friend who worked in the Red Cross and often went to the wharves to meet the incoming boats. This friend promised to find out when Dick's division was to land, hunt him up herself and see that he received the invitation at once. "See that he *came*," she put it, with a wise reservation in her heart that the dear, loving soul shouldn't be disappointed.

And now, the very night before, this friend had called Marilla on the telephone to say she had information that Dick's ship would dock at eight in the morning. It would probably be afternoon before he could get out to Springhaven; she'd better have dinner ready about half past five.

So Marilla, with shining eyes and heart that throbbed like a young girl's, had thrown her cape over her shoulders and hastened in the twilight through the hedge to tell Mary Amber.

Mary Amber, concealing her inward doubts, congratulated her and promised to come over the first thing in the morning to help get dinner. Promised also, after much urging, almost with tears on Marilla's part, to stay and help eat the dinner afterward with her and the young lieutenant. From this part of her promise Mary's soul recoiled, for she didn't believe the young leopard she'd played with at the age of nine could have changed his spots in a few years—or even covered them with a silver bar. But Mary soon saw that her presence at that dinner was an intrinsic part of Marilla's joy in anticipating the dinner. Much as she disliked being flung at the young lieutenant in this way, she promised. After all, what did it matter what he thought of her anyway, since she had no use for him? Besides, she could freeze him whenever Marilla's back was turned. And Mary Amber *could* freeze with her hazel eyes when she tried.

So early in the morning Miss Marilla and Mary Amber began a cheerful stir in Marilla's big sunny kitchen. Steadily there grew an array of salads, pies, cakes, puddings, cookies, doughnuts, biscuits, pickles, olives and jellies. Meanwhile a great stuffed bird passed through the seven stages of its final career to the oven.

But now it was five o'clock. The bird with brown and shining breast was waiting in the oven, "done to a turn." Mashed potatoes, sweet potatoes, squash, succotash and onions were finished and needed only to be taken up. Cranberries, pickles, celery and jelly gave the final touches to a perfect table, and the sideboard fairly groaned under its load of pies and cakes. One might have thought a whole regiment was to dine with Miss Marilla Chadwick that day, from the sights and smells that filled the house. Up in the spare room the fire glowed in the Franklin heater, and a geranium glowed in a west window between spotless curtains to welcome the guest. Now there was nothing left for the two women to do but experience the final anxiety.

Mary Amber had her part in that, perhaps even more than her hostess and friend; for she was jealous for Marilla and youthfully incredulous. She didn't trust Dick Chadwick, even though he was an officer and had patrolled an enemy country for a few months after the war was over.

Mary Amber had slipped over to her own house when she finished mashing the potatoes and changed her dress. She was putting little squares of butter on the bread-and-butter plates now, and the setting sun cast a halo of burnished light over her gold hair, brightening up the silk of her brown gown with its touches of wood-red. Mary Amber was beautiful to look upon as she stood with her butter knife deftly cutting the squares and dropping them in just the right spot on the plates.

But her eyes held a troubled look as she glanced from time to time at the older woman by the window. Marilla had given up all thought of work and was intent only on the road toward the station. It seemed as if not until now had her great faith failed her and the thought occurred to her that perhaps he might not come.

"You know, of course, he might not get that train," she said meditatively. "The other leaves only half an hour later. But she said she'd tell him to take this one."

"That's true," said Mary cheerily. "And nothing will be hurt by waiting. I've fixed those mashed potatoes so they won't get soggy by being too hot, and I'm sure they'll keep hot enough."

"You're a good, dear girl, Mary Amber," said Marilla, giving her a sudden impulsive kiss. "I only wish I could do something great and beautiful for you."

Marilla caught up her cape and hurried toward the door.

"I'm going out to the gate to meet him," she said with a smile. "It's time he was coming in a minute now, and I want to be out there without hurrying."

She clambered down the steps, her knees trembling with excitement.

She hoped Mary hadn't looked out of the window. A boy was coming on a bicycle. If he was a boy with a telegram or a special-delivery letter, she wanted to read it before Mary saw her. Oh, how awful if anything had happened that he couldn't come today! Of course, he might come later tonight or tomorrow. A turkey would keep, though it was never as good as the minute it was taken out of the oven.

The boy was almost to the gate now, and—yes, he was going to stop. He was swinging one leg out with that long movement that meant slowing up. She panted forward with a furtive glance back at the house. She hoped Mary was looking at the turkey and not out of the window.

Her fingers seemed suddenly tired while she was writing her name in that boy's book, and they almost refused to tear open the envelope as he swung onto his bicycle again and vanished down the road. She had enough presence of mind to keep her back to the house and the telegram in front of her as she opened it, trying to appear to be still looking eagerly down the road, while the brief typewritten message got across to her tumultuous mind.

> *Impossible to accept invitation. Have other engagements. Thanks just the same.*
>
> *Lieutenant Richard H. Chadwick*

Marilla tore up the yellow paper quickly and crumpled it into a ball in her hands as she stared down the road through brimming tears. She managed an upright position. But her knees were shaking under her, and a tight knot was growing in her stomach. Across the sunset skies, in letters of accusing size, seemed to blaze the paragraphs from *The Springhaven Chronicle*, copied afterward in the country *Gazette*. It stated that Miss Marilla Chadwick's nephew, Lieutenant Richard H. Chadwick, was expected at his aunt's home as soon as he landed in this country after a long and glorious career in other lands and would spend the weekend with his aunt and "doubtless be heard from at the Springhaven Clubhouse before he left."

Her throat caught with an odd little sound like a groan. Still, with her hand grasping the front gate, Marilla stood and stared down the road, trying to think what to do, how to word a paragraph explaining why he didn't come and how to explain to Mary Amber so that that look of sweet incredulousness wouldn't come into her eyes.

Then suddenly, as she stared through her blur of tears, a straggling figure appeared, coming around the bend of the road by the Hillis house. And Marilla, with only the thought of escaping from Mary Amber's watchful, loving eyes a moment longer, till she could think what to tell her, staggered through the gate and down the road toward the person, whoever it was, that was coming slowly up the road.

Marilla stumbled on, nearer and nearer to the oncoming man, till suddenly through her tears she noticed he wore a uniform. Her heart leaped, and for a moment she thought it must be Dick; he had been playing a joke by the telegram and was coming on immediately to surprise her before she had a chance to be disappointed. It was wonderful how the years had done their halo work for Dick with Miss Marilla.

She stopped short, trembling, one hand to her throat. Then, as the man drew nearer and she saw his halting gait—saw, too, his downcast eyes and whole dejected attitude—she somehow knew it wasn't Dick. He would never have walked to her home that way. Little Dick had had a swagger that couldn't be forgotten. The older Dick, crowned now with many honors, wouldn't have forgotten to hold his head high.

Unconscious of her apparent interest she stood with her hand still fluttering at her throat and her eyes on the man as he advanced.

When he was almost opposite her, he looked up. He had fine eyes and good features. But his expression was bitter for one so young, and in his eyes was a look of pain.

"Oh, excuse me," said Marilla, glancing around to be sure Mary Amber couldn't see them so far away. "Are you in a hurry?"

The young man looked surprised, amused and slightly bored, but paused politely.

"Not 'specially," he said. There was a tone of dry sarcasm in his voice. "Is there anything I can do for you?"

He lifted his trench cap and paused to rest his lame knee.

"Why, I was wondering if you would mind coming in and eating dinner with me," Marilla said eagerly from a dry throat of embarrassment. "You see, my nephew's a returned soldier, and I've just got word he can't come. The dinner's all ready to be dished up, and it needn't take you long."

"Dinner sounds good to me," said the young man with a grim glimmer of a smile. "I guess I can accommodate you, madam. I haven't had anything to eat since I left the camp last night."

"Oh! You poor child!" said Marilla, beaming on him with a welcoming smile. "Now isn't it fortunate I should have asked *you?*" she added, as if a throng of soldiers had passed from which she might have chosen. "But are you sure I'm not keeping you from someone else who is waiting for you?"

"If anyone else is waiting anywhere along this road for me, it's news to me, madam. Anyhow, you got here first, and I guess you have first rights."

He had lapsed into the soldier's easy vernacular now. For the moment his bitterness was held in abeyance, and the nice look in his eyes shone forth.

"Well, then, we'll just go along in," said Marilla, casting another quick glance toward the house. "I think I'm most fortunate to have found you. It's so disappointing to get dinner ready for company and then not have any."

"Must be almost as disappointing as to get ready for dinner and then not have any," said the soldier affably.

Marilla smiled.

"I suppose your name doesn't happen to be Richard, does it?" she asked with that childish appeal in her eyes that had always kept her a young woman and good company for Mary Amber, even though her hair had long been gray.

"Might just as well be that as anything else," he responded, willing to step into whatever role was set for him in this most unexpected game.

"And you wouldn't mind if I call you Dick?" she asked with a wistful look in her blue eyes.

"Like nothing better," he assented and found his own heart warming to this confiding stranger.

"That's beautiful of you!" She put out a shy hand and laid it lightly on the edge of his cuff. "You don't know how much obliged I am. You see, Mary Amber hasn't ever quite believed he was coming—Dick, I mean—and she's been so kind and helped me get the dinner and all. I just couldn't bear to tell her he isn't coming."

The young soldier stopped short in the middle of the road and whistled.

"Oh, no! Are there other guests? Who's Mary Amber?"

"Why, she's just my neighbor, who played with you—I mean with Dick when he was here visiting as a child many years ago. He wasn't always as polite to her then as a boy should be to a little girl. And—well, she's never liked him very well. I was afraid she would say, 'I told you so,' if she thought he didn't come. It won't be necessary for me to tell any lies, you know. I'll just say, 'Dick, this is Mary Amber. I suppose you don't remember her.' And that'll be all. You don't mind, do you? It won't take long to eat dinner."

"But I'm a terrible mess to meet a girl!" he exclaimed, looking down at himself. "I thought it was just you. This uniform's three sizes too large and needs a drink. Besides," he passed a speculative hand over his smoothly shaven chin, "I don't *care* for girls!" There was a deep frown between his eyes, and the bitter look had returned to his face.

Marilla thought he looked as if he might run away.

"Oh, that's all right!" said Marilla anxiously. "Mary Amber doesn't like men either. She says they're all a selfish, conceited lot. You don't need to have much to do with her. Just eat your dinner and tell anything you want to about the war. We won't bother you to talk much. Come—this is the house. The turkey must be on the table getting cold by now."

She swung open the gate and laid a persuasive hand on the shabby sleeve. The young man reluctantly followed her up the path to the front door.

Chapter 2

When Lyman Gage set sail for France three years before, he left behind him a modest interest in a promising business enterprise, a girl who seemed to love him dearly and a debt of several thousand dollars to her father, who had advised him to go into the enterprise and furnished the funds for his share in the capital.

When he returned from France three days before, he was met with news that the business enterprise had gone to smash during the war, the girl had become engaged to a dashing young captain with a well-feathered nest, and the debt had become a galling yoke.

"Father says to tell you you don't need to worry about the money you owe him," wrote the girl sweetly, concluding her revelations. "You can pay it at your leisure when you get started again."

Lyman Gage lost no time in gathering together every cent he could scrape up. This was more than he at first hoped, because he owned two houses in the big city in which he'd landed. These houses, though old and small, were located near an industrial plant that had sprung up since the end of the war, and houses were going at soaring prices. They were snapped up at once at a sum that was fabulous in comparison with their real value. This, with what he brought home and the bonus he received on landing, exactly covered his indebtedness to the man who was to have been his father-in-law. When he turned from the window where he telegraphed the money to his lawyer in a far state with instructions to pay the loan at once, he had just forty-six cents left in his pocket.

Suddenly, as he realized he had done the last thing left on earth he now cared to do, the noises of the great city got hold of his nerves and tore and racked them.

He was filled with a great desire to get out and away from it. He didn't care where—just so the piercing sounds and rumbling grind of city traffic wouldn't press upon the raw nerves and torture them.

With no thought of getting any food or providing for a shelterless night that was fast coming on, he wandered out into the train area of the great station and idly read the names over the gates. One caught his attention—Purling Brook. It seemed as if it might be quiet there, and a fellow could think. He followed the impulse and strode through the gates just as they were about to be closed.

Dropping into the last seat in the car as the train was about to start, he flung his head back and closed his eyes wearily. He didn't care whether he ever got anywhere or not. He was weary in heart and spirit. He wished he might just sink away into nothingness. He was too tired to think, to bemoan his fate, to touch with torturing finger of memory the beautiful hopes he had woven about the girl he thought he loved better than anyone else on earth. Just in passing he wished he had a living mother he could go to for healing his sick heart. But she had been gone long years, and his father even longer. He had no one to whom he cared to show his face, now that all he had counted dear on earth had been taken from him.

The conductor roused him from a profound sleep, demanding a ticket. He was awake enough to remember the name he'd seen over the gate: "Purling Brook. How much?"

"Fifty-six cents."

Gage reached into his pocket and displayed the coins on his palm with a wry smile.

"Guess you better put me off here, and I'll walk," he said, stumbling wearily to his feet.

"That's all right, son. Sit down," said the conductor half roughly. "You pay me when you come back sometime. I'll make it good." And he glanced at the uniform kindly.

Gage looked down at his shabby self helplessly. Yes, he was still a soldier, and people weren't over the habit of being kind to the uniform. He thanked the conductor and sank into sleep again, to be roused by the same kindly hand a few minutes later at Purling Brook. He stumbled off and stood looking dazedly about him at the village. The sleep wasn't yet gone from his eyes nor the ache from his nerves. But the clear quiet of the little town seemed to wrap him about like salve, soothing him, and the crisp air entered his lungs and gave him heart. He realized he was hungry.

The afternoon train he'd traveled on appeared to be a popular one. He looked beyond the groups of happy home comers to where it hurried away down the track, even then preparing to stop at the next near suburban station to deposit a few more home comers. There on that train went the only friend he felt he had in the world at present, that grizzly conductor with his kind eyes looking through bifocals like a pleasant old grasshopper.

Well, he couldn't remain here any longer. The air was biting, and the sun was going down. Across the road the drugstore even then was twinkling out with lights behind its blue and green glass urns. Two boys and a girl were drinking something through straws at the soda fountain and laughing. It turned him sick; he couldn't tell why. He had done things like that many times.

A little stone church stood down the street, with a spire and bells. The sun touched the bells with burnished crimson till they looked like Christmas cards. A youthful rural football team crossed the road, talking noisily about how they would come out that night if their mothers would let them. And the station cab came down the street full of passengers and waited for a lady at the meat market. He could see the legs of a chicken sticking out of the basket as the driver helped her in.

He began to wonder why he hadn't stayed in the city and spent his forty-six cents for something to eat. It would have bought a great many crackers or even bananas. He passed the bakery, and a whiff of fresh-baked bread greeted his nostrils. He cast a wistful eye at the window. Of course he might go in and ask for a job in payment for his supper. He was in his soldier's clothes. But no. That was equivalent to begging. He couldn't bring himself to do that. Here in town they would have all the help they wanted. Perhaps, farther out in the country—he didn't know what—but he couldn't bring himself to ask for food, even with the offer to work. He didn't care enough for that. What was hunger? A thing to be satisfied and come again. What would happen if he didn't satisfy it? Die, of course, but what did it matter? What was there to live for?

He passed a house with many windows, where children were gathered about a piano and one was clumsily playing an accompaniment. They had an open fire, and the long windows reached down to the piazza floor. They were singing at the top of their lungs, the old, timeworn song made familiar to them by community singsongs, still good to them because they all knew it so well.

> *There's a long, long trail a-winding*
> *Until my dreams all come true. . .*

It gripped his heart like a knife. He had sung that song with *her* when it was new and tender, just before he sailed away, and the trail had seemed so long! Now he'd reached the end of it, and she hadn't been there to meet him! It was incredible! She so fair! And false! After all those months of waiting! That was the hardest part of it, that she could have done it and then explained so lightly that he was away so long she was sure he would understand, and they both must have lost their childish attachment—and so on, through the long, nauseating sentences of her repeal. He shuddered as he said them over to his tired heart and then shuddered again with the keen air; his uniform was thin, and he had no overcoat.

What had she said about the money? He needn't worry about it. A sort of bone to toss to the lonely dog after he was kicked out. Ah, well! It was paid. He was glad of that. He was even grimly glad for his own destitution. It gave him a sense of satisfaction to go hungry and homeless in order to pay it all in one grand lump, at once, and through his lawyer, without any word to her or her father. They shouldn't be even distant witnesses of his humiliation. He would never cross their path again if he had his way. They should be as completely wiped out of his existence and he out of theirs as if the same universe didn't hold them.

He passed down the broad, pleasant street in the crisp air, and every home on either hand gave him a thrust of memory that stabbed him to the heart. He'd hoped to have a home like one of these someday, although it might have been in the city, for she always liked the city. He had hoped to persuade her to the country, though. Now he saw as in a revelation how futile such hopes had been. She would never have come to love the sweet, quiet ways he loved. She couldn't ever have really loved him, or she would have waited and not changed.

Over and over again he turned the bitter story, trying to settle it in his heart so the sharp edges wouldn't hurt, to accustom himself to the thought that the one he'd cherished through the dark years that were past was not what he'd thought her.

He stopped in the road beside a tall hedge that hid the Hillis house from view and snatched out the picture he'd carried in his breast pocket till now—snatched it out, gazed at it with a look that wasn't good to see on a young face and tore it across! He took a step forward, and every step he tore a tiny fragment from the picture and flung it into the road bit by bit till the lovely face was mutilated in the dust where the feet of passersby would grind upon it and those great blue eyes gazing back at him from the picture for so long would be destroyed forever. That picture was the last thread binding him to her. When the last scrap of picture had fluttered away, he put his head down and strode forward like one who has cast off his last hope.

The voice of Miss Marilla roused him like a homely, pleasant sound about the house on a morning when one has had an unhappy dream. He lifted his head and, soldier-like, dropped into the old habit of hiding his emotions.

Her kind face comforted him, and the thought of dinner was a welcome one. The ugly tragedy of his life seemed to melt away for the moment, as if it couldn't stand the light of the setting sun and her wholesome presence. An appeal in her eyes reached him; somehow he didn't feel like turning down her naïve, childlike proposition. Besides, he was used to being cared for because he was a soldier, and why not once more now when everything else had gone so rotten? It was an adventure, and what was left for him but adventure? he asked himself with a bitter sneer.

But when she mentioned a *girl*—that was a different thing! Girls were all treacherous. It was a new conviction with him. But it had gone so deep that it extended not only to a certain girl or class of girls, but to all girls everywhere. He had become a woman-hater. He wanted nothing more to do with any of them. And yet at that moment his tired, disappointed, hurt man's soul was really crying out for the woman of the universe to comfort him, to explain to him this awful circumstance that had come to all his bright dreams. A mother, that was what he thought he wanted—and Marilla looked as if she might make a nice mother. So he turned like a tired hungry boy and followed her, at least until she said "girl." Then he almost turned and fled.

Yet, while Marilla coaxed and explained about Mary Amber, he stood facing again the lovely vision of the girl he had left behind at the beginning of the long, long trail and whose picture he had just trampled underfoot on this end of the trail—which it now seemed would wind on forever alone for him.

As he paused on Marilla's immaculate front steps, he prepared himself to face the enemy of his life in the form of woman. The one thing that made him enter that house and submit to being Marilla's guest was that his soul had risen to battle. He would fight Girl in the concrete! She would be his enemy from henceforth. And this strange, unknown girl, who hated men and thought them conceited and selfish, this cold, inhuman creature, was likely false-hearted, too, like the one he had loved and who hadn't loved him. He would show her what he thought of such girls, of all girls—what all men who knew anything thought of all girls! Thus reasoning, he followed Marilla into the pleasant oilcloth-covered hall and up the front stairs to the spare room. There she smilingly showed him the towels and brushes prepared for his comfort and left him, calling cheerily back that dinner would be on the table as soon as he was ready to come down.

He bathed his tired, dirty face and cold, rough hands in the warm, sweet-scented soapsuds and wiped them on the fragrant towel. Then he stood in front of the mirror all polished to reflect the visage of Lieutenant Richard H. Chadwick and brushed his close-cropped curls till no hint of wave was left in them. And all the while he was hardening himself to meet Girl in the concrete and seek revenge for what she had done to his life.

With a final polish of the brush and a flick of the whisk broom over his discouraged-looking uniform, he set his lips grimly and went downstairs, folding his cap and putting it in his pocket. He might want to escape at any minute, and it was best to be prepared.

Chapter 3

Mary Amber was carrying in the platter of golden-brown turkey when he first saw her. She hadn't heard him come down and was entirely off her guard, intent upon her work, with a stray wisp of gold hair across the kitchen-flushed cheek. She looked so sweet and serviceable and true, with her lips parted in the pleasure of the final completion of her task, that the soldier was taken by surprise and thrown entirely off his guard. Was this the false-hearted creature he had come to fight?

Then Mary Amber felt his eyes on her as he stood staring from the open hall door and, lifting her own clear ones, froze into the opponent at once. A very polite opponent with the grace of a young queen, but nevertheless an opponent, cold as a young icicle.

Marilla, with bright eyes and preternaturally pink cheeks, spoke into the vast pause that suddenly surrounded them all, and her voice sounded strangely unnatural to herself.

"Dick, this is Mary Amber. I suppose you don't remember her."

And the young soldier, not yet recovered from that first vision of Mary Amber, went forward with his belligerence to woman somewhat held in abeyance.

"You—have changed a good deal since then, haven't you?" he managed to ask, with his native quickness, the right thing in an emergency.

"A good many years have passed," she said, coolly putting out a reluctant hand to please Marilla. "You don't look at all as you did. I never would have known you."

The girl was looking keenly at him, studying his face closely. If a soldier just home from an ocean trip could get any redder, his face would have grown so under her scrutiny. Also, now that he was face to face with her, he felt his objection to Girl in general receding before the fact of his own position. How did that ridiculous old woman expect him to carry off a situation like this without giving it away? How was he supposed to converse with a girl he had never seen before, about things he had never done—with a girl he was supposed to have played with in his youth? Why had he been such a fool to get into this corner for the sake of one more dinner? Why, tomorrow he would need another dinner and all the tomorrows through which he might have to live. What was one dinner more or less? He felt in his hip pocket for the comforting assurance of his cap and glanced toward the hall door. It wouldn't be far to bolt back to the road, and what would be the difference? He would never see either of them again.

Then the sweet, anxious eyes of his hostess met his with an appealing smile, and he felt himself powerless to move.

The girl's eyes had swept over his ill-fitting uniform, and he could almost feel every crease and stain.

"I thought they told us you were an officer, but I don't see your bars." She laughed and searched his face again accusingly.

"This is another fellow's uniform," he answered lamely. "Mine got shrunk so I could hardly get into it, and another fellow who was going home changed with me."

He lifted his eyes frankly, for he told the truth, and looked into her eyes. But he saw she didn't believe him. Her dislike and distrust of the little boy Dick had come to the front. He saw she believed Dick had been boasting to his aunt of honors that weren't his. A wave of anger swept over his face; yet somehow he couldn't summon his defiance. Somehow he wanted her to believe him.

They sat down at the beautiful table, and the turkey got in its work on his poor human sensibilities. The delicate perfume of the hot meat as it fell in large, flaky slices from Marilla's sharp knife, the whiff of the summer savory and sage and sweet marjoram in the stuffing, the smoothness of the mashed potatoes, the brownness of the candied sweet potatoes—all cried out to him and held him prisoner. The odor of the food brought a giddiness to his head, and the faintness of hunger attacked him. A pallor grew under the tan of his face, and the dark shadows under his eyes touched Marilla and almost softened the hard look of distrust growing around Mary Amber's lips.

"This certainly is great!" he murmured. "I don't deserve to get in on anything like this, but I'm no end grateful."

Mary Amber's questioning eyes recalled him in confusion to his role of nephew in the house, and he was glad to bow his head while Marilla softly asked a blessing on the meal. He had been wont to think he could get away with any situation. But he began to feel now as if his recent troubles had unnerved him, and he might make a mess of this one. It seemed as if that girl could see into a fellow's heart. Why couldn't he show her how he despised the whole race of false-hearted womankind?

They heaped his plate with good things, poured him coffee rich with cream, gave him cranberry sauce and pickles and olives, and passed little delicate biscuits and butter with the fragrance of roses. With all this before him he suddenly felt as if he couldn't swallow a mouthful. He lifted his eyes to the opposite wall, and a neatly framed sentence in Old English lettering met his eye: "Who crowneth thee with lovingkindness and tender mercies, so that thy youth is renewed like the eagle's."

An intense desire to put his head down on the table and cry came over him. The warmth of the room and the fragrance of the food had made him conscious of an ache in every part of his body. His head was throbbing, too, and he wondered what was the matter with him. After all the bitterness of the world, to meet a kindness like this seemed to unnerve him. But gradually the food got in its work, and the hot coffee stimulated him. He rose to the occasion. He described France, spoke of the beautiful cathedrals he had seen, the works of art, the little children, the work of reconstruction that was going on. He spoke of Germany, too, when he saw they expected him to have been there, although this was a shoal on which he almost wrecked his role before he realized. He told of the voyage over and the people he met, and he kept most distinctly away from anything personal, at least as far away as Mary Amber would let him.

She with her keen, questioning eyes was always bringing up some question that was almost impossible for him to answer directly without treading on dangerous ground, and it required skill indeed to turn her from it. Mary listened and marveled, trying continually to trace in his face the lines of the fat-faced, arrogant child who used to torment her.

Mary rose to take the plates, and the young soldier insisted on helping. Pleased to see them getting along so nicely, Marilla sat smiling in her place, reaching out to brush away a stray crumb on the tablecloth. Mary lingered in the kitchen a moment, to be sure the fire wasn't being neglected, and lifted the stove lid. With the draught a little flame leaped up around a crumpled, smoldering yellow paper with the familiar "Western Union Telegraph" heading. Three words stood out distinctly for a second, "Impossible to accept," and then were enveloped by the flame. Mary stood and stared with the stove lid in her hand, and then, as the flame curled the paper over, she saw "Lieutenant Richard—" revealed and immediately licked up by the flame.

It lay, a little crisp, black fabric with its message utterly illegible, but still Mary stood and stared and wondered. She had seen the boy on the bicycle ride up and go away. She had also seen the approaching soldier almost immediately, and the thought of the telegram was at once erased. Now it came back forcefully. Dick, then, sent a telegram, and it looked as if he declined the invitation. Who, then, was this stranger at the table? Some comrade working Miss Marilla for a dinner, or Dick himself, having changed his mind or playing a practical joke? In any case Mary felt she should disapprove of him utterly. It was her duty to show him up to Miss Marilla. Yet how could she do it when she didn't know anything herself?

"Hurry, Mary, and bring the pie," called Marilla. "We're waiting."

Mary put the stove lid down and went slowly, thoughtfully back to the dining room carrying a pie. She studied the face of the young soldier intently as she passed him his pie, but he seemed so young and pleasant and happy she hadn't the heart to say anything just yet. She would bide her time. Perhaps it was all explainable. So she set to asking him questions.

"By the way, Dick, whatever became of Barker?" she asked, fixing her clear eyes on his face.

"Barker?" said Lyman Gage, puzzled and polite, then remembering his role. "Oh, yes, *Barker!*" He laughed. "Great old Barker, wasn't he?" He turned in troubled appeal to Marilla.

"Barker certainly was the cutest little guinea pig I ever saw," said Marilla, beaming, "although at the time I really wasn't as fond of it as you were. You wanted it around in the kitchen so much."

There was covert apology in Marilla's voice for the youthful character of the young man he was supposed to be.

"I must have been a good deal of a nuisance in those days," hazarded the soldier, feeling he was treading on dangerous ground.

"Oh, no!" sighed Marilla, trying to be truthful and at the same time polite. "Children will be children, you know."

"All children are not alike." It was as near to snapping as sweet Mary Amber ever came. She had memories which time hadn't dimmed.

"Was it as bad as that?" laughed the young man. "I'm sorry!"

Mary had to laugh. His frankness certainly was disarming. But there was that telegram! And Mary grew serious again. She didn't intend to have her gentle old friend deceived.

Mary insisted on clearing off the table and washing the dishes, and the soldier insisted on helping her. So Marilla, much disturbed that domestic duties should interfere with the evening, put everything away and made the task as brief as possible. Every trip back from the refrigerator and pantry she looked anxiously at Mary Amber to see how she was getting on with the strange soldier and how the strange soldier was getting on with her.

At first she was a little troubled lest he shouldn't be the kind of man she would want to introduce to Mary Amber. But after she heard him talk and express such thoroughly wholesome views on politics and national subjects she almost forgot he wasn't the real Dick, and her doting heart couldn't help wanting Mary to like him. He was, in fact, the personification of the Dick she had dreamed out for her own, as different in fact from the real Dick as could have been imagined and a great deal better. His frank eyes, pleasant manner and cultured voice pleased her. She couldn't help feeling he was Dick come back as she'd have liked him to be all the time.

"I'd like to have a little music before Mary has to go home," Marilla said wistfully.

Mary Amber was just hanging up the dish towel with an air that said plainly without words that she felt her duty toward the stranger was over and she was going to depart at once.

"Sure!" said the stranger. "You sing, don't you, Mary?"

Mary resigned herself to another half hour. They went into the parlor, and she sat down at the old square piano and touched its asthmatic keys that sounded the least bit tin-panny even under such skilled fingers as hers.

"What shall I play?" she asked. " 'The long, long trail'?" She had a bit of sarcasm in her tone. Mary was a real musician and hated ragtime.

"No! *Never!*" said the soldier quickly. "I mean—not that, *please.*"

A look of such bitter pain swept over his face that Mary glanced up surprised and forgot to be disagreeable for several minutes while she pondered his expression.

"Excuse me," he said. "But I loathe it. Give us something else. Sing something *real*. I'm sure you can."

There was a hidden compliment in his tone, and Mary was surprised. The soldier was acting as he might have in his own social sphere.

Mary struck a few chords tenderly on the piano and then broke into the delicious melody of "The Spirit Flower." Lyman Gage forgot he was playing a part in a strange home with a strange girl, forgot he hadn't a cent in the world and his girl was gone, and sat watching her face as she sang. For Mary had a voice like a thrush in the summer evening, that liquid appeal that always reminds one of a silver spoon dropped into a glass of water. And she had a face like the spirit flower itself. As she sang she couldn't help living, breathing, being the words she spoke.

Absolutely nothing about Mary Amber reminded him of the girl he had lost. Something in her sweet, serious demeanor as she sang called to his better nature—a wholesome, serious sweetness that was an antiseptic against bitterness and sweeping denunciation. Lyman Gage was lifted out of himself and set in a new world where men and women thought of something besides money, position and social prestige. He seemed to be standing off apart from himself and seeing himself from a new angle. And he saw he wasn't the only one who mattered in this world and got a hint that his plans might be only hindrances to a larger life for himself and everyone else. Not that he exactly thought these things in so many words. It was more as if while Mary sang a wind blew freshly from a place where such thoughts were crowding and made him seem smaller in his own conceit than he'd thought he was.

"And now sing 'Laddie,' " pleaded Marilla.

A wave of annoyance swept over Mary Amber's face. It was plain she didn't wish to sing that song. Nevertheless she sang it, forgetting herself and throwing all the pathos and tenderness into her voice that belonged to the beautiful words. Then she turned from the piano and rose. "I must go home at once" was written in every line of her attitude.

Marilla rose nervously and looked from one of her guests to the other.

"Dick, I wonder if you haven't learned to sing."

Her eyes were so pathetic that they stirred the young man to her service. Besides, something contemptuous in the attitude of that human spirit flower standing on the wing, as it were, in that done-with-him-forever attitude spurred him into a faint desire to show her what he could do.

"Why, sure!" he answered lazily.

With a stride he transferred himself to the piano stool and struck a deep, strong chord or two. Suddenly there poured forth a wondrous baritone such as was seldom heard in Purling Brook and indeed is not common anywhere. He had a feeling he was paying for his wonderful dinner and must do his best. The first song that had come to mind was a big, blustery French patriotic song, and the very spirit of the march was in its cadence.

Out of the corner of his eye he could see Mary Amber still poised, but waiting in her astonishment. He felt he'd already scored a point. When he came to the grand climax, she cried out with pleasure and clapped her hands. Marilla had sunk into the mahogany rocker but was sitting on the edge, alert to prolong this gala evening. Two bright spots of colorful delight shone on her faded cheeks.

He didn't wait for them to ask him for another. He dashed into a minor key and began to sing a wild, sweet, sobbing song of love and loss till Mary Amber, entranced, slipped into a chair and sat breathless with clasped hands and shining eyes. That song was such an artistic, perfect thing that she forgot everything else while it was going on.

When the last sob died away, and the little parlor was silent with deep feeling, he whirled about on the piano stool and rose briskly.

"Now that I've done my part, am I allowed to see the lady home?"

He looked at Marilla instead of Mary Amber for permission, and she smiled, half frightened.

"It isn't necessary at all," spoke Mary crisply, rising and going for a wrap. "It's only a step."

"Oh, I think so, surely!" answered Marilla as if a great point of etiquette had been decided. She gave him a look of perfect trust.

"It's only across the garden and through the hedge," she said in a low tone, "but I think she'd appreciate it."

"Certainly," he said and turned with perfect courtesy.

Just then Mary looked in at the door and called, "Good night."

He didn't make a fuss about attending her. He simply was there close beside her as she sped through the dark without a word to him.

"It's been very pleasant to meet you," he said. She had turned with a motion of dismissal at her own steps. "Again," he added lamely. "I–I've enjoyed the evening more than you can understand. I enjoyed your singing."

"Oh! *My* singing!" flung back Mary. "Why, I was like a sparrow beside a nightingale. It wasn't quite fair of you to let me sing first without knowing you had a voice. It's strange. You never used to sing."

Her glance seemed to go deep as she looked at him through the shadows of the garden. He thought about it as he crept back through the hedge, shivering now, for the night was keen and his uniform was thin. Well, what did it matter what she thought? He would soon be far away from her and never likely to see her again. Yet he was glad he had scored a point, one point against Girl in the concrete.

Now he must go in and bid his hostess good-bye, and then away to—where?

Chapter 4

As Lyman Gage walked up the steps to Marilla's front porch a sick tremor of cold and weariness passed over his big frame. Every joint and muscle seemed to cry out in protest, and his very vitals seemed sore and racked. The bit of bright evening was over, and he was facing his own gray life again with a future that was void and empty.

But the door wasn't shut. Marilla was hovering anxiously inside with the air of just having retreated from the porch. She gave a little relieved gasp as he entered.

"Oh, I was afraid you wouldn't come back," she said eagerly. "And I did so want to thank you and tell you how we—how I—yes, I mean *we,* for I know she loved that singing—how very much we enjoyed it. I'll always thank God He sent you along just then."

"Well, I certainly have cause to thank you for that wonderful dinner," he said earnestly, as he might have spoken to a dear relation, "and for all this"—he waved his big hand toward the bright room—"this pleasantness. It was like coming home, and I haven't any home to come to now."

"Oh! Haven't you?" said Marilla. "Oh, *haven't* you?" she said again wistfully. "I wonder why I can't keep you a little while then. You seem just like my own nephew—as I'd hoped he would be—I haven't seen him in a long time. Where were you going when I stopped you?"

The young man lifted heavy eyes that were bloodshot and sore to the turning and tried to smile. To save his life he couldn't lie blithely when it seemed so good to be in that warm room.

"Why—I was—I don't know—I guess I just wasn't going anywhere. To tell you the truth, I was all in and down on my luck and as blue as indigo when you met me. I was just tramping anywhere to get away from it."

"You poor boy!" said Marilla, putting her small blue-veined hands on the old khaki sleeve. "Well, then you're just going to stay with me and get rested. There's no reason in the world why you shouldn't."

"No, indeed!" said Lyman Gage, drawing himself up. "I couldn't think of it. It wouldn't be right. But I certainly thank you with all my heart for what you've done for me tonight. I really must go at once."

"But where?" she asked, as if he belonged to her, grasping hold of his big rough hands with hers.

"Oh, anywhere, it doesn't matter!" he said, holding her delicate hand in his with a look of sacred respect as if a nice old angel had offered to hold hands with him. "I'm a soldier, and a few storms more or less won't matter. I'm used to it. Good night."

He clasped her hands a moment and was about to turn away, but she held his fingers eagerly.

"You won't go that way!" she declared. "Out into the cold without any over-coat and no home to go to! Your hands are hot, too. I believe you have a fever. You're going to stay here tonight and have a good sleep and a warm breakfast. Then, if you must go, all right. My spare bed is all made up, and there's a fire in the Franklin heater. The room's as warm as toast, and Mary put a big bou-quet of chrysanthemums up there. If you don't sleep there, it will all be wasted. You *must* stay."

"No, it wouldn't be right." He shook his head again and smiled. "What would people say?"

"Say! Why, they've got it in the paper that you're to be here—at least, that Dick's to be here. They'll think you're my nephew and think nothing else about it. Besides, I guess I have a right to have company if I like."

"If there was any way I could pay you," said the young man. "But I haven't a cent to my name and no telling how long before I'll have anything. I really couldn't accept any such hospitality."

"Oh, that's all right," said Marilla cheerily. "You can pay me if you like, sometime when you get plenty. Or perhaps you'll take me in when I'm having a hard time. Anyhow, you're going to stay. I won't take no for an answer. I've been disappointed about Dick's coming, and me having no one to show for all the years of the war, just making sweaters for the world, it seemed like, with no one belonging to me. And now I've got a soldier, and I'm going to keep him at least for one night. Nobody's to know but you're my nephew, and I haven't got to go around town, have I, telling that Dick didn't care enough for his old country aunt to come out and take dinner with her? It's nothing to them, is it, if they think he came and stayed overnight too? Or even a few days. Nobody'll be any the wiser, and I'll take a lot more comfort."

"I'd like to accommodate you," faltered the soldier. "But you know I really should—"

Suddenly the big fellow was seized with a fit of sneezing, and the sick sore tremors danced down his back, slapped him in the face, pricked him in the throat and banged against his head. He dropped weakly down in a chair and pulled out the most discouraged-looking handkerchief a soldier ever carried. It looked as if it might have washed the decks on the way over, or wiped off shoes, as doubt-less it had. It left a dull streak of olive-drab dust on his cheek and chin when he polished off the last sneeze and lifted his suffering eyes to his hostess.

"You're sick!" declared Marilla with a kind of satisfaction, as if now she had something she could really take hold of. "I've thought it all evening. I first laid it to the wind in your face, for I knew you weren't the drinking kind. Then I thought maybe you'd been up all last night or something; lack of sleep makes eyes look that way. But I believe you've got the grippe, and I'm going to put you to bed and give you some homeopathic medicine. Come, tell me the truth. Aren't you chilly?"

With a half-sheepish smile the soldier admitted he was, and a big involuntary shudder ran over his tall frame with the admission.

"Well, it's high time we got to work. There's plenty of hot water. You go up to the bathroom and take a hot bath. I'll put a hot-water bag in the bed and get it good and warm. And I've got a long, warm flannel nightgown I guess you can put on. It was made for Grandmother, and she was a big woman. Come, we'll go right upstairs. I can come down and shut up the house while you're taking your bath."

The soldier protested, but Marilla swept all before her. She locked the front door and put the chain on. She turned out the parlor light and shoved the young man before her to the stairs.

"But I shouldn't," he protested again with one foot on the first step. "I'm an utter stranger."

"Well, what's that?" said Marilla crisply. " 'I was a stranger, and ye took me in.' When it comes to that, we're all strangers. Come, hurry up. You should be in bed. You'll feel like a new man when I get you tucked up."

"You're awfully good," he murmured, stumbling up the stairs. He had a sick realization that he was giving way to the chills and tremors that were dancing over him, that he was all in and in a few minutes more would be a contemptible coward, letting a lone, old woman fuss over him this way.

Marilla turned up the light and threw back the covers of the spare bed, sending a whiff of lavender through the room. The Franklin heater glowed cheerfully, and the place was warm as toast. There was something sweet and homelike in the old-fashioned room with its odd, ancient, framed photographs of people long gone and its plain but fine old mahogany. The soldier raised his bloodshot eyes and looked about with a thankful wish that he felt well enough to appreciate it all.

Marilla had pulled open a drawer and produced a long, flannel garment of nondescript fashion. From a closet she drew forth a long pink bathrobe and a pair of felt slippers.

"There! I guess you can get those on."

She bustled into the bathroom and turned on the hot water, then heaped big white bath towels and sweet-scented soap upon him. In a kind of daze of thankfulness he stumbled into the bathroom and began his bath. He hadn't had a bath like that in—was it two years? Somehow the hot water held down the sick tremors and cut out the chills for the time. It was wonderful to feel clean and warm and smell the freshness of the towels and soap. He climbed into the big nightgown which also smelled of lavender and came forth presently with the felt slippers on the front of his feet and the pink bathrobe trailing around his shoulders. A meek, conquered expression rested on his face. He crept gratefully into the warm bed according to directions and snuggled down with that sore thrill of thankfulness that everybody who has ever had grippe knows.

Marilla bustled up from the downstairs with a second hot-water bag in one hand and a thermometer in the other.

"I'm going to take your temperature," she said briskly and stuck the thermometer into his unresisting mouth.

It was wonderful to be fussed over this way, almost like having a mother. He hadn't had such care since he was a little fellow in the hospital at prep school.

"I thought so!" said Marilla, casting a practiced eye at the thermometer a moment later. "You've got quite a fever; and you've got to lie right still and do as I say, or you'll have a time of it. I hate to think what would have happened to you if I'd let you go off into the cold without any overcoat tonight."

"Oh, I'd have walked it off likely," said the old Adam faintly in the sleepy, sick soldier. But he knew as he spoke that he was lying, and he knew Miss Marilla knew it also. He would have laughed if it hadn't been too much trouble. It was wonderful to be in a bed like this and be warm, and that ache in his back against the hot-water bag! It almost made his head stop aching.

In moments he was asleep. He never realized when Marilla brought a glass and fed him medicine. He opened his mouth obediently when she told him and went right on sleeping.

"Bless his heart!" she said. "He must have been all worn out."

She turned the light low and, gathering up his chairful of clothes, slipped away to the bathroom, where presently they were all, except the shoes, soaking in strong, hot soapsuds. Then she went downstairs to stir up the fire and put on irons. But she took the precaution to close all the blinds on the Amber side of the house and pull down the shades. Mary never needed to find out what she was doing.

The night wore on, and Marilla worked with happy heart and willing hands. She was doing something for somebody who really needed it and for the time being had no one else to do for him. He was hers exclusively to be served this night. It was years since she'd had anybody of her own to care for, and she luxuriated in service.

Every hour she slipped up to feel his forehead, listen to his breathing and give him his medicine, and then she slipped down to the kitchen again to her ironing. Garment by garment the soldier's meager outfit came from the steaming suds and was conveyed to the kitchen, where it hung on an improvised line over the range and got itself dry enough to be ironed and patched. It was a work of love, and therefore it was done perfectly.

When morning dawned, the soldier's outfit, thoroughly renovated and pressed almost beyond recognition, lay on a chair by the spare-room window. And Marilla in her dark-blue serge morning dress lay down on the outside of her bed to take "forty winks." But even then she could hardly get to sleep; she was so excited thinking about her guest and wondering whether he would feel better when he awoke or whether she should send for a doctor.

A hoarse cough roused her an hour later, and she hurried to her patient and found him tossing and battling in his sleep with some imaginary foe.

"I don't owe you a cent!" he declared fiercely. "I've paid it all, even to the interest while I was in France. And there's no reason why I shouldn't tell you just what I think of you. You can go to thunder with your kind offers. I'm off *you* for life!" And then the big fellow turned with an anguished groan and buried his face in his pillow.

Marilla paused in horror, thinking she had intruded upon some secret meditation. As she waited on tiptoe and breathless in the hall, however, she heard the steady hoarse breathing keep on and knew he was still asleep. He didn't rouse, more than to open bloodshot, unseeing eyes and close them again when she loudly stirred his medicine in the glass and held the spoon to his lips. As before, he obediently opened his mouth and swallowed and went on sleeping.

She stood a moment anxiously watching him. She didn't know just what she should do. Perhaps he was going to have pneumonia! Perhaps she should send for the doctor, and yet there were complications about that. She would be obliged to explain a lot—or else lie to the neighborhood! And he might not like for her to call a doctor while he was asleep. If she only had someone with whom to advise!

On ordinary questions she always consulted Mary Amber, but by the very nature of the case the girl was out of this. Besides, in half an hour she discreetly put herself outside of any touch with Marilla's visitor by taking off in her runabout for a short visit to a college friend over in the next county. Mary Amber plainly didn't care to subject herself to further contact with the young soldier. He might be Dick, or he might not be Dick. It was none of her business while she was visiting Jeannette Clark; so she went away hurriedly.

Marilla heard the purr of the engine as the little car started down the hedged driveway and watched the flight with satisfaction. She had an intuition that Mary Amber wasn't in favor of her soldier, and she had a sense of hiding the truth from her dear young friend that made her breathe more freely as she watched Mary's flight. Moreover, it was with a certain self-reproachful relief she noted the little brown suitcase lying at the girl's feet as she slid past Marilla's house without looking up. Mary Amber was going away for the day at least, probably overnight. By that time the question of the soldier would be settled one way or the other without Mary's having to worry about it.

Marilla ordered a piece of beef and brewed a cup of the most delicious beef tea, which she took upstairs. She managed to get her soldier awake enough to swallow it. But it was plain he didn't realize where he was and seemed content to close his eyes and drowse away once more.

Marilla was deeply troubled. Some pricks from the timeworn adage beginning, "O what a tangled web we weave," began to stab her conscience. If only she hadn't allowed those paragraphs to go into the county paper! No, that wasn't the real trouble at all. If only she hadn't dragged in another soldier and made Mary Amber believe he was her nephew! Such an old fool! Just because she couldn't bear the mortification of having people know her nephew hadn't cared enough for her to come and see her when he was nearby! But she was well punished. Here she had a strange sick man on her hands and no end of responsibility! Oh, if only she hadn't asked him in!

Yet, as she stood watching the quick throb in his neck above the old flannel nightgown and the sweep of the dark lashes on his hot cheek as he slept, her heart cried out against the wish. No, a thousand times no. If she hadn't asked him in, he might have been in some hospital by this time, cared for by strangers. And she would have been alone, with empty hands, getting her own solitary dinner or sewing on the aprons for the orphanage, with nothing in the world to do that really mattered for anybody. Her heart went out to this stranger boy with a great yearning; he had come to mean her own—or what her own should have been to her. She wouldn't have him anywhere else for anything. She wanted him right where he was for her to care for, something she could love and tend, even if it were only for a few days.

And she was sure she could care for him. She knew a lot about sickness. People sent for her to help them out, and her wonderful nursing had often saved a life where the doctor's remedies had failed. She felt sure this was only a severe case of grippe that had taken fierce hold on his system. Thorough rest, careful nursing, nourishing broth and some of her homeopathic remedies would work the charm. She would try it a little longer and see. If his temperature wasn't higher than the last time, it would be safe to get along without a doctor.

She put the thermometer between his relaxed lips and held it there until she was sure it had been in long enough. Then she carried it softly over to the front window and studied it. No, it hadn't risen; in fact, it might be a fifth of a degree lower.

Well, she would venture it a little longer.

For two days Marilla cared for her stranger soldier as only a born nurse could care, and on the third morning he rewarded her by opening his eyes and looking about. Then, meeting her own anxious gaze, he gave her a weak smile.

"I've been sick!" he said as if stating an astonishing fact to himself. "I must have given you a lot of trouble."

"Not a bit of it, you dear child," said Marilla, stooping and brushing his forehead with her lips in a motherly kiss. "I'm so glad you're better!"

She passed her hand like soft old fallen rose leaves over his forehead, and it was moist. She felt of his hands, and they were moist too. She took his temperature, and it had gone down almost to normal. Her eyes were shining with more than professional joy and relief. He had become to her in these hours of nursing and anxiety as her own child.

But at the kiss the boy's eyelashes had swept down upon his cheek. When she looked up from reading the thermometer, she saw a tear glisten unwillingly beneath the lashes.

The next two days were a time of untold joy to Marilla while she petted and nursed her soldier boy back to some degree of his normal strength. She treated him as if he were a little child who had dropped from the skies to her loving ministrations. She bathed his face, puffed up his pillows, took his temperature, dosed him, fed him and read him to sleep. Marilla could read well, too. She was always asked to read the chapter at the Fortnightly Club whenever the regular reader whose turn it was failed. And while he was asleep she cooked dainty, appetizing little dishes for him. They had a wonderful time together, and he enjoyed it as much as she did. The fact was he was too weak to object, for the grippe had done a thorough work with him. He was, as he put it, "all in and *then* some."

He seemed to have gone back to his childhood days since the fever began to abate, and he lay in a sweet daze of comfort and rest. His troubles, perplexities and loneliness had dropped away from him, and he felt no desire to think of them. He was having the time of his life.

Then suddenly, wholly unannounced and not altogether desired at the present stage of the game, Mary Amber arrived on the scene.

Chapter 5

Mary was radiant as the sunny morning in a red tam, and her cheeks as red as her hat from the drive across country. She appeared at the kitchen door in her accustomed way as Marilla was lifting the dainty tray to carry her boy's breakfast upstairs, and she almost dropped it in her dismay.

"I've had the grandest time!" exclaimed Mary Amber. "You don't know how beautiful the country is, all bronze and brown with a purple haze, and a frost like silver lace this morning when I started. You've simply got to put on your wraps and come with me for a little while. I know a place where the shadows melt slowly, and the frost won't be gone yet. Come quick! I want you to see it before it's too late. You're not just eating your breakfast, Auntie Rill! And on a tray, too! Are you sick?"

Marilla glanced guiltily down at the tray, too transparent even to evade the question.

"No, why—I—he—my neph—"

She stopped in hopeless confusion, remembering her resolve not to tell a lie about the matter, whatever came.

Mary Amber stood up and looked at her, her keen young eyes searching and finding the truth.

"You don't mean to tell me *that man* is here yet? And you waiting on him!"

Both sorrow and scorn were in the fine young voice.

In the upper hall the sick soldier in a bathrobe was hanging over the banisters in a panic, wishing some kind angel would arrive and waft him away on a breath. All his perfidy in getting sick on a strange gentlewoman's hands and lying lazily in bed, letting her wait on him, was shown up in Mary Amber's voice. It found its echo in his own strong soul. He had known all along that he had no business there, that he should have gone out on the road to die rather than betray the sweet hospitality of Miss Marilla by allowing himself to be a selfish, lazy slob—that was what he called himself as he hung over the banisters.

"Mary! Why, he's been very *sick!*"

"Sick?" There was a covert sneer in Mary Amber's incredulous young voice.

The conversation was suddenly blanketed by the closing of the hall door, and the sick soldier padded disconsolately back to bed, weak and dizzy, but determined. This was as good a time as any. He should have gone before!

He trailed across the room in the big flannel nightgown that hung out from him with the outlines of a stout old auntie and dragged down from one bronzed shoulder rakishly. His hair was sticking up wildly, and he felt of his chin fiercely and realized he was wearing a growth of several days.

In a neat pile on a chair he found his few clean garments and struggled into them. His carefully ironed uniform hung in the closet. He braced himself and struggled into the trousers. It seemed a tremendous effort. He longed to drop back on the pillows but wouldn't. He sat with his head in his hands, his elbows on his knees, trying to get courage to totter to the bathroom and subdue his hair and beard, when he heard Marilla coming hastily up the stairs. The little coffeepot was sending on a delicious odor, and the glass of milk tinkled against the silver spoons as she came.

He had managed his leggings by this time and looked up with an attempt at a smile, trying to pass it off in a jocular way.

"I thought it was high time I was getting about," he said and broke down coughing.

Marilla paused in distress and looked at his hollow eyes. Everything seemed to be going wrong this morning. Oh, why hadn't Mary Amber stayed away just one day longer? But of course he hadn't heard her.

"Oh, you're not fit to be up yet!" she exclaimed. "Do lie down and rest till you've had your breakfast."

"I can't be a baby having you wait on me any longer," he said. "I'm ashamed of myself. I shouldn't have stayed here at all!" His tone was savage, and he reached for his coat and jammed it on with a determined air in spite of his weakness and the sore shivers that crept shakily up his back. "I'm perfectly all right, and you've been wonderful. But it's time I was moving on."

He pushed past her hurriedly to the bathroom, feeling he must get out of her sight before his head began to swim. The water on his face would steady him. He dashed it on and shivered, longing to plunge back into bed, yet continuing his ablutions.

Marilla put down her tray and stood with tears in her eyes, waiting for him to return, trying to think what she could say to persuade him back to bed again.

Her anxious expression softened him when he came back, and he agreed to eat his breakfast before he went anywhere. He sank gratefully into the big chair in front of the Franklin heater, where she had laid out his breakfast on a little table. She had lined the chair with a big comforter, which she drew unobtrusively about his shoulders now, slipping a cushion under his feet and quietly coddling him into comfort again. He looked at her gratefully and, setting down his coffee cup, reached out and patted her hair as she arose from tucking up his feet.

"You're just like a mother to me!" he said, trying to keep back the emotion from his voice. "It's been great! I can't tell you!"

"You've been just like a dear son," she beamed, touching the dark hair over his forehead shyly. "It's like getting my own back again to have you come for this little while and be able to do for you. You see it wasn't as if I really had anybody. Dick never cared for me. I used to hope he would when he grew up. I used to think of him over there in danger and pray for him and love him and send him sweaters. But now I know it was really you I thought of and prayed for. Dick never cared."

He looked at her tenderly and pressed her hand.

"You're wonderful!" he said. "I'll never forget it."

That precious time while he was eating his breakfast made it even harder for what he meant to do. He saw he could never hope to do it openly either. She would fling herself in his path to prevent him from going out until he was well. So he let her tuck him up carefully on the spread-up bed and pull down the shades for him to take a nap after the exertion of getting dressed. He caught her hand, kissed it fervently as she was leaving him and cherished her murmured "Dear child!" Then he closed his eyes and let her slip away to the kitchen where he knew she would be for some time preparing something delicious for his dinner.

When she was safely out of hearing, rattling away at the kitchen stove, he threw back the covers vigorously, set his grim determination against the swimming head, stalked over to the little desk and wrote a note on the fine notepaper he found there.

Dear wonderful little mother, I can't stay here any longer. It isn't right. But I'll be back someday to thank you if everything goes all right.

Sincerely,
Your Boy

He tiptoed over and laid it on the pillow. Then he took his old trench cap, neatly pressed and hanging on the corner of the looking glass, and stealthily slid out of the pleasant, warm room down the carpeted stairs and out the front door into the crisp, cold morning. The chill air met him with a challenge as he closed the front door and dared him not to cough. But with an effort he held his breath and crept down the front walk to the road, holding in control as well the long, violent shivers that seized him in their grasp. The sun met him and blinded his sensitive eyes. The wind with a tang of winter jeered at his thin uniform and trickled up his sleeves and down his collar, penetrating every seam. But he stuffed his hands into his pockets and strode grimly ahead on the way he had been going when Marilla met him, passing the tall hedge where Mary Amber lived and trying to hold his head high. He hoped Mary Amber saw him *going away!*

For perhaps half a mile past Mary Amber's house his courage and pride held him, for he was a soldier, who had slept in a muck pile under the rain, held his nerve under fire and gone on foot ten miles to the hospital after he was wounded. What was a little grippe and a walk in the cold to the neighboring village? He wished he knew how far it was, but he had to go, for it would never do to send the telegram he must send from the town where Miss Marilla lived.

The second half-mile he lagged and shivered, without enough energy to keep up a circulation. The third half-mile and the fourth were painful, and the fifth was completed in a sick daze of weakness. The cold, though stimulating at first, had been getting in its work through his uniform, and he felt chilled to the very soul. His teeth were chattering, and he was blue around the lips when he staggered into the telegraph office of Little Silverton. His fingers were almost too stiff to write, and his thoughts seemed to have congealed also, though he had been repeating the message all the way, word for word, with a vague feeling that he might forget it forever if he didn't keep it going.

"Will you send that collect?" he asked the operator when he had finished writing.

The girl took the blank and read it carefully.

Arthur J. Watkins, Esq.,
LaSalle Street, Chicago, Illinois
   Please negotiate a loan of five hundred dollars for me, using old house as collateral. Wire money immediately Little Silverton. Entirely out of funds. Have been sick.

Lyman Gage

The girl read it through again and then eyed him cautiously.

"What's your address?" she asked, giving a slow speculative chew to her gum.

"I'll wait here," said the big blue soldier, sinking into a rush-bottomed chair by the desk.

"It might be some wait," said the girl dryly, giving him another curious once-over.

"I'll wait!" he repeated fiercely and dropped his aching head into his hands.

The instrument clicked away vigorously. In his fevered brain he imagined it writing on a typewriter at the other end of the line and felt a curious impatience for his lawyer to read it and reply. How he wished it would hurry!

The morning droned on, and the telegraph instrument chattered breezily, with the monotony of a sunny child who knows no larger world and is happy. Sometimes it seemed to Gage as if every click pierced his head and he was going crazy. The shivers were keeping in time running up and down his back and chilling his very heart. The room was cold, cold, *cold!* How did that foolish girl stand it in a pink transparent blouse, showing her fat arms huskily? He shivered. Oh, for one of Miss Marilla's nice thick blankets and a hot-water bag! Oh, for the soft, warm bed, the quiet room and Miss Marilla keeping guard! But he was a man—and a soldier!

And every now and then would come Mary Amber's keen accusing voice: "Is *that man* here yet? And you *waiting on him!*" That was what kept him up when he might have given way. He *must* show her he was a man. *"That man!"* What did she mean? Did she suspect him of being a fraud and not the real nephew? Well, what did he care? Let Mary Amber go to thunder! Or, if she didn't want to go, he would go to thunder himself. He felt himself there already.

Two hours went by. Now and then someone came in with a message and went out again. The girl behind the desk got out a pink sweater she was knitting and chewed gum in time to her needles. Sometimes she eyed her companion curiously, but he didn't stir or look up. If there hadn't been prohibition, she might have thought him drunk. She began to think about his message and weave a crude little romance around him. She wondered whether he'd been wounded. If he had given her half a chance, she would have asked him questions. But he sat there with his head in his hands like a stone image and never seemed to know she was in the room.

After a while it got on her nerves. She took up her telephone and carried on a gallery conversation with a fellow laborer somewhere up the line, giggling a good deal and telling about a movie she went to the night before. She used rare slang, with a furtive glance at the soldier for developments. But he didn't stir. Finally she remarked loudly that it was getting noontime and "so-longed" her friend, clicking the receiver into place.

"I gotta go to lunch now," she remarked in an impersonal tone. "I have an hour off. This office is closed all noontime."

He didn't seem to hear her. She repeated, and Gage looked up with blood-shot, heavy eyes.

"What happens to the message if it comes while you're away?" he asked feverishly.

"Oh, it'll be repeated," she replied easily. "You c'n come back 'bout two o'clock er later, 'n' mebbe it'll be here. I gotta lock up now."

Lyman Gage dragged himself to his feet and looked about him. Then he staggered out onto the street.

The sun hit him a clip in the eyes again that made him sick, and the wind caught at his sleeves and ran down his collar gleefully. The girl shut the door with a click and turned the key, eyeing him. He seemed to her very stupid for a soldier. If he had given her half a chance, she would have been friendly to him. She watched him drag down the street with an amused contempt, then turned to her belated lunch.

Lyman Gage walked on down the road a little way and then began to feel as if he couldn't stand the cold a second longer, though he knew he must. His heart was behaving oddly, seeming to be absent from his body for whole seconds at a time and then returning with leaps and bounds that almost suffocated him. He paused and looked around for a place to sit down and, finding none, dropped down on the frozen ground at the roadside. It occurred to him he should go back now while he was able, for he was fast getting to the place where from sheer weakness he couldn't walk.

He rested a moment and then stumbled up and back toward Little Silverton. Automobiles passed him, and he remembered thinking that, if he weren't so sick and odd in his head, he would try to stand in the road and stop one and get the people to carry him somewhere. He had often done that in France or even in this country during the war. But now it seemed he couldn't do that either. He had set out to prove to Mary Amber he was a man and a soldier, and hold-ing up automobiles wouldn't be compatible with that idea.

Then he realized that all this was crazy thinking, that Mary Amber had gone to thunder and so had he, and it didn't matter anyway. All that mattered was for him to get that money and go back and pay Miss Marilla for taking care of him, and then for him to take the next train back to the city and get to a hospital. If he could only hold out long enough for that. But things were fast getting away from him. His head was hot and in a whirl, and his feet were so cold he thought they must be dead.

Without realizing it he walked by the telegraph office and on down the road toward Purling Brook again.

The telegraph girl watched him from the window of the tiny bakery where she ate her lunch.

"There goes that poor idiot *now!*" she said with her mouthful of pie a la mode. "He gets my goat! I hope he doesn't come back. He'll never get no answer to that telegram he sent. People ain't goin' round pickin' up five hundred dollarses to send to broke soldiers these days. They got 'um all in Liberty Bonds. Say, Jess, gimme one more o' them chocolate éclairs, won't you? I gotta get back."

About that time Lyman Gage found a log by the wayside and sank down on it. He had no more breath to carry him on and no more ambition. If Mary Amber had gone to thunder, why should he care whether he got an answer to his telegram or not? She was only another girl, anyway—GIRL, his enemy! And he sank into a blue stupor, with his elbows on his cold, cold knees and his face hidden in his hands. He had forgotten the shivers now. They'd taken possession of him and made him one with them. It might be, after all, that he was too hot and not too cold. And there was a strange burning pain in his chest when he tried to breathe, so he wouldn't breathe. What was the use?

Chapter 6

Marilla tiptoed softly up the hall and listened at the door of the spare bedroom. It was time her soldier boy woke up and had some dinner. She had a beautiful little treat for him today, chicken broth with rice and some little bits of tender breast meat on toast, with a quivering spoonful of currant jelly.

It was very still in the spare room, so still that a falling coal from the grate of the Franklin heater made a hollow sound when it fell into the pan below. If the boy was asleep, she could usually tell by his regular breathing. She listened with a keen ear, but she couldn't hear it today. Perhaps he was awake, sitting up. She pushed the door open and looked in. Why! The bed was empty! She glanced around the room, and it was empty too!

She passed her hand across her eyes as if they had deceived her and went over to look at the bed. Surely he must be there somewhere! And then she saw the note.

"Dear wonderful little mother!"

Her eyes were too blurred with quick tears and apprehension to read any further. "Mother!" He'd called her that. She could never feel quite alone in the world again. But where was he? She took the corner of her white apron and wiped the tears away vigorously to finish the note. Then, without pausing to think and even in the midst of her apprehension, she turned swiftly and went downstairs, out the front door, across the frozen lawn and through the hedge to Mary Amber's house.

"Mary! Mary Amber!" she called as she panted up the steps, the note grasped tightly in her trembling hand.

She hoped Mary Amber's mother wouldn't come to the door and ask questions. Mary's mother was so sensible, and Marilla always felt as if Mrs. Amber disapproved of her just a little whenever she was doing anything for anybody. Not that Mary Amber's mother wasn't kind to people. But she was always so sensible in her kindness and did things in the regular way and wasn't impulsive like Marilla.

But Mary Amber herself came to the door, with pleasant forgetfulness of her old friend's recent coolness, and tried to draw her into the hall. This Marilla firmly declined, however. She threw her apron over her head and shoulders as a concession to Mary's fears for her health.

"Oh, don't talk about me, Mary. Talk about *him*. He's gone! I thought he was asleep. I went up to see if he was ready for his dinner, and he's *gone!* And he's sick, Mary. He's not able to stand up. Why, he's had a fever. It was a hundred and three for two days and only got down to below normal this morning for the first time. He isn't fit to be out either—and that little thin uniform with no overcoat!"

The tears were streaming down Marilla's sweet Dresden-china face, and Mary Amber's heart was touched in spite of her.

She came and put her arm around Marilla's shoulder and drew her down the steps and over to her own home, closing the door carefully first so her mother didn't need to be troubled about it. Mary Amber always had tact when she wanted to use it.

"Where was he going, dear?" she asked sympathetically, with a view to making out a good case for the soldier without Marilla's bothering further about him.

"I—do—don't know!" sobbed Marilla. "He just thought he shouldn't stay and bother me. Here! See his note."

"Well, I'm glad he had some sense," said Mary with satisfaction. "He was perfectly right about not staying to bother you." She took the little crumpled note and smoothed it out.

"Oh, my dear, you don't understand," said Marilla sobbing. "He's been such a good, dear boy and so ashamed he'd troubled me! And really, Mary, he'll not be able to stand it. Why, you should see how little clothes he had! So thin, and cotton underwear! I washed them and mended them, but he should have had an overcoat."

"Oh, well, he'll go to the city and get something warm and go to a hospital if he falls sick," said Mary Amber comfortably. "I wouldn't worry about him. He's a soldier. He's stood lots worse things than a little cold. He'll look out for himself."

"Don't!" said Marilla fiercely. "Don't say that, Mary! You don't understand. He is *sick,* and he's all the soldier boy I've got—and I've *got* to go after him. He can't be gone very far, and he really isn't able to walk. He's weak. I can't stand to have him go this way."

Mary Amber looked at her with a curious light in her eyes.

"And yet, Auntie Rill, you know it was fine of him to do it," she said with a dancing dimple in the corner of her mouth. "Well, I see what you want. And, much as I hate to, I'll take my car and scour the country for him. What time did you say he left?"

"Oh, Mary Amber!" smiled Marilla through her tears. "You're a good girl. I knew you'd help me. I'm sure you can find him if you try. He can't have been gone over an hour, not much. I've only fixed the chicken and put my bread in the pans since I left him."

"I suppose he went back to the village, but there hasn't been any train since ten, and you say he was still there at ten. He's likely waiting at the station for the twelve o'clock. I'll speed up and get there before it comes. I have fifteen minutes. I"—glancing at her wristwatch—"I guess I can make it."

"I'm not so sure he went that way," said Marilla, looking up the road past Mary Amber's house. "He was on his way up that way when—"

Marilla suddenly shut her mouth and didn't finish the sentence. Mary Amber gave her another curious, discerning look and nodded brightly.

"You go in and get warm, Auntie Rill. Leave that soldier to me. I'll bring him home."

Then she dashed back through the hedge to the garage and in a few minutes was speeding down the road toward the station.

Marilla watched her in troubled silence and then, putting on her cape that always hung handy by the hall door, walked a little distance up the road, straining her old eyes, but seeing nothing. Finally in despair she turned back. Presently, just as she reached her own steps again, she saw Mary's car come flying back with only Mary in it. But Mary didn't stop or even look toward the house. She sped on up the road this time, and the purring of the engine was sweet music to Marilla's ears. Dear Mary Amber, how she loved her!

❧

The big blue soldier, cold to his soul and full of pain that reminded him of the long horror of the war, was still sitting by the roadside with his head in his hands when Mary Amber's car came flying down the road. She stopped before him with a little triumphant purr of the engine, so close to him that it roused him from his lethargy to look up.

"I should think you'd be ashamed of yourself, running away from Miss Marilla like this and making her worry herself sick!"

Mary Amber's voice was sharp as icicles, and the words went through him like red-hot needles. He straightened up, and the light of battle came back to his eyes. This was GIRL again, his enemy. His firm upper lip moved sensitively and came down straight and strong against the lower one, showing the nice line of character that made his mouth handsome.

"Thank you," he said coldly. "I'm only ashamed I stayed so long." His tone further added that he didn't know what business of hers it was.

"Well, she sent me for you. And you'll please to get in quickly, for she's very much worked up about you."

Mary Amber's tone stated that she herself wasn't in the least worked up about a great, hulking soldier who would let a woman wait on him for several days hand and foot and then run away when her back was turned.

"Kindly tell her I'm sorry I troubled her, but it isn't possible for me to return at present," he answered stiffly. "I came down to send a business telegram, and I'm waiting for an answer."

A sudden shiver seized him and rippled involuntarily over his big frame. Mary Amber was eyeing him contemptuously, but a light of pity stole into her eyes as she saw him shiver.

"You're cold!" said Mary as if she were charging him with an offense.

"Well, that's not strange—is it—on a day like this? I haven't made connections yet with an overcoat and gloves—that's all."

"Look here—if you're cold, you've simply got to get into this car and let me take you back to Miss Marilla. You'll catch your death of cold sitting there like that."

"Well, I may be cold, but I don't *have* to let you take me anywhere. When I get ready to go, I'll walk. As for catching my death of cold, that's strictly my own affair. Nobody in the world would care if I did."

The soldier had blue lights like steel in his eyes, and his mouth looked very soldier-like indeed. His whole manner showed there was no use trying to argue with him.

Mary Amber eyed him with increasing interest and thoughtfulness.

"You're mistaken," she said grudgingly. "There's one. There's Miss Marilla. It would break her heart. She's like that. And she hasn't much to care for in the world either. Which makes it all the worse what you've done. Oh, I don't see how you *could* deceive her."

"Deceive her?" said the astonished soldier. "I never deceived her."

"Why, you let her think you were Dick Chadwick, her nephew. And you *know* you're not! I knew you weren't the minute I saw you, even before I found Dick's telegram in the stove saying he couldn't come. And then I asked you a lot of questions to find out for sure, and you couldn't answer one of them right." Her eyes were sparkling, and her face had an eager look, like an appeal, almost as if she wanted him to prove what she was saying wasn't true.

"No, I'm not Dick Chadwick," said the young man with fine dignity. "But I never deceived Miss Marilla."

"Well, who did then?" Disappointment and unbelief were in Mary Amber's voice.

"Nobody. She isn't deceived. She tried to deceive you."

"What do you mean?"

"I mean she wanted you to think I was her nephew. She was mortified, I guess, because he didn't turn up, and she didn't want you to know. So she asked me to dinner to fill in. I didn't know anybody was there till I was going in the door. Then I had to go and get sick in the night and dish the whole thing. I was a fool to give in to her, of course, and stay that night, but it sounded good to have a real night's sleep in a bed. I didn't think I was such a softie as to get out of my head and be on her hands like that. But you needn't worry. I intend to make it up to her fully as soon as I can lay hands on some funds—"

He suddenly broke into a fit of coughing so hoarse and croupy as to alarm even Mary Amber's cool contempt. She reached back in the car and, grasping a big fur coat, sprang out on the hard ground and threw the coat about him, tucking it around his neck and trying to fasten a button under his chin against his violent protest.

"You're very kind," he gasped loftily, as soon as he could recover his breath. "But I can't put that on, and I'm going down to the telegraph office now to see if my wire has come yet."

"Look here," said Mary Amber in quite a different tone. "I'm sorry I was so suspicious. I see I didn't understand. I ask your pardon, and won't you please put on this coat and get into this car and let me take you home quick? I'm really very troubled about you."

The soldier looked up in surprise at the gentleness, and almost his heart melted. The snarly look around his mouth and eyes disappeared, and he seemed a bit confounded.

"Thank you," he said simply. "I appreciate that. But I can't let you help me, you know."

"Oh, please!" she said, a kind of little-girl alarm springing into her eyes. "I won't know what to say to Miss Marilla. I promised her I'd bring you back."

His eyes and lips were hardening again. She saw he didn't mean to yield, and Mary Amber wasn't used to being balked in her purposes. She glanced down the road, and a sudden light came into her eyes and brought a dimple of mischief into her cheek.

"You'll have to for my sake," she said hurriedly in a lower tone. "There's a car coming with some people in it I know. They'll think it awfully odd for me to be standing here on a lonely roadside talking to a strange soldier sitting on a log on a day like this. Hurry!"

Lyman Gage glanced up and saw the car coming swiftly. He saw, too, the dimple of mischief. But with an answering light of gallantry in his eyes he sprang up and helped her into the car. The effort brought on another fit of coughing.

As soon as he could speak he said, "You can take me down to that telegraph office, if you please, and drop me there. Then nobody will think anything about it."

"I'll take you to the telegraph office if you'll be good and put that coat on right and button it," said Mary Amber commandingly. She had him in the car now and knew she could go so fast he couldn't get out. "But I won't stop there until you promise me on your honor as a soldier that you won't get out or make any more trouble about my taking you back to Miss Marilla."

The soldier looked very balky indeed, and his firm mouth got itself into fine shape again, till he looked into Mary Amber's eyes and saw the saucy, beautiful lights there. Then he broke down laughing.

"Well, you've caught me by guile," he said, "and I guess we're about even. I'll go back and make my adieus to Miss Marilla."

A little curve of satisfaction settled about Mary Amber's mouth. "Put that coat on, please."

The soldier put it on gratefully. He was beginning to feel a reaction from his battle with Mary Amber, and now that he was defeated the coat seemed most desirable.

"Don't you think it would be a good idea if you'd tell me who you really are?" asked Mary Amber. "It might save some embarrassment."

"Why, certainly!" said the soldier in surprise. "It hadn't occurred to me— that's all. I'm Lyman Gage, of Chicago." He named his rank and regiment in the army. Then, looking at her curiously, he said, hesitating, "I'm—perfectly respectable. I don't really make a practice of going around sponging off unprotected ladies."

Her cheeks flamed a gorgeous scarlet, and her eyes looked rebuked.

"I suppose I should apologize," she said. "But really, you know, it looked rather peculiar to me—"

She stopped suddenly, for he was seized with another fit of coughing, which had such a shrill sound that she involuntarily turned to look at him with anxious eyes.

"I s'pose it did look odd," he managed to say at last. "But you know that day when I came in I didn't care a hang." He dropped his head wearily against the car and closed his eyes for just a second, as if keeping them open was a great effort.

"You're all in now!" she said sharply. "And you're shivering! You should be in bed this minute." Her voice held deep concern. "Where is that telegraph office? We'll just leave word for them to forward the message if it hasn't come, and then we'll fly back."

"Oh, I must wait for the message," he said, straightening up with a hoarse effort and opening his eyes sharply. "It's really imperative."

She stopped the car in front of the telegraph office. The operator, scenting a romance, scuttled out of the door with an envelope in her hand and a different look on her face from the one she wore when she went to lunch. She hadn't had much faith in that soldier or in the message he had sent "collect." Nor had she believed any answer would come, or at least any favorable one.

Now she hurried across the pavement to the car, studying Mary Amber's red tam as she talked and wondering whether she couldn't make one like it out of the red lining of an old army cape she had.

"Yer message's come," she announced affably. "Come just after I got back. An' I got yer check all made out fer yah. You sign here. See? Got anybody to 'dentify yah? 'Tain't necessary, see? I c'n waive identification."

"I can identify him," spoke up Mary Amber with cool dignity.

The soldier looked at her wonderingly. That was a very different tone from the one she'd used when she came after him. After all, what did Mary Amber know about him?

He looked at the check as if it weren't real. His head felt very odd. The words of the message seemed all jumbled. He crumpled it in his hand.

"Ain't yah going to send an answer?" put in the operator aggrievedly, hugging the thin muslin sleeves of her soiled shirtwaist to keep from shivering. "He says to wire him immediately. He says it's important. I guess you didn't take notice to the message."

The soldier tried to smooth out the crumpled paper with his numb fingers. Seeing he was feeling miserable, Mary Amber took it from him and placed it before him.

Am sending you a thousand. Wire me your post-office address immediately. Good news. Important.

Arthur J. Watkins

"I guess I can't answer that now," said the soldier, trying his best to keep his teeth from chattering. "I don't just know—"

"Here, I'll write it for you," said Mary with sudden understanding. "You better have it sent in Aunt Rill's care, and then you can have it forwarded anywhere. I'll write it for you."

She took a silver pencil from the pocket of her coat and wrote the telegram rapidly on a corner she tore from the first message, handing it out for his inspection and then passing it on to the operator, who gathered it in.

"Send this c'lect too, I s'pose," she called after the car as it departed.

"Yes, all right, anything," answered Lyman Gage, wearily sinking back in the seat. "It doesn't matter anyway."

"You're sick!" said Mary Amber anxiously. "We're going to get right home. Miss Marilla will be wild."

The soldier sat up holding his precious check.

"I'll have to ask you to let me out," he said, trying to be dignified under the heavy stupor of weariness that was creeping over him. "I've got to get to a bank."

"Oh, must you today? Couldn't we wait till tomorrow or till you feel better?" asked Mary anxiously.

"No, I must go now," he insisted.

"Well, there's a bank on the next corner," she said, "and it must be closing time." She shoved her sleeve back and glanced at her watch. "Just five minutes till three. We'll stop, but you'll promise to hurry, won't you? I want to get you home. I'm worried about you."

Lyman Gage cast her another of those wondering looks like a child unused to kindness suddenly being petted.

It made her feel as if she wanted to cry. All the mother in her came to her eyes. She drew up in front of the bank and got out after him.

"I'll go in with you," she said. "They know me over here, and it may save you trouble."

"You're very kind," he said almost curtly. "I dislike making you so much trouble—"

Perhaps it was because of Mary's presence that the transaction went through without question, and in a few minutes more they were back in the car again, Mary tucking up her big patient fussily.

"You're going to put this around your neck," she said, drawing a bright woolly scarf from her capacious coat pocket. "And around your head," she added, drawing a fold up around his ears and the back of his head. "And keep it over your nose and mouth. Breathe through it. Don't let this cold air get into your lungs," she finished with a businesslike air as if she were a nurse.

She drew the ends of the scarf around, completely hiding everything but his eyes, and tucked the ends into the neck of the fur coat. Then she produced another lap robe from some region beneath her feet and tucked that carefully around him.

It was wonderful being taken care of in this way; if only he weren't so cold and tired and sore all over he could have enjoyed it. The scarf had a delicate aroma of spring and violets, something that reminded him of pleasant things in the past. But it all seemed like a dream.

They were skimming along over the road he had come up at such a laborious pace, and the icy wind cut his eyeballs. He closed his eyes, and a hot curtain seemed to shut him out from a weary world. Almost he seemed to be spinning away into space. He tried to open his mouth under the woolen fragrance and speak. But his companion ordered him sharply to be still till he got where it was warm, and a sharp cough like a knife caught him. So he sank back again into the perfumed silence of the fierce heat and cold that seemed to be raging through his body and continued the struggle to keep from drifting into space. It didn't seem quite gallant or gentlemanly to say nothing, or soldierly to drift away like that when she was being so kind.

And then a curious memory of the other girl drifted around in the frost of his breath mockingly, as if she were laughing at his situation, almost as if she had put him there and was glad. He tried to shake this off by opening his eyes and concentrating on Mary Amber as she sat sternly at her wheel, driving her machine for all it was worth, her eyes anxious and the flush on her cheek bright and glowing. The notion came to him that she was in league with him against the other girl. He knew it was foolish, and he tried to drive the idea away. But it stayed till she passed her own hedge and stopped the car at Miss Marilla's gate.

Then it seemed to clear away, and common sense reigned for a few brief moments while he stumbled out of the car and into Marilla's parlor and the warmth and cheer of that good woman's almost tearful, affectionate welcome.

"I want you to take that," he said hoarsely, pressing into her hand the roll of bills he had secured at the bank. Then he slid down into a big chair, and everything whirled away again.

Marilla stood aghast, looking at the money and then at the sick soldier, till Mary Amber took command.

He never remembered just what happened or knew how he got upstairs and into the warm, kind bed again, with hot broth being fed him and hot-water bags in places needing them. He didn't hear them call the doctor on the telephone or know when Mary slipped away down to her car again and rode away.

But Mary Amber knew this was the afternoon when *The Purling Brook Chronicle* went to press, and she had an item that must get in. Quite demurely she handed the envelope to the woman editor as she was preparing to mail the last of her copy to the printer in the city. The item read:

> *Miss Marilla Chadwick, of Shirley Road, is entertaining over the weekend Sergeant Lyman Gage, of Chicago, just returned from France. Sergeant Gage is a member of the same division and came over in the same ship with Miss Chadwick's nephew, Lieutenant Richard Chadwick, of whom mention has been made in a former number, and has seen long and interesting service abroad.*

Mary Amber was back at the house almost before she was missed and just as the doctor arrived, ready to serve in any capacity whatever.

"Do you think I should introduce him to the doctor?" Marilla asked Mary in an undertone at the head of the stairs, while the doctor was divesting himself of his big fur overcoat. She had a drawn anxious look like one about to be found out in a crime.

"He doesn't look to me as if he could acknowledge the introduction," said Mary with a glance in at the spare bed, where the young man lay sleeping heavily and breathing noisily.

"But—should I tell him his name?"

"That's all right, Auntie Rill," said Mary. "I told him his name was Gage when I phoned, and I said he was in the same division with your nephew. It isn't necessary for you to say anything about it."

Marilla paused and eyed Mary strangely with a frightened, appealing look and then with growing relief. So Mary Amber knew! She sighed and turned back to the sickroom with a comforted expression growing around her mouth.

But the comforted expression changed once more to anxiety, and self was forgotten when Marilla began to watch the doctor's face as the examination progressed.

"What has this young man been doing?" he growled, rising from a position on his knees where he'd been listening to the soldier's breathing with an ever-increasing frown.

Marilla looked at Mary quite frightened, and Mary stepped into the breach.

"He had a heavy cold when he came here, and Miss Chadwick nursed him, and he was doing nicely. But he ran away this morning. He had some business to attend to and slipped away before anybody could stop him. He got very chilled, I think."

"I should say he did!" exclaimed the doctor. "Young fool! I suppose he thought he could stand anything because he went through the war. Well, he'll get his now. He's in for pneumonia. I'm sorry, Miss Chadwick, but I'm afraid you've got a bad case on your hands. Would you like to have me phone for an ambulance and get him to the hospital? I think it can be done at once with a minimum of risk."

"Oh, no, no!" said Marilla, clasping one white hand and then the other nervously. "I couldn't think of that—at least, not unless you think it's necessary—not unless you think it's a risk to stay here. You see he's my—that is, he's almost—like—my own nephew." She lifted appealing eyes.

"Oh, I beg your pardon!" he said with a look of relief. "In that case he's to be congratulated. But, madam, you'll have your hands full before you're through. He's made a very bad start—a very bad start indeed. When these big, husky fellows get sick, they do it thoroughly. Now if you'll just step over here, Mary, I'll explain to you both about this medicine. Give this every half-hour till I get back. I'll run up here again in about two hours. I've got to drive over to the Plush Mills now, to an accident case. But I'll be back as quick as I can.

I want to watch this fellow pretty closely for the first few hours."

When the doctor was gone, Mary Amber and Marilla stood one on each side of the bed and looked at each other, making silent covenant together over the sick soldier.

"Now," said Mary Amber softly, "I'm going down into the kitchen to look after things. You just sit here and watch him. I'll run over first to put the car away and tell Mother I'll stay with you tonight."

"Oh, Mary Amber, you mustn't do that," said Marilla anxiously. "I never meant to get you into all this scrape. Your mother won't like it at all. I'll get along all right. And, anyway, if I find I can't, I'll get Molly Poke to come and help me."

"Mother will be perfectly satisfied to have me help you in any way I can," said Mary with a light in her eyes. "As for Molly Poke, if I can't look after you better than she can, I'll go and hide my head. You can get Molly Poke when I fail, but not till then. Now, Auntie Rill, go sit down in the rocking chair and rest. Didn't I tell you I'd help get that turkey dinner? Well, the dinner isn't over yet—that's all. And I owe the guest an apology for misjudging him. He's all right, and we've got to pull him through, Auntie Rill—so here goes."

Mary Amber gave Marilla a loving squeeze and sped down the stairs. Marilla sat down to listen to the heavy breathing of the sick soldier and watch the dark lashes on the sunken, tanned cheeks.

Chapter 7

For three weeks the two women nursed Lyman Gage, with now and then the help of Molly Poke in the kitchen. Some days they came and went silently, looking at each other with stricken glances and at the sick man with pity. And Mary Amber went and looked at the letter lying on the bureau and wondered whether she should telegraph that man who sent the soldier the money that day. Another letter arrived and then a telegram, all from Chicago. Then Mary and Marilla talked it over and decided to make some reply.

By that time the doctor had said Lyman Gage would pull through, and he had opened his eyes once or twice and smiled weakly at them. Mary Amber went to the telegraph office and sent a message to the person in Chicago whose name was written at the left-hand corner of the envelopes, the same that had been signed to that first telegram.

> Lyman Gage very ill at my home, pneumonia, not able to read letters or telegram. Slight improvement today.
>
> Marilla Chadwick

Within three hours an answer arrived.

> Much distressed at news of Gage's illness. Cannot come because of fractured bone, automobile accident. Please keep me informed and let me know if there is anything I can do.
>
> Arthur J. Watkins

Mary wrote a neat little note that night before she went on duty in the sick-room, stating that the invalid had smiled twice that day and asked what day of the week it was. The doctor felt that he was on the high road to recovery now, and there was nothing to do but be patient. They would show him his mail as soon as the doctor was willing, which would probably be in a few days now.

The day they gave Lyman Gage his mail to read, the sun was shining on a new fall of snow, and the air was crisp and clear. Geraniums were blossoming in the spare-room windows between the sheer white curtains, and the Franklin heater was glowing away and filling the place with the warmth of summer.

The patient had been fed what he called "a real breakfast," milk toast and a soft-boiled egg, and the sun was streaming over the foot of the bed as if to welcome him back to life. He seemed so much stronger that the doctor had given permission for him to be bolstered up with an extra pillow while he read his mail.

He hadn't seemed anxious to read the mail, even when they told him it was postmarked Chicago. Marilla carried it to him as if she were bringing him a bouquet, but Mary eyed him with a curious misgiving. Perhaps, after all, there wouldn't be good news. He seemed so apathetic. She watched him furtively as she tidied the room, putting away the soap and towels and pulling a dry leaf or two from the geraniums. He was so still, and it took him so long to make up his mind to tear open the envelopes after he had them in his thin white hand. It almost seemed as if he dreaded them like a blow and was trying to summon courage to meet them.

Once, as she looked at him, his eyes met hers with a deprecatory smile. To cover her confusion she spoke impulsively.

"You don't seem deeply concerned about the news," she said cheerily.

He smiled again almost sadly.

"Well, no!" he said thoughtfully. "I can't say I am. There really isn't much left to be interested in. You see, about the worst things that could happen have happened, and there's no chance for anything else."

"You can't always tell," said Mary Amber cheerfully, as she finished dusting the bureau and went downstairs for his morning glass of milk and egg.

Slowly Lyman Gage tore the envelope of the top letter and took out the written sheet. In truth he had little curiosity. It was likely an account of how his lawyer friend had paid back the money to Mr. Harrower or else the details of the loan on the old Chicago house. Houses and loans and such things seemed far from his world just now. He was impatient for Mary Amber to come back with that milk and egg. Not so much for the milk and egg as for the comfort it gave and the cheeriness of her presence. Presently Miss Marilla would come up and tell over some incident of Mary's childhood exactly as if he were Dick, the villain! He found himself hopelessly jealous of him sometimes. Yet he knew in a feeble faraway sense that this was only a foolish foible of an invalid, and he would get over it and laugh at himself when he got well.

He smiled at the pleasantness of it all, this getting-well business, and then turned his indifferent attention to the letter.

Dear Lyman,

Why in the world did you hide yourself away in that remote corner of the world? I've scoured the country to get trace of you without a single result till your telegram came.

There's good news to tell you. The unexpected has happened, and you're a rich man, old fellow. Don't let it turn your head, for there's plenty of business to occupy you as soon as you're able to return.

To make a long story short, the old tract of land in which you put all you had and a good deal more has come to the front in great shape at last. You'll remember that the ore was found in such a state when they came to mine it that it would cost fabulous sums for the initial operations, and it fell through because your company couldn't afford to get the proper machinery.

Well, the government has taken over the whole tract and is working it. I'm enclosing the details on another paper. You'll see, when you've looked it over, how much you're needed now at home to decide numerous questions which have taxed my ingenuity to the limit to know what you would want done.

There's a great deal of timber on those lands also—valuable timber, it seems. And that's another source of wealth for you.

Oh, this war has been a great thing for you, young man. You certainly should give extra thanks that you came out alive to enjoy it all. Properly managed, your property should keep you on Easy Street for the rest of your life, and then some.

I took pains to let Mr. Harrower know how the wind blew when I paid him the money you had borrowed from him. He certainly was one surprised man. And of course I don't speak officially, but from what he said I should judge that this might make a big difference with Elinore. So you better hurry home, old man, and get busy. The sun is shining, and the war is over.

> *Yours fraternally as well as officially,*
> *Arthur J. Watkins*

Over the first part of the letter Lyman Gage dallied comfortably as he might have with his grapefruit or the chicken on toast they'd promised him for lunch. He had lost his sense of world values for the time being, and just now a fortune was no more than a hot-water bag when one's feet were cold. It merely gave him the sense he needn't be in a hurry to get well; he could take things easy because he could pay for everything and give his friends a good time after he was on his feet again. In short, he was no longer a beggar on Miss Marilla's bounty with only a thousand dollars between him and debt or even the poorhouse.

But, when he came to that last paragraph, his face suddenly hardened, and into his eyes came a glint of steel as of old, while his jaw set sternly, and lines formed around his mouth—hard, bitter lines.

So that was what had been the matter with Elinore, was it? She didn't grow tired of *him* so much but wanted more money than she thought he could furnish for a long time. He stared off into the room, not seeing its cozy details for the first time since he began to get well. He was looking at the vision of the past trying to conjure up a face whose loveliness had held no imperfections. He was looking at it squarely now as it rose dimly in vision against the gray of Marilla's spare-room wall. For the first time he saw the petted underlip with the selfish droop at its corners, the pout when she couldn't have her own way, the frown of the delicate brows, the petulant tapping of a dainty foot, the proud lifted shoulder, the haughty stare, the cold tones and crushing contempt that were hers sometimes. These had seldom been for him. And when he had seen them, he had called them beautiful, gloried in them, fool that he was! Why had he been so blind, when there were girls in the world like—well—Mary Amber?

Misjudging Elinore? Well, perhaps, but somehow he didn't believe he was. Something had cleared his vision. He began to remember things in Elinore

Harrower he had never called by their true names before. It appeared Elinore had deliberately left him for a richer man, and it was entirely possible under the changed circumstances that she might leave the richer man for him if he could prove he was the richer of the two. Bah! What a thing to get well to! Why did there have to be things like that in the world? Well, it mattered very little to him what Elinore did. It might make a difference with her, but it would make no difference to him. Some things in her letter had cut too deep. He could never forget them, no, never, not even if she came crawling to his feet and begged him to come back to her.

As for going back to Chicago, business be hanged! He was going to stay right here and get well. A smile melted out on his lips, and comfort settled about him as he heard Mary Amber's step on the stairs and the soothing clink of the spoon in the glass of milk and egg.

"Good news?" asked Mary as she shoved up the little table and prepared to serve the milk and egg.

"Oh, so-so!" he answered with a smile, sweeping the letters away from him and looking at the foaming glass with eager eyes.

"Why! You haven't opened them all!" laughed Mary Amber.

"Oh! Haven't I?" he said impatiently, sweeping them up and tearing them open wholesale with only a glance at each, then throwing them back on the coverlet again.

"Nothing but the same old thing. Hounding me back to Chicago," he grinned. "I'm having much too good a time to get well too fast, you may be sure."

Somehow the room seemed cozier after that, and his sleep the sweeter when he took his nap. He ate his chicken on toast slowly to prolong the happy time. And he listened and smiled with deep relish at the little stories Marilla told of Mary Amber's childhood, the gingerbread men with currant eyes and the naughty Dick who stole them. This world he was in now was such a happy, clean world, so simple and good! Oh, if he could have known a world like this earlier in his life! If only he could have been the hapless Dick in reality!

Molly Poke was established in the kitchen downstairs now. Marilla hovered over her anxiously, leaving the entertaining of the invalid much to Mary Amber, who wrote neat business letters for him, telling his lawyer friend to do just as he pleased with everything till he got back. She also read stories and bits of poems and played chess with him as soon as the doctor allowed. Oh, they were having a happy time, the three of them! Marilla fluttered about the two as if they had been her own children.

And then one lovely winter afternoon, when they were discussing how they might take the invalid out for a ride in the car one day next week, the fly dropped into the ointment!

It was as lovely a fly as ever walked on tiny French heels and came in a limousine lined with gray duvetyn, heated electrically and graced with hothouse rosebuds in a slender glass behind the chauffeur's right ear. She picked her way daintily up the snowy walk, surveyed the house and grounds as far as the

Amber hedge and rang the bell abruptly.

Marilla herself went to the front door, for Molly Poke was busy making cream puffs and couldn't stop. When she saw the fly standing haughtily on the porch, swathed in a gorgeous moleskin cloak with a voluminous collar of tailless ermine and a little toque made of coral velvet embroidered in silver, she thought right away of a spider.

And, when the beautiful red lips opened and spoke, she thought so all the more.

"I have come to see Lyman Gage," she announced, looking at Marilla with the glance one gives to a servant.

Marilla cast a frightened glance of discernment over the beautiful face. For it was beautiful, no mistaking that, perfectly beautiful, though it might have been only superficially so. Marilla wasn't used to seeing a skin that looked like soft rose leaves in baby perfection on a person of that age. Great baby eyes of blue, set wide, with curling dark lashes, eyebrows that seemed drawn by a fairy brush, lips of such ruby-red pout and nose chiselled in warm marble. Peaches and cream floated through her startled mind, and it never occurred to her it wasn't natural. Oh, the vision was beautiful—there was no doubt about that.

Marilla closed the door and stood with her back to the stairs and a look of defense on her face. She had a fleeting thought of Mary and whether she should be protected. She had a spasm of fierce jealousy and a frenzy as to what she should do.

"You can step into the parlor," she said in a tone that she hoped was calm, although she knew it wasn't cordial. "I'll go up and see if he's able to see you. He's been very sick. The doctor hasn't let him see any"—she paused and eyed the girl defiantly—"*any strangers.*"

"Oh, that'll be all right," laughed the girl with a disagreeable tinkle. "I'm not a stranger. I'm only his fiancée."

But she pronounced "fiancée" in a way Marilla didn't recognize at all, and she looked at her hard. It wasn't "wife," anyway, and it hadn't sounded like "sister" or "cousin." Marilla looked at the snip—that was what she began to call her in her mind—and decided she didn't want her to see Lyman Gage at all. But of course Lyman Gage must be the one to decide that.

"What did you say your name was?" she asked bluntly.

For answer the girl brought out a ridiculous little silk bag with a clattering clasp and chain and took from it a tiny gold card case, from which she handed Marilla a card.

Marilla adjusted her spectacles and studied it a moment with one foot on the lower stairs.

"Well," she said reluctantly, "he hasn't seen anyone yet. But I'll go and find out if you can see him. You can sit in the parlor." She waved her hand again toward the open door and started upstairs.

The blood was beating excitedly through her ears, and her heart pounded in pitiful thuds. If this "snip" belonged to her soldier boy, she was sure she could never mother him again. She wouldn't feel at home. Her thoughts were so excited she didn't know the fur-clad snip was following her close behind until she was actually in the spare bedroom and holding out the card to her boy with a trembling hand.

The boy looked up with his wide, pleasant smile like a benediction and reached out for the card with interest. He caught the look of panic on Marilla's face and the inscrutable one on Mary Amber's. Mary had heard the strange voice below and arisen from reading aloud to glance out of the window. She now beat a precipitate retreat into the little sewing room just off the spare bedroom. Then Lyman Gage realized there was another presence in the room and looked beyond to the door where Elinore Harrower stood, her big eyes watching him jealously from her swathing of gorgeous furs, while he slowly took in the situation.

It had been a common saying among his friends that no situation, however unexpected, ever found Lyman Gage off his guard or ever saw him give away his own emotions. Like lightning a sudden cloud like a curtain flitted over his face now, shutting out all he was the moment before, putting under lock and seal any like or dislike he might be feeling, allowing only the most cool courtesy to appear in his expression. Marilla, watching him like a cat, couldn't tell whether he was glad or sorry, surprised or indignant or pleased. He seemed none of these. He glanced with cool indifference toward the lovely vision smiling in the doorway now and ready to gush over him, and a stern dignity grew in the set of his jaws. Otherwise he didn't seem to have changed.

Most casually, as if he'd seen her the week before, he remarked, "Oh! Is that you, Elinore? Seems to me you've chosen a cold day to go out. Won't you sit down?"

He motioned toward a stiff chair that stood against the wall, though Mary Amber's rocker was still waving back and forth from her hasty retreat.

Marilla simply faded out of the room, although Gage said politely, "Don't leave us, please." But she was gone before the words were out of his mouth, and with a sudden feeling of weakness he glanced around the room wildly and realized Mary Amber was gone too.

Mary Amber stood in the sewing room and wondered what she should do. For the other door of the sewing room was closed and barred by a heavy iron bed that had been put up for convenience during the soldier's illness, and the only spot that was long enough to hold it was straight across the hall door. Obviously Mary couldn't get out of the sewing room without moving that bed, and she knew by experience of making it every morning that it squeaked unmercifully when it was moved. Neither could she go out through the spare bedroom, for she felt that her appearance would cause no end of explanations. Equally of course she dared not shut the door because it would make a noise and call attention to her presence.

So Mary Amber tiptoed softly to the farthest end of the little room and stood rigidly silent, trying not to listen, yet all the more attuned and sensitive to whatever was going on in the next room. She fairly held her breath lest they should hear her and pressed her fingers on her hot eyeballs as if that would shut out the sound.

"That's scarcely the way I expected you to greet me, Lyme," Elinore Harrower said in the sweet lilt of her petted voice.

"I was scarcely expecting you after what has happened," said Lyman Gage chillingly, his voice a bit high and hollow from his illness and all the cooler for that.

"I couldn't stay away when I knew you were ill, Lyme, dear!" The voice was honeyed sweet now.

"What had that to do with it?" The tone was almost vicious. "You wrote that we had grown apart, and it was true. You're engaged to another man."

"Well, can't I change my mind?" The tone was playful, kittenish.

It smote Lyman Gage's memory that he had called it teasing and enjoyed it once upon a time.

"You've changed your mind once too often!" The sick man's voice was tense in his weakness, and his brow was dark.

"Why, Lyme Gage! I think you are *horrid!*" cried the girl with a hint of indignant tears in her voice. "Here I come a long journey to see you when you're sick. And you greet me that way and *mock* me. It's not like you. You don't seem a bit glad to see me! Perhaps there's someone else." The voice had a taunt in it now and an assurance that expected to win out in the end, no matter to what she might have to descend to gain her point.

But she had reckoned without knowledge, for Lyman Gage remembered the picture he had torn to bits in the dying light of the sunset and trampled in the road. Those same brilliant eyes, that soft tinted cheek, those painted lips, had smiled impudently up to him that way as he had ground them beneath his heel. And this was GIRL, his natural enemy, who would play with him at her pleasure and toss him away when he was no longer profitable to her, expecting to find him ready at a word again when circumstances changed. He straightened up with sudden strength and caught her words with a kind of joyful triumph.

"Yes, there is *someone else!* Mary! Mary *Amber!*"

Mary Amber, trying not to hear, had caught her name, heard the sound in his voice like that of the little chick who calls its mother when the hawk appears. Suddenly her fear vanished. She turned and walked with steady step and bright eyes straight into the spare bedroom, a smile on her lips and a rose on her cheek that needed nothing to enhance its beauty.

"Did you call me—Lyman?" she said, looking straight at him with rescue in her eyes.

He put out his hand to her, and she went and stood by the bed across from the visitor, who had turned and was staring in amazement and insolence at her now.

Lyman Gage put out his big, wasted hand and gathered Mary Amber's hand in his, and *she let him!*

"Mary," said Lyman Gage possessively, with both boldness and appeal in his eyes as he looked at her. "I want Miss Harrower to know you. Mary Amber, Elinore Harrower."

Elinore Harrower had risen with one hand on the back of her chair. Her crimson lips parted, a startled expression in her eyes. Her furs had fallen back, revealing a rich and vampish little dress beneath. But she wasn't thinking of her dress just then. She was looking from one to the other of the two before her.

"I don't understand!" she said. "Did you know her before?"

Lyman Gage flashed a look at Mary for indulgence and answered happily: "Our friendship dates back to when we were children and I spent a summer with my aunt Marilla teasing Mary and letting the sawdust out of her dolls."

He gave a daring glance at Mary Amber and found the twinkles in her eyes playing with the dimples at the corner of her mouth. His fingers clung more warmly around hers.

The two were so absorbed in this little comedy they were enacting that they failed to notice its effect on the audience. Elinore Harrower had gathered her fur robes about her and was fastening them proudly at her throat. Her dark eyes were two points of steel, and the little white teeth that bit into the pouting crimson underlip looked vicious and suggestive.

"I didn't understand," said Elinore haughtily. "I thought you were among strangers and needed someone. I will leave you to your friends. You always did like simple country ways, I remember." She cast a withering glance around.

"Why, where is Aunt Rilla, Mary?" asked Lyman, innocently ignoring the sneer of his guest. "Aunt Marilla!" he raised his voice, looking toward the door. "Aunt Marilla, won't you please come here?"

Marilla, her heart a tumult of joy to hear him call her that way, straightened up from her ambush outside the door and entered, just as the haughty guest was about to stalk from the room, if one so small and exquisite as Elinore could be said to stalk. The result was a collision that quite spoiled the effect of the exit, and the two ladies looked at each other for a brief instant much as two cats might have done under similar circumstances.

Mary Amber's eyes were dancing, and Lyman Gage wanted to laugh, but he controlled his voice.

"Aunt Marilla, this is Miss Harrower, a girl who used to be an old friend of mine, and she thinks she can't stay any longer. Would you mind taking her down to the door? Good-bye, Elinore. Congratulations! And I hope you'll be very happy!"

He held out his free hand—the other still held Mary Amber's, and the smile on his lips was full of merriment. But Elinore Harrower ignored the hand and the congratulations. Drawing her fur mantle once more about her small haughty shoulders, she sailed from the room, her coral and silver toque held high and her little red mouth drooping with scorn and defeat.

Marilla, all hospitality now that she understood, offered tea and cake but was given no answer whatever. So in joyous, wondering silence she attended her soldier's guest to the door.

Lyman Gage lay back on his pillows, his face turned away from Mary Amber, listening. But his hand still held Mary's. And she, standing quietly by his side, listening too, seemed to understand that the curtain hadn't fallen yet, not quite, upon the little play. For a smile wove in and out among the dimples near her lips, and her eyes were dancing happy lights of mirth. It wasn't until the front door shut on the guest and they heard the motor's soft purr as the car left the house that they felt the tension of the moment relax, and consciousness of their position stole upon them.

"Mary, Mary Amber!" whispered Lyman Gage softly, looking up into her face. "Can you ever forgive me for all this?"

He held her hand, and his eyes pleaded for him.

"But it's all true. There is another one. I *love you!* And, oh, I'm so tired. Mary Amber, can you forgive me—and—and love me, just a little bit?"

Down on her knees went Mary Amber beside that bed and gathered her soldier boy within her strong young arms, drawing his tired head onto her firm, sweet shoulder.

When Marilla trotted back upstairs on her weary, glad feet and put her head in at the door to see how her boy had stood the strain of the visitor—and to berate herself for having allowed a stranger to come up without warning—she found them so. Mary Amber was soothing her patient to sleep by kisses on his tired eyelids, and the soldier's big hand enfolded Mary's little one contentedly.

And the man's low voice growled tenderly, "Mary, you're the only girl I ever really loved. I didn't know there was a girl like you when I knew her."

So Marilla closed the door softly, lest Molly Poke should come snooping around that way, and trotted off to the kitchen to see about some charlotte russe for supper. A great thankful gladness was growing in her heart, for—oh, suppose it had been that—hussy!

The Witness

Chapter 1

L ike a sudden cloudburst the dormitory became a frenzy of sound. Doors
slammed, feet scurried, hoarse voices reverberated, heavy bodies flung
themselves along the corridor—the very electrics trembled with the
cataclysm. One moment all was quiet with a contented after-dinner peace
before study hours; the next it was as if all of Earth's forces had broken forth.

Paul Courtland stepped to his door and threw it back.

"Come on, Court! See the fun!" called the football halfback, who was slop-
ping along with two dripping fire buckets of water.

"What's going on?"

"Swearing match! Going to make Little Stevie cuss! Better get in on it.
Some fight! Tennelly sent Whisk for a whole basket of superannuated cackle
berries." He motioned back to a freshman bearing a basket of ancient eggs.
"We're going to blindfold Steve and put oysters down his back and then finish
up with the fire hose. Oh, the plagues of Egypt are nothing compared to what
we're going to do! And when we get done, if Little Stevie don't let out a string
of good, honest cusswords like a man, I'll eat my hat. Little Stevie's got good
stuff in him if it can only be brought out—and we're going to bring it out. Then
we're going to celebrate by taking him over to the theater and making him see
The Scarlet Woman. It'll be a little old miracle, all right, if he has any of his
whining puritanical ideas left in him after we get through with him. Come on!
Get on the job!"

Drifting along with the surging tide of students, Courtland sauntered down
the corridor to the door at the end where the victim roomed.

He rather liked Stephen Marshall. There was good stuff in him—all the fellows recognized that. Only he was woefully unsophisticated, abnormally innocent, frankly religious and a little too openly fine in his life. It seemed to
rebuke the other fellows, unconscious though it might be. He felt with the rest
that the fellow needed a lesson. Especially with how he'd dared to stand up for
the old-fashioned view of miracles in biblical lit class that morning. Of course
an ignorance like that wouldn't go down, and it was best he should learn it at
once and get to be a good fellow right away. A little gentle rubbing off of the
"mamma's good little boy" veneer would do him good. Then Marshall might
even be eligible for the frat that year.

He ambled along with his hands in his pockets—a handsome, capable, powerful figure; not taking part in the preparations but mildly interested in the
plans. His presence lent enthusiasm to the gathering. He was high in authority—a star athlete, an A student, president of his fraternity, having made the
Phi Beta Kappa in his junior year and now in his senior year being chairman
of the student exec. They'd have no trouble with the college authorities if Court
was along.

Courtland stood opposite the end door when it was thrust open, and the hilarious mob rushed in. From his position with his back against the wall he could see Stephen lift his head from his book and rise to greet them. Surprise and a smile of welcome were on his face. Courtland thought it almost a pity to reward such openheartedness as they were about to do; but such things were necessary in the making of men. He watched developments with interest.

A couple of belated participants in the fray arrived breathlessly, shedding their mackinaws as they ran and casting them down at Courtland's feet.

"Look after those, will you, Court? We've got to get in on this," shouted one as he tossed a noisy bit of flannel headgear at Courtland.

Courtland kicked the garments behind him and stood watching.

There was a moment's tense silence while they told the victim why they'd come. The light of welcome in Stephen Marshall's eyes melted and changed into lightning. A dart of it went with a searching gleam into the hall and seemed to recognize Courtland as he stood idly smiling, watching. Then the lightning was withheld in the gray eyes, and Marshall seemed to conclude that, after all, it must be a huge joke, since Courtland was out there. Courtland had been friendly. He mustn't let his temper rise. The kind light entered his eyes again, and for an instant Marshall almost disarmed the boldest of them with his brilliant smile. He would be game as far as he understood. That was plain. It was equally plain he didn't understand yet what was expected of him.

Pat McCluny, with his thick neck, brutal jaw, low brow, red face and blunt speech, the finest, most unmerciful tackler on the football team, stepped up to Stephen and said a few words in a low tone. Courtland could hear only that they ended with an oath, the choicest of Pat McCluny's choice collection.

Instantly Stephen Marshall drew himself back and up to his great height, with lightning and thunderclouds in his gray eyes, his powerful arms folded, his fine head crowned with its wealth of beautiful gold hair thrown a trifle back and up, his lips shut in a thin, firm line and his whole attitude that of the fighter. But he didn't speak. He only looked from one to another of the wild young mob, searching for a friend. And finding none, he stood firm, defying them all.

Something splendid in his bearing sent a thrill of admiration down Courtland's spine as he watched, his habitual half-cynical smile of amusement still lying unconsciously about his lips, while a new respect for the country student was being born in his heart.

Pat, lowering his bullet head and twisting his ugly jaw, came a step nearer and spoke again, with a low rumble like the menace of a bull or a storm about to break.

With a sudden unexpected movement Stephen's arm shot forth and struck the fellow in the jaw, reeling him across the room into the crowd.

With a snarl like a stung animal Pat recovered himself and rushed at Stephen, hurling himself with a stream of oaths and calling curses down upon himself if he didn't make Stephen worse before he was finished with him. Pat was the "man" who was in college for football. It took the united efforts of his classmates, his frat and the faculty to keep his studies within decent hailing distance of eligibility for playing. He came from a race of bullies whose culture was in their fists.

Pat went straight for his victim's throat. Nobody could give him a blow like that in the presence of others and not suffer for it. What had started as a joke had now become real with Pat, and the frenzy of his own madness quickly spread to those daring spirits about him who disliked Stephen for his strength of character.

They clinched, and Stephen, fresh from his father's remote western farm, matched his mighty, untaught strength against the trained bully of a city street.

For a moment there was dead silence while the crowd in breathless astonishment watched and held in check their own eagerness.

Then the mob spirit broke forth as someone called out, "Pray for a miracle, Stevie! Pray for a miracle! You'll need it, old boy!"

The mad spirit which had incited them to the reckless fray broke forth anew, and a medley of shouts arose.

"Jump in, boys! Now's the time!"

"Give him a cowardly egg or two—the kind that hits and runs!"

"Teach him we'll be obeyed!"

The latter came as a sort of chant and was reiterated at intervals through the pandemonium of sound.

The fight raged on, and still Stephen stood with his back against the wall, fighting, gasping, struggling, but bravely facing them all—a disheveled object with rotten eggs streaming from his face and hair, his clothes plastered with offensive yolks. Pat had him by the throat, but still he stood and fought as best he could.

Someone seized the bucket of water and deluged both. Someone else shouted, "Get the hose!" More fellows tore off their coats and threw them down at Courtland's feet. Someone tore Pat away, and the great fire hose was turned on the victim.

Gasping at last and all but unconscious, he was set upon his feet and harried back to life again. Overpowered by numbers, he could do nothing, and the petty torments applied amid a round of ringing laughter seemed unlimited. But still he stood, a man among them, his lips closed, a firm set about his jaw that showed their labor was in vain. Not one word had he uttered since they entered his room.

"You can lead a horse to water, but you can't make him drink!" shouted one onlooker. "Cut it out, fellows! It's no use! You can't get him to cuss. He never learned how. Better cut it out!"

More tortures were applied, but still the victim was silent. The hose had washed him clean again, and his face shone from the drenching. Someone suggested it was getting late and the show would begin. Someone else suggested they must dress up Little Stevie for his first play. There was a mad rush for garments. Any garments, no matter whose. A pair of sporty trousers, socks of brilliant colors—not mates, an old football shoe on one foot, a dancing pump on the other, a white vest and a swallowtail put on backward, collar and tie also backward, a large pair of white cotton gloves commonly used by workmen for rough work—Johnson, who earned his way in college by tending furnaces, furnished these.

Stephen bore it all, grim, unflinching, until they stood him before his mirror and let him see himself, completing the costume by a high silk hat crammed down on his wet curls. He looked, and suddenly he turned upon them and smiled his broad, merry smile! After all that he could see the joke and smile! He never opened his lips or spoke—just smiled.

"He's a pretty good guy! He's game, all right!" murmured someone in Courtland's ear. And then, half shamed, they caught him high upon their shoulders and carried him down the stairs and out the door.

The theater was some distance off. They bore down upon a trolley car and took a wild possession. They sang their songs and yelled themselves hoarse. People turned and watched and smiled, considering this one more prank of those university fellows.

They swarmed into the theater, with Stephen in their midst, and took noisy occupancy. Opera glasses were turned their way, and girls nudged one another and talked about the man in the middle with the odd garments.

The persecutions had by no means ceased because they had landed their victim in a public place. They took off his hat, arranged his collar and smoothed his hair as if he were a baby. They wiped his nose with flourishing handkerchiefs and pointed out objects of interest about the theater in open derision of his supposed ignorance, to the growing amusement of those of the audience who were their neighbors. And when the curtain rose on the most notoriously flagrant play the city boasted, they added to its flagrance by their whispered explanations and remarks.

Stephen, in his ridiculous garb, sat in their midst, a prisoner, and watched the play he would not have chosen to see; watched it with a face of growing indignation, so that those about who saw him turned to look again and somehow felt condemned for being there.

Sometimes a wave of anger would sweep over the young man, and he would look about him with an impulse to break away and defy them all. But his every movement was anticipated, and he had the whole football team about him! He must stand it in spite of the tumult of rage in his heart. He wasn't smiling now. His face had that set, grim look of the faithful soldier taken prisoner and tortured to give information about his army's plans. Stephen's eyes shone true, and his lips were pressed firmly together.

"Just one nice little cussword and we'll take you home," whispered a tormentor. "A single little word will do, just to show you're a man."

Stephen's face was gray with determination. His yellow hair shone like a halo about his head. They'd taken off his hat, and he sat with his arms folded fiercely across the back of Andy Roberts's evening coat.

"Just one real little cuss to show you're a man," sneered the freshman.

Suddenly a smothered cry arose. A breath of fear stirred through the house. The smell of smoke swept in from a sudden open door. The actors paused, grew pale and swerved in their places; then one by one they fled out of the scene. The audience rose and turned to panic, even as a flame swept up and licked the curtain while it fell.

Confusion reigned!

The football team, trained to meet emergencies, forgot their cruel play and scattered over seats and railings, everywhere, to fire escapes and doorways, taking command of wild, stampeding people, showing their training and courage.

Stephen, thus suddenly set free, glanced about him and saw a few feet away an open door, felt the fresh evening breeze on his hot forehead and knew the upper back fire escape was nearby. By some strange whim of a panic-driven crowd few had discovered this exit, high above the seats in the balcony; for all had rushed below and were struggling in a wild, frantic mass, trampling one another underfoot in a struggle to reach the doorways. The flames were sweeping over the platform now, licking out into the pit of the theater, and people were terrified.

Stephen saw in an instant that the upper door, being farthest from the center of the fire, was the place of greatest safety. With one frantic leap he gained the aisle, strode up to the doorway and glanced out into the night to take in the situation—cool, calm, quiet, with the still stars overhead, down below the open iron stairway of the fire escape and a darkened street with people like tiny puppets moving on their way. Then turning back he tore off the grotesque coat and vest and the confining collar and threw them from him. He plunged down the steps of the aisle to the railing of the gallery and, leaning over in his shirtsleeves and the odd striped trousers, put his hands like a megaphone about his lips and shouted.

"Look up! Look up! There's a way to escape up here! Look up!"

Some poor struggling ones heard him and looked up. A little girl was held up by her father to the strong arms reached out from the low front of the balcony. Stephen caught her and swung her up beside him, pointing her up to the door and shouting to her to go quickly down the fire escape, even while he reached out his other hand to catch a woman whom willing hands below were lifting up. Men climbed upon the seats and vaulted up when they heard the cry and saw the way of safety. Some stayed and worked bravely beside Stephen, wrenching up the seats and piling them for a ladder to help the women up. More just clambered up and fled to the fire escape, out into the night and safety.

But Stephen had no thought of flight. He stayed where he was, with aching back, cracking muscles and sweat-grimed brow, and worked, his breath coming in quick, sharp gasps as he frantically helped man, woman, child, one after another like sheep huddling over a flood.

Courtland was there.

He had lingered a moment behind the rest in the corner of the dormitory corridor, glancing in the disfigured room—water, eggshells, ruin everywhere! A small object on the floor, a picture in a cheap oval metal frame, caught his eye. Something told him it was the picture of Stephen Marshall's mother he had seen on the student's desk a few days before, when he sauntered in to look the new man over. Something unexplained made him step in across the water and debris and pick it up. It was the picture, still unscarred, but with a great streak of rotten egg across the plain, placid features. He recalled the tone in which the son had pointed out the picture and said, "That's my mother!" Again he followed an impulse and wiped off the smear, setting the picture high on the shelf, where it looked down upon the depredation like some hallowed saint above a carnage.

Then Courtland ambled on to his room, finished getting ready and followed to the theater. He hadn't wanted to get too mixed up in the matter. He thought the fellows were going a little too far with a good thing perhaps. He wanted to see it through, but still he wouldn't quite mix with it. He found a seat where he could watch what was going on without being part of it. If anything should come to the faculty's ears he wanted to be on the side of conservatism. That Pat McCluny wasn't just his sort, though he was fun. But he always put things on a lower level than college fellows should go. Besides, if things went too far a word from Court would check them.

Courtland was rather bored with the play and was about to return to study when the cry arose and panic followed.

Courtland was no coward. He tore off his handsome overcoat and rushed to meet the emergency. On the opposite side of the gallery, high up by another fire escape, he rendered efficient assistance to many.

The fire was gaining in the pit; and still swarms of people were down there, struggling, crying, lifting piteous hands for help. Still Stephen Marshall reached from the gallery and pulled up, one after another, poor creatures, and still the helpless thronged and cried for aid.

Dizzy, blinded, his eyes filled with smoke, his muscles trembling with the terrible strain, he stood at his post. The minutes seemed interminable hours, and still he worked, with heart pumping painfully and a mind that seemed to have no thought except to reach down for another and another and point them up to safety.

Then into the confusion arose an instant of great and awful silence—one of those silences that come even into much sound and claim attention from the most absorbed.

Paul Courtland, high in his chosen station, working eagerly, successfully, calm, looked down to see the cause of this sudden arresting of the universe. There, below, was the pit full of flame, with people struggling and disappearing into fiery depths below. Just above the pit stood Stephen, lifting aloft a little child with frightened eyes and long streaming curls. He swung him high and turned to stoop again. With his stooping came the crash—the rending, grinding, groaning, twisting of all that held those great galleries in place, as the fire licked hold of their supports and wrenched them out of position.

One instant Stephen was standing by that crimson-velvet railing, with his lifted hand pointing the way to safety for the child, the flaming fire lighting his face, his hair a halo about his head, and in the next instant, even as his hand was held out to save another, the gallery fell, crashing into the fiery, burning furnace! And Stephen, with his face shining like an angel's, went down and disappeared with the rest, while the consuming fire swept up and covered him.

Paul Courtland closed his eyes on the scene and caught hold of the nearby door. He didn't realize he was standing on a tiny ledge—all that was left him of footing, high, alone, above that burning pit where his fellow student had gone down—or that he had escaped as by a miracle. There he stood and turned away his face, sick and dizzy with the sight, blinded by the dazzling flames, shut in to that tiny spot by a sudden wall of smoke that swept in about him. Yet in all the danger and the horror the only thought that came was, "God, *that was a man!*"

Chapter 2

Paul Courtland never knew how he was saved from that perilous position high up on a ledge in the top of the theater, with the burning, fiery furnace below him—whether his senses came back sufficiently to guide him along the narrow footing that was left, to the door of the fire escape, where someone rescued him or whether a friendly hand risked all and reached out to draw him to safety.

He only knew that back there in that blank daze of suspended time, before he recognized the whiteness of the hospital wall and the rustle of the nurse's starched skirt along the corridor, for a long period he was shut in with four high walls of smoke. Smoke that reached to heaven, roofing him away from it, and had its foundations down in the fiery pit of hell where he could hear lost souls struggling with smothered cries for help. Smoke that filled his throat, eyes, brain, soul. Thick smoke—yellow, gray, menacing! Smoke that shut his soul away from the universe, as if he were suddenly blotted out, and made him feel how alone he had been born and would be forever.

He seemed to have lain within those slowly approaching walls of smoke a century or two before he became aware that he was not alone after all. A Presence was there beside him. Light and a Presence! Blinding light. He reasoned that other men, the men outside the walls of smoke, the firemen, perhaps, and bystanders, might think that light came from the fire down in the pit, but he knew it didn't. It radiated from the Presence beside him. And a Voice was calling his name. He seemed to have heard the call years back in his life somewhere. Something about it made his heart leap in answer and brought that strange thrill he had as a boy in prep school when his captain called him into the game, though he was only a substitute.

He couldn't look up, yet he could see the face of the Presence now. What was there so familiar, as if he'd been looking upon that face only a few moments before? He knew. It was that brave spirit come back from the pit. Come, perhaps, to lead him out of this smoke and darkness.

He spoke, and his own voice sounded glad and ringing. "I know you now. You're Stephen Marshall. You were in college. You were down there in the theater just now, saving men."

"Yes, I was in college," the Voice spoke, "and I was down there just now, saving men. But I'm not Stephen Marshall. Look again."

And suddenly he understood.

"Then you're Stephen Marshall's Christ! The Christ he spoke of in class that day!"

"Yes, I'm Stephen Marshall's Christ! He let me live in him. I'm the Christ you sneered at and disbelieved!"

He looked, and his heart was stricken with shame.

"I didn't understand. It was against reason. But I hadn't seen You then."

"And now?"

"Now? What do You want of me?"

"You'll be shown."

The smoke ebbed low and swung away his consciousness, and even the place grew dim about him, but the Presence was there. Always, through suspended space as he was carried along, and after, when the smoke gave way and air, blessed air, was wafted in, the Presence was there. If it hadn't been for that he couldn't have borne the awfulness of nothing that surrounded him. Always the Presence was there!

A bandage covered his eyes for days, and people spoke in whispers. And when the bandage was taken away the white hospital walls were there, so like the walls of smoke at first in the dim light, high above him. When he understood it was only hospital walls, he looked around for the Presence in alarm, crying out, "Where is He?"

Bill Ward and Tennelly and Pat were there, huddled in a group by the door hoping he would recognize them.

"He's calling for Steve!" whispered Pat and turned with a gulp while the tears rolled down his cheeks. "He must have seen him go!"

The nurse laid him down on the pillow again, replacing the bandage. When he closed his eyes the Presence came back, blessed, sweet—and he was at peace.

The days passed; strength crept back into his body, consciousness to his brain. The bandage was taken off once more, and he saw the nurse and other faces. He didn't look again for the Presence. He had come to understand he couldn't see it with his eyes; but always it was there, waiting, something sweet and wonderful. Waiting to show him what to do when he was well.

The memorial services had been held for Stephen Marshall many days earlier; the university had been draped in black, with its flag at half-mast, for the proper time and its mourning folded away before Paul Courtland could return to his room and his classes.

They welcomed him back with touching eagerness. They tried to hush their voices and temper their noisiness to suit an invalid. They told him the news, what games had been won, who had made Phi Beta Kappa and what had happened at the frat meetings. But they spoke no word of Stephen!

Down the hall Stephen's door always stood open, and Courtland, walking that way one day, found fresh flowers on his desk and wreathed around his mother's picture. A quaint little photograph of Stephen taken several years back hung on one wall. It had been sent at the class's request by Stephen's mother to honor her son's chosen college.

The room was set in order, with Stephen's books on the shelves and his few college treasures tacked up about the walls; and conspicuous between the windows hung framed the resolutions concerning Stephen, the hero-martyr of the class, telling briefly how he had died and giving him this tribute, "He was a man!"

Below the resolutions, on the table covered with an old-fashioned crocheted cotton tablecloth, lay Stephen's Bible, worn, marked, soft with use. His mother had wished it to remain. Only his clothes had been sent back to her who had sent him forth to prepare for his lifework and received word in her distant home that his lifework was already swiftly accomplished.

Courtland entered the room and looked around.

No traces remained of the fray that had marred the place when he last saw it. Everything was clean and orderly. The simple saint-like face of the plain farmer's wife-mother looked down upon it all with peace and resignation. This life was not all. There was another. Her eyes said that. Paul Courtland stood a long time gazing into them.

Then he closed the door and knelt by the table, laying his forehead reverently upon the Bible.

Since he had returned to college and life had become more real, Reason had returned to her throne and was crying out against his "notions." What was that experience in the hospital but the fantasy of a sick brain? Wasn't the Presence but a fevered imagination? He'd become ashamed of dwelling on the thought, of liking to feel that the Presence was near when he was falling asleep at night. Most of all he felt a shame and a kind of perplexity in the biblical literature class where he faced "FACTS," as the professor called them, spoken in capitals. Science was another force which mocked his notions. Philosophy cooled his mind and wakened him from his dreams. In this atmosphere he was beginning to think he'd been delirious and was gradually returning to his normal state, albeit with a restless dissatisfaction he'd never known before.

But now in this calm, rose-decked room, with the quiet eyes of the simple mother looking down upon him, the resolutions in their chaplet of palm framing, the age-old Bible thumbed and beloved, he knew he'd been wrong. He knew he would never be the same. That Presence, whoever, whatever it was, had entered his life. He could never forget it; never be convinced it was not; never be entirely satisfied without it! He believed it was the Christ. Stephen Marshall's Christ!

By and by he lifted up his head and opened the worn Bible, reverently, curiously, just to touch it and think how the other one had done. The soft, much-turned pages fell open on their own to a heavily marked verse. There were many marked verses throughout the book.

Paul Courtland's eyes followed the words.

He that believeth on the Son of God hath the witness in himself.

Could it be that this strange new sense of the Presence was "the witness" mentioned here? He knew it like his sense of rhythm or the look of his mother's face or the joy of a summer morning. It wasn't anything he could analyze. One might argue no such thing existed—science might prove it didn't—but he *knew* it, had *seen* it, *felt* it! He had the witness in himself. Was that what it meant?

With troubled brow he turned the pages again.

If any man will do his will, he shall know of the doctrine, whether it be of God.

Ah! There was an offer—why not close with it?

He dropped his head on the open book with the age-old words of self-surrender: "Lord, what will You have me do?"

A moment later Pat McCluny opened the door, cautiously, quietly. Then, with a nod to Tennelly behind him, he entered with confidence.

Courtland rose. His face was white, but a light of something they didn't understand glowed in his eyes.

They went over to him as if he were a lost child found on some perilous height needing to be coaxed gently away from it.

"Oh, so you're here, Court," said Tennelly, slapping his shoulder with gentle roughness. "Great old room, isn't it? The fellows' idea to keep flowers here. Kind of a continual memorial."

"Great fellow, that Steve!" said Pat hoarsely. He couldn't yet speak lightly of the hero-martyr he'd helped send to his fiery grave.

But Courtland stood calmly, almost as if he hadn't heard them. "Pat, Nelly," he said, turning from one to the other gravely, "I want to tell you fellows I've met Steve's Christ, and after this I stand for Him!"

They looked at him curiously, pityingly. They spoke with soothing words and humored him. They led him away to his room and left him to rest. Then they walked with solemn faces and a dejected air into Bill Ward's room and threw themselves down on his couch.

"Where's Court?" Bill looked up from the theme he was writing.

"We found him in Steve's room," said Tennelly gloomily and shook his head.

"It's a deuced shame!" burst forth Pat. (He'd cut out swearing for a time.) "He's batty in the bean!"

Tennelly answered the shocked question in Bill's eyes with a nod. "Yes, the brightest fellow in the class, but he sure is batty! You should've heard him talk. Say! I don't believe it was all the fire. Court's been studying too hard. He's been an awful shark for a fellow who went in for athletics and everything else. He's studied too hard, and it's gone to his head!"

Tennelly sat gloomily staring across the room. It was the old cry of the man who cannot understand.

"He needs a little change," said Bill, putting his feet up on the table comfortably and lighting a cigarette. "Pity the frat dance is over. He needs to get himself a girl. Be a great stunt if he'd fall for some jolly girl. Say! I'll tell you what. I'll get Gila after him."

"Who's Gila?" asked Tennelly. "He won't notice her any more than a fly on the wall. You know how he is about girls."

"Gila's my cousin. Gila Dare. She's a good sport and a winner every time. We'll put Gila on the job. I've got a date with her tomorrow night, and I'll put her on to it. She'll enjoy that kind of thing. He met her, too, over at the navy game. Leave it to Gila."

"What style is she?" asked Tennelly, still skeptical.

"Oh, tiny and striking, with big eyes. A perfect little peach of an actress."

"Court's too keen for acting. He'll see through her in half a second. She can't put one over on him."

"She won't try," said the ardent cousin. "She'll just be as innocent. They'll be buddies in half an hour, or it'll be the first failure for Gila."

"Well, if any girl can put one over on Court, I'll eat my hat. But it's worth trying. If Court keeps on like this we'll all be buying prayer books and singing psalms before another semester."

"You'll eat your hat, all right," said Bill Ward, rising in his irritation. "I tell you Gila never fails. If she gets on the job Court'll be dead in love with her before the midwinter exams!"

"I'll believe it when I see it," said Tennelly, rising, too.

"All right," said Bill. "Remember you're in for a banquet during vacation. Fricasseed hat the *pièce de résistance!*"

Chapter 3

It was a sumptuous library in which Gila Dare awaited Paul Courtland's arrival.

Great, deep, red-leather chairs stood everywhere invitingly; the floor was spread with a magnificent specimen of Royal Bokhara; the rich recesses of the noble walls were lined with books in rare editions, a heavily carved table of dull black wood from some foreign land sprawled in the center of the room and held a bronze lamp of curious pattern, bearing a ruby light. Ornate bronzes lurked on pedestals in shadows and caught the eye, like grim ones set to watch. A throbbing fire burned in a massive fireplace of grotesque tiles, as though it opened into depths of unquenchable fire to which this room might be only an approach.

Gila herself, slight, dark-eyed, with pearl-white skin and dusky hair, was dressed in crimson velvet, soft and clinging like chiffon, catching the light and shimmering it with a strange effect. The dark hair was curiously arranged and stabbed just above her ears with two daggerlike combs glittering with jewels. A single jewel burned at her throat on an invisible chain, and jewels flashed from the little pointed crimson-satin slippers, setting off the slim ankles in their crimson-silk covering. The whole effect was startling. One wondered why she chose such an elaborate costume to waste on a single college student.

She stood with one dainty foot poised on the brass trappings of the hearth. In her short skirts she seemed almost a child—so sweet the droop of the pretty lips, so innocent the dark eyes as they looked into the fire, so soft the shadows that played in the dark hair! And yet, as she turned to listen for a step in the hall, the red lips held something mocking. She might have been a daughter of Satan as she stood, the firelight picking out those jeweled horns and slippers.

"Leave him to me," she'd said to her cousin when he told her how the brilliant young athlete and intellectual star of the university had been stung by the religious bug. "Send him to me. I'll take it out of him, and he'll never know it's gone."

Paul Courtland entered, unsuspecting. He had met Gila a number of times before at college dances and the games. He wasn't exactly flattered but was pleased she'd sent for him. Her brightness and seeming innocence had attracted him.

The contrast from the hall with its blaze of electric lights to the library's lurid light affected him strangely. He paused on the threshold and passed his hand over his eyes. Gila stood where the ruby light of hearth and lamp would set her vivid dress on fire and light the jewels at her throat and hair. She knew her clear skin, dark hair and eyes would bear the startling contrast and how her white shoulders gleamed from the crimson velvet. She knew how to arrange the flaming scarf of gauze deftly about those white shoulders so it would reveal more than it concealed.

The young man lingered unaccountably. He had a sense of leaving something behind him. Almost he hesitated as she came forward to greet him and looked back as if to rid himself of some obligation. Then she put her bits of confiding hands out to him and smiled her wistful, engaging smile.

He thrilled with wonder over her delicate, dazzling beauty and felt the luxury of the room about him, responding to its lure.

"So good of you to come to me when you're so busy after your long illness." Her voice was soft and confiding, its cadences like soothing music. She motioned him to a chair. "You see, I wanted to have you all to myself for a little while, just to tell you how perfectly fine you were at that awful fire."

She dropped upon the couch drawn out at just the right angle from the fire and settled among the cushions gracefully. The flicker of the firelight played on the jeweled combs and gleamed at her throat. The pointed slippers cozily crossed looked innocent enough to have been meant for the golden street. Her eyes looked up into his with that intimate lure that thrills and thrills again.

Her voice dropped softer, and she turned half away and gazed pensively into the fire on the hearth. "I wouldn't let them talk to me about it. It seemed so awful. And you were so strong and great."

"It was nothing!" He didn't want to talk about the fire. There was something incongruous, almost unholy, in discussing it here. It jangled on his nerves. For there in front of him in the fireplace burned a mimic pit like the one into which the martyr Steve had fallen, and there before him on the couch sat the girl! What was so familiar about her? Ah! Now he knew. *The Scarlet Woman!* Her gown was an exact reproduction of the one the great actress had worn on the stage that night. He was conscious of wishing to sit beside her on that couch and revel in her ravishing color. What about this room made his pulses beat?

Playfully, skillfully, she led him on. They talked of the dances and games, little gossip of the university, with now and then a telling personality and a sweep of long lashes over pearly cheeks or a lifting of innocent eyes of admiration to his face.

She offered wine in delicate gold-encrusted ruby glasses, but Courtland didn't drink. He scarcely noticed her veiled annoyance at his refusal. He was drinking in the wine of her presence. She suggested he smoke and wouldn't have hesitated to join him, perhaps, but he told her he was in training. She cooed softly of his wonderful strength of character in resisting.

By this time he was in the coveted seat beside her on the couch, and the fire burned low and red. They had ceased to talk of games and dances. They were talking of each other, those intimate nothings that mean a breaking down of distance and a rapidly growing familiarity.

The young man was aware of the fascination of the small figure in her crimson robing, sitting demurely in the firelight, the gauzy scarf dropped away from her white neck and shoulders, the lovely curve of her baby cheek and tempting neck showing against the background of the shadows behind her. He was aware of a distinct longing to take her in his arms and crush her to him, as he'd pluck a red berry from a bank and feel its stain on his lips. Stain! A stain was hard to remove. There were bloodstains sometimes and agonies, and yet men wanted to pluck the berries and feel the stain on their lips!

He wasn't under the hallucination of suddenly falling in love with this girl. He didn't name the passionate outcry in his soul love. He knew she had charmed many, and in yielding himself to her recognized power he was for the moment playing with a new and interesting force, with which he'd felt altogether strong enough to contend for an evening or he wouldn't have come. That it should thrill his senses with this unreasoning rapture was astonishing. He'd never fallen for every girl he met, and now he felt himself gradually yielding to the beautiful spell about him with a kind of wonder.

The lights and coloring of the room that smote his senses unpleasantly when he first entered had thrown him now into a delicious fever. The neglected wine sparkling dimly in the glasses seemed part of it. He felt an impulse to reach out, seize a glass and drain it. What if he should? What if he flung away his ideals and let the moment sway him as it would, just once? Why shouldn't he try life as it presented itself?

These notions fled through his brain like phantoms that dared not linger. His was no callow mind, ignorant of the world. He had thought and read and lived his ideals well for such a young man. He had vigorously protested against weakness of every kind. Yet here he was feeling the pull of things he had always despised; reveling in the wine-red color of the room, in the pitlike glow of the fire; watching the play of smiles and wistfulness on the girl's face. He'd often wondered what others saw so attractive in her beyond a pretty face. But now he understood. Her childlike speech and cute ways fascinated him. Perhaps she was really innocent of her own charms. Perhaps a man might lead her to give up some of her ways that caused her to be criticized. What a woman she'd be then! What a friend to have!

This was the last sop he threw to his conscience before he consciously began to yield to the spell that was upon him.

She had been speaking of palmistry, and she took his hand in hers, innocently, impersonally, with large, inquiring eyes. Her breath was on his face; her touch had stirred his senses with a madness he had never felt before.

"The lifeline is here," she said coolly and traced it delicately along his palm with a seashell tinted finger. Like cool delicious fire it spread from nerve to nerve and set aside his reason in a frenzy. He would seize the berry and feel its stain on his lips now, no matter what!

"Paul!"

It was as distinct to his ear as if the words had been spoken—as startling and calming as a cool hand on his fevered brow, the sudden entrance of a guest. He had seized her hands with sudden fervor and now, almost in the same moment, flung them from him and stood up, a man in full possession of his senses. "Listen!" he said, and as he spoke a faint cry broke forth above them, with the sound of rushing feet. A frightened maid burst into the room unannounced.

"Oh, Miss Gila, I beg pardon, but Master Harry's got his father's razor, an' he's cut hisself something awful."

The maid was weeping and wringing her hands helplessly, but Gila stood frowning angrily.

Courtland sprang up the stairs. In the tumult of his mind he would have rejoiced if the house had been on fire or a cyclone had struck the place—anything so he could fling himself into service. He drew in long, deep breaths. It was like mountain air to get away from that lurid room into the light once more. A sense of lost power returned was over him. The spell was broken.

He bent over the little boy, grasped the wrist and stopped the spurt of blood. The frightened child looked up into his face and ceased crying.

"You should have telephoned for the doctor at once and not made all this fuss in the presence of a guest," scolded Gila as she came up the stairs.

She looked garish and out of place with her red velvet and jewels in the brilliant light of the white-tiled bathroom. She stood helplessly by the door, making no move to help Courtland, while the maid was at the telephone, frantically calling for the family physician.

"Hand me those towels," Paul commanded and saw the look of disgust on Gila's face as she reluctantly picked her way across the bloodstains. It struck him that they were the color of her dress. The stain of the crushed berry. He moistened his dry lips. At least the stain was not on his lips. He had escaped. Yet by how narrow a margin.

The girl felt the man's changed attitude without understanding it. She thought the cry of the child made him jump up and fling her hands from him with that sudden "Listen!" in the moment when he had almost yielded. She didn't know an inner voice had called him. She only knew she'd lost him for the time.

He gathered the little boy into his arms when he had bound up the cut and talked to him cheerfully. The boy's curly head rested trustfully against the big shoulder.

"Floor all bluggy!" he remarked. "Wall all bluggy!" Then his eyes fell on his sister in her scarlet dress. "Gila all bluggy, too!" He laughed and pointed with his well hand.

"Be still, Harry!" said Gila.

When Courtland looked up in wonder he saw the delicate brows drawn blackly, and the mouth had lost its innocent sweetness. The child shrank in his arms, and he put a reassuring hand on the little head that snuggled against his coat. This love of little children was one of Courtland's strong points. He grew fine and gentle in their presence. It often drew attention on the athletic field when some little fellow strayed toward him and Courtland would turn to talk to him. People would stop their conversation and look his way, and a whole grandstand would come to silence just to see him walk across the diamond with a little golden-haired boy on his shoulder. There was something beautiful about his attitude toward a child.

Gila saw it now and wondered. What unexpected trait was this that sat upon the young man like a crown? Here, indeed, was a man worth cultivating, not merely for the caprice of the moment. Something in his face and attitude commanded her respect and admiration; something drew her as she hadn't been drawn before. She would win him now for his own sake, not just to show how she could charm away his morbid notions.

She continued to stare at the young man with eyes that saw new things in him, while Courtland sat petting the child and telling him a story. He paid no further attention to her.

When Gila set her heart upon a thing she had always had it. This had been her father's method of bringing her up. Her mother was too busy with her clubs and social functions to see the harm. And now Gila suddenly became aware of setting her heart upon this young man. The eternal feminine in her that was almost choked with selfishness was crying out for a man like this one to comfort and pet her the way he was comforting and petting her little brother. That he had not yielded too easily to her charms made him all the more desirable. The interruption had come so suddenly that she couldn't even be sure he had been about to take her hands in his when he flung them from him. He had sprung from the couch almost as if he had been under orders. She couldn't understand it, but she knew she was drawn by it all.

But he must yield! She had power, and she would use it. She had beauty, and it should wound him. She would win that gentle deference and attention for her own. In her jealous, spoiled heart she hated the little brother for lying there in his arms, interrupting their evening just when she'd had him where she wanted him. Whether she wanted him for more than a plaything she didn't know, but her plaything he should be as long as she desired him—and more if she chose.

When Courtland lifted his head at the sound of the doctor's footsteps on the stairs he saw the challenge in Gila's eyes. Drawn up against the white enamel of the bathroom door, all her brilliant velvet and jewels gleaming in the brightness of the room, her regal head up, her chin lifted haughtily, her innocent mouth pursed softly with determination, her eyes wide with an inscrutable look—something more than challenge—something soft, appealing, alluring, stirred and drew and repelled him all in one.

With a sense of something stronger back of him, he lifted his own chin and hardened his eyes in answering challenge. He didn't know it, of course, but he wore the look he always had when about to meet a foe in a game—a look of strength and concealed power that nearly always made the coming foe quake when he saw it.

He shrank from going back to that red room again or from being alone with her. When she wanted him to return to the library he declined, urging studies and an examination the next day. She received his somewhat brusque reply with a hurt look; her mouth drooped, and her eyes took on a wide, childlike look of distress that gave an impression of innocence. He went away wondering if, after all, he hadn't misjudged her. Perhaps she was only an adorable child who had no idea of the effect her artlessness had upon men. She certainly was lovely—wonderful! And yet the last glimpse he had of her had left that impression of jeweled horns and scarlet, pointed toes. He had to get away and think it out calmly before he went again. Oh, yes, he was going *again*. He had promised her at the last moment.

The sense of having escaped something fateful was passing already. The cool night and quiet starlight calmed him. He thought he was a fool not to have stayed longer when she asked him so prettily. He must go again soon.

Chapter 4

I think I'll go to church this morning, Nelly. Do you want to go along?" announced Courtland the next morning.

Tennelly looked up aghast from the sports page of the morning paper he was lazily reading.

"Go with him, Nelly. That's a good boy!" put in Bill Ward agreeably, winking at Tennelly. "It'll do you good. I'd go with you, but I've got to get that condition made up or they'll fire me from the varsity, and I only need this one more game to get my letter."

"Go to thunder!" growled Tennelly. "Why do you think I'd want to go to church on a morning like this? Court, you're crazy! Let's go and get two horses and ride in the park. It's a perfect morning for a ride."

"I think I'll go to church," said Courtland, with his old voice of quiet decision. "Do you want to go or not?"

Something about Courtland's voice and the way Bill Ward kept winking at him subdued Tennelly.

"Sure, I'll go," he growled reluctantly.

"You old crab, you," chirped Bill when Courtland had left. "Can't you see you've got to humor him? He needs homeopathic treatment. 'Like cures like.' Give him a good dose of religion and he'll get tired of it. Church won't hurt him any—just give him a pious feeling so he'll feel free to do as he pleases during the week. I had a phone call from Gila this morning. She says he's made another date with her after exams. He fell, all right, so go get your hat and toddle off to Sunday school. Try to lead him into a big, stylish church. They're safest; but 'most any of 'em are cold enough to freeze the eyeteeth out of a stranger as far as my experience goes."

"Well, this isn't my funeral," sulked Tennelly, going to his closet for suitable attire. "I s'pose you get your way, but Court's keen intellectually, and if he happens to strike a good preacher he's liable to fall for what he says, in the mood he's in now."

"Well, he won't strike a good preacher. There isn't one nowadays. There are plenty of orators in the pulpit, but they're all preaching about politics these days or raving about uplifting the masses, and that sorta thing won't hurt Court. Most of 'em are dry as punk. If Court keeps awake through the service he won't go again, mark my words."

These two who had decided to go up to the house of God chose a church at random. High-arched and Gothic were its massive walls, with intricate carving in the stonework. Softly swung leather doors shut the sanctuary from the outer world. The fretted gold and blue and scarlet ceiling stretched away for miles, it seemed, in the space above them, and rich carving in dark, costly wood met the wonderful frescoes at lofty heights. The carpets were soft, and the pews were upholstered in tones to match. A great silence brooded over the place, making itself felt above and beneath the swelling tones of the wonderful organ. People trod the aisles softly, like puppets playing their parts. They bent in a form of prayer for a moment and settled into silence. The minister came stiffly into the pulpit, casting a furtive eye about the congregation.

They noticed almost at once that the most popular professor in the university was acting as usher on the other side of the church. Tennelly frowned and looked at Courtland, who sat watching the usher as he showed people to their seats, wondering if that man had what he called religion and was in any way related to Stephen Marshall's Christ. This visit to a Christian church was a voyage of discovery for Courtland. He had scarcely been to religious services since he entered the university. He considered them a waste of time. Now he'd come to see if anything was in them. It didn't occur to him they might have a connection with those verses he read in the Bible about "doing the will" or with one who allied himself with Christ. The church stood to him as to many other young pagans such as he was, for a man-made institution, to be attended or not as one chose.

The music wasn't uplifting. It was well done by paid choir members, who had good voices and sang wonderful music, but they had no heart in their singing. The congregation, not large, attempted no more than a murmur of the hymns.

The sermon was a dissertation on the book of Jonah, a sort of résumé of the argument, on both sides, that has torn the theological world in these latter days. Not a word of Stephen Marshall's Christ, except a side reference to a verse about Jonah being three days and three nights in the whale and the Son of Man being three days in the heart of the earth. Courtland wasn't even sure this reference meant the Christ, and it never entered his head that it touched at the heart of the great doctrine of the resurrection of the dead. As far as he could understand the reverend gentleman, the arguments quoted against the book of Jonah were far stronger and more plausible than those put forth in its defense. What was it all about anyway? What did it matter whether Jonah was or was not, or whether anybody accepted the book? How could something like that affect a man's life?

Tennelly watched the expressive face beside him and decided that perhaps Bill Ward had been half right after all.

On their way back to the university they met Gila Dare. Gila all in gray like a dove—gray suit of soft, rich cloth; gray furs of the depth and richness of smoke; gray suede boots laced high to meet her brief gray skirts; silver hat with a single velvet rose on the brim to match the soft rose-bloom on her cheeks. Gila with eyes as wide and innocent as a baby's; cupid mouth curved in a sweet, shy smile; and dainty prayer book in gray suede held devoutly in her little gloved hand.

"Who's that?" queried Tennelly, when they'd passed a suitable distance.

"Why, that's Bill Ward's cousin, Gila Dare," announced Courtland. He was still basking in the pleasure of her smile and thinking how different she looked from last evening in this soft, gray, silvery effect. Yes, he'd misjudged her. A girl who could look like that must be sweet and pure and unspoiled. It was that unfortunate dress last night that reminded him unpleasantly of *The Scarlet Woman* and the awful night of the fire. If he ever got well enough acquainted he'd ask her never to wear red again; it made her appear sensual. Even she, delicate and sweet as she was, couldn't afford to cast a thought like that into the minds of her beholders. It was then he began to idealize Gila.

"Gila Dare!" Tennelly straightened up and took notice. So that was the invincible Gila! That soft-eyed, exquisite thing with the hair like a midnight cloud.

"Some looker!" he commented and wished he were in Courtland's shoes.

"She's got in her work all right," he commented to himself. "Old Court's fallen already. Guess I'll have to buy a straw hat—it'll be more edible."

Courtland was like his cheerful old self when he got back to the dormitory. He joked a great deal. His eyes were bright and his color better than it had been since he was sick. He said nothing about the morning service, and by and by Bill Ward ventured a question.

"What kind of a harangue did you hear this morning?"

"Rotten!" he answered and turned away. Somehow that question recalled him to the uneasiness within his soul for which he'd sought solace in the church service. He became silent again and strolled away into Stephen's room and, closing the door, sat down.

Something was strange about that room. The Presence seemed always there. It hadn't made itself felt in the church at all, as he'd hoped. He'd taken Tennelly with him because he wanted something tangible, friendly, sane, from the world he knew, to give him ballast. If the Presence had been in the church, with Tennelly by his side, he would have been sure it wasn't a hallucination connected with his memory of Stephen.

It was strange, for now that he sat there in that quiet room that had once witnessed the trying out of a manly soul and saw the plain mother's calm eyes on the wall opposite and the true eyes of the dowdy schoolboy on the other wall, he was feeling the Presence again!

Why hadn't he felt its power in the church? Was it because of the presence of such people in the temple as that mean-souled professor, whom everybody knew from experience to be insincere? Was it because the people were cold and careless and didn't sing even with their lips, let alone their hearts, but hired it to be done for them?

And then he thought of that call of his name when he was with Gila Dare, as clear and distinct, like a friend he'd left outside who had grown tired of waiting and worried about him. Why hadn't the sense of the Presence gone with him into the room? Would a Presence like that be afraid of hostile influences? No. If it was real and a Presence at all it would be more powerful than any other influence in the universe. Then why?

Could he have gone deliberately into an influence that would make it impossible for the Presence to guide?

Or could his own attitude toward that girl have been at fault? He had gone to see her regarding her somewhat lightly. As a gentleman he should regard no woman with disrespect. He should honor her womanhood even if she chose to dishonor it herself. If he'd gone to see Gila with a different attitude toward her, expecting high, fine things of her, rather than to be amused by one he scarcely regarded seriously, perhaps all this strange mental phenomena wouldn't have come to pass.

Finally he locked the door and knelt down with his head on the worn Bible. He had no idea of praying. To him prayer meant only a repetition of a form of words. There had been prayers in his childhood, brought about by the maiden aunt who kept house for his father after his mother's death and assisted in bringing him up until he was old enough to go away to boarding school. They were a bore, coming as they did when he was sleepy. He recalled a long, vague one beginning, "Our Father which art," in which he always had to be prompted, and "Now I lay me" and "Matthew, Mark, Luke and John, bless the bed I lay upon. Wish I may, wish I might, get the wish I wish tonight!" Or *was* that a prayer? He never could remember as he grew older.

He didn't know why he was drawn to kneel there with his eyes closed and his cheek on that Bible. Strange that when he was in that room all doubt about the Presence vanished, all uneasiness about reconciling it with realities, laws and science fled.

Later he stood in his own room by the window, watching the red sun go down in the west and light a ruby fire behind the long line of tall buildings that stretched beyond the campus. The glow in no way resembled, yet reminded him of, the fire in the glowing grate of the Dare library. Why had that room affected him so strangely? And Gila, little Gila, how sweet and innocent she looked when they met her that morning with her prayer book. How wrong he must have been to take people's idle talk about her and let it influence his thoughts of her. She couldn't be all they said and yet look so sweet and inno-cent. What had she reminded him of in literature? Ah! He had it. Solveig in *Peer Gynt!*

How fair! Did ever you see the like?
   Looked down at her shoes and her snow-white apron!—
And then she held onto her mother's skirtfolds
   And carried a psalmbook wrapped up in a 'kerchief!—

That ample purple person by her side, with the dark eyes, the double chin and the hard lines in her painted face, must be Gila's mother. Perhaps people talked about the daughter because of her mother, for *she* looked it fully. But then a girl couldn't help having a foolish mother. She was to be pitied more than blamed if she seemed silly and frivolous now and then.

What a thing for a man to do, to teach her to trust him and then guide and uplift her till she had the highest standards formed! She was so young and tiny and so sweet at times. Yes, she was, she must be, like Solveig.

If a man with a good moral character, a decent reputation of good taste and respectability, no fool at his studies, no stain on his name, should go with her, help her, get her to give up certain daring things she had the name of doing— if such a fellow should give her the protection of his friendship and let the world see that he considered her respectable—wouldn't it help a lot? Wouldn't it stop people's mouths and make them see that Gila wasn't what they'd been saying?

It came to him that this would be a pleasant mission for his leisure hours during the rest of that winter. All thought of any danger to him through such interaction had disappeared.

Half a mile away Gila was pouring tea for two extremely ardent youths who scarcely occupied half her mind. With the other half she was planning a little note which should bring Courtland to her side early in the week. She had no thoughts of God. She was never troubled with much pondering. She knew exactly what she wanted without thinking any further about it, and she meant to have it.

Chapter 5

I t was a great puzzle to Courtland afterward, just why he was the one who carried that telegram over to the west dormitory to Wittemore, instead of any one of a dozen other fellows who were in the office when it arrived and might just as well have gone. Did anything in the world *happen,* he wondered?

He couldn't tell why he'd held out his hand and offered to take the message.

It wasn't because he wasn't trying hard and studying for all he was worth that "Witless Abner," as Wittemore was called, had won his nickname. He worked night and day, plunged in a maze of things he didn't quite understand until long after the rest of the class passed them. He was majoring in sociology through the advice of an uncle who had never seen him. He had told Abner's mother that sociology was the coming science, and Abner was faithfully carrying out the course of study he suggested. He was floundering through hours of lectures on the theory of the subject and conscientiously working in the college settlement to get the practical side of things.

He had the distressed look of a person with very short legs who's trying to keep up with a procession of six-footers, although there was nothing short about Abner. His legs were long, his body was long, and his arms were too long for most of his sleeves. His face was long; his nose and chin were painfully long and accompanied by a sensitive mouth that was always aquiver with apprehension, like a rabbit's, and little light eyes with whitish eyelashes. His hair was like licked hay. There was nothing attractive about Wittemore except his smile, and he so seldom smiled that few of the boys had ever seen it. He had almost no friends.

He had apparently just entered his room when Courtland reached his door and was stumbling about in a hurry to turn on the light. He stopped with trembling lips and a dart of fear in his eyes when he saw the telegram. Only his mother would send him a telegram, and she would never waste the money for it unless something dreadful was the matter. He looked at it fearfully, holding it in his hand and glancing up again at Courtland, as if he dreaded to open it.

Then, with that set, stolid look of plodding ahead that characterized Abner's movements, he clumsily tore open the envelope.

"Your mother is dying. Come at once" were the terse, cruel words he read, signed with a neighbor's initials.

The young man gasped and stood gaping up at Courtland.

"Nothing's the matter, I hope," said Courtland kindly, moved by the gray, stricken look that had come over the poor fellow's face.

"It's Mother!" he groaned. "Read!" He thrust the telegram into Courtland's hand and sank down on the side of the bed with his head in his hands.

"Tough luck, old man!" said Courtland, with a gentle hand on the bowed shoulder. "But maybe it's only a scare. Sometimes people get better when they're pretty sick, you know."

Wittemore shook his head. "No. We've been expecting this, she and I. She's been sick a long time. I didn't want to come back this year. I thought she was failing. But she insisted. She'd set her heart on my graduating!"

"Well, cheer up!" said Courtland. "Very likely your coming will rally her again. What train do you want to get? Can I help you any?"

Wittemore lifted his head and looked about his room helplessly.

Courtland looked up the train, phoned for a taxi and gathered from around the room what he thought would be needed for the journey, while Wittemore was trying to get dressed. Suddenly he stopped short and drew something out of his pocket with an exclamation of dismay.

"I forgot about this medicine!" he gasped. "I'll have to wait for the next train! Never mind that suitcase. I haven't time to wait for it! I'll go up to the station as soon as I land this."

He seized his hat and would have gone out the door, but Courtland grabbed him by the arm.

"Hold on, old fellow! What's up? Surely you won't let anything keep you from your mother now."

"I must!" The words came with a moan of agony. "It's medicine for a poor old woman down in the settlement district. She's suffering horribly, and the doctor said she should have it tonight, but there was no one else to get it for her, so I promised. She's lying there waiting for it now, listening to every sound till I come. Mother wouldn't want me to come to her, leaving a woman suffering like that when I'd promised. I only came up here to get carfare so I could get there sooner than walking. It took all my change to get the prescription filled."

"What do you think I am, Wittemore? I'll take the medicine to the old lady—ten old ladies if necessary! You get your train! There's your suitcase. Do you have plenty of money?"

A blank look crossed the poor fellow's face. "If I could find Dick Folsom I'd have about enough. He owes me something. I did some copying for him."

Courtland's hand was in his pocket. He always had plenty of money about him. That had never been one of his troubles. He'd been to the bank that day, fortunately. Now he thrust a handful of bills into Wittemore's astonished hands.

"There's fifty! Will that see you through? And I can send you more if you need it. Just wire me how much you want."

Wittemore stood looking down at the bills, and tears began to run down his cheeks and splash on them. Courtland felt his own eyes filling. What a pitiful, lonely life this had been! And the fellows had let him live that way! To think that a few paltry dollars should bring *tears!*

A few minutes later he stood looking after the whirling taxi as it bore Wittemore away into the darkness of the evening street, his heart pounding with several new emotions. Witless Abner for one! What a surprise he'd been!

Would everybody you didn't fancy turn out that way if you got hold of the key to their souls and opened the door?

Then the little wrapped bottle in his hand reminded him to hurry if he would perform the mission left for him and return in time for supper. Something wouldn't let him wait until after supper. So he plunged forward into the dusk and swung himself on board a downtown car.

He had no small trouble finding the street, or rather court, in which the old woman lived.

He stumbled up the narrow staircase, lighting matches as he went, for the place was dark as midnight. By the time he'd climbed four flights he was wondering why in thunder Wittemore came to places like this? Just to major in sociology? Didn't the nut know he'd never make a success in a thing like that? What was he doing it for anyway? Did he expect to teach it? Poor fellow!

He knocked, with no result, at several doors for the old woman, but at last a feeble voice answered, "Come in," and he entered a dark room. There didn't even appear to be a window, though he afterward discovered one opening into an air shaft. He stood hesitating within the room, blinking and trying to see what was about him.

"Be that you, Mr. Widymer?" asked a faint voice from the opposite corner.

"Wittemore couldn't come. He had a telegram that his mother is dying, and he had to get the train. He sent me with the medicine."

"Oh, now ain't that too bad!" said the voice. "His mother dyin'! An' to think he should remember me an' my medicine! Well, now, what d' ye think o' that?"

"If you'll tell me where your gas is located I'll make a light for you," said Courtland politely.

"Gas!" The old lady laughed aloud. "You won't find no such thing as gas around this part o' town. There's about an inch o' candle up on that shelf. The distric' nurse left it there. I was thinkin' mebbe I'd get Mr. Widymer to light it fer me when he come, an' then the night wouldn't seem so long. It's awful, when you're sufferin', to have the nights long."

He groped till he found the shelf and lit the candle. By degrees the flickering light revealed to him a small bare room with no furniture except a bed, a chair, a small stove and a table. A box in the corner apparently contained a few worn garments. Some dishes and provisions were huddled on the table. The walls and floor were bare. The district nurse had done her best to clear up, perhaps, but with no attempt at good cheer. A desolate place indeed to spend a weary night of suffering, even with an inch of candle sending weird flickerings across the dusky ceiling.

His impulse was to flee, but somehow he couldn't. "Here's this medicine," he said. "Where do you want me to put it?"

The woman motioned with a bony hand toward the table. "There's a cup and spoon over there somewhere," she said weakly. "If you could get me a pitcher of water and set it here on a chair I could take it durin' the night."

He could see her better now, for the candle was flaring bravely. She was little and old. Her thin, white hair straggled pitifully about her small, wrinkled face; her eyes looked almost burned out by suffering. He saw she was drawn and quivering with pain, even now as she tried to speak cheerfully. Something rebellious in him yielded to the old woman's nerve, and he quieted his impatience. Sure he'd get her the water!

She explained that the hydrant was down on the street. He took the doubtful-looking pitcher and stumbled out onto those narrow, rickety stairs again.

Way down to the street and back in that inky blackness! Was this the kind of thing one was up against majoring in sociology?

"I be'n thinkin'," said the old lady, when he stumbled, blinking, back into the room again with the water. "Ef you wouldn't mind jest stirrin' up the fire an' making' me a sup o' tea, it would be real heartenin'. I ain't et nothin' all day 'cause the pain was so bad, but I think it'll ease up when I git a dose of the medicine, and p'r'aps I might eat a bite."

Courtland was appalled, but he went vigorously to work at that fire, although he had never laid eyes on anything so primitive as that stove in all his life. Presently, by using common sense, he had the thing going and a forlorn little kettle steaming away cheerfully.

The old woman cautioned him against using too much tea. There must be at least three drawings left, and it might be a long time before she got anymore. Yes, there was a little mite of sugar in a paper on the table.

"There's some bread there, too—half a loaf 'most—but I guess it's pretty dry. You don't know how to make toast, I 'spose," she added wistfully.

Courtland had never made toast in his life. He abominated it. She told him how to hold it up on a fork in front of the coals, and he managed to do two very creditable slices. He'd forgotten his own supper now. There was something quite fresh and original in the whole experience. It would be interesting to tell the boys, if some features about it weren't almost sacred. He wondered what the gang would say when he told them about Wittemore! Poor Wittemore! He wasn't as nutty as they'd thought. He had good in his heart. Courtland poured the tea, but the sugar paper had proved quite empty when he found it; likewise a plate that had once contained butter.

The toast and tea, however, seemed to be quite acceptable without their usual accessories.

"Now," he said with a long breath, "is there anything else you'd like before I go? I must be getting back to college."

"If you just wouldn't mind makin' a prayer before you go," responded the old woman, her feeble chin trembling with her boldness. "I be'n wantin' a prayer this long while, but I don't seem to have good luck. The distric' nurse, she ain't the prayin' kind; an' Mr. Widymer says he don't pray no more since he's come to college. He said it so kind of ashamed-like I didn't like to bother him again, and nobody else's come my way for three months back. You seem so kind-spoken and pleasant-like, as if you might be related to a preacher, and I thought mebbe you wouldn't mind just makin' a little short prayer 'fore you go. I dunno how long it'll be 'fore I get a chancet of one again."

Courtland stood rooted to the floor in dismay. "Why—I—," he began, growing red enough to be apparent even by the inch of flickering candle.

Suddenly the room which had been so empty seemed to grow hushed and full of breathless spectators, with One, waiting to hear whether he would respond to the call. Before his alarmed vision came the memory of that wall of smoke and that Voice calling him by name and saying, "You'll be shown." Was this what the Presence asked of him? Was this that mysterious "doing His will" the Book spoke about, which would presently give the assurance?

He saw the old woman's face glow with eagerness. It was as if the Presence waited through her eyes. Something leaped up in his heart in response, and he took a step forward and dropped on his knees beside the wooden chair.

"I'm afraid I'll make a worse bungle of it than I did of the toast," he said, as he saw her folding her hands with delight. She smiled with a serene assurance, and he closed his eyes and wondered where to find words to use in such a time as this.

"Now I lay me" would not do for the poor creature who had been lying down many days and might never rise again. "Matthew, Mark, Luke and John" was more appropriate, but there was the uncertainty about its being a prayer at all. "Our Father"—Ah! He caught at the words and spoke them.

"Our Father which art"—but what came next? That was where he'd always had to be prompted, and now, in his confusion, the rest had fled his mind. But it seemed that with the words the Presence had drawn near and was standing close by the chair. He became aware that he might talk with this invisible Presence, unfold his own perplexities and restlessness, and perhaps find out what it all meant. With scarcely a hesitation his clear voice went on eagerly.

"Our Father, which art in this room, show us how to find and know You." He couldn't remember afterward what else he said. Something about his own longing, and the old woman's pain and loneliness. He wasn't sure if it was really a prayer at all, that halting petition.

He got up from his knees greatly embarrassed—but more by the Presence he'd dared to speak to for the first time on his own account than by the old woman, whose hands were still clasped in reverence and down whose withered cheeks the tears were coursing. The smoky walls, the cracked stove, the stack of discouraged dishes, seemed to fade away, and the room was somehow full of glory. He was choking with the oppression of it and with a sinking lest the prayer had been only an outbreak of his own desire to know what this Force or Presence was that seemed to dominate him these days.

The old woman was blessing him. She held out her hands like a patriarch. "Oh, that was such a beautiful prayer! I'll not forget the words all night through and for many a night. The Lord Himself bless ye! Are you a preacher's son perhaps?"

He shook his head. But he wore no smile on his face at the thought, as he might have had five minutes before.

"Well, then, yer surely goin' to be a preacher yerself?"

"No," he said, then added, "not that I know of." The suggestion struck him curiously as one who hears for the first time he may be selected for some important foreign embassy.

"Well, then, yer surely a blessed child o' God Himself, anyhow, and this is a great night fer this poor little room to be honored with a pretty prayer like that!"

Scarcely hearing her, he said good night and went down the dark stairs, a strange sense of peace upon him. Oddly enough, while he felt he'd left the Presence up in that dismal room, it yet seemed to be moving beside him, touching his soul, breathing upon him! He was so engrossed with this thought that it never occurred to him he'd given the woman every cent in his pocket. He'd forgotten his hunger. A great wonder was moving within his spirit. He couldn't understand himself. He went back with awe over the last few minutes and the strange new world into which he'd been suddenly plunged.

Scarcely noticing how he went, he got out of the court into a neighborhood a shade less poverty-stricken and stood on the corner of a busy thoroughfare in an utterly unfamiliar district, pausing to look about him and discover his whereabouts.

A little child with long, fair hair rushed suddenly out of a door on the side street, pulling a ragged sweater about his small shoulders, and stood on the curbstone, watching the coming trolley. The car stopped, and a young girl in shabby clothes got out and walked toward him.

"Bonnie! Bonnie! I've got supper ready!" the child called in a clear voice and darted from the curb across the narrow side street to meet her.

Courtland, standing on the corner in front of the trolley, saw, too late, the automobile bearing swiftly down upon the child, its headlights flashing on the golden hair. With a cry the young man sprang to the rescue, but the child was already crumpled up, and the relentless car was speeding onward, its chauffeur darting glances behind him as he plunged his machine forward over the track, almost in the teeth of the up-trolley. After the trolley passed there was no sign of the car, even if anyone had had time to look for it. There in the road lay the broken child, his hair spilling like gold over the pavement, the still, white face looking up like a flower suddenly torn from the plant.

The girl was beside the child almost instantly, dropping her parcels, gathering him into her slender arms, calling in frightened, tender tones: "Aleck! Darling! My little darling!"

The child was too heavy for her to lift, and she tottered as she tried to rise, lifting a frightened face to Courtland.

"Let me take him," said the young man, stooping and gathering him gently from her. "Now show me where!"

Chapter 6

Into the narrow brick house he had run out of so eagerly only a few minutes before, they carried him, up two flights of steep stairs to a small room at the back of the hall.

The gas was burning brightly at one side, and something sending forth a savory odor was bubbling on a little two-burner gas stove. Courtland was hungry, and it struck his nostrils pleasantly as the door swung open, revealing a tiny table covered with a white cloth, set for two. A window was curtained with white, and a red geranium sat on the sill.

The girl entered ahead of him, sweeping back a bright chintz curtain that divided the room, and drew forth a child's cot. Courtland gently laid the little inert figure on it. The girl was on her knees beside the child at once, a bottle in her hand. She was dropping a few drops in a teaspoon and forcing them between the child's lips.

"Will you please get a doctor, quick," she said in a strained voice. "No, I don't know who; I've only been here two weeks. We're strangers! Bring somebody—anybody—quick!"

Courtland was back in a minute with a weary, seedy-looking doctor who fitted the street. All the way he was seeing the beautiful agony of the girl's face. It was as if her suffering had become his. Somehow he couldn't bear to think what might be coming. The little form had lain so limply in his arms!

The girl had undressed the child and put him between the sheets. He was more like a broken lily than ever. The long dark lashes lay still upon the cheeks.

Courtland stood back in the doorway, looking at the small table set for two and pushed to the wall now to make room for the cot. He could almost hear the echo of that happy, childish voice calling down in the street: "Bonnie! Bonnie! I've got supper ready!"

He wondered if the girl had heard. And there was supper! Two blue and white bowls set on two blue and white plates, obviously for the something hot that was cooking over the flame, with two bread-and-butter plates to match; two glasses of milk; a plate of bread, another of butter; and for dessert an apple cut in half, the core dug out and the hollow filled with sugar. He took in the details, as if they were a word picture by Wells or Shaw in his contemporary prose class at college.

"Go over to my house and ask my wife to give you my battery!" commanded the doctor in a low growl.

Courtland was off again, glad of something to do. He carried the memory of the doctor's grizzled face lying on the child's bared breast, listening for the heartbeats, and the girl's anguish as she stood over them. He pushed aside the curious throng that had gathered around the door, looking up the stairs, whispering dolefully and shaking their heads.

"An' he was so purty and so cheery—bless his heart!" wailed one woman. "He always had his bit of a word an' a smile!"

"Aw! Them ottymobeels!" he heard another murmur. "Ridin' along in their glory! There'll be a day o' reckonin' for them rich folks what rides in 'em! They'll hev to walk! They may even have to lie abed an' hev their wages get behind!"

The whole weight of sorrow of the world seemed suddenly pressing upon Courtland's heart. How had he been so unexpectedly taken out of the pleasant monotony of the university and whirled into this vortex of anguish? Was it a coincidence he was the one to go to the old woman and make her toast and then be called upon to pray, instead of Tennelly or Bill Ward or any of the other fellows? And was it again coincidence he stood at that corner at that particular moment and participated in this later tragedy?

Oh, the beautiful face of the suffering girl! Fear and sorrow and suffering and death everywhere! Wittemore hurrying to his dying mother! The old woman lying on her bed of pain! But there was glory in that dark old room when he left it, the glory of a Presence! Ah! Where was the Presence now? How could *He* bear all this? The Christ! And couldn't He change it if He would—make the world a happy place instead of so dark and dreadful? For the first time the horror of war surged over his soul in its blackness. Men dying in the trenches! Women weeping at home for them! Others suffering and bleeding to death out in the open, the cold or the storm! How could God let it all be? His wondering soul cried out, "Lord, if Thou hadst been here!"

It was the old question that used to come up in the classroom. Yet now, strangely enough, he began to feel there was an answer to it somewhere—an answer he would be satisfied with when he found it.

He seemed to pass through an eternity of thought as he crossed and recrossed the street and was back in the tiny room where life waited on death. It was another eternity while the doctor worked again over the boy. But at last he stood back, shaking his head and blinking the tears from his kind, tired, blue eyes.

"It's no use," he said gruffly, turning his head away. "He's gone!"

The girl brushed him aside and sank to her knees beside the little cot. "Aleck! Aleck! Darling brother! Can't you speak to your Bonnie just once more before you go?" she called, clearly, distinctly, as if to a child who was far on his way. Then once again she cried pitifully, "Oh, darling brother! You're all I had left! Let me hear you call me Bonnie just once more before you go to Mother!"

But the childish lips lay still and white, and the lips of the girl looking down on the quiet little form grew whiter also as she looked.

"Oh, my darling! You have gone! You'll never call me anymore! And you were all I had! Good-bye!" And she stooped and kissed the boy's cheek with a finality that wrung the hearts of the onlookers. They knew she had forgotten their presence.

The doctor stepped into the hall. The tears were rolling down his cheeks. "It's tough luck!" he said in an undertone to Courtland.

The young man turned away to hide the sudden convulsion that seemed coming to his own face. Then he heard the girl's voice again, lower, as if she were talking confidentially to One who stood close at hand.

"O Christ, will You go with little Aleck and see that he's not afraid till he gets safely home? And will You help me somehow bear his leaving me alone?"

The doctor was wiping away the tears with a great, soiled handkerchief. The girl rose calmly, pale and controlled, facing them as if she remembered them for the first time.

"I want to thank you for all you've done!" she said. "I'm only a stranger, and you've been very kind. But now it's over, and I won't hinder you any longer."

She wanted to be alone. They could see that. Yet it wrung their hearts to leave her so.

"You'll want to make some arrangements," offered the doctor.

"Oh! I'd forgotten!" The girl's hand fluttered to her heart, and her breath gave a quick catch. "It will have to be simple," she said, looking from one to another of them anxiously. "I haven't much money left. Perhaps I could sell something!" She looked desperately around on her little possessions. "This little cot! It was new just two weeks ago, and he won't need it anymore. It cost twenty dollars!"

Courtland stepped gravely toward her. "Suppose you leave that to me," he said gently. "I think I know a place where they'd look after the matter reasonably and let you pay later or take the cot in exchange—anything you wish. Would you like me to arrange things for you?"

"Oh, if you would!" said the girl wearily. "But it's asking a great deal of a stranger."

"It's nothing. I can look after it on my way home. Just tell me what you wish."

"Oh, the very simplest there is!" She caught her breath. "White, if possible, unless it's more expensive. But it doesn't matter anyway now. There'll have to be a *place* somewhere, too. Sometime I'll take him back and let him lie by Father and Mother. I can't now. It's two hundred miles away. But there'll only need to be one carriage. There's only me to go."

He looked his compassion but only asked, "Is there anything else?"

"Any special clergyman?" asked the doctor kindly.

She shook her head. "We hadn't been to church yet. I was too tired. If you know of a minister who would come. . . ."

"It's tough luck," said the doctor as they went downstairs together, "to see a nice, likely little chap like that taken away so. And I operated this afternoon on a hardened old reprobate around the corner here, that's played the devil to everybody, and he's going to pull through! It does seem strange. It ain't the way I'd run the universe, but I'm thundering glad I ain't got the job!"

Courtland walked on through the busy streets, thinking that sentence over.

He perceived dimly there might be another way of looking at the matter; that the wicked old reprobate might yet have something more to learn of life before he went beyond its choices and opportunities; a conviction that if he were called to go he'd rather be the little child in his purity than the old man in his deviltry.

The sudden cutting down of this lovely child had startled and shocked him. The girl's bereavement cut him to the heart as if she belonged to him. It brought the other world so close. It made what until now seemed big and worthwhile look so small and petty, so ephemeral! Had he always given himself to things that didn't count, or was this a perspective distorted through nervous strain and overexertion?

He came more presently to a well-known undertaker's and, stepping in, felt more than ever the borderland sense. In this silent house of sadness men stepped quietly, politely, and served you with courteous sympathy. What was the name of the man who rowed his boat on the River Styx? Yes! Charon! These wise-eyed grave men who continually plied their oars between two worlds! How did they look at life? Were they hardened to their task? Was their gravity acting? Did earthly things appeal to them? How could they bear this continual settled sadness about the place? The awful hush! The tear-stained faces! The heavy breath of flowers! Not the lofty marble arches or the beauty of surroundings or the soft music of hidden choirs and a distant organ up in a hall above, where a service was even then in progress, could take away the fact of death—the settled, final fact of death! One moment here on the curbstone, golden hair afloat, eyes alight with joyous greeting, voice of laughter; the next gone, irrevocably gone, "and the place thereof shall know it no more." Where had he heard those words? Strange, sad house of death! Strange, uncertain life to live. Resurrection! Where had he caught that word in carved letters twined among lilies above the marble staircase? Resurrection! Yes, there must be if there was ever to be any hope in this world!

It was a strange duty he had to perform, for a college boy to whom death had never come very close since he'd been old enough to understand. He wondered what the fellows would say if they could see him here. He felt half a grudge toward Wittemore for having let him in for all this. Poor Wittemore! By this time tomorrow night he might be doing this same service for his own mother!

Death—everywhere! It seemed as if everybody was dying!

He made selections with a memory of the girl's beautiful, refined face. He chose simple things and everything white. He asked about details and gave directions so all would move in an orderly manner, with nothing to annoy. He even thought to order flowers, valley lilies and some bright rosebuds, not too many to make her feel under obligation. He took out his checkbook and paid for the whole thing, arranging so the girl wouldn't know how much it really cost and that a small sum might be paid by her as she could, to be forwarded by the firm to him—to make her feel comfortable about it all.

As he went out into the street again a great sense of weariness overcame him. He had lived—how many years!—in experience since he left the university at half past five o'clock. How little his past life looked to him as he surveyed it from the height he had just climbed. Life! Life was not all basketball and football and dances and fellowships and frats and honors! Life was full of sorrow and bounded on every hand by death. The walk from where he was up to the university looked impossible. In the next block was a store where he was known. He could get a check cashed and ride.

He found himself studying the faces of the people in the car in a new light. Were they all acquainted with sorrow? Yes, lines of hardship or anxiety or disappointment were more or less on the older faces. And the younger ones! Did their bright smiles and eagerness have to be frozen on their lips by grief someday? Life was a terrible thing! Take that girl now, Miss Brentwood—Miss R. B. Brentwood, the address had been. The name her brother had called her fitted better: "Bonnie." What would life mean to her now?

He wondered if anyone would feel such sorrow and emptiness of life if he were gone. The fellows would feel bad, of course. There would be speeches and resolutions, a lot of black drapery and that sort of thing in college, but what did that amount to? His father? Oh, yes, of course, he would feel it some, but he had been separated from his father for years, except for brief visits during vacations. His father had married a young wife, and they had three young children. No, his father wouldn't miss him much.

He swung off the car in front of the university and entered the dormitory at last, too engrossed in his strange new thoughts to remember he'd had no supper.

"Hello, Court! Where've you been? We've looked everywhere for you. You didn't come to the dining hall! What's wrong with you? Come in here!"

It was Tennelly who hauled him into Bill Ward's room and thumped him into a great leather chair.

"Why, man, you're all in! Give an account of yourself!" he said, tossing his hat over to Bill Ward and pulling away at his mackinaw.

"P'raps he's in love!" suggested Pat from the couch where he was puffing away at his pipe.

"P'raps he's flunked his Greek exam," suggested Bill Ward, with a grin.

"He looks as if he'd seen a ghost!" said Tennelly, eyeing him critically.

"Cut it out, boys," said Courtland with a weary smile. "I've seen enough. Wittemore's called home. His mother's dying. I ran an errand for him down in some of his slums, and on the way back I just saw a little kid get killed. Pretty little kid, too, with long curls!"

"Say, that is going some!" said Pat from his couch.

"Ferget it!" exclaimed Bill Ward, coming to his feet. "Had your supper yet, Court?"

Courtland shook his head.

"Well, just you sit still there while I run down to the pie shop and see what I can get."

Bill seized his cap and mackinaw and went roaring off down the hall.

Courtland's eyes were closed. He hadn't felt so tired since he left the hospital. His mind was still struggling with the questions his last two hours had flung at him to be answered.

Pat sat up and put away his pipe. He made silent motions to Tennelly, and the two picked up the unresisting Courtland and laid him on the couch. Pat's face was unusually sober as he put a pillow under his friend's head. Courtland opened his eyes and smiled.

"Thanks, old man," he said, gripping his hand. Something in Pat's face he had never noticed before. As he shut his eyelids he had an odd sense that Pat and Tennelly and the Presence were all taking care of him. A sick fancy of worn-out nerves, of course, but pleasant all the same.

Down the hall a nasal voice twanged at the telephone, shouting each answer as though to make the whole dormitory hear. Then loud steps and a thump on the door as it was flung open:

"Court here? A girl on the phone wants you, Court. Says her name is Miss Gila Dare."

Chapter 7

The three young men looked at one another in silence.

"Shouldn't I go and get a message for you, Court?" asked Tennelly. For Courtland's face was ashen gray, and the memory of it lying in the hospital was too recent for him not to feel anxious about his friend. He had been permitted to return to college so quickly only with strict orders not to overdo.

"No, I guess I'll go," said Courtland indifferently, rising as he spoke.

They listened anxiously to his tones as he talked over the phone.

"Hello. . . . Yes! . . . Yes! . . . Oh! Good evening! . . . Yes. . . . Yes. . . . No-o-o—it won't be possible. . . . No, I've just come in, and I'm pretty well all in. I have a lot of studying yet to do tonight. This is exam week. . . . No, I'm afraid not tomorrow night either. . . . No, there wouldn't be a chance till the end of the week, anyway. . . . Why, yes, I think I could by that time, perhaps—Friday night? I'll let you know. . . . Thank you. Good-bye!"

The listeners looked from one to the other knowingly. This wasn't the tone of one who had "fallen" very far for a girl. They knew the signs. He had actually been indifferent! Gila Dare hadn't conquered him as easily as Bill Ward thought she would. And the strange thing about it was that something in the atmosphere that night made them feel they weren't so very sorry. Somehow Courtland seemed unusually close and dear to them just then. For the moment they seemed to have perceived something fine in his mood that held them in awe. They didn't tease him when he came back, as they would ordinarily have done. They received him gravely, talking together about the examination the next day, as if they'd scarcely noticed his going.

Bill Ward came back presently with his arms laden with bundles. He looked at the tired face on the couch but whistled a merry tune to let on he hadn't noticed anything amiss.

"Got a great spread this time," he declared, setting forth his spoils on two chairs beside the couch. "Hot oyster stew! Sit by, fellows! Cooky wrapped it up in newspapers to keep it from getting cold. Bowls and spoons are in the basket. Nelly, get 'em out! Here, Pat—take that bundle out from under my arm. That's celery and crackers. Here's a pail of hot coffee with cream and sugar mixed in. Look out, Pat! That's jelly roll and chocolate éclairs! Don't mash it, you chump! Why didn't you come with me?"

It was pleasant to lie there in that warm, comfortable room with the familiar pennants, pictures and trophies and hear the fellows talking of everyday things; to be fed with food that made him begin to feel like himself again; to have their kind fellowship about him like a protection.

They were grand fellows—full of faults, too, but true at heart. Life-friends he knew, for a cord bound their four hearts together with a tenderer tie than bound them to any of the other fellows. They'd been together the four years, and if all went well and Bill Ward didn't flunk anything more, they would all four go out into the world as men together at the end of that year.

He lay looking at them quietly as they talked, telling foolish jokes, laughing immoderately, asking one another anxiously about a tough question in the exam that morning and what the prospects were for good marks for them all. It was all so familiar and beloved. So different from those last three hours amid suffering and sorrow! It was all so natural and happy, as if the world held no sorrow. As if this life would never end! But he wasn't yet over that feeling of the Presence in the room with them, standing somewhere behind Pat and Tennelly. He liked to feel its consciousness in the back of his mind. What would the fellows say if he tried to tell them about it? They'd think he was crazy. He felt he'd like to be the means of making them understand.

He told them gradually about Wittemore—not as he might have told them directly after seeing him off nor quite as he'd expected to tell them. What he said gave them a kinder, keener insight into a character they had all but condemned and ignored before. They didn't laugh! It was a revelation to them. They listened with respect for the student who had gone to his mother's dying bed. They had all been away from their own mothers long enough to feel a mother's worth quite touchingly. Moreover, they perceived that Courtland had seen more in Wittemore than they had ever seen. He had a side, it appeared, that was wholly unselfish, almost heroic in a way. They'd never suspected him of it before. His long, horselike face, with the light china-blue eyes always anxious and startled, appeared to their imaginations with a new appeal. When he returned they would be kinder to him.

"Poor old Abner!" said Tennelly thoughtfully. "Who'd have thought it? Carrying medicine to an old bedridden crone! And was going to stick to his job even when his mother was dying! He's got some stuff in him, if he hasn't much sense!"

Courtland was led to go on talking about the old woman, picturing in a few words the room where she lay, the pitifully few comforts, the inch of candle, the tea without sugar or milk, the butterless toast. He told it simply, unaware that he told how he'd made the toast. They listened without comment as to one who had been set apart to a duty undesirable but greatly to be admired.

Afterward he spoke again about the child, telling briefly how he was killed. He barely mentioned the sister, and he told nothing whatever of his own part in it. They looked at him curiously, as if to read between the lines, for they saw he was deeply stirred, but they asked nothing. Presently they fell to studying, Courtland with the rest, for the next day's work was important.

They made him stay on the couch and swung the light around where he could see. They broke into song or jokes now and then as was their wont; but over it all was a hush and a quiet sympathy that each one felt, and none more deeply than Courtland. At no other time during his college life had he felt so keenly and so finely bound to his companions as this night.

When he went at last to his own room across the hall, he looked about on its comforts and luxuries with a kind of wonder that he had been selected for all this, while that poor woman down in the tenement had to live with bare walls and not even a whole candle! His pleasant room seemed so satisfying. And that girl was alone in her tiny room with so little about her to make life easy, and her beautiful dead brother lying stricken before her eyes! He couldn't get away from the thought of her when he lay down to rest, and in his dreams her face of sorrow haunted him.

Not until after the examinations the next afternoon did he realize he was going to her again—had been going all along. Of course he was only a passing stranger, but she had no one, and he couldn't let her need a friend. Perhaps— why, he surely *had* a responsibility for her when he was the only one who happened by!

She opened the door at his knock, and he was startled by the look on her face, so drawn and white, with great dark circles under her eyes. She hadn't slept or wept since he saw her, he felt sure. How long could human frame, especially one so young and frail, endure like that? He longed to take her away somewhere out of it all. Yet, of course, there was nothing he could do.

She was full of quiet gratitude for what he'd done. Without his kind intercession, she said, she would have had to pay far more. She'd been through it too recently before and understood that such things were expensive. He rejoiced that she judged only by the standards of a small country place, didn't know city prices and therefore little suspected how much he'd done to smooth her way. He told her of the preacher he secured that afternoon by telephone— a plain, kind man recommended by the undertaker. She thanked him again, apathetically, as if she hadn't the heart to feel anything keenly.

"Have you eaten anything today?" he asked suddenly.

She shook her head. "I couldn't eat! It would choke me!"

"But you must eat, you know," he said, as if she were a little child. "You can't bear all this. You'll break down."

"Oh, what does that matter now?" she asked, with her hand fluttering to her heart again and a wave of anguish passing over her pale face.

"But we must live, mustn't we, until we are called to come away?"

He asked the question shyly. He didn't understand where the thought or words came from. He wasn't conscious of evolving them from his own mind.

She looked at him in sad acquiescence. "I know," she said, "and I'll try pretty soon. But I can't just yet. It would choke me!"

Even while they were talking, a door in the front of the hall opened, and an untidy person with unkempt hair appeared, asking the girl to come into her room and have a bite. When she shook her head the woman said, "Well, then, child, go out a few minutes and get something. You'll not last through the night at this rate! Go, and I'll stay here until you come back."

Courtland persuaded her at last to come with him down to a little restaurant around the corner and have a cup of tea—just a cup of tea. With a weary look, as if she thought it was the quickest way to get rid of their kindness, she yielded. He thought he never would forget the look she cast behind her at the white, sheet-covered cot as she walked out the door.

It was an odd experience, taking this stranger to supper. He'd met all sorts of girls during his young career and had many different experiences, but none like this. Yet he was so filled with sympathy and sorrow for her that it wasn't embarrassing. She didn't seem like an ordinary girl. She was set apart by her sorrow. He ordered the daintiest and most attractive that the plain menu of the little restaurant afforded, but he only succeeded in getting her to eat a few mouthfuls and drink a cup of tea. Nevertheless it did her good. He could see a faint color coming into her cheeks. He spoke of college and his examinations, as if she knew all about him. He thought it might give her a more secure feeling if she knew he was a student at the university. But she took it as a matter that didn't concern her in the least, with an aloofness that showed him he was touching only the surface of her being. Her real self was just bearing it to get rid of him and return to her sorrow alone.

Before he left her he felt moved to tell her how he'd seen the child coming out to greet her. He thought perhaps she hadn't heard those last joyous words of greeting and would want to know.

The light leaped up in her face in a vivid flame for the first time, her eyes shone with the tears that sprang mercifully into them, and her lips trembled. She put out a small, cold hand and touched his sleeve.

"Oh, thank you! That is precious," she said, and, turning her head, she wept. It was a relief to see the strained look break and the healing tears flow.

He left her then, but he couldn't escape the thought of her all night with her sorrow alone. It was as if he had to bear it with her because there was no one else to do so.

When he left her he looked up the minister he'd made brief arrangements with over the telephone. He had to confess to himself that his real object in coming had been to make sure the man was "good enough for the job."

The Reverend John Burns was small, sandy, homely, with kind, twinkling red-brown eyes, a wide mouth, an ugly nose and freckles. But he had a smile that was cordiality itself and a big hand that gripped a real welcome.

Courtland explained he'd come about the funeral. He felt embarrassed because he hadn't anything to say. He'd given the details over the phone, but the kind, attentive eyes were sympathetic, and he found himself telling the story of the tragedy. He liked the way the minister received it. It was the way a minister should be to people in their need.

"You're a relative?" asked John Burns as Courtland stood up to go.

"No." Then he hesitated. For some reason he couldn't bear to say he was an utter stranger to the lonely girl. "No, only a friend," he finished. "A—a—kind of neighbor!" he added, trying to explain the situation to himself.

"Sort of a Christ-friend perhaps?" The kind eyes seemed to search into his soul and understand. The freckled face lit with a smile.

Courtland gave the man a keen, hungry look. He felt strangely drawn to him, and a quick light of brotherhood darted into his eyes. His fingers answered the other's friendly grasp as they parted, and he went out feeling that somehow *there* was a man who was different—a man he'd like to know better and study carefully. That man must have had some experience. He must know Christ! Had he ever felt the Presence?

He threw himself into his studies again when he got back to the university, but in spite of himself his mind kept wandering back to strange questions. He wished Wittemore would come back and say his mother was better. Wittemore started this odd sidetrack that sent him off to make toast for old women and manage funerals for strange young girls. If Wittemore would get back to his classes and plod off to his slums every day, with his long horselike face and scared little apologetic smile, why, perhaps his own mind would let him get back to his work. And with that he sat down and wrote a letter to Wittemore, brief, sympathetic, inquiring, offering any help that might be required. When it was finished he felt better and studied half the night.

As soon as he woke up the next morning he knew he would have to go to that funeral. He hated funerals, and this would be a terrible ordeal, he was sure. Such a pitiful funeral, and he an utter stranger, too! But the necessity presented itself like a command from an unseen force, and he knew it was required of him—that he would never feel quite satisfied with himself if he shirked it.

Fortunately, his examination began at eight o'clock. If he worked fast he could finish in plenty of time, for the funeral had been set for eleven o'clock.

Tennelly and Pat gazed after him aghast when, after the exam, he declined their suggestion that they all go down to the river skating for an hour and try to get their blood up after the strain so they could study better after lunch.

"I can't! I'm going to that kid's funeral!" he said and strode up the stairs with his arms full of books.

"Good night!" said Pat in dismay.

"Morbid!" exclaimed Tennelly. "Say, Pat, I don't guess we better let him go. He'll come home all in again."

But when they found Bill Ward and went up to stop Courtland, he'd left by the other door and was halfway down the campus.

Chapter 8

The third-story back room was neat and pretty. The gas stove and other things had disappeared behind the chintz curtain. Before it stood the small white coffin, with the boy lying as if he were asleep, the roses strewn about him, and a mass of valley lilies at his feet. The girl, pale and calm, sat beside him, one hand resting across the casket protectingly.

Three or four women from the house had brought in chairs, and some of the neighbors had slipped in shyly, half in sympathy, half in curiosity. The minister was already there, talking in a low tone in the hall with the undertaker.

The girl looked up when Courtland entered, thanking him for the flowers with her eyes. The women huddled in the back of the room watched him curiously. The doctor came in and walked over to stand beside the coffin, looking down for a minute, and then turned away with the frank tears running down his face. He sat beside Courtland. The stillness and strangeness in the bare room were awful. It was only bearable to look toward the peace in the small, white, dead face, for the calm on the sister's face cut one to the heart.

The minister and the undertaker stepped into the room, and then it seemed to Courtland as if One other entered also. He didn't look up to see; he merely sensed it. It stayed with him and relieved the tension in the room.

Then the minister's voice, clear, gentle, ringing, triumphant, stole through the room and out into the hall, even down through the landings, where some of the neighbors were clustered, listening.

" 'And I heard a voice from heaven saying unto me, "Write, Blessed are the dead which die in the Lord from henceforth" . . .But I would not have you to be ignorant, brethren, concerning them which are asleep, that ye sorrow not, even as others which have no hope. For if we believe that Jesus died and rose again, even so them also which sleep in Jesus will God bring with him. . . . For the Lord himself shall descend from heaven with a shout, with the voice of the archangel and with the trump of God: and the dead in Christ shall rise first: Then we which are alive and remain shall be caught up together with them in the clouds, to meet the Lord in the air: and so shall we ever be with the Lord. Wherefore comfort one another with these words.' "

The words were utterly new to Courtland. If he'd heard them before at funerals, they had never entered his consciousness. They seemed almost uncannily to answer the question of his heart. He listened with painful attention. Most remarkable statements!

" 'But now is Christ risen from the dead, and become the firstfruits of them that slept!' "

He glanced instinctively around where it seemed the Presence had entered. He couldn't get away from feeling that He stood just to the left of the minister there, with bowed head. It was as if He'd come to take the child away with

Him. Courtland remembered the girl's prayer the night the child died: "Go with little Aleck and see that he's not afraid till he gets safely home." He glanced up at her calm, tearless face. She was drinking in the words. They seemed to give strength under her pitiless sorrow.

" 'The last enemy that shall be destroyed is death!' "

Courtland heard the words with a shock of relief. He'd been under the depression of death—death everywhere and always—threatening every life and earthly project! And now this confident sentence that looked toward a time when death should be no more! He had to face it and think it out, as something presenting itself for him to believe. It was as if the Christ Himself were having it read just for him alone, and only Christ and the dead child were there waiting to walk into another, more real life while Courtland stood on the threshold of another world to learn a great truth.

" 'But some will say, How are the dead raised up? And with what body do they come?' "

Courtland looked up, startled. The very thought dawning in his mind! The child, presently to lie under the ground and return to dust! How could there be a resurrection of that little body after years perhaps? How could there be hope for that wide-eyed sister with her sorrow?

" 'Thou fool, that which thou sowest. . .thou sowest not that body that shall be, but bare grain, it may chance of wheat, or of some other grain.' "

He listened through the wonderful nature-picture, dimly understanding the reasoning, and on to the words, " 'So also is the resurrection of the dead. It is sown in corruption, it is raised in incorruption; it is sown in dishonor, it is raised in glory; it is sown in weakness, it is raised in power; it is sown a natural body, it is raised a spiritual body.' "

He looked at the child lying among the lilies. Was that the thought? The little child laid under the earth like the lily bulb, to see corruption and decay, would come forth, even as the lilies came up out of the darkness and decay of their underground tomb and burst into beautiful blossoms, the perfection of what the ugly brown bulb was meant to be. All the possibilities come to perfection! No accident or sin stain to mar the glorified character! A perfect soul in a perfect, glorified body!

The wonder of the thought swelled within him and sent a thrill through him with the minister's voice.

" 'So when this corruptible shall have put on incorruption, and this mortal shall have put on immortality, then shall be brought to pass the saying that is written: Death is swallowed up in victory. O death, where is thy sting? O grave, where is thy victory? Thanks be to God, which giveth us the victory through our Lord Jesus Christ!' "

If Courtland had been asked before he came there whether he believed in a resurrection he might have given a doubtful answer. During the four years of his college life he'd passed through various stages of unbelief along with many of his fellow students. With them he'd constructed a life philosophy he supposed he believed. It was founded partly upon what he *wanted* to believe and partly upon what he could *not* believe, because he'd never been able to reason it out. Up to this time even his experience with the Presence hadn't touched this philosophy he'd built like a fancy scaffolding inside of which he expected to fashion his life. The Presence and his partial surrender to its influence had been a matter of the heart, and until now it hadn't occurred to him that his allegiance to the Christ was incompatible with his former philosophy.

The doctrine of the resurrection suddenly stood before him as something that must be accepted along with the Christ, or the Christ was not the Christ! Christ *was* the resurrection if He was at all! He *had* to be that, *had* to have conquered death, or He would not have been the Christ; He would not have been God humanized for the understanding of men unless He could do godlike things. He wasn't God if He couldn't conquer death. He wouldn't be a man's Christ if He couldn't come to man in his darkest hour and conquer his greatest enemy—death.

A great fact had been revealed to Courtland: There was a resurrection of the dead, and Christ was the hope of that resurrection! It was as if he had just met Christ face-to-face and heard Him say so and had it explained to him fully and satisfactorily. He doubted if he could tell the professor in the biblical literature class how, because perhaps *he* hadn't seen the Christ that way, but others understood. That girl wasn't hopeless. The light of a great hope glowed in her eyes; she could see far away over the loneliness of the years to come, up to the time when she should meet the little brother again, glorified, without stain.

Courtland suddenly thought how Stephen Marshall would look with that glorified body. His last glimpse of him standing above the burning pit of the theater with the halo of flames about his head had given him a vision. Gladness welled up within him that someday he'd surely see Stephen Marshall again, grasp his hand and make him know how he repented of his own part in the persecution that led to his death; make him understand how in dying he'd left a path of glory behind and given life to Paul Courtland.

In the prayer that followed, the minister seemed to be talking with dear familiarity to One he knew well. The young man wondered that any dared come so near and longed for such assurance and comradeship.

They took the casket out to a quiet place beyond the city, where the little body might rest until the sister wished to take it away.

As they stood on that bleak hillside, dotted with white tombstones, the city looming in the distance, Courtland recognized the group of buildings belonging to his university. He marveled at the closeness of life and death in this world. Out there the busy city, everybody tired and hustling to get, to learn, to enjoy; out here everybody lying quiet, like the corn of wheat in the ground, waiting for the resurrection time, the call of God to come forth in beauty! What a difference it would make in the working and getting and hustling and learning and enjoying if everybody remembered how near the lying-quiet time might be! How unready some might be and how much difference it must make what one had done with the sojourn in the city, when the stopping time came! How much better it would be if one could live remembering the Presence, always being aware of its nearness! To live Christ! What would that mean? Was he ready to surrender a thought like that?

The minister had an urgent call in another direction. He must take a trolley that passed the cemetery gate and leave at once. It fell to Courtland to look after the girl, for the doctor hadn't been able to leave his practice to take the long ride to the cemetery.

Courtland led her to the carriage and put her in. "I suppose you'll want to go directly back to the house?"

She turned to him as if she were coming out of a trance. She caught her breath and gave him one wild, beseeching look, crying out with something like a sob: "Oh, how can I *ever* go back to that room *now?*" And then her breath seemed to leave her, and she fell back against the seat almost lifeless.

He sprang in beside her, took her in his arms and laid her head against his shoulder. Then he loosened her coat about her throat and chafed her cold hands, drawing the robes closely about her slender shoulders. But she lay there pale and without a sign of life. He thought he'd never seen anything so ghastly white as her face.

The driver came around and offered a stimulant. They forced a few drops between her teeth, and after a moment her eyelids fluttered faintly. She came to herself, looked about her, realized her sorrow and dropped off again.

"She's in a bad way!" murmured the driver, looking worried. "I guess we'd better get her somewheres. I don't want to have no responsibility. My chief's gone back to the city, and the other man's gone across county. I reckon we'd better go on and stop at some hospital if she don't come to pretty soon."

The driver vanished, and the carriage started at a rapid pace. Courtland sat supporting his silent charge in growing alarm, alternately chafing her hands and trying to force more stimulant between her lips. He was relieved when at last the carriage stopped again and he recognized the stone buildings of one of the city's great hospitals.

Chapter 9

When Paul Courtland returned to the university, the afternoon exam had been in progress about half an hour. Explaining briefly to the professor, he settled to his belated work regardless of Bill Ward's anxious glances from the back of the room and Pat's lifted eyebrows from the other side. He knew he had yet to meet those three beloved antagonists. He seemed to have passed through eons of experience since last night. The political science exam questions he was working on seemed paltry beside the facts of life and death.

He'd remained at the hospital until the girl came out of her long semiconsciousness and the doctor said she was better, but the thought of her pale face was continually before him. When he closed his eyes for a moment to think how to phrase some answer he saw that still, beautiful face as it lay on his shoulder in the carriage. It had filled him with awe to think that he, a stranger, was her only friend in that great city, and she might be dying! Somehow he couldn't cast her off as a common stranger.

He had arranged for her to be placed in a small private room at a moderate cost and had paid for a week in advance. The cost was a trifle to Courtland. The new overcoat he'd meant to buy this week would more than cover it. Besides, if he needed more than his ample allowance his father was always ready to advance what he wanted. But having paid for the girl's comfort and care, he still couldn't forget her. His responsibility seemed doubled with everything he did for her. He was perplexed about how she was going to live all alone with her tragedy—or tragedies—for it was apparent from the little hints she had dropped that the small brother's death was only the climax of a series of sorrows that had come to her young life. And yet she, with all that sorrow surrounding her, could still believe in the Christ and call upon Him in her trouble! He felt a kind of triumph in his heart when he reached that conclusion.

He lay on the couch in Tennelly's room that night after supper and tried to think it out, while the other three rattled on about their marks and expressed indignation over the way the professors were blacklisting Pat just when he was trying so hard. He didn't know the fellows were keeping it up to get his mind away from the funeral; he was thinking about that girl.

The doctor had told him she was very run down and had been for some time. Her heart action wasn't what it should be, and she showed symptoms of poor nutrition. What she needed was rest, utter rest. Sleep if possible most of the time for at least a week, with careful feeding every two or three hours, and after that a quiet, cheerful place with plenty of fresh air, sunshine and more sleep; no anxiety and nothing to call on the exhausted energies for action or hurry.

Now how was that to be brought about for a person who had no home, no friends, no money and no time to lie idle? Moreover, how could there be any cheerful spot in the world for a girl who had passed through the fire as she had?

Presently he went out to the drugstore and telephoned the hospital. They said she'd had only one more slight turn of unconsciousness but had rallied from it quickly and was resting quietly now. They hoped she would have a good night.

Then he went back to his room and thought about her some more. He had an important English examination the next day; yet try as he would to concentrate on Wells and Shaw, that girl and what would become of her kept getting in between him and his book.

After ten o'clock he sauntered down the hall and stood in Stephen Marshall's room for a few minutes, as he was getting the habit of doing every night. The peace of it and the uplift the room always gave him were soothing to his soul. If he'd known a little more about the Christ to whose allegiance he'd declared himself he might have knelt and asked for guidance; but as yet he hadn't heard of the promise to the man who "abides" and "asks what he will." Nevertheless, when he entered that room his mind took on the attitude of prayer and he felt that somehow the Presence got close to him, so that perplexing questions were made clear.

As he stood that night looking about the plain walls, his eyes fell upon that picture of Stephen Marshall's mother. A mother! Ah! If there were a mother somewhere to whom that girl could go! Someone who would understand her; be gentle and tender with her; love her, as he thought a real mother would do—what a difference that would make!

He thought over the women he knew—the mothers. There weren't so many. Some of the professors' wives who had sons and daughters of their own? Well, they might be fine for their own sons and daughters, but not one seemed likely to want to mother a stranger like this girl. They were nice to the students, polite and kind enough for one tea or reception a year, but that was about the limit.

Well, there was Tennelly's mother—dignified, white-haired, beautiful, dominant in her home and clubs, charming to her guests, but—he could just fancy how she would raise her lorgnette and look Bonnie Brentwood over. There would be no room in that grand house for a girl like Bonnie.

Bonnie! How the name suited her! He had a strange protective feeling about that girl—not as if she were like the other girls he knew. Perhaps it was a "Christ-friend" feeling, as the minister suggested.

But to go on with the list of mothers—wasn't there one anywhere to whom he could appeal? Gila's mother? Pah! That painted, purple image of a mother! Her own daughter needed to find a real mother somewhere. She couldn't mother a stranger! Mothers! Why weren't there enough real ones to go around? If he had only had a mother, a real one, who had lived, he could have told Bonnie's story to her, and she would have understood.

He looked into the pictured eyes on the wall, and an idea came to him, like an answer to prayer. Stephen Marshall's mother! Why hadn't he thought of her before? She was that kind of mother, of course, or Stephen Marshall wouldn't have been the man he was! If the girl could only get to her for a little while!

But would she take her? Would she understand? Or might she be too overcome with her own loss to have rallied to life again? He looked into the strong motherly face and was sure *not*.

He would write to her and test whether there was a mother in the world or not. He went back to his room and wrote her a long letter from the depths of his heart—a letter he might have written to his own mother if he'd ever known her, but one he'd never written to any woman before.

Dear Mother of Stephen Marshall:

I know you're a real mother because Stephen was what he was. And now I'm going to let you prove it by bringing you something that needs a mother's help.

There's a little girl—about nineteen or twenty years old, I think—lying in the hospital, worn out with hard work and sorrow. She recently lost her father and mother and brought her five-year-old brother to the city a couple of weeks ago. They were living in a very small room, boarding themselves, and she was working all day somewhere downtown. Two days ago, as she was coming home on the trolley, her little brother, crossing the street to meet her, was knocked down and killed by a passing automobile. We buried him today, and the girl fainted on the way back from the cemetery and only recovered consciousness when we got her to the hospital.

The doctor says she's exhausted her strength and needs to sleep for a week and be nurtured and then go to some cheerful place where she can just rest for a while and have fresh air, sunshine and good, plain, nourishing food.

Now she hasn't a friend in the city. From the few things she's told me there's no one in the world she'll feel free to turn to, and she isn't the kind of girl who'll accept charity. She's refined, reserved and independent. Another thing, too—she prays to your Stephen's Christ—that's why I dared write you about it.

You see, I'm an entire stranger to her. I just happened along when the boy was killed and had to stick around and help. Of course she hasn't any idea of all this, and I haven't any real business with it. But I can't see leaving her this way.

You wonder why I didn't find a mother closer by. I haven't one of my own living, except a stepmother, who wouldn't understand, and all the other mothers I know wouldn't qualify for the job any better. I've been looking at your picture, and I think you would.

My thought is this (if it doesn't strike you right, maybe you can think of some other way): I'm pretty well fixed for money, and I've got a lump I've been intending to use for a new car. My old car is plenty good enough for another year, so I'd like to pay this girl's board till she gets rested and strong and cheered up. I thought perhaps you'd see your way

*clear to write a letter and say you'd like her to visit you—you're lonely
or something. I don't know how a real mother would fix that up, but I
guess you do.*

*Of course the girl mustn't know I have a thing to do with it except that
I told you about her. She'd be up in the air in a minute. She wouldn't
stand for me doing anything for her. She's that kind.*

*I'm sending a check for two hundred dollars now because I thought,
in case you take up with my suggestion, you might send her enough
money for the journey. I don't believe she has any. We can fix it about
the board any way you say. Please tell me how much it's worth. I don't
need the money for anything. But whatever's done has to be mighty
quick or she'll go back to work again, and she won't last three days if
she does. She looks as if a breath would blow her away.*

*I'm sending this special delivery to hurry things. Her address is Miss
R. B. Brentwood, Good Samaritan Hospital. The boy called her Bonnie.
I don't know what her full name is.*

*So now you have the whole story, and it's up to you to decide. Maybe
you think I've got a lot of crust to propose this, and maybe you won't see
it this way. But I have the nerve because Stephen Marshall's life and
death have made me believe in Stephen Marshall's Christ and Stephen
Marshall's mother.*

> *I am, very respectfully,*
> *Paul Courtland*

He mailed the letter that night and then studied hard till three o'clock in the
morning.

The next morning's mail brought a dainty note from Gila's mother, inviting
him to a quiet family dinner with them Friday evening. He frowned when he
read it. He didn't care for the large, painted person, but perhaps she had more
good than he knew. He'd have to go and find out. She might even be a help in
case Stephen Marshall's mother didn't pan out.

Chapter 10

Mother Marshall stood by the kitchen window with her cheek against a boy's old soft felt hat and looked out into the gathering dusk for Father. The hat was so old and worn that its original shape and color were scarcely distinguishable, and in one spot her tears had washed some of the grime into deeper stains about it. Only on days when Father was off to town on errands did she allow herself a momentary weakness of tears.

So she had stood in former years looking out into the dusk for her son to come whistling home from school. So she stood the day the awful news of the fiery death came, while Father sat in his rush-bottomed chair and groaned. She'd laid her cheek against that old felt hat and comforted herself with the thought of her splendid boy, who had lived his short life so intensely and wonderfully. When she felt the old scratchy cloth against her cheek it brought back the memory of his strong young shoulder, where she used to lay her head sometimes when she felt tired and he would fold her in his arms and pat her shoulder. It comforted her to feel it now—one of those little tangible things our poor souls have to tether to sometimes when we lose the vision and get fainthearted.

Mother Marshall wasn't morbid one bit. She always looked on the bright side of everything, and she'd had much joy in her son as he was growing up. She'd seen him strong of body, soul and mind. He had won the scholarship of the whole Northwest to the big Eastern university. It was hard to pack him up and have him go so far away, where she couldn't see him soon, where she couldn't listen to his whistle coming home at night, where he couldn't even come back for Sunday and sit in the old church pew with them. But those things had to come. It was the only way he could grow and fulfill his part of God's plan. And so she put away her tears till he was gone and kept them for the old felt hat when Father was out about the farm.

Then the news came that Stephen had graduated and gone up higher to God's eternal university to live and work among the great. Even then her soul had been big enough to see the glory of it behind the sorrow and say with trembling, conquering lips, "I shall go to him, but he shall not return to me. The Lord gave, and the Lord hath taken away. Blessed be the name of the Lord!"

That was the kind of nerve Mother Marshall was built with, and it was only in such times as these, when Father had gone to town and stayed a little later than usual, that the tears in her heart got the better of her and she laid her face against the old felt hat.

Down the road in the gloom moved a dark speck. It couldn't be Father, for he'd gone in the machine—the nice, comfortable car Stephen had made them get before he went away to college, because he said Father needed to have things easier now—and by this time the lights would be lit, for it was dusk.

The speck grew larger. It made a chugging noise. It was one of those horrible motorcycles. Mother Marshall hated them, though she'd never let on. Stephen had said he intended to get one with the first money he earned after he came out of college, but she'd hoped in her heart they would go out of fashion by then and there would be something less fiendish-looking and safer to take their place. She hated the idea of Stephen ever sitting on one, flying through space. But now he was gone beyond all such fears. He had wings, and there were no dangers where he was.

The motorcycle came on like a comet now and thundered in at the big gate. A sudden alarm filled Mother Marshall's soul. Had something happened to Father? That was the only terrible thing left in life to happen now. An accident! And this boy had come to prepare her for the worst? She opened the kitchen door wide before the boy had stopped his machine and set it on its feet.

"Sp'c'l d'liv'ry!" fizzed the boy, handing her a fat envelope, a book and the stub of a pencil. "Si'n 'eer!" he said, indicating a line on the book.

She managed to write her name in cramped characters, but her hand was trembling so she could hardly form the letters. A wild idea that perhaps they discovered that Stephen escaped death somehow flitted through her brain and out again, controlled by her strong common sense. Such notions always came to people after death had taken their loved ones—frenzied hopes for miracles! Stephen had been dead for four months now. There could be no such possibility, of course.

To calm herself she opened the slide of the range and shoved the teakettle a little farther on so it would begin to boil, before she opened that fat letter. She lit the lamp, too, put it on the supper table and changed the position of the bread plate, covering it with a fringed napkin so the bread wouldn't dry. Everything must be ready when Father returned. Then she sat down with her gold spectacles and tore open the envelope.

She was so absorbed in the letter that she failed for the first time since they got the car to hear it purring down the road, and the headlights sent their rays out without anyone at the kitchen window to see. Father was getting worried that the kitchen door didn't open as he drew in beside the flagstone, when Mother suddenly came flying out with a smile lighting her face. He hadn't seen her look that way since Stephen went away.

She'd left a trail of paper from her chair to the door and held the envelope in her hand. She rushed out and buried her face in his rough coat collar.

"Oh, Father! I've been so worried about you!" she declared, but she didn't look worried a bit.

Father looked down at her tenderly and patted her plump shoulder. "Had a flat tire and had to stop and get her pumped up," he explained. "And then the man found a place needed patching. He took a little longer than I expected. I was afraid you'd worry."

"Well, hurry in," she said eagerly. "Supper's ready, and I've got a letter to read to you."

If Mother liked a thing in that home, Father would too. His sun rose and set on her, and they'd lived together so long and harmoniously that the thoughts of one reflected the other. It didn't matter which you asked about a thing, you were sure to get the same opinion as if you'd asked the other. One didn't give way to the other; they just had the same habits of thought and decision, the same principles to go by.

After she passed the hot johnnycake, saw that Father had the biggest pork chop and the mealiest potato, and gave him his cup of coffee creamed and sugared just right, Mother got out the letter with the university crest and began to read. She had no fears Father wouldn't agree with her about it. She was sure of his sympathy in her pleasure; sure he'd think it was nice of Stephen's friend to write to her and pick her out as a real mother, saying all those pleasant things about her; sure he'd be proud that she, with all the women they had in the East, should have so brought up a boy that a stranger knew she was a real mother. She had no fear Father would frown and declare they couldn't be bothered with a stranger around, that it would cost a lot and Mother needed to rest. She knew he'd be touched at once with the poor, lonely girl's position and want to help her. She knew he'd fall in with anything she would suggest. And Father's eyes lighted with tenderness as she read, watched her proudly and nodded in strong affirmation at the phrases touching her ability as mother.

"That's right, Mother. You'll qualify for a job as mother better'n any woman I ever saw!" said Father, as he reached for another helping of butter.

His face kindled with interest as the letter continued, but he shook his head when it came to the money part.

"I don't like that idea, Mother. We don't keep boarders, and we're plenty able to invite company for as long as we like. Besides, it don't seem just the right thing for that young feller to be paying her board. She wouldn't like it if she knew it. If she was our daughter we wouldn't want her to be put in that position, though it's very kind of him, of course—"

"Of course!" said Mother. "He couldn't very well ask us, you know, without saying something like that, especially as he doesn't know us, except by hearsay."

"Of course," agreed Father. "But then equally, of course, we won't let it stand that way. You can send that young feller back his check and tell him to get his new ottymobeel. He won't be young but once, and I reckon a young feller of that kind won't get any harm from his ottymobeels, no matter how many he has. You can see by his letter he ain't spoiled yet, and if he's got hold of Steve's idea of things he'll find plenty of use for his money, doing good where there ain't a young woman about that's bound to object to being took care of by a young man she don't know and don't belong to. But I guess you can say that, Mother, without offending him. Tell him we'll take care of the money part. Tell him we're real glad to get a daughter. You're sure, Mother, it won't be hard for you to have a stranger around in Steve's place?"

"No, I like it," said Mother with a smile, brushing away a bright tear that burst out unawares. "I like it 'hard,' as Steve used to say! Do you know, Father, what I've been thinking—what I thought right away when I read that letter? I thought, suppose that girl was the one Stephen would have loved and wanted to marry if he'd lived, and suppose he'd brought her home here. What a fuss we'd have made about her! And I'd have loved to fix up the house and make it look pleasant for her and love her as if she were my own daughter."

Father's eyes were moist too. "H'm! Yes!" he said, trying to clear his throat. "I guess she'd be com'ny for you when I have to go to town, and she'd help around with the work some when she got better."

"I've been thinking," said Mother. "I've always thought I'd like to fix up the spare room. I read in my magazine how to fix up a young girl's room when she comes home from college, and I'd like to fix it like that if there's time. You paint the furniture white and have two sets of curtains, pink and white, and little shelves for her books. Do you think we could do it?"

"Why, sure!" said Father. He was so pleased to see Mother interested like this. She'd been so still and wistful ever since the news came about Stephen. "Why, sure! Get some pretty wallpaper, too, while you're 'bout it. S'posen you and I take a run to town again in the morning and pick it out. Then you can pick your curtains and paint, too, and get Jed Lewis to come in the afternoon and put on the first coat. How about calling him up on the phone right now and asking him about it? I'm real glad we've got that phone. It'll come in handy now."

Mother's eyes glistened. Stephen insisted upon that phone before he left home. They hadn't used it half a dozen times except when the telegrams came, but they hadn't the heart to have it disconnected, because Stephen had taken so much pride in having it put in. He said he didn't like his mother left alone in the house without a chance to call a neighbor or send for the doctor.

"Come to think of it—hadn't you better send a telegram to that chap tonight? We can phone it down to the town office. He'll maybe be worried about how you'll take that letter. Tell him he's struck the right party all right, and you're on the job writing that girl a letter tonight that'll welcome her. But tell him we'll finance this operation ourselves, and he can save the ottymobeel for the next case that comes along—words to that effect, you know."

The supper things were shoved back and the telephone brought forth. They called up Jed Lewis first before he went to bed and got his reluctant promise to be on hand at two o'clock the next afternoon. They had to tell him they were expecting company or he mightn't have come for a week in spite of his promise.

It took nearly an hour to reduce the telegram to ten words, but at last they settled on:

Bonnie welcome. Am writing you both tonight. No money necessary.
Stephen's Mother and Father

The letters were happy achievements of brevity, for it was getting late, and Mother Marshall realized they must be up early in the morning to get the shopping done before two o'clock.

First was the letter to Bonnie, written in a cramped, laborious hand.

Dear Little Girl:

You don't know me, but I've heard about you from a sort of neighbor of yours. I'm just a lonely mother whose only son has gone home to heaven. I've heard about your sorrow and loneliness, and I've taken a notion that maybe you'd like to come and visit me for a while and help cheer me up. Maybe we can comfort each other a bit, and, anyhow, I want you to come.

Father and I are fixing up your room for you, just as we would if you were our own daughter coming home from college. For we've quite made up our minds you'll come, and Father wants you just as much as I do. We're sending you mileage and a check to get any things you may need for the journey, because we wouldn't want to put you to expense to come this long way just to please two lonely old people. It's enough for you that you're willing to come, and we're so glad about it that it almost seems as if the birds must be singing and the spring flowers going to bloom for you, even though it's only the middle of winter.

Don't wait to get any fixings. Just come as you are. We're plain folks.

Father says be sure you get a good, comfortable berth in the sleeper and have your trunk checked right through. If you've got any other things besides your trunk, have them sent along by freight. It's better to have your things here where you can look after them than stored away off there.

We're so happy about your coming that we can't wait to hear what time you start. So please send a telegram as soon as you get this, saying when the doctor will let you come, and don't disappoint us for anything.

Lovingly, your friend,
Rachel Marshall

The letter to Paul Courtland was more brief, but just as expressive.

Dear Friend—You're a dear boy, and I'm proud my son had you for a friend.

(When Courtland read the letter he winced at that sentence and saw himself once more standing in the hall in front of Stephen Marshall's room, with the garments of his persecutors.)

I've written Bonnie Brentwood, telling her how much we want her, and I'm going to town in the morning to get some things to fix up a pretty room for her.

Thank you for thinking I was a good mother. Father and I are both quite proud about it. We're very lonely and are glad to have a daughter for as long as she'll stay. But even if we hadn't wanted her, we couldn't have said no when you asked for Christ's sake.

Father says we're returning the check because we want to do this for Bonnie ourselves; then there won't be anything to cover up. Father says if you've begun this way you'll find plenty of ways to spend that money for Christ and let us look after this one little girl. We've sent her mileage and some money, and we're going to try to make her happy.

Someday we'd be very happy if you'd come out and visit us. I'd like to know you for my dear Stephen's sake. You're a dear boy. I'm glad you've found our Christ. Father thinks so too. Thank you for thinking I would understand.

Lovingly,
Mother Marshall

But after all that excitement Mother Marshall couldn't sleep. She lay quietly beside Father in the old four-poster and planned the room. She must get Sam Carpenter to put in some little shelves on each side of the windows and a wide locker between for a window seat, and she'd make some pillows like those in the magazine pictures. A dozen times she pictured how the girl would look and what she would say, and once her heart was seized with fear that she hadn't made her letter cordial enough. She went over the words of the young man's letter as well as she could remember them and let her heart soar and be glad Stephen had touched one life and left it better for his being in the university that little time.

Once she stirred restlessly, and Father put out his hand and touched her in alarm. "What's the matter, Rachel? Aren't you sleeping?"

"Father, I believe we'll have to get a new rug for that room."

"Sure!" said Father, relaxing sleepily.

"Gray, with pink rosebuds, soft and thick," she whispered.

"Sure! Pink, with gray rosebuds," murmured Father as he dropped off again.

They made little of breakfast the next morning—they were both too excited about getting off early—and Mother forgot to caution Father about going at a high speed. If she suspected he was running a little faster than usual she winked at it, for she was anxious to get to the stores as soon as possible. She'd risen early to read over the magazine article again and knew just how much pink and white she'd need for the curtains and cushions. She also meant to get little brass handles and keyholes for the bureau. She was like a child getting ready for a new doll.

Not until they were on their way back home again, with packages about their feet and an eager light in their faces, did an idea suddenly come to them—an idea so chilling that the eagerness left their eyes for a moment and the old, patient look of sorrow returned. Mother Marshall put it into words.

"You don't suppose, Seth, that perhaps she mightn't *want* to come!"

"Well, I was thinking, Rachel, we'd best not be getting too set on it. But, anyhow, we'd be ready for someone else. You know Stevie always wanted you to have things fixed nice and fancy. But you fix it up. I guess she's coming. I really do think she must be coming! We'll just pray about it, and then we'll leave it there!"

So with peace in their faces they arrived home, just five minutes before the painter was due, and unloaded their packages. Father lifted out the big roll of soft, velvety carpeting, gray as a cloud, with moss roses scattered over it. He was proud to think he could buy things like this for Mother. Of course now they had no need to save and scrimp for Stephen the way they had during the years, so it was well to make the rest of the way as bright for Mother as he could. And this "Bonnie" girl! If she would only come, what a bright, happy thing it would be in their desolate home!

But suppose she shouldn't come?

Chapter 11

T he telegram reached Paul Courtland Friday evening, just as he was going to the Dare dinner, and filled him with an almost childish delight. Not for a long time had he had anything as nice as that happen; not even when he made Phi Beta Kappa in his junior year had he been so filled with exultation. To think there was a woman in the world who would respond in that cordial way to a call from the great unknown!

He presented himself in his most sparkling mood at the house for dinner. Nothing at all was blue about him. His eyes fairly danced with pleasure, and his smile was rare. Gila looked and dropped her eyes demurely. She thought the sparkle was all for her, and her wicked heart gave a throb of exultant joy.

Mrs. Dare was no longer a large, purple person. She was in full evening dress, explaining that she and her husband had an engagement at the opera after dinner. She resembled the dough people the cook used to fashion for him in his youth. Her arms reminded him of those shapeless cookie arms, as he watched her bejeweled hands moving among the trinkets at her end of the glittering table. Her gown, what there was of it, was of black gauze emblazoned with darting sequins of deep blue. An aigrette in her hair twinkled above her coarse, painted face. Courtland, as he studied her more closely, rejoiced that the telegram had arrived before he left the dormitory, for he never could have come to this woman seeking refuge for his refined Bonnie girl.

The father of the family was a wisp of a man with a nervous laugh and a high, thin voice. Kind lines formed around his mouth and eyes, indulgent lines—not self-indulgent either, and insomuch they were noble—but his face had a weakness that showed he was ruled by others to a large extent. He said, "Yes, my dear!" quite obediently when his wife ordered him affably around. A cunning look in his eye might explain the impression current that he knew how to turn a dollar to his own account.

Courtland wondered what would happen if he suddenly asked Mr. Dare what he thought of Christ or if he believed in the resurrection. He imagined they'd look aghast as if he'd spoken of something impolite. One couldn't think of Mrs. Dare in a resurrection; she'd seem so out of place, so sort of unclothed for the occasion, in those doughy arms with her glittering jet shoulder straps. He realized these thoughts racing through his head were only fantasies occasioned no doubt by his own nervous condition, but they kept crowding in and bringing mirth to his eyes. How, for instance, would Mother Marshall and Mother Dare hit it off if they happened together in the same heaven?

Gila was in white, from the tip of her pearly shoulders down to the tip of her pearl-beaded slippers—white and demure. Her skin looked even more pearly than when she wore the brilliant red-velvet gown. It had a pure, dazzling whiteness, different from most skins. It perplexed him. It didn't look like flesh but more like some ethereal substance meant for angels. He drew a breath of satisfaction that not even a flush was upon it tonight. No painting there at least! He wasn't master of the rare arts that skins are subject to these days. He knew artificial whiteness only when it was glaring and floury. This pearly paleness was exquisite, delicious. In contrast the dark eyes, lifted pansylike for an instant and then dropped beneath those long curling lashes, were almost startling in their beauty. The hair was simply arranged with a plain narrow band of black velvet around the white temples, with the soft loops of cloudy darkness drawn out on her cheeks. There was an attempt at demureness in the gown; soft folds of transparent nothing seemed to shelter what they couldn't hide, and more such folds drooped over the lovely arms to the elbows. Surely this was loveliness undefiled. The words of *Peer Gynt* came floating back disconnectedly, more as a puzzled question in his mind than as they stand in the story.

Is your psalm-book in your 'kerchief?
    Do you glance adown your apron?
Do you hold your mother's skirt-fold?
    Speak!

But he only looked at her admiringly and talked on about the college games, making himself agreeable to everyone and winning more and more the lifted pansy-eyes.

When dinner was over they drifted into a large white and gold reception room, with inhospitable chairs and settees whose satin slipperiness offered no inducements to sit down. Gold-lacquered tables stood near a concert grand piano, also gold inlaid with mother-of-pearl cupids and flowers. Everything was most elaborate. Gila, in her soft transparencies, looked like a wraith amidst it all. The young man chose to think she was too rare and fine for a place so ornate.

Presently the mother's cookie arms were enfolded in a gorgeous blue-plush evening cloak loaded with handsome black fur. With many bows and kind words the husband toddled off beside her, reminding Courtland of a big cinnamon bear and a small black and tan dog he'd once seen together in a show.

Gila stood in the great gold room and asked shyly if he'd like to go to the library, where it was cozier. The red light glowed across the hall, and he turned from it with a shudder of remembrance. The glow seemed to beat upon his nerves like something striking his eyeballs.

"I'd like to hear you play, if you will," he answered, wondering if a dolled-up instrument like that was really meant to be played upon.

Gila pouted. She didn't want to play, but she wouldn't refuse the challenge. She went to the piano and rippled off a brilliant waltz or two, just to show him she could do it, and played "Humoresque" and a few catchy melodies that were in the popular ear just then. And then, whirling on the gilded stool, she lifted her eyes to him.

"I don't like it in here," she said with a little shiver. "Let's go into the library by the fire. It's pleasanter there to talk."

Courtland hesitated. "Look here," he said. "Wouldn't you just as soon sit somewhere else? I don't like that red light of yours. It gets on my nerves. I don't like to see you in it. It makes you look—well—something different from what I believe you really are. I like a plain, honest white light."

Gila gave him one swift glance and walked laughingly over to the library door. "Oh, is that all?" she asked. Touching a button, she switched off the red table lamp and switched on what seemed like a thousand tapers concealed softly about the ceiling.

"There!" she cried half mockingly. "You can have as much light as you like, and when you get tired of that we can cut them all off and sit in the firelight." She touched another button and let him see the room in the soft dim shadows and rich glow of the fire. Then she turned the full light on again and entered the room, dropping into a big leather chair at the side of the fireplace and indicating another chair on the opposite side. She had no notion of sitting near him or luring him to her side tonight. She had read him right. Hers was the demure part to play—the reserved, shy maiden, the innocent, childlike woman. She would play it, but she would humble him! So she had vowed with her white teeth set in her red lips as she stood before her dressing table mirror that night when he fled from her red room and her.

With a sigh of relief he dropped into the chair and sat watching her, talking idly, as one who is feeling his way to a pleasant intimacy of whose nature he isn't quite sure. She was sweet and sympathetic about the exams, told how she hated them herself and thought they should be abolished; said he was a wonder, that her cousin had told her he was a regular shark, and yet he hadn't let himself be spoiled by it. She flattered him with that deference a girl can pay to a man which makes her appear like an angel of light. She sat so quietly, with big eyes lifted now and then, talking earnestly of fine and noble things, that his best thoughts about her were confirmed. He watched her, thinking what a lovely, lovable woman she was, what gentle sympathy and keen appreciation of fine qualities she showed, child though she seemed to be! He studied her, thinking what a friend she might be to that other poor girl in her loneliness and sorrow if she only would.

He didn't know he was yielding again to the lure the red light had made the last time he was there. He didn't realize that, red light or white light, he was being led on. He only knew it was a pleasure to talk to her, be near her and feel her sympathy, and that something had unlocked the depths of his heart, the place he usually kept to himself, even from the fellows. He'd never opened it to a human being before. Tennelly had come nearer to glimpsing it than anyone. But now he was going to open it, for he'd at last found another human being who could understand and appreciate.

"May I shut off the bright light and sit in the firelight?" he asked, and Gila acquiesced sweetly. It was just what she'd been leading up to, but she didn't move from her reticent yet sympathetic position in the retired depths of the great chair, where she knew the shadows and the firelight would play on her face and show her serious pose.

"I want to tell you about a girl I met this week."

A chill fell on Gila, but she didn't show it; she never even flickered those long lashes. Another girl! How dared he! The white teeth set down sharply on the red tongue out of sight, but the sweet, sympathetic mouth remained placid.

"Yes?" The inflection, the lifted lashes and the whole attitude were perfect.

He plunged ahead. "You're so wonderful yourself that I'm sure you'll appreciate and understand her, and I think you're just the friend she needs."

Gila stiffened in her chair and turned her face to the fire, so he could see her lovely profile.

"She's all alone in the city—"

"Oh!" broke forth Gila in almost childish dismay. "Not even a chaperon?"

Courtland stopped, bewildered. Then he laughed. "She didn't have any use for a chaperon," he said. "She came here with her little brother to earn their living."

"Oh, she *had* a brother then!" sighed Gila with evident relief.

It occurred to Courtland to be pleased that Gila was so particular about the conventionalities. He'd heard it rumored more than once that her own conduct overstepped the most lenient rules. That must have been a mistake. It was a relief to know it from her own lips.

But he explained gravely, "The little brother was killed on Monday night. Just run down in cold blood by a passing automobile."

"How dreadful!" shuddered Gila, shrinking back into the depths of the chair. "But you know you mustn't believe a story like that! Poor people are always getting up such tales about rich people's automobiles. It isn't true at all. No chauffeur would do a thing like that! The children just run out and get in the way of the cars to tantalize the drivers. I've seen them myself. Why, our chauffeur has been arrested three or four times and charged with running over children and dogs, when it wasn't his fault at all. The people were just trying to get money out of us! I don't suppose the little child was run over. It was probably his own fault."

"Yes, he was run over," said Courtland gently. "I saw it myself! I was standing on the curbstone when the boy—he was a beautiful little fellow with long golden curls—rushed out to meet his sister, calling out to her, and the automobile came whirring by without a sign of a horn and crushed him like a broken lily. He never lifted his head or moved again, and the automobile never even slowed up to see—just shot ahead and was gone."

Gila was still for a minute. She had no words to meet a situation like this. "Oh, well," she said, "I suppose he's better off, and the girl is too. How could she take care of a child in the city alone and do any work? Besides, children are an awful torment, and very likely he would have turned out bad. Boys usually do. What did you want me to do for her? Get her a position as a maid?"

Her tone held something almost flippant. Strange that Courtland didn't recognize it. But the firelight, the white gown, the profile and the dropped lashes had done for him once more what the red light had done before—taken him out of his normal senses and made him see a Gila that wasn't really there—soft, sweet, tender, womanly. The words, though they didn't satisfy him, merely meant she hadn't yet understood what he wanted and was striving hard to find out.

"No," he said, "I want you to go and see her. She's sick and in the hospital. She needs a friend, a girlfriend, such as you could be if you would."

Gila answered in her slow, pretty drawl, "Why, I hate hospitals! I wouldn't even go to see Mama when she had an operation on her neck last winter, because I hate the odors they have around. But I'll go if you want me to. Of course I won't promise how much good I'll do. Girls of that stamp don't want to be helped, you know. They think they know it all, and they're usually insulting. But I'll see what I can do. I don't mind giving her something. I've three evening dresses I hate, and one of them I've had on only once. She might get a position to act somewhere or sing in a café if she had good clothes."

Courtland hurried to impress her with the fact that Miss Brentwood was a refined girl of good family and that it would be an insult to offer her second-hand clothing. But when he gave it up and yielded to Gila's plea that he drop these horrid, gloomy subjects and talk about something cheerful, he had a feeling of failure. Perhaps he shouldn't have told Gila. She simply couldn't understand the other girl because she'd never dreamed of such a situation.

If he could have seen his gentle Gila a few hours later, standing before her mirror again and setting those sharp teeth into her red lip, with the ugly frown between her angry eyes; if he could have heard her muttered words and, worse still, guessed her thoughts about him and that other girl—he certainly would have gone out and gnashed his teeth in despair. If he could have known what was to come of his request to Gila Dare he would have rung up the hospital and had Miss Brentwood moved to another one in hot haste or, better still, have taken strenuous measures to prevent that visit. But instead of that he read Mother Marshall's telegram over again and lay down to forget Gila Dare utterly and think pleasant thoughts about the Marshalls.

Chapter 12

G ila Dare, in her most startling costume, plastered with costly fur, and
wearing high-laced, French-heeled boots, came tripping down her
father's steps to the limousine. She carried a dangling little handbag
and a muff big enough for a rug. Her two eyes looked forth from the rim of the
low-squashed, bandagelike fur hat like the eyes of a small, sly mouse about to
nibble someone else's cheese.

By her side sauntered a logy youth, with small, blue eyes fixed adoringly on
her. She wore a large bunch of pale yellow orchids, evidently his gift, and was
paying for them with her glances. One knew by the excited flush on the young
man's face that he'd rarely been paid so well. His eyes took on a glint of intelligence, one might almost say of hope, and he smiled egregiously, egotistically.
As he opened the door of the luxurious car for her he wore an attitude of one
who might possibly be a fiancé. Her mouse eyes—you wouldn't have dreamed
they could ever be large and wistful or innocent—twinkled pleasurably. She
was playing her usual game for which she was becoming notorious, young as
she was.

"Oh, now, *Chaw*-ley! *Ree*-ally! Why, I never dreamed it was that bad! But
you mustn't, you know! I never gave you permission!"

The chauffeur, sitting stolidly in his uniform, awaiting the word to move,
wondered idly what she was up to now. He was used to seeing the game played
all around him day after day, as if he were a stick or a stone or one of the metal
trappings of the car.

"Chawley" Hathaway looked unutterable things, and the mouse eyes looked
back unutterable things, with that lingering, just-too-long-for-pardoning
glance that certain men and women employ when they want to loiter near the
danger line and toy with vital things. An impressive handclasp, another long,
languishing look, just a shade longer this time; then he closed the door, lifted
his hat at the mouse-eyed goddess, and the limousine swept away. They'd
parted as if something momentous had occurred, and both knew in their hearts
that neither had meant anything at all except to play with fire for an instant.

Gila swept on in her chariot. The young man with whom she'd played was
well skilled in the game. He understood her, as she him. If he got burned, it
was up to him. She meant to take care of herself.

Around another corner she spied another acquaintance. A word to the automa-
ton on the front seat and the limousine swept up to the curb where he was passing. Gila leaned out with the sweetest bow. She was the condescending lady
now; no mouse eyes in evidence this time—just a beautiful, commanding presence to be obeyed. She would have him ride with her, so he got in.

He was a tall, serious youth with credulous eyes, and she swept his soulful
nature as one sweeps the keys of a familiar instrument, drawing forth timeworn

melodies that, nevertheless, were new to him. And just because he thrilled under them and looked in her eyes with startled earnestness, she liked to play upon his soul. It would have been boring if he'd understood, for he was dull and young—though his years numbered two more than hers. She liked to see his eyes kindle and his breath come quick. Someday he'd tell her with impassioned words how much he loved her, and she would turn him neatly and comfortably down for awhile, till he learned his place and promised not to be troublesome. Then he might join the procession again as long as he behaved. But at present she knew she could sway him as she would, and she touched the orchids at her belt with tender little caressing movements and melting looks. She knew he'd have a box of something rarer waiting for her when she reached home, if the city afforded such.

She set him down at his club, well satisfied with her few minutes. She was glad it didn't last longer, for it would have grown tiresome; she'd carried him just far enough on the wave of emotion to stimulate her own soul.

Sweeping away from the curb again, bowing graciously to two or three other acquaintances who were going in or out of the curb building, she gave an order for the hospital and set her face to the duty before her.

A little breeze of expectation, a stir among the attendants about the door, preceded her entrance into the hospital. Passing nurses apprized her furs and orchids; young interns took account of her eyes—the mouse eyes had returned, but they lured with something unspeakable and thrilling in them.

She waited with a superb air that made everybody hurry to serve her, and presently she was shown up to Bonnie Brentwood's room. Her chauffeur had followed, bearing a large pasteboard suitbox which he set down at the door, and then departed.

"Is this Miss Brentwood's room?" she asked of the nurse who opened the door.

Her patient had just awakened from a refreshing sleep, and she had no notion this lofty person came to see the quiet, sad-eyed girl who had arrived in such shabby garments. The visitor had made a mistake, of course. The nurse grudgingly admitted that Miss Brentwood roomed there.

"Well, I've brought some things for her," said Gila, indicating the large box at her feet. "You can take it inside and open it."

The nurse opened the door a little wider, looked at the small, imperious personage in fur trappings and then down at the box. She hesitated a moment in a kind of inward fury, then swung the door a little wider open and stepped back.

"You can set it inside if you wish or wait till one of the men comes by," she said coolly and walked back into the room and busied herself with the medicine glasses.

Gila stared at her a moment, but there wasn't much satisfaction in wasting her glares on that white linen back, so she stooped and dragged in the box. She came and stood by the bed, looking down at the sick girl.

half-annoyed expression. She hadn't noticed the altercation at the door. Her apathy toward life was great. She was lying on the borderland, looking over and longing to go where all her dear ones had gone.

"Is your name Brentwood?" asked Gila in a sharp, high key so alien to a hospital.

Bonnie recalled her spirit to this world and focused her gaze on the girl as if to recall where she'd ever met her. Bonnie's hair was spread out over the pillow, as the nurse had just prepared to brush it. It fell in long, rich waves of brightness and rings of gold about her face. Gila stared at it jealously, as if it were something stolen from her. Her own hair, cloudy and dreamy and made much of with what skill and care could do, was pitiful beside this.

The girl's face was perfect in form and feature—delicate, refined, and lovely. Gila knew it would be counted rarely beautiful, and she was furious! Why did that upstart of a college boy send her here to see a beauty?

By this time the girl on the bed had summoned her soul back to earth and answered in a cool, distant tone, "Yes, I'm Miss Brentwood."

"Well, I've brought you a few things!" declared Gila. "Paul Courtland asked me to come and see what I could do for you." She swung her moleskin trappings about and pointed to the box. "I don't believe in giving money," she said with a tilt of her chin, "but I don't mind giving a lift in other ways to persons who are truly worthy. I've brought you a few evening dresses I'm finished with. They may help you get a position playing for the movies; or if you don't know ragtime, you might act—they'll take almost anybody with good clothes. Besides, I'm going to introduce you to a girls' employment club. They have a hall and hold dances once a week, and you get acquainted. It only costs ten cents a week and will give you a place to spend your evenings. If you join, you'll need evening dresses for the dances. Of course I understand some of the girls go in their street suits, but you stand a much better chance of having a good time if you're dressed attractively. And then they say men often go there evenings to look for a stenographer or an actor or some kind of worker, and they always pick out the prettiest. Dress goes a long way if you use it right. Now there's a dress in here—." Gila stooped and untied the cord on the box. "This dress cost $150, and I wore it only once!"

She held up a tattered blue net adorned with straggling, crushed, artificial rosebuds, its sole pretension to a waist being a couple of straps of silver tissue attached to a couple of rags of blue net. It looked for all the world like a bedraggled butterfly.

"It's torn in one or two places," continued Gila's ready tongue, "but it's easily mended. I wore it to a dance, and somebody stepped on the hem. I suppose you're good at mending. A girl in your position should know how to sew. My maid usually mends things like this with a thread of itself. You can pull one out along the hem, I'd think. Then here's a pink satin. It needs cleaning. They don't charge more than two or three dollars—or perhaps you might use cleaning fluid. I had slippers to match, but I found only one. I brought that along. I thought you might do something with it. They were horribly expensive—made to order, you know.

"Then this cerise chiffon, covered with sequins, is really too showy for a girl in your station, but in case you get a chance to act you might need it, and anyhow I never cared for it. It isn't becoming to me. Here's an indigo Charmeuse with silver trimmings. I got horribly tired of it, but you'll look stunning in it. It might even help you catch a rich husband—who knows? There're half a dozen pairs of white evening gloves. I might have had them cleaned, but if you can use them I can get new ones. And there's a bundle of old silk stockings! They haven't any toes or heels much, but I suppose you can darn them. And of course you can't afford to buy expensive silk stockings!"

One by one Gila had pulled the things out of the box, rattling on about them as if she were selling corn cure. She was excited, to be sure, now that she was fairly launched on her philanthropic expedition; the fact that the two women in the room were absolutely silent and gave no hint of how they were going to take this tide of insults was also disconcerting. But Gila wasn't easily disconcerted. She was very angry, and her anger had been growing in force all night. The greatest insult man could offer her had been heaped upon her by Paul Courtland, and no punishment was too great for the unfortunate innocent who had occasioned it. Gila didn't care what she said and didn't fear the consequences. No man lived, as far as she knew, who couldn't be humbled after she punished him sufficiently for any offense he might knowingly or unknowingly commit.

That she really had begun to admire Courtland, and to desire him in some degree for her own, only added fuel to her fire. This girl he pitied should be burned and tortured; she should be insulted and extinguished utterly, so that she'd never lift her head again within recognizable distance of Paul Courtland, or she would know the reason why. Paul Courtland was *hers*—if she chose to have him. Let no other girl dare look at him!

The nurse stood, starched and stern, with growing indignation at the stranger's audacity. Only absolute astonishment took her off her guard for the moment and prevented her from ousting the young lady from the premises instantly. She'd also heard the magic name of the handsome young gentleman used as password and realized this might be some rich relative of the lovely young patient that she wouldn't like to have put out. The nurse looked from Bonnie to the visitor in growing wrath and perplexity.

Bonnie lay there wide-eyed, with growing dignity in her face. Two soft, pink spots of color bloomed out in her cheeks, and her eyes twinkled with amusement. She was watching the visitor as if she were a passing Punch-and-Judy show come to entertain her. She regarded her and her display with a quiet disinterest that was getting on Gila's nerves.

"You can have my flowers, too, if you want them," said Gila, seeing that her insults brought no response from either listener. "They're rare orchids. Did you many flowers, and these were given me by a young man I don't care in the least about."

She unpinned the flowers and held them out to Bonnie, but the sick girl lay still a moment and regarded her with that quiet, half-amused gravity.

"I presume you can find a wastebasket down in the office if you want to get rid of them," said Bonnie suddenly, in a clear, refined voice. "I really shouldn't care for them. Isn't there a wastebasket somewhere about?" she asked, turning toward the nurse.

"Down in the hall by the front entrance," answered the nurse grimly.

Gila stood holding her flowers and looking from one woman to the other, unable to believe that any other woman had the insufferable audacity to meet her on her own ground. Were they ridiculing her, or were they innocents who thought she didn't want the flowers or didn't know enough to think orchids beautiful? Before she could decide, Bonnie was speaking again, still in that quiet tone that gave her command of the situation.

"I'm sorry," she said, as if she must let her visitor down gently, "but I'm afraid you've made some mistake. I don't recall ever meeting you before. You must be looking for some other Miss Brentwood."

Gila stared, and her color suddenly began to rise under the pearly tint of her flesh. Had she made some blunder? This certainly was the voice of a lady. And the girl on the bed had the advantage of absolute self-control. Somehow that angered Gila more than anything else.

"Don't you know Paul Courtland?" she demanded.

"I never heard the name before!"

Bonnie's voice was steady, and her eyes looked coolly into the other girl's. The nurse looked at Bonnie and marveled. She knew Paul Courtland's name well; she telephoned to that name every day. How was it the girl didn't know it? She liked this girl and the man who had brought her here and been so anxious about her. But who on earth was this hussy in fur?

Gila looked at Bonnie with an expression that said as plainly as words could have: "You lie! You *do* know him!" But her lips uttered scornfully, "Aren't you the poor girl whose kid brother got killed by an automobile in the street?"

Across Bonnie's stricken face flashed a spasm of pain, and her lips grew white.

"I thought so!" sneered Gila. "And yet you deny you ever heard Paul Courtland's name! He picked up the kid and carried it in the house and ran errands for you, but you don't know him! That's gratitude for you! I told him the working class were all like that. I have no doubt he's paid for this very room you're lying in!"

"Stop!" cried Bonnie, sitting up, her face white to the very lips. "You have no right to come here and talk like that! I can't understand who could have sent you! Certainly not the courteous stranger who picked up my little brother. I don't know his name or anything about him, but I can assure you I won't allow him or anyone else to pay my bills. Now will you take your things and leave my room? I'm feeling very—tired!"

The voice suddenly trailed off into silence, and Bonnie dropped back limply upon the pillow.

The nurse sprang like an angry bear who's seen someone troubling her cubs. She touched a button in the wall as she passed and swooped down on the tawdry finery, stuffing it into the box. Then she turned to the fur-trimmed lady, placed an arm firmly about her slim waist and scooped her out of the room. Flinging the bulging box down at her feet, where pink, blue, cerise and silver gushed forth, she shut the door and flew back to her charge.

The emergency doctor was hurrying down the hall, formidable in his white linen uniform. When Gila looked up from the confusion at her feet she encountered grave, disapproving eyes behind a pair of tortoise-shell goggles.

"What does all this mean?"

"It means that I have been insulted, sir, by one of your nurses!" declared Gila, tilting her chin up. "I'll see that she's removed at once from her position."

The doctor eyed her mildly, as though she were a small bat squeaking at a mighty hawk. "Indeed! I think you'll find that rather difficult! She's one of our best nurses! Henry," he said to a passing attendant, "escort this person and her—belongings—down to the street!"

Then he entered Bonnie's room, closing and fastening the door behind him.

Henry, with an ill-concealed grin, stooped to his task. Thus Gila, with brows pulled together in a deep scowl and lips pouting, descended to her waiting limousine.

Tears of anger fell on her cheeks as she leaned back against her cushions. She wiped them away with a cobweb of a handkerchief, while she sat and hated Courtland and the whole tribe of college men, her cousin Bill Ward included, for getting her into a scrape like this. Defeat was something she couldn't brook. She had never, since she stopped wearing short dresses, felt so defeated! But it shouldn't be defeat. She would take her full revenge for all that had happened. Courtland would bite the dust! She would show him he couldn't go around picking up stray beauties and sending her after them to pet them for him.

She didn't watch for acquaintances during that ride home but remained behind drawn curtains. At home she stormed up to her room, ordering her maid not to disturb her, and sat down angrily to write an epistle to Courtland that would bring him to his knees.

Meanwhile the doctor and nurse worked silently, skillfully, over Bonnie until the weary eyes opened again and a long-drawn sigh showed that the girl had returned to the world.

When the doctor had left the room and the nurse had given her some beef tea, Bonnie raised her eyes and asked, "Would you mind finding out for me just what this room costs?"

The nurse had thought about what she'd say when this question came. "Why, I'm under the impression you won't have to pay anything," she said pleasantly. "Sometimes when patients leave, they're especially grateful and leave an where strangers come in for a few days and need quiet—real quiet they can't get in the ward. I believe someone paid something for this room in some kind of way like that. I guess the doctor thought you'd get well quicker if you had it quiet, so he put you in here. You needn't worry a bit about it."

Bonnie smiled. "Would you mind making sure?" she asked. "I'd like to know just what I owe. I have a little money."

The nurse nodded and slipped away to whisper the story to the doctor, who grew more indignant and contemptuous than he had been to Gila and sent the nurse promptly back with an answer.

"You don't have to pay a cent," she said cheerfully. "This bed is endowed temporarily, the doctor says, to be used at his discretion, and he wants to keep you here till someone comes who needs this room more than you do. At present there isn't anyone, so you needn't worry. We're not going to let any more little feather-headed spitfires in to see you either. The doctor bawled the office out for letting that girl up."

Bonnie tried to smile again but only sighed. "Oh, it doesn't matter." After a minute she added, "You've been very good to me. Sometime I hope I can do something for you. Now I'm going to sleep."

The nurse left to look after some of her duties. Half an hour later she came back to Bonnie's room and entered softly, so as not to waken her. She was worried she'd left the window open and the wind might be blowing on her, for it had turned a good deal colder since the sun set.

She tiptoed to the bed and bent over in the dim light to see if her patient was all right, then drew back sharply. The bed was empty! Turning on the light, she looked around, but no one else was in the room. Bonnie was gone!

Chapter 13

The nurse searched the room, throwing open the wardrobe. Bonnie's shabby clothes were no longer hanging on the hooks. She rushed to the window and looked helplessly along the fire escape into the courtyard below, where the ambulance was bringing in a new patient, but she didn't see the girl. Turning back, she noticed on the table a bit of paper from the daily record-sheet folded up and pinned together with a quaint little circle of old-fashioned gold in which were set tiny garnets and pearls. The note was addressed, "Miss Wright, Nurse." A five-dollar bill fell from the paper. She picked up the note.

Dear Miss Wright—I'm leaving this little pin for you because you've been so good to me. It isn't very valuable, but it's all I have. The five dollars are for the room. I know it's worth more, but I haven't any more just now. You've all been very kind. Please give the money to the doctor and thank him for me. Don't worry about me; I'm all right. I just need to get back to work.
Good-bye, and thank you again.

Sincerely,
Rose Bonner Brentwood

The nurse rushed down to the office. A search was instituted at once. Everyone in the office and halls was questioned. Only one elevator man remembered a person, dressed in black, going out of the nurses' side door. He thought it was one of the probation nurses.

They searched the streets for several blocks around. It had been only a few minutes, and the girl was weak. She couldn't have gone far.

The evening mail came and with it a letter bearing a Western postmark addressed to Miss R. B. Brentwood. The nurse looked at it sadly. A letter for the poor child! What hope and friendliness mightn't it contain! If it had only come a couple of hours sooner!

Later that evening, when they finally decided the patient had disappeared, the nurse went to the telephone.

Courtland was in Tennelly's room. They'd been discussing the question of woman suffrage that had come up in political science class that day. Tennelly held that most women were too unbalanced to vote; you could never tell what a woman would do next. She was swayed entirely by her emotions, mainly two—love and hate; sometimes pride and selfishness. *Always* selfishness. All women were selfish!

Courtland thought of Mother Marshall's true eyes and the telegram that had come the day before. He held that all women were not selfish. He said he knew one woman who was not. All women were not flighty and unbalanced or swayed by their emotions. He knew two he thought were not swayed by their emotions. Just then he was called to the telephone.

The nurse's voice broke into his thoughts: "Mr. Courtland, this is the nurse from Good Samaritan Hospital. I thought you should know Miss Brentwood's disappeared. We've searched everywhere but can't get any clue to her whereabouts. She wasn't fit to go. She'd fainted again and was unconscious a long time. She had a very disturbing call this afternoon from a young woman who mentioned your name and got up to the room somehow without the usual formalities. Of course I thought she had the doctor's permission, and she came right in. She brought a lot of dirty evening gowns, tried to give them to my patient and called her a working girl; spoke of her little dead brother as 'the kid' and was very insulting. I thought perhaps you could give us a clue as to where the patient might be. She was much too weak to be out alone—and in this bitter cold! Her jacket was very thin. I'm afraid she could get pneumonia. I thought she was sound asleep. She left a little note for me, with a pin she wanted me to keep, and five dollars to pay for her room. You see, she got the notion from what that girl said that she was on charity in the room and wouldn't stay. I thought you'd want me to let you know."

There was almost a sob in the nurse's voice as she ended. Courtland's heart sank.

Poor Gila! She hadn't understood. She'd meant well but hadn't known how. He was a fool to ask her to go! She had no experience with sorrow and poverty. How could she understand?

His anger rose as he listened to a few more details concerning Gila's remarks. Of course the nurse was exaggerating, but how crude of Gila! Where was her womanly intuition? Her finer sensibilities? But, after all, perhaps the nurse hadn't understood fully. Perhaps she'd taken offense and misconstrued Gila's intended kindness. Well, the main thing was that Bonnie was gone and must be hunted up. It wouldn't do to leave her without friends, sick and weak, this cold night. She had, of course, gone home to her room. He could easily find her. He wouldn't mind going out, though he'd intended doing other things that evening; but he'd undertaken this job and must see it through. Then there was that telegram from Mother Marshall! And her letter on the way! Too bad! Of course he must make Bonnie go back to the hospital. He'd have no trouble coaxing her back when she knew how she'd distressed them all.

"I'll go right down to her old place and see if she's there," he told the nurse. "She's probably gone back to her room. I'll insist she return to the hospital tonight."

As he hung up the receiver Pat touched his elbow and pointed to a messenger boy waiting for him with a note.

It was Gila's violet-scented missive over which she'd wept those angry tears. He signed for the letter with a frown. Somehow the perfume annoyed him. He put the thing in his pocket, having no patience to read it at once, and hurried down the hall.

As he passed the office Courtland found a letter in his box, noting with comfort that it bore a Western postmark. As he waited for his trolley at the corner, he reflected how strange it was that this young woman he'd never seen or heard of before should suddenly be flung upon his horizon and seem, in a measure, his responsibility. He'd been shaking free from that sense of accountability since she was reported getting better—especially since he'd put her on the hearts of Mother Marshall and Gila. Gila! How the thought of her annoyed him just now!

In the trolley he opened Mother Marshall's letter and read, marveling at the revelation of motherhood it contained. Motherhood and fatherhood! How beautiful! A sort of Christ-mother and Christ-father, these two who had been bereft of their own, were willing to be. And Bonnie! How she needed them—and had left before she knew! He must persuade her to go to Mother Marshall! For, after all, this whole bungle was his fault. If he'd never brought Gila into it this wouldn't have happened.

A factory girl shivered into the car in a thin summer jacket and stood beside a girl in furs and a handsome coat. Courtland thought of Bonnie in her shabby black summer suit. He remembered noticing how thin it looked as they stood beside the grave on the bleak hillside and wondering if she weren't cold. But it was mild that day compared to this, and the sun was shining then. She must have half frozen in that long ride. And had she enough money to buy something to eat? She'd left a five-dollar bill at the hospital—probably her last, he thought.

He grew more and more nervous and impatient as he neared his destination.

He sprang up the narrow stairs that had grown so familiar to him the past week, watching the crack under the door anxiously to see if a light was shining. But it was dark. He tapped at the door lightly. But of course she'd have gone to bed at once after the journey. He tapped louder and held his breath to listen. But no answer came.

Then he tapped again and called in subdued tones, "Miss Brentwood! Are you there?"

He heard a stir at the other end of the hall and the scratching of a match. A light appeared under the door of the front room, the door opened a crack, and a frowsy head was thrust out, with a candle held high above it and sleepy eyes peering into the darkness of the hall.

"Has Miss Brentwood returned? Have you seen her?" he asked.

"Not as I knows of, she ain't come," said a woman's voice. "I went to bed early. She might ov and I not hear her—she's so softly like."

"I wonder if we could find out? Would you mind coming and trying?"

The woman looked at him keenly. "Oh, you're the young feller what come to the fun'rul, ain't you? Well, you jest wait a bit, an' I'll throw somethin' on an' come an' try." The woman came in an amazing costume of many colors and called and shook the door. She got her key and unlocked the door, stepping cautiously inside and looking about. She advanced, holding the candle high, with Courtland waiting behind. He could see one withered white rosebud on the floor—but no sign of Bonnie. Her room was as she'd left it the day of the funeral.

Chapter 14

Suddenly, as Courtland stood in the narrow dark street alone and uncertain, he was no longer alone. As clearly as if he'd felt a touch on his sleeve he knew that One was there beside him and that his errand had the sanction of that Presence which had met him once in the fiery way and promised to show him what to do.

"God, show me where to find her!" he exclaimed.

Then, as if someone had said, "Come with me!" he turned, as certainly as if a passerby had directed him to where he'd seen her, and walked up the street—that is, *they* walked up the street.

Always in thinking of that walk afterward he thought of it as "they walking up the street"—he and the Presence.

The first thing he remembered about it was that he'd lost his uncertainty and anxiety. How long the route was or where it was to end didn't seem to matter. Every step of the way was companioned by One who knew what He was about. It came to him that he'd like to go everywhere in such company; that no journey would be too far or arduous, no duty too unpleasant, if all could be as this.

He stepped into the telephone office and called up hospitals. One or two reported young women brought in, but the description was not at all like the girl he was searching for. He jotted them down in his notebook, however, feeling they might be a last resort.

As he turned the pages of the phone book his eye caught the name of the city morgue, and a sudden horror confronted him. What if something had happened to her and she'd been taken there? What if she'd ended the life that had looked so lonely and impossible to her? No, she would never do that, not with her faith in Christ! And yet, if her vitality was low and her heart taxed with sorrow, she could scarcely be responsible for what she did.

He rang up the morgue.

Yes, a young woman had been brought in about an hour ago. . .Yes, dressed in black—had long light hair and was slender. "*Some looker!*" the man said.

Courtland shuddered and hung up. He must go to the morgue.

When they entered the gruesome place of the unknown dead, the Presence entered with him; yet he felt that it was there already, standing close among the dead—had been there when they came in!

Courtland's face was pale and set as he passed between the silent dead laid out for identification. He shuddered inwardly as he was led to the spot where the latest one lay, a slim young girl with golden hair, sodden from the river where she was found, her pretty face sharpened and coarsened by sin.

He drew a deep breath of relief and turned away quickly from the sight of her poor drowned eyes, rejoicing that they weren't Bonnie's eyes. He was glad he might still think of her alive and continue searching for her. But a dart of pain pierced his heart as he looked again at this little wreck of womanhood, leaving a hard life, where she'd reached for brightness and pleasure and found ashes and bitterness instead, and going into a beyond of darkness. What would the resurrection mean to a poor soul like that? Perhaps it hadn't all been her fault. Perhaps others had helped push her down, smug in self-righteousness, to whom the resurrection would be more of a horror than to the pretty, ignorant child whose untaught feet had strayed into forbidden paths! Who knew? He was glad to look up and feel the Presence there. Who knew what might have passed between the soul and God? It was safe to leave that soul with Him who had died to save. It was good to know that the hardened girl, the grizzled sot, the toothless crone and the little newsboy who lay in the same row were guarded alike and beloved by the same Presence that would go with him.

Around the newsboy huddled a group of street gamins, counting out their few pennies and talking excitedly of how they would buy him some flowers. Tears had stained their grimy cheeks, and it was plain they pitied him—they who might yet tread the paths of sin and deprivation and sorrow for many long years. And the Presence was there. So near them, with the pitying eyes! The young man knew the eyes were pitying. If the children could only see! He felt an impulse to turn back and tell them as he passed into the street, yet how could he make them understand—he who understood so feebly and intermittently himself? He felt a great ache to go out and shout to the world to look up and see the Presence in their midst.

He was entirely aware that his present mental state would have seemed to him little short of insanity twenty-fours hours before; that it might pass again as it had before—and a kind of mental frenzy seized him lest it would. He didn't want to lose this assurance of One guiding him through such a sorrowful world as this one now seemed to be.

With the age-old anguished cry of "Give me a sign!" he spoke aloud once more: "God, if You're really there, let me find her!"

Yet if any had asked him just then if he ever prayed he would have told them no. Prayer was to him a thing utterly apart from this cry of his soul, this longing for an understanding with God.

He walked on through unfamiliar streets, passing men and women with worn and haggard faces, tattered garments and discouraged mien. And always that cry came in his soul, "Oh, if they only knew!" The Presence walked by his side, and men passed by and saw Him not.

He was walking in the general direction of the Good Samaritan Hospital, just as anyone would walk with a friend through a strange place and accommodate his going to the man who was guiding him. All the way a sort of intercourse took place between him and his Companion. His soul was putting forth questions he would someday take up in detail; but now he was working them out, becoming satisfied that this was the only way to solve the otherwise unanswerable problems of the universe.

the most part through narrow streets crowded full of small houses interspersed with cheap stores and saloons. The night darkened, and a cold wind from the river swept around corners, reminding him of the dripping yellow hair of the girl in the morgue. It cut like a knife through Courtland's heavy overcoat and made him wish he'd brought his muffler. He stuffed his gloved hands into his pockets. Even in their fur linings they were stiff and cold. He thought of the girl's thin jacket and shivered visibly as they turned into another street where vacant lots on one side left a wide sweep for the wind and sent it along with stinging bits of sand. The clouds were heavy as with snow, but it was too cold to snow. Only biting steel could fall from clouds like that on such a bitter night.

Any moment he might have turned back, gone a block to one side and caught the trolley across to the university, where warmth and friends were waiting. And what was this one lost girl to him? A stranger? No, she was no longer a stranger! She had become something infinitely precious to the whole universe. God cared, and that was enough. He couldn't be God's friend unless he cared as God cared!

The lights were out in most of the houses they passed, and there were fewer saloons. The streets loomed wide ahead, the line of houses dark on the left and the stretch of vacant lots with the river beyond on the right. Across the river a line of dark buildings with an occasional blink of lights blended into the dark sky, and the wind blew merciless over all.

On ahead a couple of blocks the light was flung out on the pavement and marked another saloon. Bright doors swung back and forth. The intermittent throb of a piano and twang of a violin made merry with the world's misery, and voices came at intervals above it all.

The saloon doors swung again, and four or five dark figures jostled noisily out and came haltingly down the street. They walked crazily, like ships without a rudder, veering from one side of the walk to the other, shouting and singing uncouth, ribald songs, hoarse laughter interspersed with scattered oaths.

"O! Jesus Christ!" came distinctly through the quiet night. The young man felt a distinct pain for the Christ by his side, like the pressing of a thorn into the brow. For these were among those for whom He died.

Courtland realized he was seeing everything on this walk through the eyes of Christ. He remembered Scrooge and his journey with the Ghost of Christmas Past in Dickens's *Christmas Carol*. It was like that. He was seeing everyone's real soul. He was with the architect of the universe, noting where the work had gone awry from the mighty plans. He suddenly knew these figures coming giddily toward him were created for mighty things!

The men paused before one of the dark houses, pointed and laughed, then drew nearer the steps and bent over. He couldn't hear what they were saying; the voices were hushed in ugly whispers, broken by harsh laughter. Only now and then he caught a syllable.

"Wake up!" floated out into the silence once. "No, you don't, my pretty little chicken!"

Then a girl's scream pierced the night, and something darted out from the dark doorstep, eluding the drunken men, but slipped and fell.

Courtland broke into a noiseless run.

The men had scrambled tipsily after the girl and clutched her. They lifted her unsteadily and surrounded her. She screamed again, dashing this way and that blindly, but they met her every time and held her.

Courtland knew at once he'd been brought here for this crisis. Lowering his head and crouching, he moved swiftly forward, watching carefully where he steered, and came straight at two of the men with his powerful shoulders. It was an old football trick and bowled the two assailants on the right straight out into the gutter. The other three made a dash at him, but he sidestepped one and tripped him; a blow on the chin sent another sprawling on the sidewalk. But the last one, who was perhaps the most sober of them all, showed fight and called to his comrades to come on and get this stranger who was trying to steal their girl. The language he used made Courtland's blood boil. He struck the fellow across his foul mouth and then, clenching with him, went down on the sidewalk. His antagonist was heavier than he; but the steady brain and the trained muscles had the better of it from the first, and in a moment more the drunken man was choking and limp.

Courtland rose and looked about. The two fellows in the gutter were struggling to their feet with loud threats, and the fellow on the sidewalk was staggering toward him. They would be upon the girl again in a moment. He looked toward her, as she stood trembling a few feet away from him, too frightened to run, not daring to leave her protector. A streetlight fell directly upon her pale face. It was Bonnie Brentwood!

With a kick at the man on the ground who was trying to rise, and a lurch at the man on the sidewalk who was coming toward him, Courtland dived under the clutching hands of the two in the gutter who couldn't get on the curb again. Snatching up the girl like a baby, he fled up the street and around the first corner, and all the cursing, drunken, reeling five came howling after!

Chapter 15

Courtland ran three blocks and turned two corners before he stopped and set the girl on her feet again. He looked anxiously at her pale face and frightened eyes. She was shivering. He tore his overcoat off, wrapped it about her and, before she could protest, caught her up again and ran another block or two.

"Oh, you mustn't!" she cried. "I can walk perfectly well, and I don't need your coat. Please, please put on your coat and let me walk! You'll catch a terrible cold!"

"I can run better without it," he explained briefly, "and we can get out of the way of those fellows quicker this way!"

So she lay still in his arms till he put her down again. He looked up and down either way, hoping to see the familiar red and green lights of a drugstore open late. But none greeted him; all the buildings seemed to be residences.

Somewhere in the distance he heard the whir of a late trolley. He glanced at his watch. It was half past one. If only a taxicab would come along. But no taxi was in sight. The girl was begging him to put on his overcoat. She'd drawn it from her own shoulders and was holding it out to him insistently. With the rare smile he was noted for, Courtland took the coat and wrapped it firmly about her shoulders again, this time putting her arms in the sleeves and buttoning it up to the chin.

"Now," he said, "you're not to take that off again until we get where it's warm. You needn't worry about me. I'm used to going out in all kinds of weather without my coat as often as with it. Besides, I've been exercising. When did you have something to eat?"

"When I left the hospital this evening, I had some strong beef tea," she answered airily, as if that had been only a few minutes before.

"How did you happen to be where I found you?" he asked, looking at her keenly.

"Why, I must have missed my way, I think," she explained, "and I felt a little weak from having been in bed so long. I sat down on a doorstep to rest a minute before I went on, and I'm afraid I must have fallen asleep."

"You were *walking*?" His tone was stern. "Why were you walking?"

A desperate look entered her face. "Well, I hadn't any carfare, if you must know the reason."

They were passing a streetlight as she said it, and he looked down at her profile in wonder. He felt a sudden choking in his throat and a mist in his eyes. He had it on the tip of his tongue to say, "You poor little girl!"

Instead he said, in a tone of intense admiration, "Well, you certainly are the pluckiest girl I ever saw! You have your nerve with you all right! But you're not going to walk another step tonight!"

And with that he stooped, gathered her up again, and strode forward. He could hear the distant whir of another trolley and determined to take it, no matter which way it was going. It would take them somewhere he could telephone for an ambulance. So he sprinted forward, regardless of her protests, and arrived at the next corner in time to catch the car going to the city.

Nobody else was in the car, and he made her keep the coat about her. He couldn't help seeing how worn and thin her shoes were and how she shivered now even in the great coat.

"Why did you run away from the hospital?" he asked suddenly, looking straight into her eyes.

"I couldn't afford to stay any longer."

"You made a big mistake. It wouldn't have cost you a cent. That room was free. I made sure of that before I secured it for you."

"But that was a private room!"

"Just a little more private than the wards. That room was paid for and put at the doctor's disposal to use for anyone he thought needed quiet. Now are you satisfied? And you're going back there till you're well enough to go out again. You raised a big row in the hospital, running away. They've had the whole force of assistants out hunting you for hours, and your nurse is awfully upset. She seems to be crazy over you. She nearly wept when she telephoned me. And I've been out for hours hunting you, stirred up the old lady on your floor at your home and a lot of hospitals and other places, and then just found you in the nick of time. I hope you've learned your lesson, to be good after this and not run away."

He smiled indulgently, but the girl's eyes were full of tears.

"I didn't mean to make all that trouble for people. Why should you all care about a stranger? But, oh! I'm so thankful you came! Those men were terrible!" She shuddered. "How did you happen to come there? I think God must have led you."

"He did!" said Courtland with conviction.

When they reached the big city station he stowed his patient into a taxi and sent a messenger up to the restaurant for hot chicken broth, which he administered himself.

After the broth was finished she lay back with her eyes closed. He realized she'd reached her limit of endurance. She hadn't even protested wearing his overcoat any longer.

It was a strange ride. The girl sat closely wrapped in her corner, asleep. The car bounded over obstacles now and then or swung around corners and threw her about like a ball, but she didn't awaken. Finally Courtland drew her head down on his shoulder and put his arm about her to keep her from being thrown out of her seat, and she settled down like a tired child. He couldn't help thinking of that other girl lying stark and dead in the morgue and being glad this one was safe.

Nurse Wright was hovering about the hallway when the taxi drew up to the hospital entrance, and Bonnie was tenderly cared for at once.

Courtland began to realize that this hospital was an evidence of the presence of Christ in the world. He wasn't the only one who had felt the Presence. Someone moved as he was tonight had established this house of healing. There on the opposite wall was a stained-glass window representing Christ blessing the little children and the people bringing the sick, lame and blind to Him for healing.

The night routine went on about him: the strong odor of antiseptics; the padded tap of nurses' rubber soles as they walked softly on their rounds; the occasional click of a glass and a spoon somewhere; the piteous wail of a suffering child in a distant ward; the sharp whir of an electric bell; the thud of the elevator on its errands up and down; even the controlled yet ready spring to service of all concerned when the ambulance rolled up and a man on a stretcher, with a ghastly cut in his head and face, was brought in. All made him feel how little and useless his life had been before now. How suddenly he'd been brought face-to-face with realities!

He began to wonder if the Presence was everywhere or if in some places His power was not manifest—the red library, that church last Sunday.

The office clock chimed softly out the hour of three o'clock. It was Sunday morning. Should he go to church again and search for the Presence or decide the churches were out of it entirely and that He came only in places of need and suffering? Still, that wasn't fair to the churches, perhaps, to judge all by one. What an experience the night had been! Did Wittemore, majoring in philanthropy, ever spend nights like this? If so, Wittemore's nature must have depths worth sounding.

He drew his handkerchief from his inner pocket, and as he did so a whiff of violets reminded him of Gila's letter, still unread; but he paid no heed. The antiseptics were at work on his senses, and the violets couldn't reach him.

Dark circles lay under his eyes, and his hair was in a tumble, but he looked good to Nurse Wright as she hurried down the hall at last to give him her report. She almost thought he was good enough for her Bonnie now. She wasn't given to romances, but she felt that Bonnie needed one about now.

"She didn't wake up except to open her eyes and smile once," she reported. "She coughs a little now and then, with a nasty sound in it, but I hope we can ward off pneumonia. It was great of you to put your overcoat around her. That saved her, if anything could, I guess. You look pretty well used up yourself. Wouldn't you like the doctor to give you something before you go home?"

"No, thank you. I'll be all right. I'm hard as nails. I'm only anxious about her. She's had a pretty tough pull of it. She started to walk to the city! Did you know that? She must have gone about two miles. I found her somewhere near the river. She sat down on a doorstep to rest and must have fallen asleep. Some tough fellows came out of a saloon—they were full, of course—and discovered her. I heard her scream, and we had quite a scuffle before we got away. She's a nervy little girl. Think of her starting to walk to the city at that time of night, without a cent in her pocket!"

"The poor child!" said Nurse Wright, with tears in her eyes. "And she left her last cent here to pay for her room. My! When I think of it I could choke that young snob who called on her in the afternoon! You should have heard her sneers and insinuations. Women like that are a blight on womanhood. And she dared to mention your name—said you'd sent her!"

The color heightened in Courtland's face. He felt uncomfortable. "Why, I— didn't exactly send her," he began. "I don't really know her very well. I'm a student at the university, and of course I don't know many girls in the city. I thought it would be nice if some girl would call on Miss Brentwood; she seemed so alone. I thought another girl would understand and be able to comfort her."

"She isn't a girl—that's what's the matter with her. She's a little *demon!*" snapped the nurse. "You meant well, and I daresay she never showed *you* her demon side. Girls like that don't—to young *men.* But if you take my advice you won't have anything more to do with *her!* She isn't worth it. She may be rich and fashionable and all that, but she can't hold a candle to Miss Brentwood. If you'd just heard how she went on, with her nasty little chin in the air and her nasty phrases and insinuations and her patronage! And then Miss Brentwood's gentle, refined way of answering her. But never mind—I won't go into that! It might take me all night, and I've got to get back to my patient. But you're not to blame yourself. I hope Miss Brentwood's going to get through this all right in a few days, and she'll probably have forgotten about it, so don't you worry. It would be good if you came in to see her tomorrow afternoon for a few minutes. It might cheer her up. You really have been fine. No telling where she might have been by this time if you hadn't gone out after her!"

He shuddered involuntarily and thought of the faces of the five young fellows who had surrounded her.

"I saw a girl in the morgue tonight, drowned!" he said. "She wasn't any older than Miss Brentwood."

The nurse gave an understanding look. On her way back to her rounds she said to herself: "I believe he's a real *man!* If I hadn't thought so I wouldn't have told him he might come and see her tomorrow."

Then she stepped into Bonnie's room, took the letter with the Western postmark and stood it up against a medicine glass on the table beside the bed, where she could see it first thing when she opened her eyes.

little after four o'clock, when Courtland came plodding up the dormitory hall to his room, a head emerged from Tennelly's door, followed by Tennelly's shoulders attired in a bathrobe. The hair on the head was tumbled, and the eyes were full of sleep. Moreover, an anxious, yet relieved frown furrowed the brows.

"Where in thunder've you been, Court? We were thinking of dragging the river for you. I must say you're the limit! Do you know what time it is?"

"Five minutes after four by the library clock as I came up," answered Courtland. "Say, Nelly, go to church with me again this morning? I've found another preacher I want to sample."

"Go to thunder!" growled Tennelly. "Not on your tintype! I'm going to get some sleep. What do you take me for? A night nurse? Go to church when I've been up all night hunting for you?"

"Sorry, Nelly, but it was an emergency call. Tell you about it on the way to church. Church doesn't begin till somewhere 'round eleven. You'll be calm by that time. So long! See you in church!"

Tennelly slammed his door hard, and Courtland went smiling to his room. He knew Tennelly would go with him to church. For Courtland had seen among the advertisements in the trolley on his way back to the university the notice of a service to be held in a church in the lower part of the city, to be addressed by the Reverend John Burns, and he wanted to go. It might not be *the* John Burns, of course, but he wanted to see.

Worn out with the night's events, he slept soundly until ten. Then, as if he were an alarm clock set for a certain moment, he awoke.

He lay there for a moment in the peaceful awareness of something good that had come to him. Then he knew it was the Presence—there, in his room. It would always be his. It was wonderful to know the possibility of that companionship all the days of one's life.

He couldn't reason out why something like that should give him so much joy. It didn't seem sensible in the old way of reasoning—and yet, didn't it? If it could be proved to the fellows that there was really a God like that, companionable, reasonable, just, loving, forgiving, ready to give Himself, wouldn't they all jump at the chance of knowing Him personally, provided there was a way for them to know Him? They claimed it had never been proved, never could be. But he knew it could. It had been proved to him. That was the difference. That was the greatness of it. And now he was going to church again to find out if the Presence was ever there.

With a bound he was out of bed, shaved and dressed in an incredibly short space of time, and shouting to Tennelly, who took his feet reluctantly from the window seat and lowered the Sunday paper.

"Thunder and blazes! Who woke you up, you nut! I thought you were good for another two hours!"

But they went to church.

Tennelly sat down on the hard wooden bench and accepted the worn hymn-book a small urchin presented him, with an amused stare that finally bloomed into a full grin at Courtland.

"What's eating you, you blooming idiot! Where in thunder did you rake up this dump anyway? If you've got to go to church, why in the name of all that's a bore can't you pick out a place where the congregation takes a bath once a month, whether they need it or not?" he whispered in a loud growl.

But Courtland's eyes were already fixed on the bright, intelligent face and red hair of the man who stood behind the small pulpit. He was the same John Burns! A window just behind the platform, set with crude red and blue and yellow lights of cheap glass, sent its radiance down on his head, and the yellow bar lay across his hair like a halo. Behind him, in the colored lights, the Presence seemed to stand. It was so vivid to Courtland at first that he drew in his breath and looked sharply at Tennelly, as if he, too, must see, though he knew nothing was visible, of course, but the lights, the glory and the freckled, earnest man giving out a hymn.

And the singing—if one were looking for discord, well, it was there, every shade of it the world had ever known! There were quavering old voices and piping young ones; off key and on key, squeaking, grating, screaming, howling, with all their earnest might. But the melody lifted itself in a great voice on high and seemed to bear along the spirit of the congregation.

I need Thee every hour.
    Stay Thou nearby;
Temptations lose their power
    When Thou art nigh.
I need Thee, oh, I need Thee,
    Every hour I need Thee;
O bless me now, my Savior,
    I come to Thee!

These people, then, knew about the Presence, loved it, longed for it, understood its power. They sang of the Presence and were glad! Others in the world knew, then, besides him and Stephen and Stephen Marshall's mother! Without knowing what he was doing, Courtland sang. He didn't know the words, but he felt the spirit and groped along in syllables as he caught them.

Tennelly sat gazing around him, highly amused, not attempting to suppress his mirth. His eyes fairly danced as he observed first one absorbed worshipper and then another, intent upon the song. He imagined himself taking off the old elder on the other side of the aisle and the intense young woman with the large mouth and the feather in her hat. Her voice was killing. He could make the fellows die laughing, singing as she did, in a high falsetto.

He looked at Courtland to enjoy it with him, and, lo! Courtland was singing with as much earnestness as the rest. On his face sat a high, exalted look he'd never seen there before. Was it true the fire and sickness had really affected Court's mind? He seemed so like his old self lately that they'd hoped he was getting over it.

During the prayer Courtland dropped his head and closed his eyes. Tennelly glanced around and marveled at everyone's serious attitude. Even a row of tough-looking kids on the back seats had at least one eye apiece squinted shut during the prayer and almost an atmosphere of reverence upon them.

Tennelly prided himself upon being a student of human nature, and before he knew it he was interested in this mass of common people about him. But now and again his gaze returned uneasily to Courtland whose eyes were fixed intently on the preacher, as if the words he spoke were of real importance to him.

Tennelly sat back in wonder and tried to listen. It was all about a mysterious companionship with God, stuff that sounded like rot to him—uncanny, unreal, mystical, impossible! Could Court, their peach of a Court, whose sneer and criticism alike had been dreaded by all who came beneath them—could he with such a sensible, scholarly, sane mind take up with a superstition like that? It was foolishness to Tennelly.

He owned to a certain amount of interest in the sermon's emotional side. The little man could sway that uncouth audience mightily. He felt himself swayed in the tenderer side of his nature, but of course his superior mind realized it was all emotion—interesting as a study, but not to be taken seriously. It wasn't healthy for Court to see much of this. All this talk of a cross and one dying for all! Mere foolishness and superstition! Very beautiful, and perhaps allegorical, but not at all practical.

The minister was by the door before they got out and grasped Courtland's hand as if he were an old friend. Then he turned and took hold of Tennelly's. Something was so genuine and sincere about his face that Tennelly decided he must really believe all that junk he was preaching. He wasn't a fake; he was merely a good, wholesome fanatic. He bowed pleasantly and said a few commonplaces as he passed.

"Seems to be a good sort," he murmured to Courtland. "Pity he's tied down to that!"

Courtland looked at him. "Is that the way you feel about it, Nelly?"

Tennelly returned the look sharply. "Why, sure! I think he's a bigger man than his job, don't you?"

"Then you didn't feel it?"

"Feel what?"

"The presence of God in that place!"

There was something so simple and majestic about the way Courtland made the extraordinary statement—not as a common fanatic would make it or even as one who was testing for confirmation of a hope, but as one who knew it to be a fact beyond questioning, which the other merely hadn't seen—that Tennelly was almost embarrassed.

"Why—I—why—no! I can't say I noticed any particular manifestation. I was too much taken up by the smell to observe the mystical. Say, what's eating you anyway, Court? Such foolishness isn't like you. You should cut it out. You know a thing like this can get on your nerves if you let it, just like anything else, and make you a monomaniac. You should go in for more athletics and cut out some of your psychology and philosophy. Suppose we go and take a ride in the park this afternoon. It's a great day."

"I don't mind riding in the park for a while after dinner. I've got a date about four o'clock. But I'm not a monomaniac, Nelly, and nothing's getting on my nerves. I never felt better or happier in my life. I feel as if I'd always been blind and groping along, and now my eyes are open to see how wonderful life is."

"Do you mean you've got what they used to call 'religion,' Court? 'Hit the trail,' as it were?" Tennelly asked as if he were delicately inquiring about some insidious tubercular or cancerous trouble. He seemed half ashamed to connect such a perilous possibility with his honored friend.

Courtland shook his head. "Not that I know of, Nelly. I never attended one of those big evangelistic meetings in my life, and I don't know exactly what 'religion,' as they call it, is, so I can't lay claim to anything like that. What I mean is, simply, I've met God face-to-face and found He's my friend. That's about the size of it, and it makes everything look different. I'd like to tell you how it happened sometime, Tennelly, when you're ready to hear."

"Wait awhile, Court," said Tennelly, half shrinking. "Wait till you've had a little more time to think it over. Then if you like I'll listen."

"Very well," said Courtland quietly. "But I want you to know it's something real. It's no sick notion."

"All right!" said Tennelly. "I'll let you know when I'm ready to hear."

Late that afternoon, when Courtland entered the hospital, the sunshine was flooding the great stained-glass window and glorifying the face of the Christ with outstretched hands. Off in a nearby ward someone was singing to the patients, and the corridors seemed hushed to listen:

The healing of the seamless dress
    Is by our beds of pain.
We touch Him in life's throng and press
    And we are whole again!

All this recognition of Christ in the world, and somehow he'd never been aware before! He felt abashed at his blindness. And if he'd taken so long, surely there was hope for Tennelly to see, too. Somehow he wanted Tennelly to see.

Chapter 17

B onnie Brentwood was awake and expecting him, the nurse said. She lay
propped up by pillows, draped about with a dainty, frilly dressing gown
that looked too frivolous for Nurse Wright yet could surely have come
from no other source. The golden hair was lying in two long braids, one over
each shoulder, and a faint flush of expectancy colored her pale cheeks.

"You've been so good to me!" she said. "It's been wonderful for a stranger
to go out of his way so much."

"Please don't let's talk about that," said Courtland. "It's been only a pleasure
to be of service. Now I want to know how you are. I've been expecting to hear
you had pneumonia or something dreadful after that awful exposure."

"Oh, I've been through a good deal more than that," said the girl, trying to
speak lightly. "Things don't seem to kill me. I've had a lot of hard times."

"I'm afraid you have," he said. "Somehow it doesn't seem fair you've had
such a rotten time, and I'm lying around enjoying myself. Shouldn't everybody be treated alike in this world? I don't understand it."

Bonnie smiled. "Oh, it's all right!" she said with conviction. " 'In the world
ye shall have tribulation: but be of good cheer; I have overcome the world.' It's
our testing time, and this world isn't the only part of life."

"I don't see how that answers my point," said Courtland pleasantly. "What's
the idea? Don't you think I'm worth the testing?"

"Oh, surely, but you may not need the same kind I have."

"You don't appear to me to have needed any testing. So far as I can judge,
you've showed the finest kind of nerve on every occasion."

"Oh, but I do. I've needed it dreadfully! You don't know how hard I was getting—sort of soured on the world. That's why I left the old home where my
father's church was and where all the people I knew were. I couldn't bear to
see them. They'd been so hard on my dear father that I thought they caused his
death. I began to feel there weren't any real Christians left in the world. God
had to bring me off here into trouble again to find out how good people are.
He sent you—and Nurse Wright—to help me, and now today the most wonderful thing has happened! I've had a letter from an utter stranger, asking me
to come and visit. I want you to read it, please."

While Courtland read Mother Marshall's letter Bonnie studied him. Truly he
was a good sight. No girl in her senses could look a man like that over and not
know he was a fine one. But Bonnie had no romantic thoughts. Life had dealt
too harshly with her for her to have any illusions left. She had no idea of her
own charms or any thought of making much of the situation. That was why
Gila's insinuations had cut so deep.

"She's a peach, isn't she?" he said, handing the letter back. "How soon does
the doctor think you can travel?"

"Oh, I couldn't possibly *go*," said the girl, lapsing into sadness. "But I think it was lovely of her."

"Go? Of course you must go!" cried Courtland, springing to his feet, as if he'd been accustomed to managing this girl's affairs for years. "Why, Mother Marshall would be just brokenhearted if you didn't!"

"Mother Marshall!" exclaimed Bonnie, sitting up from her pillows in astonishment. "You know her?"

Courtland stopped suddenly in his excited march across the room and laughed ruefully. "Well, I've let the cat out of the bag, haven't I? Yes, I know her. I told her about you. And I had a letter from her two days ago, saying she was crazy to have you come. Why, she's just counting the minutes till she gets your telegram! You *haven't* sent her word you aren't coming, have you?"

"Not yet," said Bonnie. "I was going to ask you the best way to do. I have to send back that money and the mileage. Don't you think it would do to write? It costs a great deal to telegraph and sounds so abrupt when one has had such a royal invitation. It was lovely of her, but of course I couldn't be under obligation like that to entire strangers."

The stiffness in Bonnie's last words and a cool withdrawal in her eyes brought Courtland to his senses and made him remember Gila's insinuations.

"Look here," he said, calming down and taking his chair again. "You don't understand, and I guess I ought to explain. In the first place get it out of your head that I'm acting fresh or anything like that. I'm only a kind of big brother that happened along two or three times when you needed somebody—a—a kind of Christ-friend, if you want to call it that," he added, snatching at the minister's phrase. "You believe He sends help when it's needed, don't you?"

Bonnie nodded.

"Well, I hadn't an idea in the world of interfering with your affairs at all. But when I heard you needed rest, I wished I had a mother of my own or an aunt or someone who'd know what to advise. Then all of a sudden I thought I'd just put the case up to Mother Marshall. This is the result. Now wait till I tell you what Mother Marshall has been through, and then if you don't decide God sent that invitation I've nothing else to say."

Courtland had a reputation at college for eloquence. In rushing season his frat always counted on him to bowl over the doubtful and difficult fellows, and he never failed. Neither did he fail now, although he found Bonnie difficult enough. But he had her eyes full of tears of sympathy before he was through with the story of Stephen.

"Oh, I would love to see her and put my arms around her and try to comfort her!" she exclaimed. "I know how she must feel. But I really couldn't use a stranger's money, and I couldn't go away with all this debt, the funeral and everything!"

Then he set out to plan for her. He read Mother Marshall's letter over again and asked what things she'd need if she should go. He listed the things she'd like to sell and promised to look after them.

"Suppose you just leave that to me," he said. "I can probably get enough out of your furniture to pay all the bills, so you won't leave any behind. Then if I were you I'd use the check they've sent for your expenses and trust to getting a position in that neighborhood when you're strong enough. There're always openings in the West."

"Do you really think I could do that?" asked Bonnie, her eyes bright. "I'm a good stenographer. I've had a fine musical education, and I could teach a number of other things."

"Oh, sure! You'd get more positions than you could fill at once!" he declared joyously. Somehow it gave him great pleasure to be succeeding so well.

"Then I could pay them back soon."

"Sure! You could pay back in no time after you got strong. That would be a cinch! It might even be that you could help Mother Marshall about something in the house pretty soon. And I'm sure you'll find she needs you. Now suppose we write up that telegram. There's no need to keep the dear lady waiting any longer."

"He thinks I should go," said Bonnie to the nurse, who had just returned.

"Didn't I tell you so, dear?" asked the nurse.

"How soon would the doctor let her travel?" asked Courtland.

"Why, I'll go ask him. You want to put it in your message, don't you?"

"She's a dear!" said Bonnie, with a tender look after her.

"*Isn't* she a peach!" seconded Courtland.

The nurse was back almost at once, reporting that Bonnie might travel by the middle of the week if all went well.

"But could I get ready so soon?" asked the girl, a shade of trouble coming into her eyes. "I must go back and pack up my things and clean the room."

Courtland and the nurse exchanged meaningful glances.

"Now look here!" began Courtland with an engaging smile. "Why couldn't the nurse and I do all that's necessary? How about tomorrow afternoon? Could you get off awhile, Miss Wright? I don't have any basketball practice till Tuesday, and I could get off right after dinner. Miss Brentwood, you could tell the nurse just what you want done with your things, and I'll warrant she and I have sense enough to pack up one little room."

After some persuasion Bonnie half consented, and then they attended to the telegram.

Your wonderful invitation accepted with deep gratitude. Will start as soon as able. Probably Wednesday night. Will write.

Rose Bonner Brentwood

Bonnie had been divided between saving words and showing her appreciation of the kindness.

But the strangest thing of all was that, in his eagerness, the paper Courtland fumbled out from his pocket to write on was Gila Dare's unopened letter, reeking with violets. He frowned as he realized it and stuffed it back in his pocket again.

Courtland enjoyed sending that telegram. He enjoyed it so much that he sent another along with it on his own account.

Three cheers for the best mother in the United States! She's coming, and you should see her eyes shine!

On his way back to the university he remembered Gila's letter.

Chapter 18

The very first line translated Courtland into another world from the one he'd been living in during the past three days. Its perfumed breath struck harshly on his soul.

My dear Courtland,

I'm writing to report on the case of the poor girl you asked me to help. I was very anxious to please you and did my best. But you remember I warned you that persons of that sort were likely to be most ungrateful—indeed, quite impossible sometimes. And so, perhaps, you'll be somewhat prepared for the disappointing report I have to give.

I went to the hospital this afternoon, putting off several engagements to do so. I was quite surprised to find the girl in a private room, but of course your kindness made that possible for her, which makes her ingratitude even more unpardonable.

I took with me several of my own pretty dresses, some of them scarcely worn at all, for I know girls of that sort care more for clothes than anything else. But I found her sullen and disagreeable. She wouldn't look at the things I'd brought, although I suggested several ways in which I intended to help her and make it possible for her to have a few friends of her own class who would make her forget her troubles. She just lay and stared at me and said, quite impertinently, that she didn't remember ever meeting me. And when I mentioned your name she denied ever seeing you. She even dared to ask me to leave the room. And the nurse was most insulting.

But don't worry about it in the least, for Papa has promised to have the nurse removed at once from her position and blacklisted so she can't ever get another place in a decent hospital.

I'm afraid you'll be disappointed in your protégé, and I'm awfully sorry, for I would have enjoyed doing her good. But you see how impossible it was.

You're not to feel put out that I was treated that way, for I really enjoyed doing something for you; and you know it's good for one to suffer sometimes. I'll be delighted to go slumming for you anytime again, and please don't mind asking me. It's much better for me to look after any girls that need help than it is for you, because girls of that sort are so likely to impose upon a young man's sympathies.

My cousin has been telling me how you've been looking after some of the work of a student who is majoring in sociology, so I understand why you took this girl up. I hope you'll let me help. Suppose you run over this evening and we can talk it over. I'm giving up two whole engagements to stay home for you, so I hope you'll properly appreciate it, and if anything hinders your coming, would you mind calling up and letting me know?

Hoping to see you this evening,

Your true friend and fellow worker,
Gila Dare

The letter struck a false note in the harmony of the day. It annoyed Courtland beyond expression that he'd made such a blunder as to send Gila after Bonnie. He couldn't understand why Gila hadn't had better discernment than to think Bonnie an object of charity. His indignation was still burning over the trouble and danger her action brought to Bonnie. Yet he hated to have his opinion of Gila shaken. He'd arranged it in his mind that she was a sweet and lovely girl, one in every way similar to Solveig the innocent, and he didn't care to change it. He tried to remember Gila's conventional upbringing and realize she couldn't conceive of a girl out of her own social circle other than as a menial. The vision of her loveliness in rose and silver, with her prayer book in her kerchief, was still dimly forcing him to be at least polite and accept her letter of apology for her failure, as he could only suppose it was sincerely meant.

Then all at once a new fact dawned on him. The invitation had been for Saturday evening! This was Sunday evening! And now what must he do? He might call her up and apologize, but what could he say? Bill Ward might have told her by this time he knew the letter had been received. A blunt confession that he'd forgotten to read it might offend, yet what else could he do? It was most annoying.

He went to the telephone as soon as he reached the college. The fellows had already gone down to the evening meal. He could hear the clink of china and silver in the distant dining room. It was a good time to phone.

A moment, and Gila's cool contralto answered: "*Hello-oo!*" Something about the way Gila said that word conveyed a lot of things, instantly putting the caller at a distance but placing the lady on a pedestal before which it became desirable to bow.

"This is Paul Courtland."

"Oh! Mr. Courtland!" Her voice was freezing.

But Courtland wasn't used to being frozen out. "I owe you an apology, Miss Dare," he said. He didn't care how blunt he sounded now. It always angered him to be frozen. "Your letter reached me as I was leaving here last evening on an important errand. I put it in my pocket, but I've been so occupied that it escaped my mind until now. I hope I didn't cause you much inconvenience."

"Oh, it really didn't *mattah* in the *least!*" answered Gila. Nothing could be colder or more distant than her voice, and yet there was something in it this time, a subtle lure, that exasperated. A teasing little something at his spirit demanded to be set right in her eyes—to have her the suppliant rather than him.

"I really am awfully ashamed," he said in a boyish, humble tone and then gasped at himself. What was there about Gila that always got a fellow's goat?

After that Gila had the conversation where she wanted it and finally told him sweetly he might come over this evening if he chose. She had other engagements, but she would break them all for him.

"Suppose you go to church with me this evening," he temporized. "I've found a minister I'd like you to hear. He's quite original!"

There was a distinct pause at the other end of the phone, while Gila's white teeth dug into her red underlip, and her pearly forehead drew the straight, black, pencilled brows naughtily. Then she answered, in honeyed tones, "Why, that would be lovely! Perhaps I will. What time do we start?"

Something in her tone annoyed him, despite his satisfaction at having induced her to be friends again. Almost it sounded like a false note in the day again. He hadn't expected her to go. Now that she was going, he was sure he didn't want her.

"I warn you it's among common people in the lower part of the city," he said almost severely.

"Oh, that's all right!" she declared. "I'm sure it will be dandy! I certainly do enjoy new experiences!"

He hung up the phone with far greater misgivings than when he asked her to call on Bonnie.

Bill Ward was called out of the dining room to the telephone almost as soon as Courtland came down to the table.

It was Gila on the phone. "Is that you, Bill? Well, this is Gila. Say, what in the name of peace have you let me in for now? I hope to goodness Mama won't find it out. She'd have a pink fit! Say! Is this a joke or what? I believe you're putting one over on me!"

"Search me, Gila! I'm in the dark! Give me a line on it, and I'll tell you."

"Well, what do you think that crazy nut has pulled off now? Wants me to go to church with him! Of all things! And down in some old slum, too! If I get into a scrape you'll have to promise to help me out, or Mama'll never let me free from a chaperone again. And I had to make Art Guelpin and Turner Bailey sore, too, by telling them I was sick and they couldn't come and try those new dance steps tonight as I'd promised. If I get into the papers or anything I'll have a long score to settle with you."

"Oh, cut that out, Gila! You'll not get into any scrape with Court. He's all right. He's only nuts about religion just now and seems to be set on sampling all kinds of churches. Say! That's a good one, though, for you to go to church with him. I must tell the fellows. Keep it up, Gila, old girl! You'll pull the fat out of the fire yet. You're just the one to go along and counteract the pious line. You should worry about Art Guelpin and Turner Bailey! You can't keep either of them sore; they haven't got backbone enough to stay that way. If it's the same dump Court took Tennelly to this morning you'll get your money's worth. Nelly said it was a scream."

Bill Ward came back, grinning from ear to ear. Every few minutes during the rest of the meal he broke out in a broad grin and looked at Courtland, who was absorbed in his own thoughts. Then he would slap Tennelly on the shoulder and say, "Ho, boy! It's a rare one!" But it wasn't until Courtland had hurried away that Bill gave his information.

"Oh, Nelly!" he burst forth. "Court's going to take Gila to church! You don't suppose he'll take her to that dump where he led you this morning, do you? I can see her nose go up now. I thought I'd croak when she told me! Wait till you hear her call me up on the phone when she gets home! She'll give me the worst bawling out I ever had! And Aunt Nina would have apoplexy if she knew her darlin' pet was going into that part of town! Oh, boy! Set me on my feet, or I'll die laughing!"

Tennelly regarded Bill with solemn consternation. "Do you mean to tell me Court has asked your cousin to go to that camp-meeting hole where he took me this morning? Cut out the kidding and tell me straight! Well, then, Bill, it's serious, and we've got to do something! We can't have a fellow like Court spoiled for life. He's gone stale—that's what's the matter. He needs strenuous measures to pull him up."

"He sure does," said Bill, getting up from the couch where he'd been rolling in his mirth. "What can we do? What about his business ambitions? Couldn't we work him that way? Court's got a great head on him, you know. I thought Gila would do the business, but if he's rung in religion on her it's all up, I'm afraid. But business is a different thing. Not even Court could mix business and religion, for they won't fit together!"

"That's the trouble," said Tennelly. "If it gets out about Court he won't stand half a chance. I was thinking of my uncle Ramsey, out in Chicago. He has large financial interests in the West. He often wants promising men to take charge of some big thing, and it means a fine opening—big money and no end of social and political pull to get into one of the berths. He's promised me one when I finish college, and I was going to talk to him about Court. He's twice the man I am and just what uncle Ramsey wants. He's coming east next week and likely to stop over. I might see what I can do."

"That's just the thing, Nelly. Go to it, old man! Write your uncle a letter tonight. Nothing like giving a lot of dope beforehand."

"That's an idea. I will!"

Meanwhile Gila awaited Courtland's arrival, attired in blue velvet and ermine, with high-laced white kid boots and a hat that resembled a fresh, white setting-hen, tied down to her pert face with a veil whose large-meshed surface was broken by a single design, a large black butterfly anchored just across her dainty nose. A most astonishing costume in which to appear in the Reverend John Burns's unpretentious church crowded with the canaille of the city!

It was the first time Courtland felt that Gila was a little loud in her dress.

Chapter 19

Mother Marshall pulled herself up from the low hassock on which she'd been sitting to sew the carpet and trotted to the head of the stairs.

"Father! Oh, Father! It's all done! I just set the last stitch. You can bring your hammer and tacks. Better bring your rubbers, too. You'll need them when you stretch it."

Father hurried up so quickly that it was clear he had the hammer and rubbers all ready.

"You'll need a saucer to put the tacks in." She hustled away to get it. When she came back the carpet was spread out, and Father stood surveying the effect.

"Say, now, it looks real pretty, don't it?" he said, looking up at the walls and down at the floor.

"It certainly does! And I'm real glad the man made us take this plain pink paper. It didn't look like much to me when he first brought it out, I must confess. I'd set my heart on stripes with pink roses in it. But when he said 'felt,' why, that settled it because the magazine article said felt papers were the best for general wear and satisfaction. And when he brought out that roll with the cherry blossoms on it for a stripe around the top, I was happy down my spine. It looked so kind of bridelike and pretty, like our cherry orchard on a spring evening when the pink is in the sky. And that white molding between 'em is going to be real handy to hang the pictures on. The man gave me some little brass picture hooks. See—they fit right over the molding. Of course, there's only one picture, but she'll maybe have some of her own and like it all the better if the wall isn't cluttered. The magazine said have 'a few good pictures.' I mean to hang it up right now and see how it looks! There! Doesn't that look pretty against the pink? I wasn't sure about the white frame—it was so plain— but I like it. Those apple blossoms against that blue sky look real natural, don't they? You like it, don't you, Father?"

"Well, I should say I do," said Father, as he scuffed a corner of the carpet into place with his rubbered feet. "Say, this carpet is some thick, Mother, as I guess your fingers will testify after sewing all those long seams. 'Member how Stevie used to sit on the carpet ahead of your seams when he was a baby and laugh and clap his hands when you couldn't sew any further because he was in the way?"

"Yes, wasn't he the sweetest baby!" said Mother Marshall with a bright tear glinting suddenly down her cheek. "Why, Father, sometimes I can't make it seem true that he's done with this life and gone ahead of us into the next one. It won't be hard for us to die because he's there, and we won't have to think of leaving him behind to go through trials and things."

"Well, I guess he's pretty happy seeing you chirk up so, Mother. You know what he'd have thought of this! Why, he'd have rejoiced! He hated so to have you left alone all day. Don't you mind how he used to wish he had a sister? Say, Mother, you just stand on the corner there till I get this tack in straight. This edge is so tremenjus thick! I don't know as the tacks are long enough. What was you figuring to do with the bookshelves, put books in or leave 'em empty for her things?"

"Well, I thought about that, and I made out we'd better put in some books so it wouldn't look so empty. We can take them out again if she has a lot of her own."

"We could put in some of Steve's that he set such store by. There's that set of Scott, and then there's Dickens and those other fellows he wanted us to read evenings this winter. By the way, Mother, we ought to get at that! Perhaps she'll like to read aloud when she comes. That would about suit us. We're rather old to begin reading aloud; Steve's always read to us so long. I don't know but I'd buy a few new books, too. She's a girl, and you might find something written lately that she'd like. It wouldn't do any harm to get a few. You could ask the bookstore man what to pick out—say a shelf or two."

"Oh, I shouldn't need to do that!" said Mother, hurrying to get her magazine, which was never far away these last two or three days. "There's a whole long list here of books 'your young people will want to have in their library.' Wells and Shaw and Ibsen, and a lot of others I never heard of; but these first three I remembered because Stephen spoke of them in one of his first letters about college. Don't you know he was studying a course with those men's books in it? He said he didn't know as he was always going to agree with all they said, but they were big, broad men and had some fine thoughts. He thought sometimes they didn't just have the inner light about God and the Bible and all, but they were the kind of men who were getting there, striving after truth, and would likely find it and hand it out to the world again when they got it—like the wise men hunting everywhere for a Savior. Don't you remember, Father?"

"I remember!" Father tried to speak cheerily, but his breath ended in a sigh, for the carpet was heavy. Mother looked at him sharply and changed the subject. It wasn't always easy to keep Father cheerful about Stephen's going.

"You don't suppose we could get those curtains up tonight, too, do you?"

"Why, I reckon!" said Father, stopping for a puff of breath and looking up to the white woodwork at the top of the windows. "You got 'em all ready to put up, all sewed and everything? Why, I reckon I could put up those rods after I get across this end, and then you could slip the curtains on while I'm doing the rest. You don't want to get too tired, Mother. You know you been sewing a long time today."

"Oh, I'm not tired! I'm just childish enough to want to see how it's all going to look. Say, Father, that wasn't the telephone ringing, was it? You don't think we might get a telegram yet tonight?"

"Not scarcely!" said Father, with his mouth full of tacks. "It's been bad weather, and like as not your letter got storm-stayed a day or so. You mustn't count on hearing 'fore Monday, I guess."

They both knew the letter should have reached the hospital where Bonnie Brentwood was supposed to be about six o'clock that evening, for so they'd calculated the time between Stephen's letters to a nicety. But each was engaged in trying to keep the other from getting anxious about the telegram that didn't come. It was now half past eight by the kitchen clock, and both of them were as nervous as fleas listening for that telephone to ring that would decide whether the pretty pink room was to have an occupant or not.

"These white madras curtains look like there's been a frost on a cobweb, don't they?" said Mother Marshall, holding up a pair arranged on the brass rod ready to hang. "And just see how pretty this pink stuff looks against it. I declare it reminds me of the sunset light on the snow in the orchard out the kitchen window evenings when I was watching for Steve to come home from school. Say, Father, don't you think those bookshelves look cozy on each side of the bay window? And wasn't it clever of Jed Lewis to think of putting hinges to the covers on the window seat? She can keep lots of things in there! Wait till I get those two pink silk cushions you made me buy. My! Father, but you and I are getting extravagant in our old age! And all for a girl who may never even answer our letter!"

She tried to disguise a sob at the end of her words, but Father caught it and flew to the rescue.

"There now, Mother!" he said, pulling himself up from the carpet, hammer in hand, and putting his arms around her. "Don't you go fretting! Like as not she was asleep when the letter got there, and they wouldn't wake her up, or mebbe it would be too much excitement for her at night that way. And then again if the mail train was late it wouldn't get into the night deliv'ry. You know that happened once for Steve, and he was real worried about us. Then they might not have deliv'ry at the hospital on Sunday, and she couldn't *get* it till Monday morning. See? And there's another thing you got to calc'late on, too. She might be too sick yet to read a letter or think what to say to it. So just be patient, Mother. We'll have that much more time to fix things; for, so to speak, now we don't have any limitations on what we think she is. We can plan for her like she was perfect. When we get her telegram we'll get some idea and begin to know the real girl, but now we've just got our own notion of her."

"Why, of course!" choked Mother, smiling. "I'm just afraid, Seth, that I'm getting set on her coming, and that isn't right at all, because she mightn't be coming."

"Well, and then again she might. It doesn't matter. We'll have this room fixed up company fine, and if she don't come we'll just come here and camp for a week, you and me, and pretend we're out visiting. How would that do? Say, it's real pretty here, like spring in the orchard, ain't it, Mother? Well, now, you figure out what you're going to have for bureau fixings, and I'll get back to my tacking. I want to get done tonight and get that pretty white furniture moved in. You're sure the enamel is dry on that bed? That was the last piece Jed worked on. I think he made a pretty good job of it, for such quick work.

Don't you? Got a clean counterpane and one of your pink and white patchwo
quilts for in here, haven't you, and a posy pincushion? My, but I'd like to kn
what she says when she sees it first!"

And so the two old dears jollied each other along till far past their bedtir
When at last they lay quiet for the night Mother raised up in the moonli,
flooding her side of the room and looked cautiously over to the other side
the bed.

"Father! You awake yet?"

A sleepy yes came forth.

"What'll we do about going to church tomorrow? The telegram might co
while we're gone, and then we'd never know what she answered."

"Oh, they'd call up again until they got us. And anyhow we'd call them
when we got back and ask if any message had come yet."

"Oh! Would we?" She lay down with a sigh of relief, marveling, as she of
did, at the superior knowledge in technical details men often displayed.
course in the vital things of life women had to be on hand to make things mo
smoothly. But a little thing like that now, that needed a bit of what seem
almost superfluous information, a man always knew—and you wondered h
he knew, because nobody ever seemed to have taught him. So at last Mot
Marshall slept.

Anxious inquiry of the telephone after church brought forth no telegra
Dinner was a strained and artificial affair, preceded by a wistful but submiss
blessing on the meal. Then the couple settled down in their comfortable cha
one on each side of the telephone, and tried to read; but somehow the ho
dragged slowly by.

"There's that pair of Grandmother Marshall's andirons up in the attic!" s
Mother Marshall, looking up suddenly over the top of the *Sunday School Tin*

"I'll bring them down first thing in the morning!" said Father, with his f
ger on a promise in the psalms. Then there was silence for sometime.

Mother Marshall's eyes suddenly fell on an article headed "My Class of Boy

"Seth!" she said, with a light in her eyes. "You don't suppose she'd be w
ing to take Stephen's class of boys in Sunday school when she gets bette
can't bear to see them stay away, and Deacon Grigsby admits he don't kn
how to manage them."

"Why, sure!" said Father. "She'll take it, I've no doubt. She's that kind,
think. And if she isn't now, Mother, she will be after she's been with you awhil

"Oh, now, Father!" said Mother, turning pink with pleasure. "Come, let's
up and see how the room looks at sunset!"

So arm in arm they climbed the front stairs and stood looking about on the g
rified rosy background with its wilderness of cherry bloom about the frieze. S
a transformation of the dingy old room in such a little time! Arm in arm tl
went over to the window seat and sat leaning stiffly against the two pink
cushions and looking out across the rosy sunset snow in the orchard, think
wistfully of the boy that used to come whistling up that way and would ne

come to them so again. Then, just as Father drew a sigh and a tear crept out on Mother's cheek (the side next to the window), a long-hoped-for, unaccustomed sound burst out downstairs. The telephone was ringing! It was Sunday evening at sunset, and the telephone was ringing!

They both sprang to their feet and clutched each other for a moment.

"I'll go, Mother," said Father in an agitated voice. "You sit right here and rest till I get back."

"No! I'll go, too!" declared Mother, trotting after him. "You might miss something, and we should write it down!"

In breathless silence they listened for the magic words, Mother leaning close to catch them and trying to scratch them down on a corner of the telephone book with a stump of a pencil she kept for writing recipes.

"Your wonderful invitation accepted with deep gratitude."

"What's that, Father? Make him say it over again!" cried Mother, scribbling away. " 'Your wonderful invitation (oh, she liked it, then!) accepted'—she's coming, Father!"

"Will start as soon as able."

("Then she's really coming!")

"Probably Wednesday night."

("Then I'll have time to get some pink velvet and make a cushion for the little rocker. They do have pink velvet, I'm sure!")

"Will write."

("Then we'll know what she's like if she writes!")

Mother Marshall's happy thoughts were in a tumult, but she had her head about her yet.

"Now make him say it all over from the beginning, Father, and see if we've got it right. You speak the words out as he says 'em, and I'll watch the writing."

And so at last the message was verified and the receiver hung up. They read the message over together and looked at each other with glad eyes.

"Now let's pray, Rachel!" said Father, with a solemn, shaken voice of joy. And the two lonely old people knelt down by the little table on which the telephone stood and gave thanks to God for the child He was about to send to their empty home.

"Now," said Father Marshall, when they'd risen, "I guess we better get a bite to eat. Seems like a long time since dinner. Any of that cold chicken left, Mother? And a few doughnuts and milk? And say, Mother—we better get the chores done up and get to bed early. I don't think you slept much last night, and we've got to get up early. There's a whole lot to do before she comes. We need to chirk up the rest of the house a bit. Somehow we've let things get down since Stephen went away."

As she placed her platter of cold chicken on the table, Mother asked, "How soon do you s'pose she'll write? I'm just aching to get that letter!"

Chapter 20

Gila had counted on an easy victory that evening. She had furnished for the occasion her keenest wit, her sweetest laughter, her finest derision and her most sparkling sarcasm. As she and her escort joined the motley throng who were patiently making their way into the packed doorway she brought them forth eagerly.

Even while they took their turn among the crowd she began to make sharp little remarks about the company they were keeping, drawing her velvet robes about her.

Courtland, standing head and shoulders above her, his fine profile outlined against the brightness of the lighted doorway, was looking about with keen interest on the faces of the people and wondering why they'd come. Were they searching for the Presence? Had they, too, felt it within those dingy walls? He glanced down at Gila with a hope that she, too, might see and understand tonight. What friends they might be—how they might talk things over together—if only she'd understand!

He wished she'd had better sense than to array herself in such startling garments. He could see the curious glances turned her way—glances that showed she was misunderstood. He didn't like it and reached down a protecting hand and took her arm, speaking to her gravely, just to show the bold fellows behind her that she was under capable escort. He didn't hear her retorts at the expense of their fellow worshippers. He was annoyed and trying by his serious mien to shelter her.

The singing was already going on as they entered—plain old gospel songs, sung as badly, though with even more fervor, than in the morning. Courtland accepted the tattered hymnbook and put Gila into the seat the usher indicated. He was in the spirit of the gathering and anxious only to feel once more what had been about him in the morning. But Gila was so amused with her surroundings that she could scarcely pay attention to where she was to sit and almost tripped over the end of the pew. She openly stared and laughed at the people around her, as though that was what Courtland had brought her there for, and kept nudging him and calling his attention to some grotesque figure.

Courtland was singing, joining his fine tenor with the curious assembly and enjoying it. Gila recalled him each time from a realm of the spirit, and he would give attention to what she said, bending his ear to listen, then look seriously at the person indicated, try to appreciate her amusement with a nod and absent smile, and go on singing again. He was so absorbed in the gathering that her talk scarcely penetrated to his real soul.

If he had been trying to baffle Gila he could not have used a more effective method, for the point of her jokes seemed blunted. She turned her eyes at last to her escort and studied him, astonishment and chagrin in her countenance.

Gradually both gave way to a kind of admiration and curiosity. One couldn't look at Courtland and not admire. The strength in his handsome young face and figure was always noticeable among a company anywhere, and here among these foreigners and wayfarers it was especially so. She was conscious of a thrill in his presence that was new to her. Usually her attitude was to make others thrill at her presence. No man before had caught her fancy and held it like this rare one. What secret lay behind his strength that made him resist the arts that had lured other victims?

She watched him while he bowed his head in prayer and noted how his rich, close-cut hair waved and crept about his temples; she noted the curve of his chin and the curl of his lashes on his cheek. More and more she coveted him. She must set herself to find and break this other power that had him in its clutches. She recognized she might not care for him after the other power was broken and might have to toss him aside after he was fully hers. But what of that? Hadn't she thus tossed many a hapless soul that had come like a moth to singe his wings in her candle flame, then laughed at him as he lay writhing in pain—and tossed after him, torn and trampled, his own ideals of womanhood, too—so that all other women might henceforth be blighted in his eyes. Ah! What of that, so that unquenchable flame in her soul, that restlessly pursued and conquered and cast aside, might be satisfied? Wasn't that what women were made for, to conquer men and toss them away? If they didn't, wouldn't men conquer them and toss them away? She was only fulfilling her woman-hood as she'd been taught to look upon it.

But something puzzling about Courtland interested her deeply. She thought it might be half his charm. He seemed to *want* to be good, to resist evil. Most of the other men she knew had been ready to fall as lightly with as little earnestness as she into whatever doubtful paths her dainty feet had led. Many of them would have led further than she would go, for she had her own limi-tations and conventions, strange as it may seem.

So Gila sat and meditated, with a thrill in the thought of a new experience; for, young as she was, the pleasures of her existence had palled upon her many times.

Suddenly her ear was caught by the sermon. The ugly little man in the pul-pit, with the strange eyes that seemed to look through you, was telling a story of a garden, with One calling and a pair of naked souls guilty and in fear before Him. It was as if she were one of them! What right had he to flaunt such truths before a congregation?

She wasn't familiar enough with Bible truths to know where he got the story. It didn't seem to be a story. It was just her Eden where she walked and ate what fruit she desired every day without thinking of any command that might have been issued. She recognized no commands. What right had God to command her? The serpent had whispered early to her, "Thou shalt not surely die." Her only question was whether the fruit was pleasant to the eyes and a tree desired to make one wise. Till now no Lord God had been walking in her garden in the cool of the day. Only her mother, and she was easy to evade. She had never been afraid or felt her soul naked till now, with the ugly man's bright brown eyes upon her and his words shivering through her like winds about the unprotected. Hideous things she'd forgotten came into view and confronted her, and somewhere in the room One seemed to call her to account. She looked back to the speaker, her delicate brows drawn darkly, her blue-black eyes fierce, her whole face and attitude a challenge to the sermon. Courtland, absorbed as he was in what the speaker had to say and welcoming the message into his soul, became aware of the tense figure by his side and, looking down, was pleased she'd forgotten her nonsense and was listening—and somehow missed the defiance in her attitude.

Gila didn't smile when the service was over. She went out haughtily, impatiently, looking about on the throng with contempt. When Courtland asked her if she'd like to stop a minute and meet the preacher she pulled up her chin and uttered a "No, indeed!" with no doubt left for lingering.

Out in the street, away from the crowd somewhat, she suddenly stopped and stamped her foot. "I think that man is perfectly *disgusting!* He should be *arrested!* I don't know why such a man is allowed at large!"

She was almost panting in her anger, as if he'd put her to shame before an assembly.

Courtland turned toward her.

"He's outrageous!" she went on. "He has no *right!* I *hate* him!"

Courtland watched her in amazement. "You can't mean the minister!"

"Minister! He's no minister!" declared Gila. "He's a fanatic! One of the worst kind. He's a fake! He's uncanny! The idea of talking about God that way as if He's always around everywhere! I think it's *awful!* I would think he'd have everybody in hysterics!"

Gila's voice sounded as if she were almost there herself. She strode by his side with a vindictive click of her high-heeled boots and a prance of her elaborate person that showed she was bristling with wrath.

But Courtland's voice was sad with disappointment. "Then you didn't feel it! I was hoping you did."

"Feel what?" she asked sharply. "I felt something, yes. What did you mean?" Her voice softened, and she drew near him and slipped her hand again within his arm. There was an eagerness in her voice that Courtland wholly misinterpreted.

"Feel the Presence!" he said gently, reverently, as if it were a magic word, a password to a mutual understanding.

"Presence?" she asked. "Yes, I felt a presence, but what presence did you mean?" Her voice was soft with meaning.

"The presence of God."

She turned upon him and jerked her arm away. "The presence of God in that place?" she demanded. "No! *Never!* How dreadful! That is irreverent!"

"Irreverent?"

"Yes! Very irreverent!" said Gila piously. "And a man like that is profaning holy things. If you care for religious things you should come to my church, where everything is quiet and orderly and decent people are there. Why, those people looked as if they might all be thieves and murderers! And outlandish! My soul! Some of their things must have come out of the ark! Did you see that girl with the tight green skirt? Imagine! A whole year and a half out of date! I think it is immodest to wear things when they get out of style like that. And the idea of that man talking to those people about God coming down to live with them! That's the limit. As if God cared anything about people like that! That man ought to be arrested, putting notions into poor people's heads. It's just such talk as that that makes riots and things. My father says so. Getting common, stupid people all worked up about things they can't understand. It's wicked!"

Gila raved all the way home. Courtland, for the most part, let her talk and was silent.

Seated finally in the library, for he couldn't go away yet, somehow, he had something he must ask her. He turned to her, calling her for the first time by her name.

"But, Gila, you said you felt a Presence. What did you mean?"

Gila was silent. The tumult in her face subsided.

She dropped her lashes and played with the frill on the wrist of the long chiffon sleeve of her blouse. Her eyes beneath their concealing lashes kindled. Her mouth grew sweet and sensitive; her whole attitude became shy and alluring. She sat before the fire, casting now and then a wide, shy, innocent look up, her face half turned away.

"Does she look adown her apron!" floated the words through his brain. Ah! Here at last was the Gila he'd been seeking! The Gila who would understand!

"Tell me, Gila!" he said in an eager, low appeal.

She stirred, drooped a little more toward him, her face turned away till only the charming profile showed against the rich darkness of a crimson curtain. Now at last he was coming to it!

"It was—*you*—I meant!" she breathed softly.

He sat up. Her tone held subtle flattery. He couldn't fail to be stirred by it.

"Me!" he said almost sternly. "I don't understand!" But his voice was gentle. She looked so small and scared and "Solveig"-like.

"You meant *me!*" he said again. "Won't you please explain?"

Chapter 21

Courtland went back to college that night in a tender, exalted mood. He thought he was in love with Gila.

That had been a wonderful scene before the fire, with the soft, hidden yellow lights above and Gila with her delicate, fervid little face, dark eyes and shy looks. She'd risked a tear upon her pearly cheek and another to hang upon her long lashes, and he'd had a curious desire to kiss them away; but something held him from it. Instead, he took his clean handkerchief, wiped them softly and thought Gila was shy and modest when she shrank from his touch.

He didn't take her in his arms. Something held him from that, too. He had a feeling she was too scared, and he mustn't lightly snatch her for himself. Instead, he put her gently in the big chair by his side, and they sat and talked together quietly. He didn't realize he'd talked the most. He didn't know what they talked about, only that her reluctant whispered confession somehow entered him into a close intimacy with her that pleased and half awed him. But when he tried to tell her of a wonderful experience he'd had she lifted up her hand and begged, "Please not tonight! Let's not think of anything but each other tonight!" And so he let it pass, knowing she was all wrought up.

He hadn't asked her to marry him or even told her he loved her. They had talked in quiet, wondering ways of feeling drawn to each other; at least *he* had talked, while Gila sat watching him with deep, dissatisfied eyes. She knew she couldn't win him with the arts that had won others. His was a deeper, stronger nature. She must bide her time and be coy. But her spirit chafed beneath delay, and dark passions lurked behind and brooded in her eyes.

Perhaps this was what held him in uncertainty. It was as if he waited permission from some unseen source to take what she was so evidently ready to give. He thought it was the sacredness in which he held her. Almost the sermon and the feeling of the Presence were out of mind as he went home. A phantom joy hovered now like a will-o'-the-wisp above his heart and danced, giving him a strange, inexplicable exhilaration. Was this love? Was he in love?

He flung himself down on Tennelly's couch when he got back to the dormitory. Bill Ward was deep in a book under the droplight, and Tennelly was supposed to be finishing a paper for the next day.

"Nelly, what is love?" asked Courtland suddenly, in the silence. "How do you know when you're in love?"

Tennelly dropped his fountain pen in his surprise and had to crawl under the table after it. He and Bill Ward exchanged one lightning glance of relief as he emerged from the table.

"Search me!" said Tennelly, as he sat down again. "Love's an illusion, they say. I never tried it, so I don't know."

Silence again filled Tennelly's room. Presently Courtland got up and said good night. In his own room he stood by the window, looking out into the moonlight. The preacher had said prayer was talking with the Lord face-to-face. That was a new idea. Courtland dropped on his knees and talked aloud to God as he had never opened his heart to a living creature before. If prayer was that, why, prayer was good!

Gila, studying her pretty, discontented face in the mirror, with all its masks laid aside, would have shivered in fear and been all the more uncertain of her success if she could have known that the man she would have for a lover was on his knees talking about her to God. Her naked soul in a garden all alone with the Lord God, and a man who was set to follow Him!

Tennelly looked up and raised his eyebrows as Courtland closed the door. "Guess you didn't need to write that letter!" offered Bill Ward. "I thought Gila would get in her work!"

"Well, it's written and mailed, so that doesn't do any good now. And, anyway, it's always good to have more than one string to your bow!" added Tennelly. Courtland in love! He wasn't sure he liked it. Courtland and Gila! What kind of girl was Gila? Was she good enough for Court? He must look into this.

"Say, Bill, why don't you introduce me to your cousin? It's about time I had a chance to judge for myself how things are getting on," growled Tennelly presently.

"Sure!" said Bill. "Good idea! Why didn't you mention it before? How about going now? It's only half past ten. Court didn't stay very late, did he? No, it isn't too late for Gila. She never goes to bed till midnight, not if there's something interesting going on. Wait. I'll call her up and see. I'm privileged anyway. Cousins can do anything. I'll tell her we're hungry."

So it came about that an hour after Gila sat in the firelight with Courtland and listened, puzzled, to his reverent talk of a soul-friendship, she ushered into the same room her cousin and Tennelly. She met Tennelly with a challenge in her eye.

Tennelly had one in his. Their glances lingered, sparred and lingered again, and each knew this was a notable meeting.

Tennelly was tall and strikingly handsome. He had those deep black eyes that hold a maiden's gaze and dare a devil. Yet behind his look was something strange, dashing, scholarly. Gila saw at once that he was distinguished in his way, and though her thoughts were strangely held by Courtland she couldn't let one like this go unchallenged. If Courtland didn't prove corrigible, why, good fish were still in the sea. It was well to have more than one hook baited. So she received Tennelly graciously, boldly, impressively, and in three minutes was talking with that daring intimacy young people of her style love to affect.

And Tennelly, fascinated by her charms, yet seeing through them and letting her know he saw through them, was fencing with her delightfully. He told himself it was his duty for Courtland's sake. Yet he was interested for his own sake and knew it. But he didn't like the idea of Court and this girl! They didn't fit. Court was too genuine. Too tenderhearted. Too idealistic about women. With him it was different. He knew women—understood this one at a glance. She was a peach in her way, but not the perfect little peach Court should have. She'd flirt all her life and break old Court's heart if he married her.

So he laughed and joked with Gila, answering her challenging glances with glances just as ardent, while Bill Ward sat and watched them both, chuckling to himself.

And Courtland, on his knees, talked with God!

The next morning Courtland awoke with an eagerness to see what life had in store for him. Was this the experience of love into which he was entering? He thought of Gila all in halos now. The questions and unpleasantnesses were forgotten. He told himself she'd one day see and understand the wonderful experience through which he was passing. He'd tell her as soon as possible. Not today, for he'd be busy, and she had engagements Tuesday evening and all day Wednesday.

He hadn't noticed the subtle withdrawing as she told him, the quick, furtive calculation in her glance. She knew how to make coming to her a privilege. Just because she'd let him think he saw a bit of her heart that night, she meant to hold him off. Not too long, for he was sufficiently bound to her to be safe from forgetting, but just long enough to whet his eagerness. She expected him to call and beg to see her sooner, when she might relent if he was humble enough.

And she hadn't misjudged him. He was looking forward to Thursday as a bright, particular goal, planning what he'd say to her, wondering if his heart would bound as it had when she looked at him Sunday night and if the strange sweetness that seemed about to settle upon him would last.

Before he left his room that morning he did something he'd never done before in college; he locked his door and knelt beside his bed to pray, with a strong, sweet sense of the Presence standing beside him and breathing power into his soul.

He didn't have much to ask for himself. He simply craved that Presence, and it had never seemed so close. As he unlocked his door and hurried down the hall to the dining room he marveled that a thing so sweet had been so long neglected from his life. Prayer! How he'd sneered at it! Yet it was a reasonable thing after all, now that he'd come to it believing.

Nurse Wright was on hand promptly at the appointed place. She was armed with a list of written instructions. They set to work at once, putting aside the things to be sold; folding and packing the scanty wardrobe and placing nearby the clothes and things that had belonged to little Aleck. One incident brought tears to their eyes. In moving out the trunk a large pasteboard box fell, and the contents dropped on the floor. The nurse stooped to pick up the things, some pieces of an old overcoat of fine, dark blue material, cut into small garments, basted, ready to be sewed, and a tissue paper pattern in a printed envelope marked "Boy's suit." Courtland lifted up the cover to put it on again, and there they saw, in a child's stiff printing, the inscription, "Aleck's new Sunday suit," and underneath in smaller letters, "Made out of Father's best overcoat."

"Poor little kid!" said Courtland. "He never got to wear it!"

"He's wearing something far better!" said the nurse. "And think what he's been spared. He'll never know the lack of a new suit again!"

Courtland looked at her thoughtfully. "You believe in the resurrection, don't you?"

"I certainly do! If I didn't I would get another job. I couldn't see lives go out the way I do and those left behind, suffering, and not go crazy if I didn't believe in the resurrection. You're a college student. I suppose you're beyond believing things. It isn't the fashion to believe in God and the Bible anymore, I understand, not if you're supposed to have any brains. But I thank God He's left me the resurrection. And when you face the loss of those you love you'll wish you believed in it, too."

"But I do," said Courtland quietly, making his second confession of faith. "I never thought much about it till lately. It goes along with a Christ, of course. There had to be a resurrection if there was a Christ!"

"Well, I certainly am glad there's one college student with some sense!" said the nurse, looking at him with admiration. "I guess you had a good mother."

"No," said Courtland, shaking his head. "I never knew my own mother. That'll be one of the things for me to look forward to in the resurrection. I was like all the rest of the fellows—thought I knew it all and didn't believe anything till something happened. I was in a fire, and one of the fellows died. And then, afterward—maybe you'll think I'm nuts when I tell you—Christ came and stood by me in the smoke and talked with me, and I knew Him! He's been with me ever since."

The nurse looked at him curiously, a strange light in her eyes. Then she turned suddenly and looked out the window over the gray roofs.

"No, I don't think you're nuts," she said brusquely. "I think you're the only sensible man I've met in a long time. It stands to reason if there is a Christ He'd come to people that way sometimes. I never had any vision or anything I know of, but I've always known in my heart there was a Christ and He was helping me. I couldn't answer their arguments, those smart young doctors and nurses who talked so much. But I always felt nobody could upset my belief, even if the whole world turned against Him, for I *knew* there was a Christ! I don't know *how* I know it, but I *know* it, and that's enough for me. I don't boast of being much of a Christian myself, but if I didn't know there was a Christ I couldn't stand the life I have to live or the disappointments I've had."

Tears were rolling down her cheeks, but her eyes were shining when she turned around.

"Say, I guess we're sort of relations, aren't we?" Courtland said, holding out his hand. "You've described my feelings exactly."

She took the offered hand and gripped it warmly. "I knew you must be different when you hunted for my patient so late at night that way," she said.

Courtland went out presently, bringing back a secondhand man with whom he made a quiet bargain that not even the nurse could hear, and the surplus furniture was carted away. It was not long before the little room was dismantled and empty.

They visited a department store together and purchased a small bag with traveling accessories in plain compact form, light enough for an invalid to carry. Courtland begged to be let in on the gift, but the nurse was firm.

"This is my picnic, young man," she said. "You're doing enough! You can't deny it. For pity's sake, wait till you know her better before you do anymore!"

"Do you think I'll ever know her any better?" asked Courtland, laughing.

"If you have any sense you will!" snapped the nurse and waved a grim but pleasant good-bye as she took the trolley back to the hospital.

Wednesday night Courtland was on hand with his car in plenty of time to take Bonnie and the nurse down to the station. He was almost startled at the girl's beauty as she walked slowly down the steps. Certain details of her outfit showed the nurse's hand: a soft white collar; a floating, sheltering veil, gathered up now about the black sailor hat; well-fitting gloves; shoes polished like new. All these things made a difference and set off the girl's lovely face in its white resignation to an almost unearthly beauty. He found himself wanting to turn back often and look again as he drove his car through the crowded evening streets. She looked so frail and sweet that he couldn't help thinking of Mother Marshall and how she'd feel when she saw her. Surely she couldn't help but take her to her heart! He felt a certain pride in her, as if she were his sister. He was half sorry she was going away. He'd like to know her better. The nurse's words "until you know her better" floated through his mind. What a strange thing for her to say! It wasn't in the least likely he'd ever see Bonnie again.

They left her in the sleeper, giving special instructions to the porter to look after her and surrounding her with magazines and fruit.

"She looks as if a breath might blow her away!" said Courtland, speaking out of a troubled thought, as he and the nurse stood on the platform watching the train leave. "Do you think she'll get through the journey all right?"

"Sure!" said the nurse, furtively wiping away a tear. "She's got lots of pep. She'll rally and get strong pretty soon. She's had a pretty tough time the last two years. Lost her mother, father, a sister and this little brother. Her father's heart was broken when he was asked to leave his church because he preached temperance too much. The martyrs in this world didn't all die in the Dark Ages! They're having them yet!"

"But she looks so ethereal!" continued Courtland. "I wish I'd thought to suggest that you go along. We could have trumped up some reason why you needed a vacation."

"Couldn't do it!" said the nurse, smiling and patting his arm. "I thought of it, but it wouldn't work. I have to be at the hospital tomorrow for an important operation. Nobody else in the hospital could very well take my place. Besides, she's sharp as a tack, and you needn't think she doesn't see through a lot of the things you've done for her. Mark my words—you'll hear from her someday! She means to know the truth about those bills and pay every cent back. But don't worry about her. She'll get through all right. She's got more nerve than any dozen girls I know, and she doesn't go alone through this world either. She's had a vision, too, or you would never see her wearing that calm face with all she has had to bear!"

"Did it ever seem strange to you that good people have so much trouble in this world?" said Courtland, voicing his old doubt.

"Well, now *why?* What's *trouble* going to be in the resurrection? We won't mind then what we passed through, and this world isn't forever, thank the Lord! If it's serving His plan any for me to get more than what seems my share of trouble, why, I'm willing. Aren't you? The trouble is that we can't see the plan, and so we go fretting because it doesn't fit our ideas. If it was our plan now we'd patiently bear everything, I suppose, to make it come out right. We aren't up high enough to get the whole view of the finished plan, so of course lots of things look like mistakes. But if we trust Him at all, we know they aren't. And sometime, I suppose, we'll see the whole, and then we'll understand why it was. But I never was one to do much fretting because I didn't understand. I always know what my job is, and that's enough. I'm content to trust the rest to God. It's a God-size job to run the universe, and I know I'm not equal to it."

Her simple logic calmed his restless thoughts, but he still felt a strange wistfulness in his heart about Bonnie. She looked so pale and resigned and sad! He wished she hadn't gone quite so far out of his life.

Meanwhile, out in the dark night Bonnie's train whirled along. And sometime during the long hours between midnight and dawn rushed the express that was bearing back to Courtland another menace to his peace of mind.

Chapter 22

Uncle Ramsey was large and imposing, with an effulgent complexion and a prosperous presence. He wore a double-jeweled ring on his arthritic finger and a scarab scarfpin. His eyes were keen and shifty; his teeth had acquired the habit of clutching his fat black cigar viciously while he snarled his loose lips about them in conversation. Uncle Ramsey never looked someone in the face when he was talking. He looked off into space, where he appeared to have the topic under discussion in visible form before him. He never took up with the conversation his host offered. He furnished the topics himself and pinned one down to them. It was of no use to start any subject unless it had been previously announced, because it never got further than the initiative. Uncle Ramsey always went on with whatever he had in mind. Tennelly knew this tendency and realized that in writing the letter he took the only way of bringing Courtland to his uncle's notice.

After an exceedingly good dinner at the frat house, where Tennelly didn't usually dine, and being reinforced by one of the aforesaid fat black cigars, Uncle Ramsey leaned back in Tennelly's leather chair.

"Now, Thomas!" he began.

Tennelly stirred uneasily. He despised that "Thomas." His full name was Llewellyn Thomas Tennelly. At home they called him "Lew." Nobody but Uncle Ramsey ever dared the hateful Thomas. He liked to air the fact that his nephew was named after him, the great Ramsey Thomas.

"Suppose you tell me about this man you have for me? What kind of looking man is he?"

Uncle Ramsey screwed up his eyes, looked to the middle distance where the subject should be and examined him critically.

"Has he—ah—*personality?* Personality is a great factor in success, you know."

Tennelly, in the brief space allowed him, declared his friend would pass this test.

"Well! And can he—ah!—*lead men?* Because that is a very important point. The man I want must be a leader."

"I think he is."

"Ah! And does he—?" on down through a long list of questions.

At last, after once more relighting his cigar, which had gone out frequently during the conversation, he turned to his nephew and fixed him sharply with a fat pale blue eye.

"Tell me the worst you know about him, Thomas! What are his faults?" he snapped and settled back to squint at his imaginary stage again.

"Why—I—why, I don't think he has any," declared Tennelly, shifting uneasily in his chair. He had a feeling Uncle Ramsey would get it out of him yet.

"Yes, I perceive he has! Out with it!" snapped the keen old bird, flinging his loose lips about restively.

"It's only that he's got a religious twist lately, uncle. I don't think it'll last. I really think he's getting over it!"

"Religion! Ah! Well, now that might not be so bad—not for my purpose, you know. Religion really gives a confidence sometimes. Religion! Ah! Not a bad trait. Let me see him, Thomas! Let me see him *at once!*"

Tennelly had said nothing to Courtland about the approaching uncle, and therefore it was a surprise when Tennelly knocked on his door and dragged him from his books to meet a Chicago uncle.

"He's come East looking for the right man to fill an important position. It's something along your line, I guess, so I spoke to him about you," whispered Tennelly, as they crossed the hall together.

Face-to-face they stood, the financier and the young senior, and studied each other for the fraction of a second. Courtland wasn't afraid of any man, and his natural attitude toward all men was challenge till he knew them. He stood straight and tall and looked Uncle Ramsey in the eye, critically, questioningly, courteously, but with no attempt to propitiate—and not the slightest apparent conception of the awesomeness of the occasion or the condescension of the august personage he was thus permitted to meet.

And Uncle Ramsey liked it. True, he tried to fix the young man much as a cook fixes a roast with a skewer, to be put over the fire; but Courtland didn't skew. He just sat down indifferently and looked the man over, smiled pleasantly now and then, and listened; but he didn't give an inch. Even when the marvelous proposition was made which might change the course of his future life and bring him glory, Courtland never flickered an eyelash.

"He took it as calmly as if I'd offered him toast with his tea when he already had bread and jam, the young whelp!" marveled Uncle Ramsey, after Courtland thanked him, promised to think it over and went back to his room. "He's got the personality all right! He'll do! But what's his idea in being so reluctant? Didn't the offer strike him as big enough, or what's the matter? I must say I don't like to wait. When I find a man I like to nail him. What's the idea, Thomas? Does he have something else up his sleeve?"

"Not that I know of," said Tennelly, looking troubled. "I guess he's just got to think it over. That's Court. He never steps into a position until he knows exactly what he thinks about it."

"M-m-m! Another good trait! You're sure it isn't anything else?"

"I don't know of anything unless some of his religious notions are standing in his way. I'm sure I can't make him out lately. He had a shock a few months ago—one of the fellows killed in a fire—and he can't seem to get over it."

"Oh, well, we'll fix him up all right," said Uncle Ramsey. "We'll just send him down to our model factory here in the city and let him see how things are run. Convince him he's doing good, and that'll settle him. All white marble, with vines over the place, and a big rest room and reading room for the hands, gymnasium on the roof, model restaurant, all up to date. Cost a lot of money, too, but it pays! When some whining idiot of a woman, without enough business of her own, goes blabbing down there in Washington about the 'conditions' in the factories and all that rot, we run a few senators up here for the day and show 'em that model factory. Oh, it pays in the long run. You take your man there, and you'll land him all right!

"By the way, there's a rat of a preacher around that factory I'd like to throttle! He's making all sorts of trouble, stirring up folks to ask for things. He's putting it in their heads to demand an eight-hour day and no telling how much more! He's undertaken to tell us how we should run our business. Tell us which doors we'll lock or leave unlocked, how often we'll let our hands sit down and what kind of machines we'll get! He's a regular little rat! Know him? His name's Burns. And he's got pull down there in Washington that's making us a lot of trouble, too! That's one thing I want this new man for. I want to train him to spy on that sort of interference and by and by do some lobbying. We must stop business like that. What time is it? I guess I better hunt out that little rat and give him a good scare."

Uncle Ramsey departed to "rat-hunt," and Tennelly repaired to Courtland's room. He sat down and began to tell what a wonderful opportunity this was and how unprecedented in Uncle Ramsey to offer such a thing to a young man still in college. It showed how he was taken with Courtland. It was most flattering.

Courtland admitted it was and that he was grateful to his friend for mentioning his name. He said it looked good—like the kind of thing he'd hoped would turn up when he finished college, but he couldn't decide it immediately.

Tennelly urged that Uncle Ramsey was insistent; his business was urgent, and he must know one way or the other immediately. He tried to give Courtland an adequate idea of Uncle Ramsey's greatness and the audacity of anybody, especially a college upstart, keeping him waiting. But Courtland only shook his head and said he couldn't give his answer at once. If that was the condition of the offer he'd have to let it pass.

Tennelly talked and talked but finally went back to his room baffled. He couldn't understand what was the matter with Courtland.

When Uncle Ramsey returned from a fruitless search for the "rat," he was enraged to find Courtland wasn't awaiting his coming in trembling eagerness to accept his munificent offer.

Another personal interview that evening brought nothing more satisfactory than a promise to look into the matter carefully and to have another talk the next evening. Uncle Ramsey raged and swore. He blamed the rat of a preacher and declared he must leave for Boston that evening; but he finally sent a telegram instead and decided to remain until the next night. He'd intended to look after matters in the city on his return, and of course he could do it now instead. He felt it important to land the young man before he could think too much. Moreover, he was piqued that a youngster like that would consider turning down a job like the one he was offering him.

If Courtland had tried to explain to Tennelly and his uncle why this offer, which would have delighted him three months earlier, was hanging in the balance of his mind, they would scarcely have understood. He would have to tell them of the Presence by his side, which was very real to him as he stood in Tennelly's room listening to Uncle Ramsey that afternoon and which had hovered by him since, close, strong, with that pervading, commanding nearness that demanded his utmost attention. He would have to tell them he was under orders now, being led, and that every step was new and untried; he must look into the face of his Companion and Guide and find out if this was the way he was to go.

Something somewhere was holding him back. He didn't know why or for how long. He simply couldn't make that decision tonight. He must await permission before moving.

Possibly the trip to the factory the next day, which he promised to take, might shed some light on the matter. Possibly he'd find counsel somewhere. But where? He thought of Gila. He took out a lovely photograph she gave him before he left her Sunday night—a charming, airy, idealistic thing that had lain innocently open on the library table where "someone" had left it earlier in the day. He stood it up on his desk and studied the spirited will-o'-the-wisp face. Then he turned away sadly and shook his head. She wouldn't understand because she hadn't seen for herself.

Tennelly and his uncle went downtown in the morning and took lunch together. Courtland was to meet them at the factory at three o'clock, but somehow he missed them. Perhaps it was intention. He went early. He wanted to see things for himself and went alone first. Afterward he could go the rounds to satisfy Mr. Thomas, but first he would see it alone.

Then, after all, it was the Reverend John Burns who met him at the door and took him through the factory, bent on seeing some parishioner on an errand of love. And he had that strange sense of the Presence having been there before them, walking about among the machinery, looking at the tired face of one, sorrowing over the wrinkles in another forehead, pitying the weary hands that toiled, blessing the faithful! It reminded him of the morgue. For a minute he thought that if the Presence was here in this peculiar sense, then, of course, it was an indication he was needed here to work for these people, as Uncle Ramsey had tried with strange worldly wisdom to make him understand. But then, suddenly, he glimpsed the minister's face, white under its freckles, with a righteous wrath as he fixed his gaze sternly on the door at the end of the long room. He looked up quickly to hear the click of a key in a lock as the foreman passed from one room to another.

He glanced at the minister, and their eyes met.

"They lock them in here like sheep in a pen. If a fire broke out they'd all die!" said the minister under his breath.

"You don't say!" said Courtland, startled. It was his first view of conditions like this. He looked about with eyes alive to things he hadn't seen before. "But

I thought this was a model factory. Isn't it fireproof?"

"Somewhat so, on the *outside!* It's a whited sepulcher, that's what it is. Beautiful marble and vines; beautiful rest room and library—for the *visitors* to rest and read in; beautiful restaurant where the girls must buy their meals at the company's prices or go without; beautiful outside everywhere—but it's *rotten* all through!

"Look at the width of that staircase! That's the one the employees use. The visitors see only the broad way you came up. Look at those machines—all painted and gilded! They're old models and twice as heavy to work as the new ones, but we can't get them to make changes. Look at those seats, put there to impress the visitors! The fact is not one of the hands dare use them, except a minute now and then when the foreman happens to leave the room. They know they'll get docked in their pay if they're caught sitting down at their work. And yet it's always flaunted before the visitors that the workmen can sit down when they like. So they can, but they can go home without a pay envelope if they do, when Saturday night comes.

"Oh, there's enough here to make one's blood boil! You're interested in these things? I wish you'd let me tell you more sometime. And the long hours, the stifling air in some rooms and the little children working in spite of the law! I wish men like you would come down here and help clean this section out and make conditions different. Why don't you come and help me?"

The minister laid his hand on Courtland's arm, and instantly it seemed as if the Presence stood beside him and said, "Here! This is your work!"

With great conviction in his heart Courtland turned and followed Burns down the broad marble stairs out to the office, where he left word for Tennelly and his uncle that he'd been there and had to go but would see them again that evening. Then he headed down the street to Burns's common boardinghouse, where they sat down and talked the rest of the afternoon. Burns opened Courtland's eyes to many things he hadn't known were in the world. It was as if he laid his hands upon him and said, as in days of old, "Brother Saul, receive thy sight!"

When Courtland returned to the university his decision was made. He felt he was under orders, and the Presence was not leading him into any such commission as Uncle Ramsey proposed. His only regret was that Tennelly wouldn't understand. Dear old Tennelly, who had tried to do his best for him!

The denouement began in Tennelly's room after supper, when Courtland courteously and firmly thanked Uncle Ramsey but *declined* the offer.

Uncle Ramsey grew apoplectic in the face and glared at the young man, finally bringing out an explosive "What! You *decline?*"

Uncle Ramsey spluttered and swore. He tore up and down the small confines of the room like an angry bull, bellowing forth anathemas and arguments in a confused jumble. He enlarged on the insult he'd been given and the opportunity being lost never to be offered again. He called Courtland a "trifling idiot" and a few other gentle phrases and demanded reasons for such an unprecedented decision.

Courtland's only answer was, "I'm afraid it isn't going to fit in with my views of life, Mr. Thomas. I've thought it over carefully, and I can't accept your offer."

"Why not? Isn't it enough money?" roared the mad financier. "I'll double your salary!"

"Money has nothing to do with it," said Courtland quietly. "That would make no difference." He was sorry for this scene, for Tennelly's sake.

"Well, have you something else in view?"

"No, not definitely."

"Then you're a fool!" said Uncle Ramsey, further stating what kind of fool he was several times *vigorously*. After that he mopped his beaded brow with trembling, agitated hands and sat down. The old bull was baffled at last.

Uncle Ramsey blustered all the way to the train with his nephew. "I've got to have that young man, Thomas. There're no two ways about it. A fellow who can stand out the way he did against Ramsey Thomas is just the man I want. He's got personality. Why, a man like that at work for us would be worth millions! He'd give confidence to everyone. Why, we could make him a senator in a few years, and there's no telling where he wouldn't stop! He's the kind of man who could be put in the White House if things shaped themselves right. I've *got* to have him, Thomas, and no mistake! Now I'm going to put it up to you to find out the secret. Get his number, and we'll meet him on any reasonable proposition he puts up. Say, Thomas, isn't there a girl anywhere who could convince him?"

"Yes, there's a girl!"

"The very thing! You make her wise about it, and when I come back next week I'll stop off again and see what I can do with her. You can take me to call on her. Can you work it, Thomas?"

Tennelly said he'd try and went to see Gila on his way back to the university.

Gila listened to the story of Uncle Ramsey's offer with bated breath and averted gaze. She wouldn't show Tennelly how much this meant to her. But in her eyes grew a determination that would not be denied.

She planned a campaign with Tennelly coolly and with a glee that fooled him completely. He saw she was entering into the spirit of the thing and had no idea she had any other interest than to please her cousin and achieve a kind of triumph herself in making Courtland do the thing he'd vowed not to do.

But long after Tennelly had gone home she stood before her mirror, looking with dreamy eyes into the pictures her imagination drew there for her. She saw herself Courtland's bride after he succeeded in the big business enterprise to which Uncle Ramsey had opened the door. She saw Washington with its domes and Capitol looming ahead of her ambition, senators and great men bowing before her and even the White House like a fantasy of possibility. All this and more were hers if she played her cards right. Never fear! She would play them. Courtland *must* be made to accept Uncle Ramsey's proposition.

Chapter 23

Bonnie's letter reached Mother Marshall Wednesday afternoon while Father was off in the machine arranging for a man to do the spring plowing. She knew it by heart before he got back. She was standing at her trysting window with her cheek against the old hat, watching the sunset and thinking it over when the car came chugging down the road.

Father waved his hand boyishly as he turned in at the gate, and Mother was out on the side doorstep waiting as he came to a halt.

"Heard anything yet?" he asked eagerly.

"Yes. A nice, dear letter!" Mother held it up. "Hurry up and come in, and I'll read it to you."

But Father couldn't wait to put away the machine. He bounded out like a four-year-old and came right in then, regardless of the fact that it was getting dark and he might run into the doorjamb putting away the machine later.

He settled down, overcoat and all, into the big chair in the kitchen to listen; and Mother put on her spectacles in such a hurry she got them upside down and had to begin over again.

You dear Mother Marshall and dear Father Marshall, too!

Inviting a stranger like me to visit you is the most wonderful thing I ever heard of. At first I thought it wasn't right to accept such a great kindness from people I never saw and who didn't know whether they could even like me or not. But afterward Mr. Courtland told me about your Stephen and that you suffered, too. And then I knew I might take you at your word and come for a little while to get the comfort I need so much. Even then I couldn't have done it if Mr. Courtland and my nurse hadn't told me they were sure I could get something to do and repay you for your kindness.

If I can comfort you in your loneliness I'll be so glad. But I'm afraid I could never even half fill the place of such a fine son. Mr. Courtland has told me how grandly he died. He saw him, you know, at the very last minute and saw all he did to save others.

But if you'll let me love you both I'll be so grateful. All I had on earth are gone home to God now, and the world looks so hard and sad to me. I hope you can love me a little while I stay and not let me make you any trouble. Please don't go to any work to get ready for me. I'll gladly do anything necessary when I get there. I'm quite able to work now, and if I have a place where someone cares whether I live or die it won't be so hard to face the future. A great, strange city is an awful place for a girl with a heavy heart.

I'm so glad you know Jesus Christ. It makes me feel at home before I get there. My dear father was a minister.

They wouldn't let me pack up, so I did the best I could with directing the kind friends who did it for me. I've taken you at your word and had Mother's sewing machine and a box of my little brother's things sent with my trunk. But if they're in the way I can sell them or give them away. And I don't want you to feel I'm going to presume upon your kindness and settle down on you indefinitely. As soon as I get a chance to work I must take it, and I'll want to repay you for all you've done for me. You've sent me a great deal more money than I need.

I start Wednesday evening on the through express. I've marked a timetable and am sending it because we can't find out just what time I can make connections from Grant's Junction, where they say I have to change. Perhaps you'll know. But don't worry about me. I'll find my way to you as soon as I can get there. I'm praying I won't disappoint you. And now till I see you,

> *Sincerely and gratefully,*
> *Rose Bonner Brentwood*

"It couldn't be improved on," declared Mother, beaming. "It's just what I'd have wanted her to say if I'd planned it all out, only more so!"

"It's all right!" said Father. "But that's one thing we forgot. We should have sent her word we'd meet her at the station and what time the train left Grant's Junction and all! Now that's too bad!"

"Now don't worry, Father. She'll find her way. Like as not the conductor will have a timetable and tell her all about the trains. But I certainly wish we had let her know we'd meet her."

They were still worrying about it that night at nine o'clock while Father wound the kitchen clock and Mother put a mackerel soaking for breakfast. Suddenly the telephone in the next room gave a whir, and both Father and Mother jumped as if they'd been shot, looking at each other as they hurried to the phone.

It was Father who took down the receiver. "A telegram? For Mr. Seth Marshall! Yes, I'm listening. Write it down, Mother. A telegram!"

"Mercy! Perhaps she wasn't well enough to start!" gasped Mother, putting her pencil in place.

Miss Brentwood left tonight at nine-fifteen on express number 10, car Alicia lower berth number 8. Please let me know if she arrives safely.

> *Paul Courtland*

"Now isn't that thoughtful of him!" he said, as he hung up the receiver. "He must have sensed we wanted to send her word, and now we can do it!"

"Send her word!" said Mother.

"Why, sure! Haven't you read in the papers how they send messages to trains that're moving? It's great, isn't it, Mother? To think this little dinky telephone puts you and me out here on this farm in touch with all the world."

"Do you mean you can send a telegram to her on board the train, Seth?"

"Sure!" said Father. "We've got all the numbers. Just send to that express train that left tonight. What was it—express number 10 and so on, and it'll be sent along and get to her."

"Well, I'd ask her to answer then, to make sure she got it. That's a mighty uncertain way to send messages to people flying along on an express train. If you don't get any word from her you'll never know whether she got it or not, and then you won't know whether to meet her at Sloan's or Maitland," said Mother, with a worried pucker on her forehead.

"Sure!" said Father, taking down the receiver. "I can do that."

"It's just wonderful, Seth, how much you know about important things like that!" sighed Mother when the telegram was sent. "Now I think we better go right to bed, for I've got to get to baking early in the morning. I want to have bread and pies and doughnuts fresh when she comes."

While they were eating breakfast the answer came.

Telegram received. Will come to Sloan's Station. Having comfortable journey.

R. B. B.

"Now isn't that wonderful!" said Mother, sitting back weakly behind the coffeepot and wiping away an excited tear with the corner of her apron. "To think that can be done! Now wouldn't it be beautiful if we had telephones to heaven! Think, if we could get word from Stephen today, how happy we'd be!"

"Why, we have!" said Father. "Wait!" He reached over to the little stand by the window and grasped the worn old Bible. "Here, listen to this!"

For this we say unto you by the word of the Lord, that we which are alive and remain unto the coming of the Lord shall not prevent them which are asleep. For the Lord himself shall descend from heaven with a shout, with the voice of the archangel and with the trump of God: and the dead in Christ shall rise first: Then we which are alive and remain shall be caught up together with them in the clouds, to meet the Lord in the air: and so shall we ever be with the Lord. Wherefore comfort one another with these words.

"There, Mother! Ain't that just as good as any telegram from a moving train? And it's signed with His own seal and signature! It means He's heard our sorrow about Stephen's leaving us, and He heard it ages before we felt it ourselves and wrote this down for us. Sent us a telegram this morning, just to comfort us! I reckon that meeting with Stephen and the Lord in the air is going to knock the spots clean out of this little meeting tomorrow morning down at Sloan's

Station. We won't need our ottymobeel anymore after that. We'll have *wings,* Mother! How'll you like to fly?"

Mother gave a gasp of joy and smiled at Father like a rainbow through her tears. "That's so, Father! We don't need telephones to heaven, do we? I guess His words cover all our needs if we'd only remember to look for them. Now, Father, I must get at those doughnuts! Are you going to take the machine and run down to town and see if those books have come yet? They should be here by now. Then don't forget to fix that fire up in the bedroom so it'll be ready to light when she gets here. Isn't it funny, Father—we don't know how she looks! Not in the least. And if two girls should get off the train at Sloan's Station we wouldn't know which was the right one!"

"Well, *I* would!" declared Father. "I'm dead certain there ain't two girls in the whole universe could have written that letter, and if you'd put any other one down with her, and I saw them side by side, I could tell first off which she was!"

So they helped each other through that last exciting day, finding something to do up to the very last minute the next morning before it was time to start to Sloan's Station to meet the train.

Mother would go along, of course. She pictured herself standing for hours beside that kitchen window with her cheek against the old hat, waiting and wondering what had happened that they hadn't come, and she couldn't see it that way. So she left the dinner in such stages of getting ready that it could soon be completed and then wrapped herself in her big gray cloak.

Father went faster than he'd ever gone since he got the car, and Mother never even noticed. He panicked lest his watch might be running slow and the train arrive before they got there. So they arrived at the station almost an hour ahead of the train.

"Oh, I'm so glad it's a pretty day!" said Mother Marshall, slipping her gloved hands in her sleeves to keep from shivering with excitement.

She sat in the automobile till the train drew up to the platform and people began to get out. But when Bonnie stepped down from the car she forgot her doubts as to how they'd know her and jumped out on the platform without waiting to be helped. She rushed up to Bonnie, saying, "This is our Bonnie, isn't it?" and folded her arms about the girl, forgetting entirely that she hadn't meant to use the name until the girl gave her permission; that she had no right to know the name even, wasn't supposed to have heard of it and was giving the young man away.

But it didn't matter! Bonnie was so glad to hear her own name called in that endearing tone that she put her face down in Mother Marshall's comfortable neck and cried. She couldn't help it, there while the train was still at the station and the other travelers were peering curiously out of the sleeper at the beautiful pale girl in black who was being met by that nice old couple with the automobile. Somehow it made them all feel glad; she'd looked so sad and alone on the journey.

What a ride that was home again to the farm, with Mother Marshall cuddling and crooning to her, "Oh, my dear pretty child! To think you've really come all this long way to comfort us!" And Father was running the old machine at an unheard of speed, slamming along over the road and reaching back now and then to pat the old buffalo robe that was tucked snugly around Bonnie.

Bonnie herself was fairly overcome and couldn't get her equilibrium. She thought these must be wonderful people to invite a stranger and do all they were doing, but such a reception as this she never dreamed of.

"Oh, you're so good to me!" cried Bonnie, with a smile through her tears. "I know I'm acting like a baby, but I can't help it. I've had nobody so long, and now to be treated like this! It seems as if I'd come home!"

"Why, sure! You have!" said Father in his big, hearty voice.

"Put your head right down on my shoulder and cry if you want to, dear," said Mother Marshall, pulling her softly toward her. "You can't think how good it is to have you here! Father and I were so afraid you wouldn't come! We thought you mightn't be willing to come so far to utter strangers!"

So it went on all the way, all of them so happy they scarcely knew what they were saying.

Then, when they reached the house, even Father was so far gone he couldn't let them go upstairs alone. He had to leave the machine standing by the kitchen door and carry that handbag up as an excuse to see how she'd like the room.

Bonnie, pulling off her gloves, entered the room when Mother opened the door. She looked around confused, as if she'd stepped from the middle of winter into a summer orchard.

Then she cried out with delight, "Oh! How beautiful! You don't mean for me to have this lovely room? It isn't right! A stranger and no money!"

"Nothing of the kind!" growled Father, patting her on the shoulder. "Just a daughter come home!"

Then he beat a hasty retreat to the fireplace and touched a match to the fire already laid, while Mother, purring like a contented mother cat, pushed the bewildered girl into the big flowered chair in front of the fire.

In the midst of it all Mother remembered dinner should be eaten at once and that Bonnie must have a chance to wash her face and straighten her hair before dinner.

So Father and Mother, with reluctant lingerings and last words, as if they weren't going to see her for a month, finally bustled off together. In no time at all Bonnie was down there, too, begging to help and declaring herself perfectly able, although her pale face and the dark rings under her eyes belied her. Mother Marshall thought, after all, she should have put Bonnie to bed and fed her with chicken broth and toast instead of letting her come downstairs to eat stewed chicken, little fat biscuits with gravy, and the most succulent apple pie in the world, with a creamy glass of milk to make it go down.

Father had just finished trying to make Bonnie take a second helping of everything, when he suddenly dropped the carving knife and fork with a clatter and sprang from his chair.

"I declare to goodness, Mother, if I didn't forget!" he said and rushed over to the telephone.

"Why, that's so!" cried Mother. "Don't forget to tell him how much we love her!"

Bonnie looked from one to the other of them in astonishment.

"It's that young man!" explained Mother. "He wanted us to telegraph if you got here safe. You know he sent us a message after he put you on the train."

"How very thoughtful of him!" said Bonnie. "He's the most wonderful young man! I can't tell you all he did for me, a mere stranger. So that explains how you knew where to send your message. I puzzled over that."

Four hours later Courtland, coming up to his room after basketball practice, a hot shower and a swim in the pool, found the telegram.

Traveler arrived safely. Bore the journey well. Many thanks for the introduction. Everybody happy. If you don't believe it come and see for yourself.

Father and Mother Marshall

Courtland read it and looked dreamily out the window, trying to picture Bonnie in her new home. Then he said aloud, with conviction, "Sometime I'll go out there and see!"

Just then someone knocked at his door and handed him a note from Gila.

Dear Paul—Come over this evening. I want to see you about something very special.

Hastily,
Gila

Chapter 24

Gila's note came to Courtland as a happy surprise. He hadn't expected to see her until the next evening. Not that he'd brooded much over the matter. He was too busy and too sanely healthy to do that. Besides, he was as yet only questioning within himself whether he was going to fall in love. The sensation so far was exceedingly pleasurable, and he was ready for the whole thing when it should arrive and prove itself. But at present he was in the quiescent stage when everything seemed significant and delightfully interesting.

He had firmly resolved that the next time he saw Gila he would tell her of his own heart experience with the Presence. He realized he must go carefully and not shock her, for he'd begun to see that her prejudices would be against taking any stock in such an experience. He had only recently come from a like position that he could well understand her extreme views, her almost repugnance toward hearing anything about it. But he would make her see the whole thing, just as he'd seen it.

Now Gila had no notion of allowing any such recital as Courtland was planning. She'd set her stage for another scene and had on her most charming mood. She was wearing a little dress of pale blue wool, so simple that a child of ten might have worn it under a white ruffled apron. The neck was decorated with a soft kerchieflike collar. Not even a pin marred the simplicity of her costume. Her hair, too, was simpler than usual, almost carrying out the childish idea with its soft looping away from the face. Little heelless black satin slippers were tied with narrow black ribbons quaintly crossed and recrossed over the slim, blue silk ankles, carrying out the charming idea of a modest, simple maiden. Nothing could be more coy and charming than the way she swept her long black lashes down upon her pearly cheeks. Her great eyes when they were lifted were clear and limpid as a baby's.

Courtland was fairly carried off his feet at sight of her and felt his heart bound in reassurance. This must be love! He'd fallen in love at last! He who had scorned the idea so long and laughed at the other fellows, until he doubted in his own heart whether the delightful illusion would ever come to him! The glamour was about Gila tonight and no mistake! He looked at her with his heart in his eyes.

She dropped her lashes to hide a glint of triumph, knowing she'd chosen her setting right at last. Softly, dreamily, in the back of her mind floated the nation's Capitol and her standing amid admiring throngs receiving homage. She would succeed. She had achieved her first triumph with the look in Courtland's eyes. She could carry out Mr. Ramsey Thomas's commission and win Courtland to anything that would forward ambitious hopes for him. She was sure of it.

The important business she wished to see Courtland about was to ask him if he'd be her partner in a bazaar and pageant that was to be given shortly for some charitable purpose by the folks in her society. She wanted Courtland to march with her and to consult him about the characters they should choose and costumes they should wear.

As if she were a child desiring him to play with her, he yielded to her mood, watching her with delighted eyes, that anything so exquisite and lovely should ask for his favor. Of course he would be her partner! He entered into the arrangements with zest, though he let her do all the planning and heeded little what character she chose for him or what costume, so she was pleased. Indeed, his part in the matter seemed slight so he might go with her—his sweet, shy, lovely maiden! For so she seemed to him that night. A perfect Solveig!

The reason for the little slippers became apparent later, when she insisted upon teaching him dancing steps to be used in a final assembly after the pageant. He felt intoxicated in the delight of moving with her through the dreamy steps to the music of the expensive Victrola. Just to watch her little feet full of lightness and grace; to touch her small, warm hand; to be so near those drooping lashes; to feel her breath on his hand; to think of her as trusting her lovely self to him—made him almost deliriously happy. And she, with her lashes, her delicate way of barely touching his arm and her seeming unaware-ness of his presence, was so exquisite and pure and lovely tonight. She didn't dream, of course, of how she made his pulses thrill and how he was longing to gather her into his arms and tell her how lovely she was.

Afterward he was never quite sure what kept him from doing it. He thought at the time it was a wall of purity and loveliness surrounding her and making her sacred, so that he felt he must go slowly, mustn't startle her or make her afraid of him. It never occurred to him that the wall might be surrounding him. He had entirely forgotten the first visit to Gila in the Mephistophelian gar-ments, with the red light filling the unholy atmosphere. There had never been so much as a hint of red light in the room since he said he didn't like it. The lampshade seemed to have disappeared. In its place was a great wrought metal thing of old silver jeweled with opalescent medallions.

But it was part of Gila's intent to lead him on and yet hold him at a distance. She'd read him right. He possessed an old-fashioned ideal of woman, and the citadel of his heart was only to be taken by such a woman. Therefore, she would be such a woman until she won. After that? What did it matter? She would have attained her desire!

But the drooping lashes hid no unconscious sweetness. Those eyes held a sinister gleam as she looked at herself over his shoulder when they passed the great mirror set in a cabinet door. The little hand lay lightly in the strong one with deliberate intention. Every movement of the dreamy dance she was teach-ing him, every touch of the satin slipper, had its nicely calculated intention to draw him on. The sooner she could make him yield and crush her to him, the sooner he declared his passion for her, that much nearer would her ambitions be to their fulfillment. Yet she must be sure she had him close in her trap before she disclosed her purpose to him.

So the blue puritanlike spider threw her silver gossamer web about him, entangling his fine manly heart and flinging diamond dust and powder made of charms in his eyes to blind him. But as yet she knew not of the Presence that was now his constant companion.

They had danced for some time, floating about in the delight of the motion together and the nearness of each other, when it seemed to Courtland as if a cooling hand was suddenly laid on his feverish brow and a calm came to his spirit like a beloved voice calling his name with the accent that is certain of quick response.

Thus he remembered what he'd come to tell Gila. Looking down at that bit of humanity almost within his embrace, a great tenderness for her and longing came over him to make her know now what the Presence was becoming to him.

"Gila," he whispered, and his voice was full of thrill. "Let's sit down awhile! There's something I want to tell you!"

Instantly she responded, lifting innocent eyes to his face and gliding toward the couch where they might sit together, settling down on it, almost nestling to him, then remembering and drawing away shyly to play her part. She thought she knew what he was going to say. She thought she saw the love-light in his eyes so dazzling it almost blinded her. It frightened her a little, too, unlike the light in other lovers' eyes. She wondered if it was because she cared herself so much now that it seemed so different.

But he didn't take her in his arms as she'd expected him to do, though he sat quite near and spoke in a low tone. His arm lay across the back of the couch behind her; he sat sideways, turned toward her, and still touched reverently the little hand he was holding as they danced together.

"Gila, I have a story to tell you," he said. "Until you know it you can never understand me fully, and I want with all my heart to have you understand me. It's something that has become a part of me."

She sat quivering, wondering, half fearful. Was he going to tell her about another girl? A fierce, unreasoning anger shot across her face. She wouldn't tolerate the thought that anyone had had him before her. Was it—it couldn't be that baby-face pauper in the hospital? She drew her slim body up tensely and waited for the story.

Courtland told the story of Stephen, told it well and briefly. He pictured Stephen so that the girl must admire him. No woman could have heard that description of a man like Stephen and not bow her woman's heart and wish she might have known him.

Gila listened, fascinated, even up to the moment of the fire and the tragedy when Stephen fell into the flames. She shuddered visibly several times but sat tense and listened. She even was unmoved when Courtland told of finding himself on a ledge above the burning mass, creeping somehow into a small haven, shut in by a wall of smoke, and feeling this was the end. But when he began to tell of the Presence, the Light, the Voice, the girl gave a sudden start and gripped her cold hands together. Almost imperceptibly she drew her body away from him and turned slowly till she faced him, horror and consternation in her eyes, unbelief and scorn on her lips. But still she didn't speak, still held her gaze on him and listened, while he told of coming back to life, the hospital walls, the strange emptiness and the Presence; the recovery and the Presence still with him; the going here and there and finding the Presence always before him and yet with him!

"He's here in this room with us, Gila!" he said simply.

Then suddenly Gila sprang away from him to her feet, uttered a wild scream of terror and burst into angry tears!

Courtland sprang to his feet in dismay and instant contrition. He made the horror of the fire too dramatic. He didn't realize how dreadful it would be to a woman's delicate sensibilities. This gentle, loving girl had felt it to her soul, and her nerves gave way before the reality of it. He was an idiot to tell the story in that bald way. He should have gone about it more gently. He wasn't used to women. He must learn better. Would she forgive him?

And now indeed he had her in his arms, although he was unaware of it. He was trying to comfort and soothe her, as he'd soothe a frightened child. Not only his handkerchief but his hands were needed to charm away those tears and comfort the pitiful face that looked so helpless against his shoulder. He wanted to stoop and lay his lips on those trembling ones. Perhaps Gila thought he would. But he wouldn't take advantage of her helplessness. Not until she was herself and could give him permission would he avail himself of that sacred privilege. Now it was the part of a man to comfort her without any element of self in the matter.

When he drew her down upon the couch again, with the sobs still shaking her soft blue and white frilly breast, her blue-black hair damp and tossed on her temples, and tried to tell her how sorry he was for putting her through the horrors of that fire, she protested. It was *not* the fire. She shivered. It was not the horror and the smoke. It was *not* Stephen's death or the danger to him. It was not *any* of those that unnerved her. It was that other awful thing he said: that ghostly, ghastly, uncanny, dreadful story of a Presence! She almost shrieked again as she said it and shivered away from him, as if something cold and clammy were still in his touch that gave her the horrors.

A cold disappointment settled down on him. She hadn't understood. He looked at her, troubled, disappointed, baffled. He couldn't, then, bring her this knowledge he wished so much for her to have. One could only tell about it to one's friends but couldn't give it to them. It was something they must take for themselves, must feel and see by themselves.

With new illumination he turned to her and said in a voice wonderfully tender for a man so young: "Listen, Gila! I've been clumsy in telling you. You can't see it just from my poor story. But He'll come to *you,* and you'll see Him for yourself. I'll ask Him to come to you as He has to me."

Again that piercing scream, and with a quick movement, almost like a serpent, she slid from his side and stood quivering in the middle of the room, her eyes flashing, her body shrinking, both hands clenched to her throat.

"Stop!" she cried. "Stop!" she screamed again, stamping her foot. "I won't hear such horrible things! I *won't have* any spirits coming around me! I *won't see* them! Do you understand? I *hate* that Presence, and I *hate you* when you talk like that!"

She'd worked herself into a fine tantrum, but behind it was a horrible fear and shrinking from the Christ he described, the shrinking of the naked soul in the garden from its God. The childlike eyes were wide with horror now; the sweet, innocent mouth was trembling with emotion. She was anything but Solveig-like. If Courtland caught a glimpse of the real Gila through it all he laid it to his own clumsy way of handling the delicate mystery of a girl's shy nature. He saw she was wrought up beyond her own control, and he was so far under the illusion that he blamed himself only and set himself to calm her.

He coaxed her to sit down again, put his strong hand over her trembling one, marveling at its smallness and softness. He talked to her in quiet, reassuring tones. He promised he would talk no more about the Presence till she was ready to hear. He was leaning toward her in his strength, his arm behind her, his hand on her shoulder, with a sheltering, comforting touch when he told her this, as one would treat a child in trouble. Suddenly, like the sun flashing out from behind the clouds, she lifted up her teary face and smiled, nestling toward him, her head falling down on his shoulder with a sigh like a tired, satisfied child, her face lifted temptingly so very close to his.

It was then he did the thing that bound him to what followed. He stooped and laid his lips upon her warm trembling ones and kissed her. The thrill that shot through him was like the click of shackles snapping shut about one's wrist, like the turning of the key in a prison house, the shooting of the bolt to one's dark cell. He held her there and touched her soft hair with his fingertips; touched her cool forehead with his lips; touched her warm, soft lips again and felt the thrill. But something was the matter. He felt the surging forces within him rise and batter at the gate of his self-control. He wanted to say, "Gila, I love you!" But the words stuck in his throat.

What had he done? Where did this sense of defeat and loss come from? The Presence! Where was the Presence? Yes—there—but withdrawn, standing apart in sadness, while he sat comforting and caressing one who had just said she hated Him! But that was because she hadn't seen Him yet. She was frightened because she didn't understand. He could yet make her see. He would implore the Presence to come to her, to break down her prejudice, to let her have the vision also!

So he sat and comforted her, yet longed to get away and think it out. This sense of depression and bitter disappointment hung about him like a burden—now, of all times, when he should be happy!

But Gila was nestling close, patting his sleeve, saying sweet nonsensical words as if she were really the child she seemed. He looked down at her and smiled. How small she was. He must remember she was very young and probably never had much bringing up. Serious things frightened her. He must lead her gently. It made him feel old and responsible to look at this tender, beautiful girl enveloped as she was in the garment of his ideal of womanhood.

Yet something about it all drove him from her. He must think it out and come to some clear understanding with himself. As it was, it seemed to him as if he were trying to make peace within himself while before him lay his own broken vows. He had vowed to himself to bring her to the Christ and hadn't accomplished it. Instead she declared she hated him and the Presence both; yet here he sat expressing love to her, ignoring it all! He felt a distinct weakness in himself but didn't know how to remedy it.

When he finally got away from Gila and walked feverishly toward the university, he felt as if his soul was crying out within him for a solution to his perplexities. By his side walked a Friend, but a veil seemed to hang between them. Ever mingling with his thoughts came the sweet, tear-wet face of Gila, with its Solveig-look, pleading up at him from the evening mist, luring him as it were to forget the Christ. He passed his hand wearily over his eyes, and told himself he'd been through a good deal that evening and his nerves weren't as strong as they were before the fire.

He was surprised to find it was still early when he got back to his room, barely half past nine. Yet it seemed near midnight; so much had happened.

What would he think if he knew that at that very minute Tennelly was seated in the chair in the library he had just vacated and Gila, posing bewitchingly in the firelight, was merrily talking about him?

Not that they were saying anything against him—of course not! Tennelly would never have stood for that, and Gila knew better. But Gila had no intention of giving Tennelly any idea how far matters had gone between her and Courtland. As for Tennelly, he would have been the most amazed of the three if he'd known all. He'd been Courtland's intimate friend for so many years that he thought he knew him perfectly. He would have sworn Courtland's friendship with Gila hadn't progressed further than a mere first stage of friendship. He admitted Gila had an influence over his friend, but that it had gone heart-deep seemed impossible. Courtland was a man of too much force, even young as he was, and too much maturity of thought, to be permanently entangled with a girl like Gila. That was what Tennelly thought before Gila turned her eyes toward him and flung a few of her silver gossamer threads about his soul. For always in those early days of visiting Gila it had been in Courtland's behalf: first to see if she was good enough for his friend, and next to get her partnership in the scheme of turning Courtland's thoughts away from "morbid" things.

But that night for the first time Tennelly saw the Solveig in Gila and was stirred on his own account. The childish blue frock and the simple frilled kerchief did their work with his high soul as well, and he sat charmed and watched her. After all, there was more to her than he'd thought, or else she was a consummate actress. So Tennelly sat late before the fire, till Gila knew he'd turn aside again often to see her for himself, and then she let him go.

Chapter 25

Gila went to a house party the next day, with only a tinted, perfumed note, like a flutter of painted wings, to explain that the butterfly had melted into the pleasant sunshine to taste honey in other flowers for a time.

In a way her going was a relief to Courtland. He didn't understand himself. Something was wrong, and he wanted to find out what before he saw her again.

While he was in this troubled state he stumbled upon the Bible as something that might bring light.

He'd studied it in his biblical literature classes and found it much like other books—a literary classic, a wonderful gem of beauty in its way, a rare collection of legends, proverbs, allegories and the like. But looking at it now, with the possibility it was the Word of God, all was changed.

He remembered once seeing a tray of gems in an exhibit and among them one that looked like a common pebble. The man who had charge of the exhibit took the pebble and held it in the palm of his hand, when it suddenly began to glow and sparkle with the colors of the rainbow and rival all the other gems. The man explained that only the warmth of the human hand could cause this marvelous change. You might lay the stone under the direct rays of a summer sun; yet it would have no effect until you took it in your hand, when it would give forth its beauty once more.

It was like this when he began to read the Bible with the idea that it was the Word of God. Things flashed out at him that dazzled his thoughts; living, palpitating things, as if they were hidden to be discovered only by one who searched. Hidden truths came to light that filled his soul with wonder. Gradually he understood that belief was the touchstone by which all these treasures were to be revealed. Everywhere he found it, belief in Christ was a condition to all the blessings promised. He read of hearts hardened and eyes blinded because of unbelief and saw that unbelief was something a man was responsible for, not a condition which settled down upon him and he couldn't help. Belief was a deliberate act of the will. It wasn't a theory or an intellectual affirmation; it was a position taken, which necessarily must pass into action of some kind. He began to see that without this deliberate belief it was impossible for people to know purely spiritual things. It was the condition necessary for revelation. He was fascinated with the pursuit of this new study.

Wittemore came to his room one evening, his face grayer, more strained than ever. Wittemore's mother had made another partial recovery and insisted on his return to college. He was plodding patiently, breathlessly along in his classes, trying to catch up. He'd paid Courtland back part of the money he borrowed and was paying the rest in small installments. Courtland hated to take it but saw it would hurt him to refuse it. So he would stop now and then to talk about his settlement work, to show a friendly interest in him. Wittemore had responded with a quiet wistfulness and a patient hovering in the background that touched the other man's heart deeply.

"I've just come from my rounds," said Wittemore, sitting down on the edge of a chair. "That old lady you carried the medicine to—she's been telling me how you made tea and toast!" He paused and looked embarrassed.

"Yes," said Courtland, smiling. "How's she getting on? Any better?"

"No," said Wittemore, the hopeless gray look settling about his mouth. "She'll never be any better. She's dying!"

"Well," said Courtland, "that'll be a pleasant change for her, I guess."

Wittemore winced. Death had no pleasant associations for him. "She told me you prayed for her. She wants you to do it again."

He plainly thought the praying had been a joke with Courtland.

Courtland looked up, the color rising slowly in his face. He saw the accusation in Wittemore's sad eyes.

"Of course I know what you think of such things. I've heard you in class. I don't believe in them anymore myself." Wittemore's voice had a trail of hopelessness in it. "But somehow I couldn't bring myself to make a mockery of prayer, even to please that old woman. You see, *my mother still believes in prayer!*" He spoke apologetically, as of a dear one who lacked advantages.

"But I *do* believe in prayer!" said Courtland. "What you heard me say in class was before I understood."

"Before you understood?" Wittemore looked puzzled.

"Listen, Wittemore. Things are all different now. I've met Jesus Christ, and my eyes are open. I was blind before, but since I've felt the Presence everything has been different."

And then he told the story of his experience. He didn't make a long story out of it. He gave brief facts, and when it was finished Wittemore dropped his face into his hands and groaned.

"I'd give anything if I could believe that again," he said between his long bony fingers. "It's breaking my mother's heart for me to leave the faith!"

The slick haylike hair fell in wisps over his hands; his high, bony shoulders were hunched over Courtland's study table. He was a great, pitiful object.

"Why don't you then?" said Courtland, going to the closet for his overcoat. "It's up to you, you know. You *can!* God can't do it for you, and of course nothing's doing till you've taken that step. I found that out!"

"But how do you reconcile things—calamities, disasters, war, suffering, that poor old woman lying on her attic bed alone? How do you reconcile that with the goodness of God?"

"I don't reconcile it. It isn't my business. I leave that to God. If I understood all the whys and wherefores of how this universe is run I'd be great enough to be a god myself."

"But if God knows everything I can't see how He can let some things go on. He must be limited in power, or He'd never let some things happen if He's a good God!" Wittemore's voice had a plaintive sound.

"Well, how do you know that? In the first place, how can you be sure what a calamity is? And, say, did it ever strike you that some of the things we blame on God are really up to us? He's handed over His power for us to do things, and we haven't seen it that way; so the things go undone, and God is charged with the consequences."

"I wish I could believe that!" said Wittemore.

"You can! When you really want to enough, you will. Come on—let's get that prayer down to the old lady! I'm sort of an amateur yet, but I'll do my best."

They went out into the mist and murk of a spring thaw. Wittemore never forgot that night's experience—the prayer and the walk home again through the fog. The old woman died at dawn.

Courtland spent much time thinking about Gila these days. His whole soul was wrapped up in the desire that she might understand. He was longing for her; idealizing her; thinking of her in her innocent beauty, her charming ways; wondering how she would meet him the next time, what he would say to her; living on her brief, alluring notes that came to him from time to time like fitful rose petals blown from a garden where he longed to be. Yet in a way it was a relief to have her gone until he could settle his great perplexity concerning her.

Gila prolonged her absence by a trip south with her father, and so it was several weeks before Courtland saw her again.

A settled sadness seemed to be over his soul when he prayed about her, and when at last she returned and summoned him to her he was no nearer a solution to his difficulty than when he'd left her.

The hour before he went to her he spent in Stephen's room, turning over the pages of Stephen's Bible. When he rose at last to go he turned again to a verse that had caught his eye among the marked verses that were always so interesting to him because they seemed to have been landmarks in Stephen's life.

My presence shall go with thee, and I will give thee rest.

It almost startled him that it suited his need so well. He read on a few verses.

And he said unto him, If thy presence go not with me, carry us not up hence. For wherein shall it be known here that I and thy people have found grace in thy sight? is it not in that thou goest with us? so shall we be separated, I and thy people, from all the people that are upon the face of the earth.

Wonderful words those, implying a close relationship that shut out to a certain extent all others who were not one with that Presence. He wished he knew what it all meant. In that moment was born a desire to understand the Bible and know how believing scholars explained things.

But as he went from the room and on his way, he felt that to some extent he had a solution to his trouble. He was to be conducted personally by the presence of God wherever he went, whatever he did! This was to make life less complex, and in some mysterious way the power of the Christ with him was to be manifested to others. Surely he might trust this in Gila's case and feel sure he would be guided aright; that she would come to see for herself how this guiding power was always with him. Surely she would come to know it and love it also.

Gila met him with fluttering delight, reproaching him with a pout for not writing oftener, calling him to order for looking solemn, pretty herself in a frilly pink dress that gave her the look of a pale anemone, windblown and sweet and wild.

She talked about the "fine times" she'd had and the "peachy" men and girls she'd met; flattered him by saying she saw none handsomer or more distinguished than he. She accepted as a matter of course the loverlike attitude he adopted, let him tell her of his love as long as he wasn't too solemn about it, teased and played with him, charmed him with every art she knew, dancing from one mood to another like a sprite, winding her gossamer chains about him more and more, until, when he went from her again, he was fairly intoxicated with her beauty.

He had lulled his anxiety with the thought that he must wait and be patient until Gila saw. But it was growing harder to approach her about the things most important to him. Sometimes when he was wearily trying to find a way back from her frothy conversation to the real things he hoped she would enjoy with him someday, she'd call him an old crab and summon to her side other willing youths to stimulate his jealousy—youths of sometimes unsavory reputation whose presence gave him deep anxiety for her. Then he'd tell himself he must be more patient, that she was young and must learn to understand gradually.

Gila developed a great interest in Courtland's plans for a career, of which she chattered much to him, suggesting ways in which her father might help him into a position of prominence and power in the political world. But Courtland, with a shadow of trouble in his eyes, always put her off. He admitted he'd thought of politics but wasn't ready to say what he would do.

So spring came with its final examinations, and commencement drew nearer.

Through it all Courtland found much time to be with Gila; often in company or flashing through a crowded thoroughfare by her side; following her whims; excusing her follies; laying her mistakes and indiscretions to her youth and innocence; always trying to lead up to his great desire, that she might see his Christ.

Tennelly watched the whole performance anxiously. He wanted Courtland to be drawn out of what he considered his "morbid" state, but not at the price of his peace of mind. He was sure Courtland shouldn't marry Gila. He was equally sure she meant nothing serious in her present relation to Courtland. He felt responsible in a way because he'd agreed in the plot with his uncle to start her on this campaign. But if Courtland should come out of it with a broken heart, what then?

A week before commencement the crisis came.

Gila had summoned Courtland to her.

In her most imperial mood, wearing an imported dress whose intricacies and daring contrasts were calculated to strengthen a determined spirit in combat, Gila awaited his coming impatiently. She knew that day he'd received another offer from Ramsey Thomas, tempting and baited with alluring possibilities that dazzled her if not her friend. She meant to make him tell her about the offer, accept it that afternoon and clinch the contract by telephoning the acceptance to the telegraph office before he left her home.

Courtland was tired. He'd been through a hard week of exams, was on several committees and had a number of important class meetings. He'd attended various functions and spent many unavoidably late hours. He'd come to her hoping for a rest and the joy of her society. Just watching her dainty grace as she moved about a room, handling the tea things and giving him a delicate sandwich or a crisp cake, filled him with joy and soothed his troubled spirit; it was so like his ideal of what a woman should be.

But Gila wasn't handing out tea that afternoon. She had other fish to fry and went at her business with a determination that very soon showed there was no rest to be had there.

Very prettily, but efficiently, she pressed him about his plans. Had he no plans about what he would do when he finished college? Of course she knew he had money of his own (he'd never told her how much, and she hadn't any way of asking a man like Courtland when he didn't choose to tell a thing like that), but nowadays that was nothing. Even rich men did *something*. One wasn't anything unless one was in something big! Hadn't he had any offers? It was odd, a brilliant man as he was. She knew lots of young fellows who had no end of chances to get into big things when they finished their education. Didn't his father know of something? Hadn't he ever been approached?

Goaded at last by her delicate but determined insinuations, Courtland told her. Yes, he'd had offers; one in particular was fine from a worldly point of view, but he didn't intend to take it. It didn't fit his ideal of life. Things about it weren't square. He wasn't sure how his own plans were going to work out yet. He must talk with his father first. Possibly he'd study awhile longer somewhere.

Gila frowned. She had no idea of letting him do that. She wanted him to get into something big right away, so she might begin her career. So that had been standing in his way. Study—how stupid! No, indeed! She wanted no scholar for a husband, who would bore her with dull old books and lectures and never want to go anywhere with her. She must switch him from this idea at once. She returned to the rejected business proposition with zeal. What was it? What were its future possibilities? Great! What could he object to in that? How ridiculous! How long ago had that been offered to him? Was it too late to accept? What? He'd had the offer repeated more flatteringly that very day? Where was the letter? Would he let her see it?

She bent over Uncle Ramsey's brusque sentences with a hidden smile of triumph and pretended to be surprised. "How perfectly wonderful! All that responsibility and all those chances to get to the top! Even a hint of Washington!"

She dimpled and opened her eyes imploringly at him. She pictured herself going with him and holding court among the great of the land. She wheedled and coaxed and all but commanded, while he sat and watched her sadly, realizing how well fitted she was for the things she was describing and how she loved them all.

So shall we be separated, I and thy people, from all the people that are upon the face of the earth!

He started upright! It was as if a voice had spoken those strange words from the Bible. Was this what they meant? Separation! But Gila was "his people" now. Wasn't she one day to be his wife? He must explain it. He must let her know he'd chosen a way of separation that didn't include the paths in which she was longing to wander. Would she shrink and wish to turn back? Nevertheless, he must make it plain to her.

Gently, quietly, he tried to make her understand. He told her of Ramsey Thomas's visit and his own decision in the winter. He told her of the factory that was built to blind the eyes of those who were trying to help men. He tried to describe how girls as young as she, with similar hopes and fears and ambitions and perhaps as much sweetness and native beauty as she had, were obliged to toil long hours amid surroundings that must crush the life out of any pure soul and turn sweetness to bitterness and beauty to peril. He hinted at dreadful things of which she knew nothing and from which she'd always been shielded—and how he could not, for the sake of those crushed souls, accept a position that would close his mouth and tie his hands forever from doing anything about it. He told her he could not accept honor founded upon dishonor; that he'd taken Christ for his pattern and guide and could do nothing to drive God's presence from him.

She had been sitting with her face averted, her clasped hands dropped straight down at the side of her lap, the fingers interlaced and tense in excitement, her bosom heaving with agitation under the Paris gown. But when he reached this point she sprang to her feet and away from him, standing with her shoulders drawn back, her head thrown up, her chin out, her whole body stiff.

"It is time this stopped!" she said. Her voice was cold like a frozen dagger and went straight through his heart. "It is time you put away forever this ridiculous idea of a Presence and of setting yourself up to be better than everyone else. This isn't religion; it's fanaticism! And it has got to stop now and *forever,* or I will have nothing whatever to do with you. Either you give up this idea of a ghost following you around all the time and accept Mr. Ramsey Thomas's offer this afternoon, or you and I part! You can choose *now* between me and your Presence!"

Chapter 26

Gila had never been more beautiful than when she uttered her terrible ultimatum to Courtland. Her head sat on her lovely shoulders royally; her attitude was perfect grace. Her spirited face with its dark eyes and lashes in its setting of blue-black hair was fascinating in its exquisite modeling. She looked like a proud young cameo standing for her portrait. But her words shot through Courtland's heart like icy swords dividing his soul from his body.

Suddenly white and stern, he rose to his feet and stood looking at her as if his own heart had turned traitor and slain him. A moment they stood in battle array, two forces representing the two great powers of the universe. Looking straight into each other's souls they stood, plumbing the depths, seeing as in a revelation what each really was!

To Courtland it was suddenly made plain that this girl had no part or lot in the things that had become vital to him. She had not seen, *would* not see! Her love wasn't great enough to carry her over the bridge that separated them, nor might he go back over that bridge after her!

Gila in her fierce haughtiness looked into Courtland's eyes and saw, as never before, the strength of his character. Saw that here was a man she would not likely meet again in her life, and she was about to lose him forever. Saw he would never give in about a matter of principle and that his love was worth all the more to any woman because he would not; knew which way he would choose, from the first word of her challenge. Yet the fury within her would not let her withdraw. She stood with haughty mien and cold, flashing eyes, watching him suffer the blow she dealt him; knew it was more than his love for her she was killing with that blow. Yet she did not withdraw it while she might.

"Gila! Do you mean that?"

She looked him straight in the eye and thrust her sword in deeper with a steady hand. "I do!"

He stood for a moment looking steadily at her with that cold, observant gaze, as if he wanted this last picture of her to erase all tender memories that might cause pain in the future. Then he turned as if to One who stood by his side.

Not looking back again, he said, clearly and distinctly, "I choose!"

And with that he passed through the door.

Gila stood, white and furious, her clenched fists down at her sides, the sharp teeth biting into the red underlip until the blood came. She heard the front door shut in the distance, and her soul cried out within her; yet she stood still and held her ground. She turned her face toward the library window. Between the curtains she could presently see his tall form walking down the street. He wasn't disheartened. He held his head up and walked as if in company with One he was proud to own. There was nothing dejected about the determined young back. Fine, noble, handsome as a man could be! She glimpsed his figure that one moment; then he passed beyond her sight, and she knew in her heart he would never come to her again. She had sent him from her forever.

She dashed up to her room in a fury and locked herself in. She wept and stormed and denied herself to everyone. She waited for the telephone to ring; yet she knew he would not call.

Courtland never knew where he was walking as he went out that day to meet his sorrow and face it like a man. He passed some of his professors but didn't see them. Pat McCluny came up, and he looked him in the eye with an unseeing stare and walked on.

Pat looked after him, puzzled.

"Holy Mackinaw! What's eating the poor stew now?" he exclaimed.

He stood a moment looking back after Courtland as he walked straight ahead, passing several more university fellows without even a nod of recognition. Then he turned and slowly followed, on through the city streets, out into the quieter suburbs, out farther into the country, mile after mile; out a bypath where grass grew thick and wildflowers straggled underfoot, where presently a stream wound soft and deep between steep banks, and rocks loomed high on either hand; under a railroad bridge and up among the rocks, climbing and puffing till at last they stood upon a great rock, with McCluny a little way behind and out of sight.

In a crevice, where the natural fall of the crumbling rocks had formed a shelter, Courtland dropped upon his knees—not as a spot he'd been seeking, but as a haven to which he'd been led. As he knelt, all Pat, standing, awed, a few feet below, heard was, "O God! O *God!*"

He knelt there a long time, while Pat waited below, trying to think what to do. The sun was sinking, and a soft, pink summer light was glinting over the brown rocks and bits of moss and grasses. The young leaves waved lightly overhead like children dancing in the morning, and something of the beauty of the scene crept into Pat McCluny's soul as he stood and waited before this Gethsemane gate for a man he loved to come forth.

At last he stepped up the rocks quietly and stood by Courtland, laying a gentle hand on his shoulder. "Come on, old man—it's getting late. About time we were getting back!"

Courtland got up and looked at him dazed, as if his soul had been bruised and he was just recovering consciousness. Without a word he turned and followed Pat back to the city. They didn't talk on the way. Pat whistled a little; that was all.

When they reached the university gates Courtland turned and put out his hand, speaking in his own natural tone. "Thanks awfully, old chap! Sorry to have made you all this trouble!"

"That's all right, pard," said Pat huskily, grasping the hand in his big fist. "I saw you were up against it and stuck around—that's all!"

"I won't forget it!"

They parted to their rooms. It was long past supper time. Pat went away by himself to think.

Over and over to himself Courtland was saying, as he realized what had come to him, "It isn't so much that I've lost her. It's that *she should have done it!*"

Pat said nothing even to Tennelly about his walk with Courtland. He figured Courtland would rather they didn't know. He simply hovered near like a faithful dog, ready for whatever might turn up. He was relieved to see that his friend came down to breakfast next morning, with a pale, resolute face, and went about the day quietly, as if everything was usual.

Tennelly and Bill Ward were on the alert. They'd missed Courtland at the festivities the night before but were so occupied with their own part in the busy week that they had little time to question him. Later in the day Tennelly wondered why Courtland hadn't brought Gila, as he'd intended, for the class play. But a note from Gila informed him she was finished with Paul Courtland forever and he'd have to get someone else to further his uncle's schemes, for she wouldn't. She intimated she might explain further if he called, and Tennelly made a point of calling in between things and found Gila inscrutable. All he could gather was that she was very angry with Courtland, hopelessly so, and considered him worth no more effort on her part. She was languidly interested in Tennelly and accepted his invitation to the dance that evening most graciously. She'd expected to go in Courtland's company, but now if he repented and came to claim his right she'd ignore it.

But Courtland took Gila at her word. He had no idea of claiming any former engagement with her. She cut him off forever, and he must abide by it. Courtland spent the night on his knees in the sacred room at the end of the hall. He was much stronger to face things than when he left her. So when he met Gila walking with Tennelly he lifted his hat courteously and passed on, his face grave and stern as when she last saw him, but in no way showing any other sign he'd suffered or repented his choice. Pat, walking beside him, looked furtively at Gila then keenly at his companion and winked to his inner consciousness.

"She's the poor simp who did the business! And she looks her part," he told himself. "But he'll get over that. He's too big to miss *her* long!"

Although Courtland felt pain in the days following his choice, he also felt great peace in his heart. He seemed to have grown older, counting days as years, and to have a wider vision on life. Love of woman was gone out of his life, he thought, forever! Love wasn't an illusion quite as he'd thought. No! But Gila hadn't loved him, or she never would have made him choose as she did. That was plain. If she hadn't loved, then it was better he should go out of her life. He was glad the university days were over, and he might begin a new environment somewhere. He felt something strong in his soul pushing him on to a decision. Was it the Voice calling him again, leading to what he was to do?

This thought was uppermost in his mind during commencement, which before had meant so much to him and all four years had been the goal he'd been aiming for. Now that it was here he seemed to have gone beyond it and found it to be but a little detail by the way, a very small matter not worth stopping and making so much fuss about. Of course, if Gila had loved him and would be there watching for him when he stepped forward to take his diploma; if she would be listening when he delivered that oration he had spent so much time on and received so much commendation for, that would have meant everything to him a few brief days ago—of course, it would have been different then. But as it was he wondered why everyone took so much trouble for a lot of nonsense.

Courtland was surprised to see his father come into the hall as he went up on the platform with his class. He hadn't expected his father. He was a busy man who didn't get away from his office often.

It touched him that his father cared to come. He changed his plans and took the train home with him after the exercises, instead of waiting a day or two to pack up, as he'd expected to do. The packing could wait awhile. So he went home with his father.

They had a long talk on the way, one of the most intimate they'd ever had. During the conversation it came out that Mr. Courtland had heard of the offer made to his son by Ramsey Thomas and that he was not unfavorable to its acceptance.

"Of course, you don't really need to do anything of the sort, you know, Paul," he said. "You've got what your mother left you now, and on your twenty-fifth birthday there will be two hundred and fifty thousand coming to you from your grandfather Courtland's estate. You could spend your life in travel and study if you cared to. But I guess, with your temperament, you wouldn't be satisfied with an idle life like that. What's your objection to this job?"

Courtland told the whole story carefully, omitting no detail of the matter concerning conditions at the factory and the matters he was not only expected to wink at, but also sometimes to help along by his influence. He realized, as he told it, that his father would look at the thing fairly but very differently.

"Well, after all," said the father, comfortably settling himself to another cigar, "that's all a matter of sentiment. It doesn't do to be too squeamish, you know, if you have ambitions. Besides, with your income you could have helped out and done a lot of good. You should have thought of that."

"In other words, earn my salary by squeezing the life out of them and then toss them a penny to buy medicine. I don't see it that way! No, Dad, if I can't work at something clean I'll go out and work in the ground or do *nothing*, but I *won't* oppress the poor."

"Oh, well, Paul, that's all right if you feel that way about it, of course. Ramsey Thomas wanted me to talk it over with you—promised to do the square thing by you and all that—and he's a pretty good man to get in with. Of course I won't urge you against your will. But what are you going to do, son? Have you thought of anything?"

"Yes," said Courtland, leaning back and looking steadily at his father. "I've decided I'd like to study theology."

"Theology!" The father started and knocked an ash from the end of his cigar. "H'm. Well, that's not a bad idea! Rather odd, perhaps, but still there's always dignity and distinction in it. Your great grandfather on your mother's side was a clergyman in the Church of England. Of course it's rather a surprise, but it's always respectable, and with your money you'd be independent. You wouldn't have any trouble getting a wealthy, influential church either. I could manage that, I think."

"I'm not sure I want to be a clergyman, Father. I said *study* theology. I want to know what scholarly Christians think of the Bible. I've studied it with a lot of scholarly heathen who couldn't see anything in it but literary merit. Now I want to see what has made it a living power throughout the ages. I've got to know what saints and martyrs have founded their faith on."

"Well, Paul, I'm afraid you're something of an idealist and a dreamer like your mother. Of course it's all right with your income, but, generally speaking, it's as well to have an object in view when you take up study. If I were you I'd look into the matter carefully before I made any decisions. If you really think the ministry is what you want, why, I'll just put a word in at our church for you. Our old doctor Bates is getting a little out of date and will be about ready for the retired list by the time you've finished your theological course. Let's see, how long is it, three years? Had you thought where you'll go? What seminary? Better make a careful selection; it has so much to do with getting a good church afterward."

"Father! You don't *understand!*" said Courtland desperately and then wondered how to begin. His father had been a prominent member of the board of trustees in his own church for years, but had he ever felt the Presence? In the days when Courtland used to sit and kick his heels in the old family pew and be reproved for it by his aunt, he never remembered any Presence. Doctor Bates's admirable sermons had droned on over his head like bees humming on a summer day. He couldn't remember a single thought that ever entered his mind from that source. Was that all that came of studying theology? Well, he would find out, and if it was, he'd *quit* it!

They were comfortably glad to see him at home. His stepmother beamed graciously on him between her social engagements, and his young brothers swarmed over him, demanding all the athletic news. The house was big, ornate, perfect in its way. It was good to eat superior cooking—if he'd cared to eat anything then—and he knew he should enjoy the freedom in life out of college. But he was restless. The girls he used to know reminded him of Gila or else had grown old and stout. The country club didn't interest him in the least, nor did the family's plans for the summer. It didn't suit him to be lionized because of his brilliant career at college. It bored him to go into society.

Sometimes, alone in his room, he would think of the situation and try to puzzle it out. He and the Presence seemed to be there on a visit which neither of them enjoyed very much and were enduring for the sake of his father, who seemed gratified to have his eldest son at home again. But all the time Courtland was chafing at the delay. He felt there was something he should be about. There was nothing here. Not even the young brothers presented a hopeful field, or perhaps he didn't know how to go about it. He told them stories one day when he wheedled them off in the car with him, and they listened eagerly when he described the fire in the theater, Stephen Marshall's wonderful part in rescuing people, and his death. But when he tried to tell them in boy language of his own experience he could see them look strangely, critically, at him, and finally the oldest one said, "Aw, rats! What kinda rot are you giving us, Paul? You were nutty then, o' course!" He saw that, young as they were, their eyes were held like the rest.

In the second week Courtland made his decision. He'd return to the university and pack up. Gila would be away from the city by then; he would have no chance of meeting her and having his wound opened afresh. The fellows would be gone, and he could do almost as he pleased.

The second day after he went back he met Pat on the street, and from him he learned that Tennelly and Bill Ward had gone down to the shore to a house party given by "that fluffy-ruffles cousin of Bill's."

Pat drew his own conclusions from the white look on Courtland's face when he told him. He would enjoy throttling the girl if he had a chance just then, when he saw the look of suffering in Courtland's eyes.

Pat clung to Courtland that week, helped him pack and dogged his steps. Except when he visited the sacred room at the end of the hall in the dormitory, Courtland was never sure of freedom from him. He was always on hand to propose a hike or a trip to the movies when he saw he was tired. Courtland was grateful, and something about him was so loyal that he couldn't give him the slip. So when he went down after Burns and whirled him away in his big gray car to the seashore Friday morning to stay until Saturday evening, Pat went along.

Chapter 27

They were an odd trio, the little Scottish preacher, the big Irish athlete and the cultured aristocrat! Yet they managed to have a good time those two days at the shore and came back the warmest of friends. Pat proved his devotion to Burns by attending church the next day with Courtland and listening attentively to every word. He did it much as the fellows used to share one another's stunts in college, sticking by and helping out when one had a hard task to perform. But it pleased both Courtland and Burns that he came. Courtland wondered, as he shared the hymnbook with him and heard him growl out a few bass notes to old "Rock of Ages," why it lifted him up so to hear Pat sing. He hadn't yet recognized the call to fish for men or know it was the divine angler's delight in his employment that was lifting him. While they were singing that hymn he stole a look at Pat and wondered suddenly whether he would understand about the Presence or not; he felt a burning desire to tell him about it if the right opportunity arose.

The days at the shore did a lot for Courtland. He carefully selected a spot many miles removed from the popular resort where Mr. Dare had a magnificent cottage, and nothing in the whole two days reminded him of Gila. It was a quiet place, with a long, smooth beach and no boardwalks or crowds to shut out the vision of the sea. He leaped along the sand and dived into the water with his old enthusiasm. He played like a fish in the ocean. He taught Burns several things about swimming and played pranks like a schoolboy. He basked in the sun and told jokes, laughing at Pat's brilliant wit and Burns's dry humor. At night they took long walks on the sand and talked of things Pat could scarcely understand. He was satisfied to stride between them, listening to the vigorous ring of Courtland's old natural voice again. He heard their converse high above where he lived and loved them for the way they searched into things too deep for him.

Out in the wildest, loneliest part of the beach that night he heard the first hint of what had come to Courtland's soul. Pat was of Catholic ancestry and had inherited a reverence for the unseen. He had shed religion like a shower, but he respected it.

Courtland spent much time near the factory and John Burns's church during the next few weeks. He helped Burns a good deal, for the man had heavily taxed himself with the burdens of the poor. Courtland found ways to relieve necessity privately and put a poor soul now and then on his feet and able to face the world again by loaning a few cents or dollars. It took so little to open heaven's gate to some lives! With his keen intellect and fine perceptions Courtland helped the older man sometimes in his perplexities.

Once, when Burns was greatly worried over a bill that was hanging fire during a prolonged session of Congress, Courtland went down to Washington for a weekend and hunted up some of his father's congressional friends. He told them a few facts concerning factories in general and a certain model, white marble, bevined factory in particular that at least opened their eyes if it didn't make much difference in the general outcome. Though the bill failed to pass that session, being skillfully sidetracked, Courtland managed to stir up trouble for Uncle Ramsey Thomas that made him storm about the office wrathfully and wonder who that "little rat of a preacher" had helping him now!

Late in September Pat, with a manner of studied indifference, told Courtland of a rumor that Tennelly was engaged to Gila Dare.

The very next Sunday night Tennelly turned up at Courtland's apartment after he and Pat had gone to the evening service and then followed them to church. He dropped into a seat beside Pat, amazed to find him there.

"You here!" he whispered, grasping Pat's hand with the old friendly grip. "Where's Court?"

Pat grinned and nodded up toward the pulpit.

Tennelly looked forward and for a minute didn't comprehend. Then he saw Courtland sitting in a pulpit chair by the red-headed Scottish preacher.

"What in thunder!" he growled, almost out loud. "What's the joke?"

Pat's face was on the defensive at once, though he was plainly enjoying Tennelly's perplexity. "Court's speaking tonight!" Pat probably never enjoyed giving any information as much as that sentence in his life.

"The deuce he is!" said Tennelly out loud, during the preacher's prayer. "You're lying, man!"

Pat frowned. "Shut up, Nelly. Can't you see the game's called? I'm telling you straight. If you don't believe it wait and see."

Tennelly looked again. That surely was Courtland sitting there. What could it mean? Had Courtland taken to itinerant preaching? Consternation filled him. He loved Courtland as his own brother. He'd have done anything to save his brilliant career for him.

He hadn't intended staying for the service. He planned to slip in, get Courtland to come away with him, have a talk and return to the shore on the late train. But the present situation altered his plans. He could only stay and see this thing through. Pat was a whole lot deeper than the rest had ever given him credit for being.

Pat was enjoying the service's psychological effect on Tennelly. He'd never been much of a student in psychology class, but when it came to looking into another man's soul and telling what he was thinking about and would do next, Pat was there. That was what made him such an excellent football player. When he met his opponent he could always size him up and tell just about what kind of plays he'd make and know how to prepare for them. Pat was no fool.

That was a most unusual service. The minister read the story of the martyr Stephen and the conversion of Saul of Tarsus, from the sixth, seventh, eighth and ninth chapters of Acts. The reading was brief and dramatic. Even Tennelly was caught and held as Burns read in his clear, direct way that made Scripture seem to live again in modern times.

"I've asked my friend Mr. Courtland to tell you the story of how he met Jesus one day on the Damascus road," said Burns, as he closed the Bible and turned to Courtland, sitting still with bowed head just behind him.

Courtland had made many speeches during his college days. He'd been the prince among his class for debate, proud of his ability as a speaker and delighted in being able to hold and sway an audience. He'd never known stage fright or dreaded appearing before people. But ever since Burns asked him to tell the story of the Presence to the people in the church before he left for his theological studies, Courtland had been frightened. He consented. Somehow he couldn't do anything else; it was so obviously to his mind a "call." But if he were a coward in any sense he'd have run away that Saturday afternoon and got out of it all. Only his horror of being "yellow" had kept him to his promise.

Since ascending to the platform he'd been overcome by the audacity of the idea that he, a mere babe in knowledge, a recent scorner, should get up and tell a roomful of people, who knew far more about the Bible than he did, how he found Christ. He had no words to tell anything. They'd fled from his mind!

He dropped his head on his hand to pray for strength, and a calm came to his soul. The prayer and Bible reading had steadied him, and he got hold of what he had to say as the story of the young man Saul progressed. But when he heard himself being introduced so simply and knew his time had come, he seemed to hear the words he read that afternoon.

Fear thou not; for I am with thee: be not dismayed; for I am thy God: I will strengthen thee; yea, I will help thee; yea, I will uphold thee with the right hand of my righteousness.

Courtland lifted his head and stood. All at once Tennelly's face stood out from the others, intent, curious, and Courtland knew his opportunity had come to tell Tennelly about the Presence.

Tennelly, the man he loved above all other men! Tennelly, the man who perhaps loved Gila and was to be close to her through life! His fears vanished; his soul burned within him.

Fixing his eyes on the fine, vivid face, Courtland began his story. Truly his words must have been drawn red-hot from his heart, for he spoke as one inspired. As if he were alone in the room with his friend, Courtland looked into his friend's eyes and told his story, forgetting all others, intent only on making Tennelly see what Christ had been to him, what He was willing to be to Tennelly—and Gila—if they would!

The young man kept his eyes on the speaker. It was curious to see him so absorbed—Tennelly, who was so conventional, so careful what people thought, so conscious of all elements in his environment. It was as if his soul were sitting in his eyes for the first time in his life, and things unsuspected, perhaps, even by him, showed themselves: traits, weaknesses, possibilities, longings, too, and pride.

When Courtland finished and sat down he didn't drop his head on his hands again. He had spoken in the Lord's strength. He had nothing to be ashamed of. He was looking now at the audience and no longer at Tennelly. He realized it was given to him to bear the message to these other people also. He was filled with humble exaltation that this great opportunity was entrusted to him.

The people, too, were hushed and filled with awe. They showed by the quiet way they reached for the hymnbooks, the reverent bowing of their heads for the final prayer, that they'd felt the power of Christ with the speaker. Many lingered and pressed about him, to touch his hand and make mute appeal with their troubled eyes. Some asked him eagerly for reassurance of what he'd said; others thanked him for the story. They were humble, sincere, eager, like the ones of old who crowded around the Master and heard him gladly. Paul Courtland was filled with humility. He stood there half embarrassed as they pressed about him. He took their hands and smiled his brotherhood but scarcely knew what to say to them. He felt like an awkward boy who'd made a great discovery and was too shy to talk about it.

Pat and Tennelly stood back against the wall and waited, silently. Tennelly watched the people as they went out: common people, subdued, wistful, even tearful; some with illumined faces as if they'd seen a light in the darkness.

When at last Courtland drifted to the back of the church and reached Tennelly, the two met with a look straight into each other's soul, while their hands gripped in the old clasp. No smile or commonplace expression crossed either face—just that strong, steady look of recognition and understanding. It was Tennelly looking at Courtland, the new man in Christ Jesus; Courtland looking at Tennelly after he'd heard the story.

They walked back to Courtland's apartment almost in silence, a kind of holy embarrassment on them. Pat whistled "Rock of Ages" softly under his breath most of the way.

They sat talking stiffly, as if they hardly knew one another, and told the news. Bill Ward had gone to California to look into a big land deal his father was interested in. Wittemore's mother had died, and he wasn't returning next year for his senior year. It was surface talk. Pat put in a little about football. He discussed which of last year's scrubs were most hopeful candidates for the varsity team this year. Not one of the three cared then whether the university had a football team or not. Their thoughts were on deeper things.

But the recent service wasn't mentioned or Courtland's extraordinary part in it. By common consent they shunned the subject. It was too near each one's heart.

Finally Pat took himself off, professedly in search of ice water, as the cooler in the hall had for some reason run dry. He was gone for some time.

When he left the room Tennelly sat up. He had something to say to Courtland alone. It must be said now before Pat returned.

Courtland got up, crossed the room and stood looking out the window on the city's myriad lights. In his face was a distant yearning and something too deep for words. It was as if he were waiting for a blow to fall.

Tennelly looked at Courtland's back and gathered up his courage. "Court," he said hoarsely, trying to summon the nomenclature of the dear old days. "I wanted to ask you something. Was there anything—is there—between you and Gila Dare that makes it disloyal for your friend to try to win her if he can?"

It was still in the room. The whir of the trolleys could be heard below as if they were out in the hall. They grated harshly on the silence. Courtland stood as if carved out of marble. It seemed ages to Tennelly before he answered, with the sadness of the grave in his tone.

"No, Nelly! It's all right. Gila and I didn't hit it off. It's over between us forever. Go ahead! I wish you luck!"

There was an attempt at the old loving understanding in the answer, but somehow the last words had almost the sound of a sob in them. Tennelly had a feeling he was wringing his own happiness out of his friend's soul.

"Thanks awfully, Court! I didn't know," he said awkwardly. "I think she likes me a lot, but I couldn't do anything if you had the right of way."

When Pat returned with a tray of glasses clinking with ice and the smell of crushed lemons, they were talking of the new English professor and the chances he'd be better than the last, who was "punk." But Pat wasn't deceived. He looked from one to the other and knew the blow had fallen. He might have prevented it, but what was the use? It had to come sooner or later. They talked late. Finally Tennelly rose and came toward Courtland, with his hand outstretched, and they all knew the evening's real moment had come at last.

"That was a great old talk you gave us this evening, Court!" Tennelly's voice was husky with feeling. One sensed he'd kept the feeling out of sight all evening. He was holding Courtland's hand in a painful grip and looking again into his eyes as if to search his soul to the depths. "You sure have something there that's worth looking into. You had a great hold on your audience, too. Why, you almost persuaded me there was something in it!"

Tennelly tried to finish his sentence in a lighter vein, but the feeling was in his voice yet.

Courtland gripped his hand and revealed his eagerness with a sudden light of joy and hope. "If you only would, Nelly! It's what I've longed for—!"

"Not yet!" said Tennelly, almost pulling his hand away from the detaining grasp. "Sometime, perhaps, but not now! I have too much else on hand. I must beat it now! Man alive! Do you know what time it is? See you soon!" Tennelly was off in a whirl of words.

"Almost thou persuadest me!" Had someone whispered the words behind him as he went?

Courtland stood looking after him till the door closed, then he turned and stepped to the window again. He was so long standing there that Pat went at last and touched him on the shoulder.

"Say, pard," he said in a low, gruff voice. "I'm nothing but a roughneck, I know, and not worth much at that. But if it's any satisfaction to you to know you've bowled a bum like me over to His side, why, *I'm with you!*"

Courtland turned and grasped his hand, throwing the other arm about Pat's shoulder. "It sure is, Pat, old boy," he said. "It's the greatest thing ever! Thanks! I needed that just now. I'm all in!"

They stood so for some minutes with their arms across each other's shoulders, looking out of the window to the city, lying needy before them; down to the street below, where Tennelly hastened on to win his Gila; up to the quiet, wise old stars above.

Chapter 28

Tennelly didn't come back as he promised. Instead he wrote a cheerful note telling of his engagement to Gila. He said it wasn't to be announced publicly yet, as Gila was so young. They'd wait a year perhaps before announcing it to the world, but he wanted Courtland to know. At the bottom he added: "That was a great old speech you made the other night, Court. I haven't forgotten it yet. Your reference to Marshall was a crackerjack! The faculty should have heard it."

Courtland read it, closed his eyes for a minute, passed his hand over his brow and then handed the note to Pat. The understanding between the two was deep and tender now.

Pat read without comment, but the frown on his brow matched the set of his jaw. When he spoke again he told Courtland of the job he was offered as athletic coach in a preparatory school in the same neighborhood as the theological seminary where Courtland had decided to study. Courtland listened without hearing and smiled wearily. He was entering his Gethsemane. Neither of them slept much that night.

In the early dawn Courtland arose, dressed and stole silently out of the room, down through the sleeping city, out to the country, where he'd gone once before when trouble struck him. He felt he must get away to breathe, to go where he and God could be alone.

Pat understood. He waited till Courtland was gone to fling on his clothes and be after him. He noted the direction from the window and guessed where he'd be.

On and on Courtland walked with the burning sorrow in his soul; out through the heated city, over the miles of dusty road, his feet finding their way without apparent direction from his mind; out to the stream and the path where wildflowers and grasses had strewn the ground in springtime; bright now with white and purple asters. The rocks wore vines of crimson, and the goldenrod was full of bees and yellow butterflies. Gnarled roots bore creeping tufts of squaw berry with red berries dotting thick between. But Courtland passed on and saw it not.

Above, the deep blue sky was flecked with summer clouds. Birds called loudly of the summer's ending. The bees droned on, and the bullfrogs gave forth a deep thought or two, while the stream flowed brown beside the path.

But Courtland heard and saw nothing but the dark of his Gethsemane. For every nodding goldenrod and saucy purple aster only brought back Gila's saucy, lovely face. She belonged to another now. He hadn't realized before how fully he'd chosen, how lost she was to him, until another, and that his best friend, had taken her for his own. Not that he repented his decision. Oh, no! He couldn't have chosen otherwise. Yet now, face-to-face with the truth, he realized he'd always hoped, even when he walked away from her, that she would find the Christ and one day they'd come together again. Now that hope was gone forever. She might find the Christ; he hoped and prayed she would— yet it was a wish apart from his personal loss. But she could never summon him now, for she'd given herself to another.

He gained at last the rock-bound refuge where he knelt once before. Pat, coming later from afar, saw his old panama lying down on the moss and knew he was there. Creeping softly up, he assured himself all was well, then crept away to wait. He'd brought a basket of grapes and a bag of luscious pears for when Courtland would have fought his battle and come forth. What those hours of waiting meant to Pat might be found written in the lives of some of the boys in that school where he coached athletics the next winter. But what they meant to Courtland will only be found written in the records on high.

Sometime a little after noon peace came to Courtland's troubled soul.

When thou passest through the waters, I will be with thee; and through the rivers, they shall not overflow thee!

It was as near to him as whispers in his ear, and peace was all about him.

He stood up, looked afar off, saw the beauty of the day, heard the dreaminess of the afternoon coming on, heard louder God's call to his heart and knew he had strength for all his need. Then Pat came with his refreshment like a ministering angel.

When they returned to the city that evening a note had come from Bonnie, the first Courtland had received since the formal announcement of her arrival and her gratitude to him for being the means of bringing her to that dear home.

This letter was almost as brief as the first, but it breathed a spirit of peace and contentment. She enclosed a check for the funeral account. She was well and happy. She was teaching in the grammar school where Stephen Marshall used to study when he was a little boy and giving music lessons in the afternoons. She could soon pay back everything she owed and to do a daughter's share in the home where she was treated like an own child. She closed by saying that his kindness to her would never be forgotten; that he seemed to her, and always would, like the Lord's messenger sent to help her in her despair.

The letter held such a fresh, strong, true ring to it. He sighed and thought how strange it was that he almost resented it, coming as it did in contrast with Gila's falseness. Gila who professed to love him so deeply and then so easily laid that love aside and put on another. Perhaps all girls were the same. Perhaps this Bonnie, too, would do the same if a man turned out not to have her ideals.

He answered Bonnie's note in a day or two with a cordial one, returning her check, assuring her everything was fully paid and expressing his pleasure that she'd found a real home and congenial work. Then he dismissed her from his mind.

A week later he went to the seminary, and Pat accompanied him as far as the preparatory school where he was to enter upon his duties as athletic coach.

Courtland found the atmosphere of the seminary quite different from college. The men were older. They'd chosen their work in the world. Their talk was of things ecclesiastical. The day's events were spoken of with reference to the religious world. It was a new viewpoint in every sense of the word. Yet he was disappointed he didn't find a more spiritual atmosphere among the young men who were studying for the ministry. If anywhere in the world the Presence might be expected to be moving and apparent it should be here, he reasoned, where men had given themselves to studying the gospel of Christ and where all were supposed to believe in Him and to have acknowledged Him before the world. He found himself the only man there who wasn't a member of any church, and yet he felt he could speak to only three or four about the Presence and not be considered strange.

There was a great deal of gossip about churches and ministers; what this or that one was paid; and the chances of a man being called to a city church when he was just out of the seminary. It was how his father had talked when he told him he wanted to study theology. It turned him sick at heart to hear them and seemed so far from the attitude he thought a servant of the Lord should have. He was losing his ideal of ministers as well as of women. He mentioned it one day bitterly to Pat when he came over to spend a spare evening, as he frequently did.

"I think you're wrong," said Pat in his abrupt way. "From what I can figure only a few of those guys got around Christ and knew what He really was! You didn't suppose it would be any different now, did you? Guess you'll find it that way everywhere—only a few *real* folks in *any* gang!"

Courtland looked at Pat in wonder. He was a constant surprise to his friend, in that he grew so fast in the Christian life. He'd bought a little Bible before he left the city. It was small and fine and expensive, utterly unlike Pat, and he always carried it with him and apparently read it often. He hadn't been given to reading anything more than was required at college, so it was even more surprising. He told Courtland he wanted to know the rules of the game if he was going to get in it. His sturdy common sense often gave Courtland something to think about.

Pat was bringing his new religion to bear upon his work. He already had a devoted bunch of boys he was dealing out wholesome truths to in the school. The headmaster looked on in amazement, for morality hadn't been one of the chief recommendations the university faculty had given Pat. They had, in fact, privately cautioned the school they'd have to watch out for such things themselves. But instead of finding a somewhat lawless man in their new coach, the headmaster was surprised to discover a purity campaign on foot and a ban on swearing and cigarette smoking such as they could never establish before. It came to their ears that Pat had personally conducted an offender along these lines out to the school boundaries and administered a good thrashing on his own account. The faculty watched anxiously to see the effect of such summary treatment on the student body but were relieved to find the new coach's following wasn't diminished and that better conduct became the order of the day.

Pat and Courtland were often together these days, and one Sunday afternoon in late October, while the sun was still warm, they took the athletic teams on a long hike in the country. When they rested, Pat asked Courtland to tell the boys about Stephen and the Presence.

That was the real beginning of Courtland's ministry, those unexpected, spontaneous talks with the boys, where he could speak his heart and not fear being misunderstood.

Two or three professors in the seminary struck Courtland as being profoundly spiritual and sincere in their lives. They were old men, noted the world over for their scholarship and strong faith. They taught as Courtland imagined a prophet might have taught in Old Testament days, with their ears open to hear what the Lord would have them speak to the children of men. At their feet he sat and drank in great draughts of knowledge, going away satisfied. Other professors, some extremely brilliant, seemed to have an undertone of flippancy in their attitude toward the Bible and Christ and to delight in finding an inauthentic portion over which they might haggle away the precious hours of the classroom. They lacked the reverent attitude toward their subject which only could save the higher criticism from being destructive rather than constructive.

As the year passed he came to know his fellow students better and to find among them a few earnest, thoroughly consecrated ones, most of them plain men like Burns, who had turned aside from the world's allurements to prepare themselves to carry the gospel to those in need. Most of them were poor men also and of humble birth, with a rare one now and then of brains and family and wealth, like Courtland, to whom God had come in some peculiar way. These stood apart from others, whom the rest respected and admired, yet laughed at in a gentle, humoring way, as if they wasted more energy on their calling than there was any real need to do. Some of them were going to foreign lands when they were through, had already been assigned to their mission stations and were planning for the needs of the locality. Courtland felt an idler and drone among them that he didn't yet know what he was to do.

As the men came to know him better, they predicted great things for him: wealthy churches falling at his feet, brilliant openings at his disposal. But Courtland took no part in any such discussions. He had the heart attitude that he was to be guided, when he was through his studies, to where he was most needed. It didn't matter where, as long as it was the place God wanted him to be.

In February Burns had a farewell service in his church. He'd resigned his pastorate and was going to China. Pat and Courtland went down to the city to attend the service and Monday saw him off to San Francisco for his sea voyage to China.

As he stood on the platform watching the train move away with his friend, Courtland wished he could be on that train going with Burns to China. He was to take up Burns's work around the settlement and in the factory section, to see some of his friend's plans through to completion. He was almost sorry he'd promised. He felt utterly inadequate.

Spring came, and with it the formal announcement of Tennelly and Gila's engagement. Courtland and Pat each read it in the papers but said nothing of it to each other. These days Courtland worked harder.

He tried to plunge into the work and forget self, and to an extent he was successful. He found plenty of distress and sorrow to contrast with his own, and his hands and heart were presently full to overflowing.

Like the faithful fellow worker he was, Pat stuck by him. Both looked forward to the week Tennelly had promised to spend with them. But instead of Tennelly came a letter. Gila's plans interfered, and he couldn't come. He wrote joyously that he was sorry, but he couldn't possibly make it. It shone between every line that Tennelly was overwhelmingly happy.

"Good old Nelly!" said Courtland with a sigh, handing the letter to Pat.

Courtland stood staring out the window at the roofs and tall chimneys. The blistering summer sun simmered hot and sickening over the city. Red brick and dust and grime were all around him. His soul was weary of the sight and faltered in its way. What was the use of living? What?

Then suddenly he straightened up and leaned from the window. The fire alarm was sounding. Its sinister wheeze shrilled through the hot air. It sounded again. One, two! One, two, three! It was in the neighborhood.

Without waiting for a word, both men sprang out the door and down the stairs.

Chapter 29

T he Whited Sepulcher," as some of the bitterest of her poorly paid slaves called the model factory, stood coolly, insolently, among her dirty, red-brick, grime-stained neighbors—like some dainty lady appareled in sheer muslins and jewels appearing on the threshold of the hot kitchen where her servants were sweating and toiling to prepare her a feast.

The vines were green and abundant, creeping about the white walls, befring-ing the windows, clinging to the eaves and straying out over the roof. No mat-ter how parched the ground in the district parks, no matter how yellow the leaves on the few stunted trees nearby, no matter how low the city's supply of water or how many public fountains had to be temporarily shut off, that vine was always watered. Its root lay deep in soft, moist earth fertilized and cared for; its leaves were washed each evening with a refreshing spray from the hose that played over it.

"Seems like I'd just like to lie down there and sleep with my face clost up to it, all wet and coollike, all night!" sighed one poor bony victim of a girl, scarcely more than a child, as the throng pressed out the wide door at six o'clock and caught the moist fragrance of the damp earth and growing vine.

"You look all in, Susie!" said her neighbor, pausing in her gum-chewing to eye her friend keenly. "Say, you better go with me to the movies tonight! I know a nice cool one for a nickel."

"Can't!" sighed Susie. "Ain't got ther nickel, and besides I gotta stay with Gran'mom while Ma goes up with some vests she's been makin'. Oh, I'm all right. I jus' was thinkin' about the vine; it looks so cool and purty. Say, Katie, it's somepin' to b'long to a vine like that, even if we do have it rotten sometimes. Don't you always feel kinda proud when you come in the door, 'most as if it was a palace? I like to pretend it's all a great house where I live, and there's carpets and lace curtings to the winders, and a real gold sofy with pink-velvet cushings. And when I come down and see one of the company's ottymobeels standin' by the curb waitin', I like to pertend it's mine—only I don't ride 'cause I've been ridin' so much I'd *ruther* walk! Don't you ever do that, Katie?"

"Not on yer *life,* I don't!" said Katie, with a frown. "I hate the old dump! I hate every stone in the whole pile! I could tear that nasty green vine down an' stamp on it. I'd like to strip its leaves off an' leave it bare. I'd like to turn the hose off and see it dry up an' be brown an' ugly an' dead. It's stealin' the water they oughtta have over there in the fountain. It's stealin' the money they oughtta pay us fer our work. It's creepin' round the winders an' eatin' up the air. Didn't you never take notice to how they let it grow acrost the winders to hide folks from lookin' in from the visitors' windows there on the east side? They don't care how it shuts away the draught and makes it hotter 'n a furnace where we work! No, you silly! I'm never proud to come in that old marble door. I'm always mad, away down inside, that I have to work here. I had to go crawlin' and askin' fer a job an' take all their insults an' be locked in a trap.

"Take it from me—there's goin' to be some awful accident happen here someday. If a fire should break out how many d'you s'pose could get out before they was burned to a crisp? Did you know them winders was nailed so they wouldn't go up any higher 'n a foot? Did you know they ain't got 'nouf fire escapes to get half of us out ef anythin' happened? Did you never take notice to the floor roun' them three biggest old machines they've got up on the sixth? I stepped acrost there this mornin'—Mr. Brace sent me up on a message to the forewoman—an' that floor shook under my feet like a earthquake! Sam Warner says the building ain't half strong enough fer them machines anyway. He says they'd oughtta put 'em down on the first floor. But they didn't want to 'cause then they don't show off good to visitors, so they stuck 'em up on the sixth, where many don't see 'em. But Sam says someday they're goin' to bust right through the floor, an 'f they do, they ain't gonta stop till they get clear down to the cellar, an' they'll wipe out everythin' in their way when they go! B'leeve me! I don't wanta be workin' here when that happens!"

"*Good night!*" said Susie, turning pale. "Them big machines on the sixth is right over where I work on the fifth! Say, Katie, le's ast Mr. Bruce to put us on the other side o' the room. Aw, what's the use o' livin'? I'd most be willin' to be dead just to get cool! Seems zif it's allus either awful hot er awful cold!"

They went to their stifling tenements and unattractive suppers. They dragged their weary feet over the hot, dark pavements, laughing and talking boisterously with their comrades, or crowded into amusement places to forget for a little while. Then they crept back to toss the night out on a hard cot in breathless air or to fire escape or flat roof for a few brief hours of relief, till it was time to return to the vine-clad factory and its hot, noisy slavery for another day.

Three girls fainted on the fifth floor and two on the sixth next morning. They weren't carried to the cool, shaded rest rooms to revive but lay on the floor with their heads huddled on a pile of waste and had a little warmish water from the rusty "cooler" in the back stairway poured on them as they lay. No white-clad nurse with palm leaf and cooling drinks attended their unconscious state, although one was in attendance in the rest room to look after the comfort of any chance visitors. When any worker stooped to comfort another, she fanned her neighbor with her apron, casting an anxious eye on her own silent machine and knowing she was losing "time."

Susie fainted three times that morning, and Katie lost an hour, bringing water and making a fan out of a newspaper. She also had an angry altercation with the foreman. He said if Susie "played up" this way she'd have to quit; plenty of girls were waiting to take her place, and he had no time to fool with kids who wanted to lie around and be fanned. It was his last few words as she was reviving that stung Susie to life again and put her back at her machine for the last time in nervous panic, with the thought of what would happen at home if she lost her job. Up above her the great heavy machines thrashed on, and the floor trembled with their movement. The air around her was black and thick and hot, and she could scarcely see the machinery for dizziness. She worked it from habit, as she stood swaying in her place, and wondered if she could hold out till the noon whistle blew.

Down in the basement, near one of the elevator shafts, a pile of waste lay smoldering, out of sight. A boy from the lumberyard in the next block had stopped to light his cigarette as he passed into the street after bringing a bill to the head manager. He tossed his match away, not seeing where it fell. The factory thundered on in full swing of a busy, driving morning, while the match nursed its flame.

How long it crept and smoldered no one knew. The smell of smoke and cry of fire seemed to come from every floor at once. More smoke in volumes poured up through cracks and burst from the elevator shaft; a lick of flame darted out like a serpent ready to strike, menacing against the heat of the big rooms. Cries and clashing machinery thundered on like a storm above an angry sea.

The girls rushed together in fear or, screaming, ran desperately to windows they knew they couldn't raise! They pounded at the locked doors and crowded in the narrow passages, frantically surging this way and that. There was no one to quiet them or tell them what to do. If someone would only stop that awful machinery! Was the engineer dead?

The cool vines crept in about the windowsills and over the imprisoning panes, as if to taunt the victims caught in the death trap.

"At any rate, if we die you'll die too!" cried Katie Craigin, shaking her fist at the long green tendrils that swept across the window nearest her machine. "Oh, you! You'll burn to a crisp at the roots! You'll wither up an' die. You'll be dead an' brown an' ugly! An' I'm glad! I *hate* you! Do you hear?" She stamped her foot, then turned to look for Susie.

But Susie had fallen once more by her machine leaving it unguarded while it thrashed on uselessly. Her pinched face looked up from the dirty floor in pitiful unconsciousness amid the wild rush and whirl of the fear-maddened company. If terror drove them they'd pass blindly over her.

The room seemed about to burst with the heat. Timbers were cracking. All the stories they'd heard of the frailty of the building goaded them as they hurtled from one end of their pen to the other, while intermittent clouds of smoke and darting flames conspired to bewilder their senses.

Katie seized her friend and drew her out of the path of the stampede. As she lifted her a cry arose, like the wail of a lost world facing the judgment. The floor swayed, the machines almost tottered, and the floor above seemed bending down with some great weight. There was a cracking, wrenching, twisting, as of the whole building in mortal pain, and just as Katie drew her unconscious friend to the window the floor gave way and down crashed three awful machines, like great devouring juggernauts, to crush and bear away whatever came in their way.

After that, hell itself could scarcely have presented a more terrible spectacle of writhing, tortured souls, pinned anguishing amid the flames; of white faces below looking up to ghastly ones above that gazed down with horror into the awful cavern, closed their eyes, clung to walls and windows, and didn't know what to do.

The fearful noise of machinery had suddenly ceased and been succeeded by a calm in which the soft sound of rushing flames, the babble of the crowd outside, the gong of fire engines and the cry of firemen seemed like music to the ears. Water hissed on hot machinery and burning walls. It splashed inside the window and on Susie's pale face. It touched Katie's hot hands as she lifted her friend nearer the spray. A shadow of a ladder crossed the window. Splintered glass fell about her, and a hand reached in and crushed the window frame.

Pat lifted out the limp Susie and handed her down to Courtland, just below, while Katie looked back at the pit of fire beneath her, knowing that in a few seconds, without help, she too would be part of that writhing, awful heap. She saw the white face and staring eyes of the gray-haired woman who ran the machine next to hers lying beneath a pile of dead. She reeled and felt her senses going. Her hot hands clung to the hotter window ledge. The flames were leaping nearer! She couldn't hold out—

Then a strong hand grasped her and drew her out into the air, and she felt herself being carried down, wondering, as she went, if the vine was roasted yet or if it still smirked greenly outside this holocaust and wishing she had strength to shake a mocking finger at it. And then she knew no more.

For three long hours Courtland and Pat worked side by side, bringing out the living, searching for the dead and dying, carrying them to an improvised hospital in an old warehouse in the next block. Grim and soiled and gray, with singed hair, blistered hands and faces, and sickened hearts, they toiled on.

To Courtland the experience was like walking with God and being shown the way he might have gone and how he was saved. If he'd accepted Ramsey Thomas's proposition he would have shared in the sin that caused this catastrophe. He would have been a murderer, almost as much responsible for that charred body lying at his feet, for all those dead and dying, as if he owned the place.

The whited sepulcher lay a heap of blackened ruins. Only one small corner of blackened marble rose, to which clung a green fragment to show what was only a few short hours before. The morning's sun would see it, too, withered and black like the rest. The model factory was gone. But the money that built it, the money it made, still existed to rebuild it, a perpetual blind to the lawmakers who might have stopped its abuses. It would undoubtedly be built again, more whited, more sepulchral than before.

As he looked on the ruin he resolved to give his life to fight the power that was setting its heel upon humanity and putting a price on its blood. He would devote all his powers to lifting up people downtrodden and oppressed in the simple act of earning their daily bread.

Ramsey Thomas, happening to be in a nearby city and answering a summons by telegraph, arrived at the scene in an automobile as Courtland stood there, grimed and tattered from his fight with death.

Ramsey Thomas, baffled, angry, distressed, wriggled out of his car to the sidewalk and faced Courtland, curiously conspicuous and recognizable with all his disarray. Courtland towered above the great man with righteous wrath in his eyes. Ramsey Thomas cringed and looked embarrassed. He'd come to look over the ground to see how much trouble they would have getting the insurance and hadn't expected to be met by a giant Nemesis with blackened face and singed eyebrows.

"Oh, why—I," he began. "It's Mr. Courtland, isn't it? They tell me you've been very helpful during the fire. I'm sure we're much obliged. We'll not forget this, I assure you—"

"Mr. Thomas," broke in Courtland in a clear, decisive voice, "you wanted to know a year ago why I wouldn't accept your proposition, and you couldn't understand my reason for refusing. There it is!"

He pointed to the heap of ruins.

"Go over to that warehouse and see the rows of charred bodies! Look at the agonized faces of the dead and hear the groans of the dying. See the living who are scarred or crippled for life. You're responsible for all that! If I'd accepted your proposal I would have been responsible, too. And now I mean to spend the rest of my life fighting the conditions that make such a catastrophe as this possible!"

Courtland turned and, in spite of his tatters and grime, walked majestically away from him down the street.

Ramsey Thomas stood rooted to the ground, watching him, a mingling of emotions chasing one another over his rugged countenance: astonishment, admiration and fury in quick succession.

"Hang him!" he said under his breath. "Now he'll be a worse pest than that little rat of a preacher, for he's got twice as much brains and education!"

Chapter 30

The summer passed in hard, earnest work.

Courtland had been back at his studies four weeks when another letter from Tennelly arrived. Gila had gone to her aunt's at Beechwood for a two-week stay. She was worn out with the various summer functions and needed a complete rest. They were to be married soon, perhaps in December, and would have a lot to do to prepare for that. She was going to rest absolutely and had forbidden him to follow her, so he had some leisure on his hands. Would Courtland like to spend a weekend somewhere along the coast halfway between? They could each take their own cars and meet wherever Courtland said.

Courtland received the letter Saturday morning. Pat had gone down to the city for over Sunday. An inexpressible longing to see Tennelly filled him, before his marriage completed the wall separating them. He wanted to have a real talk, to look into his friend's soul and see the old loyalty shining there. He wanted more than all else to come close to him again and, if possible, tell him about the Christ.

He took down his road book, turned to the map and let his finger fall on the coastline about midway between the city and the seminary. Looking it up in the book, he found Shadow Beach described as a quiet and exclusive resort with a good inn, excellent service and fine sea bathing. Well, that would do as well as anywhere. He telegraphed Tennelly:

Meet me at Shadow Beach, Howland's Inlet, Elm Tree Inn, this evening.
Court

It was dark when he reached Elm Tree Inn. The ocean rolled, a long black line flecked with faint foam along the shore and luminous with a coming moon. From the road he could see two dim figures, like moving shadows, walking down the sand picked out against the moon's path. All else was lonely up and down. Courtland shivered slightly and almost wished he'd selected a more cheerful spot for the meeting. He hadn't realized how desolate a sea can be when it's growing cold. Nevertheless, it was majestic. It seemed like eternity in its limitless stretch. The lights in far harbors glinted out in the distance down the coast. The vast emptiness filled him with sadness. He felt as if he were entering upon anything but a pleasant reunion and half wished he hadn't come.

Courtland ran his car up to the entrance and sprang out. He was glad to get inside, where a log fire was crackling. The warmth and light dispelled his sadness. Things took on a cheerful aspect again.

"I suppose you haven't many guests left," he said pleasantly, as he registered.

"Only them, sir!" said the clerk, pointing to the entry just above Courtland's.

"James T. Aquilar and wife, Seattle, Washington," Courtland read idly and turned away.

"They been here two days. Come in nerroplane!" went on the clerk.

"Fly all the way from Seattle?" asked Courtland. He was looking at his watch and wondering if he should order supper or wait until Tennelly arrived.

"Well, I can't say for sure. He's mighty uncommunicative, but he's given out he flies 'most anywhere the notion takes him. He's got his machine out in the lot back o' the inn. You oughtta see it. It's a bird!"

"H'm!" said Courtland. "I must have a look at it in daylight. I'm looking for a friend up from the city pretty soon. Guess it would be more convenient for you if we dined together. I'll wait a bit. Meanwhile, let me see what rooms you have."

When Courtland came back to the office and sat down before the fire to wait, the spell of sadness seemed to have vanished.

He sat for half an hour, with his head thrown back in the easy chair, watching the flames, thinking back over old college memories the thought of Tennelly made vivid again. In the midst of it he heard steps on the veranda. Someone from outside unlatched the door and flung it open. A wild, careless laugh floated in on the cold breath of the sea. Courtland came to his feet as if he'd been called! That laugh had gone through his heart like a knife, with its heartless babylike mirth. It was Gila! Had Tennelly played him false and brought her along? Was this some kind of ruse to get them together? He knew Tennelly was distressed over their alienation and that he understood to some extent it was because of Gila he refused the many invitations pressed upon him to come down to the city and be with his friends.

The door swung wide on its hinges, and Gila entered in a stylish suitcoat of homespun, leather-trimmed and short-skirted, high boots, leather leggings and a jaunty leather cap with a bridle under her chin. Only her petite figure and baby face saved her from being taken for a tough young sport. She swaggered in, chewing gum, her gauntleted hands in her pockets, her young voice flung almost coarsely into the room by the wind. The innocent look was gone from her face; the eyes were wide and bold, the exquisite mouth in a sensuous curve.

Behind her lounged a man older than her by many years, with silver at his temples, daredevil eyes and a handsome, voluptuous face. He kicked the door shut behind him and leaned against it while he lit a cigarette.

Gila's laugh rang harshly in the room again, following some quiet remark, and the man laughed coarsely in reply. Then, suddenly, she looked up and saw Courtland standing there with folded arms, regarding her steadily, and her eyes grew wide with horror.

It was Courtland's great disillusionment.

Never had he seen such fear in a human face.

Gila's skin grew gray beneath its pearly tint; her whole body shrank and cringed; her eyes were fixed upon him with terror in their gaze.

"Papers haven't come in yet, Mr. Aquilar," called the clerk. "Train's late tonight. Be in pretty soon, I reckon!"

The man growled out an imprecation on a place where the papers didn't come till that hour in the evening and lounged on toward the elevator. Gila slid along by his side, her eyes on Courtland, with the air of hiding behind her companion. Her face was drooped, and when she turned toward the elevator she dropped her eyes also, and a wave of shame rolled up and covered her face and neck and ears with a dull red beneath the pearl. Her last glance at Courtland was the look Eve must have had as she walked past the flaming swords with Adam out of Eden. Her eyes, as she stood waiting for the elevator boy to come, seemed to grovel on the floor.

Was this the sweet, wild, innocent flower that had held him in its thrall all the sorrowful months and separated him from his dearest friend?

Tennelly! Courtland had forgotten until that instant that Tennelly would be there in a few minutes—perhaps was even then at the door!

He strode forward, and Gila quivered as she saw him coming. She looked up in terror, putting out a fearful hand to her companion's arm.

The elevator boy had arrived and was slamming back the steel grating. The man stood back to let Gila enter, and she slunk past him, her gaze still held in horror on Courtland.

"Will you do me the favor of stepping into the reception room to the right for a moment?" asked Courtland, addressing the man but looking at Gila.

"The devil we will!" said the man, glaring at him. "What right do you have to ask a favor like that?"

But Courtland was looking at Gila, with command in his eyes. As if she dared not disobey she stepped out of the elevator, her eyes still on him, her face gray with apprehension. Without further word from him she walked slowly before him into the room he indicated.

"You're a fool!" said Aquilar, regarding her contemptuously.

But she went as if she didn't hear him. She entered the room, walked halfway across and turned about, facing the two who had followed. Courtland was inside the room, with Aquilar lounging in the door, as if the matter were of little consequence to him. He had a smile of contempt still on his lips.

Courtland's manner was grave and sad. He had the commanding presence of an avenging angel.

"Gila, are you married to this man?" he asked, looking at her, as if to search her soul.

Gila kept her dark, horrified gaze on his face. She was beyond trying to deceive now. She slowly gave one shake to her head, and her white lips formed the syllable no, though it was almost inaudible.

"And yet you are registered in this hotel as his wife?"

Her eyes suddenly flamed with shame. She dropped them before his gaze and seemed to try to assent, but her head was too low to bow. She lifted miserable pleading looks to his face twice but couldn't stand the clear rebuke of his gaze. It was like the whiteness of the reproach of God, and her sinful soul could not bear it. She lifted a handkerchief and uttered something like a sob, as the sound of a lost soul looking back at what might have been.

"What the devil have you got to say about it? Who the devil are you anyway?"

roared the man from the doorway.

The elevator boy and clerk were all agog. The latter had come out of his pen and was standing on tiptoe behind the boy to get a good view of the scene. The room was tense with stillness.

Aquilar's voice was not one to pass unnoticed when he spoke in anger, but Courtland did not even lift an eyelid toward him.

Perhaps Aquilar's words had given Gila courage, for she suddenly lifted her eyes to Courtland's face again, with a flash of vengeance in them.

"I suppose you'll tell Lew about it?" she flung out bitterly. "I suppose you'll make up a story to tell him. But you don't suppose he'll believe *you* against *me,* do you?"

Her eyes were flashing fire now. Her imperious manner was upon her. She'd driven him from her once. She would defeat him again.

He watched her without a change of countenance. "No, I won't tell him," he said quietly. "But *you will!*"

"I?" Gila turned a contemptuous glance upon him. "Some chance! And I warn you that if you tattle anything about it I'll turn the tables against you in a way you little suspect."

"Gila, you will tell Lew Tennelly *everything,* or you will never marry him! It is his right to know! And now, sir"—Courtland turned to Aquilar, who was leaning amusedly against the doorway—"if you will step outside I will *settle with you!*"

But suddenly Gila screamed and covered her face with her hands, for there, just behind Aquilar, stood Tennelly, looking like a ghost. He had heard it all!

Chapter 31

Tennelly stepped inside the room, gave one questioning look at Aquilar as he passed him, searching straight into his startled, shifty eyes, and stood before the crouching girl. She had dropped into a chair and was sobbing as if her heart would break.

"What does this mean, Gila?"

Tennelly's voice was cold and stern.

Courtland glanced at his shocked face and turned away from the pain of it. But when he looked for the man who had wrought this havoc he had suddenly melted from the room. The front door was blowing back and forth in the wind, and the clerk and elevator boy stood, open-mouthed, staring. Courtland closed the reception room door and hurried out on the veranda, but he saw no sign of anyone in the wind-swept darkness. The moon had risen enough to make a bright path over the sea, but the earth as yet was wrapped in shadow.

Down in the field, beyond the outbuildings, he heard a whirring sound, and as he looked a dark thing rose like a great bird high above his head. The bird had flown while the flying was good. The lady might face her difficulties alone!

Courtland stood below in the courtyard, while the moon rose and shed its light through the sky, and the great black bird executed an evolution or two and whirred off to the north, doubtless headed for Seattle or some equally inaccessible point. Helpless wrath was upon him. Dolt he'd been to let this human leper escape from him into the world again! A kind of divine frenzy seized him to capture him yet and put him where he could work no further harm to other willing victims. Yes, he thought of Gila as a willing victim. An hour earlier he would have called her just plain innocent victim. Now something in her face, her attitude, as she saw him and walked away with her guilty partner, had made him know her at last for a sinful woman. The shackles had burst from his heart, and he was free from her allurements forever. He understood now why she bid him choose between her and Christ. She had no part or lot in things pure and holy. She hated holiness because she was sinful.

It was midnight before Gila and Tennelly came forth, Tennelly grave and sad, Gila tear-stained and subdued.

Courtland was sitting in the big chair before the fireplace, though the fire was smoldering low, and the elevator boy had long ago retired to slumbers on a bench in a hidden alcove.

Tennelly came straight to Courtland, as though he knew he'd be waiting there for him. "I'm taking Gila down to Beechwood. You'll come with us?" The tone held quiet entreaty.

"Shall I take my car?"

"No. You'll ride with me on the front seat. Is there a maid here I can hire to go with us? We can bring her back in the morning."

"I'll find out."

That was a silent ride through the late moonlight. The men spoke only when necessary to keep the right road. Gila, huddled sullenly in the backseat beside a dozing, gray-haired chambermaid, spoke nothing at all. And who shall say what her thoughts were as hour after hour she sat in her humiliation and watched the two men she had wronged so deeply? Perhaps her spirit seethed the more violently within her silent, angry body because she wasn't yet sure of Tennelly. Her tears and explanations, her pleading story of deceit and innocence, hadn't wrought the charm upon him they might have if Aquilar hadn't been known to him in the past two weeks, a stranger hanging about Gila, encouraged against her lover's oft-repeated warnings. A mysterious story of an unfaithful wife put an air of romance about him that Tennelly hadn't liked. Gila had never seen him so serious and hard to coax as tonight. He spoke to her as if she were a naughty child and commanded her to go at once to her aunt in Beechwood and remain there the allotted time. She simply had to obey or lose him. Tennelly's fortune and prospects made him quite desirable as a husband. Moreover, she felt that through marrying Tennelly she could better hurt Courtland, the man she now hated with all her heart.

They reached Beechwood at not too unearthly an hour. The aunt was surprised, but not unduly so, for Gila was a girl of many whims, and that she came at all to quiet Beechwood to rest was shock enough for one day. She asked no troublesome questions.

Tennelly wouldn't remain for breakfast but started on the return trip at once, with only a brief stop at a wayside inn for something to eat. The elderly attendant in the back seat was disappointed. She had no chance to get a bit of gossip with anyone; but she received good pay for the night's ride and made up some thrilling stories to tell that were better than the truth might have turned out to be, so nothing was lost after all.

Tennelly broke the silence when he and Courtland were at last alone together. "She only went for a ride in his aeroplane," he said sadly. "She had no idea of staying more than an afternoon. He promised to set her down at the next station in Beechwood, where her aunt was to meet her. She was filled with horror when she found she must be away overnight. But even then she had no idea of his purpose. She says nobody ever told her about such things; she was ignorant as a child! She's full of repentance and feels this will be a lesson for her. She says she intends to devote her life to me if I'll only forgive her."

So that was what she told Tennelly behind the closed doors!

Before Courtland's eyes floated a vision of Gila as she first caught sight of him in the inn. If ever soul was guilty in full knowledge of her sin she had been! Again she passed before his vision with shamed head drooping and her proud manner gone. The mask had fallen from Gila forever as far as Courtland was concerned. Not even her pitiful, teary face that morning, when she crept from the car at her aunt's door, could deceive him again.

"And you *believe* all that?" asked Courtland. He couldn't help it. His dearest friend was in peril. What else could he do?

"I—don't know!" said Tennelly helplessly.

There was silence in the room. Then Tennelly did realize a little. Perhaps Tennelly had known all along, better than he!

"And—you will forgive her?"

"I *must!*" said Tennelly in desperation. "Court, my life is bound up in her!"

"So I once thought!" Courtland was only musing out loud.

Tennelly looked at him sadly.

"She almost wrecked my soul!" went on Courtland.

"I know," said Tennelly in profound sorrow. "She told me."

"She *told you?*"

"Yes, before we were engaged. She told me she'd asked you to give up preaching, that she could never bear to be a minister's wife. I began to realize what that would mean to you then. I respected your choice. It was great of you, Court! But you never really loved her, man, or you couldn't have given her up!"

Courtland was silent for a moment, then he burst out: "Nelly! It was not that! You *shall* know the truth! She asked me to give up *my God* for her!"

"*I have no God,*" said Tennelly dully.

A great yearning for his friend filled Courtland's heart. "Listen, old man, you *mustn't* marry her!" he burst out again. "I believe she's rotten all the way through. You didn't see and hear all last night. She *can't* be true! She doesn't have it in her! She'll be false to you whenever she takes the whim! She will lead you through hell!"

"You don't understand. I would *go* through hell to be with her!"

Tennelly's words rang through the room like a knell, and Courtland could say no more. Silence again filled the room. Courtland watched his friend's haggard face anxiously. There were deep lines of agony about his mouth and dark circles under his eyes.

Suddenly Tennelly lifted his hand and laid it on his friend's. "Thanks, Court. Thanks a lot. I appreciate it more than you know. But this is my job. I guess I've got to undertake it! And, *man*—can't you see I've *got* to believe her?"

"I suppose you have, Nelly. God help you!"

When Courtland returned to the seminary he found a letter from Mother Marshall.

Chapter 32

Courtland opened Mother Marshall's letter with a feeling of relief and anticipation. Here at least would be a fresh, pure breath of sweetness. His soul was worn and troubled with the experience of the past two days. A great loneliness possessed him when he thought of Tennelly or looked forward to his future, for he was convinced he should never turn to the love of woman again. So the dreams of home and love and children that had had their normal part in his thoughts of the future were cut out, and the days stretched forward in one long round of duty.

> *Dear Paul:*
>
> *This is Stephen Marshall's mother, and I'm calling you by your first name because it seems to bring my boy back again to be writing so familiarlike to one of his comrades.*
>
> *We've been wondering, Father and I, since you said you didn't have any real mother of your own, whether you mightn't like to come home Christmas to us for a little while and borrow Stephen's mother. I've got a wonderful hungering in my heart to hear a little more about my boy's death. I couldn't have borne it just at first, because it was all so hard to give him up, especially when he was just beginning to live his earthly life. But now since I can realize him over by the Father, I'd like to know it all. Bonnie says you saw Stephen go, and I thought perhaps you could spare a little time to run out West and tell me.*
>
> *Of course, if you're busy and have other places you mustn't let this bother you. I can wait till sometime when you're coming West and can stop over for a day. But if you care to come home to Mother Marshall and let her pretend you are her boy for a little while, you'll make us all very happy.*

When Courtland finished reading the letter he put his head down on his desk and shed the first tears his eyes had known since he was a little boy. To have a home and mother-heart open to him like that in the midst of all his sorrow and perplexity fairly undid him. By and by he lifted up his head and wrote a hearty acceptance of the invitation.

That was in November.

In the middle of December Tennelly and Gila were married.

It wasn't Courtland's choosing that he was best man. He shrank from even attending that wedding. He tried to arrange for his western trip early enough to avoid it. Not that he had any more personal feeling about Gila, but because he dreaded to see his friend tied up to such a future. It seemed as if the wedding was Tennelly's funeral.

But Tennelly had driven up to the seminary on three successive weeks and begged Courtland to stand by him.

"You're the only one in the world who knows all about it and understands, Court," he pleaded.

And Courtland, looking at his friend's wistful face, feeling, as he did, that Tennelly was entering a living purgatory, could not refuse him.

It did not please Gila to have him take that place in the wedding party. He knew her shame, and she couldn't trail her wedding robes as guilelessly before him now or lift her hand, with its costly blossoms, before the envious world without realizing she was but a whited sepulcher, her rotten heart death beneath the spotless robes. For she was keen enough to know she was defiled forever in Courtland's eyes. She might fool Tennelly by pleading innocence and deceit, but never Courtland. For his eyes had pried into her very soul that night he discovered her in sin. She had a feeling that he and his God were in league against her. No, Gila did not want Courtland to be Tennelly's best man. But Tennelly had insisted. He had given in on almost every other thing, and Gila had had her way; but he would have Courtland for best man.

She drooped her long lashes over her lovely cheeks and trailed her white robes up a long aisle of white lilies to the steps of the altar. But when she lifted her miserable eyes in front of the altar she couldn't help seeing the face of the man who discovered her shame. It was a case of her naked, sinful soul walking in the Garden again, with the voice and the eyes of God upon it.

Lovely! Composed! Charming! Exquisite! All these and more they said of her as she stood before the white-robed priest and went through the ceremony, repeating, parrot-like, the words: "I, Gila, take thee, Llewellyn—." But in her heart were wrath and hate—and no more repentance than a fallen angel feels.

When at last the agony was over and the bride and groom turned to walk down the aisle, Gila lifted her pretty lips charmingly to Tennelly for his kiss and leaned lovingly upon his arm, smiling saucily at this one and that as she pranced out into her future. Courtland, coming just behind with the maid of honor, one of Gila's friends, lolling on his arm, felt that he should be inexpressibly thankful to God he was only best man in this procession and not bridegroom.

When at last the bride and groom departed, and Courtland had shaken off the kind but curious attentions of Bill Ward, who persisted in thinking Tennelly had cut him out with Gila, he turned to Pat and whispered softly, "For the love of Mike, Pat, let's beat it before they start anything else!"

Pat, anxious and troubled, heaved a sigh of relief and hustled his old friend out under the stars with almost a shout of joy. Nelly was caught and bound for a season. Poor old Nelly! But Court was free! Thank the Lord!

Courtland was almost glad he went back to hard work again and would have little time to think. The past few days had wearied him. He looked on life as a passing show and felt left out of any pleasure in it.

On a cold, snowy night Courtland came down to the city and took the western express for his holiday.

Snow, deep, vast, glistening, was everywhere when he arrived at Sloan's Station on the second morning. But the sun was out, and nothing could be more dazzling than the scene that stretched on every side. They'd come through a blizzard and left it traveling eastward at a rapid rate.

Courtland was surprised to find Father Marshall waiting for him on the platform, in a great buffalo-skin overcoat, beaver cap and gloves. He carried a duplicate coat which he offered to Courtland as soon as the greetings were over.

"Here, put this on—you'll need it," he said heartily, holding out the coat. "It was Steve's. I guess it'll fit you. Mother and Bonnie's over here, waiting. They couldn't stand it without coming along. I guess you won't mind the ride, will you, after them stuffy cars? It's a beauty day!"

And there were Mother Marshall and Bonnie, swathed to the chin in rugs and shawls and furs, looking like two red-cheeked cherubs!

Bonnie was wearing a soft wool cap and scarf of knitted gray and white. Her cheeks glowed like roses; her eyes were as bright as two stars. Her gold hair rippled out beneath the cap and caught the sunshine around her face.

Courtland stood still and gazed at her in wonder and admiration. Was this the sad, pale girl he'd sent west to save her life? Why, she was a beauty, and she looked as if she'd never been ill in her life! He could scarcely bear to take his eyes from her face long enough to get into the front seat with Father Marshall.

As for Mother Marshall, nothing could be more satisfactory than the way she looked like her picture, with those calm, peaceful eyes and that tendency to a dimple in her cheek where a smile would naturally come. Apple-cheeked, silver-haired and plump. She was ideal!

That was a merry ride they had, all talking and laughing in their happiness at being together. It was so good to Mother Marshall to see another pair of strong young shoulders beside Father on the front seat again.

Mother Marshall took him up to Stephen's room when they reached the old rambling farmhouse set in the snowy landscape. Father Marshall had taken the car to the barn, and Bonnie was hurrying to put dinner on the table.

Courtland entered the room as if it were a sacred place and looked around on the plain comfort: the homemade rugs, the fat pincushion, the quaint pictures on the walls, the bookcase with its rows of books, the white bed with its quilted counterpane of delicate needlework, the neat marble-topped washstand with its appointments and its wealth of large old-fashioned towels.

"It isn't very fancy," said Mother Marshall apologetically. "We fixed up Bonnie's room as modern as we could when we knew she was coming"—she waved an indicating hand toward the open door across the hall, where the rosy glow of pink curtains and cherry-blossomed wall gave forth a pleasant sense of light and joy—"and we meant to fix this over for Steve the first Christmas when he came home, as a surprise. But now he's gone we sort of wanted to keep it as he left it."

"It's great!" said Courtland. "I like it just like this. Don't you? It's fine of you to put me in it. I feel as if it's almost a desecration, because, you see, I didn't know him very well. I wasn't the friend to him I might have been. I thought I should tell you that right at the start. Perhaps you wouldn't want me if you knew all about it."

"You would have been his friend if you'd had a chance to know him," said the mother. "He was always a real brave boy!"

"He sure was!" said Courtland, deeply stirred. "But I did get to know what a man he was. I saw him die, you know. But it was too late then."

"It's never too late!" said Mother Marshall, brushing away a bright tear. "There's heaven, you know!"

"Why, surely there's heaven! I hadn't thought of that. Won't that be great?" Courtland spoke the words reverently. It came to him he might make up in heaven for many things lost down here. He'd never thought of that before.

"I wonder if you would mind," said Mother Marshall wistfully, "if I was to kiss you, the way I used to do Steve when he'd been away?"

"I wouldn't mind a bit," said Courtland, setting his suitcase down suddenly and taking the plump little mother reverently into his arms. "It would be *great*, Mother Marshall," he said and kissed her twice.

Mother Marshall reached her short arms up around his neck and laid her gray head for just a minute on the tall shoulder, while a tear hurried down and fitted itself invisibly into her dimple. Then she ran her fingers through his thick brown hair and patted his cheek.

"Dear boy!" she breathed contentedly but suddenly roused herself. "Here I'm keeping you, and that dinner'll spoil! Wash your hands and come down quick! Bonnie will have everything ready!"

Courtland first realized the deep, happy, spiritual life of the home when he came down to the dining room and Father Marshall bowed his head to ask a blessing. Strange as it may seem, it was the first time in his life he'd ever sat at a home table where a blessing was asked on the food. They had the custom in the seminary, of course, but it was observed perfunctorily, the men taking turns. It never seemed the holy recognition of the presence of the Master, as Father Marshall made it seem.

Bonnie was like a daughter of the house, getting up for a second pitcher of cream, running to the kitchen for more gravy. It was so ideal that Courtland felt like throwing his napkin up in the air and cheering.

Mother Marshall arranged it all that Bonnie and he should go to the woods after dinner for greens and a Christmas tree. Bonnie looked at Courtland almost apologetically, wondering if he was too tired for a strenuous expedition like that.

No, he wasn't tired. He'd never been so rested in his life. He felt like hugging Mother Marshall for getting up the plan, for he could see Bonnie never would have proposed it; she was too shy. He donned a pair of Stephen's old leather leggings and a sweater, shouldered the ax as if he'd carried one often, and they started.

He thought he'd never seen anything so lovely as Bonnie in that fuzzy woolen cap, with the sunshine of her hair straying out and the fine glow in her beautiful face. He knew he'd never heard music half as sweet as Bonnie's laugh as it rang through the woods when she saw a squirrel sitting on a high limb scolding at their intrusion. He never thought of Gila once the whole afternoon or even his lost ideals of womanhood.

They found a tree just to their liking. Bonnie had picked it out weeks beforehand, but she didn't tell him so, and he thought he discovered it himself. They cut masses of laurel and ground pine and strung them on twine. They dragged the tree and greens home through the snow, laughing and struggling with their fragrant burden, getting so well acquainted that at the doorstep they had to lay down their greens and have a snow fight, with Father and Mother Marshall watching delightedly from the kitchen window. Mother's cheek was pressed against the old gray hat. She was thinking how Stephen would have liked to be here with them; how glad he'd be if he could hear the happy shouts of young people ringing around the lonely old house again!

They set the tree up in the parlor and made a great log fire on the hearth to give good cheer—for the house was warm as a pocket without it. They colored and strung popcorn, gilded walnuts, cut silver-paper stars and chains for the tree, and hung strings of cranberries, bright red apples and oranges between. They trimmed the house from top to bottom, even twining ground pine on the stair rail.

Those were the speediest two weeks Courtland ever spent in his life. He'd planned to remain with the Marshalls perhaps three or four days, but instead of that he delayed till the last train that would get him back to the seminary in time for work—and missed two classes at that. He'd never had a comrade like Bonnie, and he knew, from the first day almost, that he'd never known a love like the love that flamed up in his soul for this sweet, strong-spirited girl. The old house rang with their laughter from morning to night as they chased each other upstairs and down, like two children. Hours they spent tramping through the woods or over country roads. More hours they spent reading aloud to each other, or rather most of the time Bonnie read and Courtland devoured her lovely face with his eyes from behind a sheltering hand, watching every varying expression, noting the straight, delicate brows, the beautiful eyes filled with holy things as they lifted now and then in the reading, and marveling over the sweetness of the voice.

The second day of his visit Courtland made an errand with Bonnie to town to send off several telegrams. As a result a lot of things arrived for him the day before Christmas, marked "Rush!" They were smuggled into the parlor behind the Christmas tree, with great secrecy after dark by Bonnie and Courtland, and covered with the buffalo robes from the car till morning. There was a big leather chair with air cushions for Father Marshall; its mate in lady's size for Mother; a set of encyclopedias he'd heard Father say he wished he had; a lot of silver forks and spoons for Mother, who apologized for the silver being rubbed off some of hers. There were two sets of books in wonderful leather bindings he'd heard Bonnie say she longed to read, and there was the tiniest gold watch, about which he'd been in terrible doubt ever since he sent for it. Suppose Bonnie thought it wrong to accept it when she'd known him such a short time! How would he make her see it was all right? He wouldn't tell her she was sort of his sister, for he didn't want her for a sister. He puzzled over that question whenever he had time, which wasn't often, because he was so busy and happy every minute.

Then there were five-pound boxes of chocolates, glacéd nuts and bonbons, and a crate of foreign fruits, with nuts, raisins, figs and dates. There was a long, deep box from the nearest city filled with the most wonderful hothouse blossoms: roses, lilies, sweet peas, violets, gardenias and even orchids. Courtland had never enjoyed spending money so much in his life. He only wished he could get back to the city for a couple of hours and buy a lot more things.

To paint the picture of Mother Marshall when she sat on her new air cushions and counted her spoons and forks—real silver forks beyond all her dreams! To show Father Marshall, as he wiped his spectacles and bent, beaming, over the encyclopedias or rested his gray head back against the cushions! Ah! That would be the work of an artist who could catch the glory that shines deeper than faces and reaches souls. As for Courtland, he was too much taken up watching Bonnie's face when she opened her books; looking deep into her eyes as she looked up from the velvet case where the watch ticked softly into her wondering ears; seeing the breathlessness with which she lifted the flowers from their bed among the ferns and placed them reverently in jars and pitchers around the room.

It was a wonderful Christmas! The first real Christmas Courtland had ever known. Sitting in the dim firelight between dusk and darkness, watching Bonnie at the piano, listening to the tender Christmas music she was playing, joining his sweet tenor in with her clear soprano now and then, Courtland suddenly thought of Tennelly, off at Palm Beach, doing the correct thing in wedding trips with Gila. Poor Tennelly! How little he would be getting of the real joy of Christmas! How little he would understand the wonderful peace that settled down in the heart of his friend when, later, they all knelt in the firelight, and Father Marshall prayed, as if he were talking to One who stood there close beside him, whose companionship had been a life experience.

There were so many pictures Courtland had to carry back with him to the seminary. Bonnie in the kitchen, with a long-sleeved, high-necked, gingham apron on, frying doughnuts or baking waffles. Bonnie at the organ on Sunday in the little church in town or sitting in a corner of the Sunday-school room surrounded by her seventeen boys, with her Bible open on her lap and in her face the light of heaven while the boys watched and listened, too intent to know they were doing it. Bonnie throwing snowballs from behind the snow fort he built her. Bonnie with the wonderful mystery upon her when they talked about the watch and whether she might keep it. Bonnie in her window seat with one of the books what was the matter with the automobile and then came back to his room unexpectedly after his knife and caught a glimpse of her through the open door.

And that last one on the platform of Sloan's Station, waving him a smiling good-bye!

Courtland had torn himself away at last, with a promise to return the minute his work was over and with the consolation that Bonnie would write to him. They'd arranged to pursue a course of study together. The future opened up rosily before him. How had skies ever looked dark? How had he thought his ideals vanished and womanhood a lost art when the world held this one pearl of a girl? Bonnie! Rose Bonnie!

Chapter 33

The rest of the winter sped by. Courtland was happy. Pat looked at him enviously sometimes, yet he was content. His old friend didn't have as much time to spend with him, but when he came for a walk and a talk it was with a heartiness that satisfied. Pat had long ago discovered a girl was at Stephen Marshall's old home, and he sat wisely quiet and rejoiced. What kind of girl he could only imagine from Courtland's rapt look when he received a letter and from the exquisite photograph that presently took its place on Courtland's desk. He hoped to have opportunity to judge more accurately when summer came, for Mother Marshall had invited him to come out with Courtland in the spring and spend a week, and he was going. Pat had something to confess to Mother Marshall.

Courtland went out twice that summer, once for a week as soon as his classes were over. It was then Bonnie promised to marry him.

Mother Marshall had a lot of sense and took a great liking to Pat. One day she took him up to Stephen's room and told him about Stephen's boyhood. Pat, great baby giant that he was, knelt beside her chair, put his face in her lap and blurted out the tale of how he'd led the mob against Stephen and indirectly caused his death.

Mother Marshall heard him through with tears of compassion running down her cheeks. It wasn't quite news to her, for Courtland had told her something of the tale, without any names, when he confessed he'd looked after the garments of those who did the persecuting.

"There, there!" said Mother Marshall, patting his dark head. "You never knew what you were doing, laddie! My Steve always wanted a chance to prove he was brave. When he was a little fellow and read about the martyrs, he used to say: 'Would I have that much nerve, Mother? A fellow never can *tell* till he's been *tested!*' So I'm not sorry he had his chance to stand up before you all for what he thought was right. Did you see my boy's face, too, when he died?"

"Yes," said Pat, lifting his head. "I'd just picked up a kid he sent up to the fire escape and saw his face lit up by the fire. It looked like the face of an angel. Then I saw him lift up his hands and look up like he saw somebody above, and he called out something with a sort of smile, as if he was saying he'd be up there pretty soon! And then—he fell!"

The tears were raining down Mother Marshall's cheeks by now, but a smile of triumph shone in her eyes.

"He wanted to be a missionary, but he was afraid he couldn't preach. My Stephen was always shy before folks. But I guess he preached his sermon!" she sighed contentedly.

"He sure did!" said Pat. "I never forgot that look on his face or the way he took our roughneck insults. None of the fellows did. It made a big impression on us all. And when Court began to change, came out straight and said he believed in Christ and all that, it knocked the tar out of us all. Stephen hasn't finished preaching yet. You should hear Court tell the story of his death. It bowled me over when I heard it, and everywhere he tells it people believe! Wherever Paul Courtland tells that story, Stephen Marshall will be preaching."

Mother Marshall stooped over and kissed Pat's astonished forehead. "You have made me a proud and happy mother today, laddie! I'm glad you came."

Pat, suddenly conscious of himself, stumbled to his feet, blushing. "Thanks, Mother! It's been great! Believe me, I won't ever forget it. It's like looking into heaven for this poor bum. If I'd had a home like this I might have stood some chance of being like your Steve, instead of just a roughneck athlete."

"Yes, I know," smiled Mother Marshall. "A dear splendid roughneck, doing a big work with the boys! Paul has told me all about it. You're preaching a lot of sermons yourself, you know, and going to preach some more. Now shall we go down? It's time for evening prayers."

So Pat put his strong arm around Mother Marshall's plump waist and drew one of her hands in his, and together they walked down to the parlor, where Bonnie was already playing "Rock of Ages." It seemed to Pat the kingdom of heaven could be no sweeter, for this was the kingdom come on earth.

When he and Courtland were upstairs in their room, and the house was quiet for the night, Pat spoke. "I've sized it up this way, Court. There ain't any dying! There's only an imaginary line like the equator on the map. It's heaven or hell, both now and hereafter! We can begin heaven right now and live it on through, and that's what these folks have done. You don't hear them sitting here fighting like the professors used to do, about whether there's a heaven or a hell. They know there's both. They're living in one and pulling out of the other, hard as they can. And they're too blamed busy, following out the Bible and seeing it prove itself, to listen to the twaddle to prove it ain't so! I'm sure glad you gave me the tip and I got a chance to get in on this game. It's the best game I know, and the best part about it is it lasts forever!"

Tennelly was away all that summer, doing the fashionable summer resorts and taking a California trip. The next winter he spent in Washington. Uncle Ramsey had him at work, and Courtland ran into him in his office once, when he took a hurried trip down to see what he could do for the eight-hour workday bill. Tennelly looked grave and sad. He was touchingly glad to see Courtland. They didn't speak of Gila once, but when Courtland lay sleepless in his sleeper on the return trip that night Tennelly's face haunted him and the wistfulness in it.

A few months later Tennelly wrote a brief note announcing the birth of a daughter, named Doris Ramsey after his grandmother. The tone of his letter seemed more cheerful.

Courtland was so happy that winter he could scarcely contain himself. Pat had great times kidding him about the Western mail. Courtland was supplying a vacant church down in the old factory district in the city, and Pat often went along. On one of these Sunday afternoons late in the spring they were walking down a street they didn't often take, and suddenly Courtland stopped with an exclamation of dismay and looked up at a great blaring sign wired on a big old-fashioned church:

CHURCH OF GOD
FOR SALE

Pat looked up at the sign and then at Courtland's face, figuring out, as he usually could, what was the matter with Court.

"That's tough luck!" he said sympathetically.

"It's terrible!" Courtland said.

"Whose fault do you s'pose it is? Not God's. Somebody fell down on his job, I reckon! Congregation gone to the devil, likely!"

"Wait!" said Courtland. "I must find out."

He stepped into a cigar store and asked some questions. "You were right, Pat," he said, when he came out. "The congregation has gone to the devil. They moved up into the more fashionable part of town, and the church is for sale. There's only one member of the old church left down here. I'm going around to see him. Pat, that sign mustn't stay up there! It's a disgrace to God."

"What could you do about it?" Pat was puzzled.

"Do about it? Why, man, I can buy it if there isn't any other way!"

They went to see the church member, who proved to be a good old soul, but deaf and old and very poor. He said they had to give the church up; they couldn't make it pay. All the rich people had moved away. He shook his head sadly and told how he and his wife were married there. He hobbled over and showed them how to get in a side door.

The yellow afternoon sun was sifting through cheap stained-glass windows and fell in mellow quiet on the faded cushions and musty ingrain carpet. The place had that look of having been abandoned. Yet Courtland, as he stood in the shadow under the old balcony, seemed to see the presence of the eternal God standing up there behind the pulpit, seemed to feel the hallowed memories of long ago and smell the lingering incense of all the prayers that had gone up from all the souls who had worshipped there in years past.

"They think an iron foundry's going to buy it, or else someone may make a munitions factory out of it," the old man offered. "This war's bringing a big change over things."

"Their plowshares into swords, their pruning hooks into spears," repeated an unseen voice behind Courtland.

His face set sternly. He turned to Pat. "I can't let that happen, old man! I'm going to buy it if I can. Let's go and look it up!"

Pat looked at his companion with awe. He'd always known he was rich, but—to purchase a church as if it were a jackknife. That sure was going some!

Courtland didn't return to the seminary until Tuesday morning. By that time he had bought his church. It didn't take him long to come to an agreement. The

Church of God was in a bad way and was willing to take up with almost any offer that would cover their liabilities.

"Well," said Pat, "that sure was some hustle! There's one thing, Court. You don't have to candidate for any church like those other guys in your seminary. You just went out and bought one—though I surmise you and I'll have to do some scrubbing if you calculate to hold services there very soon."

"I hadn't thought of that, Pat. Maybe that would be a good idea!"

"Holy Mackinaw, man! What did you buy it for then, if you didn't intend to use it? Just to tear down that blooming sign?"

"That's about the size of it," said Courtland, smiling, as he halted in front of his newly acquired church and looked up at it with interest. "But now I've got it I might as well use it. Suppose we start a mission here, Pat, you and I? Let's cut the sign down first, and then, I'm going to hunt up a stonecutter. This church needs a new name. 'Church of God for sale' has killed this one! This means a church that used to belong to God and doesn't anymore. They've sold the Church of God, but His presence is still here."

A few weeks later, when the two came down to look things over, the granite arch over the old front doors bore the inscription in stone letters:

CHURCH OF THE PRESENCE OF GOD

Courtland stood looking for a moment, and then he turned to Pat eagerly. "I'm going to get possession of the whole block if I can—maybe the opposite one, too, for a park—and you've got to be physical director! I'll turn the kids and the older boys over to you, old man!"

Pat's eyes were full of tears. He had to turn away to hide them. "You're an old dreamer!" he said in a choking voice.

So the rejuvenation of the old church went on from week to week. The men at the seminary grew curious as to what took Pat and Courtland to the city so much. Was it a girl? It finally got around that Courtland had a rich and aristocratic church in view and was soon to be married to the daughter of one of its prominent members. But when they congratulated him, Courtland grinned.

"When I preach my first sermon you may all come down and see," he replied, and that was all they could get out of him.

Courtland found a lot had to be done to that church. Plaster was falling off in places, and the pews were getting rickety. The pulpit needed doing over, and the floor had to be recarpeted. But what a difference it made when it was done! Soft greens and browns replaced the faded red. The carpet was thick and soft, and the cushions matched. Bonnie had given careful suggestions about it all.

"You could've managed without cushions, you know," said Pat, as he seated himself in appreciative comfort.

"I know," said Courtland, "but I want this to look like a *church*. Someday when we get the rest of the block and can tear down the buildings and have a little sunlight and air, we'll have some *real windows* with wonderful gospel stories on them, but these will do for now. There has to be a pipe organ some-day, and Bonnie will play it!"

Pat always glowed when Courtland spoke of Bonnie. He never had ceased to be thankful that Courtland escaped Gila's machinations.

But that very afternoon, as Courtland was preparing to hurry to the train, a note came from Pat, who had gone ahead on an errand.

Dear Court—Tennelly's in trouble. He's up at his old rooms. He wants you. I'll wait for you down in the office.

Pat

Chapter 34

Tennelly was pacing up and down the room. His face was white; his eyes were wild. He had the haggard look of one who's come through a series of harrowing experiences up to the supreme torture where nothing worse can happen.

Courtland's knock brought him at once to the door. With both hands they gave the fellowship grip that meant so much to each in college.

A moment they stood, looking into each other's eyes, with Courtland, wondering, startled, questioning. It was Gila, of course. Nothing else could reach the man's soul and make him look like that. But what had happened? Not death! No, not even death could bring that look of shame and degradation to his high-minded friend's eyes.

As if Tennelly had read his question he spoke in a voice so husky with emotion that his words were scarcely audible: "Didn't Pat tell you?"

Courtland shook his head.

Tennelly's head went down, as if he were waiting for courage to talk. Then he spoke. "She's gone, Court!"

"Gone?"

"Left me, Court! She sailed at daybreak for Italy with another man."

Tennelly fumbled in his pocket and brought out a crumpled note, blistered with tears. "Read it!" he muttered, turning to the window.

Dear Lew,

I'm sure when you come to your senses and get over some of your narrow ideas you'll be as much relieved as I am over what I've decided to do. You and I were never suited for each other, and I can't stand this life another day. I'm perishing! It's up to me to do something, for I know, with your strait-laced notions, you never will! So when you read this I'll be out of reach, on my way to Italy with Count von Bremen. They say there's going to be war in this country anyway, and I hate such things, so I had to get out of it. You won't have any trouble getting a divorce, and you'll soon be glad I did it.

As for the kid, if she lives she's much better off with you than with me, for you know I never could stand children; they get on my nerves. And, anyhow, I never could be all the things you tried to make me, and it's better in the end this way. So good-bye, and don't try to come after me. I won't come back, no matter what you do, for I'm bored to death with the last two years, and I've got to see some life!

Gila

Courtland read the flippant note twice before he trusted himself to speak, and then he walked over to the window, slowly smoothing and folding the crumpled paper. A baby's cry in the next room pierced the air, and the father gripped the window seat and quivered as if a bullet had struck him.

Courtland put his hand on his friend's arm. "Nelly, old fellow," he said, "you know I feel with you—"

"I know, Court!" he said with a weary sigh. "That's why I sent for you. I had to have you!"

"Nelly! There aren't any words delicate enough to handle this thing without hurting. It's raw flesh and full of nerves. There's just One who can do anything here. I wish you believed in God."

"I do!" said Tennelly in a dreary tone.

"He can come near you and give you strength to bear it. I know, for He did it for me once!"

Courtland felt as if his words were falling on deaf ears, but Tennelly, after a pause, asked bitterly, "Why did He do this to me, if He's what you say He is?"

"I'm not sure He did, old man! I think perhaps you and I had a hand in it!"

Tennelly looked at him keenly for an instant and turned away, silent. "I know what you mean," he said. "You told me I'd go through hell, and I have. I knew it in a way myself, but I'm afraid I'd do it again! I loved her! I'm afraid—I *love her yet!* Man! You don't know what an ache such love is."

"Yes, I do," said Courtland with a sudden light in his face, but Tennelly didn't notice.

"It isn't entirely that I've lost her or must give up hoping she'll sometime care and then settle down to knowing she's gone forever. It's the way she went! The—the—the *disgrace!* The humiliation! The awfulness of it! We've never had anything like that in our family. And to think my baby has to grow up to know that shame! To know her mother was a disgraceful woman! That I gave her a mother like that!"

"Now, look here, Tennelly! You didn't know! You thought she'd be all right when you were married!"

"But I *did know!*" wailed Tennelly. "I knew in my soul! I think I knew when I first saw her, and that was why I worried about you when you used to go and see her. I knew she wasn't the woman for you. But, blamed fool that I was! I thought I was more of a man of the world and would be able to hold her. No, I didn't either, for I knew trusting my love to her was like trying to enjoy a sound sleep in a powder-magazine with a pocketful of matches. But I did it anyway! I dared trouble! And my child has to suffer for it!"

"Your child will perhaps be better for it!"

"I can't see it that way!"

"You don't have to. If God does, isn't that enough?"

"I don't know! I can't see God now; it's too dark." Tennelly put his forehead against the windowpane and groaned.

"But you have your child," said Courtland, hesitating. "Doesn't that help?"

"She breaks my heart," said the father. "To think of her worse than motherless!

That little bit of a helpless thing! And it's my fault she's here with a future of shame!"

"Nothing of the sort! It'll be your fault if she has a future of shame, but it's up to you. Her mother's shame can't hurt her if you bring her up right. It's your job, and you can get a lot of comfort out of it if you try!"

"I don't see how," he said dully.

"Listen, Tennelly. Does she look like her mother?"

Tennelly's sensitive face quivered with pain. "Yes," he said huskily. "I'll send for her, and you can see." He rang a bell. "I brought her and the nurse up to town with me this morning."

An elderly, kind-faced woman brought the baby in, laid her in a big chair where they could see her and then withdrew.

Courtland drew near, half shyly, and looked in startled wonder. The baby was strikingly like Gila, with all her grace and delicate features and wide, innocent eyes. The sweep of the long lashes on the little white cheeks, too white for baby flesh, seemed old and strange in the tiny face. Yet when the baby looked up and recognized her father she crowed and smiled, and the smile was wide and frank and lovable, like Tennelly's. There was nothing artificial about it; Courtland drew a long sigh of relief. For a moment he looked at the baby as if she were Gila grown small again; now he suddenly realized she was a new little soul with a life and a spirit of her own.

"She will be a blessing to you, Nelly," he said, looking up hopefully.

"I don't see it that way!" said the hopeless father, shaking his head.

"Would you rather have her—taken away—as her mother suggested?" he hazarded suddenly.

Tennelly gave him one quick, startled look. "No!" he said and staggered back into a chair. "Do you think she looks as sick as that? I know she's not well. I know she's lost flesh! But she's been neglected. Gila never cared for her and wouldn't be bothered looking after things. She was angry because the baby came at all. She resented motherhood because it limited her pleasures. My poor little girl!"

Tennelly dropped on his knees beside the baby and buried his face in her soft little neck.

The baby swept her dark lashes down with the old Gila trick and looked with a puzzled frown at the dark head so close to her face. Then she put up her little hand and moved it over her father's hair with an awkward attempt at comfort. The great big being with his head in her neck was in trouble, and she was vaguely sympathetic.

A wave of pity swept over Courtland. He dropped to his knees beside his friend and spoke aloud: "O Lord God, come near and let my friend feel Your presence now in his terrible distress. Somehow speak peace to his soul and help him to know You, for You are the only One who can help him. Help him tell You all his heart's bitterness now, alone with You and his little child, and find relief."

Softly Courtland arose and slipped from the room, leaving them alone with the Presence.

Gila had been gone two months when the day was finally set for Bonnie's wedding.

They had consulted long and much about telling Tennelly, for even Bonnie saw the event could only be painful to him, coming as it did on the heels of his own deep trouble. And Tennelly had long been Courtland's best friend—at least until Pat grew so close as to share that privilege with him. It was finally decided Courtland should tell Tennelly about the approaching wedding at his first opportunity.

Bonnie had long ago heard all about Gila, gone through the bitter throes of jealousy and come out clear and trusting, with the whole thing happily relegated to that place where all such troubles go from the hearts of those who truly love each other and know that no one else in the universe could take the place of the beloved.

Courtland had been preaching in the Church of the Presence of God for four Sabbaths now, and the congregation was growing steadily. He told a few friends in the factories nearby of the service. He put up a notice on the door saying the church would be open for worship regularly and everyone was welcome. He didn't wish to force anything. He was following the leading of the Spirit. If God really meant this work for him, He would show him.

Courtland's preaching was not the usual cut-and-dried order of the young theologue. He had studied theology to help him understand his God and his Bible, not give him a set of rules for preaching. So when he stood up in the pulpit it wasn't to follow any conventional order of service or try to imitate the great preachers he'd heard, but to give the people something to help them live during the week and realize the presence of Christ in their daily lives.

The men at the seminary got wind of it and came down by twos and threes and finally dozens, as they could get away from their own preaching to see what that closemouthed Courtland was doing, and went away thoughtful. It wasn't what they'd expected of their brilliant classmate, ministering to these common working people right in the neighborhood where they lived and worked.

At first they didn't understand how he came to be in that church and asked what denomination it was anyway. Courtland said he really didn't know what it had been, but he hoped it was the denomination of Jesus Christ now.

"But whose church is it?" they asked.

"Mine," he said simply.

Then they turned to Pat for explanation.

"That's straight," said Pat. "He bought it."

"*Bought it!* Oh!" They were silenced. Not one of them could have bought a church and wouldn't have if they could. They would have bought a good mansion for themselves in their retirement. Few of them understood it. Only the man who was going to darkest Africa to work in the jungles, and a couple who were bound, one for the leper country and another for China, had a light of understanding in their eyes and gripped Courtland's hand with reverence and ecstatic awe.

"But, man alive!" said one, unwilling to leave his brilliant friend in such a hopeless hole. "Don't you realize if you don't hitch onto some denomination or board of trustees or something, your work won't count in the long run? Who's to carry on your work and keep up your name and what you've done, after you're gone? You're foolish!" He'd just received a flattering call to a city church himself and knew he wasn't half as well suited for it as Courtland.

But Courtland flung up his hat in a boyish way and smiled. "I should worry about my name after I'm gone. And as for the work, it's for me to do, isn't it? Not for me to arrange for after I'm dead. If my heavenly Father wants to keep it up after I'm gone He'll find a way, won't He? My job is to look after it while I'm here. Perhaps it won't be needed any longer after I'm gone. God sent me here to buy His church when it was for sale, didn't He? Well, then, if it's for sale again He'll find somebody else to buy it, unless He's finished with it. The New Jerusalem may be here by then, and we won't have to have any churches. God Himself will be the tabernacle! So you see I'm just going to run my little church the best I can with what God gives me, and I won't trouble any boards at present, not as long as I have enough money to keep the wheels moving."

They went away then with doubtful looks, and Courtland heard one say to another, shaking his head in a dubious way, "I don't like it. It's very irregular!"

And the other replied, "Yes! It's a pity about him. He might do something big if he weren't so impractical."

"The poor stews!" said Pat, looking after them.

Courtland wrote to Bonnie about the happenings at seminary and church and what the theologues said about his being impractical and irregular. And Bonnie, with a tender smile, leaned down and kissed the words in the letter and murmured softly to herself, "Dear impractical beloved!"

Bonnie was very happy. To possess great wealth that must be spent in the usual way, surrounded by social distinction, attended by functions and society duties, would have burdened her. But to have money to use without limit in helping other people was a miracle of joy. To think it should have come to her!

Yet something was greater than the money and the new interests opening up before her, and that was the wonder of the man who had chosen her to be his wife. That such a prince among men, such a friend of God, would have passed by others of rank, of beauty and attainments far greater than hers, and come out West to take her, fairly overwhelmed her with wonder when she had time to think about it. For she was as busy as she was happy these days, with her school work and music, the home duties she could get Mother Marshall to leave for her, her beautiful sewing on the simple bridal garments, and stealing time from all to write the most wonderful letters to the insatiable lover in the East.

Bonnie passed through these days with a song on her lips whenever she went about the house and a tender touch for the dear old people who had been father and mother to her in her loneliness. She realized only vaguely what it would be to them when she was gone and they were alone again, for her heart was so full of her own joy that she couldn't think a sad thought.

But one afternoon she came home from school earlier than usual. Opening the door softly so she might surprise Mother Marshall, she heard voices in the dining room and paused to see if they had company.

"It's going to be mighty hard when Bonnie leaves us," said Father Marshall with a quaver.

There was a sigh over by the window, then Mother Marshall said, "Yes, Father, but we mustn't think about it, or the next thing we know we'll let her see it. She's the kind of girl that would turn around and say she couldn't get married, if she got it in her head we needed her. She's got a grand man, and I'm just as glad as I can be about it." There was a gulp like a sob over by the window. "I wouldn't spoil her happiness for anything in the world!" The voice took on a forced cheerfulness.

"Sure! We wouldn't want to do that!"

"It's 'most as bad as when Stephen was going away, though. I have to shut my eyes when I go by her bedroom door and think about how we fixed it up for her and counted on how she'd look and all. I couldn't stand it. I had to shut the door and hurry downstairs."

"Well, now, Mother, you mustn't feel that way. You know the Lord sent her first. Maybe He has some other plan."

"Oh, I know!" said Mother briskly. "I guess we can leave that to Him—only seems like I can't bear to think of anybody else coming to be in her room."

"Oh, no! We couldn't stand for that!" said Father quickly. "We'd have to keep it for her—for them—when they come home to visit. If any other party comes along I reckon we'll just build out a bay window on the kitchen chamber and fix that up. Now don't you worry, Mother. You know he promised to bring her home a lot, and it ain't as if he didn't have enough money to travel, let alone an ottymobeel. I shouldn't wonder maybe if we could go see them sometime. We could get to see the university then, too, and look at Steve's room. You'd like that, wouldn't you, Mother?"

Bonnie didn't go into the dining room to surprise them. Instead, she stole away down in the orchard to hide her tears.

A little later she saw the postman ride up to the letter box on the gatepost and drop in a letter, and all else was forgotten.

Yes, from Paul! A lovely, thick letter!

Mother and Father Marshall and their sadness suddenly vanished from her thoughts, and she hurried back to a big stump in the orchard, where she often read her letters.

Chapter 35

*D*ear Bonnie Rose [she smiled tenderly; he was always giving her a new name]:

I've been to see Tennelly at last, and he's great! What do you think? He's not only coming to the wedding, but he asked if I'll let him be best man, unless I'd rather have Pat. I told Pat, and you should have heard him roar. "Fat chance! Me best man, with you two fellows around!" he said.

Father and my stepmother will come. But please tell Mother Marshall she needn't worry because they'll only stay for the ceremony. I know she was a little troubled about my stepmother, lest things would seem plain to her—bless her dear heart! But she needn't worry at all, for she's a kindly soul. They'll come in their private car, which will be dropped off from the morning train and picked up by the night express at the junction. So you see they'll have to leave for Sloan's Station early in the afternoon.

But the greatest news of all I heard tonight! Pat brought it as usual. It beats all how he finds out pleasant things. You remember how we wished John Burns hadn't gone to China yet, so he could marry us? Well, he's coming back. He's been sent on some errand for the government with two Chinese men and is due in San Francisco a week before the wedding. I've sent a wireless to ask him to stop over and take part in the ceremony. I was sure this would meet with your approval. Of course, we'll ask your minister out there to assist. You don't know how this pleases me. Only one of the professors I'd have cared to ask, and he's with his wife, who's very ill at a sanitarium. It seems somehow as if Burns belongs to us, doesn't it, dear?

I stood tonight on the steps of the church and looked at a ray of the setting sun that was slanting between buildings and laying a finger of gold on the old dirty windows across the street till they blazed into sudden glory. As I looked the houses faded away, as they do in a moving picture, and gradually melted into a great open space that stretched a whole big block, all clear and green with thick velvety grass. A lot of trees were in the space, and hammocks under some of them, with little children playing about. At the farthest end were tennis courts and a baseball diamond. And who do you think I saw teaching some boys to pitch, but Pat! On the other side of the street a big, old warehouse had been converted into a gymnasium with a swimming pool.

All around the block were model tenements, with thousands of windows and light and air and cheerfulness. Between the curbing and the pavement were flowers in little beds that the children could water and cultivate and pick. A fountain of filtered water stood in the center of the green, and a drinking fountain at each corner of the block, but there wasn't a saloon in sight!

I looked to my right, and the old stone house with its grimy face had changed into a beautiful home with vines and flowers. Everywhere were windows jutting out and lovely green grass and more trees all the way to the corner! On the left, the old foundry had been cleansed and transformed and become a hospital belonging to the church. I couldn't help thinking then what a grand doctor Tennelly would have made if he only hadn't been an aristocrat. The hospital was white, and an ambulance belonged to it, with nurses who worked not only for money but for the love of Christ. Not a doctor in it didn't know what the presence of God meant or couldn't point the way for a dying sinner to be saved.

Back of the church block, in place of the old shackly factories, was a great model factory with the best modern equipment, and the eight-hour system in full swing. No little children working for a scanty living! No tired girls and women standing all day long! No foremen who didn't love humanity and have some kind of idea what it was to have the presence of the living God in the factory!

I went back to the stone house and discovered a big living room with a grand piano at one end and a stone fireplace large enough for logs. A wide staircase led up to a gallery where many rooms opened off, rooms enough for everyone we wanted and a big special one for Father and Mother Marshall, winters, opening off in a suite, so they could be to themselves when they got tired of us all. Of course, in summers they might want to go home sometimes and take us all with them, or maybe run down to the shore with us in an off year now and then. Break the news to them gently, darling, for I've set my heart on that house just as I saw it, and I hope they won't object.

Other rooms were there but vague, because I saw that you must have the key to them yet, and I must wait till you come, to look into them.

Then I heard sweet sounds from the church, and, turning, I went in. Someone was playing the organ, high up in the dusky shadows of the gallery, and I knew it was you, Bonnie Rose, my darling! So I knelt in a pew and listened, with the Presence standing there between us. And as I knelt, another vision came to me, a vision of the past!

I remembered the days when I didn't know God; when I sneered and argued and did all I could in my young, conceited way against Him. I remembered, too, when He came to me in my illness and I began to believe, and the day I read that verse marked in Stephen's Bible: "He that believeth on the Son of God hath the witness in himself." I suddenly realized that had been made true to me. I have the witness in my own heart that Christ is the Son of God, my Savior! That His presence is on earth and manifest to me at many times.

No seeming variance of science, no quibble of the intellect, can ever disturb this faith on which my soul rests. It is more than a conviction; it is a perfect satisfaction! I KNOW! I may not be able to explain all the mysteries, but I can never doubt again, because I know. The more I meet with modern skepticism, the more I'm convinced that's the only answer to it all: "He that doeth His will shall know of the doctrine," and that promise is fulfilled to all who have the will to believe.

All that came to me quite clearly as I knelt in the church in the sunset, while you were playing—was it "Rock of Ages"?—and a ray of setting sun stole through the old yellow glass of the window in the organ loft and lay on your hair like a crown, my Bonnie darling! My heart overflowed with gratitude for the great way life has opened up to me. That I, the least of His servants, should be honored by the love of this pearl of women!—

There was more of that letter, and Bonnie sat long on the stump reading and rereading, with her face glowing with wonder and joy. But at last she stood up and went to the house, bounding into the dining room where Mother and Father Marshall were pretending to be busy about a lamp that didn't work right.

Down she sat with her letter and read it—at least as much as we have read—to the two sad old dears who were getting ready for loneliness. But after that no more sadness was in that house. No more tears or wistful looks. Father whistled everywhere he went, till Mother told him he was like a boy again. Mother sang about her work whenever she was alone. For why should they be sad anymore? Good times were still going in the world, and *they were in them!*

"Father!" whispered Mother that night, when she was supposed to be well on her way to slumber. "Do you suppose the Lord heard us grumbling this afternoon and sent that letter to make us ashamed of ourselves?"

"No," said Father tenderly, "I think He just smiled to think what a big surprise He had already for us. It doesn't pay to doubt God—it really doesn't!"

Chapter 36

Pat was out with the ambulance. He'd been taking a convalescent from the hospital down to the station and shipping him home to his mother in the country, to be nursed back to health. Pat often did little things like that that were utterly out of his province, just because he liked to.

He had seen his patient off and was threading his way through a crowded thoroughfare when a bright red racer passed him at a furious rate, driven by a woman with a reckless hand. She shot by the ambulance like a rocket and at the next corner came face to face with a great motortruck that was thundering around the corner at a tremendous speed. From the first glance there was no chance for the racer. It crumpled like paper and lay in the bright splinters on the street, the lady tossed aside and motionless, with her head against the curb.

The crowd closed in about her, and someone called for the police. The crowd opened again as an officer signed to the ambulance to stand by, and kind hands put the lady inside. Pat sped to the home hospital, which wasn't far away, and was soon inside its gates with the house doctor and nurse rushing out in answer to his signal.

A light was shining in the church close by, although it wasn't yet dark. Bonnie was playing softly on the organ. Pat knew the hymn she was playing.

> At evening, ere the sun was set,
> The sick, O Lord! around Thee lay;
> Oh, with what divers ills they met,
> Oh, with what joy they went away!
>
> Once more 'tis eventide, and we,
> Oppressed with various ills, draw near—

Pat was following the melody in his mind with the words that were so often sung in the Church of the Presence of God at evening service. He jumped down from his driver's seat and went around to the back of the ambulance, where they were preparing to carry the patient into the building. He wondered what sort he'd brought to the House of Healing this time. Then suddenly he saw her face and stopped short, with a suppressed exclamation.

There, huddled on the stretcher, in her costly sporting garments, with her long, dark lashes sweeping over her hard, painted face and a pinched look of suffering about her loose-hung baby mouth, lay Gila!

He knew her at once and drew back in horror. What had he done! Brought her here, this evil viper that had crept into his friends' garden and despoiled them of their joy! Why hadn't he looked at her before they started? He might easily have taken her to another hospital instead of this one. He could do so yet.

But Courtland was standing on the steps, looking down at the huddled figure on the stretcher, with a strange expression of pity and tenderness in his face.

"I didn't know! I didn't see her before, Court!" stammered Pat. "I'll take her somewhere else now before she's been disturbed."

"No, Pat, it's all right! It's fitting she should come to us. I'm glad you found her. You must have been led! Call Bonnie, please. And, Pat, watch for Nelly and take him into my study. He was coming down on the Boston express. Let me know as soon as he gets here."

Courtland hurried into the hospital. Pat looked after him for a moment with a light of love in his eyes and realized for the first time what was meant by the power of a new affection. Court hadn't minded seeing Gila on his own account. He was thinking only of Tennelly. Poor Nelly! What would he do?

There was no hope for Gila from the first. There had been an injury to the spine, and it was only a question of hours how long she had to stay.

It was Bonnie's face upon which the great dark eyes first opened in consciousness again. Bonnie in soft, white garments was sitting beside the bed, watching. A strange contraction of fear and hate passed over her face as she looked, and she spoke in an insolent, sharp little voice, weak as a sick bird's chirp.

"Who sent you here?" she demanded.

"God," said Bonnie gently, without an instant's hesitation.

A startled look came into Gila's eyes. "God! What does He want with me? Has He sent you here to torment me? I know who you are! You're that poor girl Paul picked up in the street. You've come to pay me back!"

Bonnie's face was full of tenderness. "No, dear, that's all passed. I've just come to bring you a message from God."

"God! What do I have to do with God?" A quiver of anguish passed over her face. "I hate God! He hates me! Am I dead, then, that He sends me messages?"

"No, you're not dead. And God doesn't hate you. Listen! He says, 'I have loved you with an everlasting love.' That's the message He sends. He's here now. He wants you to pay attention to Him."

The blanched face o۱ the pillow tightened and hardened in fear once more. "That's that awful Presۜۑce again! The Presence! The Presence! I've been trying to get away from it for three years, and it's pursued me everywhere! Now I'm caught like a rat in a trap and can't get away! If I'm not dead, then I must be dying, or you wouldn't dare talk to me this awful way! *I am dying!* And *you* think *I'm going to hell!*" Her shrill voice rose almost to a scream.

Above the sound, Bonnie's calm, clear voice dominated with a sudden quieting hush. Courtland, standing with the doctor and Tennelly just outside the partly open door, was thrilled with the sweetness of it, as if some supernatural power were given to her at this trying time.

"Listen, Gila! This is what He says: 'God sent not his Son into the world to condemn the world; but that the world through him might be saved. . . . God so loved the world that he gave his only begotten Son, that whosoever believeth in him should not perish, but have everlasting life.' He wants you to *believe now* that He loves you and wants to save you."

"But He couldn't!" said Gila with the old petulant tone. "I've hated Him all my life! I *hate Him now!* And I've never been good! I couldn't be good! I don't *want* to be good! I want to do just what I *please!* And I *will!* I won't hear you talk this way! I want to get up! Why does my body feel so strange and numb, as if it wasn't there? Am I dying now? Answer me quick! Am I dying? *I know I am.* I'm dying, and you won't tell me! I'm dying, and I'm afraid! I'M AFRAID!"

One piercing scream after another rang out through the corridors. In vain Bonnie and the nurse sought to soothe her. The high, excited voice raved on.

"I'm afraid to die! I'm afraid of that Presence! Send Paul Courtland! He tried to tell me once, and I wouldn't hear! I made him choose between me and God! And *now I'm going to be punished!*"

"Listen, dear," continued Bonnie in a steady, tender voice. "God doesn't want to punish. He wants to save. He's waiting to forgive you if you'll let Him!"

Something in her low-spoken words caught and held the attention of the soul in mortal anguish. Gila fixed her great, anguishing eyes on Bonnie.

"Forgive! Forgive! How could anybody forgive all I've done! You don't know anything about such things," she said with contempt. "You've always been a goody-good! I can see it in your look. You don't know what it is to have men making fools of themselves over you. You don't know all I've done. I've been what they call a sinner. I sent away the only man I ever loved because I was *jealous of God!* I broke the heart of the man who loved me because I got tired of him and his everlasting perfection. I hated the idea of being a mother, and when my child came I deserted her. I would have killed her if I'd dared! I went away with a bad man. And when I got tired of him I took the first way that opened to get away from him. God doesn't forgive things like that! I didn't expect Him to when I did them. But it isn't fair not to let me live out my life. I'm too young to die! And I'm afraid! I'm AFRAID!"

"Yes, God forgives all those things! There was a woman once like that, and Jesus forgave her. He'll forgive you if you ask Him. But He can't forgive you unless you're sorry and really want Him to. He says, 'Though your sins be as scarlet they shall be as white as snow; and though they be red like crimson, they shall be as wool.' But you have to be sorry first that you sinned. He can't forgive you if you aren't sorry."

"Sorry! *Sorry!*" Gila's laugh rang out mirthlessly and echoed in the high, white room. "Oh, I'm *sorry* all right! What do you think I am? Do you think I've been *happy?* Don't you know I've suffered torments? Everything I've touched has turned to ashes. I've gone everywhere and done everything to try to forget myself, but that awful Presence was always chasing me. Standing in my way everywhere I turned! Driving me! Always driving me toward hell! I've tried drowning my thoughts with cocktails and dope, but always when they wore off, that Presence was pursuing me! Do you mean to tell me there's forgiveness for me with Him?"

Her breath was coming in painful gasps as she screamed out the words, and the nurse leaned over and gave her a quieting draught.

Bonnie, in a low, clear voice, began to repeat Bible verses:

The blood of Jesus Christ his Son cleanseth us from *all* sin!

As far as the east is from the west, so far hath he removed our transgressions from us.

I, even I, am he that blotteth out thy transgressions for mine own sake, and will not remember thy sins.

If we confess our sins, he is faithful and just to forgive us our sins, and to cleanse us from all unrighteousness.

Gila listened with wondering, incredulous eyes, like the eyes of a frightened, naughty child who scarcely understood what was being said and was in a frenzy of fear.

"Oh, if Paul Courtland were here he'd tell me if this is true!" Gila cried at last.

Instantly, from the shadow of the doorway, stepped Courtland and stood at the foot of the bed where she could see him, looking steadily at the dying girl for a moment and then lifting his eyes, as if to One who stood just beside her.

"O Jesus Christ, who came to save, come close to Your poor little wandering child and show her she's forgiven! Take her gently by the hand and help her see You and how loving You are. Help her understand how You came to earth and died to take her place of punishment so she might be forgiven! Open her eyes to see what love like that can be!"

Gila turned startled eyes on Courtland as she heard his voice, strong, beseeching, tender, intimate with God! She listened, watching his illumined face as he prayed. Watched and listened as one who suddenly sees a ray of light where all was darkness; till gradually the tenseness and pain faded from her face and a surprised calm took its place.

The strong voice went on, talking with the Savior about what He'd done for this poor erring one, till with a sigh, like a tired child, the eyelids dropped over her frightened eyes and a look of peace began to dawn.

While the prayer had been going on, Tennelly, with his little girl in his arms, had slipped into the room and stood with bowed head looking with anguished eyes at the wreck of the beautiful girl who was once his wife.

Suddenly, as if alive to subtle influences, Gila opened her eyes again and looked straight at Tennelly and the baby! A dart of consciousness entered her gaze, and something like a wave of anguish passed over her face.

She made a piteous, helpless movement with the small jeweled hands that lay limply on the coverlet and murmured one word, with pleading in her eyes, "Forgive!"

Courtland had ceased praying, and the room was very still till Bonnie, just outside the door, began to sing softly:

Rock of Ages, cleft for me,
> Let me hide myself in Thee!
Let the water and the blood
> From Thy riven side which flowed
Be of sin the double cure,
> Save me from its guilt and power!

Suddenly little Doris, who had been looking down with wondering baby solemnity on the strange scene, leaned forward and pointed to the bed.

"Pitty Mama dawn as'eep!" she said softly, and with a groan Tennelly sank with her to his knees beside the bed.

Courtland, kneeling a little way off, spoke out once more.

"Lord Jesus, Savior of the world, we leave her with Your tender mercy!"

As if a visible sign of assent had been asked, the setting sun suddenly dropped lower, blazing into glory the golden cross on the church and throwing its reflection upon the wall at the head of the bed just over the white face of the dead.

The baby saw and pointed once again. "Pitty! Pitty! Papa, see!"

The sorrowing father lifted his eyes to the golden symbol of salvation, and Courtland, standing at the foot of the bed, spoke softly.

" 'I am the resurrection, and the life: he that believeth in me, though he were dead, yet shall he live.' "

As in a Mirror

Chapter 1

The day was so warm that irregular Sabbath worshippers remained at home, and even regular ones found the weather sufficient excuse for not attending. Two young men, of the latter group, were exceptions. Possibly they went to church because the stone building looked darker and cooler than their rooms. At least, they met in the pew they owned together and smiled listlessly at each other.

The only person who didn't seem listless was the pastor. The heat must have produced energy in him, for his voice rang out among the half-empty pews and echoed down the aisles, startling sleepy members into sitting straight. Perhaps the pastor was energetic to keep himself awake. Or perhaps something occurred recently to stir his heart with sympathy for certain persons to whom little sympathy is usually given.

His text, "I was a stranger and ye took me not in," was followed by his first sentence: "The negative form of that statement fits today's experiences." After that, he described the ordinary method of dealing with the modern tramp. The sermon couldn't be called a plea for the tramp, for he frankly acknowledged the tramp's general worthlessness and deplored the habit a "few lazy people" had of giving him money. But he declared that the average man today used neither judgment nor charity in dealing with tramps.

Certain men and women would dive into filthy streets and alleys searching for the lost; give whole afternoons to seeking out and ministering to tenement-house sufferers; go to jails and prisons and other poorly ventilated places to teach the depraved. These same men and women would turn away from their doors a hungry man asking for food, with a harsh refusal and without asking what brought him to that state or trying to win him to a better life. The next day or week, when his desperate need had made a criminal of him, they would visit him in his cell and do what they could toward his reformation. But not one crumb of prevention would they give to the poor tramp at their doors, whose worst crimes, so far, might have been poverty and laziness!

The pastor grew eloquent as he continued, citing some thrilling instances he'd recently learned about. He affirmed that the Lord Jesus Christ, who came to save the lost, would be ashamed to meet in their own homes two-thirds of the people who bore His name, because of their treatment of His starving tramps. He didn't plead for indiscriminate giving; he begged the listeners not to go away and say he'd urged giving tramps money or even clothing that could easily be exchanged for liquor. But a bit of bread to be eaten on one's doorstep, followed by a drink of cool water and a few words of inquiry or sympathy or exhortation, couldn't drag any tramp lower than he was. Who would say the opportunity might be blessed of God and the seed dropped bear such fruit that bread-giver and bread-eater might rejoice together through eternity? Wasn't it worthwhile at least to think about this army of hungry, half-clad opportunities that tramped annually past our doors? Were we ready today to give account to Him who said, "I was hungry and ye gave me no bread"?

The two young men who had met in church weren't sleepy. One, in fact, sat up and looked steadily at the speaker, his eyes kindling with deepened interest as the sermon grew more emphatic.

"How that man can get up so much energy on a day like today is beyond me," his companion said, following a brief prayer and a single verse of a hymn, as the organist roared and thundered them out of church.

"The subject energized him," said the young man who had listened intently. "He handled it well and in an original manner."

"Dr. Talbert is nothing if not original. But why did he choose a regular broadside for such a melting day? Something quiet and soothing would have been more in keeping."

"So people wouldn't be disturbed in their slumbers, eh? Oh, I looked around and saw they slept very well. What a trial it must be to the doctor to pour out eloquence and energy on sleepers! Seriously, Fletcher, weren't you impressed with his way of dealing with the problem? He didn't seem to have new ideas so much as he spoke out on an unpopular side and told the individual his duty. We deal with this matter through organizations nowadays, like Associated Charities. Then the average man and woman, who know these organizations by name only and never lift a finger toward their work, feel that their responsibility has been shouldered and they can simply moralize."

"Oh, he talked well—Dr. Talbert always does. I told you he was more worth hearing than any other man in town. You aren't used to his style, and it's impressive. He didn't come until after you went abroad, did he?"

"He came the Sunday before, but I didn't hear him. I went with my mother to Dr. Pendleton's church that day. No, I've heard Dr. Talbert very little. Is he always so stirring?"

"He's always high pressure, if that's what you mean. I haven't decided yet whether he's more so than a quieter man would be. Doesn't some of it seem like mere oratory?"

"What do you mean by that? He's an orator, but I wouldn't think of using that word 'mere' with him. Do you think he doesn't feel what he says?"

"Oh, some of it he feels, probably. But—I'd like to be a tramp tomorrow morning and call at his door, to see how he'd apply his sermon."

"How do you think he would?"

"With his Monday morning shoes," Fletcher replied with an indolent laugh. "Not as bad as that," he added, seeing his friend was expecting something more serious. "But I wouldn't expect any more consideration from him because of that sermon. You see, King, you've got to take a certain amount of—shall I call it idealism?—into consideration when you listen to a sermon, especially when the speaker is an enthusiast like Dr. Talbert. You can't pin him down to hard facts; he has to soar—make statements one day that the next he'd naturally tone down a little."

"I don't believe it," said King emphatically. "There's a lot of surface talking, I know. But I like to think that from the pulpit we get truth, not only in doctrine, but in statements regarding everyday life. I like to believe the speaker is in earnest. I may disagree and think he's mistaken, but I want him to believe every word he utters, to the depths of his being. Nothing less than that could command my respect."

The young man Fletcher politely covered a yawn with his hand. "It's too hot to argue, and there's no need. Dr. Talbert is in earnest enough. I only mean I don't believe he'll serve the next tramp who calls on him a dinner of turkey and pound cake and give him a solid silver fork to eat them with."

"Who's idealizing now?" laughed his friend. "I thought his views stayed within the bounds of common sense."

King halted before an apartment house and, after his invitation to Fletcher to enter was declined, seated himself in the elevator and was taken to the fourth floor front, where he lived in luxurious rooms alone. Fletcher sauntered three squares further and let himself into a fine house on the corner, where his father and sisters were awaiting him.

Changing into cooler clothes King drew an easy chair in front of the window where a faint suspicion of a breeze hovered and, contrary to his habit, without book or paper. The walls were lined with shelves containing every choice book of the season, as well as the standard volumes of the past. A bookcase was crowded with standard magazines, and the large study table strewn with the latest newspapers. Evidently the occupant was an avid reader; yet none of his silent companions appealed to him. He didn't look sleepy; on the contrary, that intent look in the church remained on his face. Some problem had confronted him. It kept him working during that entire afternoon, with the thermometer in the nineties. He went to his boarding house to dinner as usual but carried that preoccupied air and came away again without lingering for music or conversation as he sometimes did. He lay down for his Sunday afternoon nap, but sleep didn't come. Instead, he stared at the ceiling and thought.

He'd dropped into that same easy chair again, still without book or paper, when he heard a tap at his door, and his friend Fletcher appeared.

"Awake, old fellow? I knocked very softly for fear of disturbing a nap; it was so hot earlier in the day a fellow couldn't sleep. Don't you want to go around and hear Dr. Waymouth this evening?"

"Take a seat," said King, glancing about for another easy chair and motioning his friend toward it. "No, to be entirely frank, I don't. I've had sermon enough for one day. I can't get away from the morning one; it's stayed with me all afternoon."

Fletcher laughed genially. "Dr. Talbert is going to be too strong a tonic for you, I'm afraid. You'll have to change your church relations and go to Dr. Pendleton's. You're high pressure yourself and need soothing, as I said this morning."

"We're all searching too much for soothing potions at church. No, in fact, I need rousing. Wheel that chair up here and let me talk to you. I've thought a lot this afternoon. Fletcher, that sermon needs to be thought about—it dealt with a problem demanding solution. Do you know how many tramps are in our country annually? The figures are appalling! I was reading some statistics on the subject only last night, but they didn't impress me much until I heard Dr. Talbert. What do we know about them? As he said, we pass them by with a smile or a sneer, go on our well-fed way and forget them. Who's trying to reach them? We have no idea how we'd feel if we were put for a single week in their places—homeless, moneyless and without decent clothing."

"Many of them leave good homes to tramp about the country," said his friend. King sat up straight and confronted him.

"Don't you believe it," he said. "Some are scamps searching for adventure, no doubt. But most tramp from stern necessity. How can we help them unless we enter into their lives? I'm planning to write a book with a tramp in it. I've been gathering materials all spring, and I thought I was nearly ready to begin work, before I heard that sermon. Now I'm sure I know nothing about the fellow. I'll tell you what, Fletcher—I'm going to turn tramp."

Fletcher leaned back in his easy chair and laughed—not loud, just low, amused chuckles that died down and bubbled up again, as though he couldn't get away from the absurdity of the idea.

"Laugh as much as you please," said his friend good-humoredly, "but I'm serious. Since hearing Dr. Talbert this morning, I decided I've studied one side of the problem, and it would be impertinent to write about it before studying the other side. Do you remember Charles Reade's old book *Put Yourself in His Place*? There's common sense in that title. I'm going to attempt just that thing. I have the summer before me. Mother and Elizabeth are in Europe and want to remain there until next spring. There's nothing to hinder my turning tramp tomorrow, and in all seriousness I mean to do it."

Fletcher ceased laughing and tried to dissuade his friend from taking such an erratic step, but with little hope of succeeding. In all the years he'd known John Stuart King, that young man had been noted for carrying out his projects, many of them seemingly unreasonable. The subject was thoroughly canvassed that evening; the church bells tolled in vain; the hot day reached its ending; darkness and a measure of coolness fell upon them, and still the two sat and talked.

"Well," said Fletcher at last, "if you will, you *will*. I knew that before I began. But you'll be tired of your bargain before the season is half over and know no more about the 'true inwardness' of tramp life than now. It's a farce, you see—you can't be a tramp. A man who knows he has a fortune to fall back on can't feel as the tramp does, and it's folly to try."

"There's truth in that," he repeated. "I can only approximate the conditions. But it won't be a farce. I won't use one penny of my money while I tramp over the country. I'll be hungry and ragged if necessary, if I can't find work to feed and clothe myself. It's the honest tramp doing the best he can with his environment who interests me, and an honest tramp I'm going to be. Anyway, I'll help myself in writing my own book, and that's a great point."

Chapter 2

The third day following that Sunday, a tramp was seen walking down one of the city's principal business streets in a slouching gait common to those people. He avoided looking directly into the eyes of anyone he met, another characteristic of that class. His hair, brown and plentiful, was tossed about wildly, and his slouch hat was pushed well down over his head. His clothes were cleaner than many tramps', suggesting he'd made an almost painful effort to be clean and belonged to the better class of unfortunates. Still, the clothes had many defects. The sleeves were much too short and badly frayed; they'd been out at the elbow but were patched with a different material. A calico shirt was buttoned high about the throat, and that also was clean but collarless. The shoes were the worst part of the outfit, unless the shabby trousers dangling above them were worse.

On the whole, John Stuart King looked furtively at himself as he lounged along, uncertain whether to feel elation or dismay at the success of his disguise. He'd chosen an unfamiliar street; yet he met from time to time people he knew well in society. For the most part they passed him without a glance. He was of a world different from theirs and too common to awaken their curiosity. As he grew bolder, once or twice he asked for work from men whose name and position he knew. They knew his name perfectly, would have recognized it anywhere but didn't know him by sight. Without exception they answered him curtly in the negative, without question or remark. They had no work for such as he. He might be hungry, but it was doubtless his fault. Anyway there were charities, breakfast missions and what not for wretches of his stamp. If their faces expressed any thought of him, the tramp concluded it took that form.

One young lady startled him and made him feel his best course would be to strike out into the country as soon as possible. He'd met her at receptions and parties, and as she passed him she started, even turning her head.

He heard her say, "How much that fellow looks like"— the name dropped from his hearing, but he couldn't be sure it wasn't his own.

"The idea!" laughed her louder companion.

The tramp moved on more rapidly, his face flushing. This incognito walk through the city of his birth gave him strange sensations. He wasn't well known, except in certain circles; long absences from home during the years when people change the most kept him from being recognized. But to pass those who would gladly call themselves his friends if they recognized him, and to receive no knowing nod or glance, had its startling side. Did mere clothes count for so much?

His speculations ceased suddenly. Approaching quickly was his closest friend, Arnold Fletcher. Now for the crucial test: If Fletcher passed him, then he couldn't be himself. But he hadn't intended to test this on a public thoroughfare. Why was Fletcher on this street and at this hour? He was evidently hurrying, for he walked with long strides, looking neither to the right nor the left. Yes, he was passing without a glance. Suddenly the tramp became courageous.

"Could you help me, sir, to find work, enough to earn my breakfast?" he said in the desperate tone he thought a fellow in his situation should use.

"Work?" repeated Fletcher, slackening his pace and recalling his thoughts from—the tramp couldn't decide where. "There's work enough in the world—too much to suit me! Your trouble probably is that you can't do any of it decently. What kind of work do you want?"

"Any kind," said the tramp.

But it was an unguarded moment. He felt such a thrill of satisfaction that his friend hadn't passed him with a frown and a coldly shaken head that he looked at him and smiled his own rich smile.

"What!" said Fletcher, dazed. "Who in—upon my word! It can't be! And yet—why, John, your own mother wouldn't recognize you!"

"Hush!" said John. "You talk too loud in public, and you're too familiar. The question is, do you have any work for me?"

"Yes," said Fletcher, laughing heartily. "What a scarecrow you are, to be sure. At first I didn't dream it was you, and yet I was expecting to see you. I'll give you something to do: Call on Dr. Talbert—that's a good fellow. He'll have work for you—or a cup of coffee and a sandwich or something like it, which is better. He's bound to, according to your theories. Just try it. I'll give a thousand dollars to home missions if you will, when I earn it."

"Hush!" said John again. Two men they knew were approaching.

Fletcher took the hint and, as they passed, was saying in dignified tones, "There's an Associated Charities station less than a mile from here. Go down there—I don't know exactly where it is, but you can inquire."

One man glanced back with a superior smile, "Being victimized, Fletcher? Don't waste your time—the fellow needs the lockup more than charity."

"You knew as much about the station as most of them," said King, when they were alone again. "Never mind—I'll do without breakfast. I'm leaving town. I'll tramp as far as Circletown today. Remember that one John Stuart will be looking there for letters. Good-bye. Thank you for your sympathy—it's done me good."

"John," his friend said, detaining him with a hand and looking anxious, "give up this absurdity. What would your mother say? Above all, what would Elizabeth think of you? At least, don't go away without any money. Have you really no money with you?"

"Not a cent," he said with a genial smile. "I'm honest, you see, and am doing nothing I need to be ashamed of. I'm simply testing a phase of life that's only too common. As for the anxiety of my mother and other friends, they're to know nothing about it, so they won't be troubled. If I come to downright grief, I'll remember you and your bank account."

"You'll be back looking after your own within the month."

"Possibly—in which case I'll have accomplished all I care to. I haven't become a tramp for the remainder of my natural life. Good-bye, Fletcher. Wish me success, for you can't dissuade me."

Alone, our tramp considered for the first time following his friend's advice and calling on Dr. Talbert. True, he was a member of his church, but not well acquainted with him. He'd recently returned from abroad and met his pastor two or three times at crowded gatherings. He doubted he'd be recognized now. Why not test the practical nature of the discourse that had moved him? Not that Dr. Talbert must devote himself to every tramp he saw because he'd spoken unusual words in their behalf, but a word of sympathy or exhortation, possibly advice, would likely be given him. How did such men as Dr. Talbert advise such men as he was representing himself to be? It was worth risking discovery to learn. Without delay he turned toward Dr. Talbert's residence.

He chose an unfortunate day. That evening was Dr. Talbert's regular midweek lecture, and he prepared as carefully for that as he did the Sabbath services. He was late in reaching his study and didn't like to be disturbed there. No one in his employ would ever call him down to see a tramp, but an imperative summons had called him to the parlor. He had to show his visitor out, and the visitor had come on church business with an edge in it for the pastor. There is much such business outsiders know nothing of.

The good man frowned as his eyes rested on the forlorn tramp who humbly asked for work, and he replied harshly, "No, I have no work. And if I had I wouldn't give it to a fellow who doesn't know enough to go to the back door."

The tramp's face reddened. He hadn't remembered there were back doors; he wasn't used to them. He stammered an apology and repeated his willingness to work for breakfast.

"Breakfast!" repeated Dr. Talbert, glancing irritably at his watch. "It's much nearer dinner than breakfast! My whole morning frittered away—it's a shame! No, sir, I have no work or breakfast for you—or a moment's time to waste on you. My morning is gone already." And the door was literally slammed in his face. It wasn't Dr. Talbert's ordinary manner. He was sincere and on almost any other occasion would have tried to live up, in a measure at least, to his Sunday morning eloquence.

He'd have been dismayed if he'd known with what disappointment the tramp turned from his door, saying to himself as he did so, "I believed in him, and he's spoiled it."

John Stuart King, scholar and author, was not wont to make sweeping deductions on slight proof. But with a tramp's garb he'd apparently taken on something of his surface character; at least, his heart felt very sore and sad at this rebuff.

He moved away slowly, moralizing as he went. Were Fletcher's cynical views of life nearer right? Was there no downright sincerity in this world? He believed himself to be a lover of truth to a marked degree. He had personified

Truth, admired her, worshipped her and written about her in a way others had well-nigh worshipped.

Fletcher assured him it was all fine on paper and important too; people must have ideals. But as for finding flesh-and-blood specimens, that wasn't to be expected.

And he contended the world held many whose daily lives were as carefully patterned after Truth as were his ideals. Had he been mistaken? He looked down at himself and sighed. Then, as he caught his own reflection in a plate-glass window, he laughed—a laugh already touched with bitterness. His very costume, that he'd made such pains to secure, taught him the same hateful lesson. He'd visited pawnbrokers' shops and second-hand clothing shops without number, almost in despair. The wardrobe of the decent poor wasn't apparently what he needed. Where was he to find it? Then he thought of those furnishing shops for amateur theatrical entertainments and found exactly what he needed.

"Private entertainment?" the attendant asked as he studied his customer. He complimented him on his character selection and assured him his part would be perfect.

How humiliating to think that to a degree everybody was playing a part; no one was strictly, solemnly and continually himself.

The bitterness left his laugh after a little. The matter had its comic side. Surely he shouldn't be at war this morning against all shams, when he had for the first time in his life made himself up for as complete a sham as possible.

"But I have a purpose," he told himself, "one that justifies the method. Neither am I planning to be a continuous sham. I'll probably lay this aside very soon. Am I half tired of it already? John Stuart, you need to get away from the city. You've always contended the truest people are in the country. Now tramp out and prove it."

Perhaps in all his cultured years filled with opportunities, during no single day did John Stuart King learn more about human nature than on that first one of his new life. Men, women and children contributed to his education. It was new to have young, pretty women look at him with curious, distrustful eyes and cross the street to avoid contact. Before twelve o'clock he was genuinely hungry and offered to bring water pails from the "wells" that dotted the country through which he traveled, or to do anything else he could think of, for dinner. Five times he was refused—once with hesitation and a lingering regret in the eyes of a woman who "hadn't anything to spare"; three times with cold indifference; and once with fiery tongue and slammed door. Being very hungry he tried again, though he admitted to himself it would be easier to steal something.

The sixth woman gave him two pieces of stale bread in a not-too-clean paper bag and added a bone that once had meat on it.

"I'm afraid to refuse 'em," he heard her explain to someone inside, "for fear they'll fire the buildings or do something ugly. I've read of such things."

So even this wasn't charity! But the receiver ate it with a relish daintier fare hadn't always found.

The woman evidently watched him from some pinhole, for she continued her remarks. "He ain't bad looking, as tramps go. He don't look real mean, and his clothes is pretty clean and patched up decent. I shouldn't wonder if he had a mother somewheres, who did her best to make him look decent."

Visions of his mother patching the clothes he wore were almost too much for the tramp's risibles. He ate the last mouthful hastily and moved on, philosophizing over his power to describe the value of stale bread and bones where meat had been. For a full hour his sympathies were entirely on the tramp's side. Then he met one so repulsive in appearance he instantly justified the woman who feared him. It was a new experience to be accosted as he was.

"Any luck that way, pal?" the man asked, nodding in the direction from which he'd come.

"I haven't found any work yet, if that's what you mean," he replied, in the tone that in his former circumstances would have been called cold.

The man sneered. "Oh, that's your dodge, is it? I've had worse trials in life than not finding work. Did you spot any of the houses?"

"Did I what?"

"Mark the houses where they treated you decent and gave you coffee or lemonade or something? You must be green! Don't you carry no chalk or nothin' with you to mark the places? You're a hard-hearted wretch. If you can't do so much for your fellow tramps as that, you should go to the lockup."

The young man found himself shrinking from this specimen with loathing. Could he fraternize with someone like him, even to study human nature?

Then, curiously enough, for almost the first time since he started out, he thought of the Lord Jesus Christ. What a lonely man He must have been!

Chapter 3

The Elliotts had just risen from the tea table—that is, most of them had. Colin, the son, who was late, still lingered, helping himself to cream and pouring it over his sweet baked apple.

Ellen, gathering the dishes and passing them out to Susan, the hired help, was always in a hurry and tried to hasten the laggard.

"Come, Col—you've had enough supper. And if you haven't, you should have been here when the rest of us began. I'm clearing off the table."

"All right," was the good-natured reply. "Just so you leave the apples and cream. These apples are prime. I'm glad there's a big yield this year. Father."

"Yes," said Mr. Elliott in an absent-minded tone. He held the evening paper in his hand and, before sitting down to enjoy it, stood reading a paragraph that had caught his eye.

"Speaking of the harvest apples," said Colin, "makes me think of Jim. Who will we get to take his place? I called there coming out, and he won't be ready for work again this season, if ever."

"Is that so?" said his father, in a tone of deep concern. "I'm very sorry to hear it. Jim was a faithful fellow and did as well as he knew how, which can be said of few. As to filling his place, I don't know. It's a bad time of year to be looking for extra help."

"We need someone right away," said Colin, with his mouth full of apple and cream.

A knock sounded at the side door, and the farmer, paper in hand, stepped forward to respond. A man's voice was heard asking something, and Mr. Elliott stepped out to him.

Ellen, meanwhile, made rapid progress with the dishes, although she stopped from time to time to admire an illustration in the new magazine her sister, Hilda, was examining. The Elliotts' summer dining room was also their family sitting room, and Mrs. Elliott already had her sewing basket and was waiting to settle at her end of the table.

Hilda glanced up from her magazine. "Don't hurry, Ellie—the only rest Mother gets is while you're preparing the table."

"El is too eager for her finery to heed that hint," said the brother, laughing.

Then the door opened again, and the father returned. He walked over to Mrs. Elliott and spoke half-apologetically.

"Mother, an unusually decent-looking fellow's out there, hunting for work. He didn't ask for supper, but I got out of him he's had nothing since breakfast. You can manage something for him, can't you?"

"It's one of father's unusual tramps!" exclaimed Colin. "I knew it was. I saw it in his face." Both he and Ellen laughed, and the father's face relaxed into a smile as he waited for Mrs. Elliott to speak.

"Of course, Roger, if you say so. Only you know you decided—"

"I know," he interrupted quickly, "but this man is—"

"This man is unusual," said Colin, taking the words from his father. "Don't you know that, Mother?"

Mrs. Elliott laughed too. Every one of "father's tramps" was unusual and must be considered exceptions to the stern rule that provided only a ticket to the Associated Charities Bureau in the city two miles away. No matter how emphatically he'd agreed with the board at their last meeting that it fostered vice to feed tramps at one's door, without inquiring into their condition, and explained to Susan and his family it mustn't be done at his house anymore, when Mr. Elliott answered a call from one, he was fed. And if necessary he was clothed and made as comfortable as circumstances permitted. The young Elliotts invariably laughed at their father's trait and were always proud it existed. Not one of them cared to turn deaf ears to a hungry appeal.

"I'll have him go around to the kitchen door," Mr. Elliott said, turning to go back to his tramp. "Give him some of that stew and a cup of coffee. Remember that he's had no dinner."

Ellen grumbled a little. "Dear me! Susan is working in the milk room, and I'll have to feed him myself."

"Perhaps Colin will go out with you," suggested Mrs. Elliott anxiously.

Hilda closed her magazine and rose. "I'll feed the tramp, Mother," she said. She didn't care to have her pretty young sister, sometimes inclined to be reckless, gazed upon by a tramp's bold eyes.

"Is he to have some of the gingercake and cheese?"

"Oh, yes," said Colin, speaking for his mother, "and a napkin, Hilda, and some of the choice grapes and a finger bowl. Remember: He isn't the common kind."

Hilda went away laughing and prepared a corner of the kitchen table for the stranger. She laughed again as she got out a small linen square and laid it across the end for a tablecloth. It probably was foolish, as Colin thought, but she really had to make things neat and comfortable when a human being was to sit down before them. From the window she could see the tramp scrubbing his face at the pump-trough. He used the water like a luxury, tossing his hair back and bathing his head also.

Ellen came out with a message from her mother and stood looking. "He acts like a great Newfoundland dog who's been away from the water for a week!" she said, laughing. "Hilda, he has fine eyes," she added. "Just look at them. I don't wonder Father was taken with him."

"Run back, dear, and finish fixing the table for Mother. She's in a hurry to work. You can hem that ruffle I was working on. Then I can baste it on your skirt when I come in." She had no desire for her younger sister to study a pair of fine eyes.

But Mr. Elliott had no mind to leave his tramp to either daughter's care. He saw Susan stepping briskly about the milk room and came to the kitchen with the tramp. By this time the table was set and a generous portion of the appetizing stew dished up for him. The stranger glanced at the young woman in a neat dress, with fair hair curling about her temples, then plunged into eating.

"What's your name?" asked Mr. Elliott, when the first hunger pangs had evidently been appeased.

"John Stuart," was the quick reply.

"A good name. Are you a Scotchman?"

"My great-grandfather was."

"And a good, honest, hard-working man, I daresay. How was his great-grandson reduced to such straits?"

"Well, sir, you know the times are very hard. I've been looking for work as faithfully as a man could for the last two months and have found nothing but odd jobs here and there, enough to keep me alive."

"What can you do? What have you been brought up to do?"

The red mounted slowly in the young man's face. This question had been asked before but never embarrassed him as much. Was it because the young woman was looking at him just then with earnest eyes?

On John Stuart King's study table stood a small easel containing a picture of a young woman with holy eyes and an expression that captivated the student. The sketch was named "Truth." Its owner, studying it with his friend Fletcher, once declared the artist should have reached fame with that picture, for it embodied truth.

"The embodiment of a notion," his friend replied. "You'll never find a face like that in real life."

Yet here was the face before him! A striking likeness, anyway, and in its presence the tramp felt he could speak only truth. He answered presently in lowered tones.

"Nothing."

"That's frank, at least," said Mr. Elliott with a little laugh. "I suspect you ran away from a respectable home sometime. Is that it?"

"No, sir. My father is dead, and Mother knows I'm out on a tramp."

"Poor Mother!" It was Hilda's voice, low and pitiful. She hardly meant to speak the words aloud; they breathed themselves out of her sympathy and reached his ear.

Under the circumstances the tramp should have felt nothing but amusement. The woman least needing pity of almost any person he knew was his mother. Yet he glanced at the speaker with gratitude. He was grateful for its womanliness and the effect he felt sure it would have had on him if he'd been what he seemed. He resolved suddenly to secure work at this house if possible; if not, as near it as possible.

"How do you expect to get work if you don't know how to do anything?" was the farmer's next searching question. But he followed it with another. "Do you know anything about horses?"

John Stuart's eyes brightened. Here at least he could speak truth. Almost since his babyhood he'd dealt with horses. He owned two, a well-matched span, the admiration and envy of all his friends. He loved almost any horse, and his success in dealing with refractory ones had caused surprised comment even when he was a mere boy.

"Yes, sir, I do," he said, his eyes kindling. "I know a good deal about them. I like them, and they like me. I can drive any horse."

The supper, meanwhile, had been disappearing. Despite the figure of Truth that had stepped out of its frame and was looking at him with human eyes, the tramp was hungry. Nothing so good had fallen to his lot for many days, and he was determined to make the most of it. Hilda silently refilled his plate and cup. Then her father stepped to the dining room door, called his son and motioned him to stay in the kitchen while he went to consult. Hilda followed him from the room.

"I've a mind to try him, Mother," Mr. Elliott said to his wife who was sewing. "We need help now; and we'll need it worse when Colin begins school again. He says he understands horses, and something about the fellow makes me feel he's telling the truth. How does he impress you, Hilda?"

"As very hungry," said Hilda, smiling. But she added, "He hasn't a bad face, Father. I don't believe he's very wicked."

"But isn't it rather risky, Roger, a perfect stranger and a tramp at that? You know the boy who drives the horses will have to take Hilda back and forth, as well as Colin and Ellen."

"Oh, of course I won't trust him with that until he's been tested. He might drive the farm wagon, though, for a few days. I can tell in five minutes whether he really knows anything about horses. You can see he's tired. We should give him shelter for the night, at least. If he wants work I don't know how he'll ever get it unless somebody trusts him. Will it be much trouble to get the wood-house chamber ready?"

"Oh, Father! You won't let a tramp sleep there, will you? He might set the house on fire and burn us up!"

His younger daughter looked up from her ruffles to ask this. Her father laughed.

"You must've been reading dime novels, Ellie. Tramps don't do that sort of thing much, outside certain books. I doubt they do it when they're treated like human beings. If this fellow wants work, he'll have every motive for behaving himself. If he doesn't, he can easily slip away early without setting any fires. Do you object, Sarah?"

"Oh, no," said his wife quickly, "not if you think it best. Susan can get the woodhouse chamber ready, or if she doesn't finish in time, Hilda will look after it. Can't you, dear?"

"Yes'm," said Hilda, with a quiet smile she hid from her giddy sister. These young people were often amused with the deferential manner in which their father appealed to his wife, apparently leaving everything to her judgment. But they couldn't remember a time when she hadn't answered as now, "If you think it best."

"Your father thinks so" was the law of life by which they'd been brought up.

"When I get married," Ellen once remarked, "I mean to have a husband just like Father, who'll always say, 'What do you think, my dear?' "

"That'll be all right," said her brother cheerfully, "provided you'll be a woman just like Mother, who'll always say, 'Just as you think best, my dear.' "

Yet at times in Farmer Elliott's life, unknown to these children, the quiet-faced, gentle-voiced woman had set herself like granite against some plan of his and held herself firmly to "No, Roger, I don't think that would be right," until she won him to see with her eyes, and he lived to thank her for clearer vision. The mother felt no need to explain these things to her children.

Susan benefitted the woodhouse chamber with her strong arms and executive ability, but before its new occupant was invited in, the elder daughter visited the room. It was severely clean—a matter of course with Susan—and the bed was made up comfortably. But Hilda spread a white cloth over the small table, laid a plainly bound Bible on it and pinned above it a cheap print of a cheerful home scene.

Susan sneered at it all, with the familiarity of country hired help. "Land sakes, Hilda! Them kind don't care for pictures. As for the Bible, he prob'ly can't read a word. If he can, he'd rather have a weekly story paper or something."

"We can't be sure, Susan. I think he can read. Most young fellows here learn to read and write in their childhood. Perhaps his mother used to read the Bible to him. She may have sat in a chair like that mother in the picture, and it may all speak to his heart. Who can tell?"

Susan sneered again. "I can. Them kind o' things only happen in storybooks. Look how you fixed up for that Joe Wilkins, and he ran away with the horsewhip and hatchet first chance. If I was your father I wouldn't have no such truck around. But you'll get your reward for trying, you and him too, doubtless."

Chapter 4

The sensations of the "tramp" who finally took possession of that wood-house chamber may be better imagined than described. Susan had remarked that he "probably never saw anything so nice and comfortable in his life as that room." If she could have peeped into his bachelor apartments her remarks would beggar even imagination. An old-fashioned, high-backed rocker stood in this room. Its cushion was stuffed with sweet-smelling hay that could be renewed for each new occupant, and a chintz cover found its way to the washtub an hour after the last one sitting on it had departed.

Into this chair John Stuart dropped, gazing about him with tender curiosity. He'd tramped long enough to appreciate the room's cleanliness, coolness and pleasant odors. When he occupied the "Sleepy Hollow chair" in his city home and planned this extraordinary outing, it was early July. Before that, certain business matters had held him in town through June, and he'd intended to start his vacation that next week; so he'd started. Now the first days of September were upon them, and by ordinary calculations his vacation should be over. But he told himself it had just commenced, although the experiences through which he'd passed were enough to fill a volume.

He saw and studied all sorts of men. He was hungry, with nothing to satisfy that hunger; he was weary, with no resting place in sight. For the first time in his life he suffered for want of these common necessities. He found work, but because he hadn't been brought up to do any of it he couldn't stay in the same place more than a day or two. In truth, this part of the experience hadn't troubled him, for he found no place he felt willing to tarry. Each day as he tramped he rejoiced that his plan didn't include long stays anywhere. But this evening he felt differently; at the Elliott farm he was willing to stay.

He looked down at himself. One of the hardest features of his self-imposed exile had been the difficulty of procuring a bath. He'd tied a change of clothing in a bundle and slung it on a stick, as he noticed tramps sometimes did. He assured himself a self-respecting tramp, as he meant to be, could do no less than that. But the difficulty of getting his clothes washed, dried and mended became appalling as the weeks passed and more than once had threatened the entire abandonment of the scheme. But for a perseverance peculiar to his nature, he would have given up long before. Perhaps he would have done so anyway, if he hadn't had such interesting days when he felt he learned more about that strange, troublesome "other half" than any reading or statistics could give him. On this evening, for the first time since his new life began, he was offered the use of a bath.

"There's a place in the stable," Farmer Elliott had said, "where you can wash up and be fresh and clean before you go to your room. My folks are particular about that room; they keep it as clean as they do the parlor and don't want anything ugly brought into it. Do you have clean clothes in your bundle?

All right—I like that. When a fellow wants to be clean and takes a little trouble for it, it shows he hasn't lost his self-respect. There's a bundle of clothes in the stable closet for times like this. If you need anything while your clothes are being mended, why, help yourself—you're welcome to anything there. I'll give you work enough to earn them for yourself, if you choose to do it."

John Stuart, as he listened, had felt his heart glow with a feeling deeper than gratitude. Here at last was a chance for a tramp to become a man. It was the first genuine effort at helpfulness he'd met. No, perhaps that wasn't fair; it was the first common-sense effort. Others had tried. Tracts had been given him, and advice, but not water, soap and towels. These he found in abundance in the stable closet, with certain garments he much needed. He was dismayed to discover clothes wear out. He thought he had theories on that subject before; but having theories and realizing them are two different things. He sat in the sweet-scented chair and surveyed himself with satisfaction. He looked and felt better. Dr. Talbert was right; tramps were horrid. He wondered how anybody could endure them. But the treatment they received by the Christian public was calculated to drop them lower in the social scale. It seemed an occasional Farmer Elliott existed, however, and he thanked God for him.

He looked over at the white-covered table. Susan was wrong; he appreciated it. Perhaps no table ever looked purer to him. Some of the places he'd slept in since July he didn't wish to describe even on paper. Tired as he was, he walked to the table and studied the print, with a smile Ellen would have declared made him handsome. Then he lifted the large Bible and took it back to the easy chair. The difference between this Christian home and other homes he knew of was undoubtedly rooted in this old-fashioned book. He was accustomed to somewhat regular reference to the book, but not daily Bible reading. Wasn't he a church member? Two months of his grown-up life had never passed without his resorting to its teachings.

He turned the pages at random as was his habit. The book seemed to open of itself to Ezekiel. He wasn't familiar with that part of the Bible; its imagery had been too dense for easy understanding, and he'd never seemed to have time to study it. He paused now over a sentence: "And the word of the Lord came unto me again." He smiled at the imagined appropriateness of the phrase. Probably Ezekiel hadn't been so long without that word as he had. What message did it have for him? "Saying, Son of man, set thy face toward Jerusalem." He read no further.

He wasn't given to imaginary interpretations of writings; yet he confessed to a slightly startled feeling. It wasn't impossible the Lord had him in mind that evening and meant him to get his word from the book. Was it a hint to him that while he was studying human nature in new forms, to write a book with some startling facts in it, he'd forgotten Jerusalem? Not that he'd been distinctly irreligious. He rarely lay down to sleep at night, even in the strangest surroundings, without going through the form of prayer. But more than once he'd been conscious of its being a mere form and excused himself on the ground that a man in his strange circumstances could be pardoned for wandering thoughts.

Dr. Talbert's sermon in July was the last he'd heard. Each succeeding Sabbath he'd been within sound of the church bell, but he couldn't get himself to appear in church in his present costume. He told himself he would attract too much attention and detract from others' comfort. And as he thought of it this evening, he confessed that the woods, the fields, and the sermons he found in stones, with the music of birds and brooks, had seemed more than he could imagine the homely little church services being. So without much consideration he stayed away and enjoyed it. "Son of man, set thy face toward Jerusalem." Was it a message for him? Had he drifted away from the church and from—

"Nonsense!" he said. "You're growing too imaginative. That would do for an interpretation of some of those dyspeptic divines of the past century."

He closed the book, replacing it on the white table. He was too weary for Bible reading now, he said. But he got down on his knees and tried to hold his thoughts to something like real prayer.

And in her room across the yard, inside the farmhouse, Hilda Elliott, on her knees, was asking at that moment that the stranger within her father's gates might not leave them without a reminder of the bread of life waiting for his hand to grasp. She'd placed the Bible in his room with a purpose and asked that it might have a message for him.

Neither did Farmer Elliott forget the stranger who slept in his woodhouse chamber. Had the tramp heard himself prayed for when they knelt around the family altar, his heart would have warmed as never before. The son of the house was impressed by the fervent prayer.

"That old fellow out there won't fire the house tonight, El—you needn't be afraid," he said to his younger sister. "He can't, after that prayer. He'd have to be good in spite of himself, if he heard Father."

"Why?" said Ellen, trying to cover the feeling the prayer had awakened in her. "You've had Father's prayers all your life, and they don't seem to have affected you that way."

"It's different with you and me," said Colin, laughing. "We're not lost sheep, wandering about on the bleak mountains. We're supposed to be safely tucked up inside the fold." And he went away whistling,

> Away on the mountains wild and bare,
> Away from the tender Shepherd's care.

It seemed strange and at times sad that, with such a father and mother, and elder sister, Ellen and Colin Elliott hadn't learned how to pray for themselves.

"He takes hold of the horses as though he'd been brought up with them, and Blixen took to him at once like a friend," said Farmer Elliott. "I never saw a stranger who could do much with Blixen. He must be kind-hearted—she let him pat her nose and turned her head to look after him. Jet likes him too. I told him Jet was inclined to be surly with strangers. He laughed and said he never saw a dog who didn't like him. Sure enough, Jet walked right up and let him pat her."

"Father has set out to make his tramp perfect," interposed Colin, "so correct even the horses and the dog recognize it. Confess, Father—you think of keeping him all winter and trusting him to go to the bank and everywhere."

Mr. Elliott looked at his son and laughed good-naturedly. Neither son nor daughters in this household seemed to hesitate about making merry over both father and mother's peculiarities, and the parents seemed ready to meet them halfway, joining in the laugh at their own expense. Yet both father's and mother's opinions were genuinely respected. Perhaps the fact that the parents weren't too dignified to laugh at their own weaknesses increased their influence over their children, who were keen to observe not only weaknesses, but sterling worth.

"We must have someone to take your place, Colin, when you return to school—why not John?"

"The idea!" said Ellen, with her nose curled. At that they all laughed.

Yet it soon became evident that every family member liked John and that the farmer increasingly trusted him. Certainly no hired man had ever given so much satisfaction with the horses, and Farmer Elliott confessed that with him that meant a great deal. Mrs. Elliott remarked on his excellent memory; he hadn't forgotten a single commission given him, though some were small and troublesome. Hilda said it was comforting to have a man who brought the horses to the door at the exact moment and was always on hand to receive them when reaching home.

And Ellen said he was their only hired man who knew enough to say "Miss Ellen." The family laughed at this, but Ellen stoutly affirmed that was how they always did in books, and she liked it. She thought it would be much nicer if Susan were directed to say "Miss Ellen," instead of shouting out "El" as she actually sometimes did.

"Dear," Mrs. Elliott said, laughing, "remember that Susan is a farmer's daughter, like you, and only comes to accommodate us. I imagine she'd say 'Miss Ellen' if you would say 'Miss Susan,' but certainly not otherwise."

"Then," said Ellen, "I wish we had a tramp for a kitchen girl, and I hope Father will always keep John."

Even Susan contributed to the verdict in his favor. "He's more particular to clean his feet when he comes into the kitchen," she said, as she passed back and forth, "than any fellow we ever had. I wish Colin was as particular."

John Stuart was plainly trying to do his best. Just what his motive was in lingering in this farmhouse and learning a daily work routine that could only be distasteful to him, he might have found it difficult to explain to his or his friends' satisfaction.

He could hardly insist he was studying human nature, for the sphere seemed too narrow. Yet every day he grew more interested in the phase of humanity spread before him.

"I'm studying Truth," he said to himself with a smile, and the form his thought took justifies the capital letter. "I believe I've found Truth. Her likeness to the ideal increases as I see more of her. She embodies the idea—Truth in its purity and simplicity. Such a life should be an influence in the world. I wonder if it is?

Yet how can it be in such a confining circle? I'd like to have her, or perhaps my conception of her, for the heroine of my next book. What could I make her accomplish for good? Indeed, I'd like to see the girl herself set where she could reach people. I wonder if she's satisfied with her present sphere? Does she realize she has a sphere or should? How does one learn? I profess to be studying her; yet an hour of conversation with her in the dining room, with me properly introduced, would tell me more about her than weeks of this life. But would it? I know hundreds of young women that way—not one looks like her. But the home life, though confining, should tell something. I'll wait and see."

Chapter 5

John Stuart was in the farmhouse kitchen working on a door that didn't want to open or shut easily. Playing with tools had been one of his boyhood pleasures, and he handled hammer, screwdriver and saw in a way that commanded the respect of even critical Susan, who could wield those implements herself.

Others were in the kitchen also. It was Saturday, and Ellen was washing the breakfast dishes, a task she hated, while Susan worked elsewhere. Mrs. Elliott was attending to the bread, and Hilda was hovering between kitchen and pantry with a mixture requiring eggs, flour, sugar and—the observant John couldn't decide what else. A young girl from a neighboring farm, with the pleasant unconventionality of the country, was chatting with them all in the kitchen.

Her errand was with Hilda.

"I'm so sorry!" she was saying. "Can't you go, Hilda? It'll be such fun for us all to be together in that house. What engagement can you have that can't be postponed?"

The freedom of country life has its annoying side. Perhaps in no other place are personal questions urged upon someone. Hilda's face flushed a little, and she hesitated, making a journey to the pantry before she replied.

"I have no engagement, Winnie. I simply don't think it's best for me to go."

"How horrid!" exclaimed the young lady. "Do you mean you don't want to go? I thought you'd be the one to complete it. Nannie Marvin's going. And Rex Hartwell—that's clear, after mentioning Nannie. Oh, Hilda, why won't you join us? Oh, I know why you won't—you don't like the games they play. There! That's it—you're blushing like a peony. Now that's being too particular, don't you think, Mrs. Elliott? If Nannie Marvin and Rex Hartwell can tolerate them, I think the rest of us might. You don't have to play unless you choose. Please go, Hilda. It will spoil things if people won't join heartily."

Hilda found her voice at last. "I'm sorry to 'spoil things,' " she said with an attempt at playfulness. "But since I'm only one, I don't expect such a disastrous result."

"But why won't you go? You haven't told me yet. Is it because Rob Sterritt is to be there?"

"Certainly not," said Hilda. Then she added, "You said you guessed a reason—why aren't you satisfied with it? It's well known I don't enjoy those games the young people play, and I don't care to go where I'll be urged to join what I don't like, and argued with and pressed for reasons. I have no desire to force my views on others, and so, to be frank, I've decided to stay home."

"How foolish! Isn't she, Mrs. Elliott? You'll have to turn nun, I'm afraid—you're growing so particular. What's wrong with those little games anyway? Our grandmothers must have played some of them. They're better than dancing—at least people like you always think so, though I could never see any harm in dancing."

If Hilda Elliott did, she kept her views to herself—much to the regret of the man mending the door.

"Did you ever hear me say I considered the games better than dancing," she said at last, still speaking lightly. "But I didn't mean to force you into a discussion. People have to agree to differ, you know. Does Jamie return to college next week?"

"Yes, of course. Life's a failure to people who aren't in college. Ellie can come on Tuesday anyway, can't she? Aunt Annie sent a special invitation for her, and Kate will be awfully disappointed if she doesn't come. Kate's having a dozen or so of her young friends for her special benefit. You won't keep Ellie from joining them, I hope?"

The dishwasher's eyes flashed with interest in the reply, and Hilda looked at her mother, who, intent on her bread, said nothing. Hilda was forced to speak.

"You must appeal to Mother in such matters, Winnie. I don't pretend to manage my sister."

"Ah, but everyone knows you do. Everything goes in this house just as Hilda Elliott wants it to—doesn't it, El? Mrs. Elliott, Ellie can come to the annual meeting, can't she? We want her especially; there'll be special fun for the young ones."

"Ellen doesn't generally go out evenings without her sister," Mrs. Elliott said gently. "Her father doesn't think it best for her."

"There!" said the caller. "I told you it would be as you said, Hilda. You're horrid, and I'll tell the others so."

She arose and to Hilda's evident relief soon departed.

This, however, signalled an outburst from Ellen. She hardly waited for the doors to close after their caller. "I don't see how you can bear to talk that way before Winnie! You know she'll spread all over town everything you said and a lot you didn't say. Why couldn't you just have said you couldn't go to the meeting and were sorry?"

"Because, Ellie, I could go if I chose, and I'm not sorry not to go. How could I make statements that weren't true?"

The girl flung her drying cloth impatiently. "You've run wild about truth. Everybody says such things and understands them. It's common courtesy to say you're sorry when you can't do something people want you to do."

"So do I, dear. But in this case I had no previous engagement or anything else to plead; I simply decided not to go. As for the reasons, she forced them from me by her persistent questions."

"Yes, you had," said the girl, answering the first part of this statement. "You could have said you were having company on Tuesday. Then you could have sent for Hattie and Rick to come and spend the day. It's easy enough to get out of things politely."

"Ellie, do you really mean that would have been getting out of things truthfully?"

"Yes, it would have been true enough. An engagement you plan in your mind is as much an engagement as though you'd carried it out. Hattie and Rick are glad enough to come whenever sent for. Everybody does such things. At the Marvins' the other day, Nannie saw the Wilson boys driving in and knew they were coming to call. She ran up to the meadow where her father was working and told Nell to say she wasn't home. I suppose you wouldn't have done it to save the entire farm. But it was true enough—Nannie's home isn't in the meadow lot."

"I'm sorry that's Nannie's idea of truth," said Hilda.

"It's everybody's but yours," persisted the excited girl. "I wouldn't be tied to your notions for anything; it's slavery. And you don't always speak the truth either, for all your worship of it. You said you didn't pretend to manage me. It would have been much nearer true if you admitted you managed me all the time as if I were a baby—and I must say I don't like it."

"Ellen!" said Mrs. Elliott in warning tones.

But the girl, with flashing eyes, set down with a thud the glass pitcher she was drying. "Well, Mother, I can't help it. Father would let me go Tuesday night, if Hilda wouldn't interfere. All the girls my age are going. Kate invited them and is having a room especially for them while the club is having reports and things. She has a secret that's being told that night, and there'll be lots of fun. I don't see how Hilda can stop my fun all the time with her notions. If that's how religion works, I hope I'll never have any."

"John," said Mrs. Elliott suddenly, "will you get a stick of wood for the sitting-room fire—one of those large hickory chunks from the far end of the woodhouse?"

And John, much to his regret, had to leave his unfinished door and do her bidding. Of course he knew why the wood was required just then. As he selected it, he reflected that Hilda Elliott evidently had a sphere and a hard-to-manage one. It interested him that this encounter largely concerned truth. It would still do to compare her with his ideal picture. Perhaps the artist who sketched it had understood, having seen what outlines a careful adherence to the soul of Truth would carve on the human face.

Yet he confessed he was in sympathy with both the elder and younger sister. He resolved to learn if possible why the club meeting was such an objectionable place. He could imagine surroundings that wouldn't conform to that pure-faced girl's tastes, but why shouldn't the younger one indulge the tastes belonging to her unformed, rollicking years? Was Hilda prudish about it, desiring to make a staid young woman, like her, of a girl who couldn't be more than sixteen and had eyes dancing with fun, even at their quietest?

It was growing interesting. He had theories regarding this subject. On what subject didn't he have theories? He believed young people in their unformed years were often injured by being held too closely to occupations and interests befitting only their elders. He'd like to talk with Hilda about this; he could convince her very soon that—and then he pulled himself up sharply. Who was he to talk over education theories with Hilda Elliott or anybody else? How certainly people would stare if they heard him attempt it. He had deliberately put himself outside the pale of all such efforts. What efforts could he make now to better the world? But that was nonsense. Did he mean the laboring man had no opportunity in his sphere for benefitting others?

On the contrary, he'd held that nothing was more needed in the laboring world than men who were examples to their fellows in all departments of moral life. "If we could persuade even a few of our laboring men to be true to their higher instincts, to be clean and strong in every fiber of their being, we'd see what leaven would be placed in that grade of life. We'd recognize it soon as the power that makes for righteousness."

He expressed this thought in a careful paper presented before the Citizens' League in a certain town in his own state. He'd believed in it thoroughly and urged it in favor of hand-to-hand effort among the working classes. He believed in it still. But—and his face flushed—his trouble was that he wasn't a laboring man. He didn't belong to the sphere in which he'd placed himself— he wasn't true to himself. Did the motive relieve the shadow of falseness? He thought of "Nannie," whoever she was, running to the meadow lot so it might be said she wasn't at home. Did his ideas of truth lie parallel with hers, instead of with the ideal head he still insisted was real?

He put those thoughts away and gave himself to the business at hand. He mustn't be too particular about truth—not now. He must rather take Ellen for his model. Poor bright-eyed girl! Could a frolic in which apparently the best people were engaged be objectionable for her?

The kitchen had changed considerably during his temporary absence. The dishwasher had vanished, as had the work. The breadmaker was tucking the last loaf under blankets, and Hilda was receiving a cheerful girl at the side door.

"I'm receiving calls in the kitchen," she was saying. "I intend to hover around my cake until it's baked. Susan has a talent for burning cakes, so come right in. Oh, John, I can't have that great stick put in now; the oven is right for baking. My cake will be out in a bit; then you can build up the fire. Sit down, Nannie. What a pretty hat! It's very becoming."

"Now don't begin on my new hat and turn my head with compliments," the caller said, laughing. "You know I've come to scold you. I met Winnie Houston down by the lower gate. Not that I hadn't planned my campaign before I saw her. I had an idea how it would be and came to talk sense into you. Haven't you heard that when people are in Rome they must do a little as the Romans do? We really mustn't remove ourselves from these good people because we've had a few more advantages than they have. Even Rex agrees with that, and he knows nothing about the country."

"Now, Nannie! Hold to common sense, won't you? The idea of removing myself from my neighbors! You know I don't. You mean to talk about the club meeting, I suppose. You're wasting your breath. I told you two months ago I'd attended that club for the last time, and I've seen nothing since to lead me to change my mind."

"Oh, I don't blame you for not wanting to attend all the gatherings. But this is the annual meeting, and Winnie Houston's aunt has opened her house, which is unusual, you know. You might want to go this time, just to see that old house at its best. They'll be very disappointed, and I'm afraid offended, if you don't honor them."

For the last fifteen or twenty minutes John hadn't worked rapidly. But despite his slowness the door was finished, and he had no pretext for lingering. He left reluctantly. He'd heard enough about Nannie to want to study her. Besides, he was growing deeply interested in this club meeting. He should be present; evidently it would afford unusual opportunities for studying the social conditions in this region. But how impossible it would probably be to bring about such an event.

Chapter 6

Yet the opportunity was being prepared. John Stuart discovered early that schools formed an important part of the Elliott family life. Colin was a sophomore in a small college about thirty miles from his home. He had to be driven to the station two miles away Monday mornings and brought from it Friday evenings. Ellen was in the village high school and must be taken each morning by the nine-o'clock bell, while Hilda had nearly two miles to go in the opposite direction. It made what Farmer Elliott called "lively work" of a winter morning.

However it might be in winter, it was pleasant work during September's closing days, and John Stuart looked forward to being trusted to take these drives.

It had almost shocked the hired man to discover that Truth, stepping out of her frame, taught a country district school!

After deciding this was part of her sphere, however, he had a consuming desire to see her in it. He smiled at how safely he could have conveyed her in the pony phaeton kept for her use. Occasionally he smiled almost cynically at how readily he'd probably be trusted to drive her if he were in gentleman's dress and gentleman's work. Though in this he didn't do Farmer Elliott justice. He wouldn't have entrusted his daughters to strangers' care, no matter how well dressed they might have been. On Monday mornings and Friday afternoons, when Colin Elliott was at hand, the hired man was allowed to drive the double-seated carriage to the high school and the station. Otherwise, the father himself drove into town, while Mrs. Elliott sometimes, and sometimes Susan, drove the pony phaeton out to the little white schoolhouse.

But on Monday afternoon preceding the club meeting a difficulty arose. Ellen must be brought from school, a man was coming to see Mr. Elliott on important business, and neither Mrs. Elliott nor Susan drove the span of fine horses. John, going in and out on duties, knew the husband and wife were in anxious consultation.

"I have great confidence in him," he heard the farmer say. His cheeks flushed, and he wondered if he deserved the confidence. "He does his work with painstaking care and shows himself to be thoroughly conscientious."

"Susan might go along and do some errands," his wife said. "But that would seem absurd." Then her face brightened. "Why, Laura Holcombe is coming out with Ellen tonight to visit at the Houstons'. Winnie spoke to her about it yesterday. It will be all right for John to drive them out."

So John let the horses walk leisurely up the long hill, while the two girls chattered in the back seat, growing so interested in their subject that they talked louder than they realized.

"It's a shame you can't go tomorrow night! Everybody says it will be the nicest entertainment we'll have this winter. I tell you what, El—I'd go if I were you! Everybody says it's odd you allow Hilda to manage you as you do. She couldn't do more if she were your mother. Why don't you insist upon going?"

"It isn't Hilda!" said Ellen with a touch of indignation. "Father said I couldn't go."

"Oh, your father! As if everybody didn't know it was Hilda behind your father! He'd let you go fast enough if it wasn't for her. People say you're a slave to Hilda."

"I'd be obliged if people would mind their own business!" was the haughty answer. "It isn't any such thing."

"Then if I were you I'd prove it. Why don't you go anyway? Spend the night with me—you've been promising to come for a long time. Then we can go over to Mrs. Pierce's together and come back again when we get ready, and Hilda needn't be any wiser. Come, El—we'll have such fun! Kate Pierce says it's the only entertainment she expects to give this winter, and she means to make the most of it. A lot of college boys will be there too. Colin isn't one of them, so you needn't worry about meeting him; he was invited, but he said he had another engagement. Will you, El? I can plan it beautifully, if you will."

The driver couldn't see the young girl's face, which was turned from him, but her voice quivered with eagerness.

"Oh, dear! I'd like to—nobody knows how much. But it's out of the question."

"Well, now, why, I'd like to know? It isn't as though it's a disreputable place. All the young people around are to be there. It isn't simply that silly club. Why shouldn't you be in the fun as well as the rest. Don't you see it's just Hilda's notion that keeps you at home? Your father and mother wouldn't think of such a thing if not for her. She doesn't like the games the silly ones gather in a room by themselves and play, so she won't have anything to do with any of it! I call that silly, don't you? She isn't obliged to play them. I know the problem with her. Rob Sterritt caught her in a game of forfeits one night and tried to kiss her. It was all in the game, but Hilda has been mad about it ever since—Winnie says so. El, I know your sister is as good as gold, but don't you think she has a few old-maid notions? What harm would it do for Rob Sterritt to kiss her in fun? He worships the ground she treads on."

The spirited horses at that moment gave such a sudden start that even preoccupied Ellen turned her head to see what was the matter. The driver had flourished his whip without knowing it. His eyes were flashing over the thought that such a woman as Truth, even though out of her frame, should be subjected to a kiss from Rob Sterritt—whoever he was—in the name of fun. What a surprising country this must be into which he'd dropped!

His desire to be present at the club meeting grew stronger every moment. Before they reached the farmhouse he decided he must be there, if only to protect Ellen from the Rob Sterritts who might be present. To his indignation and shame the young girl had been persuaded at last to help plan a deception to bring about the desired result. He couldn't hear all the talk, but he gathered from Ellen's voice and sometimes her words that she was not easy to persuade and more than once was about to abandon the idea.

Once she exclaimed indignantly, "I can't do it, Laura. You know I don't tell wholesale falsehoods."

"Falsehoods! Who wants you to? I'm sure I don't, and you're not polite to hint at such a thing. I'd like to know what's false! I invite you to spend the night with me. You've been promising me for a year that you'd stay all night sometime. Then I invite you to go over to Kate's with me. I can't stay late. Father says I must be home before twelve o'clock, so we'll come back together, and you'll be doing exactly what you said—spending the night with me. And if they ask you if I'm going to the club, you can say no because I'm not going regularly, like the others. Mother doesn't want me to stay late. I've been sick, you know, and she's afraid I'll get too tired. I'm to come away early, so it isn't like real going. I never saw anything better planned for you, El! Even if your sister finds out, she can't complain of such an innocent thing as that."

And the sister of Truth was deceived by the film of truth thrown over a network of falsehood! The man on the front seat marveled but was more sure he must somehow be among the revellers. Also, had the elder sister been wise? Wasn't she straining at a gnat? Wouldn't it have been better to accompany her young sister and so be there to shield her from anything undesirable, rather than by her fastidiousness drive the girl to such straits?

Another thought made his face flush. Could he do anything? No. In his own sphere in life, as a boarder at the Elliott farmhouse, even with the slight acquaintance with the family two weeks would allow, he could imagine himself saying, "Be careful, Miss Elliott, for your young sister. I think a plan is forming you wouldn't approve of." Or some words to that effect, which might put her on her guard. But he understood his present position well enough to realize such a course now would probably be considered an insult.

In the farmyard someone was waiting to see John—a young man from the neighboring farm and a member of the planning committee for the famous club meeting. They'd been disappointed in some of their help, he said; the fellow who was to look after their horses, or help look after them, had sent word at the last minute he had to go to town that night. He wouldn't get a job from them again in a hurry. Could John Stuart come in his stead? Mr. Elliott had agreed to spare him, if John was willing, and they'd give him as good a supper as the club had and fifty cents besides. He could look on and see the games and the fun, as much as he wanted, when the horses were cared for.

Never was work more promptly accepted. Of course, Ellen's plans would probably be overturned now. He reflected that if she wished to keep them a secret from her family, she wouldn't risk his seeing her. But then part of his object in going would be attained. If he could thus shield the girl, it might be the best he could do for her. But Ellen heard nothing about his engagement. It wasn't of interest in the family circle and Ellen forgot to question what was wanted of John.

The next morning found Ellen up unusually early, preparing for her evening's sport. It wasn't easy to smuggle all she needed into her small handbag.

Several times she gave up and declared to herself it wasn't possible. Moreover, Hilda made her nervous by sisterly offers to pack her bag for her.

So far her way had been easy. The invitation to spend the night with Laura Holcombe had been renewed so often in the past that it occasioned no surprise when it came again. The Elliotts, being careful parents, hadn't encouraged the neighborhood fashion of exchanging homes for a night, so such outings were limited. But the Elliotts knew Laura had been ill and kept from the night air for several weeks. They judged she begged for Ellen's company as a consolation for not being able to attend the club party.

Mrs. Elliott's only remark had been, "Laura must content herself with you instead of the party, must she?"

Ellen muttered some unintelligible reply and congratulated herself on not having to "even *look* any fibs."

In truth, the Elliotts were glad the invitation had come now. They proved their trust in her by not even thinking of the club party in this connection, although the Holcombes lived nearly across the street from the house thrown open for the party. Only John looked on with intelligent eyes at the girl's nervousness and wondered how many embarrassing scenes, like that he witnessed, she'd been obliged to live through and whether she escaped the falsehoods she indignantly repudiated.

"Why, child!" Mrs. Elliott exclaimed. "Must you carry such a large package? What can you be taking?"

"Oh, Mother, it's some books I've been promising Laura forever."

"Books! It doesn't look like a parcel of books. Why did you tie them so carefully? They'd have been easier laid on the seat, and John could have left them for you at the door this morning."

Ellen had hesitated, and John, waiting for her, saw the flush deepen on her excited face as she said, after a moment's thought, "To tell you the truth, Mother, I put my other dress in the package. I suppose you'll think it silly, but I thought I'd like to dress up a little after school."

If the mother thought it silly she withheld any remark, and Ellen kissed her three times, "for tonight and tomorrow morning," and went away happy that she'd told the truth. She had struggled with herself about the package, being tempted to hint at fancy work or something like it, and she congratulated herself on escaping the temptation. "I won't tell a downright lie," she assured herself, "even if the whole plan falls through."

Yet she knew what her mother believed; knew she meant her to believe the package contained, besides the books, the handsome brown suit known as her church dress; and knew she had be dismayed to know it contained, instead, the lovely pale-blue dress garnished with white lace she wore on rare occasions!

It was only the hired man's face that looked grave. He understood the world and young people's dress too well not to surmise the truth. It pained him more than seemed reasonable, even to him, to see how easily the sister of Truth could satisfy herself with its mere varnish.

Chapter 7

J ohn Stuart King, familiar as he was with the world and society, made discoveries at the Bennettville Club's annual gathering. He hadn't supposed such conditions existed. As an observer he had abundant chance for study, and he made good use of it. The gathering was large and likely representative. From country homes for miles around, young people came; many of them weren't at all old enough to be called ladies and gentlemen, even if their manners justified the terms.

Distinctly two classes of people were present: the intelligent, refined and reasonably cultured, and the "smart," handsome, slightly reckless young people whose cultural advantages had been limited. Almost none present didn't know to a certain extent how to dress. That is, they'd given thought and care and some knowledge to looking pretty and to a degree succeeded. Some of the material was flimsy and, to the observer's skilled eye, lacked details he was used to seeing, but the general effect was striking. Bright colors prevailed, but the wearers had some idea of harmony, and the blondes and brunettes had instinctively chosen their colors.

Overall it wasn't with the style of dress the critic could find most fault. But when it came to manner, he saw startling innovations on accepted ideas. Long before the evening was over, he felt his pulses beating high with indignation— because of the position of the better of the two classes. Some of these evidently moved among the guests with amused tolerance. He readily selected the young woman Nannie and her friend Rex from the others. He overheard snatches of talk when they met at the end of a game, that should instead have been called a romp.

"I don't wonder Hilda Elliott wanted to escape this!" the gentleman said half laughing, yet shaking his head. "Some of the boys are almost rough."

"Yes, but they mean only fun. It's their annual frolic and a time-honored institution. I don't think they're ever so wild on other evenings. Ellie didn't escape it, you see—or rather she did escape, I presume, and is here in all her glory. How pretty she looks tonight! Did you see her when Rob Sterritt tried to kiss her? I wouldn't think Rob would try his skill in that family again; he's the one who angered Hilda. Ellie was too much for him. I think the child bit him—I know she scratched."

The sentence ended in laughter. What would the two think if they knew that behind them, shielded from view by a portière, was the Elliotts' hired man, his face dark with indignation? Games? He had wondered what they could be like to arouse a lady's ire. Now he saw.

They seemed to be foolish games, for the most part, having the merest shred of the intellectual to commend them and that so skillfully managed that the merest child in intellect might have joined in heartily. But the distinctly objectionable features seemed connected with the system of forfeits attached to each game. These, almost without exception, involved much kissing.

Of course the participants were young ladies and gentlemen. The distributer of the forfeits seemed to exercise a certain amount of discrimination; yet occasionally such guests as Nannie and Rex and others of their class would be drawn into the vortex and seem to yield, as if to the inevitable, with what grace they could. John watched a laughing scramble between Nannie and an awkward country boy, who couldn't have been over fifteen. He came off victorious, for she rubbed her cheek violently with her handkerchief and looked annoyed, even while she tried to laugh.

But the college boys were far more annoying than the country youths. John Stuart felt his face burning, as he saw with what abandon these young men rushed into the rudest forfeits and scrambled as they would for college prizes. There was a lot of scrambling and screaming and apparent unwillingness by the ladies; yet one felt that, as they were invariably conquered, they submitted with remarkable resignation.

Occasionally there was an exception. Ellen Elliott, for instance, announced early in the evening that no one needed to put her name on for one of those silly forfeits; she would have nothing to do with them. Had she been more familiar with such scenes, she'd have known this was the signal for putting her name on continually. But the boys who came in contact with her learned that, unlike many girls present, she meant what she said. With the college boys she fared better than with her lifelong acquaintances. They discovered the prettiest girl in the room had a mind of her own. More than once her emphatic "No, indeed—I'm not to be kissed on cheek or hair or hand, and you'll be kind enough to understand it" held at a respectful distance a mustached youth who had just subdued one of her schoolmates.

But the neighborhood boys didn't understand it and thought it ridiculous for El Elliott to put on airs with them. To her encounter with the objectionable Rob Sterritt, John Stuart not only listened but participated. After the first scramble was over—an angry one on Ellen's part—during which the scratching and possible biting took place, most everyone supposed Rob Sterritt had yielded the point and acknowledged himself worsted. But he followed the girl to the hall and began again.

"Come now, El—don't be ridiculous. It's all in fun. But I must pay my forfeit, or I'll never hear the last of it. I won't be rough, honestly. I'll just give you a delicate little kiss as the minister might, if he was young enough, and let it go at that."

The young girl's eyes fairly blazed at him. "Rob Sterritt, don't you *dare* try to kiss me! If you had the first idea of what it is to be a gentleman, you'd know better than to refer to it even, after what I've said."

He mistook her for an actress.

"I don't wonder you play the tigress, El. You do it better than Hilda. But then, of course, you know I must pay my forfeit. It's double if I fail and a good deal at stake—upon my word, you must."

John Stuart then stepped from his station just behind the door. "I mean to protect this young lady from whatever she finds disagreeable."

He had never spoken more quietly. But his low-pitched voice had reserve strength in it, and his whole manner was curiously unlike that of the young fellows about him and curiously impressive.

Rob Sterritt—a sort of accepted neighborhood roughneck, tall, strong, generally good-natured, priding himself on his strength and impudence—stood back with astonishment and asked a single explosive question. "Who the dickens are you?"

"I'm Mr. Elliott's hired man and have a right to protect his daughter."

"Oh, you do! Well, you idiot, there's nothing to protect her from; it's only a game. I understood you were here to look after horses. I advise you to attend to your own business."

But he walked away at once and left Ellen to the hired man's care. Nothing had ever startled him as much as the strange sense of power held in check that the brief sentence had conveyed to him.

Ellen's face blanched. It was her first awareness of John.

"John," she whispered, "did they send you for me?"

"Oh, no, Miss Ellen. I'm here as your friend said, merely to look after the horses. Your father gave me permission to earn an extra half-dollar this way. But I saw that the man was annoying you and thought I should interfere."

The color flamed into the girl's cheeks. The strangeness of her situation impressed her. Her father's hired man trying to protect her from her "friend"!

"He didn't mean any harm," she said quickly. "It's how they play games—that is, some do. It's horrid! I never realized how horrid until tonight. Hilda's right. John, you meant well, I'm sure, so I thank you. But—"

She hesitated. Then, looking up at him half appealingly, she said, "They don't know at home that I'm here."

He didn't help her in the least. She turned from him as if in impatience, then turned back.

"There are reasons why I don't care to have them know it just now. I don't suppose you consider it part of your duty to report you saw me?"

"I don't see that it is—at least, not unless I'm questioned. Of course, if I'm asked a question, the reply to which should involve the truth, I'd have to speak it."

She was growing very angry with him; he could tell that by the flash in her eyes.

"Oh, indeed!" she said. "You worship Truth? A remarkable hired man, certainly. Don't be afraid. I'm not going to ask you to tell any falsehoods in my behalf. I don't think my family will ask you where I've been. Are you always so careful of your words? You'd do for a disciple of—well, never mind."

She whirled away from him as she spoke. He knew his face had flamed and was vexed by it. Why should he imagine himself stabbed whenever the truth was mentioned? What if he were acting a part for a little time? It was innocent, with a noble motive behind it, and with no possibility of harming anyone. Had the girl meant he'd do for a disciple of her sister? Would he? Would her pure eyes look favorably on even so laudable a simulation as his? Dissatisfaction was growing within him whenever he thought of Hilda Elliott and the bar he'd built between her and any possible friendship. Yet determination was also growing to remain in his position, until he proved certain truths to his own satisfaction—truths having nothing to do with tramps.

Some truths he proved that night. One was that certain country neighborhoods entertained themselves in ways other country neighborhoods where education and culture had permeated society didn't suspect. Another was that some of the cultured ones, either because of careless good nature, like Nannie and Rex, or far worse motives, like some of the college boys, fostered this condition by their presence.

Still another was that Hilda Elliott had begun none too early to shield her beautiful young sister from the dangerous world that surrounded her—and the shield was inadequate. He watched with a feverish sense of responsibility, as the girl paced up and down the wide, old-fashioned hall, beside a college youth, whose face he liked less than any he'd seen. Infinitely less than even Rob Sterritt's. It was refined and cold and cruel. They were talking earnestly, Ellen excitedly. The watcher could hear her every word. As the music in the next room grew louder, and her companion raised his voice, his words, too, were distinct. The hired man made no attempt to withdraw himself from hearing. He wanted to hear; he was there to learn. The tramp question was evidently not the most formidable threatening some grades of society.

Ellen was still complaining of the games in schoolgirl superlatives. They were "awfully silly" and "perfectly horrid," and she was "utterly disgusted" with it all! Her companion agreed with her. He was surprised; he used to hear his uncle tell of such things, but he didn't know the customs lingered anywhere. So bewildering that anyone preferred such obsolete entertainments to the refining amusement of dancing. She danced, of course? No? Now he was astonished; dancing was the very "poetry of motion." Not that she needed it; her every motion was grace. He singled her out from the first, for this reason among others. But she would enjoy dancing so much. Might he ask why she didn't indulge?

How could her parents approve of such amusements here tonight and yet object to dancing!

Ellen winced over this. The watcher could see she did and struggled with herself to be truthful.

"No," she burst forth at last, "they don't approve of entertainment like this! I was never at one of these club meetings."

The young man laughed pleasantly. He assured her he understood. She'd escaped, like him, for a break from constant study and found more than she sought. But she should enjoy a single dance just to convince herself of the beauty of the movements and the restfulness of the exercise, after such hoydenish experiences as they'd been through that evening.

He knew a few very good people retained some old-fashioned notions about the dance, growing out of certain past abuses, he supposed. But these were fast disappearing and in cultured regions had disappeared entirely. If he might only promenade with her to the time of that delicious music, he'd remember it all winter. Why, it made no difference, her not knowing how. He could teach her the steps in five minutes. She'd take to it naturally, as a bird does to song.

John Stuart's face darkened as he saw the two, a few minutes later, moving down the long parlor cleared for dancing, to the "time of that delicious music." He knew young men—perhaps college men and boys better than any other class. He didn't need to overhear the talk of two, a moment later, to assure him he hadn't mistaken the character.

"Look at Saylor with that bright-eyed gypsy. She belongs to an exclusive family, Rex Hartwell says. The older sister won't attend these gatherings. If her father were here, I'd tell him I'd rather she be kissed six times by every country bumpkin present than dance fifteen minutes with a fellow like Saylor. Doesn't it make you shiver to think how he'll go on about her tomorrow?"

John Stuart went out to the horses, wishing he were John Stuart King, a certified protector of Ellen Elliott.

Chapter 8

A mile away from the Elliott farm stood an old-fashioned stone mansion. It was of special interest to the villagers who lived a mile further on and to the country people for miles around. John Stuart, on first entering the neighborhood, had no difficulty in discovering its whereabouts. He too regarded it with special interest, since it was remotely connected with his own family.

In this house lived a somewhat eccentric and, if public gossip concerning him was true, a disagreeable old man, familiarly called "Squire Hartwell." For more than a quarter of a century he'd resided there alone, except for his hired attendants. In the spring of the year in which our history opens, this man died suddenly. Certain circumstances connected with the closing months of his life had roused the neighborhood to keen interest in his affairs.

Another name for him, as the younger man came to be known and liked, was "Rex Hartwell's uncle." Rex was closely connected with him during almost his entire life. The country people had it that "Squire Hartwell brought him up." That meant, however, that he paid the boy's bills as a child in his old nurse's family where he was boarded and later at boarding school and college. This he did, evidently, because the boy was the son of his only sister, who died when her child was five years old, and not because of any affection he seemed to have for him. He'd held his nephew at arm's length in his boyhood, barely tolerating short visits from him during long vacations and omitting even those as the boy grew to a companionable age.

Suddenly, however, almost immediately after Rex Hartwell's graduation from college, his uncle went abroad, taking the nephew with him as attendant. For a young man who had come up, rather than been brought up, Rex Hartwell was a model in many respects. He had a very warm heart and was so grateful to one he'd always considered his benefactor that, during their two years of travel, he devoted himself unsparingly to the old man's comfort, in a way it is fair to say had never been done before. Despite his money Squire Hartwell had lived a lonely and loveless life.

When the old gentleman suddenly returned home, he brought Rex with him, introducing him for the first time as his nephew and heir. And he made no secret of the fact he meant to leave his broad acres and railroad and bank stock to this young man.

"I've never told him so before," he said to the family lawyer, with whom he was as nearly confidential as with any person. "I had no notion of bringing up a fellow to swagger around and live to spend the money I've worked hard for. I've kept him close and taught him the value of money. I think he'll know how to take care of what I leave him. He's a very decent sort of fellow, and I'll like thinking of the property being held by one of the same name. If his mother had given him the full name, I'd have settled it all before this, I daresay. But she had a soft streak in her and gave him his worthless father's silly name. 'Reginald,' indeed! Just right for a fop. Oh, no, his father was a decent sort of man—softhearted and with no business ability. A country doctor heavily in debt and dying of overwork before he was thirty—that's his history. His son takes after the Hartwells; if he hadn't, I'd never have tried to make anything of him. Well, now we're ready for business."

So the will was drawn, duly witnessed and signed. It left not only the old stone house, almost palatial in size, and its broad acres, but factory stock and railroad stock and bank stock, with whatever bank account would be at his decease, to his nephew and namesake, Joshua Reginald Hartwell. The gossips had it the old man induced his nephew to drop his father's name, in favor of the more sensible Joshua. But Rex had firmly declared the name his father bore and his mother gave him should be his as long as he lived.

To the simple country folk around them, who counted their wealth by the very few thousands that slowly accumulated, the young man was looked up to as a prospective millionaire. They took a deep interest not only in him, but also in the fortunate young woman who had won his especial regard. This was Annette Marvin, or Nannie, as she was known in the neighborhood. Although some perhaps envied her, it was a good-natured, kind sort of envy, for Nannie Marvin was a favorite with old and young.

She was the daughter of a poor farmer, whose farm joined Mr. Elliott's but was in every respect its contrast. Farmer Marvin had never possessed what the neighbors called "knack." His wheat, oats and barley, even his potatoes, apples and other hardy fruits seemed to grow reluctantly, inviting rot and rust and weevil and worm and other enemies of goodness. As the years dragged on, the Marvin farm was never well worked, because there were no means for working it. And the only thing that grew larger was the debt, to pay the interest on the mortgage.

Years before his time, people spoke of Nannie's father as "old Mr. Marvin." Soon they began to say, "Poor old Mr. Marvin." He had such a large family to bring up and educate—and "most of them were girls, too, poor things!" They commended Nannie for her good sense and unusual spirit, when suddenly she took a new path and presented herself at the old Hartwell mansion in answer to its master's advertisement for a "young woman to wait on the housekeeper."

Nannie Marvin had graduated at the high school six months before, the best scholar in her class, and spent those months looking for a chance to teach. Boldly she declared that if there were no scholars for her to teach, she'd see about "waiting on" a housekeeper. The very girls who wouldn't have done such a thing had sense enough to commend her. Not that it was unheard of for farmers' daughters to accommodate other neighborhood farmers during busy seasons and help. Susan Appleby, who reigned in the Elliott kitchen, had come to accommodate and held herself to be as "good as any of them."

But the Marvins were considered, even among their neighbors, as "a little above the common." Though a poor farmer, Mr. Marvin had been a good Greek scholar. Failing health had driven him to the fields, and he liked now to read in his Greek testament much better than to hoe his corn. Mrs. Marvin had taught in her youth in a famous young ladies' institute. And they'd kept Nannie in school long after some people said she should be doing something to help her poor father.

For her to become a common servant under Squire Hartwell's housekeeper stirred much comment. She might better have gone to the Elliotts' or some other well-to-do farmer's family, where a mother, not a housekeeper, would look after things. But Nannie Marvin had a mind of her own. She couldn't have worked in the Elliotts' kitchen, where Hilda was her best friend. But she believed she could "wait on a housekeeper" who was a stranger and would know how to treat her as a servant. So to the stone house she went. It was prophesied she wouldn't stay a month; if she got along with the housekeeper, she wouldn't stand the old squire, reputedly disagreeable to his help.

But all these prophecies came to naught. Soon Nannie Marvin was almost a fixture at the stone house. Squire Hartwell not only tolerated her presence but, as the months passed, evidently liked to have her about and ordered the housekeeper to let Nannie fix his books and papers, dust his room, bring his tea, his gruel or whatever was wanted. He had her read aloud to him by the hour and dictated his business letters to her. Almost before anybody realized it, Nannie Marvin was established in the library as a sort of secretary to Squire Hartwell, who before scorned such help. By degrees she and the housekeeper changed places. From being summoned from dusting or egg-beating to read the news to the squire, she rose to delivering messages to the housekeeper: "Squire Hartwell wishes me to tell you," etc.

Mrs. Hodges was sensible and didn't resent the changes. On the contrary, a note of respect stole into her voice when she spoke to Nannie, and she oftener asked her help than ordered it. She even bore in silence one morning the squire's curt statement that she must "hunt up somebody else to trot around after her"; he wanted Nannie Marvin himself.

When Squire Hartwell suddenly went abroad for an indefinite period, people wondered what Nannie would do now, when they heard with surprise she was still to be in his employ. She was to have charge of the library, the conservatory and garden—the squire's special pets. She was to write him letters concerning certain interests and to receive and execute his orders. She was also to oversee the house during the housekeeper's absence. She would receive a regular salary, with the privilege of staying home.

Those who found out these details were equally divided in opinion. One part was assured Nannie Marvin was in luck; they'd never known the squire to do such a generous thing. The other part affirmed with equal assurance that doubtless he knew how to make the girl earn every cent.

With the squire's homecoming Nannie was promptly re-established in the stone house. Indeed, she was there when the housekeeper arrived and had an open letter in her hand from which she read directions for that good woman. Everybody began to realize Nannie Marvin was, as these country folk phrased it, "on the right side of the squire."

Yet many prophesied a different situation when they discovered the nephew took kindly to the quasi-secretary and treated her with the deference he'd show any lady. Surely the squire, when his eyes opened, would have none of that. They were mistaken. The squire grumbled a little when he saw his nephew's interest in Nannie Marvin. He said he didn't see why young people had to be fools. Nevertheless, Nannie had apparently won her place in his life. She had become necessary to him. Why should he complain if this was also true with his nephew?

Once it was settled how matters stood, the old man carried things with a high hand. He dismissed without warning a stable boy who dared to say "Nannie Marvin," and he told the housekeeper sternly she must teach her servants to say "Miss Marvin."

It took the neighborhood some months to get accustomed to this; and then, behold, a new surprise. One morning the neighborhood for miles around quivered with the news that Rex Hartwell and his uncle had quarreled, and the squire had changed his will and cut Rex off without a penny! The neighbors gathered in knots at the leading produce store in the village or in one another's sitting rooms and kitchens, discussing the details. The day after the quarrel, the squire's lawyer was closeted with the squire for more than two hours and, when he came out, halted on the wide piazza and swept his eyes over the rich fields, saying, "Too bad! Too bad!"

The particulars were slowly gathered, in that mysterious way news scatters through country neighborhoods. Squire Hartwell had set his heart upon his nephew and heir becoming a lawyer. He said nothing about this during their stay abroad or the first five or six months after their return. He even put his nephew off with a curt sentence about there being enough time to think of such things, when the young man tried to talk with him of his future.

Then suddenly, one morning at summer's end, he began to talk about his plans for settling the young man as a student in an eminent friend's law office. He talked as if the decree had gone forth from his birth that he was to become a lawyer. Then two strong wills clashed. Having never heard one word from his uncle regarding his profession and having, as he supposed, excellent proof it didn't matter to that gentleman what he did, Rex Hartwell had chosen for himself and chosen early. All his ideas of success were connected with the medical profession. He may have inherited the taste, as well as fostered it in his early boyhood. He'd spent many vacations with a friend in an eminent physician's family, where during his leisure he'd pored over such medical works as he could understand. When he went abroad with his uncle, having certain hours to do as he would, he'd marked out a course of study toward his chosen profession and was eager, even impatient, to begin his medical studies.

One may imagine the blow to a young man of his temperament to be informed the time had come for him to begin his law studies and that arrangements had been made for him in town. To give up his plans and force his mind to a course of study that had no attraction for him, he felt was impossible and courteously but firmly said so. He was met by a storm of indignation he hadn't supposed a gentleman could display. And he discovered that choosing the medical profession was evidently a more heinous crime than refusing the law.

His uncle was bitter against the profession and against those he declared had warped his nephew's mind in that direction. Wasn't his father's failure to earn even a decent living by his pills and powders sufficient reason why his mother shouldn't have wanted her boy to follow in such foolish footsteps? Oh, he knew the mother had wanted him to become a doctor; all women were fools where business was concerned, and his sister Alice had been one of the most sentimental fools of her sex. He should know her better than her boy who was five when she died. It was mere sentimental twaddle with her. She wanted him to inherit his father's tastes! To inherit his father's failures, she might better have said, and his skill in leaving his family paupers! He despised the whole race of pill vendors, and not a penny of his money should be turned into that channel. He'd intended from his babyhood to be a lawyer and was thwarted, not by his fault, but because of a certain doctor's meanness. He would give his nephew thirty-six hours to decide whether he'd carry out the plans for him or go his own way without a cent in the world.

Squire Hartwell didn't understand human nature very well. Perhaps no course he could have taken could have more firmly settled the young man in his purposes. He replied with outward calmness he didn't need thirty-six hours to consider. He had planned as a baby to be a doctor, like his father, and as a boy and a young man he'd kept that determination. He was sorry his uncle was disappointed. But not for millions would he sell himself to a life work he wasn't fitted for and was sure he'd only fail in. And then he left his uncle's presence, sure he'd keep his threat and "cut him off without a penny."

Chapter 9

Public opinion, represented by the little world that knew these people, was two-sided as usual. Some were sure Rex Hartwell would live to regret his folly and obstinacy. The idea of throwing away thousands just because his father had been a doctor! What was a *baby's* promise to his mother? She must have been a silly mother to think such a young child could be influenced. Logic in this was no better attended to than generally in public opinion. Others rejoiced in the young man's spirit. They said the squire had ruled people all his life; they were glad he'd found his match.

But it was hard on Nannie. Squire Hartwell found it necessary to quarrel with her also, because he couldn't make her say she thought his nephew was a simpleton and would have nothing more to do with him unless he complied with his uncle's wishes. Nannie was curtly dismissed from the house the afternoon of the day Rex received his dismissal. The squire relented sufficiently to tell her that if, in a month, she got her common sense back and could reason her "addle-pated follower" into decent behavior, he might change his mind.

It made him angry that Nannie vouchsafed no reply to this beyond a wise smile, that said as plainly as words: "I think you know your nephew, and me also, well enough to expect no such thing."

For days after that, Squire Hartwell was savage with everybody who came near him. The poor old man missed Nannie almost more than he did his nephew, and perhaps needed her more.

But it was hard on the young people. Their well-laid plans were overturned. They'd had a tacit understanding that near Christmas there would be a wedding and Nannie would assume management of the old stone house. Her husband could easily go back and forth to town every night and morning while he was studying. Both agreed that since Squire Hartwell evidently took for granted such arrangements would be made, it wouldn't be fair to him to plan otherwise.

His habit of taking things for granted was responsible for much of the trouble. Had they talked frankly and understood from the first, much sorrow might have been avoided. But Squire Hartwell assumed people could read as much of his plans as they needed to know without his help. When he became reconciled to the marriage as inevitable, he spoke, without any hint from the young people concerned, of the holiday season as the time when most foolish deeds were done, and then he'd referred casually to matters he and Nannie would attend to while her husband was away at his books. How could they know the older man meant law books, though the younger one's heart was fixed on medical books?

Scarcely could any other two people in the world have been as much together as uncle and nephew were in those days, without understanding each other's plans better. But Squire Hartwell's lifelong habit of reticence, except in certain directions, was as strong as ever, and his dislike for being questioned was well understood. His nephew had once, during an allusion to the future when Squire Hartwell and Nannie would be left together, remarked that it took money to journey daily to town and spend one's time in study. And the squire had answered sharply he saw no occasion to worry about that. Hadn't there been enough for him to spend his life thus far in study? It hadn't given out yet; when it did he'd be notified. Those poor young people took it as a hint they weren't to worry about money; so they didn't. And now they'd been notified!

Among Squire Hartwell's closing sarcasms to Nannie that afternoon was whether her excellent-brained Rex remembered it took money to "spend one's days in study," to say nothing of supporting a wife!

During those trying days Nannie Marvin took refuge in almost total silence, as far as the squire was concerned. She'd begun to have some affection for the lonely, crabbed old man—a feeling fast disappearing before his persistent unkindness to his nephew. But her memory of what had been, as well as her self-respect, kept her silent, instead of allowing her to pour out the indignant truth upon him as she wanted to do.

Those two left the stone house, then, to reconstruct their life plans as best they might. They weren't crushed. Both had been brought up on too rigid an economic basis, until very recently, to feel keenly the loss of money—at least, they thought they had. Of course it's one thing to be poor and have a father or uncle who's responsible, and quite another to be responsible for one's own expenditures and for others'. But they were too young and carefree to realize this. They talked it over cheerfully between bursts of righteous indignation.

"You don't blame me, do you, dear, for not trying to have myself ground into a lawyer at his command?" Rex would ask, having asked the same in every possible form.

And Nannie would reply, as she had a hundred times already, "Of course not, Rex! How can you ask such a question when I know your tastes and talents lie in another direction? I always hated their musty old law books, and it never seemed nice to make one's living by others' quarrels. Your uncle's just the sort of man to like such a profession though—I believe he enjoys quarrels. It's much nobler to save lives. I dream of you, Rex, coming to some home where the attending physician has failed and, as a last resort, you, the great Dr. Hartwell, are called in council, and you save a life! Just think of it, Rex—a life! Then compare that with a lawyer's work!"

He always laughed over the contemptuous tone with which she exploded that word "lawyer." Once he said, "Oh, Nannie! You're not logical. You forget that as a lawyer I might make such an eloquent plea that convinces judge and jury and saves a man from the gallows."

But she had logic for that. "No, it isn't the same. He'd probably be a miserable wretch who should be hanged, and you'd have to twist and smirch the truth to save him. But a doctor is next to God in the way he holds life and death in his hand."

She grew grave and sweet in closing her sentence. Logical or not, Rex Hartwell loved to hear her and to have her add, "Besides, a promise is a *promise*, even made by a little child. And you know you promised your mother to be a physician, like your father."

So they replanned their lives, looking bravely down the years they must be separated, and told each other they were young and strong and could endure it. They'd both work so well and wisely and overcome obstacles before they knew it. In spite of all, they were happy and sometimes pitied the lonely old man who'd banished them.

The young man found a position in a doctor's office in the city, where for certain services he would receive board and opportunity to study and the privilege of asking questions. It wasn't as easy to locate Nannie. Rex was willing to drudge, but he shrank from drudgery for her. In the abstract it was brave and beautiful of her to plan hard work. But when it came to a definite position he shrank from each one with such manifest pain that Nannie hesitated and remained at home. Meanwhile, her friend Hilda Elliott was succeeding so well with the country school where she'd taught for two seasons that Nannie envied her and wished for a similar opening.

They interested themselves somewhat in the new heir to the Hartwell estate. They knew the name was King and that a remote and almost forgotten family connection made a show of justice in the new will. Squire Hartwell, it was said, saw the young man when he was a child of seven or eight and told him that if he grew up and became a lawyer perhaps he'd leave him some money to buy law books. The boy had grown up, but he wasn't a lawyer.

Opinion was divided among the country folk as to what he was. Nannie Marvin heard somewhere he was an author and asked Rex if he might possibly be connected with that Stuart King who wrote those articles in the *Review* that created such a sensation. But Rex thought not, because he knew his uncle despised a mere writer of books, unless they were law books.

Then they wondered whether the heir would visit his acres soon, whether he would be an agreeable addition to the neighborhood and how he would treat them, if they ever met. And both of them understood the uncle so well that they hadn't thought of his relenting.

Matters were like this, with Rex Hartwell studying hard in the physician's office in town and snatching a few minutes daily to write to Nannie, who had that harder lot of waiting at home for work to come to her, when a new excitement filled the neighborhood. Suddenly, unexpectedly—as he'd done everything else in his long life—Squire Hartwell died. One morning he was driving about his grounds, giving orders in his most caustic style; the next, lying in state in his parlor, with the housekeeper wiping her eyes as she tried to give particulars.

Speculation ran high as to whether the new heir would honor the funeral with his presence. Great was the disappointment when the report circulated that he was abroad and must be represented by his lawyer.

The funeral was held, and all the village and countryside, as well as many from the city who knew Squire Hartwell in a business way, honored his dust by coming. But it was Rex Hartwell, the disinherited, who followed him to the grave as chief and only mourner. Nannie Marvin cried a little; seated in the Elliotts' carriage she followed the body to the grave and tried to remember only the days he was almost kind to her and seemed to be planning for her and Rex.

Rex Hartwell had to be more than mourner. He was so naturally associated with his uncle that people came to him for directions as to what should or shouldn't be done. He gravely assumed the responsibility and did his best. Why not, since he alone bore the name? Suppose the broad acres and bank stock had been left to someone else; he didn't intend to forget the dead man was his uncle and that during all these years he had clothed and fed and educated him. No mark of respect should be omitted. The people, looking on, said it was "real noble in the young man." And Nannie Marvin, weeping and watching furtively his every movement, felt sure this was true.

Following this excitement came another, so great as to throw all others into the background. Behold, the new will couldn't be found! The family lawyer affirmed it was made, witnessed and managed with all the law forms and that the squire had kept it, rejecting almost haughtily his lawyer's offer to take care of it for him. He wasn't in his dotage, he'd said, and could look after his own papers. Apparently he'd looked after his own so successfully that no human being could discover it.

In vain they searched the squire's private room, his library, his writing desk and closets, his large old books, some unopened for years. In vain the lawyer's young clerk, who had read books and heard several detectives talk, searched the old house curiously for some secret drawer or panel like those in books. All at last gave up the search.

The lawyer, who liked Rex Hartwell and Nannie Marvin also, but who liked better to have everything concerning legal matters done decently and in order, was at first not a little disturbed. This seemed like playing with serious interests. Why had Squire Hartwell taken hours of his valuable time and resisted his attempts at advice, if he meant to destroy the will? Or, supposing he changed his mind, why hadn't he communicated this to his lawyer so he might have been prepared for the change?

Considered from mere friendship, it had a gratifying side. The old lawyer was glad for Rex Hartwell to come into what was rightly his own. But the method of securing it was trying. After weeks had lapsed, during which no possible suggestion was overlooked and skillful hands had searched, even the lawyer admitted there was no good cause for further delay. The proper legal steps were taken, and Rex Hartwell came into formal possession of his fortune.

After that, some people thought the marriage might take place immediately. But Nannie and Rex determined to show all outward respect possible, so they and their neighbors looked forward to Christmas again with almost the same eagerness. It would be wonderful for Nannie Marvin to preside over the old stone house! Quite different from her being there under Squire Hartwell's orders, even though she was his nephew's wife. Didn't everybody know the old squire would have managed her and her husband both? But now they might hope for the house to be thrown open to company as it hadn't been for nearly a quarter of a century. They knew Nannie and Rex would be delightful people to visit.

In view of these experiences, it wasn't strange that Mr. Elliott's new hired man, by keeping his ears open and occasionally asking a question, learned the whole story. The various scenes in the drama had such intense interest for the simple country folk that they could appreciate a stranger's interest. What they would think if they discovered the would-be heir was actually "Mr. Elliott's hired tramp," that individual often amused himself by wondering.

Concerning this same heir, many wondered how he bore the news of the lost will and what he would do about it. The most he'd done was institute through his lawyer a thorough search for the missing property and then rested content. He had money enough, and his tastes didn't lie in accumulation. Why should he care because the people who should have the old man's fortune had secured it? He easily put away all personal desires with this reasoning. But, later that year, when he found himself in the very neighborhood where these curious experiences had occurred, he discovered he had a keen personal interest in all the actors.

Chapter 10

One couldn't belong to the Elliott household for long without learning the daughter, Hilda, wasn't a teacher who worked for the salary and forgot the scholars the moment the door closed for the day, remembering them with reluctance the next morning. John Stuart, in less than a month, had heard enough about her school to want to visit. Yet an opportunity seemed improbable. Although his trust in his hired man grew daily more assured, Farmer Elliott had a habit of looking after his daughter. He was overheard saying his man was so trustworthy he could get away better than he had for years. The aspirant could only bide his time.

One evening, while the family was at supper, John and Susan seated with them according to the neighborhood fashion, a discussion arose in which John was deeply interested.

"You shouldn't go out again tonight, Roger," Mrs. Elliott said, with an anxious glance. "You're hoarser than you were an hour ago. It would be a pity to get a cold—perhaps for the winter."

"Oh! There's no danger of that," the father said cheerily, though hoarsely. "It's a nice night for a ride. The air is crisp, but not disagreeable."

"Father, Nannie and Rex would like to go out with us," Hilda said. "Rex promised he'd help me this winter, and Nannie says this evening would be good to start."

Then the mother had a sudden thought involving a glance toward John and a look at her husband. She voiced it only with a tentative half-sentence, "If Nannie and Rex are along, why not—," spoken low for her husband's benefit, but loud enough for John's quick ear to catch and quick brain to understand.

"All right," said the farmer and raised his voice. "John, I believe I'll let you drive the young people out to the schoolhouse this evening. Not that it would hurt me, but Mrs. Elliott seems to think I need a little coddling."

So John's opportunity had come. Not to visit the school, but one could tell a good deal by visiting a schoolhouse. Why it was to be visited that evening, he had no idea. No one seemed to remember he was an entire stranger to the neighborhood's ways. He must learn by watching and waiting.

The long, low, uninviting building known as the Hartwell School was a revelation to him. His school life had been connected with great four-story buildings, fireproof walls and general massiveness. He knew other styles of school buildings existed, but he hadn't known any. He looked about with interest on the odd-shaped seats and wooden desks marred by more than one generation of jackknives. Yet if he'd known it, the little schoolroom wasn't typical; in a way it was a palace compared with many he might have visited.

The floor was clean and had a strip of cocoa matting down the main aisle. The lamps, set in homemade brackets fastened at regular intervals to the walls, were numerous enough to brighten the room. The teacher's platform was covered with cheerful red carpeting. On the desk was a fern growing in a pot and several other hardy plants; from being covered every night and removed on Friday nights to the sheltered closet they flourished through the long cold winter. Beside the desk chair was a little red rocker. Pictures adorned the white walls: charts and maps common to a schoolroom, several prints in colors and cheap copies of famous pictures. A Bible in blue and gilt lay open on a table. However uninviting the building might be from the outside, it was cheerful enough inside to evoke delighted exclamations from the guests privileged to speak.

Nannie Marvin, especially, was charmed.

"What a pretty place you've made of this ugly little room! I told Squire Hartwell once that I wouldn't think he'd like such a horrid old building named after him. Isn't that wall pretty, Rex? The pictures are so cheerful. If only the scholars had some comfortable seats and a carpet on the floor, it would be even prettier. I'll tell you, Rex, when—"

She stopped suddenly, glancing toward John Stuart, and flushed and laughed. He knew she was about to daydream aloud of what would be done when her name became Hartwell.

Further talk was interrupted by scholars or guests or audience arriving. It seemed an incongruous company, with sharply contrasting ages, though most were young people. Some were little boys, young enough to be in bed at that hour, while tall men of six feet and over, well proportioned, were there too. Some he recognized from the club gathering a short time before, but others were unmistakably of a lower grade than the club visitors. They shuffled in, apparently anxious to avoid observation. Yet two distinct classes were there.

Many came in briskly, as though glad to be there. They greeted Hilda eagerly but politely. This class, John discovered, was her day pupils; the others were their brothers and sisters and friends, who knew her only through these evening gatherings.

The most interested person there hadn't yet discovered what the evening's program would be, but just then Hilda walked over to him.

"John, I suppose you've never been at a gathering like this—I hardly know what to name it. During winter I've given one evening a week to this neighborhood as long as I've taught here. This is the first meeting of the season. We have two sessions: from seven to eight, and from eight to nine. For the first hour we divide into classes, whenever we can find teachers or talkers, and take up some subject the classes ask to talk over. Then at eight we have a social religious meeting; we sing and pray and then talk on some theme we hope will help them.

"These aren't all my scholars. In this neighborhood are many who can't come to school. They work all day in the woolen factory. We use these evenings for helping them any way we can. Tonight Mr. Hartwell is going to take the older boys and young men, and Miss Marvin and I will divide the girls between us for the first hour. But several boys are younger than those who usually come; they begged to come, and I couldn't deny them. Still, they can hardly be interested in what Mr. Hartwell will say. I've been wondering if—did you ever try to teach lit- tle boys or talk to them for their good?"

He suddenly recalled a winter years ago, when he taught in a mission Sunday school and became fascinated with the street children. "I did once, a good while ago," he answered with animation.

"Then would you take those five little boys over in that corner near my desk and tell them something you think may interest or help them? Usually we have subjects chosen the week before, but since this is our first session we decided to let them choose on the spot what they'd like to learn about. I haven't the least idea what those little fellows will ask of you. Are you willing to try?"

He was more than willing. The boys, with their honest faces and serious behavior, were new to him. They didn't look or act like street gamins, the type of boy in his one teaching experience. Yet they had intelligent and, in two or three instances, mischievous faces; he was eager to know what they thought and how they expressed their thoughts.

His quick consent roused vague anxieties in the young manager's mind. She'd expected him to demur, to be almost frightened over the idea and feel sure he wasn't competent to teach. She'd hoped to draw him out by it; to awaken his interest in something besides his daily work routine and perhaps do him more good than the boys. But he evidently needed no drawing out. She moved away slowly, more than doubtful about her act. The doubt increased as the hour passed, and she watched the boys' eager faces as they bent forward to catch every word. They had neither eyes nor ears for anything else in the room.

Hilda's own work suffered; she was distraught and anxious. What mischief she might have done by giving that strange young man an hour with those pure-hearted boys! What could he be telling them that held their attention? She closed the hour ten minutes early, unable to do much except regret her attempt to benefit John, and resolved to learn more about him at the first opportunity. It wasn't enough that a man was faithful in his daily work and apparently con- scientious in performing his duties; his mind might still be filled with poison, which he found pleasure in imparting. She'd read of such men.

Turning away from his boys, disappointed he had no time to add his last words, he took a seat in the farthest corner of the room, where he could watch. The hour that followed interested him deeply.

They hadn't called it a prayer meeting, and it was different from most he'd attended; yet that name fitted it as well as any.

Hilda announced that three of her pupils had asked her to take the question "What is truth?" for their talk that evening. They wanted to consider how far from the exact truth one could tread in his own or another's interest without reaching the realm named falsehood.

"In other words," said Hilda, "what is truth, and what does it demand of its followers?" Then she read from a collection of Bible verses, leaving no doubt in the listeners' minds as to the Bible's estimate of truth. Still the question remained, What is meant by truth? Or, as one of her girls put it, "How far can one keep a piece of knowledge to oneself without earning the name of being false?"

Just then John Stuart happened to glance in Nannie Marvin's direction and noticed a sudden change in her facial expression. She flushed for an instant and then paled, as she turned startled, half-frightened eyes first on the questioner, then on Hilda, and listened intently to the latter's every word. The student of human nature wondered why she was so keenly interested and if she was troubled because she often ran to the "meadow lot" and had herself reported as "not at home."

Hilda answered the question quickly. "That depends, Mary. Does the piece of knowledge concern us only? Will our silence injure anyone? Can our silence be misinterpreted in a way that brings harm? Do we sincerely believe good and not ill will result if we remain silent? If we can answer an unqualified yes to all these questions, I think we may safely keep our knowledge to ourselves."

Nannie Marvin, usually quiet, suddenly added her thought. "Sometimes great harm is done by speaking of what one may have learned by chance."

The leader turned troubled eyes on her. "Yes," she said slowly, "that's probably true. I've known a number of instances when the truth of the old proverb 'Silence is golden' was emphasized. But I think Mary has in mind another kind of harm. Perhaps I'm mistaken, but it seems to me the present danger, at least in our neighborhood, is to belittle the truth by what are called trivial departures from it. I'm afraid some of us pride ourselves on our ability to evade the truth without telling what we call falsehoods.

"I read of a boy whose father asked, 'Son, were you out late last night?' And he answered boldly that on the contrary he reached home very early. He laughed as he explained to his companion that he told the truth for once; it was very early in the morning!

"Perhaps that story illustrates my point well. Some people evade honesty in this way and yet believe they're speaking truth! It's difficult to understand how a person with ordinary common sense can deceive himself so, but it happens. The present seems full of devices for tempting young people to falseness. I heard a few days ago of a respectable girl who assumed a false name and carried on a correspondence with someone as another person! What's become of a young woman's self-respect when she stoops to such an act?"

Quick glances were exchanged between some of her scholars as Hilda said this. Their glances interpreted said, "Whom does she mean? How much does she know?"

John Stuart felt the red mounting to his temples. For the first time since he could remember, a sense of shame possessed him, against which he struggled angrily. Why should the views of this self-opinionated country girl, who in her proscribed circle thought she understood the world, disturb him? Didn't he know his own motives were beyond reproach? And wasn't he sure no harm could result from his act? Still, for a *girl* to pose in this way would be, he slowly admitted, not quite according to his ideas of—

He left the sentence unfinished. Jack Sterritt, Rob's younger brother, was asking a question.

"Miss Elliott, couldn't a girl do something like that for fun and not mean anything else?"

Hilda regarded him a moment. "I don't know, Jack," she said at last. "We'll try not to judge. Possibly she might, if she were young and ignorant and had no one to guide her. But I'd be sorry to think any of my girls could stoop so low."

Then those quick, questioning glances were exchanged again, and this time John Stuart studied them.

The talk continued in this familiar way for some time—question, answer and comment. The young medical student took much higher ground on the question of truth than most present. He seemed in hearty accord with Hilda, affirming that the infinite mischief done in the world by gossiping tongues was done chiefly because their love of talk led them to depart from the truth.

"Jack," said Miss Elliott suddenly, "will you pray?"

And then it was discovered that Jack, the awkward, blundering country boy, knew how to pray. Very simple sentences, without polish but with the ring of sincerity, voiced his desires and aspirations. John Stuart, listening with bowed head, felt again the color suffusing his face. This time it was caused by the thought, What would he have done if he'd been asked to pray? He'd been a church member for more than thirteen years; yet he'd never heard his own voice in prayer.

Chapter 11

Other prayers followed quickly. One bewildered listener was surprised so many of Hilda's pupils seemed to know how to pray. The prayers weren't long, but they had a peculiar directness, as though the petitioners felt that the Person addressed was present and prepared to give them audience.

After a little, Rex Hartwell prayed. Again the one who might be called an outsider felt astonishment. How easy it seemed for that man to pray! He felt he could speak to an audience of thousands easier than he could rise in that little room and ask God for the simplest thing.

But these experiences were nothing compared with what followed. John Stuart had never heard a woman's voice in prayer. When Hilda bowed her head and in a quiet tone and simple language, as she would speak to any of the people present, voiced her needs and the needs of others, his emotions would be hard to describe. No one else in the room evinced the slightest surprise; evidently it was an ordinary occurrence. Yet the prayer was unusual. It had a searching quality that seemed to challenge one to look into his own heart and view it, for a moment at least, as it must look to God. More searching became the sentences, more earnest the call for help, for light to see their temptations, for grace to overcome them.

And then the little schoolroom was treated to a sensation such as it hadn't known before. As soon as Hilda's voice ceased, a young girl sprang to her feet. John Stuart had noticed her several times during the evening. He told himself she was probably the star pupil and the leader among her set. She wasn't pretty, but her clear gray eyes and intelligent face were pleasant to look upon. She impressed one as a girl of marked character and ability in whatever direction she had opportunity. She was excited, and her eyes showed she'd been crying.

"Miss Elliott," she said quickly, "may I speak? There's something I must say. I thought about it before and felt I must every time I looked at you. Your face seemed to be a looking-glass in which I could see my own heart. But I told myself I couldn't do it—after that prayer, though, I *must.*"

Turning to the young people the girl said, "You know how I won the prize in that last history contest? Every question in the list was to be answered correctly, and I was the only one. But there wasn't even one. That next to the last question I—"

The girl hesitated and caught her breath. Suddenly she looked at Hilda, as if to gather strength.

"I stood near Miss Adams," she continued. "She had the history cards in her hand, and that one was on top. I—I saw the first words, two or three of them, enough to start me. I almost know I wouldn't have thought of the answer otherwise. My mind went blank. But when I saw those words, it came to me. I didn't think about its being dishonest—not as I have since. I thought at the time I earned the prize. But I know now I didn't. Oh, I've known it so long. I wanted to give the book back, but I couldn't bear to tell you I cheated! Oh, Miss Elliot, can you ever forgive me?"

With an outburst of bitter weeping she sat down.

Hilda's face was pleasant to see. "Satan has been outwitted tonight, and the truth has triumphed gloriously. I'm sure you all think so. I feel like closing this meeting with the doxology."

At its close she hurried to the girl, who still sat with bowed head.

On the homeward ride, a lively discussion ensued. On the trip out, the two ladies occupied the back seat, and Rex Hartwell sat with the driver. But Hilda had determined to better her acquaintance with her father's hired man and so changed the arrangements by a word.

"Rex, you may take care of Nannie going home. I'm going to sit with John."

Then she sprang lightly to her seat and directed the driver to give her the reins while he looked after the others' comfort. But her opportunity for growing acquainted was to be limited. Nannie Marvin was in full tide of talk, and not chiefly to Rex Hartwell.

"Hilda, I think you were horrid tonight. I never heard you go on so, working up those ignorant young people so they didn't know what they were about. I was never more sorry for anybody in my life than that poor girl. The idea of her getting so excited because she happened to see a word on a card! What did you say to her? I hope you told her she was a simpleton and that her poor little copy of Tennyson, or whatever it was, was honestly hers."

"I didn't," said Hilda quietly. "I was glad with her that she overcame the temptation to silence and was her own truthful self."

"Then I think you were cruel! I don't know how you can be so hard. It's enough to turn one away from religion entirely. Think what you've done for that girl! All those ignorant boys and girls making fun of her, looking down on her and raving over her story until it becomes a public disgrace. And a word from you—that she was excited, no harm had been done, and she really had nothing to confess—would have smoothed everything over. Jesus Christ wouldn't crush a girl that way, I know."

"Why, Nannie, dear," Rex said in low, wondering tones. He'd never seen her so excited about such a slight cause.

Hilda, too, turned and regarded her in the moonlight. "You're mistaken, Nannie," she said earnestly. "Those girls will rally about her, and the boys will stand up for her bravely. Didn't you see how they waited for her tonight, eager to say what they thought? They'll all be proud of her. I rejoice in her. When we have a generation of young people as true to their convictions of right as that, as unswerving in their truth, the world will be a better place."

"Oh, 'truth'!" exclaimed the girl. "I'm growing to hate the word. It's narrowness, not truth. All you said tonight was narrow and bigoted. Your very prayer was hard. Hilda Elliott, you'll drive people away from religion if you let it make you as severe and opinionated as that."

"My dear," said Rex, drawing a wrap carefully about his charge, who had shivered as she spoke. "You've worn yourself out tonight. I don't think you're well."

In truth, it was a strange exhibition from the usually genial, winsome girl. Hilda considered her excitement in perplexity. Why was she so disturbed by what occurred? Didn't she suppose the teacher knew her pupils better than an outsider could? Hilda was sure the confession that evening would work for good, not ill. She rejoiced in it as evidence of growing character. She tried to express her thought, repeating with more earnestness what she'd already said, but Nannie had subsided into almost total silence. Even Rex could secure only the briefest responses from her. To his tender inquires she replied almost petulantly that her head ached and added in what she tried to make a playful tone that she needed to be left alone. Hilda left her alone after a while and gave her attention to John.

"How did you get on with the little boys?" she asked kindly. "Did they have a question for you?"

"Oh, yes, indeed!" he said, smiling over the memory of their faces. "Several questions. One of the little chaps said he'd been puzzling all his life over the mysteries of his own shadow—sometimes long, sometimes short, other times racing ahead of him and again lagging behind. He expressed his puzzle so well that the others became interested. We were just getting from the actual shadows to their moral representatives when you called us to order. I'm afraid I left their inquiring minds somewhat in a fog."

For the moment he forgot himself. Those little boys puzzling over their shadows took him into his past, as if he were John Stuart King reporting to Fletcher or another close friend. He was recalled to the present when he realized Hilda Elliott was looking steadily at him, a wondering, pained look. What could she think of the hired man who addressed such language to her, with a familiarity his position didn't warrant? How should he correct such a blunder? She didn't wait for him.

"John," she said, "sometimes it seems that—that there's something about you we don't understand. I wish you felt that we—that my father was enough your friend to confide in him, if you have anything to tell."

In John Stuart King's sphere he'd never lacked for words. But now there was nothing he felt willing to say. He kept thinking how exactly her eyes in the moonlight were like those in his picture of Truth!

After a moment she began again. "That subject we talked about tonight is so important. If we could get all lives centered in absolute truthfulness, so we'd be true to our inner selves as well as to those we come in contact with, all moral problems would doubtless be solved. John, I hope you're not being false to anybody—to your mother especially. Does she know where you are?"

"Yes," he said, "I write often to my mother." He hurried his answer. What if the question was extended to "Does she know what you're doing?" He almost expected that.

"That's good," she said, evidently relieved. "Did you have a chance to go to school when you were a boy?"

The "honor man" of a distinguished university hesitated and was glad the moon was in shadow just then. It was growing almost as difficult for him to speak the exact truth as it had been for Ellen Elliott. At last he said, "I was always kept in school when I was a boy."

"I've thought from your language you must have had opportunities. I've wondered if you were one of those boys whose father and mother sacrificed a great deal and to whose manhood they looked forward as bringing their reward. Your father's gone, but I hope you're not disappointing your mother."

He'd disappointed her in several ways. She was annoyed with him now because he wasn't loitering through Europe with her and Elizabeth. She'd been vexed with him for years because he wrote for the press and for pay when he had enough money to be a gentleman of elegant leisure.

"You might as well be a day laborer," she said to him once, when he insisted upon regular, uninterrupted hours for study. Suppose he should tell all this to Hilda Elliott! How was he to continue this conversation? He must generalize.

"Mothers and sons don't always think alike," he said, trying to speak stolidly, "and everyone has to think for himself."

"Ah, but, John, mothers are so often right, and sons live long enough occasionally to find themselves mistaken. If I were an honest, well-intentioned young man, I'd think very carefully before I took any steps contrary to my mother's wishes."

"That's true," he said meekly. It was the only reply under the circumstances he felt was allowable. Plainly his questioner wasn't satisfied. He felt she was trying to study his face in the moonlight, now uncertain and fitful.

At last she spoke again, hesitantly. "John, I don't want to force your confidence, of course, but I'd like to be your friend in the truest sense of the word. So I'd like to help you think of the best friend a man can have. If you knew Jesus Christ intimately He'd help you to a better life than you're living. I don't mean," she hastened on, "that I find any fault with your life. Only—at times I've thought you might have fallen from some place you once held and aren't now filling the place God intended for you. Am I right?"

Was she? Had he fallen? How was he to answer her? He felt his face burn over the thought of what he must seem to her, and he could find no words at all.

She didn't wait long but continued gently. "Have you ever given thought to these things? I mean, have you ever thought you'd like to be a real Christian, like your mother perhaps. Is she a Christian?"

"I believe so," he said at last.

He found, poor fellow, that he hesitated even over that question! His fashionable mother, with her days spent in indolent luxury and her evenings given to opera, theater or kindred amusements—how would her religion look to Hilda Elliott? Yet she'd been a member of the church ever since he could remember and was careful not to let engagement or fatigue prevent her being present at church on communion Sundays. Wasn't she as much of a Christian as he was? Their tastes lay in different directions, but perhaps in God's sight his were no more religious than hers. Evidently in this girl's estimate he had no religious character. How sure she seemed that the whole matter was something he had yet to settle. Should he tell her he was a church member?

"Hilda," said Rex just then, "may I ask you to let John drive as rapidly as possible? Nannie's cold. She seems chilled. I'm afraid she's going to be ill."

"No, I'm not!" said Nannie in a petulant voice, very unlike her own. "Why do you insist upon in drawing attention to me? I don't know what's the matter with everyone tonight."

But attention had been effectually drawn to her. From then on Hilda tried to make her friend more comfortable and gave the word that sent the horses skimming over the road with such speed they soon drew up before Mr. Marvin's gate.

Chapter 12

The woodhouse chamber lamp at the Elliott farm burned late that night, though the sheets of carefully written manuscript spread over the table didn't increase. The room's occupant had thoughts he didn't care to commit to paper. He'd added to the furniture since his occupancy. One was a strong box that locked with a padlock; he kept certain books and all his papers there during the day, safe from Susan's inquiring eyes. Another was a lamp he bought with his first earnings, explaining carefully to Susan he had some copying to do evenings that required a strong light.

"He's got a girl somewhere he writes to," commented Susan, after describing the lamp. "I found sheets of paper throwed away the other day, filled full of stuff I couldn't make head nor tail to. I got at him about it. I said I'd think he'd throw them away, and if he couldn't write better sense than that to his girl, she'd throw them away for him."

After that John Stuart was more careful what he did with rejected manuscript pages.

But on this particular evening, as was said, the story he was writing didn't grow. Instead he established himself in the rocking chair and stared out of his one window on the fields lying white in the moonlight. His face was grave. Certain words heard that evening repeated themselves with the persistency of a phonograph set to make a single statement. For instance, "What is truth?" said itself over and over, always in Hilda Elliott's voice and with her searching eyes. If she understood his position fully, would she call him an embodied falsehood? Could he ever explain to her his reasons for this false position? Would she consider the reasons adequate? Well, suppose she didn't—must he justify himself in her eyes?

As often as the round of questions reached this one, he moved uneasily in his chair and avoided considering the answer. He'd rather consider that other question which was growing almost as persistent, whether he was satisfied with his false position. It was a false position, of course; he looked the moon boldly in the face and told it gloomily there was no use in mincing words. He forgot himself for two minutes that evening and talked as he did in his ordinary life—with what result? She looked puzzled and pained. More than once that evening, she brought a flush of shame to his face by words she hadn't imagined applied to him. When had John Stuart King blushed for his acts? It was all questionable, shading the truth, intending to deceive. "If we could get all lives centered in absolute truthfulness"—he seemed to hear again her voice speaking those words. He went on, mentally finishing the sentence. Had he committed to memory all her words? They seemed to cling to him. Could he ever make her understand? There he was, back to that question he didn't intend to think about!

Why not give it up at once? He wasn't accomplishing what he'd set out for. Rather, in a sense, that had been accomplished sometime ago, and now he was simply—not wasting time; he assured himself he was securing material every day, in a new line, that would serve him well for the future. But he wasn't satisfied.

"I suppose," he said to himself, "if I committed arson and got sent to prison, I'd learn a new lesson. But I doubt if the end would justify the means! But that's nonsense."

Still he knew he was growing daily more dissatisfied. Not with the humble life—that amused him. It was still a relief to feel no trammels of society upon him. To be free of engagements to call or dine or attend a friend to a reception. The plain fare, more excellent than he'd supposed people of that class enjoyed, far from being a cross to him, he'd eaten with a relish he hadn't known for years. Moreover, the weary nights he'd spent tossing on his bed trying to woo sleep were things of the past. On his hard, clean bed he dropped to sleep the moment his head touched the pillow and knew nothing more until the morning. Oh, there were blessings connected with this experience!

What, then, was at fault? It couldn't be the social position that chafed him. He laughed when he thought of the patronizing tone in which Rex Hartwell said: "Well, John, you keep your horses in first-class order. I wish I could find as careful a man as you to look after mine." Rex didn't mean to be patronizing; he meant simply to be kind. "John" wasn't the least annoyed, only amused. He laughed even more when he thought of Susan Appleby's honest attempts to civilize him. He was equally indifferent to Ellen's grown up, superior airs and to Nannie Marvin's efforts to be friendly with him as she tried to be with all the farm employees.

But he looked serious when he thought of Colin Elliott. He saw in the boy great possibilities. Stuart King, the scholar, might do much for him; John Stuart, his father's hired man, was powerless. It was so with the boys he met that evening. The rudest and most ignorant among them, by being a factory hand or struggling at home on a worn-out farm, considered himself a grade above a hired man and wouldn't take help or hint from him. Yet let him be perfectly frank with himself. It wasn't simply being somebody's hired man that kept him from being helpful. If this were his legitimate position in life, he felt sure he could build up gradually a character that would command the respect of every boy in the neighborhood.

"It's because I'm a sham," he told himself gloomily. "The boys don't half believe in me. They eye me with suspicion and feel the difference between what I profess to be and what I am. I'm a growing object of suspicion. I could see it tonight in her eyes. I shouldn't be surprised to hear I'm a fugitive from justice! It's as Fletcher said—I can't do it. No man can be successfully, for any length of time, what he is not."

Should he drop the whole thing? He could tell Mr. Elliott he'd decided to go home, take his month's wages due the next day, and telegraph Fletcher to express his trunk to Bennettville. He could stop with it at an obscure downtown hotel where none of his set penetrated, engage a room and change his clothes, and appear at his rooms on Chester Square as Stuart King, the author, returned at last from his summer wanderings. Within forty-eight hours he could take up his dropped life and make everything as it was before.

Could he? His startled consciousness asked this question with a force he hadn't suspected. What about that picture of Truth on his study table that had interested him? Would he ever again be satisfied with the pictured eyes, when he knew that not far away their counterpart gazed in reality upon her world— and read it apparently, as she would an open book? In plain language did he care to return to his cultured, refined, rich life and leave Hilda Elliott secure in her father's farmhouse, never to see her again, never to make her understand he was true and earnest and had a purpose in life as she had?

"If I don't," he said aloud at last, "then I'd better go tomorrow. Let me retain at least the semblance of manhood. But I couldn't go so soon. It wouldn't be right. I should give Mr. Elliott opportunity to replace me."

He was ashamed over the pleasure this thought gave him—that an honest reason for a week's delay could set his heart beating faster! It was high time he went. He rose abruptly at last, refusing to come to any decision or think longer on certain themes that kept wanting consideration.

"I'll go to work," he said with a laugh, "and try to forget myself in the troubles of Reuben and Hannah. I wonder what that precious couple intend doing with me next? The idea an author creates his situations is nonsense. Witness how these two wind me about their fingers, compelling me to let them do and say what I didn't intend should be said or done."

Then he walked over to his table for the first time that evening and found a bulky package addressed to "John Stuart." It was from Fletcher, of course. But where did it come from? He'd driven to the office at five o'clock and found nothing. Some neighbor must have been ahead of him and brought the mail. He looked troubled. This had occurred once or twice before, and each time he received a suspiciously heavy packet.

Outspoken Susan had said once, "Seems to me you get an awful lot of letters. I'd think it would take all you could earn to pay the postage, if you answer them all."

It was evidently one of the things that looked suspicious. Perhaps it helped create that pained, puzzled look he saw in Hilda's eyes that night. Oh, to look into those eyes with perfectly honest ones, with nothing to conceal or explain! If he, John Stuart King, student and author, were back at his rooms tonight with his present knowledge and could start out tomorrow morning, he'd come out to Bennettville by train and to the Elliott farm by public conveyance and boldly ask to be boarded for a few weeks while he studied the conditions of country life for his next book. Why, then the tramp question that started him on his quest might be investigated by anyone; he wouldn't care. But how would he have known of such a being as Hilda Elliott? No, his experience had been too rich to give up easily. Besides, he couldn't have come to the farmhouse and boarded with such ideas. Being a man of honor, this couldn't have—pshaw! What "ideas"? What was he talking about? And what was the matter with him tonight? It was that remarkable meeting that had upset him. No, it was that remarkable talk during the drive home. How troubled she looked!

And then he opened his letter. It enclosed others, bearing foreign postmarks. Fletcher's was brief.

> See here, my boy, isn't it time you gave up this folly and came home? If you don't appear soon I'll get up a search party and come after you. Dr. Wells asks all sorts of questions as to what you're about; and even Dickson from your bank stopped me on the street to ask if you were ill, because he hadn't been called upon to cash any of your checks lately. I'll not promise to keep the peace much longer. How many tramps can you study, pray, staying forever in one place?
>
> I looked up Bennettville yesterday, and it's an insignificant place, not even large enough for a money order office. Is it headquarters for tramps? Do come home, John. I'm tired of this, even if you're not.

"John" laid down the letter with a faint smile on his face and turned the two foreign ones over, apparently to study their postmarks. Then he opened one, written in a delicate hand.

> My dear son,
>
> I've delayed writing for several days, hoping to hear you're back in town. What can you be doing in the country so late? And why don't you give me your correct address, instead of my having to send letters in care of Fletcher? Don't you stay long enough in one place to receive any mail? If not, I don't see why you might not as well be with us. We've been in the same place now for three weeks. A quieter place, with better opportunities for you to continue with your interminable writing, I'm sure you couldn't find.
>
> I think Elizabeth is rather hurt with your conduct, though she wouldn't say so for the world. She's certainly cheerier than she was. But that isn't strange—a girl her age must have some amusement. I told her yesterday that, if you were within a thousand miles of her and would hear about it the same season, I'd almost accuse her of flirting. Be careful, Stuart. Elizabeth is young and beautiful and accustomed to attention. She won't endure neglect of any sort patiently. And if you're not attentive now, what can she expect for the future?

More followed in the same strain. The reader's face gathered in a frown. He skipped to the next page and glanced over its contents, then took up the other letter with a sigh. It was shorter than his mother's, and the hand was even more feminine and difficult to read.

My dear Stuart,

We're still to address you nowhere in particular, it seems. Your friend Fletcher is certainly very kind. Does he have the privilege of reading the letters before he forwards them, to pay for his trouble? It seems sometimes as though you were nowhere. We wonder daily what you can find to hold you to the country so late. The most I could endure the country was a very few weeks in the summer. But you always raved over it— another illustration of how startlingly our tastes differ.

We're quite domesticated now. There's talk of our remaining all winter, so it would have been a delightful place for you to indulge your scribbling propensities. There's a certain Mr. Capen here, an English gentleman with a prospective title, I believe, who's very attentive, chiefly to your mother, though of course he has to let me share his courtesies for propriety's sake. How would you enjoy a step-papa, my dear boy? He isn't old, but neither is your mother. It might be a good idea. If you say so, I'll encourage it to the best of my ability.

At this point the letter was tossed angrily down, and the frown on the reader's face deepened. He couldn't have told what irritated him so painfully. He had for years contemplated the possibility of his mother's marrying again. Not exactly with satisfaction—they were so different that they weren't, in the truest sense of the word, close companions. Still, the young man had been wont to tell himself mournfully that his mother was all he had. At the same time he'd schooled himself in the possibility of her assuming closer ties than his. So it wasn't astonishment over the unexpected that deepened the frowns. It was rather, perhaps, the absence of feeling, of heart, in either letter that struck home with a dull pain.

Mother and Elizabeth—the two names had always been associated in his life. Elizabeth was a second cousin, left early to his mother's care. For at least four years he'd thought of her as his promised wife. This had seemed a natural and reasonable outgrowth of their closeness. His mother had desired it, and neither he nor Elizabeth had been averse to the arrangement. He'd been somewhat tried lately by her apathy regarding his literary studies and her indifference to his success as an author. But he'd told himself she was like all young women. Now as the frowns deepened until his face seemed scarred with them, he admitted to himself that all young women weren't like her.

"What is truth? What is truth?" repeated the wretched phonograph in his brain, over and over and *over!*

He was angry even with that. He swept all the papers and letters—Reuben and Hannah, his brain's creations; Fletcher with his cheerful nothings; his mother and Elizabeth with their empty nothings—into his padlock box and turned the key. Then he went to bed. But it was late that night, or rather it was early in the morning, before he forgot his perplexities in sleep.

Chapter 13

Colin Elliott was tilted back in an easy chair in one of the small reading rooms connected with the college. Several other young fellows were sitting or standing about in leisurely positions also. Two were discussing a topic of considerable interest, involving a difference of opinion.

"Why don't you two fellows let me settle that dispute for you?" Colin asked.

"How should you know anything about it?" one of them asked. "You don't even know the person we're talking about."

"Don't I! What makes you so sure of that?"

"Well, do you? He's been in town about a week and hasn't been out to the college at all, despite the fact he has a dear cousin in this neighborhood."

"It's never safe to jump to conclusions, Harry, my boy. I know the color of his hair and eyes as well as I do my own father's, not to mention several other important items of information I could give you about him."

Harry was about to enlist him for his side of the debate when the other, gazing meditatively at Colin, suddenly turned their thoughts into a new channel.

"I say, Elliott, you weren't—upon my word, I believe you were—one of those fellows the other night!"

The color instantly flamed into Colin's face. But he answered with his easy laugh. "What a definite question! What a lawyer you'll make, Al! Imagine pitching such carefully planned and lucid queries as that at the head of a trembling witness! Let me see. I was a 'fellow' of some sort the other night? Undoubtedly. And I was one of a lot of fellows, no doubt. But how shall it be determined which lot you refer to?"

"He wouldn't chaff like that if he'd been with them last night," volunteered Harry. "You've heard of the precious scrape they got into at the Belmont House, haven't you?"

"Oh! Some more gossip? That's right, Hal. Lawyers have to be on the lookout for all such little things. What did we do at the Belmont House to create a sensation?"

"So you were one of them?" chimed in the other.

"I'm surprised we never thought of you. We knew you were out somewhere last night. Tell us about it, Col. If you hadn't been out of town today, you'd know there's been considerable excitement over it. Lots of stories afloat—one is that the prex is going to expel all of you. It isn't true, is it? We think it would be mean for a little fracas like that and gotten up in honor of a stranger too. We'll stand by you, Col, if that's it—though we thought it was mean of Bliss not to invite us all. It was Bliss's spread, wasn't it? What did you break? They always exaggerate those yarns."

The young men in the room closed about him, all talking at once, asking questions about the Belmont House. They'd evidently talked about it earlier in the day and thought they'd gleaned all possible information. Behold, here was a new and unexpected vein to work!

"I'm sorry you were with them, Col," said one of the older boys. "It isn't simply that one evening's performance. But that fellow Traverse has a bad name, if he is from Oxford. I don't care to be associated with him. How do you know him so well?"

"Oh, hold on!" shouted another. "Dick's green with envy, Col, because he wasn't invited. Don't listen to his preaching. But tell us about the scrape and how you'll get out of it. We heard they found only three they were sure of, and those three wouldn't even hint about the others. You weren't one of the three, were you?"

"My dear fellow, how will I know, unless you tell me who the three were?" This was Colin's laughing rejoinder. Then his face suddenly grew grave. "It's a bad business, boys. I'm glad you weren't in it—though we had no end of fun and didn't mean any harm. What's that? Traverse? Oh, he isn't as bad as his reputation; hardly anyone is. No, we haven't been expelled yet—at least I haven't. But there's no telling what'll come. You fellows will stand by us, won't you, whatever happens?"

In this way he parried rather than answered their questions for several minutes. At the time they thought they were acquiring a great deal of information. But after it was over, they reviewed the interview and realized Colin had told them nothing about the famous Belmont House trouble. In the midst of one of his half-serious, half-comic responses, a click like a closing door sounded in the alcove just behind him. He was separated from it only by a portière. He stopped suddenly and turned toward the portière.

"Is someone in there, boys?" he asked. "I glanced in when I sat down here and thought it was vacant."

One of the boys pushed back the curtain and looked in. "No," he said, "there's no one here. It's that old door. It clicks every now and then."

Colin sighed with relief. "I was preparing to be scared," he said cheerfully. "It would have been hard for me to have the prex, for instance, hiding there, listening to my confessions."

Then the questions and answers continued eagerly.

In fact, President Chambers had been standing in the corner of the alcove, almost concealed by the heavy curtains, looking thoughtfully at a book whose pages he didn't turn. He'd clicked the door as he went out.

Fifteen minutes later, while Colin Elliott was still alternately astonishing and irritating his small audience, Jackson, the dignitary who managed the important affairs of the college, appeared with his courtly bow to say President Chambers would like Mr. Elliott to come to his office immediately.

"Now for it!" exclaimed the boys, while Colin suddenly and in silence tilted his chair forward and sprang to his feet.

"I'm glad I'm not in your shoes," said Harry sympathetically.

"But remember," added another voice, "we'll stand by you."

Then Colin Elliott moved away, wondering what President Chambers could want with him.

The president gave no time for consideration. Glancing up as the young man entered, he began without other recognition than the slightest bend of his stately head.

"Elliott, you doubtless remember I gave you fifty dollars yesterday morning and asked you to step in at Wellington's and pay the bill?"

"Certainly, sir," said Colin politely.

"Very well. What did you do with the money?"

"Paid the bill, of course." And now Colin's voice had taken on both a questioning and a haughty tone.

"And secured a receipt for it?"

"No, sir. The receiving clerk was very busy and told me I might leave the bill with the money, and he'd mail the receipt. I knew the college had constant dealings at Wellington's and supposed it would be all right. Is anything wrong?"

"Yes, many things are wrong. This is by no means the worst feature. Words can't express my astonishment, rather dismay, at learning you were involved in the disgraceful scene at the Belmont House last night. If my information had come from any other source than the one it did, I'd have indignantly denied it, on the ground that your father's son couldn't have been guilty of such a lapse. To find you were not only a participant, but remembering it simply amuses you and gives you something to boast of, almost staggers my belief in young men. I hadn't imagined it of you. I've decided you perhaps anticipated the result, in dollars and cents, and now know your share will amount to more than fifty dollars. Plate glass and decorated china are expensive articles to play with, young man."

By now Colin Elliott's face was aflame. His anger, which had been steadily rising since the first words were spoken to him, had reached white heat. Yet he kept his voice low as he said, "May I ask what informant against me is so trustworthy that, on the strength of his words, you accuse me falsely and further insult me by insinuations I'd think beneath you?"

President Chambers looked steadily and sternly at the flushed face. But his voice was sorrowful. "Elliott, if you were innocent, I'd pass over the impudence of your language. I believe I'd even rejoice in it. But my informant was none other than you. I was in the lower reading room this evening, in the alcove just back of where you sat, and heard your lighthearted admissions to your classmates, as well as your avowal of close acquaintance with a man I believe to be bad in every sense of the word. After that, can you wonder at my suspicions?"

The young man caught his breath in a sudden gasp and stifled what sounded like a groan. For a moment he stared almost vacantly at the stern face before him, as though he felt unable to gather his thoughts into words.

"President Chambers," he exclaimed, "there wasn't a word of truth in that. I was just chaffing the fellows, to show them how easy it was to trick them. I hadn't heard anything about the trouble at the Belmont House until they told me, and I don't know any of the details even now. I've been away all day, by permission of the authorities. The boys were so excited and so gullible I couldn't help having a little fun at their expense. Besides, I had reasons for wishing—"

He came to a sudden stop. It was clear his listener didn't believe him. The stern look never left his face. Instead it deepened.

"Can I believe a self-respecting young man, deliberately and without any other motive than fun, would tell as many lies as I heard you tell your classmates, if what you're now saying is true? Elliott, don't you see this way of trying to evade disgrace is only a deeper disgrace?

"Listen!" he commanded, lifting his hand as the impetuous young voice was about to burst forth. "You accused me of insulting you by an insinuation. I spoke words to you that nothing but your own language, as I heard it, could have wrung from me. But I should speak plainer. The receiving clerk at Wellington's says he never received the fifty dollars you say you left with him. I came home from there, firmly believing you could explain the matter as soon as you reached here. I thought perhaps the hour was later than you realized, and you felt compelled to let the errand wait until another time, or maybe it slipped your mind. But when I heard you tonight and learned you were one of those who had, just the evening before, defied authority and disgraced yourself and the college, and could laugh over it, I believed you were tempted into other lines of disgrace.

"I don't wish to be hard upon you," he added in tones less stern, as he saw the paling face. "I'd be glad to help you and shield you from public disgrace. Regarding this affair at the Belmont House, the trustees and faculty are agreed that public examples must be made of those who dared college sentiment so flagrantly. Every student knows our position. None of you can sin ignorantly. But concerning this other, Elliott, you may have been led into sudden temptation. If you'll be honest and state everything exactly as it is, I'll shield you and give you a chance to recover yourself."

"You're very kind indeed," said Colin. "But I don't wish any shielding from you or any 'chances,' as you call them. It will go hard with me if I don't make you repent this night's work."

Turning he strode from the room. He'd never been so angry in his life. The veins in his temples seemed swelling into cords, and the blood beat against them as though determined to burst forth. Without hat or overcoat, he walked into the chill night air, not caring which way he went or what became of him. The idea that he, Colin Elliott, son of a father whose word was accounted as good as a bond, grandson of a man noted for his unswerving fidelity to truth and honor, should have it hinted to him he spoke falsely, acted falsely, actually descended to the place of a common thief! It was almost beyond belief. Thus far, no thought of the immediate consequences of the matter had entered his mind. That people would hear of it, that he'd be expelled from college in disgrace, that his mother's heart would break and his father's be wrung with agony hadn't occurred to him. It was simply the sense of personal outrage he felt and the overwhelming desire to punish President Chambers for the insults he heaped on him. In that mental state he was, of course, incapable of connected thought. Twice he circled the grounds, raging inwardly so much he was unconscious of the cold night.

When at last he came to himself sufficiently to ask what to do under the extraordinary circumstances surrounding him, the strongest feeling he had was to escape from college authority. Not that he feared it. Not he! Rather he scorned it. The very grounds had suddenly become hateful to him. If he could only be at home that minute, in his mother's room, telling her the story of his wrongs, with his hand slipped into both of hers, while his father sat opposite with his keen, searching, yet sympathetic eyes resting upon him, and Hilda leaning over the back of his chair listening intently and planning even then how to help him!

In the distance he heard the whistle of an outbound train. He stopped under a lamppost and looked at his watch. In less than an hour would be another, going westward, and in two hours more he could be at home. Why not! Not in that state, hatless and coatless! No, he could venture into the hateful building long enough to secure what he needed. Should he go and without a word to anyone? What right had those who outraged him to expect courtesy from him? He still had no thought of consequences for himself. To be sure, it was less than two days to Friday, when he should go home as usual. But two days under some circumstances are an eternity.

He rushed toward the building where he roomed. Jackson was carrying the mail to the various rooms and held out a letter for him. It was from Hilda. He stopped under the hall lamp to read it.

Dear Colin,
   Father says it's foolish, but he really isn't well this evening. He's been feverish and somewhat flighty all day and has asked frequently for you. We think he might have a more restful night if you could come down and sit with him. Could you? He isn't seriously ill, but he has enough fever to make us anxious. We'll send John to the station in the hope you can come. But Father says if you cannot, you're not to worry; and he bids me tell you he's only sending for you to please Mother and me.

Colin groaned as he finished. He'd forgotten his father was ill.

"Not bad news, I hope, sir," Jackson said with respectful sympathy.

But Colin didn't answer him. Professor Marchant was walking down the hall. Colin turned toward him. "Professor Marchant, my father is ill. Can you excuse me from college for tomorrow. I want to take the eight o'clock train."

Professor Marchant was prompt with his sympathy. He hadn't heard the latest news and took it for granted the father's illness was very serious. How else should he account for the son's evident distress?

Chapter 14

John Stuart didn't leave the Elliott farm the following week, nor did he give notice he intended to. Before he'd settled that this must be the next step, an event occurred, pushing it into the background. Farmer Elliott fell ill. Not seriously so—at least the doctor spoke cheerily and hoped the tendency toward a fever would be broken before it could get seated. But the fact that Farmer Elliott was ill at all was sufficient to awaken almost consternation in his family. Never, since the children could remember, had their father been unable to attend to his usual duties. That he was ill enough to call a physician and later be sat up with at night was a startling innovation on the home life. Of course John Stuart wouldn't talk of leaving under such circumstances. Instead, he assumed Mr. Elliott's outdoor duties entirely and made himself so steadily necessary in the house that even Susan said she didn't see how they'd ever get on without him when he took a notion to leave, as hired folks always did.

In addition to his regular duties, John had other cares he alone knew. Quite unexpectedly he found himself painfully associated with the Elliott family affairs. During her father's illness Hilda was dependent upon him for her trips to and from her schoolhouse for the weekly evening gathering. They were generally accompanied either by Rex Hartwell or Ellen Elliott, sometimes both. Rex had given himself earnestly to helping the young men and older boys who gathered there.

But Nannie Marvin, much to Hilda's disappointment, had steadily refused to make a second attempt. She had a dozen excuses. She said she didn't know how to teach girls, especially of that stamp, and it was much better for them all to be under Hilda's lead. No, indeed, she wouldn't take boys instead. Rex could do better for them than she could. She was very busy; perhaps later in the season, when she'd settled down, she might be able to help.

Hilda was puzzled. Could Nannie's approaching marriage be making her seem so unlike herself? Of course she was busy, but not to give a single evening in a week to a work in which Rex was both engaged and absorbed seemed strange.

As for Ellen, she frankly stated she went for the fun in the going and coming and not for any interest in the gatherings.

John Stuart had been accepted doubtfully and with many misgivings as the present leader of the five little boys who had first interested him, mainly because they begged to be under his care and showed the keenest interest in the meeting and in studying to the best of their small abilities the subject he'd talked to them about. Hilda, watching, anxious, could find nothing to object to. Evidently John had more general knowledge than she supposed, but as yet he seemed to be doing no harm. As soon as her father was well enough to be talked to, she must ask his advice, and together they must arrange this thing differently. There, for the time being, the matter rested.

The father didn't get well. Instead, the slow fever took obstinate hold of him. At no time was he seriously ill. At least the doctor didn't call it serious; but he needed constant care and caused some anxiety.

To one evening class Rex went alone with John Stuart and took Hilda's place as well as he could, being helped out by the watchful John in ways that surprised him. He commended that person warmly on the way home and then cross-examined him in a manner that made it painfully difficult to answer with even the semblance of truth. He was kind, assuring John that, with the education he evidently had, he should be able to get work better suited to him than what he was doing now. He said he could imagine circumstances that might have led, in desperation perhaps, to taking the first thing offered. The times were very hard, and he honored him for doing anything honest, rather than living off others. When Mr. Elliott recovered his health, they'd talk it over together and see what could be done. Mr. Elliott, he was sure, would be the last person to try to hold a man to a place lower than he was fitted to fill. Under existing circumstances what could a self-respecting young man do but mumble something that was intended to sound like gratitude and then remain silent?

After that conversation Rex told Hilda there was some mystery about the man; he was afraid all wasn't quite right with his past. He seemed averse to frankness and didn't respond kindly to sympathy. Of course this made Hilda more anxious and more careful.

Nearly a week afterward John was driving rapidly home from town one evening when he met one of the boys belonging to Hilda's, or rather to Rex Hartwell's, evening class, a clumsy, dull-eyed boy, who seemed to John to have no distinctive character.

"Evening," he said, stopping close to the wagon wheel, with the evident intention of arresting its progress. "I was comin' t' meet you."

"So I see. Can I do something for you?"

"I dunno. Maybe you can try, and maybe you can't. I went to see Rex Hartwell, but he's gone into town and won't be back in time, I reckon."

"In time for what, Thomas? Jump in, and we can talk while we ride. I'm in a hurry to get home. If I can help you, I'll be glad to."

"I dunno as it's helping me," said the boy, clambering into the wagon. "Only I feel as though anything that would help her would kind of help me somehow. You're a friend of hers, ain't you?"

"I hope so. Who is she?"

"Well, it's that El Elliott. I ain't much of a friend to *her;* she's always laughing and poking fun at us. But bein' she's her sister, I thought something should be done."

"Thomas," said John Stuart sharply, "tell me, in as few words as you can, what you're talking about."

Thus admonished, Thomas told with some idea of brevity the piece of gossip stirring him to action.

He'd learned, through listening to others who considered him too dull to join them or report their sayings where harm might result, of a company of "fellows and girls" who were to spend that very evening at the Wayside House. One of the boys had a brother working at Wayside; he said supper had been ordered at ten o'clock, and a dance would be held before and after.

"They're a lot of college fellows," explained Thomas, "and as mean a lot as they can get up, even there." From that verdict it will be understood what estimate Thomas was getting of higher education. "And they're going to bring a lot of girls with them from the city. Some have been there before, and Dick says no sister of his should have anything to do with them girls. But one of them they're going to get here, and that's El Elliott."

"Take care, Thomas!" exclaimed John Stuart, and he felt the blood flushing his face. "Miss Elliott wouldn't like to hear you using her young sister's name in that connection. If you're her friend, you should remember that."

"I'm taking care," said the boy impatiently. "If I hadn't been, do you think I'd have tramped out here to tell you about it? I thought maybe it could be stopped and you could do something about it. If you can't, why, I'll find somebody else."

"Yes," said John Stuart soothingly, ashamed of his unnecessary outburst. "I see your motive is good. Tell me all you know about it. Something must be done. Why do you think Miss Ellen is connected with it?"

"Two girls from our neighborhood go to her school, and they overhear talk. They know El Elliott and one or two other girls have been writing letters to some of the college boys. They don't sign their own names or anybody's that really is, and they just do it for fun. You heard her a few weeks ago, didn't you, talk about that in the meetin'? Some of the girls looked at one another then. They saw she didn't know her own sister was doin' it. Well, the college fellow she's been writin' to plans to come out here, get her and go for a ride, and bring up at the Wayside House and introduce her to them other girls. They're a set, Jack says. Not a decent one among 'em, he says. It seems awful, don't it, to have her sister among 'em?"

"Tell me how you learned this last, Thomas."

"Why, one of our girls that goes up there to school sets right behind El Elliott and that Holcombe girl, and she heard them talking it over. El don't know about being taken to the Wayside House. She just thinks she's going to have a ride with him, and I s'pose she don't see no great harm in it. But Jack says she's one of 'em; he heard the two fellows who came out to order the supper and room and everything, talking and laughing about it."

Thomas must certainly have been satisfied with the close attention his story received. John Stuart listened, questioned and went over the main points again, approaching them skillfully from another angle, to be sure the narrator didn't contradict himself. He felt sure at the close that the story he'd heard had some foundation, enough to give it attention and that immediately.

He looked at his watch. The hour was later than he'd supposed; what was done must be done quickly. Then he hurried his horses and got rid of Thomas, assuring him he'd done all that was necessary and that the matter would receive prompt attention. He also directed him not to mention what he told him to another human being. This last was earnestly impressed.

"Remember, Thomas—Miss Elliott would be seriously injured if this story got out. Since very few of us know it, and all of us are to be trusted, we may hope to save her sister from unpleasant consequences and at the same time shield her. I'm sure I can depend on you to make the others feel the same."

Thomas went away believing he was being depended upon to do an important work and also with the vague feeling, which had come to him before, that John Stuart was a "real smart man."

Yet John Stuart had no such realization of his power. He drove rapidly, under the impression haste was needed. But just what could be done hadn't occurred to him. Had he heard this remarkable story earlier, he might have proceeded with caution and accomplished results without frightening anybody. Then again, for the hundredth time, came that dreary second thought that, were he himself, instead of a man masquerading under an assumed name and character, his way would be infinitely plainer.

But the first step was to learn whether Ellen was at home and, if so, whether she had an appointment for the evening away from home. Susan could help him.

"No, she ain't to home," said Susan, speaking in a crisp tone, "and it's my opinion she should be. I think her pa's a good deal sicker than they tell about. He ain't no hand to lie abed for common things."

"Can you tell me where to find Miss Ellen? I have an errand to do for her."

"Oh, you'll find her, I s'pose, down to that Holcombe girl's house. At least that's where she's gone to spend the night. I told Hilda I'd keep her home if I was her. But Hilda said she was so nervous and not like herself that her mother thought she'd better go. They think she's worryin' about her pa. But it's odd worryin' that's willing to go off and leave him all night. I don't see, for my part, what she's so fond of in that Holcombe girl; they ain't a mite alike."

John left her moralizing and hurried out to think. He had been gone all day on business that Mr. Elliott felt important. He'd heard nothing about plans, but Ellen often walked home in pleasant weather. Now it appeared she must have left in the morning intending to spend the night with Laura Holcombe. John didn't like "that Holcombe girl" any better than Susan did.

Without any clear idea as to what to do next, he went to Mrs. Elliott for permission to drive to the village on important business. It distressed him that she gave reluctant consent and evidently wondered what business could call him back to the village, leaving work long waiting for him. She was, however, too preoccupied to ask close questions. Not so Hilda—she came out to the wagon with a troubled face.

"John, must you really go back to town tonight? There are so many things to be done to get ready for the night. Why didn't you stop and attend to the business when you came through?"

"This is something I thought of since," said John lamely enough. He went away angry with himself that he seemed to be living a life which made it necessary to give every sentence a double meaning.

The way of the dissembler is hard, he told himself bitterly as he drove away. What did he mean to do next? He would drive at once to the Holcombes' and learn if Ellen was there. Then what? He sped on, uncertain of his next move. Should he have told Hilda what he heard? No, he answered emphatically; he'd shield her as long as he could from any added anxiety.

He wondered if he should tell Ellen he had a message for her and then take her home—telling her, by the way, the story. Even if no word of truth was in it, it might open her eyes to the importance of taking care of her movements, lest they be construed as evil. This was the only course he'd thought of when he reached the Holcombes', only to be informed Miss Ellen had taken a short drive with a friend.

"Did Miss Laura go with her?" he ventured to ask.

"Oh, no!" Mrs. Holcombe said. Laura wasn't well enough to go out evenings. Didn't he know she'd been sick again? An old friend of Ellen's had called for her, a college friend of her brother, she believed. Then she, too, questioned closely in return and hoped Mr. Elliott wasn't worse. Laura would be dreadfully disappointed if Ellie had to go home.

He got away as soon as he could, taking the direct road to the Wayside House, but he overtook no one. A lively company was at the Wayside House and among them undoubtedly several wild young women and some college men; that much of the story was true. But Ellen Elliott, so far as he could learn, wasn't present. He told the host he called with a message for a person he'd expected to meet there. Declining to leave any word, he was departing when he glimpsed Colin Elliott in the small room opening from the main reception room, leaning against a mantel and gazing moodily into the fire. He went out with a new trouble knocking at his heart. Was sorrow coming to Hilda through this young man also? And could he do nothing? Did the young man know his sister was to be with the questionable company in that questionable house that night?

Busy with these thoughts, he drove slowly, all the time watching. The long lane he was driving down was the private entrance to the Wayside House. At the gateway he was stopped by a handsome turnout. The driver, apparently a gentleman, was having some trouble with spirited horses, who resented the appearance of the gate post. The light from the gate lamp shone full on the carriage. It was Ellen Elliott who shrank back from the glare of light. In an instant John was at her side, speaking distinctly.

"Miss Ellen, you're needed at home immediately. I came here searching for you."

"Oh, John!" she said, her lips pale with apprehension. "Father is worse!"

He made no reply. While he helped her, frightened and weeping, from one carriage to the other, and her companion tried to express his polite regrets, meanwhile looking very annoyed, John Stuart kept silence. He would have enough to say, that he didn't under these peculiar circumstances know in the least how to say, when he'd driven away with his charge.

Chapter 15

John," said Colin Elliott, as he took his seat in the sleigh the next evening, "how ill is my father?" His voice shook, and his face appeared pale and drawn by the station lamp's dim light.

John Stuart felt pity for him and, as they hurried along, talked as cheerily as he could.

"I don't think there's cause for serious anxiety. He has a slow fever, which is exhausting, but the doctor speaks confidently of the outcome. Not sleeping has been the most trying feature for a day or two. In his semi-wakeful feverish state he's had some troubled notions about you. Your mother and sister thought, if you could be beside him, these might be dispelled and he'd rest."

John was forgetting himself again in the interest of the moment. If Colin hadn't been too preoccupied to notice, he'd have stared at hearing this address from the hired man.

Part of the sentence caused him pain. He drew a deep quivering sigh that went to John's heart. "He's troubled about me? That seems almost prophetic— poor Father! I don't know how I'm to get along without his advice; I never needed it more." Then, after a moment's silence, he said, "John, I must see Hilda tonight—alone. Can you think how?"

He was in trouble certainly, or he'd never have appealed to the hired man this way! He was always more or less interested in his father's experiment and was kind to John. But it was the kindness of condescension, as though he always said, "I'm Colin Elliott, a college student, and you're my father's hired tramp." The tremble in his voice and his appeal held a note of equality. He went on eagerly.

"The truth is, I'm in trouble. Of course I can't talk to my father, nor must my mother be disturbed now. But Hilda always has time and courage for everybody's trouble. If I can talk it over with her, I know I'll feel better at once. But I don't know how to without worrying my mother and perhaps my father."

"Oh, I think we can arrange that," John replied cheerfully. "Nights I help take care of your father. When he's enjoyed you for a while and is resting, you and your sister can disappear together for a few minutes."

No sooner was the father lying back resting from pleasure of seeing his boy, than John, who'd been moving quietly about, arranging fire and lights and doing a dozen other small things to add to everyone's comfort, came over to Mrs. Elliott, speaking low.

"Could I remain here on guard, while Miss Elliott goes out with her brother for a breath of fresh air? I heard you urging it earlier in the evening."

Mrs. Elliott responded promptly. Hilda, who had a week's vacation from school and was spending it all in her father's room, was a source of anxiety to her mother.

"Go, Hilda," she said earnestly, "and take a brisk walk with Colin out in the moonlight. It will do you good. Colin, carry her off—she hasn't been out of this room today, and there's no need. John," she added with a grateful glance toward him, "is as good as a trained nurse."

The father added feebly his desire for the same thing, and the two slipped away.

John, near the window, ready for anything that might be wanted, watched the two pacing back and forth in the moonlight with a great ache in his heart. The boy was in trouble, and he, because of his own folly, was powerless to help him. If he were occupying his proper position in this household, how naturally he could say to Colin, "Tell me all about it, my friend. It's only a few years since I was your age. I can understand most things without being told and am ready to help you in whatever direction help is needed." As matters stood, what could he say?

He puzzled over the possible trouble; if it was money, and careless boys like Colin were always getting into money scrapes, how easily John Stuart King could have drawn a check for any reasonable amount! What could John Stuart, hired farmhand, do? Yet what wouldn't he do for the merry-eyed, kind-hearted, free and easy boy? Not for his sake alone or his father and mother's, both of whom John Stuart loved, but because nothing would suit him better than to bring a happy light into Hilda Elliott's solemn and, in these days, anxious eyes. He told himself gloomily that at least to himself he'd speak the truth.

Out in the clear, cold air, Colin and Hilda paced briskly back and forth, never going out of sight of the watcher in the windows. He poured out his eager, passionate story, almost too rapidly at times for coherence; she, alert, questioning, was yet alive with tender sympathy.

"Oh, Colin!" she said once, her voice full of sadness.

He hastened to answer the unspoken reproach. "Yes, I know. It comes from my intolerable habit of joking, playing with the truth. You said it would get me into trouble someday, and it has. I didn't think it could. I thought you were over particular, but I've learned a lesson! I don't half as much as I used to, Hilda. I can almost see your eyes looking into mine and stopping the words. I wish I'd seen them that night. But I was excited and anxious, you know, that the fellows—no, you don't know that either."

"What don't I know, Colin? Let me have all the truth this time."

The boy looked annoyed and hesitated. "It involves a matter I wasn't going to mention for fear of causing you needless anxiety. But I'll have to tell it now, and it doesn't matter, since it came to nothing. You know the Wayside House, at the junction, what a bad name it has? Well, a lot of fellows in college, or not a lot either, three or four, are about as bad as they can be. Two of them, it seems, have been corresponding with some girls in this neighborhood. I don't know who the girls are; they have assumed names, or at least names I never heard. One boy named Hooper is the worst scamp in college or out of it. He's been writing letters by the volume to this girl, whoever she is, and making fun of her to the boys in his set.

"I don't hear much about their activities, for, as you may naturally suppose, I don't belong. But I overheard enough one night to interest me, and I went in where they were, just as he was showing a picture. The girl actually sent her photograph to him! Hilda, if you could have heard those fellows talk as they bent over it, I think your eyes would have blazed! I glimpsed the face, and it was taken in a fancy headdress of some sort that shaded the features. But I was almost certain it was Nell Marvin! You don't think Nell sent him her picture, do you? I tried every possible way to get another look at it. But the fellow didn't mean for me to see it at all, so I failed.

"After that, I tried to find out what their next scheme might be; they always have something on hand. I found—no matter how, it took a good while to do it—that two or three of them were meeting ladies, so-called, at this same Wayside House on Tuesday evening of this week. And that rascal Hooper was meeting the girl he'd been corresponding with at the same place!

"Imagine it, Hilda! The only thing I could think of was to rush off the next afternoon down here and spend the evening at the Wayside House. And a charming evening I had! Think of being so near home and not being able to come home! Those scamps and their so-called ladies were on hand, but I'd never seen any of the girls before. Hooper wasn't there at all. He was expected, though. I overheard all sorts of conjectures about his nonappearance. The fear he would come later held me there until the party broke up.

"Some of them had a lovely row before that time—drank too much, you know. Well, I could only get back to college, and, meanwhile, trouble was brewing there for me. This fracas at the Belmont House occurred, you understand, on that very evening. It would be easy enough for me to prove an alibi, but—how much better off would I be in proving myself to have spent the evening and into the night with questionable company at the Wayside House? For that matter only questionable companies gather there, while respectable people do frequent the Belmont. You can see why I was anxious to throw those boys off the track regarding where I was that evening. I hadn't heard any particulars about the trouble at the Belmont, and I don't know anything about it yet, except that some costly dishes and furniture were smashed. I suppose there'll be a big bill to pay, but of course I can get out of that.

"As to the fifty dollars, I'm in awful trouble. I paid it as certainly as my name is Elliott, and I paid it to the assistant bookkeeper, who stands very high. How can he say I didn't, and what's become of it?

"You see how it is, Hilda—circumstances are all against me. If I'd been at home that night in my room, working, as I should have been except for that notion I got that some of our young people were in danger, why, I could prove it in two minutes. In fact, there'd be nothing to prove. The boys wouldn't have thought of my being in that crowd if I hadn't pretended to know that wretch Traverse, whom I haven't even seen. It all comes back to that, Hilda. I've been playing with falsehoods, and they got me into a scrape, as you said they would. I don't see any way out.

"When I started for home tonight I was too angry to think—I still am. What business did President Chambers have of charging me with being a thief!

Suppose the fifty dollars can't be found—what's that to me, when I know I laid it down before the bookkeeper's eyes, and he acknowledged it? I've been treated meanly. I'm sure Father would say so. But just how to manage it I don't know. I suppose I'll have to pay it again. Do you think we could raise that amount extra, Hilda, while Father is sick? And why should I pay it? Wouldn't that look like a confession of crookedness? I can't think clearly. If only we could get someone's advice!"

"What about talking with Rex Hartwell?"

The young man shrank. "Oh, Hilda, I couldn't! He'd think I wanted to borrow the money from him. I'd rather work it out on the road than do that. Must people hear about it? There'll be so many details to explain, and all sorts of false stories will spread. But then, if I'm expelled from college, it will be out anyhow. What a miserable business it is. And I always prided myself so much on our good name. To think I should be the one to stain it!"

The poor fellow's voice quivered with pain, and his sister arose at once to the situation.

"Never mind, Colin. We'll find our way out. It isn't as though you'd really done any of the things you're charged with. If that were so, I couldn't bear it. As it is, we'll be shown a way to make the truth plain. Let me think it over tonight, and in the morning I'm sure some light for how to act will come to us."

The boy's grasp on her arm tightened. His voice had a husky note. "You trust me, Hilda, don't you? You don't believe for a moment that I'm guilty of those horrid things?"

Her reply was prompt and reassuring. "Why, of course, Colin. How can you ask such a question? I know you only play with falseness. If you'd only give that up!"

"I will, Hilda. I give you my word for it. If I get safely out of this scrape, see if after this I don't make my communications 'yea' and 'nay.' "

They were opposite the window again, and he caught sight of John standing framed in it. This reminded him of something he'd meant to say; he broke in with it abruptly.

"Hilda, does John frequent the Wayside House? Last night, when I was hanging around, watching for what might develop, I saw him walk into the reception room and look about him, like a person searching for someone. I slipped into the small room, for, as you can imagine, I didn't care to be recognized there. But I couldn't help wondering what brought him. Do you suppose he can be like that?"

Hilda drew a weary sigh. "I don't know," she said mournfully. "I confess I don't know what to think of him. I'd like to believe in him in every way—he's so kind to Father and so thoughtful of us all and faithful in his work. But some suspicious circumstances are connected with him, and sometimes I'm afraid—"

She broke off abruptly. Was it fair to speak of her suspicions, if it wasn't necessary? She recalled their talk during that ride home from her evening meeting. John's language then had been so unsuited to his position. Then she remembered his haste in returning to town the evening before, though he knew pressing duties were awaiting him at home. What could have called him to the Wayside House? He had an errand, he told her, at the Holcombes'. And Ellen had returned with him. Of course this must have occurred after he left the Wayside House. He wouldn't have taken her little sister there! Her face grew dark over the passing possibility. Not that Ellie would have allowed him to do so—that, of course, was folly.

The child's sudden resolve to return home hadn't surprised her. She had nervous fits over her father's condition that could only be accounted for by supposing she heard talk outside, which made her believe he was more seriously ill than his own family thought. The child had cried a dozen times that day, and Hilda had withheld questioning, believing this to be the cause. Probably the Holcombes had questioned her with such serious faces and foreboding sighs that the poor girl had been seized with a panic and welcomed John's appearance with joy. The utmost the sister had said to her was a gentle rebuke for coming back with John. She reminded her he was still a comparative stranger, and their father had been careful not to trust him too fully.

And Ellen had said, "Oh! You needn't be afraid of John. He's good." And then had followed another burst of tears.

What this sister said aloud, after all these reflections, was, "Oh, Colin, if everybody would be frank and sincere in all their words and ways, how much easier living would be! I can't get away from being afraid John has something to conceal."

The protective instinct came over the boy. "Poor little woman!" he said, with his arm around her. "So many of us to worry over and help. You've helped me, dear sister. The thought of looking into your true face was like a tonic. I've made fun of your truth-telling propensities, but that wasn't being honest. I always admired you for it. I'd like to have my face reflect my soul, as yours does. I feel better. You've encouraged me—I knew you would. Let's go in to Father."

Chapter 16

Colin Elliott's courage lasted well into the next morning, when he bade his father a cheerful good-bye and assured him he'd get away as early as possible on the following day and wouldn't go back at all, if it weren't for some important matters at college needing his attention.

Hilda, too, was cheerful. "Keep up a good heart, Colin," was her admonition. "The truth must conquer—it always does. And, Colin, if you find that money is needed—I mean, if you decide it will be right to pay that money again—we can raise it. Don't worry about that either."

This she said even though money was scarce and she had no idea how to raise the extra sum. Mr. Elliott was considered a successful farmer, but he wasn't wealthy. To raise even fifty additional dollars, at that season of the year, would be no small matter.

When Colin was gone, some of the brightness worn for his sake faded from Hilda's face. She was haunted now with a nameless anxiety concerning Ellen. The child was at home, having begged permission to remain there. She was well, she said, but she didn't feel like school; she felt as if she'd fly if she tried to study.

"She's worried about her father," was Mrs. Elliott's conclusion. "She certainly must have heard some serious doubts about his recovery. She cried last night whenever I mentioned his name, though I assured her the doctor, when he came last evening, pronounced the symptoms better. Do you think exaggerated accounts of his illness have gotten around?"

"Possibly," said Hilda, more reticent than usual with her mother and resolved on a quiet talk with Ellen at the first opportunity.

Late in the day the opportunity occurred; in fact, she finally had to make it. She grew more resolved to it, as Ellen distinctly avoided her or, at least, studied to avoid a moment's conversation with her in private. There was certainly a stronger, or, rather, different, disturbing force than her father's illness. The child was nervous and had been, her sister reflected, for several days. Since her nerves were naturally healthy and well-managed, it became important to learn what unsettled them. How she associated the girl's unrest with what Colin had told her about the Wayside House and the mysterious photograph, she couldn't have told. Indeed, she assured herself indignantly, she didn't associate them for a moment; but the two anxieties persisted in floating through her mind. Nevertheless, whenever she recalled Colin's words about anonymous letters written by someone in their neighborhood, a strange shiver ran through her frame.

About midafternoon Ellen came downstairs dressed for walking and announced to Susan she was going for a long walk. That young woman, sorely tried with the girl's unusual nervousness, replied tartly she hoped she'd "walk off her tantrums" and come back acting like herself.

Hilda was on duty in her father's room at the time, but as soon as she was released she followed, having noted Ellen's direction. She understood her habits and met her on her return trip, just as she'd planned, half a mile from home.

"I've been sent out to take air," she said cheerily to Ellen, who was walking with eyes bent on the ground and started like a frightened creature on seeing her.

"Is that so?" came the eager reply. "Then go on to the rocks—there'll be a lovely sunset view tonight. I thought of waiting for it myself."

"No, I don't have time for the sunset today. I must get back and help Mother. Besides, I came this way to meet you. I want to have a little visit with you. We've hardly seen each other for a week or two."

She linked her arm within her sister's as she spoke, and they walked on together. Ellen, however, had made no response. As Hilda stole a glance at her, she saw she was crying softly. Her evident misery struck to the elder sister's heart.

"What is it, dear?" she asked in tones a mother might have used. "You can't be worried about Father—at least, you needn't be. We're more hopeful of his speedy recovery than we have been for nearly two weeks. The doctor spoke positively this morning, and Father feels and looks better in every way. Everything's going all right, Ellie. What troubles you? Has someone told you Father was very ill and not going to recover?"

Ellen shook her head and cried harder.

"Then it must be some trouble of your own, dear. I've seen for several days that something was wrong. Can't you confide in me, Ellie? I thought I was your best and dearest friend, next to Mother. And she's so busy with Father—can't I take her place for a while?"

"I don't know how to tell it," said poor Ellie. Her tone was so full of abject misery that her sister was sure something was gravely wrong.

They walked on for some seconds in silence, the elder sister trying to determine how best to approach a girl who'd suddenly become a bundle of sore nerves. She'd meant to question her closely as to why John was at the Holcombes' and how she changed her plans and came home with him. But the girl was evidently too much excited now, and too miserable, to talk about personalities. She determined to try to interest her in something she'd forced herself to believe was entirely outside her sister's knowledge. Perhaps through that story Ellie would get control of herself and begin to realize there was real trouble in the world.

"Colin told me a strange thing last night," she began quietly. "He's troubled about some of the college boys, wild fellows, not his set, of course. He's especially anxious about one in particular, named Hooper—at least, he has the least hope for him of any young man in college. He says that boy is capable of planning almost any evil. He overheard through some of those boys that certain bad or foolish girls had been corresponding with them, strangers, Ellie, never having even met them!

"What especially worried Colin was that this Hooper has a correspondent in this neighborhood. Can you imagine who it can be? They use assumed names, he thinks, and she's even sent him her photograph! Would you guess a girl with enough intelligence to write a letter could do such a foolish act? Colin happened upon the fellow when he was showing it and laughing and making terrible speeches over it. He only glimpsed the picture but has been haunted ever since that it resembled Nell Marvin. It was only a resemblance, but think how dreadful! It makes me angry for all pure-hearted girls, that others can bring their class into disrepute this way.

"Then, worse than the rest," Hilda continued, "they planned to bring a party of so-called ladies out to the Wayside House night before last for supper and a dance. This Hooper was to come out here and take his correspondent to the Wayside to join them. Colin was so troubled about it, for fear some poor ignorant girl in our neighborhood would get into trouble, that he secured leave of absence and came out to the Wayside House."

"Colin came to the Wayside House!" interrupted Ellen, with intense excitement. She trembled so violently that the hand resting on Hilda's arm shook as if with an ague chill.

"Yes," said Hilda, her heart sinking. Something very serious must be the matter. She hoped, poor sister, that Ellen must have become aware of the correspondence and knew who was carrying it on and that her conscience was troubling her because she'd kept it secret. She tried to finish her story without visible agitation.

"He spent the evening at the Wayside House, in such company, he says, as he was never in before and desires never to be again. But he knew none of the people, at least none of the girls. And this Hooper didn't appear at all. He doesn't know now whether Hooper learned he was there and feared he'd recognize the girl, or what detained him. Colin is still worried and anxious. He talked with me this morning about it and suggested you might help us get at the truth. It touches home, coming right into our neighborhood. Do the schoolgirls ever talk up such ideas, Ellie? Of course none of them would go to the Wayside House. But no girl among your classmates would write an anonymous letter, would she?"

Ellen made no answer. Suppressing an anxious sigh, Hilda continued after a moment.

"There's another thing. Colin says that, while he was waiting there that evening, he saw John walking about in the large room, as though he, too, were waiting for somebody. Colin didn't speak to him, because, of course, he didn't care to be recognized there if it could be avoided. But he couldn't help wondering if John went often to the Wayside. I can't think he does, and yet I don't know. There's something suspicious about him, and I've been disappointed in many people lately."

"Is the Wayside House such a dreadful place, Hilda?"

Ellen's voice asked the question, but so hoarse and constrained her sister felt she wouldn't have known it under other circumstances. She looked anxiously at the tear-filled eyes and flushed face and spoke gently.

"Why, Ellie, dear, you hardly need to ask that question. You know the reputation of the house. Our father, you remember, wouldn't send one of us there on an errand, even in broad daylight. Why do you ask? Do you think John goes there often? Or did he have an important errand? He must have gone early in the evening, before he went to the Holcombes'. All his movements that evening looked suspicious to me. Having to drive back to town, when so many duties awaited him at home, seemed strange. I don't like to suspect people of wrong, but we should be careful about John. We're responsible for his being in this neighborhood, I suppose.

"As to this other matter," Hilda said, "we can't put it from us. One can't help fearing some poor girl, with no mother and no bringing up, has been led into evil in our midst. If it were one of my scholars, Ellie, it would almost break my heart. But I can't think of any who'd be tempted like this."

"It isn't one of them," exclaimed Ellen, bursting into tears and speaking words so choked with sobs Hilda could scarcely understand them. "It isn't one of your girls. It's your own sister—I've done it all! I didn't mean any harm. It was just for fun. The girls dared me to do it. Laura Holcombe said I wouldn't write a letter to anybody, because of you. She said, if I had a grandfather and wrote to him, I'd have to show all my letters to you before they were sent, and a lot more stuff like that. So I thought I'd show them I wasn't afraid. I thought it was fun and no harm could come of it. Oh, Hilda! Have I disgraced you all? Will Father and Mother have to be told? Oh, I wish I could die!"

She turned suddenly and threw herself down on an old log by the wayside and, burying her face in her hands, sobbed as though her heart would break. Hilda stood still, regarding her with mingled pain and wonder. She hardly realized yet that the poor, ignorant, misguided girl she'd alternately blamed and pitied ever since she heard of her could be their Ellie! Solicitude for her sister finally outweighed other feelings.

"Get up, dear," she said, bending down and reaching for the girl's arm. She tried to make her voice very kind. "You mustn't sit there—you'll take cold. We must hurry home as fast as we can. Mother will be needing me. We mustn't trouble Mother and Father with this now," she continued, as Ellen allowed herself to be helped up from the log. "We must do the best we can, until Father is well. But, Ellie, I must know all about it from the beginning, if I'm to help you. Those people who came to the Wayside House that evening—did you have anything to do with them?"

"I didn't know I had," said Ellie. "I'll tell you every bit, Hilda. We picked out the name from the catalogue because we liked the sound of it—Augustus Sayre Hooper. Laura said it had an aristocratic sound, and he might be connected to the Sayres of Boston. I just thought he'd be a nice, smart young man like Colin, and it'd be great fun to get letters from him and make him think nice things about me. I never meant to see him or let him know who I was. But— Hilda, he wrote beautiful letters. I thought he was everything good and noble, and it would be an honor to be his friend. I'll show you his letters, and you'll see how truly noble he makes himself out to be—I mean, without praising himself in the least. Colin must surely be mistaken about him."

"Go on," said Hilda. Despite her effort, her voice was cold. Her sister was both younger and older than she'd thought her.

"There isn't much more," said the poor girl meekly. "He kept wanting to call on me. He said a matter begun in jest had developed into earnest. He felt sure we'd be good friends for life and that he needed my influence and letters to help him through the temptations of college. You know it's a life of temptation, Hilda. I've often heard Mother and Father say so. He said I'd done him good already and would never know how my letters had helped him over some hard places. I wanted to do a little good, Hilda. I can never be like you, helping everybody and interested in everybody, no matter how common and uninteresting they are. But I thought I could help him, and I can't bear to think what Colin says of him is true." Another burst of tears.

Hilda felt the strangest mixture of emotions. She could have shaken the trembling girl leaning on her arm for being such an arrant simpleton, and she could have gathered her to her heart and wept over her as the innocent dupe of a villain. And she was still such a child! They'd thought her free from such temptations.

"Please, Ellie, try to control yourself and tell me about it," she said at last. It was the most she could bring herself to say. "Does the Wayside House meeting come in?"

"Why, he wanted me to take a ride with him. He was to meet me at Laura Holcombe's. And—oh, Hilda, there's something more I'm afraid you'll think is dreadful. He wanted my picture a good while before this, and I wouldn't send it to him—not my own, of course. I hunted through Colin's collection for a fancy one and came upon that one of Nell Marvin she had taken in her wedding finery when she was her Aunt Kate's maid of honor. You can hardly see her face in it because there's such a cloud of drapery. Well, I sent him that and let him think it was I."

"Oh, Ellie!" The listener couldn't repress this outcry of indignation.

"Was it awful, Hilda? I can feel it was now. It's strange how dreadful things sound, repeated to you, that seemed only fun when Laura and I planned them! I had no idea he'd ever learn whose picture it was. Then, when I began to know him better and enjoy his letters and like him, as I told you, I thought it'd be such fun to let him call on Laura and me and show him that the picture he'd raved over wasn't mine at all. We'd have a good laugh over it, and that would end the matter.

"So that night he came. Laura and I were to drive with him, but Laura wasn't well enough to go, and he insisted on my going without her. He said I'd promised. He didn't mind about the picture in the least; in fact, he said he liked my face much better than the pictured one. I didn't know we were going to Wayside until he turned in at the gate. Then he said he had an appointment there with a college friend. When I told him I didn't want to go there, he asked me if I'd just step in with him while he spoke to his friend, and then we'd come right out. He said he had no idea the house was different from other country hotels and must warn his college friends of its local reputation."

"Did you go with him to the Wayside House?" interrupted Hilda.

Chapter 17

Poor sister! She was stunned over the magnitude of these discoveries. Every sentence Ellen spoke seemed to reveal a new horror. The idea of her pure-hearted young sister, whom they'd considered hardly out of her babyhood, descending to such depths! To a nature like Hilda's an anonymous letter was in itself a poisonous thing. But an anonymous letter addressed by a young girl to a man, and that man a stranger, was a disgrace from which she shrank with the force of her strong, pure nature. Yet she must meet and face disgrace such as this and help her young sister overcome it if she could. Therefore she controlled all outward feeling as far as possible and asked that probing question, "Did you go with him to the Wayside House?"

"No," said Ellen, "I didn't. Just as we were driving into the gateway, we met John with the carriage. He told me I was wanted at home immediately. I was frightened half to death, for, of course, I thought Father must be worse. He took me out of the carriage, put me into ours and drove away quickly, without a word, until we were on the road. Then he frightened me more, telling me how dreadful it was for me to go to the Wayside House. You needn't worry about John, Hilda—he's good. He made me promise I'd tell you all about it. He heard the whole story somewhere—about the letters, I mean, and all—and I promised I'd tell you every word, and I have. It wasn't just because you came out to meet me that I told you. I've been planning all day how to do it, and I meant to do it before I slept. Oh, Hilda, do speak to me, or I shall die! Have I disgraced Father and Mother and you, and everybody, and injured Nell? Oh, dear me! If I *could* just die and be forgotten!"

It was a childish wail and for the moment didn't appeal to Hilda's heart. She felt even more humiliated by this new truth. John, the hired man, her father's tramp, taken in out of charity, must rescue her sister! And the burning question was, how did he acquire his knowledge? If only he were a simple, honest hired man, earning his honest living by daily toil; if he were one of the roughest, most uncouth of their back country neighbors come to the rescue—she could have blessed him. But what was John? For all she knew, a worse man than Augustus Sayre Hooper, knowing of evil because he was of that same evil world.

Then she thought of the humiliation awaiting her because she must talk the whole wretched business over with John, discovering how much he knew and, if possible, from what source.

Her face burned at the idea and then paled at the memory of Nell Marvin and the disgrace brought carelessly upon her. What would Nannie say if she heard of it, or *when* she heard of it? Mustn't it, as a matter of honor, be told? The poor girl found herself bewildered over these questions of right and wrong, uncertain which way to turn. If she could only appeal to her clear-headed father or her quiet, far-seeing mother! But at present it was out of the question for her father, and she couldn't feel right about adding to her mother's burdens.

Meanwhile, what must she say to Ellen? Not one word of comfort had she spoken, because she hadn't reached the point where she could sincerely speak comfort. She struggled with disappointment and angry irritation with Ellen. How could a girl who had grown up in such a home as hers, with such a father and mother, have gone so far astray? If this was what the wicked outside world did for a sheltered and carefully guarded one, how could girls who grew up without a Christian home environment ever escape? Thoughts like these made her answer the girl's last appeal so coldly.

"People cannot die, Ellie, at a moment's notice and leave the consequences of their—mistakes to others." She'd hesitated for a word and had almost said "sins," but a glance at the woebegone face beside her restrained her tongue and made her say "mistakes" instead. "It's much more noble to live and do one's utmost to set right anything that may have gone wrong through our fault." One more probing question she would ask.

"Ellie, you say you didn't at any time realize you were doing wrong. It was just fun from which no serious consequences were expected. Will you tell me, then, why you didn't explain the whole scheme to Mother and me and let us share the fun with you? We're both capable of enjoying fun and quite ready to sympathize with it. Had you thought of that, dear?"

Ellen's eyes dropped, and there was silence for several seconds. Then she said, speaking low, "Hilda, Laura Holcombe thinks you're over particular about some things, and I'm afraid she's made me feel that sometimes. I told myself that was why I said nothing to you about it. But I'm going to speak exactly the truth after this, to myself as well as to other people, and I know now that I didn't tell you because I felt that you and Mother would put a stop to the whole thing. At first I didn't want it stopped because it was such fun; he wrote such merry letters. After that I liked him so well I wanted you to meet and like him too before I told you anything about it. Then I thought he'd be a friend to all of us. He said he was going to take pains to get acquainted with Colin and, being older than he, could perhaps help him in certain ways."

Hilda's lip curled derisively. Such a creature to help Colin!

It was probably well for both girls that home duties held their attention closely for the remainder of that day. Certainly the older sister wasn't ready with advice or comfort, beyond the few words she compelled herself to speak.

When, at last, she could go over the whole trying business in her own room, she tried to shoulder calmly her perplexities and responsibilities and determine what should be done. But she found quietness of spirit hard to assume. She'd hoped to give this first hour of solitude to Colin and his troubles. And, behold, here was a much more serious matter claiming immediate and absorbing attention. The bright side to Colin's troubles was he'd brought them on himself by mere folly, not deliberate sin. What if he'd been at the Belmont House on the evening in question and forever associated with the disgraceful scene, minute particulars of which were spread out in this evening's paper for the country people to read? No names were mentioned, but such matters always got abroad, especially in the country. What if one couldn't deny Colin had had the remotest connection with it? Or what if he'd been goaded by poverty into appropriating that fifty-dollar note? Certainly there was a bright side! What rest it was to realize not even a passing suggestion of his honesty had disturbed her.

When Colin chose to consider a matter important, his word could be implicitly believed. What an infinite pity he found his amusement in exaggerations or at times, as in this case, in untruthfulness. But there was a way out for him, of course, and a speedy one. Or if not, if it came to enduring public disgrace, she could be sure he was bearing disgrace justly.

But Ellen's trouble was on another plane. The poor child had undoubtedly gone astray. Not as far as she might have gone; she was mercifully shielded from an introduction to a world outside of, and far below, her an evening at the Wayside House would have given her. Did she perhaps need such a revelation, to open her eyes to the dangers awaiting foolish feet in that cruel world? Not that Hilda would have had the experiment tried! And that it wasn't, they had John to thank!

Then she thought again of the interview she must have with him and the careful questioning to find how much or how little he knew. What did that mysterious and, at times, suspicious John know of the world? How conversant was he with the Wayside House and places like it? How much of what he'd tell her would be truth and how much invented to suit the occasion? With the falsifying that had taken hold of people, she could trust almost nobody. Never mind, she must shoulder the burden and do her best. Perhaps she shouldn't have waited until morning. Her younger sister's name might even now be tossing about among the low and coarse. And Nell Marvin's photograph—how would they get it again, or explain to Nellie and her father and mother Ellen's share in the wretched transaction?

At last she gave up trying to think, reminding herself she was simply taking counsel from her own overwrought brain. Then this sorely tried young disciple of Truth, who had been bitterly stung by falsehood, remembered her refuge and gave herself to prayer.

ঞ

Colin Elliott, as he was being driven to the train that morning, had enough cares of his own to think about. Nevertheless, he gave some attention to John. In certain lines he anticipated his sister Hilda's thoughts. Why was John at the Wayside House? Who was he? To what extent were they justified in trusting him as they had? With his young eyes recently opened to temptations and dangers waiting for the unwary, he wondered about the wisdom of leaving his sisters, especially Ellen, to the care of this unknown man, upon whom they must depend more or less now that their father was ill. Yet the fellow had a good face, and he couldn't help being interested in him. Perhaps he was weak and was being led into evil surroundings since coming into their neighborhood! He wondered if he might speak some word of warning, even though he was so much younger than John.

Certainly this young man had changed much in a single night. He had no inclination now to appeal to John for sympathy; instead, he was putting his own affairs in the background and trying to plan for others. It occurred to him his duty might be to get leave of absence from college and remain at home until his father could be about again. Then the stinging thought came that circumstances might make this unnecessary. He might be, even now, suspended or expelled from college!

The thoughts of the two crossed. John spoke first.

"Mr. Colin," he said, breaking a silence of several minutes, "you told me last night you were in trouble. I've thought about it a good deal. I wish I could help. Your father has been very kind to me. If it's anything about money, perhaps I could. I've got a little money laid up. I know young men in college sometimes need more than they thought they would."

Colin turned and regarded him suspiciously. So he had money laid up! That was strange. Not that an honest working man, getting fair wages and only himself to care for, mightn't lay up a little money. But he'd been with them so short a time and came in the regular tramp fashion, asking for food, to be supposedly paid for in work. Did that look like a man who had money laid up? It must be money he secured somehow since coming to them. Was he a professional gambler? Or was he simply a bungling gambler, trying it from time to time and occasionally winning by accident? In that case, had the Wayside House and its frequenters led him astray? Meanwhile, some reply must be made to his offer.

"That's very good of you!" he said, attempting a good-natured laugh. "College fellows always need money, it seems. But I didn't think of appealing to you. Suppose I needed—say fifty dollars? I guess that would be more than you could manage?"

"No," said John, falling unsuspecting, even eagerly, into the trap, "I could lend you fifty dollars. I could raise it in an hour's time and telegraph you a money order. I'll be glad to do it, if you'll let me, and you needn't be troubled about paying me. Anytime will be all right."

Every word he spoke increased the suspicion against him. Colin had no idea of borrowing money from him and mentioned the sum merely to learn, if possible, the extent of John's resources. He didn't know how to reply.

"It's certainly generous of you to offer to help me," he said at last, "and, of course, I'm obliged to you. But, at present at least, I won't borrow. I'll have to confess you've surprised me. I didn't imagine you had a bank account. Your circumstances when you came to my father didn't lead me to think you were a moneyed man."

John's face grew red under the taunt and the realization of his own folly; he'd made another mistake. He drove on for some seconds in silence, then said coldly, "A man can earn money, Mr. Colin, by working with his hands and be honest about it."

"Of course he can," said Colin heartily. "I don't look down on any working man or feel superior to him. But, John, an honest working man, who has money laid up, doesn't usually turn tramp and come into a neighborhood where he's an entire stranger, searching for a meal. I guess that's none of our business, as long as you do your work well. You look as though you'd like to say something like that to me, so I'll say it for you.

"I'll tell you something that may surprise you," he continued. "I went to the Wayside House on business night before last and was sorry to see you there. You may be such a stranger in the neighborhood that you don't understand the character of that place. If so, the sooner you're put on your guard the better. As far as I know, no respectable person frequents it, but some of the worst characters in this part of the country do. If you're a good honest fellow, John, as I want to think you are, you won't mind my plain speaking. I'm sure my father wouldn't like to employ a man who goes regularly to such places."

"I was never at the Wayside House before in my life," said John quickly. "Very important business took me there that evening. I saw you there, Mr. Colin, and wondered. I've heard about the house. Your father himself told me about some things that occurred there. You've been good enough to tell me you were sorry to see me in such a place. Perhaps you'll excuse me if I say I had much the same feeling about seeing Mr. Elliott's son there."

Colin laughed. "So there are two of us?" he said cheerfully. "I believe it was also my first visit to that renowned spot. Odd we chose the same night, isn't it? Do you know what I advise? That neither of us goes again. The business I thought called me didn't amount to anything; it would have been better if I hadn't gone. I daresay the same could be said of yours."

John made no audible reply to this tentative question. In his heart he said, "Indeed it couldn't! If you knew what took me there, my lofty young man, you'd go down on your knees in gratitude for my effort and its success."

They were nearing the station. The horses were restless under the passing of a freight train, giving the driver a good excuse for paying undivided attention to them.

After the passenger alighted and bowed his good-morning, he turned back to say kindly, "I don't know whether I thanked you for your kind intentions. I really am very grateful. If I ever need your help in any way, I'll remember. And if you need my help anytime, I'll be glad to give it."

Then he ran for his train.

Chapter 18

John Stuart drove home from the station in a mixed frame of mind. The interview just closed undoubtedly had a ludicrous side. He'd been thinking more or less about Colin Elliott for several weeks, partly because he seemed such a merry-hearted, easily led fellow, and he knew the temptations in some colleges for such as he. Also he knew by reputation certain students at this particular college who he guessed were Colin's friends. And mainly—this he told himself, with resolve to *think* just the truth—he was Hilda Elliott's brother and evidently precious to her, and her interests—he never let himself carry his thoughts an inch further in this direction.

But he laughed, despite the gloomy undertone, over the ludicrous side of the interview. He was troubled for Colin, and Colin was troubled for him. He suspected Colin had gotten into trouble that would bring sorrow to his sister, and Colin suspected him in a dozen different ways. Both of them were guests, at least once, at a disreputable house, and each deeply regretted it for the other!

After the laugh his face sobered. He'd failed in his attempt at helpfulness and reasonably so. He had only made his own position more suspicious.

"That's what I am," he said irritably, "an object of suspicion. The boy frankly tells me so! I'm a fool, and I get more deeply involved each day. Yet what can I do? It would be the worst ingratitude to leave them now in their trouble. But until I leave I can't help them. I've certainly put myself in a strange position."

He sighed heavily and then flicked the horses with his whip, as though they were to blame. As they quickened their steps and hurried him homeward, he continued to make himself miserable over the efforts he could make for the Elliotts, provided he was in their eyes what he was in reality.

Seated in the train, speeding toward college and trouble, Colin Elliott went over his recent interview with a half smile on his face. How ridiculous to think of *John* offering him money! But it was kind of him and showed warmheartedness. The fellow should be helped. Why wasn't Hilda trying to? Then he smiled again over the folly of that thought. Poor Hilda, who always seemed to shoulder the family burdens—hadn't he just laid a heavy one on her? Doubtless, too, she was doing what she could for John. She wouldn't be his sister Hilda if she weren't.

This thought reminded him of a note thrust into his vest pocket. Hilda had handed it to him as she bade him good-bye. "Read that when you're quite alone," she'd said. It was doubtless some added word of sympathy for him in his trouble or a suggestion as to the way out. Dear Hilda! She lay awake half the night probably, thinking of him, while he, after sitting with his father until midnight, was so tired from the day's excitement he put everything from him and slept like a schoolboy.

He glanced about him at his fellow passengers. The train was full enough;

nevertheless, he felt quite alone. Not a face there invited his attention. He would read the note and see what suggestion Hilda offered. She was level-headed, and anything she thought out was worthy of consideration.

Dear Colin,

I went over your affairs a hundred times, I think, last night and found no light or comfort until I suddenly remembered a direction I once resolved to follow: 'Casting all your care upon him, for he careth for you.' I proved it once more, taking the whole matter, with all its possible entanglements, to Jesus Christ. When I arose from my knees, no circumstance was in any way changed, of course—yet my weight of anxiety was gone! I felt sure you'd be brought safely through and that the experience would work for your good. Do you know what I thought next? 'Oh, if Colin only prayed!' It does seem strange, Colin, dear, that you're not willing to try that simple remedy for all ills, which has never been known to fail. Won't you let me ask you once more, more earnestly, if possible, than ever before, to take it all to Christ?

Now I can almost hear your old refrain about being a goat and therefore having no right to the sheep's pasturage. But you know that's simply a merry way of begging a serious question. Suppose a sheep persisted in remaining outside with the goats, though offered all the protection and privileges of the sheepfold? But I don't mean to preach. I only want to ask you earnestly if, in this crisis in your life, you won't test Jesus Christ."

The young man slowly folded the note and laid it away. Its contents were different from what he'd imagined. He couldn't tell why the simple words appealed to him so forcefully. It wasn't the first or even perhaps the hundredth time Hilda had, in one form or another, pleaded for him to become a man of prayer.

He'd always put her petitions aside with cheerful courtesy, mentally resolving to give attention to the matter sometime or other. With this concession he'd always turned his thoughts quickly into another channel. This morning he couldn't. In vain he tried to concentrate on his present problems. He must arrange an interview with President Chambers to apologize for some of his rude words the evening before and plan how to explain his absence from the city on the Tuesday evening in question, without confessing he'd spent it at the notorious Wayside House, where several college men had already encountered disgrace. Above all, he needed to plan some feasible theory concerning the disappearance of that fifty-dollar note. He couldn't think consecutively about any of these matters.

Instead, his brain kept repeating that last sentence: "I only want to ask you earnestly if, in this crisis in your life, you won't test Jesus Christ." That was a startling way of putting it! Almost irreverent, if it had come from any other pen than Hilda's. Had one a right to talk about testing God? Straightway came to mind an old verse learned in childhood: "Bring ye all the tithes into the store-house, and prove me now herewith, saith the Lord." Wasn't that a challenge to be tested?

As Hilda intimated, he and Ellen actually jested together about their being goats, while the others in the family were of the best sheep in the fold. But on this particular morning it didn't seem like a jest. He didn't want to be left out, homeless. He wanted to claim eternal kinship with that blessed father and mother of his. Then he thought of how pale his father looked after the fever went down and how the hand he'd held out to grasp his had trembled. That kind hand had never failed him in any need! If God really were like a father, how much he needed Him now! To tell his story to his blessed earthly father would be such a relief! If he only knew how to go that way to God! Certainly that was how Hilda understood religion. There was no sham to her, not the merest shadow of make-believe.

He tried to determine just what his own belief was. He'd experienced, at given times in his life, what might be called sentimentalisms. That is, his emotional nature had been reached by some powerful appeal to it in the name of religion. But he was never moved enough for action. The impression this morning was different. There was nothing in Hilda's note to excite him or awaken emotion; yet he felt himself arraigned, as before an invisible judge, to account for his position.

He believed in prayer, of course; his father's son couldn't have done less. But just what did he believe regarding it? Why, this, beyond question: A human being could secure audience with One, known in history as Jesus Christ, a divine being, infinite in wisdom and power and love—therefore, A being both able and willing to befriend him. Why, then, if he were a person of average common sense, did he hold himself aloof from the help that such a belief undoubtedly afforded? Why shouldn't this powerful Friend be his friend? Why shouldn't the promise his parents and sister leaned on, the promise of divine guidance for the asking, be his also?

He confessed that often, as he looked into his sister's pure face and earnest eyes, he was reminded of a Bible verse learned in his early boyhood about some persons who noticed certain others that they'd been with Jesus. He admitted that if he were inclined to be skeptical, his sister's consecrated life would prove an unanswerable argument.

But he wasn't skeptical. Nothing he studied in the schools seemed clearer or more certain than the fundamental verities of the Christian religion. Only a few days before, in a casual conversation with some students, during which certain skeptical sentiments had been advanced, he assured the speaker he had three volumes of the Evidences of Christianity in the persons of his father and mother and sister. Any fellow who studied them would as soon doubt the daily sunrise as question the foundations on which their living was built.

He recalled his promptness in making that response and told himself he was an inconsistent fellow, unworthy of credence. How was he proving he was any better than a boy who had no mother, a mean father and a sister without brains? He knew certain boys whose home life might be thus described. If he honestly believed what he professed to the boys, why not avail himself of the offered help? He certainly was in trouble. He might put it aside for the time with the assurance of a way out; yet he was conscious of an undertone of grave anxiety.

"That's an awfully selfish motive. You should be ashamed to go to God the first time for any such reason." He didn't recognize the enemy of souls as the speaker, but his good sense made immediate answer. "What of it?"

A selfish motive would prompt him to seek human help. Yet if a human friend were available now, one he thought had both ability and desire to help him, it wouldn't take him two minutes to decide to seek him and lay the case before him. He could conceive of a man great enough to overlook past indifference upon his part, and even slights, and come to his aid. Such people existed; undoubtedly such fathers did. Didn't he know that if he were the worthless creature President Chambers evidently considered him and yet went frankly to his father with the story of his trouble, he'd be met more than halfway and helped to the extent of that father's ability? Why was it an incredible thing that God, who had chosen to name himself Father, would do as much?

Yet let him be sincere in this matter. He wouldn't go even to his earthly father without being ready to say to him, "Father, I've done wrong. I've gone contrary to what you would advise and have brought this trouble on myself largely by my folly. I don't mean to get into this sort of scrape again. I mean to follow your footsteps after this as well as I can." Was he ready to make such a statement to a Father in heaven?

Had he counted the cost? Yet what was it? What must he do to become a member of this family and claim the privileges of sonship? It seemed wonderful afterward to remember how often words he learned in childhood appeared before him during that morning's conference, ready to answer his questions authoritatively. One came now: "What doth the Lord thy God require of thee, but to fear the Lord thy God, to walk in all his ways, and to love him, and to serve the Lord thy God with all thy heart and with all thy soul?"

They were tremendous obligations, he knew, yet reasonable, remembering who he was and what he knew of God. Hadn't he always intended to give this subject serious attention sometime? Didn't he believe it was every man's duty to use his common sense in this, as in all other matters, and act according to his best judgment? Those fellows with bad habits to give up, who didn't care to make the best they could of their lives, had excuses for delaying that he hadn't. He believed he'd simply been a fool not to settle such important questions. He didn't know why he hadn't, or why they persisted now in being thought of. It was useless to push them aside with the excuse he had other matters requiring immediate attention.

Instead of searching for President Chambers, as he'd intended to do when he reached the college grounds, he went directly to his own room and locked the door. He sat with folded arms staring straight into nothingness for an hour or longer, thinking as he'd never thought before. He recalled later losing for the time all memory even of what awaited him in college; this one subject asserted its claims. At the close of the time he arose with the air of one who had settled something, crossed over to the window, drew down the shade and dropped upon his knees.

"Jackson," said President Chambers that afternoon, "did Elliott return by the morning train?"

"Yes, sir, he came in at eleven o'clock."

"Do you know where he is?"

"He went directly to his room, sir, and I haven't seen him since. I noticed particularly that he didn't come out for his twelve o'clock hour."

"Jackson, go to his room and say I'd like to see him immediately."

Jackson bowed himself away and in a brief time returned alone.

"Well," said President Chambers, "did you find him?"

"Yes, sir, he's in his room, but—"

"Did you give him my message?"

"No, sir, I didn't. He's—engaged, sir, and I didn't think you'd like to have him disturbed. I didn't even knock at the door."

"Indeed! What's the nature of an engagement so important in your eyes that you can't deliver a message from me? Is it visible through the keyhole?"

"No, sir, I didn't see him, but I heard him. To tell you the truth, sir, he is praying."

A sudden softened look spread over the president's face; he didn't know Colin Elliott ever had engagements like that.

"Very well," he said to the waiting Jackson, "you did right. Watch your opportunity and send Elliott to me as soon as he's disengaged."

Chapter 19

As soon as he was permitted to enter the office, Colin Elliott walked straight toward the president and spoke rapidly: "President Chambers, I was just coming to ask if I might speak with you for a moment, when Jackson told me you'd sent for me. I want to ask your pardon, sir, for the disrespectful words I spoke last night. I was so excited and angry I didn't realize what I was saying. I told you the truth, sir, in every detail. But I can see on reflection that under the circumstances you're perhaps justified in not believing me. In any case, I shouldn't have said what I did."

"Sit down, Elliott," said President Chambers, motioning the young man to a seat. "I want to talk with you. There are two of us, it seems. I sent for you to tell you I evidently spoke last night without due consideration. Within an hour after my words with you, I learned information that proved the truth of your statements regarding the Belmont House disgrace. I'm more glad than I can say to find out you weren't present that evening and aren't in any way associated with it. At the same time I learned another thing that caused me pain. Will you tell me where you were on Tuesday evening?"

Elliott's face flushed, but he answered quickly, "I'll tell you, sir, though I don't like to do so. I spent the evening and greater part of the night at a country hotel called the Wayside, about five miles from my home. It's a disreputable place, and my father has never approved of my stopping there, even on business. Nevertheless, I thought I had business that evening which would justify my going."

"Will you tell me the nature of the business?"

"In part, yes. I had reason to fear a young person in our neighborhood had been led into trouble and was in danger of being led further. On the impulse of the moment I went out there to learn the truth, if possible. It came to nothing, and I'm sorry I went. But that's where I was on Tuesday night."

The president's face lighted with the semblance of a smile. "I'm very glad to hear it," he said heartily. "For one thing I'm glad to have an authentic witness to what occurred at the Wayside that evening. I'm not unaware some of our own students planned that choice entertainment, and I need hardly tell you the circumstances connected with it will be carefully inquired into. You may be able to do the college a service by helping us put down this kind of wrongdoing. I congratulate you on learning that none of the girls of your own neighborhood was implicated in the matter.

"Now," he continued, "regarding the fifty-dollar banknote you left at Wellingtons,' no light has been thrown upon its mysterious disappearance. But, in view of the light that has come to me from other sources, I'm prepared to ask your pardon for my last night's insinuations and to assure you I take your word now that you did as you said."

For the first time since his troubles had come upon him Colin Elliott felt a choking sensation in his throat and knew that, if he'd been a girl, he'd have burst into tears.

"Thank you," he said with difficulty. "It's very good of you after all the lies you overheard me tell in fun. But I assure you, sir, I never told a lie in earnest in my life. I could hardly belong to my father's family and not be true."

"I can well believe that," said the president heartily. "I know your family very well, and I knew your grandfather. But I wonder if I may remind you that when you get your sport in such ways you're playing with edged tools?"

Colin's face flushed deeply. "I'd think myself an idiot," he said, "if I hadn't learned that lesson now. But, sir, what's become of the fifty-dollar note?"

The president shook his head. "I don't know, Elliott. We won't go into that. It's one of the mysteries that may never be explained. Suffice it to say, I entirely exonerate you from all blame in the matter."

"But I can't have it left so, sir. It *must* be found! Two of us will suffer unjustly all our lives if it isn't."

"You gave it to young Esterbrook, Elliott?"

"I laid it down before his eyes, and he said he'd attend to it in a moment and would send up the receipt."

"And you have entire confidence in Esterbrook?"

"I'd as soon think of my appropriating the money as of his doing it!"

"I'm glad to hear you say so. I, too, have strong confidence in that young man. So, as I say, it must for the present remain a mystery. But let me repeat my assurance—"

Just at that moment came a knock at the door, and Jackson appeared.

"A note for you, sir, marked 'Haste!' "

The president took the note, broke the seal and glanced through the contents, with a smile growing on his face as he read. Rising, he walked over to Elliott and held out his hand.

"Let me congratulate you, my boy. I'm glad I assured you of my perfect faith in your word. The missing note is found—and without even the dignity of a thief in the matter. Esterbrook is humiliated to the dust to find it with some refuse paper in his own wastebasket!"

That afternoon John Stuart made the Elliott horses travel faster than they'd ever been known to do in their short and easy lives. He left them at the gate uncared for, while he hurried into the kitchen and intercepted Hilda on her way to her father's room with a tray of tea and toast.

"A telegram for you, Miss Elliott." As he spoke, he took the tray from trembling hands and waited while they tore open the fateful yellow messenger.

Mrs. Elliott, coming at that moment from the sickroom, waited, her face pale. Then Hilda laughed, and her mother's heart went on beating again.

"What is it, dear?"

"It's from Colin, Mother. It says, 'Ok. Halleluah!' He was having some trouble in college that he didn't want you worried with, and now he's safely out of it."

"Trouble in college!" repeated Mrs. Elliott, wonderingly. "About his studies, do you mean? Hilda, your father's calling." Hilda was spared replying.

Her way through difficulties was less bright than Colin's had been. She found it very hard to determine just what should be done. The interview with John wasn't as trying as she'd expected. She said that, if it were only one of her scholars to whom she was indebted for shielding Ellen, she could be grateful. Behold, it was Thomas, the dullard and blunderer!

John kept his share of the proceedings in the background. From his standpoint what he did was the merest commonplace that would have been done, of course, by any employee of Mr. Elliott.

Hilda felt soothed by his manner. But, no sooner had she left him, than she began to reflect that it wasn't like the average working man's. Once or twice he appeared strangely embarrassed, beginning a sentence that sounded almost helpful and suddenly ceasing before it was completed. Did he know more than he chose to tell her? No, that couldn't be; his story had been direct and explicit. He hadn't hesitated or compelled her to question him for particulars; yet there was something strange about him.

She dismissed him from her mind and took up Ellen's problem. Could she wait until her father was better and ask his advice? No. Circumstances settled that point promptly. Despite John Stuart's vigorous efforts, which she knew nothing about, painful publicity was given to the affair. A scandal, such as gossips love to feed upon, had arisen concerning that evening at the Wayside House. Reporters traveled everywhere, hungry for every detail and skillful in putting together details that needed a microscope to make them fit the central story. Under such circumstances it became impossible to keep hints about Ellen out of the daily papers. Her name was mercifully and by great effort suppressed. But certain reporters know how to prepare a dish so marked in its flavor that, although its initials aren't given, those who pass may recognize it.

They found an efficient helper in Laura Holcombe, who had been sharply reprimanded by her parents for her share in the disgrace. Sulky, she took revenge by telling all she knew about the correspondence between "El Elliott" and the unknown college boy, and the engagement to drive with him without her own family's knowledge. Laura had even discovered John's share in that evening's program, and this made a toothsome morsel for the reporters.

Laura Holcombe wasn't malicious to that extent and even cried when she found some of her talk had made it to the papers and was plain enough for all acquainted with the locality to understand. She hadn't meant to brew deep mischief for her friend, but simply to talk, while she was angry and could find interested listeners, who weren't too scrupulous in repeating what they heard.

Possibly it was a salutary and certainly a much-needed lesson for Laura. They'd selected two names from the college catalogue and written each a letter. Laura Holcombe fully understood that because the name she happened to choose belonged to a gentleman, who paid no attention to it, she wasn't in a similar plight with her friend. No, I'm wrong; it's doubtful she would, under any circumstances, have gotten herself into such a plight. She understood this wicked world much better than Ellen did and belonged to that wretched class of human beings who can urge another on to depths they themselves are too wise to descend. The one had sinned ignorantly, as a child; the other had held back like a girl who knew too much about the world of sin.

And the older sister, weeping and praying, realized what today's sisters and mothers are slow to learn, that ignorance is not a shield. If she'd only talked more plainly with Ellie, instead of trying to shelter her and keep her ignorant of the dangers lying in wait for the unwary!

Meanwhile, she worked as well as prayed. That photograph, which should never have been sent, must be recovered. After careful deliberation she resolved to write for it herself; no one else could do it. She considered putting the matter into Colin's hands and decided not to. Colin was young and not too discreet where his feelings were engaged, and he was in the same building with the offender. A serious quarrel might result if he had an interview with him.

She wrote the letter, as Hilda Elliott could write on occasion. Let us hope Augustus Sayre Hooper arose from its perusal with, for once, a true opinion of himself. He wrote a reply that made Hilda's indignation burn, but he returned the photograph. The sarcasms in his letter may have been increased because he wasn't finding the transgressor's way easy. The phials of President Chamber's wrath were poured out upon him, and prompt expulsion from college followed investigation. His only solace was he didn't suffer alone. He may also have found a drop of comfort in realizing the results of his ill-doings weren't so far-reaching or disastrous as those of two of his boon companions.

It was, of course, impossible to save Colin from knowing Ellen's share in the disgrace. The evening papers would have enlightened him, if he'd heard it from no other source. His pain and shame, when the astounding facts were revealed to him, would be difficult to describe. He told Hilda afterward that, but for President Chamber's thoughtful sympathy and unfailing kindness, it seemed to him he should have died. To think the ignorant country girl he rushed away to warn and save was his own beautiful young sister, his darling.

"It's a factory town, sir," he'd explained to the president, before he knew this terrible fact. "Dozens of girls there are densely ignorant of life's common proprieties. My sister is trying to help them every way she can, and I thought it might be one she was interested in."

"I understand," President Chambers had said. "It was noble of you, Elliott."

But his voice had had a curious, almost pitying, note in it. Colin wondered at the time, and his face burned over it afterward. Even then, probably, President Chambers had known who the girl was! Smarting under the shame of it, he wrote a letter to his young sister he regretted later, and she cried over it as nothing up to that time had made her cry.

In truth, she, poor girl, was having a lesson that might suffice for a lifetime. She had all but broken the heart of her father and mother, for the day came when they had to know, and made the faces of brother and sister flush with shame for her. But the neighborhood, that portion of it least to be respected, got hold of scraps of her story and imagined more and tossed it back and forth on rude, careless tongues. Many looked askance at her and spoke of her as "that Elliott girl" and said no wonder her father was so ill; it's a wonder he didn't die. They always thought El Elliott a bold-acting girl and guessed Hilda's pride would be taken down a little now. Other helpful and sympathetic words came, by one source and another, back to Ellen until she fairly shunned the daylight and was in such a deplorably nervous state it was judged wise to keep her out of school. This Hilda regretted for her bitterly, knowing what an ordeal it would be for her when she must return.

The day came speedily to this watchful sister when she felt only pity for the poor flower whose brightness had been crushed before time for her to bloom. Undoubtedly she'd done wrong and should have known better. But then she'd sinned so ignorantly and childishly; she honestly believed in the fine theories Augustus Sayre Hooper spun for her on paper. She thought a friend rich, wise and powerful had been introduced through her to the family and would do vaguely wonderful things for Colin and the rest of them.

Hilda, as she went carefully over the letters, anxious to know just how much poison had been scattered through them, admitted the young man had a talent for writing. Most of the letters were sparkling with fun. The compliments, though lavish, were so gracefully worded it wasn't surprising one as young Ellen had been pleased with them. To Hilda's older eyes was an offensive undertone that showed her distinctly from what depths of shame and pain their darling had probably been rescued. If the child had only shown her the letters! Why wasn't this done? Why weren't she and Ellen so intimate that nothing like this could have been carried on without her knowledge? There wasn't such a great difference in their ages that confidential relations between them should be unreasonable; she was just over four years older. Had she been too much absorbed in her more mature and cultivated tastes, so the child had instinctively drawn away from her as unsympathetic? Couldn't she have interested herself more in the merry schoolgirl's pursuits and plans if she'd tried and so shielded her?

Searching thoughts were hers while reading those letters, and strong resolves were born of them. Resolutions near breaking within the hour—it tried her so to see Ellen weeping bitterly over the burning of those same letters.

"I can't help it," sobbed the girl. "He may not be good, but his letters were lovely. Nobody will ever write such nice things to me again. People look at me as though I weren't fit to speak to, and I didn't mean any harm. I don't believe he knows he's done wrong; he wouldn't do anything to hurt me for the world."

Then the sister knew she must be wise and patient; more than mere fun was involved in her sister's dangerous escapade. The young villain had reached and awakened her girlish heart.

Chapter 20

The most bewildering of Hilda's experiences during this trying time concerned Nannie Marvin, the playmate of her childhood and the closest friend of her young womanhood.

She went over one afternoon to the Marvin farm, armed with Nell's returned photograph and the resolution strong upon her to tell both Mr. and Mrs. Marvin what occurred and make what excuse she could for her poor young sister.

Nevertheless, she admitted to herself relief that Mr. and Mrs. Marvin were away from home for the day, and therefore she could have the first talk with Nannie alone. It shouldn't be hard to talk to Nannie. The main features of the story she knew already; everybody in the neighborhood did. The trouble was, they knew much more about it than facts would justify.

Hilda, therefore, began at the beginning and told every detail as briefly as she could, shielding Ellen as much as downright honesty would permit. She wasn't a little pained over Nannie's silence during this recital. She expected to find the Marvins in a thoroughly indignant frame of mind and realized they might find it hard to forgive Ellen for placing their young daughter in such a questionable position. Of course Nannie must share this feeling; yet lurking in her heart was the hope that Nannie, being so young and merry, would understand how childishly and ignorantly it was done and how far Ellen was, even now, from understanding what a gross wrong she'd done her friend.

She thought Nannie would interrupt her with some such suggestion and possibly a sympathetic word. She did nothing of the kind. No sphinx could have sat more silently and immovably through the entire story. When at last she spoke, her words were entirely different from those her friend had expected or hoped for.

"After all, Hilda, what was the use in telling me this? It doesn't do Nell or anybody else any good, as far as I can see. You have the photograph back, and it belongs to Colin's collection. Why didn't you put it up with the others and let it go? The beloved public doesn't know the photograph part of the story so far; probably they won't. Why does anybody need to know that?"

Hilda gave her a surprised, pained look and couldn't keep reproach from her voice: "Why, Nannie! How could I do such a thing?"

"Why couldn't you? That's what I'm asking. You wouldn't harm anybody by silence, and in a sense it would have shielded Ellie. Nell cannot very well help being angry when she hears of it. As for Father and Mother, I don't know what they'll say. Father is so terribly particular about such things. He's like you. If I'd been you, I'd have kept it still. But I know you well enough to be sure your dreadful conscience will give you no rest until you tell Father and Mother every turn of the story. You should have lived in the days of the martyrs, Hilda. Did you have no temptation to a different course?"

"Temptation?" said Hilda hesitantly, with heightened color on her face. "I don't think I thought of it as a temptation, but perhaps it was. The thought came to me that, if the story of the photograph wasn't known, it might cause less pain to others to have nothing said about it. But you're quite right, Nannie. I couldn't get the consent of my conscience to such a course; it savored too strongly of deception. Besides, such things always get out. I've been expecting every hour to hear fearfully exaggerated accounts of it all. To come to you then with the truth would have been much more humiliating than now. That thought made the right course plain to me, because I realized I'd be ashamed to have it known I had the truth from the beginning. No, I've thought it over, Nannie, trying to learn the right thing to do. The more I've thought and prayed, the more firm the conviction has become that in this case, as in most others, entire frankness was the safer and wiser course. I've told you now all there is to tell. No stories, however garbled, should add to your anxiety or annoyance. Suppose I'd kept back portions of the truth and had to confess them in pieces afterward. Don't you see how instantly you'd be troubled with the thought, 'Perhaps there's still more she doesn't choose to tell'? As it is, I believe you'll trust me."

"Oh, trust you!" said Nannie impatiently. "No one ever had any doubts about that. You're fearfully frank, Hilda. If it's possible to carry sincerity into fanaticism and almost into sin, you do it. I tell you, if I'd been you, I'd have kept entirely still about Nell's photograph. Poor El has had enough to bear because of her silly little venture into a hateful world. I don't believe Nell will make life any easier for her because of it. Nell is older than I am, Hilda, already. She's inclined to be prudish, or over particular, like some other people I could mention." This last she said with an attempt at merriment. "Not that I'm sorry, of course, that she's growing up to be such a discreet young woman. But still, I confess to feeling sympathetic with the giddy ones who play with edged tools while they're children and cry about it afterward. If El had come to me with her escapades, I'd have shielded and petted her into common sense again, and neither you nor anybody else would have been the wiser."

Hilda arose to go. No good could result from prolonging such an interview. "I've helped Ellie as well as I knew how," she said sadly, "and shielded her in every way that seemed right. But I can't go contrary to my ideas of right to shield anybody. One must have 'a conscience void of offense' in God's sight if one is to have any comfort in life. Poor Ellie is having a bitter lesson. But my hope for her is that, when she fully realizes her wrongdoing, she won't shield herself at the expense of truth. I don't think I'm fanatical, Nannie. I wouldn't go up and down the streets, blazoning any story. I hope this one may be kept from the public as much as possible. Certainly I'll speak of it just to your own family; they're the only ones who have a right to know the facts.

"What I said was, things always get out in mysterious ways. Perhaps the way may not be so mysterious this time. Laura Holcombe is trying to put all the wrong on Ellie and leave herself blameless. She, of course, knows about the photographs. I presume she'll tell it. I don't know why she hasn't already. That's Ellie's misfortune. I'd gladly shield her from it if I could. But I saw no honorable way except to tell you the whole. She didn't; she agreed with me that Nell must know and that your father and mother must be told, as a matter of course. I don't think she could be happy again if it had been managed any other way."

"She's caught the disease from you," said Nannie, still trying to speak lightly. "I'm glad I'm not your sister! You may be sure I won't speak of the photograph. And, if I had my way, even now Mother and Father wouldn't be troubled with it. But I can see there's no use arguing with you."

"My father doesn't think anything other than the exact truth would be honorable treatment of your father," said Hilda coldly. Then she left, not trusting herself to say more than a muffled good-bye.

As she walked slowly homeward she went over the interview in sorrowful detail. She hadn't realized how much she'd counted on a word of real sympathy from her one intimate friend. She couldn't understand the strange change in the girl; her standard of right and wrong didn't use to be so low. As unlike as possible in general appearance and ways of speaking, she supposed that on all vital points they thought much alike. Only lately Nannie seemed to be drifting away from her old views. It couldn't be Rex Hartwell's influence; he hadn't changed, unless he stood on higher ground than he once occupied. She recalled the faithful work he was doing at the schoolhouse among her boys, giving up one of his cherished evenings, and remembered the stand certain boys had taken lately, moved by Rex's influence, and exonerated him from blame. But it was bitter to lose her girlhood friend this way.

Could she have seen Nannie within ten minutes after her departure, her bewilderment and anxiety on her account would have deepened.

That young woman, as soon as the door closed after her friend, locked it and even slipped the bolt, as though that would make her more entirely alone; then she flung herself on the bed and buried her face in the pillows with bitter weeping. Not quiet tears, but a passionate outburst like an excited child. She knew she was alone in the house and perhaps, for that reason, gave fuller vent to her emotions.

"Oh! What shall I do? What *shall* I do?" Again and again this wailing cry filled the silent room, followed by relative quiet, then excited exclamations.

"I never can! I never will! She needn't talk to me this way. What are El Elliott's babyish pranks and Nell's old photograph compared with this? She as good as told me to my face I could never be happy again. Oh! I know it! I can never respect myself again. Respect! I hate myself. And Rex would hate me, if he knew. I can never do it, and I don't believe it's the only right way. Hilda is hard! She's insane over that word 'truth.' I hate the word; I wish I'd never heard it. As if there were no other virtue except hard, cold truth! And the more mischief it could work, the more virtuous she considers it to speak! What mischief the truth could work in this case! And silence could harm nobody.

"To think my wedding day is in a few weeks, and I have such burdens to bear! If anybody but me had discovered the truth, I could have borne it. Or if it had been as we thought in the first place, I wouldn't have cared. I'd grown used to it and didn't feel so badly about it. But to think of it now, after Rex has arranged everything, drives me wild. I won't think anymore about it. Hilda Elliott may preach the rest of her days and look at me out of her eyes, as if they were plate glass and would show me my real self through them! I wish I didn't need to see her again.

"I'm doing right," she told herself. "I know I am. I'm not to be turned from it by a sentimental girl who doesn't know anything about life and has never been tried for herself. It's easy enough to confess the faults of others. Why didn't she make poor little El come and tell us? She thinks there's only what she calls Truth in the world.

"What about the fifth commandment? I must think of my poor father, who's struggled all his life under debt, and my mother, who's growing old far too fast with her cares. Can I force back the burdens Rex is ready to lift from them both?

"Oh! What *shall* I do? I'm *so wretched!* And I thought I'd be so happy! I'd like to die and get away from it all. But I don't suppose I'm ready to die; I know I'm not. I can't even pray anymore. As surely as I kneel down this hateful thing must come and stare at me and insist upon being thought about.

"It's a wonder I haven't gone insane; perhaps I shall. I know exactly how people feel who are tormented day and night with a single thought that won't leave them for a moment. I'm growing cross and hateful under the strain. I never treated Hilda as I have lately. I treat everybody badly. I've seen Mother look at me sometimes, as if she couldn't understand. I'm even cross at Rex, and he's so persistently good. What's to become of me if this continues? Will I never have happiness or peace again?" The outburst was followed by another passion of tears.

She didn't overrate her change. Interested friends had been watching her anxiously for some time and commenting on her failing health. Some of them thought Rex Hartwell should hasten the marriage and give Nannie the rest she evidently needed. She was probably trying to save her mother and so over-doing. Others thought she was killing herself trying to manage a wardrobe in keeping with her future position—so foolish! Why didn't she let Rex supply the wardrobe afterward? Still another class felt sure Rex Hartwell should have sense enough to manage the money question beforehand. It was ridiculous for a man with thousands of ready money in the bank to let his wife kill herself preparing to marry him.

The Marvins and a few intimate friends knew Nannie's bridal preparations were very simple and that Rex had exhausted his ingenuity in efforts to assist her with money. They were at a loss to understand why a girl for whom life was about to bloom in all its beauty, apparently without a thorn, had dark rings gathering under her eyes, admitted to almost sleepless nights and grew daily nervous and irritable. When trials of poverty were heaviest, her mother often said she took fresh heart whenever she saw Nannie's sunny face. But now she carried a daily anxiety that poverty had never forced upon her and could only wonder, wait, and pray.

Hilda's call that day marked a crisis in her friend's life. The girl lay prone on her bed for an hour or more, breaking the silence only by detached exclamations, specimens of which have been given. Then for another hour she lay wide awake, but so quiet that intense work of some sort must have been done. After that she arose, bathed from face and eyes as much trace of tears as possible, rearranged her disordered dress and hair, then sat down to her writing table and prepared the following brief, imperative message:

> *Dear Rex,*
>
> *I know it isn't your evening to come, but you must come nevertheless. Don't let anything hinder you. I must see you tonight without fail and as early as possible. I have something very important to tell you, something that cannot wait another day.*
>
> *Nannie*

This letter she gave to John Stuart as he drove by on his way to town, instructing him to place on it a special delivery stamp and have it go in that afternoon's mail.

Thus summoned, Rex Hartwell excused himself from an evening class at the medical college, with what skill he could, and took the six o'clock train out, arriving at the Marvin farm just before eight.

Nannie was still alone. Her father and mother were in town for a day of shopping and errands. The younger portion of the family had gone in the farm wagon to meet them at the station, not so disappointed as they might have been, under other circumstances, to have Nannie refuse to accompany them. They hadn't known until the last moment that Rex was expected that evening.

"I wonder why Rex is coming tonight? I thought he had a class. He'd better take care of himself. Nan is doing high tragedy tonight and looks as if she might shoot him." This came from Kate, the family hoyden, who always excused any unladylike conduct on her part by stating she should have been a boy and was trying to atone to her father and mother for the disappointment.

"I wonder what's wrong with Nannie?" added Lillian, her next in age and most intimate sister. "She hasn't been herself for weeks. If getting ready to be married has such an effect on everybody's nerves, I hope I'll never have to go through the ordeal."

Then Alice, more staid and thoughtful than either of her older sisters, said, "Mother's afraid Nannie isn't well. She's very anxious about her, and Nan certainly hasn't acted like herself for a long time. But I suppose, when she's married and settled down, she'll feel differently."

"Isn't it fun," said Kate, "to think of Nan as a rich woman, able to go where she likes and buy what she likes? But she doesn't seem to see much fun in it. I said a lot of stuff to her this morning about how I looked forward to talking to the girls about 'my sister, Mrs. Hartwell,' who's abroad this winter or spending the summer at Bar Harbor or Niagara or some other grand place. But she didn't laugh. I think it vexed her. Her face grew red, and that odd look she has lately came in her eyes. She just said: 'Don't be a simpleton, if you can help it. There's more to getting married than going abroad and having a good time.' "

"She acts odd," said Nell, the youngest Marvin. "I read a story about a girl who acted much as she does. But she was marrying a man she didn't like. She hated him even. That isn't the way with Nannie, is it? She just idolizes Rex. If anything happened that she couldn't marry him, it would kill her."

Chapter 21

W hile her sisters freely discussed her affairs, Nannie Marvin waited alone for her intended husband's arrival. Even a casual observer would have discovered she was in a state of intense though suppressed excitement. She was carefully dressed and had perhaps never looked prettier than on that evening she felt was such a fateful one to her. She was relieved at being alone in the house. For days her sisters' good-natured comments and her mother's anxious surveillance had all but tortured her. Yet she started nervously at every sound and, when at last she heard well-known footsteps on the walk, alternately flushed and paled, as a girl might have done watching for her lover after an absence of months, instead of one she parted from the day before. She sat quite still. She felt she hadn't strength enough to step into the hall and open the old-fashioned farmhouse door.

As it happened, he didn't wait for her. He'd met the young girls at the station and learned Nannie was alone. So he let himself into the hospitable door that, after the fashion of the neighborhood, was rarely locked and, pausing only to tap at the parlor door, opened that also and went toward her.

He recognized at once her unusual excitement; indeed, he'd read it in her hurried note. More than one perplexed hour he'd spent lately trying to determine what was troubling Nannie. Was she breaking in health just now, when the long struggle with poverty was over and he was about to place her in that position she was suited to grace? Long before this, he made it unnecessary for her to worry about the future of her parents or sisters. He insisted upon frankness regarding these matters, reminding Nannie she'd be able to give practical help to the young people. Schools, musical advantages and those perplexities called clothes, he rejoiced to remember, fell largely within the power of money. He took pleasure in impressing upon Nannie it was simply her duty to plan what she'd like for her sisters.

As for the mortgage resting heavily for years on her father's shoulders, it was a thing of the past; the prospective son-in-law flatly refused to wait until he was formally admitted into the family before disposing of it. He'd looked forward to the pleasure he'd give Nannie in presenting the cancelled papers to her father, but it wasn't a happy time. Instead of smiles and gratitude, the bewildering girl gave herself up to what were evidently bitter tears. The next morning she confessed to her mother her night had been almost sleepless, and she went about more heavy eyed and far more "nervous" than before.

All things considered, Rex Hartwell was counting the days when he could take Nannie away from surroundings that seemed to be wearing her out.

On the evening in question she didn't rise to meet him but sat erect in the straightest and most uncompromising chair the room contained. A strange pallor was on her face, despite two small spots burning on either cheek, and her eyes shone like stars.

"What is it, Nannie, dear?" he asked, bending over her. "I'm afraid you're not well tonight. I hurried after receiving your summons and was relieved to hear from the girls, whom I met at the station, that you were much as usual. But I think they're mistaken; you're not well."

"Sit down!" commanded Nannie. "No, I don't want that," she said as he drew an easy chair forward and prepared to place her in it. "I want to sit here, where I am, and you take that seat opposite me. I have something to tell you. I don't want you close beside me, Rex. I can't talk so well. I told you in my note I had something very important to tell you. I want you to sit where I can see every change on your face, and I want you to help me if you can. Oh, I need help! It is very hard!

"Rex, we cannot be married at Christmas. We can *never* be married! You won't want me to be your wife when you've heard my story. Don't interrupt me, please," she said with an imperative gesture when he would have spoken eagerly. "Wait till you hear what I have to say. I thought I couldn't tell it, but I must and will. I will if it kills me. Oh, Rex!" She stopped suddenly and placed both hands over her heart, as if to steady its beating. But when he sprang toward her she motioned him back.

"Never mind—it's nothing. I'm not sick. Don't come, please. Sit there, where I told you. It's true, as I said. We cannot be married. I can't decide what you'll think, when you hear what I've done—or haven't done. Yes, I can. You'll think it's terrible, and it is. I can see it plainly now. Yet I made myself believe it wasn't so very bad—that, in fact, it was the right thing to do.

"Perhaps I'd have kept on thinking so but for Hilda Elliott. She's awful, Rex, *awful!* Don't interrupt me. I'm going to tell you the whole as that girl did at the schoolhouse that night—do you remember? It seems as if I should have as much courage as she, doesn't it? Rex, I *found the will!* The lost one—you understand? I found it a long time ago and kept it a secret. Oh! I didn't hide it away—don't think that. I found it by accident, when I wasn't looking for or even remembering it. And I made myself believe, for a time, that because I happened upon it that way, so long after everything was settled and everybody satisfied, there could be no harm in just keeping still. Oh, Rex, don't look at me that way! Can't you look—some other way?"

"My poor little girl!" Rex Hartwell's voice, though grave, was tender. Again he arose, but she waved him back.

"No, hear the rest. I must tell it all now. I'd *die* if I had to keep it to myself another hour. That old secretary in your uncle's room—you know how many times we went through it—and the lawyer's clerk, the detective and I don't know how many more—and found nothing? Well, I wasn't even hunting, remember. I'd given up all idea of finding that will. I believed your uncle destroyed it and meant you to have his money.

"Do you remember when the housekeeper wrote asking me to go up to the house and look under the rug in your uncle's room for her lost ring? It was the only place she could think of where she hadn't looked, and she remembered pushing it back and forth on her finger that last time she talked with him. Do you remember you couldn't get away from the office to go with me, so I went alone? I found it then. Now you know how long I've waited! I had to push the old secretary out of its corner. As I pushed it and slipped behind to take up the corner of the rug—I knew that poor woman's marriage ring wasn't there, but I meant to search as thoroughly as possible for it—I saw a bit of paper sticking out from the back of the secretary. Do you know the board that was put across to strengthen the back? That's where it was. I don't know why I paid so much attention to it. I had no thought of the will. But I pulled at it and thought it odd that a paper had worked itself in there. I wondered if it came from the drawer or slipped down from the top. It probably wouldn't have shown at all except I caught my dress on a little corner sliver and loosened the board or at least shook it. I pulled at the paper until I began to see writing, your uncle's hand— 'Last will and testament'—then I knew! I don't think I fainted quite away, but the room began to whirl and then grew dark.

"When I came to my senses I pushed the paper back where it was before. It slid in so that no corner showed. Rex, I know you'll believe me when I tell you I did this mechanically, not thinking of secreting it. Then the thought came to me that no one would find it there. I got a knife, slipped it in and worked at the paper until I made a little corner of it show, just as it did before. Then I pushed the secretary into place and came away. I meant to tell you everything, of course. But the next time I saw you, those plans about your office, the case of instruments, the expensive books, had come up, and it seemed I *couldn't*.

"It wasn't for myself. You know I'm not afraid of poverty. What else have I known all my life? But for me to crush your plans and ambitions and set you back dozens of years perhaps—I couldn't bear it. If the property had been left to some poor person, I'd have felt differently about it. But that man doesn't care for it; he has enough without it. See how indifferent he acted when he believed it was his— never even coming to see it. Thinking over all this made me decide to let things go. I wasn't to blame for its not being found in the first place, and how could I be blamed now? Why did I need to blazon it to the world and spoil your beautiful plans? I saw the date, Rex, just that horrid date! I *couldn't* do it and haven't.

"All these weeks I've struggled with my horrible secret—partly feeling I had a right to keep still and let others find the will if they could, and partly feeling I must go out on the street and shout it to everybody who passed. I can truly say I haven't had a happy moment since that hour. But only this very day I reached a decision. Hilda came to see me this afternoon, and her eyes seemed to burn me. They were like the eyes of God. If I couldn't endure her eyes, how could I meet His? I determined that before I tried to sleep again and before I tried to pray, I'd tell just the truth. I knew *at last* I was doing wrong. I called upon God to be my witness that not another night should pass before I told you the whole and left it for you to decide what must be done next.

"I know, without your telling me, that I've forfeited your love and trust. I've

been mean and false, and I know they're traits you hate. You're like Hil[e]
Nothing would tempt you to falsehood or to silence where truth was at sta[k]
You cannot marry me now, Rex. You cannot want to. I despise myself, and y[ou]
cannot but despise me. I free you entirely from your engagement to me and [if]
you never speak to me again, exonerate you from all blame. I know only t[oo]
well you could never be happy with someone you couldn't trust. Now I wa[nt]
to ask of you a favor—will you go away at once, without speaking any wor[d]
and leave me alone?"

"My poor little Nannie!" said Rex Hartwell. With one stride he was besi[de]
her and gathered her into his strong arms. "I'm so sorry," he said, stroking ba[ck]
the hair from her forehead and speaking soothingly, "so sorry you bore t[he]
burden alone, instead of letting me share it with you. No wonder you've t[orn]
my heart by growing thin and pale. Hush, dear! I'll hear no more self-accusi[ng]
words from your lips." And he stopped the words she would have spoken. "I'[ve]
let you talk long enough. It's my turn now. I won't have you say you've fall[en]
You've been tempted by the devil these many days, but the truth in your so[ul]
has triumphed. It was a heavy temptation. I know you so well and understa[nd]
better than any other, how infinitely greater it was to you because it involv[ed]
me. Don't you know, Nannie, that you never think of yourself? I haven't a[ny]
idea you'd have carried your silence through to the end. The Lord takes be[tter]
care of His children than that."

She needed those soothing, trusting words, more than she realized. Her p[oor]
brain reeled, and for a second time during this strain the world grew d[ark]
before her. But this time strong arms upheld her.

The interview, begun in this startling manner, lasted well into the nig[ht]
Many questions pressed forward for consideration. In the dining room the fa[m]
ily lingered over a late tea, the younger portion chatting merrily and the we[ary]
mother exerting herself to give them all possible news, interrupting hers[elf]
once to ask anxiously, "How has Nannie been today?"

They recognized the anxiety in her voice, and Kate, who had opened her l[ips]
to reply that Nannie had been "as cross as two sticks," checked herself, say[ing]
only, "Oh! She's been much as usual. What did you do about the velv[et]
Mother? Could you match it?"

The mother sighed and glanced toward the closed parlor door, wonderi[ng]
why Nannie didn't come out for a minute to welcome them. Then, mother-li[ke]
she put herself aside and attended to the day's details. It grew late, and s[till]
Nannie didn't appear. At last Mrs. Marvin expressed her surprise. Rex was [so]
much at home with them now that he rarely passed an evening with Nan[nie]
without chatting for a few minutes with them all. And she and Father had be[en]
gone all day, an event in itself unusual. She felt as though she'd been gon[e a]
week. Then she wondered at Rex being there at all. She thought he had [an]
engagement for Thursday evening.

"He had," said Kate. "But he was ordered out here tonight for some spec[ial]
reason—I don't know what. I know Nan sent a special delivery note to him a[t]

was in the fidgets when we went away because he hadn't arrived, although she knew the train he'd have to come on wasn't due yet. Let Nan alone, Mother, and don't worry over her. She'll fume herself into good humor after a while. It's all because she's getting ready to be married, I suppose."

They had family worship presently, and the family group separated. Mrs. Marvin was the last to go upstairs. She looked hesitantly toward the parlor door, took one step in that direction and then retreated. Ordinarily, or at least before this strange new mood came upon Nannie, nothing would have been simpler or more natural than for her to go in for a little visit and a good-night to Nannie and Rex. But the mother hesitated, then decided Nannie mightn't like being interrupted—so many things nowadays she didn't like.

The house grew still; but the mother lay awake, vaguely troubled. Rex didn't usually keep late hours; he was too earnest a student for that. Something unusual must have occurred.

In truth, such unusual things as would have amazed the mother were taking place behind that closed door. Well it was for Nannie Marvin she gave her confidence to a strong character. Rex was tender and patient, unexcited, and sure from the first moment as to what to do next.

"It will be all right, Nannie." His voice was not only soothing, but cheery. "Don't worry about it anymore. Tomorrow you'll go yourself, if you wish, or I'll go for you, just as you please, and get the paper and place it in the hands of my uncle's lawyer, with the simple statement that it's been found, and ask him to take at once the proper steps to place the rightful owner in possession. As to what money has been spent already, I anticipate no trouble there. The prospective heir hasn't shown himself eager for money, and a mistake like this he'll be willing to wait for a man to rectify. A great deal hasn't been spent, Nannie, not as men of wealth count. I've been economical; my life habit asserted itself and helped me in that.

"Then, for you and me, we'll simply wait as we planned before—not so long though. I've done good work the past year and feel much more assured of my abilities than a year ago. I don't think it will be very long, Nannie. And I know you'll be brave, as you were before, and put fresh heart into me every time I see you."

He wouldn't let her speak many words. He assured her cheerfully she'd said quite enough for her good. Especially he wouldn't permit another word of self-condemnation, declaring he already bore from her in that line more than he believed possible, and he wasn't to be tried further. The only time he grew positively stern was when she tried to repeat her assurance that she couldn't hold him to his engagement with her.

"Hush, Nannie!" he said, and his face was very grave. "You mustn't speak such words. In God's sight you are to me as my wife, never more tenderly beloved than at this hour, when by His grace you've overcome a great temptation and stood bravely for truth and purity. Only God shall separate us, dear, and I believe He'll let us do our work for Him together."

How good he was! Like an angel of God! This was her thought of him.

Chapter 22

After an hour, during which time Rex Hartwell had tried earnestly to bring peace to Nannie's troubled heart and flattered himself he was succeeding, she rose up from the easy chair in which he'd placed her and stood before him resolute.

"No, Rex, listen. I must speak. You're almost exactly like what I can imagine Jesus Christ would be if He were here, as He used to be. But I've suffered enough to know, now that I can think connectedly, that I must do something more. I must be honest *now* at any cost. I've been honest to you, and you were the very hardest. But there are others, Father and Mother, and oh—everybody! Mustn't I, to be true, let everybody know the truth? It seems so to me. I wish I could do it right away. If there were a great meeting tonight, in the church or somewhere, with all the people gathered who've ever known me, I'd like to tell them I found that will many weeks ago and hid it again. I'd like to describe how it was done, so the least little thing wasn't omitted."

Her excitement had increased, and her misery was pitiful to see. In vain the young man talked low, soothing words, trying to reason with her and persuade her to trust him and let him manage the matter in the right and best way.

She shook her head. "No, I cannot trust you. You're not God, although you can forgive like Him. You're just human, and you might make a mistake. You want to shield me. You pity me and are so eager to comfort me. I bless you for it, Rex. You've saved my reason, but I cannot trust your judgment—not in this."

Suddenly a new thought came to her. "Rex, if I could see Hilda Elliott tonight —now. I *must* see her. Her love for me isn't great enough to blind her judgment, and she'll tell me what I should do. She knows, Rex, and she doesn't spare even her own sister from humiliation. Besides, I've treated her shamefully. Only today I spoke cruel words to her. I feel as though I must tell her the reason for them right away. Couldn't you go across the meadow and bring her? It wouldn't take a moment, and she'd come at once if she knew I needed her. Will you?"

He hesitated only a moment. He shrank from the ordeal. But if Hilda could quiet her friend, she was certainly needed, and he hoped she could be trusted. At least there seemed no other way. He let himself quietly out of the front door while the tide of talk was highest in the dining room and sped across lots to the Elliott farm. Wondering, Hilda obeyed the summons promptly, and she and Rex walked almost in silence across the fields.

"Nannie's very excited," he said, as they neared the house. "She has something to tell you which will doubtless surprise and pain you. I wish she didn't think it necessary or at least would let me talk for her, but—I know I can trust your good judgment. She's put herself under a terrible strain that's extremely dangerous. At almost any cost her excitement must be allayed. She seems to think, among other crimes she accuses herself of, that she's treated you badly. But I'm sure she exaggerates that."

"Why, the poor child!" said Hilda. "What an idea! I can easily relieve her mind of any such feeling. I know she's been in some trouble for a good while. I only wish to help her."

Nannie was standing at the window watching for them. She came toward them eagerly, her excitement unabated.

"I knew you'd come," she said, holding out her hand to Hilda. "You never fail me, no matter how hateful I am. Oh, Hilda, you've been a good friend to poor little Ellie, but worse than Ellie is here! The child's escapade is nothing compared with my deliberate sin. I want you to know the whole story."

She told it briefly, with almost painful frankness, not even attempting to shield herself as she had to Rex. Hilda was startled. There was no question about that. The temptation was in a form so foreign to any she could have felt. She held herself, of course, from any such expression and spoke only tender, sympathetic words. But Nannie scarcely heeded them. She hurried on.

"I had a reason for wanting to see you tonight. I can't trust Rex—not in this. He's too anxious to shield me. He can't bear to give me more pain. But at the expense of pain and humiliation, no matter how extreme, I feel I must do right. Somehow I felt that you, with your calm, quiet eyes, would see what right is. Hilda, mustn't I tell everybody about it as I told you? Father and Mother and the world? Isn't that the only way to be true?"

Rex Hartwell turned anxious eyes on Hilda. Was she to be depended upon? Or had her ideas about truth become fanaticism, demanding further martyrdom of poor Nannie?

Her reply came quickly, without an instant's hesitation. "Oh, Nannie, no, indeed! I think you did right to tell Rex the whole. I don't think you could have respected yourself otherwise. Regarding your father and mother, it seems to me you have a right to exercise your own judgment. If you want to tell them— I mean, if you'd feel better—I can understand that feeling. But as to the lawyer and all the others, what is it to them? Justice is to be done in every particular. And as I look at it, that's enough. Am I not right, Rex?"

He gave her a grateful glance as he said he offered the same advice, but Nannie was afraid his feeling for her biased his judgment.

By nightfall the following day, not only the neighboring countryside and village nearby, but the large town a few miles farther away, were in a buzz of excitement over the latest developments in Squire Hartwell's affairs. The missing will had come to light! Nannie Marvin herself found it and gave it to Rex, who took instant steps toward having the property pass into the rightful heir's hands! Many and varied were the circumstances said to be connected with this discovery. The story as it traveled grew so rapidly that both Rex and Nannie might have been excused from recognizing their share in it. Never had anything so exciting occurred in the neighborhood. Poor Ellen Elliott reaped some benefit from this sudden outburst—her own affairs were for the time forgotten. All tongues were busy trying to glean, as well as give, information as to how Nannie "bore it" and what the Marvins said and did and what Rex would do now—whether, after all, he'd try to be married.

The Marvin girls also received their share of attention. Somebody said Kate Marvin might now be cured of boasting about what her sister would do and wear and how her rooms would be furnished. Some said "pride must have a fall," and the Marvins were always too lofty for their good. But the country was mostly sympathetic and regretful. It certainly was hard lines for poor Nannie—so much harder, all agreed, than if the matter had stayed settled at first. Also they agreed it was undoubtedly an added drop of bitterness for Nannie to find the will herself. And none of them knew, either then or afterward, through what depths of terrible temptation Nannie waded before that will was really found.

Neither did those beyond their immediate family circle ever learn just how the Marvins "bore it." Very soon after the astounding announcement of the discovery was made to the family, Mrs. Marvin was closeted with Nannie for an hour or more. When she came out, her other curious daughters could see she'd been crying. Yet they couldn't resist the temptation to question her; there were so many details they wanted to know. Where was the will found and how?

Kate, the inquisitive, said in response to one item, "Why, Mother, Nan hasn't been at the stone house in so long! Why didn't she find it until now? Oh, I know! It must have been hidden among those old papers Rex brought for Nannie to look over at her leisure, and she just got to it! Was that it, Mother?"

And then Mrs. Marvin resolved not to answer more questions but issued her mandate. "Girls, you're old enough to feel deep sympathy for your sister in this trial, a very sore one to her, of course. Our own share in it is heavy enough. Yet what is it compared with Nannie's? You can understand that questioning and cross-questioning and surmising, keeping the matter constantly before her, will simply be torture. She's found the will, and it's to be placed today in the proper authorities' hands. That's all we need to know, and I want it understood there must be no talk about it. Don't mention the subject to Nannie, except, of course, a very brief word of sympathy. The poor child isn't well, remember, and this strain on her is heavy. We must help her however we can. I look to my girls to be considerate and patient.

"Furthermore," she added, "you'll come in contact with hundreds of people hungry for details about matters that are none of their business. All you need to say to them is that Nannie came across the will in an unthought-of place and it had dropped there sometime and secreted itself. So there's no mystery about it. If you refrain from annoying your sister with questions, you can perhaps suggest the same to others."

They saw the force of their mother's words, although they grumbled a little at her evident disinclination to discuss the matter with them.

"You might tell us all about it," said Kate, "then we wouldn't be so likely to bother Nannie. I'm sure I'd like to know a dozen things. It's too horrid mean! Rex should have the property. It's his by every law of common sense and decency. I declare, if I'd been Nan, I'd have pitched the old will into the grate and said nothing."

"Katherine," said Mrs. Marvin, and her face was actually pale. "I'm astonished and shocked! How can you repeat such terrible words! Don't for the world say anything like that to Nannie."

"Why, Mother!" said Kate. "I don't understand you! What possible harm could it do to repeat such utter nonsense as that, even to Nannie? She isn't so far beside herself that she can't recognize the folly of it."

Mrs. Marvin turned away hastily, glad a household matter called at that moment for attention. How could she explain to her daughters the feeling of horror the mere suggestion of such a course had given her?

Rex Hartwell didn't go to his office that day; other duties pressed upon him. The plans for his entire future had been overturned in a moment, and he must at once plan a new future. His first duty was at his old home. He came for Nannie by appointment, and they went together to the stone house where they'd spent many pleasant hours. Nannie herself led the way to his uncle's room and pointed silently to the secretary, while she seated herself on his uncle's chair nearby. She'd resolved to be where she could study every change on his expressive face during this trying scene. Neither spoke while he wheeled out the old-fashioned piece of furniture, placing it at an angle for Nannie to see. The corner of the fateful paper was peeping out just as Nannie had said. If it hadn't been peeping out, it might never have been found. And if Nannie's dress hadn't caught in the rough edge, it wouldn't have peeped out—on such trivial accidents do great events sometimes hang. Rex pulled at the paper as Nannie had and drew it out, studying the characters as she had.

"It's my uncle's handwriting," he said gravely. "And that's the correct date. It certainly hid itself away securely. Well, Nannie," he added, smiling at her, "I'm glad we found it before we complicated matters more than they are." He opened the writing desk as he spoke and took from it a large envelope, slipped the important paper in it and proceeded to seal it carefully.

"Aren't you going to look at it?" asked Nannie faintly.

"No. Why should I? We practically know its contents, and I'd rather the lawyer examine it first." He drew out his pen and supplied the proper address.

"There," he said cheerfully, "that matter's out of our hands. I'll go to town this afternoon and place it myself in our friend's keeping, with the request he hasten to the proper adjustment. And now, Nannie, let's have a talk."

As he spoke, he thrust the paper into his pocket and going over to the south windows threw open the blinds and let in a glow of sunshine. For the first time Nannie noticed a fire burning in the grate. She was too preoccupied to notice before. She looked at it wonderingly.

"Yes," he said, answering her look, "I was here before, this morning. You didn't think I'd let you come to a closed, chilly room! Are you comfortable? Let's take these two chairs we've used so often before and draw up to the grate and have a visit."

In utter silence she obeyed his directions, dropping herself into the capacious leather chair he wheeled forward. He took its counterpart and settled it close beside her. Then, as if by mutual consent, they looked about the great room furnished lavishly for comfort and convenience. It had been a favorite with them. Here Nannie wrote those numberless letters for Squire Hartwell, and here she and Rex held those long talks while his uncle was taking his afternoon nap. Here they'd expected to spend much of their time as husband and wife.

"You'll write business letters for me," Rex had told her whimsically. "Or, no, I have it—you'll write out my lecture notes for me. I'll see if you can throw as much light into them as you did for some of my uncle's obscure sentences." What plans they had in connection with this room! Now they were here to bid it good-bye.

"I'd like to have these chairs," said Rex reflectively. "We've had such good times in them. I wonder if the owner would sell them to us sometime. I wouldn't if I were he. They're splendid old-fashioned chairs. One can't buy any similar these days."

Nannie thought she had no more tears to shed, but her eyes grew dim as she listened. How could he talk about it so quietly, so brightly? Her heart was breaking for him. He turned toward her presently with a cheerful smile. Suddenly he wheeled his chair a little in front of her and, leaning forward, took both her hands.

"Nannie, dear," he said, with a kind of cheerful seriousness, "I'm glad of a quiet talk with you in this old room where we learned to love each other. I want to tell you something. It involves the reason why this doesn't break me as it might have once. Of course I'm sorry not to have immediate comfort for you and your father and mother—our father and mother, dear. They're all I have. But even that only means waiting a little longer. You and I are young and strong, and it'll be strange if we can't carry out our best plans eventually.

"Meanwhile, I've come to know of an inheritance beyond computing," he continued. "Do you know the Lord Jesus Christ has in these last few weeks become more to me than I realized He could ever be to a human? I've begun to realize dimly what it means to 'put on Christ.' I've wanted to talk it over quietly with you, dear, and above all to have you share my experience. I haven't just begun the Christian life, you know. I've been a member of the family for years and an heir to the wealth stored up for me. I've simply begun to claim my rights. By and by, when we have time, I'd like to tell you how I came to this knowledge and experience and why I've been content with a starved life for so long.

"But what I want now is for us to kneel down here together in the room we supposed would be ours and consecrate ourselves anew to His service. I thought we could use wealth for Him. But since He plans it otherwise, let's gladly accept the direction as His best for us.

"And, Nannie, one thing more: I don't want you, dear, ever to speak again as if our life, yours and mine, could be two. God has joined us. And through the blessing of Him who's overcome the power of death, even that shall not separate us. You've been for weeks the subject of a fierce temptation, and God has carried you safely through it. Your life and mine should be the stronger forever because of this exhibition of His grace. Shall we kneel together and thank Him for this and begin life all over again from this hour?"

Nannie Marvin never forgot that prayer. In some respects it was unlike any she'd ever heard. She arose from it feeling that God had sealed her forgiveness and was tender and gracious both to Rex and to her.

Chapter 23

Among those considered outsiders, the most astonished and certainly the most disturbed person over the news of the recovered will was John Stuart. Though Rex and Nannie seemed eager to have the news spread as far and as fast as possible, John, sent ten miles into the country on farm business, didn't hear of it until that evening, when he brought Hilda from the station. She'd been in town doing errands for her father. John, as soon as he reached home, was sent to meet her at the train.

She began with eager questions. Did he see Mr. Hartwell that afternoon? She expected him to be on the train, but he must have taken an earlier one. Did he know whether Mr. Hartwell waited for the lawyer? John hadn't seen Mr. Hartwell or heard of a lawyer. His face expressed so much surprise she asked if he hadn't heard the news.

"I remember you've been away today," she said with a smile. "But our little neighborhood is in such turmoil I didn't suppose you could be at home for fifteen minutes without hearing something about it. But I forget you don't belong to this neighborhood. Perhaps you didn't hear anything about the second will Squire Hartwell made?"

He'd heard people talk about a second will that was lost, and from all accounts he thought it good that it was.

"It certainly seemed so to us," Hilda said, with a little sigh. "But now that it's found again, I suppose we must change our opinions and at least hope good will result."

"What!" said John Stuart. He reined in his horses with such suddenness they resented it nervously. "Miss Elliott, you can't mean that ridiculous will has been found!"

Hilda was unreasonable enough to be a bit annoyed at his great interest. Why did it matter to him? This was carrying curiosity to the verge of impudence. She replied with cold caution. The will was found, she believed. Miss Marvin herself had discovered it and notified Mr. Hartwell.

"When did this happen, Miss Elliott? Are you sure the paper has already passed into the lawyer's hands?"

There was no mistaking John Stuart's interest, even eagerness and anxiety. Hilda was more annoyed.

"Probably it has," she answered coldly. Mr. Hartwell wasn't one to delay, when he had important matters to look after. He went into town on the same train with her for the purpose, and she had no doubt it was attended to by this time. Why did John care to know?

But for once John Stuart wasn't aware of Miss Elliott's coldness and annoyance; he was still eager and anxious.

"But you spoke of his waiting for the lawyer. Mightn't he have failed in seeing him? Excuse me, but it's important for me to know the facts."

"I cannot imagine why! Judge Barnard wasn't at home early in the afternoon. I met him at the west end of the city, but I presume he returned in time for Mr. Hartwell to see him. Whether he did or not doesn't concern me, and I can't imagine why it interests you in the least."

"It's because I won't permit such foolishness, and I might be able to avoid this offensive publicity."

He'd forgotten himself entirely and for the moment spoke John Stuart King's thought in that person's voice and manner. He was recalled to his second self by feeling, rather than seeing, Hilda Elliott's stare of astonishment, mingled with a touch of terror. Could the man driving her father's horses have suddenly become insane? How else could such remarkable words be accounted for?

Instantly he knew he'd blundered irreparably, but he was excited and annoyed. *What of it?* he asked himself recklessly. *She'll have to know the truth soon. That ridiculous will has spoiled everything.* Yet what was the truth? Or, rather, what portion of it must she know at once, and what must yet be concealed? He thought rapidly and spoke again without any perceptible delay.

"I beg your pardon, Miss Elliott. I was excited and forgot whom I was speaking to. I have reasons for being interested in this will. When you hear them, I think you'll admit the reasons are sufficient. If I may see you alone this evening for a few minutes, I can explain."

"I don't wish any explanation," she said with dignity. "I of course have nothing to do with your views of this subject, unless you mean there's something you should tell me."

That last was an after-thought pressed into words by her conscience. Should she turn from a man who perhaps needed to follow out his sudden impulse to tell something he'd concealed?

He felt her coldness and shrinking from an interview with him, but his reckless mood continued. She should see and talk with him once.

"There's something I think I should tell you," he said, speaking with as much dignity as she used.

"Very well. I'll be in the sitting room tonight after seven o'clock. I don't know anything to prevent your seeing me alone for a few minutes, if that amount of caution is necessary."

As soon as his horses were cared for, the much disturbed man went directly to the woodhouse chamber and locked himself in. He touched a match to the carefully laid fire in the small Franklin stove Farmer Elliott had suggested he set up for his comfort. Then he sat back and stared gloomily at it.

When he laid the fire in the morning, he'd looked forward to a long evening spent in this quiet retreat, doing much to further the interests of Reuben and Hannah, those creatures of his brain, whose daily living he had the privilege of fashioning and directing. Now he wanted none of them, hated them both and might with the next stroke of his pen put them both out of existence. Why play with fiction when real life stalked before him in such dreary shape?

What had he done by a few reckless words? He'd made it impossible to play this part any longer or see again the one he'd long been playing it for. This time he let the truth appear to him unrebuked. He'd carried on this deception week after week, month after month, for Hilda Elliott's sake. It wasn't because he was studying human nature in a new guise or wanting to try plain living and regular hours or because he was sleeping so well and had such a fine appetite that he didn't want to break the conditions hurriedly. It wasn't even because he thought it unkind to deprive Farmer Elliott of his services when he most needed them. He could say these things when his conscience would admit them; tonight it demanded straightforwardness. He was lingering here so he might sit opposite Hilda Elliott at the table, watch her face, hear her voice, carry wood and water for her, drive her to the station—to be daily near her. This was the naked truth. And these things were possible only because he was her father's hired man.

Given that other truth he'd offered to explain to her, he instinctively felt that, for a time at least, he couldn't hope for her friendship. Could he ever hope for it? As he answered this question, his face flushed deeply. Had John Stuart King put himself in a position he was ashamed of? What did he want of Hilda Elliott's friendship? Suppose she laughed with him over the part he'd played, admired his cleverness, approved his motives and agreed they should be good friends and comrades hereafter—would he be satisfied?

It humiliated him to realize how far from satisfied he would feel. What, then, did he expect? Oh, "expect!" He kicked an innocent stick of wood at his feet, as he told it angrily that one who made a fool of himself had no right to expect anything. Suppose he could tell her every detail of the truth; should he? What would she think of Elizabeth? And then he drew himself up sharply; he was insulting her by intruding Elizabeth into the interview. Indeed, wasn't he insulting Elizabeth? The important point was, what did he think of her? If in some directions John Stuart King wasn't strong, he certainly wasn't a weak man.

His friends attributed to him unusual strength of character. While they may have mistaken a certain obstinacy for strength, as often occurs where people aren't very intimate—and while some of his doings indicated the absence of what we really mean or should mean by strength of character—still the word "weak" would certainly not apply to him. Anyone who understands his own nature, which is a deeper thing than to suppose he understands human nature, would have pitied John Stuart King that night, as the extent of his moral degradation slowly revealed itself to him.

He was engaged to be married to one woman, and every fiber of his being was athrob with the thought of another! He permitted himself to linger in this place of temptation long after admitting to his heart he was tempted. He'd put the thought aside, laughed at his conscience, or rather placed a stern seal of silence upon it, and deliberately yielded to the desire to be near Hilda Elliott and hear her voice and watch her movements.

Studying her for a character in fiction, indeed! It had been a long time since he'd allowed that thought to stay with him. Studying her, or rather holding her as a character that had entered his life and must forever be a part of him. She was too sacred for fiction—his kind of fiction.

He felt the glow on his face deepen as he recalled certain words of hers. He was driving Rex Hartwell and Nannie Marvin and Hilda from the station, and they were discussing his work—Stuart King's—as it had appeared in a current issue of a popular magazine. Hilda was sitting beside him with her face turned slightly toward those in the back seat and every line of it visible to him.

"I don't think I like him," she'd said, "not wholly. Oh, he has talent undoubtedly. I think he'll be recognized as someone we call a great writer; perhaps he deserves the name better than most. They're all disappointing."

"In what sense does he disappoint you?" Rex Hartwell had asked, and John Stuart blessed him for it; it was the very question he desired to ask.

"Why, he ignores—they all do—the 'greatest thing in the world,' " she'd replied with a slight laugh and the subtle quotation marks in her voice. "In his great character, his 'Reuben,' we can see his omissions. For all the story indicates, he might have been born and reared among beings who have no religion—if any such beings exist—so utterly he ignores it. It's a great fact in the world, swaying lives more or less all about us—more than any other single idea ever has—and claiming to involve not only this little inch of life but an endless eternity. Is it being great to write a history of any life and leave out all reference to it?"

How distinctly he remembered her every word; they had cut deeply.

"Probably he has no religion," Rex Hartwell had replied, "and therefore can't be expected to produce any in fiction."

"Then should he profess to describe life?" Hilda had asked. "Do you believe any life in our present civilization, or at least any life ordinary fiction deals with, isn't distinctly affected by what we call religion?"

The talk had drifted then from definite authors into a general discussion of fiction and its legitimate realm. John Stuart had listened closely, with an interest that would have amazed the talkers, and carried home some sword thrusts to consider. He'd worked into the night over his chief characters, Reuben and Hannah, trying to reconstruct their lives on a basis he felt might interest Hilda, and failed. He could do nothing with them. Like many fiction writers, he learned they weren't plastic clay in his hand to be molded as he would. He created them, but they had their own wills and insisted upon carrying out their own ideas of destiny. No, it was more humiliating than that. He failed in creating them. They weren't like the great Creator's work, "made in God's image." He'd brought them thus far, dwarfed and misshapen, and they refused to be recreated.

He remembered vividly his experience and his disappointment, on this evening when he told himself that such a life as Hilda Elliott's was too sacred for his kind of fiction. Must he descend yet lower on the moral scale and admit he couldn't even retain Hilda Elliott as a friend?

He sat staring at the glowing fire a long time, until it died out and a chill crept over the room. He utterly ignored Susan Appleby's repeated calls to "come that minute if he wanted any supper at all." To sit down opposite Hilda Elliott then and try to eat, he felt sure would choke him.

Just what would he say to her in that interview he'd requested? Why was he such a fool? Yet what else could he do? If that intolerable will, that should never have been made, could have stayed hidden, he might have planned his way out less painfully than this. But at all hazards he must stop that foolishness.

He sprang up at last, suddenly realizing it was nearly seven o'clock. He must prepare for the interview, and that would require time. In an obscure corner of the woodhouse chamber stood a trunk he brought from the express office only a few days before. He'd sent for it under the vague impression a crisis might come before long that would demand its resources. He strode over to it and unlocked it. Fletcher and his city tailor had done his bidding. The articles of gentleman's clothing were presently being tossed about the room, whose whitewashed walls seemed to stare in blank astonishment.

When he was dressed completely, even to the fine handkerchief in his pocket, he looked in his twelve-inch mirror and laughed—a short, dry laugh with no pleasure. How humiliating that such a transformation should occur aided by mere clothes!

Chapter 24

Hilda was in the sitting room, waiting for her caller. She wasn't annoyed, but her face, besides being serious, was somewhat disturbed. If she'd voiced her deepest thought, she might have said she was tired of it all and almost tired of everybody in her world. The world had been so trying lately, full of petty intrigues with their serious and dangerous sides; full of twists and quibbles and prevarications of the truth, when the truth would have served every purpose better and shielded its adherents.

Colin's trouble, for instance, which was nearly serious, was born entirely of his propensity to toy with words and let others gain what impressions they would, and the more false the impressions, the more intense his enjoyment. But her face cleared for a moment at thought of Colin. The watching Father in heaven had been greater than His word. Even Colin's follies were made to "work together" for his good, and Colin's feet were securely settled at last on Rock foundation.

But poor Ellie, led astray in the first place by her love of mystery, had a secret to whisper over with Laura Holcombe; received letters from somebody who thought she was somebody else; and sent him her photograph that wasn't her photograph at all. It was "such fun!" as the poor little simpleton had expressed it. Yet what would be the outcome of such fun? Would Ellie ever recover from the shock of discovering what the great censorious, caviling world thought of such things?

She had her lesson, poor darling! She learned it wasn't her father, mother and sister alone who were "over particular." When it came to experiences like hers, the people who had hinted at "strait-laced notions," "overstrained ideas" and "fanatical theories" were among the first to hold up hands of horror and cry, "Who would believe she could do such a thing?"

Oh, yes! The child had learned a lesson she'd remember. But who could be sure the sweet flower of innocence hadn't been crushed in the learning? Certainly it was a bitter experience for them all. Hilda, who knew how fond the gossips were of talking, felt the end wasn't yet.

Then, too, Nannie, her friend since childhood, was beloved as few girlfriends are. Yet how constantly, as she grew old enough to realize and understand it, had she deplored in Nannie that marked trait which led her to appear what she wasn't! In almost babyhood she smiled and appeared pleased with attentions that were really a trial to her. This trait, which was called amiability, was perhaps unwisely admired and fostered. Certainly it grew and developed in Nannie a girl who said, "Oh, how delightful!" when she listened to a plan she thought was a bore, and, "I'll be happy to go," when she meant she'd rather do almost anything than go. Pity for Nannie she didn't, at the most formative period in her life, come in contact with someone who labeled this development "falseness," instead of "common politeness."

It grew upon her and finally bore the fruit that brought her to the depths of humiliation and almost despair.

Thinking it over and realizing she had faults probably as serious, Hilda could yet be sure temptation in this guise would never have come to her.

And now, when she was all but sinking under the weight of pain and anxiety caused by various outgrowths of this same form of sin, John comes to add his experience, whatever it was! She shrank from it all. Why did she need to hear any more? She was tired; she felt she had no more advice to give, and even vague sympathy was expecting too much of her.

She hadn't the remotest conception of what John's confidence might be. She told herself half impatiently she was too weary of it all to form a theory. Yet through her mind floated a notion he must somehow be connected with that disagreeable and unjust will. Perhaps as a witness, who for some reason known to him had connived at hiding the document.

She smiled sarcastically over the memory of his surprising statement that he wouldn't "permit such foolishness!" Probably in his ignorance he imagined he could prevent it. Yet John wasn't ignorant. She recalled abundant proof that he was remarkably well informed; he was simply a mystery, and she hated mysteries. She was almost sorry she'd permitted him to come to her with his story. Not quite—for even in this unusual irritability was still a responsibility toward every person with whom she came in contact, especially for those who asked her help.

She'd struggled with her unwillingness to shoulder any more "secrets" and concealed her annoyance, if not weariness, when she told her mother with a wan smile, "John wants to see me alone for a few minutes, Mother. I told him he might come anytime after seven."

"More burdens?" asked Mrs. Elliott. "Poor little woman! You've had to shoulder others' troubles ever since you could walk. Never mind, dear—such work has its compensations. I hope John isn't in any difficulty. I like him very much. If he's ready to confide his history to you, it may be the dawning of a better day for him. Ellie, bring your book and come to Father's room. He'll like for you to read aloud for awhile."

Poor Ellie had looked up with a quick glance the moment she heard John's request and then dropped her eyes on her book again. All sorts of incidents filled Ellie with apprehension these days. What could John want of Hilda but to impart to her some fresh gossip about her, which they needed to know? He'd naturally come to Hilda, for her father wasn't yet well enough to be troubled more than necessary, and they all shielded her mother as much as possible. They didn't need to fear John was in trouble; he was good. She felt she knew, better than any of them, how good he was.

So Hilda waited. And to banish as much disagreeable thinking as possible, she took up the last issue of a popular magazine and turned to Stuart King's serial story. She mightn't approve of him entirely, but he furnished interesting reading.

And then the sitting room door opened, and John Stuart entered unceremoniously. He'd stood in the hallway for several seconds, haunted by the silliest trivialities. In John Stuart King's garb it seemed natural to think of convention-alities. In his side pocket at this moment reposed his card case, well filled. Under ordinary circumstances the proper thing would be to ring the doorbell and send in his card by Susan Appleby. But under the circumstances in which he'd placed himself, how absurd it would be even to knock! To continue thinking this way would make it impossible for him to talk with Hilda Elliott. He hurriedly pushed open the sitting room door and as hurriedly closed it behind him.

Hilda looked up from her book, stared a bewildered second, then rose to her feet, a startled look on her face.

"I beg your pardon if I'm intruding. You gave me permission to come, you remember."

Formal expression came naturally to his lips. It belonged, apparently, with his clothes!

"I don't understand," said Hilda, faltering. She was still staring.

The ludicrous side of it became uppermost to John Stuart King and put him for the moment at his ease.

"I begged the privilege of an interview, you remember? It seemed necessary to explain something to you."

"But you're not"—she was about to add "John." But something in his strangely familiar, yet unfamiliar, face held back the word. It was ludicrous still.

"I am John Stuart at your service," he said, speaking almost merrily. "Pray be seated, Miss Elliott, and I'll try to explain as briefly as possible."

She dropped back into her chair. John Stuart drew a chair for himself unin-vited and felt the situation had already ceased to be ludicrous. He had, early in their acquaintance, imagined scenes in which he should "explain," but they were never like this one. If only he didn't care what she thought of him! He felt the perspiration starting on his forehead.

How he got through the first of it he could never afterward tell. He knew he stammered something about being a student of human nature and desiring to understand better certain social conditions, especially the tramp question, before writing about them. It was a lame defense, and he realized it. His lis-tener grew colder and more dignified.

She interrupted him at last. "You claim to be a writer then?"

"That is my business."

"What do you write?"

He hesitated, and his face flushed. Her tone was that of a person who, not believing what he said, had resolved to entrap him.

"I've written on various lines," he said at last, "travel and some purely liter-ary papers. I'm writing fiction now."

"Oh! So you thought you'd create some and act it out? It may have been a clever way. But how am I to be sure which is fiction—or, rather, where fiction ends?"

"You're hard upon me, Miss Elliott!" he said quickly. "I've done nothing to deserve your contempt." Then, for the first time, he noticed the magazine still in her hand. Her tone and manner stung him, forcing him on.

"I see you have the *American Monthly*. There is what my friends call a fair shadow of me for the frontispiece. Can't you corroborate that part of my story?"

She gave a little start of surprise—was it also of dismay?—gazed fixedly at him for a moment, then turned the pages rapidly and gazed at the picture, then back to him.

"You're Stuart King!" she said at last. It's impossible for mere words to give an idea of what her tone expressed.

"I'm John Stuart King. Was it such a crime beyond pardon to drop the last name for a time, come into the country and earn an honest living for myself, doing honest work and, I believe, in a satisfactory manner?"

She was looking steadily at him. There was no smile on her face, no indication she was other than seriously displeased.

"Pardon me," she said at last. "You must be your own conscience. Whether the end in view was worth the weeks and months of deception you've had to practice, you should be better able to tell than I. I can't pretend to fathom your motive."

"My motive, Miss Elliott, as I told you, was distinctly in line with my work as a writer for the press. I wished to study certain social conditions, untrammelled by the conventionalities of my life. In particular I wanted to understand the ordinary tramp's life and describe it from his standpoint. In doing this I had a motive even you might approve. I want, if I can, to help solve the problem of how to reach and save him."

"And you found such satisfactory conditions for studying this phase of humanity here in my father's quiet farmhouse, where a tramp rarely penetrates, that you've lingered on through a large portion of your exile?"

Stuart King felt the blood surging in great waves over his face. Once more he'd blundered!

"I used the past tense, if you noticed," he said presently, in a lower tone. "It was the end for which I started out. I won't deny that other motives have held me and shaped my later decisions."

It was still a lame defense, he knew. But something in the words or the manner of rendering them Hilda didn't care to probe further.

"Well," she said suddenly, in an altered and businesslike tone, "I have nothing to do with all this, of course. You don't have to justify yourself to *me*. May I ask what it has to do with the matter that led to this revelation? Do you have any information about Squire Hartwell's will that's just been found?"

"Pardon me, Miss Elliott, but is that quite true? From your view of life, don't you have something to do with it and with me? Am I not a human being with an immortal soul you're bound to be interested in? Would it interest you to know that, while I believe I was a Christian when I entered your home, I've received new views since I've been here of what that word should imply?"

She looked away from him at last, down at the book she still held, and toyed with the pages for a moment. Then she said, "Pardon me, Mr. King. I don't wish to be hard. But I'm compelled to tell you Christianity has its very foundations in truth."

"I understand you," he said. "You're hard on me, but I think you don't mean to be. I believe I'd agree with you after this. I've started out now for truth. You asked me a question. Don't you see my relation to that unjust, foolish will? Have you heard the name of the supposed heir?"

She looked quickly at him, catching her breath in an exclamation. "It's Stuart King! And you're—"

"And I'm John Stuart King, Squire Hartwell's distant relative. That complication, Miss Elliott, wasn't my planning. It's an accident. But I hope you don't think I'll let such an unjust will stand. It was made in passion, and the maker didn't live long enough to recover his sane mind. It's unjust, and I'll have none of it. Am I wrong in thinking I can give you a bit of pleasure by that? You'd like your friends to remain in undisturbed possession of their own?"

Before he completed the sentence, he regretted beginning it. Clearly John Stuart, her father's hired man, had been on terms of intimacy with this young woman that weren't to be accorded John Stuart King, the somewhat famous author.

He changed the subject quickly. "Miss Elliott, will you keep my secret for a few days, until I can supply my place to your father? He's entrusted certain matters to me that really require my attention, and—"

She interrupted him.

"That will be impossible, Mr. King. I'm sure my father and my brother, who'll be at home tomorrow, would undergo any inconvenience rather than trouble you further. My father will, without doubt, entertain you as Mr. King, if it isn't convenient for you to go away at once. But as for lending my aid to any form of deception, however slight it may seem to you, that's out of the question. If there were no other reason, the recent painful experience in my own family would make it impossible."

"I understand that, too. I'll go away at once—tonight if you wish. But, Miss Elliott, surely I may return? I may call on you as a friend?"

It was Hilda's turn to flush. The color flamed into her face, which was pale before. But she answered steadily: "You make me appear very inhospitable, Mr. King. I must remind you we are not friends, but strangers."

"Yet you were kind to John Stuart and friendly with him, trusted yourself to his care and accepted his help. But the moment he claims equality with you, you become strangers! Nothing is changed but the clothes, Miss Elliott. Do they count for so much?"

Indignation flashed quickly in her eyes. "You compel me to speak plainly by misunderstanding my position. It isn't a question of equality or inequality. John Stuart, an honest man, earning his living in an honest way, I respected and was ready to think and speak of him as a friend. When John Stuart went out of existence, my acquaintance with him necessarily ceased."

He stood up, thinking it was time for the interview to end.

"I won't intrude longer this evening," he said in his most dignified, yet courteous tone. "But it's perhaps fair to warn you that sometime John Stuart *King* intends to try to secure an introduction to Miss Elliott."

Chapter 25

M r. Marvin's prayer at family worship that evening revealed to Nannie that her mother had told him her story. She'd shrunk nervously from doing it herself. She didn't think she could bear her pure-eyed, unworldly father's look when he first heard of his cherished daughter's temptation and downfall. She used that pitiless word in thinking of herself. Rex might blind his eyes to it, and she blessed him for doing it. But she knew she'd sinned. And her father, who would lose every penny he could earn rather than wrong anyone, would be clear regarding this. She wanted him to know the whole. She assured her mother she couldn't sleep until he was told, but somebody else must tell him.

And the father's prayer fell like balm on her wounded, sensitive spirit. It held a touch of the divine sympathy Rex had shown and that she thought no other could. As he prayed, she found herself saying over softly the words, "Like as a father pitieth his children." Then, with a sudden rush of tears not altogether unhappy, she cast herself on her infinite Father's mercy and rested.

That dear earthly father came and kissed her after the prayer, having just opened heaven for her. And his voice trembled as he said, "God keep my daughter pure. I bless Him for keeping you this far. Trust Him, and He'll bring you through to the end in peace. Poverty isn't the worst trial."

"What a strange prayer Father gave!" Kate Marvin said, as the sisters lingered in their room before bed. "Someone who didn't understand might think Nan had just received a fortune, instead of just losing one."

"Nan seems different, too," said the thoughtful Alice. "She's been gentler and less nervous all day than I've seen her for a long time. Perhaps—"

"Well," said Kate, after waiting what seemed a reasonable length of time, "perhaps what?"

"I was only thinking perhaps Nannie, too, has discovered something Father and Mother have always had."

"What's that?"

"A mysterious power, Katie, to help them over hard places and keep them sweet and strong—some people find it by praying. Don't you know Father and Mother do?"

Blessed are those fathers and mothers of whom their children can give such testimony!

Nannie Marvin found herself more at rest that evening than in weeks, though it almost seemed to her years. The great strain was over. They were poorer by contrast than ever before. The years stretched between Rex and her, and hard work lay before them all. Nevertheless, as she knelt to pray, her first thought was of gratitude. God had brought her through. Though years might stretch between her and Rex, no gulf stood between them now.

It seems a pity dull mornings must often follow periods of mental exaltation. With the next morning's dawn, Nannie Marvin felt the prosaic side of her life more keenly than she had. Depths of misery and heights of peace are both more interesting than the middle ground of everyday duty.

Nannie was quiet, but sad. The irritable stage had passed, and her voice had recovered its gentle note. But it was hard to fold away, out of sight and mind, those pretty wedding fineries she'd prepared with such painstaking care. She didn't delay. She had an old trunk brought down from the attic almost before daylight and placed in it sundry garments and a dress or two that would be "too fine" for her now.

"It's all horrid!" said Kate, who'd helped her move the trunk. "I'd rather she'd scold. It feels as if there's been a funeral!" She turned abruptly away to hide the tears.

Perhaps Nannie had some of the same feeling. She slept quietly most of the night but awakened early to think and plan. Rex shouldn't have all the hard work this time; she'd go to work too. Hilda wanted to give up her position; her father and mother didn't want her to teach any longer, and Hilda herself wanted to go away for a year of study.

They'd talked it over together in the fall, how Hilda would teach for one winter only. Nannie had been secretly glad that, instead of leaving for study, she was planning to go to her own beautiful home and make life glad and bright for so many people. They wondered who'd take Hilda's place in the school, went over their list of acquaintances and were sure none of them would suit.

Hilda had said half mournfully, "Oh, Nannie, if it could be you, how delightful for my girls and boys!"

Nannie had laughed and blushed and declared she didn't see how she could take up even such beautiful work; now her way was clear. She'd talk with Hilda about it that very day. Hilda once said that, if a suitable person could be found, she'd like to be relieved before the spring term. If she was of the same mind now, not many weeks hence Nannie might be at work. It would help a little. In other ways, too, money might be earned. Although she was a bit sorrowful that morning, she was tingling with energy. Yet she had a tear or two for the wedding dress, as she folded it away. She dried them quickly, when she heard Rex's voice in the hall below, and went down to him in a very few minutes.

"I had to pass the house on an errand," he explained, as he held her hand. "I didn't succeed in passing, you notice. This is a bright winter morning, Nannie. How would you like a brisk walk over to Mr. Potter's place?"

She gave him a quick, regretful look. "Oh, Rex! You're going to offer your horse for sale?"

"I'm going to tell him he may have her. He's envied me for having her so long it seems a pity not to gratify him."

"But that horse is your own."

"Oh, certainly! She has nothing to do with my uncle's estate. But you know, Nannie, you and I aren't going to keep a horse yet. That's a luxury awaiting our future. Come—the walk out there will do you good."

"No," she said. "I'm not going to begin that way. I'm to work too, Rex. I have plans and must set about carrying them out this morning."

"What are your plans? Perhaps I won't agree to them. You aren't at liberty to carry them out, remember, until I give you leave. Mrs. Marvin, command your eldest daughter to accompany me for a walk. The morning's just right for it."

"Isn't she willing?" asked Mrs. Marvin, smiling, as she passed through the hall. "I'd go, Nannie. It will do you good."

"That isn't to be my motto any longer, Mother. I'm going to work."

"Ah, but the work can wait for one morning," pleaded Rex. "You want to tell me all about it, you know, and honestly, Nannie, I won't hinder you again for a long time. I have some plans to tell you about that are calculated to hasten the time." The latter part of this sentence was spoken low, for her ear. Then he suddenly changed his tone.

"Nannie, you're about to have a call, or your father is. Just hide me in the kitchen or somewhere, won't you? I don't care to be hindered by that man this morning. He'll have a dozen questions to ask if he sees me. What can he want with your father?"

"Who is it?" asked Nannie, as she followed rather than led the way to the dining room. Mrs. Marvin had disappeared.

"It's my uncle's lawyer. I placed that paper in his hands last night—had to wait until the late train before I could see him. He was absent all afternoon, so I just handed it to him stating it would explain itself. Of course I enclosed a note saying who'd found it and then left. It made me too late to come out here last night, as I'd planned. So I was more glad of this opportunity this morning. He must have taken the eight o'clock train out. His business must be urgent."

"I can't imagine what it can be," said Nannie, wondering and vaguely uneasy at the same time. "Father has no business dealings with him that I know of. I wish we'd gone out, Rex, before he came. I feel as if I don't want to see him."

"Oh! We don't need to see him," said Rex cheerfully. "I'm not ready for a business talk with him yet. There are some papers to go over first. I told him so in my note. Nannie, if you'll put on your wraps, we can slip out of this dining room door and be off."

Then Mrs. Marvin opened the door and closed it after her.

"It's Judge Barnard, Rex. He's searching for you. He says he wants to see Nannie, too, on important business."

Nannie shivered like a leaf and grew deathly pale.

"My dear," said Rex soothingly, "don't be startled or troubled. Nothing needs to annoy you—probably some absurd technicality that could have waited until another time. But the average lawyer doesn't deal in common sense. I'll go out and see him and spare you the annoyance if possible, and I have no doubt it is."

But he was too late. The door Mrs. Marvin thought she closed after her didn't latch and presently swung slowly open of its own will.

Judge Barnard, who was standing near it, turned at the sound.

"Good morning, Miss Marvin," said the judge again, turning toward Nannie. He'd met her in Squire Hartwell's library when she was a secretary. He now looked at her with extraordinary interest. He was a dignified man of more than middle age and appeared as if he could, on occasion, "deal in common sense." He stood very high in his profession, and it was a long time since he'd attended in person to minor business details.

The annoyed young man watching him could only think he was moved this morning by a vulgar desire to see how both Nannie and he "bore" the unusual fortune that had fallen to them. He had to exert himself to speak with courtesy.

"Mrs. Marvin said you wished to see me, Judge Barnard. I suppose we have no reason to detain Miss Marvin?"

"Yes," said the judge, with interested eyes still on Nannie, "the matter I've come to talk about concerns her also." Then he looked about for a seat.

Rex Hartwell controlled his inward indignation and brought forward three chairs.

"I examined with great interest the paper you left me last night," Judge Barnard began deliberately, "and following its examination some interesting developments came. May I ask if the discovery of this paper has to any extent been made public?"

Rex glanced swiftly at Nannie before he replied.

"It has, sir, to quite an extent. We were anxious for our friends to know of the discovery and our changed plans as soon as possible."

He'd adopted the plural pronoun in every reference to the subject. As a matter of fact, Nannie had insisted upon telling the news as promptly and widely as lay in her power. It was one form her nervousness took.

"It's a pity," said Judge Barnard dryly, "because some people will talk themselves ill over an affair like this, and you might have saved their tongues a good deal of work. I had a remarkable caller last night after I saw you—sometime after. I think it was nearly midnight when he came. He was none other than the young man in whose favor your uncle drew a will."

"The heir!" exclaimed Rex in surprise. "Has he heard of the discovery so soon?"

"Yes, he's been spending some time in this neighborhood, it seems, and making the acquaintance of his friends unknown to them." Judge Barnard evidently enjoyed the bewilderment he was causing. He paused between each sentence and looked from one to the other as if to give them time to absorb his statements.

"In short, he's none other than your neighbor's man of all work. Mr. Elliott's farm joins this one, I believe?"

"John Stuart!" exclaimed Rex and Nannie in almost the same breath.

"That's the name he's chosen to be known by. But the surprising part of my statement is yet to come. He called on me to say he repudiated the entire property and would have nothing to do with it in any shape, except to turn it over, as rapidly as the law would allow, to the rightful heir. He affirmed what we all believe, Mr. Hartwell—that the property by right belongs to you as your uncle in his sane mind so intended, and the other will was a freak of the moment and has no moral ground to stand on. Therefore he declares it shall not stand."

"But I can't have this!" said Rex in great excitement. "My uncle made the will and lived for weeks afterward and didn't alter it. We have nothing to do with what should have been; we must deal with what is. I decline to have my uncle's property on any such ground."

"Then we apparently have two obstinate men to deal with," said Judge Barnard, smiling as though he greatly enjoyed it all. "The other is equally obstinate."

"He'll change his mind. Who is he, Judge Barnard? And why has he been posing as a stranger? Is he a laboring man?"

"Hardly! Not, at least, in the sense you mean. I'm still reserving the climax to my story. He's John Stuart King, the scholar, traveler, author and what not."

Their astonishment seemed to satisfy the judge. It was so great as to almost drive personal matters from their minds for the moment.

"Well," said Rex at last, "he has my uncle's property to look after—that's all. You may tell him I refuse to receive as a gift from him what my uncle didn't choose to leave me."

Judge Barnard turned suddenly to Nannie.

"Do you approve of such a wholesale renunciation as that, Miss Marvin?" he asked.

Nannie's answer was quick and to the point.

"Certainly I do. Mr. Hartwell isn't an object of charity. It may be noble of the man to feel as he does; I think it is. But a will is a *will,* and, however unjust, people must abide by it."

Judge Barnard leaned back in his chair and laughed. The young people regarded him with astonishment and disapproval.

"Excuse me," he said, "this is quite a new experience to me. Not much in my profession affords enjoyment. I told you the climax to my story was to come. Now you shall have it. That paper you found, Miss Marvin, was undoubtedly the last will and testament of this young man's uncle, Squire Hartwell. It's duly signed and dated, and all the forms of law are correct. In every respect, *except one,* it's a facsimile of the one I drew up for Squire Hartwell. But instead of John Stuart King being the heir, every solitary penny of the entire property is left to Miss Annette L. Marvin, on condition she marry his obstinate nephew, Joshua Reginald Hartwell. Miss Marvin, will you consent to meet those conditions, or are you, like the gentlemen, obstinate?"

For the third time in Nannie Marvin's life the "room began to whirl," and Judge Barnard, instead of waiting to be answered, went in haste to find a glass of water.

Chapter 26

It was very well to appear dignified before Hilda Elliott, but never did a gentleman leave her presence more thoroughly uncomfortable in mind than John Stuart King on that memorable evening. He was sure he'd been a simpleton throughout the interview. He allowed himself to be misunderstood, to have his motives maligned, in short, to appear ashamed of his position, instead of explaining calmly he'd adopted an ordinary business method for the sole purpose of studying social problems. It was a scheme he had a right to be proud of, rather than ashamed. This he told himself while he was fuming. In calmer moments he admitted no man could be proud of a position that compelled him to shade the truth a dozen times in a single day. Moreover, people didn't like to be duped, even though the deception had done them no harm. Something, undoubtedly, could be said for Hilda Elliott's side.

He tramped off some of his surplus energy by hurrying to the station. One step of his future was clear to him. He would, without an hour's delay, do what he could to overturn that will, which by now he hated. He took a savage delight in the prospect of making it good for nothing. The train was late, after his haste, and he had to march up and down the little platform to keep himself warm, subject to the sleepy-eyed stare of the station agent. It was unusual for residents of Bennettville and vicinity to take a train to town at that late hour.

He came back over the road with slower step, but not more cheerful views of life. His interview with Judge Barnard had added to his general sense of being ill used. That gentleman asked many questions and imparted no information. He couldn't even learn from him whether the necessary forms of law could be managed without delay.

Before reaching the farm, however, he'd decided on the next step. He wouldn't leave town that night, despite his offer to Hilda Elliott to do so if she desired. She didn't say in words that she desired it, and he believed he owed a duty to her father, although she was in too lofty a mood to recognize it.

He hadn't exaggerated the confidence Mr. Elliott had lately placed in him. On the very next day he was to drive to a distant town to complete a certain business transaction requiring judgment and quick-wittedness. Mr. Elliott hadn't hesitated to place the matter in his hands. It should have his best attention; delay would cause embarrassment and might result in pecuniary loss. He'd start at daylight. If Hilda chose, during his absence, to arrange so he could do nothing further for her father, that was her concern. But he stood ready to give honorable warning of his change of occupation. He'd be absent all day and therefore didn't need to disturb her by his presence. This settled, he gave a few hours to restless sleep, during which he continued his interview with Hilda, with even more unsatisfactory results than attended his waking, and then roused Susan Appleby at an hour she considered unreasonable.

"Pity's sake!" she grumbled. "Why didn't you start last night? I suppose it's your supper you're hungry for, since you wouldn't condescend to come and eat it."

He'd packed away Stuart King's garments in the trunk, and the clothing he wore belonged to the man known as John Stuart. So Susan felt at home with him and, as usual, wasn't afraid to speak her mind. He was very gentle with her. Susan had been a friend to him. He could recall countless times when she'd advised him for his good. He realized she'd honestly done her best to help him.

He replied meekly that it wasn't so much breakfast he wanted as to leave some messages for Mr. Elliott. It should be explained to him that John had made a very early start because he'd learned the day before that on Saturdays the chief man he was going to see generally took the noon train to town. By starting early he believed he could reach him and transact the business before train time. Other messages followed, or suggestions rather, concerning certain matters that should receive attention during his absence.

At last Susan, who was proud of the way he evidently took the Elliott interests to heart and faithfully treasured his every word, in order to give an accurate report, grumbled again. Did he think she was a walking dictionary or something to remember all those words? Mr. Elliott had run the farm before he came there, and she thought likely enough he could do it again.

She didn't know what a thorn she thrust into John's sore heart by that last. He felt its truth. He was probably exaggerating his importance even to Mr. Elliott. It really made little difference to anyone, except possibly his mother and Elizabeth, where he went or what he did.

As he drove into the farmyard late that afternoon, having accomplished his errand in a gratifying manner, he saw, hanging on one of the bars that divided the meadow lot from the yard, an individual whose presence actually gave him a pang of something like envy. It was Jim, the man who worked for Mr. Elliott before his own arrival and fell sick. He'd heard much of this individual. Susan, who thought much better of Jim ill and away, than she did of him working on the farm, had given detailed accounts of his virtues.

Jim had fully recovered and was doubtless looking for his old place. John Stuart had met the youth several times in the village and knew he was fond of the Elliott farm; a few words with him as he sat astride the fence corroborated this idea. Jim was hoping there'd be an opening, at least in the spring, and had come around to see. He'd been "talking things over" with Mr. Elliott. He didn't want to get in any other fellow's way, but, after all, this was kind of his place. A man couldn't help getting sick.

John agreed to it all. Apparently the man had come at an opportune time. Why wasn't he glad? What step should he take next? Hilda had probably made her disclosures. Perhaps he could see Mr. Elliott at once and leave without burdening her with a further glimpse of him. And then Susan shouted at him from the kitchen doorway.

"If I was you, I'd find out what I was to do next, before I unharnessed them horses. I shouldn't wonder a mite if you'd have to drive to the station after Hilda. Her and Nannie Marvin tramped there this afternoon, but it isn't likely they mean to tramp out again. I don't know nothing about it, but it's likely Mis' Elliott does. If I was you I'd ask her, before I did a lot of work for nothing. I s'pose you've heard the news, haven't you?"

"What news?" asked John tentatively, as he came toward the house, perhaps intending to follow Susan's advice. It seemed highly improbable Hilda would let him bring her from the station, but he should inquire.

"Why, about that everlasting will. It's going to pop up in some shape or other the rest of our lives, I reckon. I don't know what it will do next to make a hubbub, I'm sure."

"What's it done this time?" John was washing his hands now at the sink and wondering if Susan had already heard of the heir's rejection of the property. Evidently she didn't know who the heir was. Susan's views might indicate how much had already been told.

"Why, that fellow, whoever he is, folks thought Squire Hartwell left his money to—you've heard of him, haven't you?"

"I've heard his name mentioned several times!" said John dryly.

"Well, I reckon he feels fine today! Only maybe he didn't hear the other story. I hope he didn't. I can't help feeling kind of sorry for the poor fellow—having money left him, then not having it, then having it again, and not having it some more, is worse than never having a notion of getting any, according to my idea. It ain't his, you see, after all—" She stopped in the act of filling her kettle to see the effect of her words. "That will Nannie Marvin found, that none of 'em had sense enough to look at but just rushed off to Judge Barnard with—he come up there this morning post-haste and told them it was Squire Hartwell's last will and testament sure enough. But not a red cent of the money's left to that fellow, whatever his name was, or to anybody else, but just Nannie Marvin herself. Only she's got to promise to marry Rex Hartwell, or she can't have it. Easy enough for her to promise that! She's been crazy after him ever since I knew her.

"For pity's sake! John Stuart, what are you dripping soapy water all over my floor for? It don't need cleaning. Didn't I finish scrubbing it not an hour ago?"

"Have I hurt the floor, Susan? I'm very sorry."

He moved the offending hands to the basin, finished in extreme haste and got out again to the yard and the horses. It had suddenly become difficult to breathe inside. All his efforts, then, had been in vain. If he'd simply kept quiet and allowed things to take their course, all would have been well, and he might be at this moment quietly driving to the station for Hilda Elliott, as a matter of course. It was a very bitter reflection. He hadn't been ready for disclosures; he'd made them badly. And now to find them worse than unnecessary!

The repentant Susan came out on the steps and called again. "Come on in and get some dinner. I kept it hot for you. You needn't wait till supper. You must be about starved by now."

He answered gently again that he didn't feel hungry and would wait. Susan went in, slamming the door a little and grumbling. "Pity's sake! If he's goin' to turn so touchy as that, what's the use in trying to do anything? Jest because I scolded a little about his drippy hands!"

He left his horses blanketed at last and went into Mr. Elliott's room. That gentleman was now improving daily. He was sitting up in his easy chair and was alone. The moment John Stuart saw his face, he knew he'd been told the news. It wasn't a disagreeable interview. Mr. Elliott didn't seem indignant, like his daughter. He said he understood something of what the motive might have been and congratulated John on his success in carrying out the scheme. He even laughed a little over his own innocence and recalled, with laughter, certain items of advice he'd given. John could sooner have cried; he felt himself parting with a friend. The truth was, he'd come in closer touch with a real home than ever in his life. Moreover, despite his kindness, in Mr. Elliott was that little undertone of feeling about being duped. Like all practical jokes it had its disagreeable side. No man likes to have his faith in other men played with.

John tried to hint at his willingness to remain until Mr. Elliott could spare him better, but there was no opening for that. Evidently it was taken for granted his reason for making the disclosure was his desire to get away. His sacrifice in connection with it was apparently forgotten. Why not, since it wasn't needed?

Mr. Elliott made light of his share of the inconvenience. Jim had come to him that very afternoon, desiring his old place. It seemed providential. And he himself should be around in a few days. Oh, no! They wouldn't think of asking John to stay; under the circumstances it would be embarrassing for all of them. He was sorry he'd felt bound to attend to that day's business but glad, of course, for its successful conclusion. Jim could hardly have managed that. If he'd like to take the train that evening, Jim could drive him to the station when he went for Hilda.

In short, John Stuart went out from that interview feeling dismissed. Despite Farmer Elliott's closing words, half serious, yet comic—"You've certainly served me faithfully. If you ever find yourself needing a recommendation as a farm hand, don't hesitate to apply to me!"—there was a sense in which he felt dismissed in disgrace. He was almost compelled to leave the farm that night, and it wasn't what he wanted to do. He hesitated, with a lingering desire to say good-bye to Susan, then thought better of it and went to the woodhouse chamber as Jim was responding with alacrity to Mr. Elliott's call.

He didn't go directly to the city he called home. Instead, he bought his ticket for the college town where Colin Elliott was staying. He was in no mood for home just now. He shrank from Fletcher's probing questions and felt he had no story to tell about his summer's outing.

A vague feeling that Colin Elliott might be in some embarrassment and a desire to help him were, as nearly as he could understand his motives, what prompted him to stop at the college town. He'd never learned what trouble sent Colin home that night so burdened or how he got out of it as triumphantly as his telegram indicated. That it had to do with money, he thought was evident, and a boy deeply involved in money difficulties didn't usually find his way out so quickly. Perhaps the telegram was only a skillful effort to lift the weight from his sister's shoulders.

The more he thought about it, the more he convinced himself the boy was in danger—in greater danger than his secluded sister could even imagine. If he, John Stuart King, could win him from dangerous companions, could gradually secure his confidence and help him practically and permanently, if debt were one form of his trouble, wouldn't that be worth stopping for? It would dignify his more than doubtful experiment and restore his self-respect. And wouldn't it, as perhaps nothing else could, soften Hilda's feelings toward him and help her understand that, although he chose to masquerade for a time as another character, he was really an honest, earnest man with a purpose in life?

This last motive he tried to put away as unworthy. Hilda Elliott had practically insulted him and shown him he was less than nothing to her, despite the kind interest she'd taken in John Stuart, an interest evidently growing lately. He owed it to his self-respect not to think about her anymore. But the boy Colin, uniformly kind to him, even when he regarded him with more or less suspicion, he'd like to win him and help.

In town he wandered about, valise in hand, in the lower, more obscure sections of the city, until he found a lodging house sufficiently humble for his needs and hired a room for the night. From this he emerged in the morning, fully attired as John Stuart King, to the unbounded astonishment and, he couldn't help feeling, suspicion of the maid who stared after him as he walked down the street. He'd paid his bill the night before and said he wanted no breakfast. But that maid's stare annoyed him; he wanted no more intrigue from this time forth.

He took a car uptown and, after inquiring, selected one of the city's best hotels, where he registered as "Stuart King," with perhaps an extra flourish of his pen about the last name. Then he unpacked his valise and settled himself, resolved to give exclusive attention to Reuben and Hannah and wait for Monday and the hope of an interview with Colin Elliott.

Chapter 27

U pon my word!" said Colin Elliott. "I don't wonder my sister was startled to the degree she confesses, when you appeared to her. I don't
think I'd have recognized you at first, if I hadn't been prepared. Have
you made no changes, except in dress?" He looked critically at hair and mustache. "It's very interesting. You should have stayed and given our neighborhood another sensation; it's fairly boiling with excitement as it is. What with
the recovered will and an entirely new heir, or rather heiress, and then your
sudden, and to them mysterious, disappearance—I don't know, though, if it
could safely have borne anymore."

They were sitting together in Stuart King's room. Colin, at home for the
Sabbath as usual, had returned by a later train than was his custom. He hadn't
visited his room until night and then found Stuart King's card. His curiosity to
see that gentleman was so great he'd restrained himself with difficulty the next
day, until college duties were over, before rushing to return the call. He was
most cordial and heartily interested in the idea that led Stuart King to sacrifice
his position in the world to a summer and fall of country life and obscurity.

"I don't understand social problems well enough to appreciate your work in
that direction," he said frankly, when Stuart King tried to elaborate them for
him. "But I can see at a glance the whole thing would be great fun, and I confess I don't see the harm in it that—some people might."

He paused noticeably before concluding, and Stuart King studied his face
for news.

"You think, then, that some people would disapprove? Is that the feeling in
your neighborhood?"

"Not to any extent," said Colin, laughing. "Susan Appleby was the only
really cross person I saw. She considers herself cheated, but she admits you did
it well. She believes the man who could cheat Susan Appleby, 'right before her
face and eyes,' as she expresses it, is a genius. My father, too, sees the jolly
side of it. He laughed over some of the advice he gave you, and he says you
have the material in you for a first-class farmer."

Stuart King tried to laugh with him and make his voice sound not too anxious as he asked, "But your mother and sisters feel differently?"

"Well," said Colin, hesitating, "my sister Hilda, as perhaps you know, is a
worshipper of Truth. If she'd lived in the old days or in some heathen country,
she'd have had a carved image named Truth and bowed down to it. I like it in
her. I used to think her too particular; perhaps she is in certain directions. But
it's grand to have a character one can trust, always and everywhere. Hilda is
oversensitive in some lines. She can't help that. She's one, you see, who looks
and thinks truth, as well as speaks it."

Stuart King felt he needn't question further. Hilda had criticized him, probably with severity, and her brother had tried to take his side. He must wait. Meanwhile, he'd cultivate this young brother's acquaintance and win him, and sometime perhaps—well, perhaps what? The mail had been brought to his room since Colin arrived, and on the table before him lay a bulky letter from Fletcher. It undoubtedly contained foreign enclosures.

He pushed aside personal matters and gave himself to entertaining Colin, with such success he presently felt he might safely say, with the most winning of smiles, "Now that you understand me better than you did, I wonder if I may renew the offer I once almost offended you by making? In that line or any other I'd be glad to be called on. In other words, I'd like you, if you're willing, to consider me a friend. I'm a few years older but not so many that I've forgotten my college experiences and the satisfaction a frank friendship with a man older than I am would have been to me. Is it too early to ask you to take me for a real friend?"

"Thank you ever so much," said Colin heartily. "I don't feel you're a new acquaintance at all. I told Hilda it scared me to think of the great Stuart King and remember I'd actually given him directions about horses and cows and the like!" He stopped to laugh merrily over the memory. "I said I hoped our roads would never cross again, because I wouldn't know what to say. But you see I rushed away in search of you as soon as possible, and I'm not at all afraid of you. I always liked John Stuart better than I thought it wise to show him." The merry, yet earnest look on the young face was pleasant.

"Poor little Ellie," he continued, "had a momentary return of her love of mystery and romance and announced she thought it would be delightful to meet you as Stuart King, the great writer! I say, Mr. King—we owe you a debt of gratitude we can never repay for your share in rescuing that poor girl. Hilda admitted you were very wise and kind about that matter, and my mother can't be grateful enough."

This certainly was comforting. Stuart King's heart warmed even more toward Hilda Elliott's brother. He contrived, before the interview closed, to renew his offer of help, approaching the subject from another side and, he flattered himself, with such adroitness it wouldn't sound like repetition.

Colin had arisen to go, but he turned back with the bright look shining on his face. "That's very good of you! I recognized it as truly good when you offered help to me before. I was only afraid John Stuart shouldn't have so much money!" His frank laugh was fascinating. "I'm glad to tell you I don't need any help in that direction. I was in a sea of trouble. But an Infinite Helper came to my aid and carried me through." There was no mistaking his reverent tone.

Stuart King waited respectfully for whatever more he might have to say along those lines.

Suddenly he changed his tone and spoke eagerly, "I do need help, however, in other directions. It seems strange to be asking you at this time. It was the last thought I had when I came. But you've been so kind. Hilda told me you're a Christian, and I know, by your energy in taking hold of anything that's to be done, what sort of Christian you must be. I wonder if you wouldn't be just the one to set me at work? I've just started on that road, Mr. King. In fact, my decision dates from the morning following my night of trouble. I was driven into the fold, one may say. A vast amount of coaxing was done beforehand, but I paid no attention to it. I'm inside at last, though. Now what I want is to get to work. I'm alive from head to foot with undirected energy. There's work enough to be done, among the boys in college, for instance, and outside in the city. But I don't know how to set about any of it. Could you give me a hint? Sort of start me? What's your line of Christian work in your own city? And what did you do in college? Did you have some system, something I can get hold of? You might not imagine it, but I'm a systematic fellow. I have definite hours for definite things and mental pigeonholes filled with them, you understand."

Poor Stuart King! Yes, he understood, but he stood silent, constrained, embarrassed, before the bright young face and earnest eyes looking up to him for guidance. What was his line of Christian work? What indeed! Would anything astonish the people in his own city more than seeing him at Christian work? How many times had he spoken to others on this subject?

Fletcher, his friend and fellow church member, and he often criticized sermons together as they walked home from church. But, aside from that, he couldn't recall holding any religious conversation even with him. He didn't usually attend the midweek prayer meeting of his church; it fell on a night when a literary lecture of importance was often held in another part of the city. Then, too, he'd been abroad a great deal and never fallen into the habit of a midweek prayer meeting or of any prayer meeting. What had he done in college in the name of Christian work? Nothing. If he spoke plain truth, as he'd told himself he meant to speak in the future, he'd have to use that word. Should he confess this to such an eager beginner, looking to him for guidance?

He didn't think all these thoughts in detail while Colin waited for his answer. Instead, they flashed through his brain, making a stinging path to his awakening conscience. He was glad Colin was on his feet and had just explained he must meet a college engagement.

"These are very important questions," he said, and he was afraid his smile was sickly. "They can't be answered hurriedly. Come and see me again, and we'll talk things over. When will you come? Can you spare an evening for me soon?"

Colin ran hurriedly over the week's program. Tuesday was lecture evening, and on Wednesday he'd promised to go with a friend to make a call at some distance.

"How would Thursday evening do?"

"Thursday," said Colin, "is our college prayer meeting evening. I've only recently begun to attend it, but I thought I wouldn't allow other activities to interfere with it. You think that's the way to begin, don't you? If someone starts out with letting other matters push in, there's always something to push."

"Undoubtedly," said the supposed guide. He hoped the blood flushing his face was unnoticeable.

Then there were no other evenings that week. On Friday Colin went home again. He couldn't know how much Stuart King envied him this privilege or how much he wished he could be invited to hold their next conference at the Elliott farm. He must wait until the following Monday, though he wanted to say certain things to this young brother that he might report to his sister.

Left alone, Stuart King let the bulky letter wait, while he gave himself to some of the most serious, as well as humiliating, thinking he'd ever done in his life.

Once more were his plans and hopes shattered! He'd earnestly hoped to be helpful to this young man, to win him from careless and probably dangerous ways, to guide him into higher lines of thought and study than his opportunities had yet suggested to him. In short, he hoped to be such a friend to him that Hilda Elliott might one day say, perhaps with grateful tears making her beautiful eyes soft and bright, "I have to thank you for saving my brother to his highest self."

And now, behold, the boy was not only safe from the common, petty temptations he'd feared for him but was tremendously in earnest and needed leading in exactly the ways he was powerless to help! The older man could feel the throb of energy and settled purpose in the boy. He was sure no ordinary decision had been reached. He could tell Colin Elliott's faith meant a force that would be known among his classmates and in his boarding house, that would grow with his growth and develop as his mental powers strengthened. He would indeed become such a Christian as Hilda Elliott already was, with Christianity an underlying test to which all acts, however trivial, must be brought.

Could he wish him to be less than this? No, indeed—he drew himself up proudly with the thought. He respected and admired such characters. But he'd been content to admire them from afar and feel, rather than reason, that such a condition was attainable only for the few. Now he discovered that, if he would be not only Hilda Elliott's friend, but also the boy's, he must search after that condition.

He sat well into the night, busy with the most serious problems that can concern the human mind. After a time he could put Hilda Elliott and then all human friendships or embarrassments aside and let conscience speak to his soul. It asked very solemn questions. Why should he, a man with unusual opportunities for education and culture, discover he was actually below a young fellow like Colin Elliott, regarding the most important matters? He might call it boyish enthusiasm and smile excusingly and give his mind to his studies. He'd been doing something like it before this, he discovered. But some new light had entered his soul, compelling him to be consistent with himself.

Did he believe this life at its longest was short compared with that eternity, only a faint conception of which even the cultured mind could grasp? Did he believe one book, claiming to be from God, told us all we actually know about that eternity? Putting aside for the moment the differing opinions of Christendom, did he believe in the general statements plainly made in that revelation? Without hesitating, his mind answered yes to all these questions. Then came the searching one. Was his life arranged and managed according to these beliefs?

Since growing to manhood he'd spent much time abroad, all but living there. Yet it always interested him that an Englishman or Frenchman recognized him at once as an American and as a sojourner rather than a resident.

"You're an American?" said, rather than asked, a man in London he'd just been introduced to. Then he added, "I suppose you're like the rest of them, planning to go home as soon as you can?"

He thought of this as he sat alone with his conscience. Did he impress any person he met as a citizen of another country planning to go home? Hadn't he always lived as though only this inch of life interested him, and religion was just an incident along the way? Colin had appealed to him, asked his help, apparently confident he could give it. But his clear-eyed sister wasn't deceived. And Colin would soon learn that, boy as he was and just started on this road, he was, by reason perhaps of his lifelong environment, already further advanced than this traveler who professed to have begun the journey years before.

What was he going to do about it? The boy had been drawn to him, had enjoyed the evening and would come again. He could win and influence him, could gradually mold him by what pattern he chose—should he try it? His own aims had been high; his life could in no ordinary sense be called a failure. Most parents and, yes, most sisters he knew would feel honored by any notice he bestowed on their sons and brothers. Would the Elliotts? Sooner than turn the boy's high aspirations into other channels, he would hold aloof from him entirely! Was there no other alternative?

After a while, as has been said, he got beyond all these and let not just his conscience, but God's voice, speak to him. It sent him to his knees.

On the next Monday evening, after talking with Colin about the home he'd just left, Stuart King laid a cordial hand on the young fellow's shoulder and said, "My friend, I have something to tell you. I'm not the one to advise you about the most important part of your life. If it were a question of Greek or mathematics, I might be of service. But I'm simply a babe in this matter of practical Christianity." A sad smile crossed his face. "I don't mind telling you," he added, "I'm ashamed of my life as a Christian. I mean to have a different record from now on. But it's only right to tell you that, much as I'd like to help you in the line you spoke of the other night, I don't know how. You'll have to go to someone who hasn't wasted his opportunities."

The younger man, wondering, touched, drawn by simple frankness, hesitated a moment, then, holding out his hand, said eagerly, "Suppose we start together then and find out what to do?"

Chapter 28

The great stone house, belonging in the Hartwell family ever since one stone was laid upon another, was ablaze with light, and from all the hospitable rooms issued the sound of merry voices. The long hoped for, long deferred social function, filling the thoughts of Bennettville and vicinity for so long, was in progress. Mr. and Mrs. Reginald Hartwell were "at home" after their wedding journey and had gathered their friends about them.

Not one person in the neighborhood who could lay claim to even a slight acquaintance with Nannie Marvin Hartwell was forgotten. Hilda's boys and girls, as the young people from her school were called, were there in force. So was Susan Appleby, in the dining room door, with her arms akimbo just then, staring about her complacently but serving efficiently in the kitchen between times.

"I had as good an invite as the best of 'em," she confided in a strong voice to Jack Sterritt. "If I hadn't I wouldn't have stirred a step to help. But they ain't the kind that looks down on folks the minute they get a little money. Ain't she sweet tonight in that bride dress? I declare, I didn't know Nannie Marvin was so pretty. It beats all what wedding finery will do!"

"We'll have them here often," said the bride in confidence to Hilda, as they watched some of the country girls who were gazing earnestly at the pictures on the walls. "We mean to have an 'evening' on purpose for our friends in this neighborhood. We'll teach them all sorts of little things that will help them, without their ever imagining they're being taught. Gradually we'll drive out of the region those games you dislike so much, along with several other objectionable things, just by showing them a better mode of entertainment. Rex says we'll try the 'expulsive power' of new entertainments. Oh, Hilda! We mean to do so many things with this dear old house! Rex has such lovely plans! You don't half know him. We knelt together in this very library, by that leather chair near the grate, and consecrated this room especially to the work. And," she said with lowered tone and a little nervous clutch of her friend's arm, "I thought then, while I listened to his prayer about what we meant to try to do, what if I'd burned that will! I was tempted to it! What if I had?"

"You never would have done it," said Hilda with quiet confidence. "Don't even think of it, dear. God takes care of His own."

She stood later near one of the leather chairs. She liked to look down into their depths and remember they'd been "consecrated." She was feeling very happy. There were lovely possibilities for Rex and Nannie, and through them her dear boys and girls would receive help. Money was a beautiful servant!

Young Dr. Warden moved toward her. He was Rex Hartwell's closest friend and had traveled at an inconvenient time to act as his best man. It hadn't been difficult to persuade him to come again and assist at this reception. He was evidently pleased to be associated with Hilda Elliott, since she was the bride's maid of honor.

"I think you told me I was to help you 'feel at home' tonight!" he said, laughing. "Are there many guests left you haven't met?"

"Oh, there must be dozens! The entire medical college has come out tonight, I think."

"Then I should be doing my duty. I've met most of the guests from the college. But others are at least equally distinguished. Of course you've met the star of the evening? He came late, though, after we stopped receiving formally. Perhaps you haven't met him? What an oversight!"

"How can I know until you name the wonder?" laughed Hilda. "Who's the star? I thought there were several."

"Ah, but this one is of the first magnitude. His last book, just out, is creating a furor. I mean Stuart King, of course."

At that instant someone tapped him on the shoulder and spoke a few words quietly.

"Certainly," said Dr. Warden. "Miss Elliott, let me introduce you to my friend, Mr. King. All right, Hartwell. Excuse me, Miss Elliott. The 'chief' is summoning me." He then disappeared in the throng.

Stuart King and Hilda Elliott stood confronting each other. There was a moment's hesitation, as though she were trying to determine what to say. Then she laughed, a low, rippling laugh full of merriment.

"I'm acquainted with you after all," she said. "Clothes aren't so important as we supposed."

"But you said we were to be strangers."

"I know I did. I was hard on you, Mr. King. I've realized it since. My brother takes care that we won't forget your name in the family. I like the work you and he are doing."

"He's doing it," said Stuart King earnestly. "I've only been able to help a little with the organization. I couldn't enter into it as I'd like to do, because I'm going home so soon."

It was a very different conversation from the numberless ones he'd tried to plan since he first knew he'd have this coveted opportunity. He'd been anxious, if she'd talk with him at all, to make her talk, or rather make her listen to his defense, of his fall campaign. He felt that, while he didn't have such a high opinion of it as he had, he could convince her he was thoroughly in earnest to understand a form of life he wished to write about. He meant to ask her if she wouldn't read his book and see if she didn't find evidence he understood some points, at least, better than he could without such aid.

But, after that first laughing sentence, she ignored their past acquaintance and went straight to his and her brother's present work. She was eager for details, for suggestions on what he'd try to do if he continued in the college town. She had certain plans of her own to propose and was anxious to learn, through him, whether they'd be feasible for her brother to add to his. In short, she showed him, plainly as words could, that the special Christian effort he'd undertaken with her brother interested her, instead of Stuart King, author of the season's most popular work of fiction—and immeasurably instead of John Stuart, the dissembler to whom she was once so kind, and so severe, but now whom she seemed to have forgotten.

For the next few weeks he had opportunities to study this phase of Hilda Elliott's character. At least he made the opportunities. His invitation to call was sufficiently cordial, and he improved it. Twice, during the week following the reception at the stone house, came invitations from certain wealthier families of the surrounding neighborhood. Of course these people had never noticed John Stuart by even a glance and were more than delighted to receive John Stuart King at their homes. On both occasions he went down by the early train and called at the Elliott farm.

Early the next week he persuaded himself that courtesy demanded making a few calls in the neighborhood—notably, of course, on the bride and groom and also at the Elliott farm. On Friday night he went down by Colin's hearty invitation and spent the Sabbath. Certainly Hilda had decided he wasn't a stranger. She was frank and cordial, deeply interested as ever in his and Colin's enterprise, and an efficient helper.

Farmer Elliott had apparently recovered from his slight annoyance at being the subject of a practical joke and was as cordial as possible. As for the quiet mother, she'd never been other than kind and friendly, and poor Ellie, who hadn't recovered from her frightened air and her timidity in the presence of others, still received him gratefully. Only Susan Appleby held aloof.

"Humph!" she said, when his position in the literary world was explained to her. "How do you know he writes books? He may have borrowed 'em, like he did his work clothes. Who knows what he'll do next? I wouldn't be surprised to see him turn out a circus man or something."

This estimate so amused Colin he couldn't resist the temptation to repeat it to Stuart King, who laughed with him genially and hid a sense of shame and pain. Did Susan voice in her rough, uncultured way something like Hilda's thought of him? In other words, did *she* trust him fully?

The time came, just as spring was opening, when Stuart King steadily, yet with infinite pain, declined Colin's earnest invitation to go home with him. The older man had held stern vigil with himself the night before and knew honor demanded his staying away from the Elliott farm. Not for Hilda's sake—and therein, with strange inconsistency, lay the deepest pain. She continued to be as indifferent to him personally as she was at their first meeting. But he knew mere friendliness was so far from satisfying him that at times he was ready to declare he'd rather they be strangers. Yet what did that state of mind prove? It was humiliating to a degree he didn't think he could endure. But he must face the facts and be a man of honor, if he could, and at the same time a man of truth.

Late in the night this decision brought him to write a letter. It was early in the morning before that letter was finished, though it wasn't long. Three times he tore the carefully written sheet into fragments and began anew. Never had he spent so much time on a letter to Elizabeth. Never had he thought to write her, or any woman, such a letter. What humiliation for a man of his years and his character to admit he made an irreparable mistake and that the woman he asked to be his wife didn't share first place in his heart. More than once he laid down the pen, hid his burning face in his hands, told himself he couldn't write it and told himself sternly a moment afterward that he must. Honesty demanded it. Elizabeth could hold him to his pledged word. He didn't deny her right to do so. He was ready to abide by his mistake. But to go with her to the marriage altar hiding the facts, would add insult to injury.

It was vain for him to go over his past and groan at the folly of a boy playing at manhood and drifting into an engagement, when, if he'd understood his own heart, he would have known he had only a friendly liking for the woman he asked to be his wife. He thought of his mother and her interest in the matter and her influence. He put those thoughts aside, assuring himself he might have been a manly man, if he'd chosen, and that he needn't call his mother to account for what he alone should have controlled.

At last the letter was written and sealed and started on its journey across the ocean. He must wait now for a reply. Worn with his night of self-humiliation, Stuart King had just enough strength left to decline Colin's invitation. Hilda Elliott might consider him the merest acquaintance. But he knew his own heart well enough now to be sure it would be dishonorable of him to try to see her.

Colin went away vexed. He enjoyed Stuart King's company, and there seemed no reason why that gentleman shouldn't prefer a visit with him at the farm, rather than a Sabbath alone in town. When the next Friday night came, and his pressing invitation was again rejected, Colin was puzzled and all but angry.

There was evidently some mystery about Stuart King, as there had been about John Stuart. He professed to be so fond of the farm and of "Father and Mother" and was so ready, even eager, to hear about every detail of their family life. And this time, at his instigation, his mother had sent a genial invitation to "John," as she still called him, to come down; yet he refused.

In the evening, while Stuart King sat alone, weakly wishing it had been right to go to the farm and sorely missing the bright-faced young man who grew daily closer to him for his own sake, the foreign mail was brought to his room. There was only one letter and that from his mother. It couldn't be in response to anything he'd written. But his face flamed as he tore it open. What would his next foreign mail have for him?

This one began ominously.

My dear Stuart,

I hope you feel satisfied now with the result of your method of managing! I'm sorry for you, of course. A mother's heart always remains the same, no matter how foolish her son may be. Yet, while I don't admit it to Elizabeth, I feel you have only yourself to thank. No girl of spirit will endure such tardy letter writing and such prolonged and unnecessary absences, as you have treated her to. She's written you all about it, I suppose. At least she promised four days ago she would.

This wretched little Englishman may be going to have a title, but he's in my opinion anything but a gentleman. He knew months ago that Elizabeth was engaged. I told him so myself; it came naturally for me to do so. But it evidently made no difference to him. I've never liked the creature; he's too fulsome. Elizabeth pretended he was paying attention to me. The idea! She knew better all the time.

Well, this is like all my other plans in life, for nothing. I must say you've thwarted me, in one way or another, ever since you were a baby. But I suppose you can't help it. You're like your father.

I'm too provoked with Elizabeth now to have heard any details, but I suppose the wedding will be soon. It's just like him to rush. I'll come home as soon as I can. I'll write again when I know what's to be done.

Your affectionate
Mother

P.S. It's just a case of pique on Elizabeth's part. I have no doubt you could make it all right again if you would, but I have no faith to believe you will.

Stuart King sat and stared at this letter like one in a dream. Elizabeth engaged to be married, and he—*free!* By degrees he took in that tremendous fact. He didn't have to wait for the foreign mail and for embarrassment and humiliation, all of which would be terrible to explain. Elizabeth had deserted him, and he was free! He didn't need to write that humiliating letter; he might have spared her so much. There seemed to be so many things he needn't have done if only he'd waited!

He sat up again that very night to write another letter. He couldn't wait. He was losing ground every day, and Dr. Warden was gaining! Twice during his calls at the Elliott farm he'd met Dr. Warden. Moreover, Hilda liked frankness. He would be frank. This letter was long. It confessed everything but was humble in its claims. It asked only for time and opportunity to prove the writer's sincerity. It was answered more promptly than he'd dared hope—a frank, kind letter; too kind.

Hilda had been sorry more than once, she wrote, for those hard words she spoke to him on that first evening. She was so astonished and so tried that she didn't realize what she was saying. She'd be glad if he could forget the part he'd called "hard" and look upon her as a friend. But as to more than that—

Stuart King sat longer over that letter than any other. He read it through a dozen times, until the words burned into his heart; read between the lines and knew the words that weren't there as well as those that were. It meant she didn't trust him, couldn't teach her heart to do so, couldn't forget John Stuart. He'd deceived her and successfully played a part. How could she be sure Stuart King wasn't simply engaged on another "study of human nature"? Oh, she didn't write those words, but he read them plainly. Within the week he went home. He'd always meant to go as soon as he saw the way clear. He saw it now.

He was settled in his old rooms, seated before his old secretary, with sheets of paper strewn around and two pictures mounted on easels in their old places, looking down on him. One was a photograph of Elizabeth. He hadn't laid it away—why should he? Elizabeth was his cousin. Her photograph had stood there ever since he occupied the room. He was entirely willing to have it there; he had only kindness in his heart for Elizabeth. The other was the pictured face of Truth. The eyes were certainly similar, he told himself, gazing at it earnestly. But they didn't do hers justice.

Seated in his old place near the south window was Fletcher. He'd been there all evening, asked a thousand questions, been answered heartily and with apparent fullness. But something about his old friend he didn't understand.

"He's taken strides," he told himself. "He's changed. It evidently improves a person to become a tramp! I feel as if he's gone out of my vision or up out of my horizon. I wonder what it means."

"Did you make any acquaintances that will last?" he asked presently, continuing his cross-examination. "Any kindred spirits, I mean?"

"A few that will last to all eternity."

Fletcher's eyes had followed his friend's and were resting on the pictured face of Truth, their old subject for discussion and disagreement.

"Did you convince yourself of the folly of finding a face like that in flesh and blood?" he asked whimsically, for the sake of recalling old times.

"Especially the eyes," he continued, as his friend was evidently not ready to answer. "They seem to look through a person. I'm glad there's no one like it in real life. They'd make someone see his own shortcomings as a fine mirror does."

Stuart King wheeled around in his chair to look at his friend.

"Fletcher," he said earnestly, "there *are* such eyes. They belong to people who do remind someone of his mistakes and failures, but who at the same time lift him up to a higher plane. I'll tell you something in confidence. The woman who becomes my wife, if there's to be a wife for me in this world, will have eyes much like those."

Classic Fiction

Readers of quality Christian fiction will love these new novel collections from Grace Livingston Hill, the leading lady of inspirational romance. Each collection features three titles from Grace Livingston Hill and a bonus novel from Isabella Alden, Grace's aunt and a widely respected author.

Collection #5 includes the complete Grace Livingston Hill books *The Enchanted Barn, Miranda,* and *The Love Gift,* plus *Agatha's Unknown Way* by Isabella Alden.

paperback, 480 pages, 5 ³⁄₁₆" x 8"

❤ ❤ ❤ ❤ ❤ ❤ ❤ 💜 ❤ ❤ ❤ ❤ ❤ ❤ ❤

❤ ❤ ❤ ❤ ❤ ❤ ❤ 💜 ❤ ❤ ❤ ❤ ❤ ❤ ❤